"Yglesias beautifully captures the double bind that this generation faces. . . . The characters in *Only Children* find out that having it all is not easy. . . . Read *Only Children* for a romp through a world of Snuglis, MacLaren strollers, and Nuk Pacifiers."

Los Angeles Times

"*Only Children* by Rafael Yglesias is a timely and true-to-life story about parenthood in urban America in the 1980s. . . . The story accurately reflects many of today's parenting dilemmas."

Associated Press

"*Only Children* is different, a refreshing study of yuppies-in-transition from their unique, have-it-all lifestyles to the more timeless stresses of parenthood, dealing doggedly with details as universal and riveting as infant constipation and the pecking order at the playground."

Milwaukee Journal

"A superlative cast . . . Yglesias turns an eagle eye on the delights and pitfalls of parenting in the 80s."

The Kirkus Reviews

ONLY CHILDREN

Rafael Yglesias

BALLANTINE BOOKS • NEW YORK

Library of Congress Catalog Card Number: 87-28939

ISBN 0-345-36031-1

This edition published by arrangement with William Morrow & Company,
Inc.

Manufactured in the United States of America

First Ballantine Books Edition: July 1989

For my sons,
MATTHEW AND NICHOLAS

Part One

1

AT LAST, SHE FELT THE PAIN. FROM OUT OF THE UNIVERSE the hurt arrived: rumbled into her belly, radiated to her pelvis, crashed into her spine, and dissolved, a terrible acid, into her bones.

And then it was gone.

Nina rose from the bed slowly—for weeks she had had to rotate herself one way, then the other, in order to gain enough momentum for rising—and waddled out of the bedroom.

Once in the hallway, she heard Eric on the phone. He was at the center of an electronic carnival. Besides using the phone, Eric had his eyes on a television broadcast of a baseball game, its volume muted, while the stereo softly played his current obsession, Handel's *Messiah*. To achieve these multiple sensory gratifications, Eric had stretched the phone wire from the kitchen wall unit all the way out, across the living room, so he could sit on the couch while chatting, his eyes on the television, his ears perfectly positioned to hear the stereo balance.

She followed orders. Quietly, although the bend down to the liquor cabinet made her want to groan, Nina took out a bottle of bourbon—Eric, his senses already overloaded, didn't notice her— and sneaked into the kitchen. She sighed and rested for a moment before getting a glass. Her eyes lit on the wall calendar above the cutting board. Today, June 10, was circled in red, by a pen whose ink had long since dried up. It's psychosomatic, she said to herself. Nobody delivers on their due date.

She poured a shot. The amber liquid looked revolting. She sipped it, felt her tongue rebel against the harsh taste, and, to get it over with, quickly tossed the rest back.

She stood there for a while, thinking nothing, waiting. When she gave up her attentiveness to her insides, she realized with dismay

3

that she had forgotten to notice the time. Mild dismay—a familiar feeling of regret at her own inefficiency. Not that she thought herself scatterbrained, simply lazily irresponsible, letting everything go until the last minute. Perhaps that was why this promptness—

Again it came. The world's colors intensified; its shapes wavered. She grabbed the counter—squeezed for the reassurance of permanence. Her bloated body seemed ready to explode—stopped up—the imprisoned pressure hardening fiercely. If it weren't for the stabbing pain in her back, it wouldn't be so bad. . . .

It was gone. Check the time. She wasn't wearing her watch; the battery had run down months ago, and she hadn't gotten around to . . . oh, well. She looked at the little clock built into the kitchen stove: eight-thirty. Since it was the middle of the afternoon, she knew that was wrong.

Nina walked laboriously back into the bedroom before it occurred to her that it didn't matter whether the clock was set right, she only needed to check the length of the intervals. Her impression was that it hadn't been very long between the first and second. Also, the shot of booze hadn't made them go away, ruling out what's his name's pains: false labor. Now that she was at the radio clock beside the bed, how much time had gone by since the attack at the counter?

I'll have to tell Eric and let him keep track. He'll bring out his stopwatch and video camera, she warned herself. He'll hover and fret and pack and take out manuals and check outside to see how available taxis were. . . . It was a nightmare really, the combination of her lazy disorganization and his nervous disorganization.

Who the hell was Eric talking to? He had spent the entire nine months on the phone. On the phone or out with friends. She hoped. Not that he wasn't involved in the pregnancy. His repeated living room concerts of the *Messiah* expressed just how dangerously fascinated he had become.

"We're kids," he'd say, supposedly joshing. "What are we doing becoming parents?"

"Most people have children in their early twenties. We're not precocious," she'd answer, meaning that since they were both over thirty—he was thirty-one, she had had the joy of turning thirty while six months gone—they were mature enough to attempt parenthood.

"I'm kidding," he'd answer, hugging her, or trying to, and then put his big hand on the basketball she had swallowed. "Is he or she moving?"

"No."

"I'm sure it's a girl," Eric would always say, convincing her that he wanted a boy desperately, so much so that he thought saying the opposite would prevent a jinx. His constant wondering made her wish her doctor, Marge Ephron, had ordered amniocentesis. Ephron hadn't, however. Eric claimed that if Nina had had the procedure, he wouldn't want to be told the sex ahead of time, but Nina knew he couldn't enjoy a self-imposed suspense.

The pains were false, she decided, feeling very comfortable and warm from the shot of alcohol. She hadn't had a drink since the first month, and this little bit was having a field day with her sober system. She felt pleasantly smashed.

"You must be having a ball," she said to her stomach out loud. That startled her. She never talked to herself. Eric did. It spooked her the first time she overheard him: mumbling to himself late at night in his study, hunched over the stock graphs, talking his gobbledygook: "It's priced at only half book value, the P/E is low. . . ."

Baby must be bombed, she decided from the dormancy below. Maybe the drink killed him. Yes, him. The restless kicking, the four reversals of positions (according to Dr. Ephron, baby was breech at the latest examination) meant it was a boy. His father's son. If it were a girl like her, she would be enjoying the dark and sleeping peacefully. No, it was a little male in there, watching television, playing music, and talking on a tiny blue telephone. "Excuse me," he could be saying. "Gotta run."

Was that a pain? This one seemed to originate with her, building slowly, no invasion from the heavens. Her middle constricted. She felt more coming and began to rub in the motion she was taught and do her breathing. For a moment or two, it worked. The pain seemed elongated by the breaths but also diminished—and then suddenly her back was breaking, something was coming out through her spine. "Damn!" she said aloud, and tried to roll onto her side. Maybe I have to take a crap, she hoped.

"What's up?" Eric asked. He stood in the doorway and she noticed his height, almost six and a half feet, his kinky hair barely clearing the top.

I'll never get his son out through my little vagina, she despaired. Now there was only a faint trace, a shadow, of the stabbing in her spine. "I think it's started," she answered.

For a moment Eric looked blank. His big brown eyes, set wide apart, were usually warm and welcoming, slightly baffled while he listened, but now they stared ahead dumbly—a cartoon character's eyes.

She rolled herself up into a sitting position. "I haven't timed them," she said, sighing.

"How many?" he asked, his voice squeaking a little.

"Three—"

"Three! Why didn't you tell me?"

"I think. I don't know. You'd better keep track of the time."

"Did you call the doctor?"

"You were on the phone."

"Honey! For this I would've hung up."

"It's too early to call anyway."

Eric remained fixed in the doorway, staring. He looked shocked, as though he had never expected this to happen. What did he think—she was going to carry the Goodyear blimp inside her forever? "When are we supposed to call?"

"I forget," she said. She straightened herself with a groan.

"Is that a pain?"

"No. Ten minutes apart."

"That's when we go to the hospital?"

"Is that what it is?" she asked quizzically.

"No, I was asking."

"No, I call at ten minutes. I think that's what it is." She decided to lie down—but she couldn't move. She suddenly felt convinced that if she kept still, the pains wouldn't come anymore. But I want them to come, she argued to herself. I want to get this over with.

"Ten minutes!" he exclaimed, and walked farther in. His nervous energy had returned, his eyes flickering with schemes, irritation, plots, and feeling; emotion appeared on his face as though he were a transparent man. She loved him because of this quality, so different from herself; often she couldn't show what trembled inside her even when she wished to. Especially happiness—the pleasant mask of her features would stubbornly resist being stretched into an ecstatic smile and she'd offend gift givers, lovers, praising parents with her content, but unexcited, face. She marveled at the rapid play of Eric's feelings—drop a tiny pebble into the pool of his soul and watch the magic ripples appear, extend, and glide out into the world, spreading his joy or his fury. When she married him and kissed his pale face, drawn at the awesome prospect of eternity with her, and saw the color return while they danced surrounded by friends, she knew she could trust him; that when he stopped loving her, the sorrowful finale would reverberate on his face's sounding board for everyone to hear. "Ten minutes!" he exclaimed again with worry and disapproval. "That doesn't sound right."

"Look in the notebook," she said, nodding at the dresser.

He opened the steno book where she had written all the information they had been told by the doctor and the midwife at the childbirth classes. He hunched over to read, lowered his head, and stared at the words. "Ten minutes." Eric was disgusted, as though he had lost a bet. "How long are they?" he asked, looking up at her.

"I told you—I don't know. You're in charge of timing them."

He nodded and pushed his sleeve away to look at his watch. "When was the last one?"

"I don't know!" she shouted.

"Sorry." He put a hand up to deflect her furious words. He leaned against the dresser and continued to glare at his timepiece.

She laughed at the sight. He was capable of remaining in that position, awaiting her next spasm, for hours.

Eric ignored her amusement. "Ten minutes doesn't seem like much time."

Now she really began to laugh and then choke as she tried to talk: "It's not—it's not how much time there is—not how much before the—"

"I know that!" he protested, looking up. "But ten minutes apart can be only an hour or so before delivery."

She shook her head no. He nodded yes. She repeated her negative motions, closing her eyes while she did, as if another contradiction would be too much to bear.

"Most of the time it's much longer, but I read that *sometimes*, sometimes, it's only an hour away."

"That's with second and third children."

"What are we arguing for?" he squealed to the ceiling, his hands out in frustration. He went back to his watch.

"I can't eat," she said after a few moments.

"I don't blame you," he said with a grunt.

"No," she corrected. Talking took too much energy. "I'm not allowed to."

Eric picked up the notebook again and flipped it open.

"Only soup," she said. "Clear soup," she added, hoping to stop him from searching for information she already knew.

It didn't. Eric leafed through the notebook deliberately until he found the right page. "Clear soup," he said, as though this were the first time it had been mentioned. "Are you hungry? Do you want me to get some?"

"Get some?" she asked, baffled.

"Is that because of anesthesia?"

"Yes."

"From the store."

"I feel like I'm stoned," she complained, and shook her head. "Is it me or you?"

Eric looked at her, smiling broadly, his big, wide mouth showing small, brilliant teeth. "It's both of us," he said, laughing. "We're scared to death. I can't remember the goddamn breathing, I can't remember the name of our doctor, I can't remember the name of the hospital—I can't remember your name!" He pushed himself off the dresser and fell to his knees in front of the bed. Eric put his head on the bedspread next to her feet and stretched his long arms out with the weird extension of an ape. He stared at her thighs; his hands ran over her knees and then moved down to her feet. The strong fingers felt good, restoring sensation and warmth to her numbed and tired legs.

"It's up to you, Bear," she called down to him softly. "You have to help."

He picked his head up slightly. His forehead crinkled when he raised his eyebrows to look at her. "Why? This was your crazy idea."

"Liar," she said pleasantly, wistfully. "I want clear soup," she added with a smile.

"Do we have any?" he asked. "What *is* clear soup?"

"Plain soup—broth with nothing in it. Nothing solid."

Eric sighed. He rose to his feet slowly and shuffled out, head bowed, shoulders hunched, his walk exaggerated to mimic a burdened old man.

He'll be fine, she thought. Eric'll be fine? she repeated, amazed. Why am I worried about him?

Please don't let me die, she said silently to the ceiling, with no panic in her, just a simple request.

There was a crack running across the middle where there had once been a light fixture. We should have painted, she sighed, before the baby came. In her mind, once the birth occurred, they would be imprisoned in the apartment, their life and things frozen in place until baby left for college. She had tried, bolstered by the so-called nesting instinct, to make a few cosmetic changes in the apartment, but she had let so many obvious things—such as painting—go undone. She imagined there would never be another chance. Motherhood seemed so awesome from reading the books, a kind of tightrope act across the chasm of time from birth to maturity: tilt to one side and the child would be cast into the gloom of permanent trauma; lean in the other direction and the abyss of self-abusive permissiveness was there to swallow her. There couldn't possibly be time left over for things like painting apartments.

Eric appeared again, a can of Campbell's chicken noodle soup in his hand. "This?"

She nodded. "You have to strain everything but the soup."

He listened to this seriously, digested it, nodding, and then walked back to the kitchen.

From the floor, reverberating through the bed, she felt the distant thunder.

Eric reappeared with the can of soup and a colander. "Strain it with this or with a strainer?"

The middle of her body went—seized by an invasion, the nerves cut from her brain's control. She started to rub the shaking territory, quelling the rebellion, breathing out, counting.

"Oh, my God," Eric said, and dropped both items. The colander clattered; the can hit with a dull thud. She glanced at the floor to see if it had burst. Eric rushed to the dresser where he had left the notebook and looked at his watch while his hand fumbled for a pen in his shirt pocket.

There was a piercing stab in her spine. "A colander *is* a strainer!" she shouted through the momentary agony. It was gone, a candle snuffed out, with no smoky trace of its fiery presence.

He was writing. "That's what I thought," he said good-naturedly. "Was that one bad?"

"Just at the end. It's hurting my back."

He paled. He had remembered from the classes, she knew, even before he asked: "You don't think it's back labor?" the way one might inquire if a lump was cancerous.

"Maybe I just have to go to the bathroom," she groaned, and began to get up.

"What?" he said, laughing. "I'm not charting constipation, am I?"

Nina smiled weakly. Eric moved next to her and offered his hands to help her up. She pushed off them and rose into his arms. She buried her head in his warm chest and listened to his anxious breathing, comforted anyway by his largeness, his size implying strength, inspiring confidence.

"I love you," he said after a while.

She lifted her head to smile at him. She was surprised to see his eyes glistened with emotion. "We'll be fine," she heard herself say, again amazed that she felt called upon to reassure him.

"Don't worry," he answered, as though she had expressed worry.

She moved out of his arms. While she shuffled off to the john, he said, "I'll make the soup."

"You're going to have to learn to cook," she said.

"I'll start tomorrow," he said.

Sitting on the toilet, she felt ludicrous and she despaired of everything. Her enormous belly was exaggerated by the position; her head was filled with disgusting images of the baby falling out into the bowl. She had a dread—from her childhood—of constipation, a condition that pregnancy had returned to her. She was afraid to strain, but she wanted to make sure—imagine going to the hospital only to discover she had to make number two. She didn't want the "fulfilling" experience of natural childbirth now that she had a taste of its emptying pain. She could tell from the look of her thighs and the painfully taut stomach skin that she would never be the same. And lastly, worst of all, she didn't want this life inside her to emerge. Squalling and needing—expecting her to provide everything from milk to moral guidance.

When she tried to move her bowels, the beginning of the effort frightened her. She worried that it might provoke a contraction. She started to laugh at herself, but the release of tension in her face loosened a sob instead.

"Honey?" Eric called out nervously. "Are you okay?"

She pressed her forehead with her fingers to hold back more; her whole body was engaged in an effort to restrain nature, fighting the overwhelming uncivilized elements with thin weather stripping and tattered insulation. Nothing could stop this hurricane; it would blow through her, the swirling force blasting her open to take what it wanted.

Suddenly she was peeing. She had no memory of receiving a request from, or of sending an order to, her bladder. Already the mutiny had succeeded: the ship's course was in the hands of the crew; she had become a bystander—locked below—forced to guess at what was going on.

Wiping herself was a joke. She caught a glimpse of the ridiculous maneuver in the mirror and winced.

Eric greeted her the moment she opened the door: "Soup's ready. Did you have any luck?"

So now every body function was going to become an item on the news. Why should she tell him if she had crapped or not? She shook her head no.

Her disgust at having to answer was then misunderstood for upset at the failure. "They give you an enema at the hospital," Mr. Information said with an encouraging smile. "Remember? They told us—"

"Thanks for reminding me," she said, not concealing her sarcasm.

Eric laughed good-naturedly. He hovered beside her, walking

awkwardly, matching her slow steps with halting ones of his own. Nina scowled at him. He scrunched his big face up: expectant, eager, ready to fulfill any request. The sight was charming and broke her irritation. She smiled at him and touched his chin with her hand. Eric caught it in his own and kissed it. "Mmmm. Warm," he commented. He led her to the kitchen table, where a bowl of chicken broth sat forlornly—no napkin, no plate underneath. She sipped it, tasting nothing. Eric disappeared for a few minutes.

When Eric reappeared at the doorway, she stared in disbelief; he had the video camera to his face, the carrying case strapped to his back. The flashing light above the lens warned her he was taping, so she didn't say the various obscenities that occurred to her. Eric wouldn't edit them, and years later her child would be doomed to watch the spectacle of his mother cursing out Dad only hours before the moment of joyous birth.

"Well?" Eric prompted, his voice muffled by the camera.

"It's a fabulous bowl of soup," she said in a flat voice.

He la_____ "That's great," he commented. "This is the big day. H_____ ___ ___ he continued.

_____ _ishly. "I feel like Greta Garbo."

_____ s hummed as he came in

_____ _l that there

_____ bo__

"A wat_____ _____ _____ ___ ___ d of soup to her lips. ___

AT TEN O'CLOCK IN THE MOR_____ _____ ___MMEL surveyed their preparations. The baby s____ ___ ___ _e having a boy—was in a ghostly state of perfection. _____ _e placed in neat rows, obviously unsullied by use: the gaily co____ hanging animals were still; the crib sheets were taut; the baby carriage's rubber wheels were white and shiny, its chrome frame glistened, and the hood yawned its emptiness.

Diane stood at the changing table and pulled at the small mattress to make sure it was securely strapped. She had a frightening thought: what if something happens and the baby is born dead? Then this sleeping room, awaiting the life to waken it, would remain in a coma—a tomb for their expectations, its perfection mocking their arrogant preparations.

Peter had no such morbid fantasies. He had praised the existence of amniocentesis: knowing the sex, they could buy clothes in advance; with the assurance that the child was healthy, anxiety was minimized; and they didn't have to go to the fuss of picking a girl's name. Peter also maintained he was happy about the fact that their doctor, once Diane was two weeks late, decided to schedule a Caesarean. He regretted that their natural-childbirth training would be wasted—they had put a lot of effort into it—but after all, there would be no pain, no exhausting vigil, only a neat scar, cleverly placed so that even if Diane wore a bikini, it would be hidden. The process would be sensible and orderly. They weren't hippies anymore—actually, they weren't when everybody else was—and this procedure seemed civilized, coordinated, and convenient. Peter had been a reluctant father (she bullied me into it, was the way he described it to himself) and had agreed only on the condition that Diane guarantee him his work and their social life wouldn't suffer. Many of their friends, when Peter told them of the conditions he had set before he agreed to have a child, had said that his vision of fatherhood, besides being coldhearted, was impossible; this scheduled birth reassured Peter that raising a child could be neat and organized.

From the window, Peter watched for the car while Diane had her premonition of disaster at the changing table. Peter remembered what his mother-in-law had said a few months ago when he confessed his worries. "When you see that beautiful angel's face," Diane's mother told him, "you won't mind giving up a little sleep." The hell I won't, he thought. He saw the limousine pull up beside the dull green awning. "It's here," he said.

They went downstairs. Peter smiled at the obsequious doorman, who made a big show of rushing to the door to open it for them. "Good luck," the doorman said in his Spanish accent. Peter smiled confidently.

Diane kept her head down and watched her big body move. She put a hand on her belly when she felt the air rush over her face. Poor thing, she thought about her child, you don't want to come out. The chauffeur had already opened the black limousine's door. Lights glowed from the interior, darkened by its green tinted windows. The chauffeur offered his hand to help her in. "Watch your step, ma'am,'' he said. She looked at his face. He was young, no sign of a beard on his clear skin. That, and his attitude toward her, made her feel ancient or, worse, finished as a sexually desirable woman. Not merely for now, in the full state of pregnancy, but forever.

Peter doesn't look at me anymore, she thought to herself as they got under way. She stared at her husband's profile, intent on the view ahead, and tried to remember the last time they had sustained eye contact. Whenever Peter glanced at her, his eyes immediately trailed down to her belly and then, guiltily, away from her altogether, as though he had been caught staring at a cripple. Diane hadn't expected Peter to remain sexually interested once she began to show, but to avoid even looking at her suggested a deep loathing and disgust. And right now he wasn't solicitous or tender. On the brink of this fateful event, just when she imagined Peter would hold her hand or put a reassuring arm around her shoulder, instead he sat a foot away, his body held rigidly, as though he feared she might touch him.

She did. She reached for Peter's hand, resting on the leather next to his leg, and covered it, her fingers arching over his knuckles—a crab climbing a rock. To her surprise, he turned his palm up and grasped her firmly. Peter's cold hand squeezed desperately as though he were drifting toward a waterfall and she were a rope to the safety of shore. But the rest of him remained aloof. He's scared, not disgusted, she thought with relief.

Peter hated hospitals. He had had an appendectomy in the middle of his sophomore year at Harvard, and all his dealings with doctors, nurses, orderlies, admissions and billing bureaucrats had been infuriating. Throughout Peter's life he had had great success dealing with institutions—indeed, he worked for a large organization—but hospitals were the exception. Because one was ill, there was no way to bargain successfully with the medical establishment. Going into a hospital was to be stripped of all civil rights, Peter often said, and having lost battle after battle in the past, he was now shy of the simplest encounter. He fully expected them not to have Diane's operation scheduled, to have no idea of who she or her doctor was, in short, to find everything in a mess. This pessimism wasn't alleviated by the precautions he had taken—namely, getting to know the chief of medicine at New York Hospital through his boss at the Stillman Foundation as well as using the top obstetrician (Dr. Stein) despite the fact that Diane didn't like Stein's manner. One of the good things about the Caesarean was that it guaranteed the presence of this hotshot. Stein's associate might have ended up doing the procedure if Diane went into labor at an inopportune time, which, in the case of Dr. Stein, seemed to be any hours after six at night and before nine in the morning on weekdays. Weekends were totally out of the question. Peter didn't say so to Diane, but he suspected Dr. Stein ordered the Caesarean because Peter, using his cultivated acquaintance with the chief of medicine as a lever, kept tilting Stein toward an agreement that he would be on call outside his normal hours.

Nevertheless, it turned out Peter's preparations *did* work. Everything was in order. Diane's private room was ready for after the procedure; the instructions to where they should proceed in the Gothic caverns were accurate; she was expected there; the forms he had filled out a week before were present; Dr. Stein arrived shortly after Diane was in her hospital gown and Peter had struggled into a smock and cap.

Dr. Stein examined Diane with his long pink hands. Peter looked away when things got too intimate, thinking what an oddly disgusting profession gynecology must be: making the mysterious mundane.

"Nothing happening," Stein said cheerfully. "We could try to induce labor, but—" he shook his head sadly—"in the end, that rarely works." He winked at Diane. "You'll never see the scar." She had complained to Peter about Stein's tendency to wink. She said it always preceded the mention of anything bad: a good-humored father chuckling and joshing his weeping children over some disappointment.

"That's easy for you to say," Peter answered Dr. Stein with a pleasant smile. Peter had learned, years ago at Harvard, to say the most challenging things with a bright smile. To show the handle of the knife, but not the blade. "Doctors are always doing that, aren't they?" he went on to Diane, almost as if Dr. Stein weren't in the room. "Being brave about their patient's misfortunes."

"I was *reassuring* my patient," Dr. Stein answered petulantly.

"It's fine, Doctor," Diane said. "I'm not worried about the scar."

"Of course not," Peter said with emphasis, appalled that he might have implied an unseemly vanity on her part.

Stein said they would be moved into the operating room in a few minutes and then left them alone. "For God sakes, Peter," Diane said. "He's about to cut my body open. Don't piss him off."

"He's an arrogant little shit," Peter mumbled, but he nodded penitently. "I'll be good," he added.

They rolled Diane into the tiled room; it reminded Peter of the huge common showers in school gymnasiums. He walked beside her horizontal body, watching his feet move in the oversized blue plastic coverings. It was all so tacky and undignified. The only thing modern medicine had left to childbirth was the fear; its spiritual mystery, its grandeur were obscured as thoroughly as if a high-rise apartment had been built on top of a cathedral.

Diane felt useless and stupid while the technicians worked around her. Dr. Stein explained what they were doing in a mumble. He was repeating information she already knew; the childbirth classes had included a long lecture and film on Caesarean sections. As promised, the spinal block didn't hurt. They put a tentlike cover above her abdomen and a stool beside her head for Peter to sit on. Peter took his place, his face white, his hand, moist with terror, clenching hers. He stared at Diane, his eyes large and unfocused, unwilling even to glance in the direction of the activity.

"Do you want to watch?" Stein asked. He nodded at a thick rectangular mirror on top of a long stainless-steel pole. Diane was reminded of the security mirrors placed on elevators and at the rear of stores. She could keep her eyes on the lower region and see if they mugged her uterus or shoplifted the baby.

"I don't think so," she answered in a querulous voice. She rolled her head to the side and gazed into Peter's eyes. "You agree?"

Peter closed his eyes and then nodded his head up and down slowly. He opened his eyes. "Oh, yeah, I agree."

"We're going to make the incision," Stein said. "You might have a vague . . . very vague sensation. But if you feel anything clearly, sing out."

"I will," she said. She tensed in anticipation. She imagined a patch of her skin slicing open—a tearing sound, blood gushing up all over Dr. Stein. But there was nothing, nothing at all. This is going to be easy, she thought, and felt glad.

ERIC BECAME AWARE OF THEIR BIZARRE POSITIONS. HIS WHALE OF a wife knelt on all fours in front of the television, her great belly sagging only an inch from contact with the living-room rug while she made the strained huffing sounds of natural-childbirth breathing. Eric sat on the coffee table in order to be above her and pressed his clenched fist into the small of her back. Eric could picture how perverse the scene might look to an observer.

Maintain steady pressure. Eric replayed the phrase of their instructor to encourage himself while his arm muscles cramped from the unrelieved exertion. Maintain steady pressure, Eric thought, watching Rock Hudson's leering eyes. Nina had selected *Pillow Talk* from the television schedule to distract them while they waited for the labor pains to be only five minutes apart. Then they could head for the hospital.

Nina moaned. In response, Eric pushed down on her back even harder. "Oh, that's better," she said, dismaying Eric, because he could never keep up this new level of effort. The blood in his arm seemed to have gelled, ready to burst through the skin.

"I'd better write the time down," he said. He had noted the time on the video recorder's digital clock, and he knew without checking the sheet that the pains were still eight minutes apart. They had been stuck at this interval for over an hour. Nina already seemed worn-out, her face drawn, her eyes scared, her voice enervated. She's not going to make it, he thought. What did *that* mean? She couldn't quit. But by the look of her, a few more hours of this seemed unimaginable. He wanted to get to the hospital. There the medical people could take over, deal with it if she couldn't finish. "Eight minutes," he said.

"I can't believe it." She sighed.

"Should we call the doctor and tell—"

"We're not supposed to call until it's five minutes!" Nina said furiously.

"But—just to tell her that they're not getting any closer—"

"No!" She sounded as if she were training a dog. "I'm not going to keep bothering Ephron when she's told me what to do."

"You mean, no matter how painful it is, no matter how long it goes on—"

"If it gets too painful, I'll call. God, Eric, don't make this any harder than it already is."

Is it me? he wondered. Or is she irritable from the pain? Everything he said grated on her. I'm supposed to be strong, he criticized himself. Supply patience and confidence—not worry.

Patience and confidence. That's what it would take to be a father. What a colossal effort—to stand on the lonely hill of responsibility, the wind whipping his hair, and clench his jaw bravely for years and years. To conceal how frightened and inadequate he really was.

He wanted to run from the room screaming. Hail a cab to the airport, board a plane to Las Vegas, and spend the rest of his days playing, whoring, and sleeping. Every time he met Nina's glazed eyes, they focused on him and came to life, burning with mute requests. For reassurance, for efficiency, for solace. And soon there would be another pair, needing even more things. Security, love (unstinting, uncritical, and absolute), and . . . money.

How could he—of all people—have entered into this enterprise without taking into account how much goddamn money was involved? If he had to cite one thing that was absent from his childhood, one gloomy cloud that darkened his parents' windows, its dense atmosphere poisoning their lungs, lidding their eyes, that was the absence of money. Eric's father, Barry, a floor manager in Gimbel's shoe department, had tried one bold move to make money: he quit his steady paycheck, borrowed from relatives and friends, and opened a place of his own in Washington Heights. But it had failed, and although Barry was taken back by his old employers, there was debt, there was a cut in pay, there was gloom and shame and fear.

Eric had sworn to himself that he would grow up to be rich, that nothing would prevent him from shooting through the black mist into the sunny life of the wealthy. And yet he had committed to the birth of his child, his heir, without knowing if he could sustain his income, if he could swell it into a mountain of capital to elevate his son effortlessly—the sweat, the climb, the danger of falling . . . all eliminated by Eric's brilliance.

What if it isn't a son? Then Eric's lack of a fortune would be even worse. After all, a daughter might inherit his features, and then it would take a trust fund of at least two million to attract a husband.

"What are you smiling about?" Nina asked, letting her body descend on the floor.

"I was hoping, if it's a girl, that she doesn't look like me. She'd need one hell of a dowry."

"Oh, Bear." Nina sighed, hurt by his cynicism. "If she looks like you, she'll be beautiful. Six feet tall, beautiful skin."

"Brown eyes?"

"She'll have my eyes," Nina said firmly, her blue eyes widening with conviction.

Eric laughed, pleased he had wrung this little admission of vanity. "Only a one-in-four-chance," he warned, shaking his finger at her.

"It'll come through."

"Will you love this baby if it doesn't?"

"What do you mean?" she protested.

"I don't know. I just hope—for its sake—that it's got blue eyes."

"That's not funny," she said, turning from him to look balefully at the television. Her thick brown hair shifted off her back, fell across her shoulder, and exposed the pale white freckled skin of her neck.

"I was kidding, for chrissakes."

"I don't feel like joking right now," Nina answered in a faint voice. "Ugh," she groaned, a hand reaching for her back.

Wearily, Eric planted his fist there and pressed. Hard. Pushing,

pushing, pushing. Hoping he could get the little bugger to come out already. To end the fantasy and begin the reality.

"ELEVATE THE BLADDER," SHE HEARD STEIN SAY. PETER WINCED. He tried to mask his reaction, but a flicker of queasy disgust peeped through. Diane felt weird about their poking around her insides like shoppers at a sale counter, but only intellectually. She couldn't picture—even to scare herself—what they were doing. And this abstracted relationship to the birth of her son was a relief. She had worried she wouldn't be up to natural childbirth, that like some scared kid on the first day of battle, she'd panic and flee, only to be dragged, crying, back to the front—humiliation following cowardice.

Instead, this seemed almost queenly. Her husband, the doctors, and the nurses attendant on her various parts, the heavy painful lower half of her body whisked away to a numbed dimension.

"Here he is!" Stein said. She strained her neck and caught a glimpse (above the tented blue sheet rising from her chest) of a slimy bald head. "Clip. All right."

The baby cried. Not the bloodcurdling scream she expected, but a feeble squeak of protest, a kitten startled from sleep.

Stein, his eyes warmer, bigger, and kinder than she had ever seen them, approached with her son. Stein's hand, covered by a transparent rubber glove, encompassed the whole of baby's skull; the fingertips spread beyond, petals open, cradling the blossom within.

"Let's say hello to Mama and then we'll check you out," Stein said to the creature—it was too much of a miniature, too strangely animate, too wet to be called anything else—and then laid it in between her swollen breasts. One of the nurses—also beaming with tranquil joy—raised Diane's head so she could look at the face.

"Hello," said a voice at her side. She was surprised to find it belonged to Peter; she had almost forgotten he was there. Peter leaned in, his hand covering baby's tiny, furiously clenched fist. By comparison, Peter's hand looked gigantic and terrible.

"Easy," she said involuntarily.

"I'm barely touching him," Peter complained.

She looked at the face. It was unreal—the skin translucent (hardly protecting the blue-green veins beneath), fine hairs everywhere, the lips full, brilliantly red against their pale surroundings. Baby's legs and arms cringed and yearned, as if finding the open air harsh—a mute appeal for cushions and warmth.

"Hello, Byron," Peter said to the baby, using the name he had urged over her plaintive objections. Too pretentious, too odd (the potential nickname—By?—sounded like a description of sexual confusion), and besides, Diane had never read Byron. (Wasn't he a sexist pig?) But Peter had, especially in adolescence, and he made no attempt to pretend it was simply a love for the name itself. "It'll guarantee one thing," Peter said. "He'll be sure to read Byron at least once—so we won't have a complete illiterate for a son."

Diane looked at her creation. That was no Byron. The brilliant whitish yellow umbilical cord, as thick as a trunk phone line into a busy office, extended from his red and swollen belly. The biggest thing about him were his testicles (maybe he *was* like Byron), but that was caused by birth or something—they had explained at the classes. The legs were retracted up almost to the stomach, a frog turned upside down, feet feeling desperately for a comforting surface.

"All right, let's give him over to Dr. Kelso," Stein said, and a young baby-faced pediatrician picked up Byron with a confidence that both impressed and irritated Diane.

"Welcome to the world," Dr. Kelso said, and carried him off.

NINA HATED THE FURNITURE. THE DARK, DREARY WOOD OF THE living-room shelves, the fat, rumpled couch, the dull red rug, the thick, oafish horizontal blinds (smudged by futile attempts to clean off New York's air)—they all seemed responsible for the pain and mistake of this birth. Her back ached with bruising hurt, like nothing she had ever felt before. The base of her torso felt sore and dented, as though someone had been striking her with a mallet over and over and over—trying to halve her. Whenever Eric removed his fist, the pain intensified, stabbing so insistently her breakage seemed only moments away.

"Oh! Oh! Press! Press!" she cried. She reached back to the wound, almost fearful, however, that her hand would find nothing where once there had been her body—her strong, young, always reliable flesh.

"Okay, okay," he said, and his strong fist shored her up, lifting her above the surging pain, just high enough for her to breathe and survive.

"Oh, God! Oh!"

"Breathe! Do your breathing!"

Nina huffed and puffed irregularly, skimming insecurely on the pain, buffeted out of her attempts to get a steady rhythm by the erratic stabs of hurt.

"Forty-five seconds," Eric said. His voice was squeezed by the effort of maintaining pressure on her back. "Contraction is subsiding."

"No, it's not!" she protested. Eric laughed, but she wasn't joking, she wanted to be accurate.

And then it was gone.

Vanished—not a tide ebbing—but whisked away by a magician's wand. Stay off my spine! she yelled internally at the thing inside her. She pictured the midwife from the childbirth classes, holding the break-apart model of a pregnant woman high enough for everyone to see, while she manipulated the fetus doll to show various positions. The midwife illustrated back labor by pressing the plastic fetus's head down on the model's spine. "The pressure here gets worse as baby's head is pushed lower by the contraction. Gravity is best for relieving the pressure. Get on all fours like a dog. Have your husband keep a ball or his fist or an ice pack pressing on the small of your back. Back labor is very difficult, but it can be handled." Oh, yeah?

"It's five minutes," Eric said. "That was five minutes. We should go."

He's terrified, she thought, disgusted. She knew it was still too early—that if they went to the hospital now, they would be stuck in the labor room for hours. And because of her back labor, being there might mean the instigation of medical procedures such as putting on the fetal monitor, forcing her to lie down on her back—the worst possible position. But Eric's smoldering hysteria at being away from medical supervision was dangerously close to ignition. "We're supposed to wait until it's consistently five minutes," she argued, risking the conflagration.

Eric looked at his notebook, reciting: "Six, five and a half, six, five and a half, five. It's getting there."

Nina struggled to get to her feet. Eric took her hand and pulled. He groaned at the effort. "Jesus," he commented.

"Now you know how I feel." Nina walked to the phone and dialed Dr. Marge Ephron's service.

"Who are you calling?"

"The doctor."

"I thought you weren't—"

The service answered. The operator immediately agreed to call Dr. Ephron. Nina hung up. "You're right," she said to Eric. "We should go to the hospital. I may need help with this pain." Once she might have expected a protest from her husband. He had been keen on doing the natural childbirth. But the pale, nervous man, already nodding his agreement, was an unlikely objector.

The phone rang. Nina picked it up. "That was fast." She put a foot forward and placed her right hand behind her on the small of

her back. She arched her watermelon stomach forward. Put a ba-
bushka on her and she could be a peasant woman in the field pausing in between harvesting the potatoes to deliver her child. For Eric,
the sight filled him with respect and guilt. "They're almost five
minutes apart. I'm having a lot of back pain, though. I may need
help." Nina pressed her thin lips together, breathing through her
nose, while she listened to her doctor's response. Eric knew that
meant Dr. Ephron was being either critical or contradictory. "We
are," Nina said. "I've been on all fours for hours and Eric's arm
has practically fallen off from keeping his fist in my back."

You'd think a woman doctor would be sympathetic, Eric thought.
After all, Ephron has had two kids herself, the last quite recently.

"Right," Nina now said, her mouth relaxing into a conciliatory
pout. "Un-huh. Okay. We'll wait. Thanks." Nina hung up. "She
says it'll be harder on us at the hospital. We're supposed to call
when it's consistently four minutes apart."

"Great. American medicine's great, isn't it? Don't go to the
hospital when you're in pain 'cause it'll only be harder on you!"

"Okay, Eric. No speeches."

Everything I do is wrong. He closed his eyes. I'm not gonna
make it. He had had that conviction all along, despite the obvious
fact that millions of other men had managed to survive this experience.

"Oh!" Nina began to pace. "It's starting," she hissed with a
sharp, fearful intake of breath.

"What! It's only been four minutes!"

Nina was walking, stiff-legged, across the living room. "My
back, my back," she shouted in between huffs and puffs. Eric
followed her, comically hunched over, attempting to place his hand
on her constantly retreating back.

"Stand still!" he pleaded.

"I can't, I can't!" she said, moving away just as he finally got
his fist pressed against her.

"Get on the floor!"

"Goddammit! Goddammit! Goddammit!" she said, scurrying
back and forth as though she could dodge the agony. She stopped
abruptly, grabbed the thick mass of her brown hair behind her head,
pulling it taut at the scalp, and screamed: "Fuck this!"

Eric seized her, one arm going about her shoulders so she couldn't
escape, and jammed his free fist into her back. "Breathe!" he
screamed right into her ear.

She jerked her head away and defensively put a hand up to her
ear. "Ow!"

"Sorry," Eric said, twisting his hand into her mercilessly, amazed that such force could relieve pain rather than cause it.

Nina tried to keep to the exercise, but she would break off to exclaim at the pain and lose the rhythm. She kept thinking (whenever the mist of hurt lifted enough for her to regain the vista of consciousness): I hate being a woman.

PETER LOOKED DOWN AT THE FEW UNCOVERED INCHES OF BYRON'S body. After Kelso's examination—"Ten, ten," the cheerful fellow announced. "He's passed his first test"—some more disgusting things were done about the umbilical cord, and then they left Byron to lie nude under an intense heating lamp while dawdling over taking his foot- and fingerprints—"He's already got a record," a nurse wisecracked—before swaddling him in two cloth blankets, leaving only the barest minimum of his face exposed. By then Byron had cried himself into a state of unconsciousness. A blissful sleep, it seemed to Peter, who had been handed the package of his child while he sat awkwardly on the stool (the lack of armrests made holding Byron wearisome) next to Diane's head. Her lower half was presumably being replaced and sewn up; Peter certainly wasn't going to look and verify that. When he occasionally glanced at the floor beneath the operating table, he saw a bucket into which they had dumped the sponges and Lord knows what else. The items inside were soaked red, and Peter was sickened by the notion that Diane had lost a pailful of blood. Rationally, he assumed that wasn't possible, but the sight argued otherwise.

"He's beautiful," Diane kept saying in a hoarse, tired voice. Every few minutes, punctuating her awed stare, she'd repeat, "He's beautiful"—each time with a tone of discovery.

Peter looked down at the uncovered oval of Byron's face. To him it seemed nothing more than a mush of uncooked flesh. The only distinguishable things (nose and mouth) were too small to be taken seriously; his closed eyes seemed to blend seamlessly into his forehead. Why, that little stub of a nose looked as though a strong dose of sunlight could melt it. And he was so light—too insubstantial to have caused the enormous fuss around them.

"He's beautiful," she said again, amazed. And then: "Isn't he?"

He's mush, Peter thought. Unmolded clay. A transparency on which she could project any fantasy.

"Don't you think he's beautiful?" Diane asked.

But *what* is he? Peter wondered. That's really a human being? From this blob a tall version of himself would grow and one day stand, dressed in a black suit, and mourn Peter's death? Peter imagined old versions of his friends passing in front of a dark, smooth young man: Byron grown. "Your father was a good man. I'll miss him." And what would Byron be feeling? Relief. Now the trust funds would dissolve and the money come directly under his control. Now he would stand at the head of the ship, no longer second-in-command, no longer peering over the old man's shoulder at the bright blue horizon.

I will become the whimsical god of his life—idol and tormentor—someone to imitate, someone to destroy.

"Yes, he's beautiful," he finally answered.

"Hold his head up," a nurse instructed, lifting the elbow that was cradling Byron's head. "They have no neck muscles. You have to support his head."

"That's not all I have to support," Peter answered.

The anesthesiologist snorted in agreement.

Peter's awareness of these attendants had been unspecific up until now—other than Dr. Stein, faceless. To think of them otherwise, for them to be real, to accept the fact that these strangers had been staring into his wife's body like commuters stuck in a line peering into the Holland Tunnel was untenable. It seemed absurd to have to share this moment, this unique and intimate experience, with a bunch of people to whom he hadn't even been introduced. He wanted to get out of this sordid tiled place, away from his new burden and back to his comfortable home, to the dignity of seclusion. After all, these next few days, while Diane and Byron were at the hospital, might be his last chance at peace for many a year.

"I'm going to go," he said.

"What?" Diane said.

"I'll take the baby." The nurse who had been hovering over him interrupted. She practically snatched Byron away. Not that Peter resisted.

"I have to tell people," Peter remonstrated, although Diane hadn't sounded argumentative. "They're all waiting."

"When will I see you?"

"This evening."

"When are visiting hours?" Peter asked Dr. Stein, glancing in his direction and catching sight of a bloody sponge as it was tossed into the pail.

"Husbands can come anytime," the nurse answered with a hint of reproach. At what? Peter wondered.

"If the wife wants them," Stein mumbled.

"I want him," Diane said.

"All right, I won't go." Peter folded his arms and stared ahead.

He felt stupid having this personal conversation in front of the hospital people.

"No. Go. You have to call people."

Peter got up quickly before she could change her mind again, kissing her perfunctorily. "Wait," she called out, her hand pleading for his return.

Peter bent over again. She urged him down and opened her pale, dry lips. He met them reluctantly. She was lying nude, her lower half not only exposed but still sliced open. This romantic embrace seemed silly under the circumstances.

"I love you," she said with the happy, spent openness of a satisfied inamorata. It was absurd, as if they had moved their bed to the Forty-second Street IRT station and were doing their lovemaking amidst the stone-faced commuters.

"Me too," he said quickly. "I'll call from the hall and come back to visit you in recovery before going home." Peter began his stride to the enormous swinging stainless-steel doors built wide and high for the gurneys and equipment. Already he felt lighter; the heavy constriction of controlling his behavior in front of those people loosened its grip. "Bye, Byron," he called to the tiny bundle, and pushed his way out. He walked faster and faster through the hall of birthing rooms, feeling more himself with each step away from them. I'm a father, he thought with growing pride. He was eager to tell everyone the news. He felt more interesting. More real.

My son is born, he thought, studying the faces of waiting fathers, arriving mothers, bored nurses, and abstracted doctors. And Byron will be a better person than every one of these people.

Actually, the whole business had gone quite well, as well as he had hoped. He dared to think, as he dialed his mother's number on the wall phone in the outer hallway, that now things would go smoothly. And it was sweet to think, no matter how embarrassing the expression of it, that Diane loved him and enjoyed becoming a mother. It would be good for his boy.

"Hello?" his mother's voice asked.

"Hello, Grandma," he said to the phone, and got the expected satisfaction of hearing her gasp with awe and pleasure.

ERIC HAD LOST ANY TRACE OF EXCITEMENT ABOUT HAVING A BABY. He had felt some trepidation in the previous few months, but this surpassed his worst fears. With every minute, Nina's pain seemed to intensify; the prospect of hours more appalled him. Surely, once they got to the hospital and Dr. Ephron examined Nina, she would give her an epidural or a Caesarean or at least some heavy pain-killers. Nothing this horrible could be natural.

At last, they had been given permission to go to the hospital. It was now three o'clock in the morning. Nina had been in labor for twelve hours. He felt absolutely spent. But the end was in sight—provided he could find a taxi.

When they got in the elevator, even Nina seemed more relaxed. "You wait in the lobby," he said. "I'll go to the avenue for a cab."

"Don't leave me with Gomez to have the baby," she said, referring to their weird night doorman.

"That's the idea," he answered as the doors opened to the lobby. She grabbed his arm. "Please."

"Are you nuts? Of course not."

The elevator doors began to close. Eric held them back. He nodded for her to exit. "I'll tell Gomez to get the cab."

"That's a good idea." She smiled like a child and moved out confidently. But once in the lobby, she stopped in her tracks. Gomez was sprawled in the tall-backed oak chair facing the doors. His head had flopped to one side, his mouth was open, and his chest rose and fell in the steady rhythm of a deep sleep.

Nina hissed as she breathed in sharply: "Oh!"

Eric looked at his watch. "Contraction begins," he said loud, hoping to arouse Gomez.

"This isn't bad," she whispered.

"You don't have to whisper," Eric said.

Nina backed herself against the wall, closed her eyes, and took deep, slow breaths.

"Fifteen seconds!" Eric almost shouted, keeping his eyes on Gomez. "Contraction is building." Gomez snorted, lifted his head slightly, yawned, and stretched his neck, apparently about to wake up. But then Gomez nuzzled his shoulder and resumed sleeping without having opened his eyes. "Great! The entire PLO could be entering the building!"

"Shhh!" Nina said, and started to pace, quickening her respiration.

"Gomez!" Eric said.

"Leave him alone—ah!" Nina rushed to the mailboxes, put her back to them, bent forward as much as she could, and pushed against them.

A long, inquisitive grunt came out of Gomez: "Hmmmm?" But no movement.

"Thirty seconds," Eric said furiously. "Contraction is peaking."

''Comeon comeon comeon comeon!'' Nina chanted, her eyes shut tight, squeezing her hands together.

''We have to get to the hospital,'' Eric said to the ceiling.

''We'll get there, we'll get there, we'll get there.'' Nina spoke through her huffs and puffs.

''Forty-five seconds. Contraction is subsiding.'' Eric cupped his hands and shouted toward the doorman, ''Gomez! Wake up!''

''Huh?'' Gomez started up, tried to right himself by grabbing the chair's arms, but his left hand slid on the polished wood and brought the weight of his body against it, so that slowly, but inevitably, despite Gomez's cry of surprise and despair, he and the chair toppled over.

Nina laughed briefly. The pain cut it short, but she laughed again after a gasp. Eric, however, ignored the calamity, calling out: ''Gomez, my wife is in labor. Get a cab.''

Gomez, a tall, lean man with a solemn face, looked up from his position. ''I can't get up.''

''Something broken?'' Jesus, Eric thought, I'm going to have to take both of them to the hospital.

''No, no. The chair. Get it off me.''

''Sixty seconds. Contraction is over.'' Eric walked over and lifted the heavy chair. Gomez crawled a few feet away before getting up. He looked at the chair suspiciously.

''I told Gary to get another one. That one's dangerous.''

''Are you all right? Listen, she's in labor. Can you get us a cab?''

''What?'' Gomez looked at Nina, alarmed. ''What?''

''We have to go to the hospital, so—''

''Right away, right away.'' Gomez hustled out the door.

Eric sighed and returned to Nina's side. She looked pale. ''Is he getting a cab?'' she asked.

''Yeah, I just hope he doesn't get run over.''

Nina laughed reluctantly, as though it hurt. ''That was funny.''

Gomez returned, jogging in, distraught. He stopped inside the lobby doors and looked at them.

''You got one?'' Eric asked.

''There are no cabs.'' Gomez said tentatively, as though trying out a lie.

''It's three in morning! You have to look longer than that. I'll go—''

''No, no.'' Gomez turned to leave again.

''We'll both go,'' Nina said. ''I'm fine.''

''Okay,'' Eric said. He picked up her bag and extended his arm for her to take.

Gomez looked agitated. "Excuse me, excuse me," he said. Gomez went up to Eric and pulled him a few feet away from Nina.

Eric was outraged by this physical familiarity. It's what I get for being a regular guy with them, he thought. "What are you doing?"

"There are bad boys out there," Gomez whispered.

He's flipped, Eric thought. He'd always suspected Gomez was the night man because he was a nut on Thorazine and couldn't handle the heavier social tasks of the day shift. "What?"

"Hoodlums."

"We won't get mugged, Gomez."

"No! Right outside now!"

Eric looked Gomez full in the face, directly into his eyes. As he did, he realized it was the first time. Although he had often been waylaid by Gomez on late-night excursions for ice cream and been forced to dawdle at the elevator discussing the fortunes of the Mets, or the Giants, Eric had managed to keep his eyes averted, away from the final bond of seeing into Gomez's eyes, to know whatever might be there: shy worry; the glitter of excitement; the dull glaze of sadness. For Eric, once that contact happened, the person became a responsibility, someone to whom one could never again be rude without the aftereffect of guilt, someone whose feelings had to be considered with each request. Obviously that would be a grave inconvenience with doormen.

Gomez's eyes were scared, and weary from the fear, as though he had conquered the dread repeatedly, only to lose to it each time, so that the challenge held no prospect for victory.

My God, for years he's been the night man living in terror. Why doesn't he keep the door locked and stay awake? He'd feel safer.

And now, on top of his cowardice, unable to get them the cab, Gomez was embarrassed. It was his job, after all, to provide them with security. Instead, he was forcing Eric to take the risk. "I'll be all right," Eric assured him, and meant it. He doubted Gomez's ability to judge danger. And besides, Eric had grown up, as he often told people, in a tough neighborhood, had had his share of street fights, and was a big man. Prowling the city at night, being six-six and two hundred pounds, he'd never been hassled. And he didn't expect to be.

"They have a knife," Gomez whispered intensely, glancing at Nina.

"Honey, what's the matter?" Nina called out.

"You'd better wait here. It'll only take a minute for me to find a cab."

"I'll stand at the door and watch you," Gomez said with enthusiasm. He obviously felt better that he could offer some help.

Nina approached, her big stomach in the lead, towing the rest of her slowly. "I want to go with you."

"Honey! It'll take a second. Stay here." Eric let go of the overnight bag (to have his hands free) and quickly walked out the inner-lobby doors to prevent any further discussion.

As he approached the exit to the street, he heard them. There was a radio playing rock music and a rhythmic tapping on something metallic and hollow. Eric decided to walk out boldly, not glance at them or move in the opposite direction, but to behave as though they were harmless—as, indeed, he assumed they were. At least to him.

The emptiness of Ninth Street was disconcerting; usually busy during the day and well into the evening with cars and cabs going crosstown, at three in the morning there was no traffic to be seen in the orange haze of the streetlamps. The only life was the presence of three black teenagers clustered around a fire hydrant. Their heads turned at the sound of Eric's exit from the building. In the harsh light their faces loomed at him, almost glowing. One backed away immediately, his arms hanging loosely, ready for flight. The tallest had a joint in his hand; yellow smoke burned from its tip directly into his right eye. He closed the lid deliberately, a puppet winking, but didn't move the joint.

"Hey, man!" he called out, greeting a friend. But his body was still, ominous.

"Any fucking cabs out here?" Eric said, and walked past them, off the sidewalk, looking east up Ninth. There were no cars in sight for more than two blocks, and only a pair of forlorn headlights in the distance promised a break. But even that wasn't a cab. Eric cursed himself for using the garage in the building. It was closed from two to six in the morning. On Tenth Street there was all-night parking, but that cost an extra thirty bucks a month. The rule of going first class—any attempt to escape its tyranny ended in punishment. This little attempt at a savings had never once been inconvenient, but what a ghastly accounting there might be tonight.

He heard the kids whisper behind him in a rapid chorus, punctuated by a contemptuous snort of laughter. "I don't take cabs, man!" the tall one said. Eric had his back to the teenagers—his shoulders tingling, as though developing radar to protect him from surprise—and he couldn't tell if the comment was seriously addressed to him. He decided to ignore it.

The traffic lights in the distance turned green, but apart from the lone car, no others appeared. He turned around to look toward the uptown avenue. Only after Eric found himself staring at the trio did he realize it seemed like a reaction to the leader's remark.

"You hear what I say?" the tall one spoke. He sucked on the joint and offered it to the others, stretching his arm behind him, the joint pinched daintily between two fingers. It was taken.

Eric didn't want to be this person standing outside a building with a wife in labor confronted by the three stoned black teenagers spoiling for an incident. The sociological logic of the situation, reducing him and them to blank numbers in a simple equation, undoing the romance, the pleasant fear, of him and Nina at the instant of his child's beginning—this was to be the memory? These stupid kids menacing him? His conversion from a young street-smart New Yorker to some timid bozo unable to get his wife to the hospital?

"Look!" Eric yelled. "My wife is in labor! I'm gonna get a fucking cab! Do you understand!" he shouted at an even louder volume than he had begun. It did him good, expelling not only tension but fear as well into the orange haze. The kids stood still, almost like statues, children absorbing an expected reproof. "Either help me, kill me, or get the fuck out of here!"

"Hey, man," the tall one said slowly.

The lobby door opened. Nina appeared, carrying the little bag, its size ludicrous by contrast with her bloated stomach. "Eric," she said in a calm, intimate voice, as if they were in bed together going over the events of the day. "Let's start walking. Maybe we'll get one on the way."

Behind her, skulking in the doorway, Gomez shouted in a tone of nervous bravado: "The cops are parked around the corner! At the deli. Maybe they give you a ride."

What a stupid transparent lie, Eric thought, disgusted.

The teenagers thought so too. The one who until now had backed away, had seemed most ready to flee laughed explosively and stepped forward to answer Gomez. "Kiss my ass, motherfucker," he said, giggling from the dope.

"Watch your language!" Gomez scolded like an old woman.

"I don't watch shit!" the giggler screamed, extending his right hand, a whooshing sound announcing the switchblade's existence before the orange light glowed on its surface.

Eric felt himself shrink, his huge frame, filled out by his studious exercising, broad at the shoulder, narrow at the waist, his long arms, powerful enough to snap the kid's arm in half, his thick thighs, and elastic calves, strong enough to bound over in a stride:

the adult renovation on the puny body of his childhood detonated in a puff of demolition, reversing history, replacing the skyscraper with frail clapboard. He was little again.

We're going to die and I can't stop it.

Gomez seemed to lose his mind, his former panic replaced with insane boldness. He came out of the lobby doors and shouted at the kids: "What's the matter with you! You crazy! You want to go to jail!"

"I'll open you up!" the kid said, and made two slashes in the air to illustrate how.

Get between them, Eric told himself.

"You punk! You don't have the *cojones*!" Gomez answered.

Nina walked away from the group, straight at Eric and the gutter. "There's a cab!" she said with delight, and no fear, in her voice.

Eric turned to see a free taxi glide across the street, its turning signal blinking, angling straight for him, a guided missile adjusting with its target's dodges. He stepped back to preserve his toes. The driver stopped and smiled at him knowingly. "What hospital?"

"Beth Israel," Nina answered, and opened the door.

"That's easy," the driver said.

"I don't want to fuck with you," Eric heard Gomez say while Eric automatically followed Nina into the cab. The leader of the teenagers had turned to face the taxi, ready to challenge it. Gomez shouted and waved his hands disdainfully at the kid with the switchblade. The knife bearer remained in a melodramatic crouch, still pointing the blade where Gomez had stood earlier, ignoring the back and forth of Gomez's angry pacing.

"Trouble?" the driver asked them, staring at the scene. "Should we do something?"

Nina leaned across Eric and rolled his window down. "We're all right, Gomez! Thank you! Go to sleep!"

The leader of the kids, his face as still as the impassive mask of a sentinel, moved his lips. "Good luck," he said.

Gomez seemed to pay no attention to Nina. He continued to lecture the switchblade holder. "What you mean making all this noise at night? People are sleeping!"

"We can go," Nina concluded. The driver nodded and pulled away, taking the turn at the corner without slowing, so the cab swung out wide. Nina toppled into Eric's lap. She smiled wanly at him.

And then her face scrunched up in pain. "Here comes another one," she said.

2

DIANE WAS AFRAID. SHE STUDIED THE BUBBLES IN THE IV line, telling herself they couldn't be air pockets that would enter her vein, travel to her heart, and stop it—but fearing anyway that they might be. And she hurt. A pain that had begun as a dull ache was now intense, pulsing from the base of her skull to her forehead, as if someone were trying to pry it off.

She complained. Slowly, very slowly, her complaints were answered. The headache (what a diagnostic understatement of her agony) was a side effect of her epidural, she was told. Sometimes during surgery it moved around, becoming, in effect, a spinal tap, and led to some sort of fluid movement that caused a severe headache. They didn't want to give her a potent painkiller; she got a part Tylenol, part codeine tablet instead. That merely reduced the wrenching, stabbing pain to a bruised, throbbing hurt—a taunting reminder of life without the top of her head coming off, thereby making the resumption of intense pain more dismaying. She always seemed to need the next dose of Tylenol/codeine an hour before she was allowed to have it.

And then, any movement of the lower half of her torso was scary. Sometimes she suspected the incision in her belly wasn't closed and her insides were spilling out. Usually her body sent a sharp order of distress, freezing her in place, wincing until the wave of nauseating weakness, soreness, and ache was overwhelmed by the oppressive pounding in her skull. It was then she felt grateful for the headache.

She hated the television in her room. It was mounted above the molding, way up in the air, positioned for a platform bed that hadn't been built. The location gave a better view of its dirty plastic bottom than the broadcast. When off, the blank screen appeared to be

31

a gray that she speculated was a layer of dust. When she turned it on, the picture looked old, the colors from another era, the shape excessively curved, reminding her of being alone on Saturday mornings watching farm programs while her mother slept late.

She dreaded visitors and phone calls. At her request, Peter had turned off the phone and told everyone but Diane's mother and his parents and stepparents not to come for a few days. But Diane also resented the absence of company. Every desire and instinct were accompanied by an equally strong reluctance and revulsion.

She felt deserted and betrayed by the world. Her doctor had refused to allow her to lie in with Byron until she felt stronger. She didn't argue or even disagree. Still, it wasn't her choice. Her baby had been carried off and was delivered only to be fed (or failing to feed) with an immediate announcement by the nurse of when he would be recollected. Even her brief times alone with Byron made her aware of her failures. Byron seemed uninterested in eating, so she was useless instead of crucial; she didn't have the strength to get up and put him back in the Lucite cart the hospital used to wheel the babies from the nursery to the rooms, so instead of being the most trustworthy caretaker, she was the least reliable. His visits were an hour long at most, so she had yet to diaper him or rock him to sleep (he never seemed fully awake anyway), and although she made the effort to hold him up against her shoulder to burp him (it hurt some muscle below), nothing like a belch had ever been heard. She longed to feel maternal, for a rising tide of sentiment to overwhelm what she thought ought to be trivialities—her discomfort, her fatigue, her loneliness—but she was dead to Byron. He seemed utterly foreign, a misdelivered package.

Her mother, Lily, appeared on the first day, looking radiant. In her old age, Lily's jowls, her thick glasses, and her crumpling skin had made her rather gargoylish—Peter once said at a drunken dinner party that he reconsidered marrying Diane after seeing what time had done to Lily—but on this day the wrinkling of age was ironed by Lily's joy in her grandchild.

"He's beautiful!" Lily exclaimed before she was halfway in the door. She had stopped off at the nursery and viewed Byron through the glass, swaddled in his blanket, his eyes closed, his mouth pursed, concentrated on rediscovering his former peace. Lily came into the room, stood still several feet away from Diane's bed, clasped her little, pudgy hands together, and repeated: "He's beautiful!"

Diane was already exhausted by her. Diane knew Lily's enthusiasm would be set on high for Diane to scale, or otherwise Diane would be left behind, watching her mother enjoy an exhilaration that, by rights, belonged only to herself. Diane tried to beam a smile, but it must have looked queasy.

"How are you, darling?" Lily asked, lowering her tone sympathetically. She moved toward the bed, took Diane's cheeks in her hands, squeezed, and made a whooshing sound of pleasure and possession. "You look pale."

"I've just had a baby."

"That was yesterday. You shouldn't be in pain now. What do the doctors say?"

"Ma, I've had a C section! That's abdominal surgery. You don't recover from that in a day." Already Diane was whining like a teenager. Barely thirty seconds gone and fifteen years had been lopped off; if her mother stayed for longer than two minutes, they might be wheeling Diane into the nursery. Where was Peter? He had promised to be there as a buffer.

"My friend Harriet's daughter had a C section—she was on her feet in three days. Maybe you should get another doctor. Doctors aren't perfect, you know. They make mistakes."

Diane closed her eyes. Why did she have a cartoon mother? It was hard to have nightmares as bad as the reality of Lily.

"Hello!" Peter entered, looking disgustingly fit. He was dressed in his festive Waspy summer clothes, ready to board the yacht at the Cape. "Hello, Lily! You look lovely"

"Your son is beautiful!" Lily said, also grabbing Peter by the cheeks and smacking her lips on his. That was a remarkable expression of warmth from Lily to Peter; she had never accepted him into her heart either publicly or privately, presumably because he wasn't Jewish. "What difference does it make?" Diane had once asked her, exasperated. "Really, Ma? What difference does it make?" "It makes a difference," Lily had said, nodding to herself, her tone heavy with accepted sorrow, going to the ovens bravely.

"You too, huh?" Peter said cheerfully.

"Don't you think he's beautiful?" Lily pleaded.

Peter laughed good-naturedly. He strolled over to Diane and kissed her. "You really are mother and daughter."

"What are you talking about!" Diane snapped at him. Peter couldn't have come up with a more infuriating remark if he'd worked on it all night.

Peter turned to Lily. "Exactly what Diane kept saying right after the birth. 'He's beautiful, he's beautiful,' " he imitated, with a hint of a Yiddish accent.

"But he is!" Lily mocked a protest. "I'm not prejudiced just because I'm his grandmother. I'm very objective."

"What do you mean?" Diane insisted to Peter. "When did I keep saying to you, 'He's beautiful, he's beautiful'?"

"At the very instant of his birth." Peter seemed full of himself, enunciating his words like a preening actor, his eyes darting from Diane to Lily to measure his effect. "You were madly in love with him the moment you saw him. I was green with envy—knew I was finished. Hopeless. I'll be lucky if you remember to set a place for me at dinner."

"Don't be jealous of your own son," Lily said, now perfectly serious.

How stupid, Diane thought. I don't even know that baby. I'm scared of it, and he's concocted the reverse to portray himself as a victim. I lie here with my head broken, my stomach split, my thighs lumpy, my breasts swollen—and he plays the jilted lover, no doubt anticipating excuses for his future indifference and neglect.

Had she made a ghastly mistake? Peter had told her no to the idea of having a baby, in his mild but utterly resolved manner, over and over, never wavering, never, in even the most hypothetical discussion, conceding that one day he might change his mind. But time was passing, faster and faster as she left thirty behind. She had wasted several years after college, trying to decide what to do (really it had been an attempt to find something besides the obvious, anything other than the law), so that she was, in general, three years behind everyone. Four in some cases, since she had gone to private schools that didn't believe in skipping, no matter how bright the student. And she had been bright—effortlessly, democratically achieving A's, without regard to the area. School had been the theater in which she always got the leading part, resounding applause, and rave reviews. She missed it.

Diane longed to be her former taut self, snapping awake, grabbing her books, her notebooks filled with her precise handwriting, to begin another long day, surrounded by friends eager to please and impress her, while she pleased and impressed her professors. She began to weep at the thought of its loss.

"Diane," Peter said.

"Darling," her mother said. Lily's big face was in front of her, the eyes swimming in the glasses, fish grown too large to be contained by their bowl. "We're all very proud of you," Lily said, and hugged Diane, the small, thick hands squeezing hard.

Diane heard herself sob. Peter stood still, his face distant and puzzled, a baffled stranger. The first year they were lovers, he liked to kiss her flat stomach, so smooth and tight that the hipbones made visible points in the air, fins gliding through her undulating sea.

Peter would surround her navel with kisses and then run his tongue into it. Tickled, she'd suck her nonbelly in even more so that the bones of her ribs appeared, impressed by her olive skin. Finally he'd put his mouth to her sex, his hands grasping her thighs, his fingers almost able to touch his thumbs, so thin were the tightly packed sausages of her legs.

All that was gone now. Gone forever. Her stomach had a tangled bulge in it, like a duffel bag sloppily stuffed with a few dirty towels, and the definition between her buttocks and her thighs had evaporated, the sausage skin made mushy by nature's fierce boiling, the meat inside now a loose jelly, unevenly distributed, imminently threatening to ooze out.

"My baby." Her mother's voice surrounded her, and her head was embraced, hidden from the world. Lily's perfume was infiltrated by other odors—decay, disinfectant—and her own skin felt clammy against her mother's roughened, hard cheeks.

"I'll be all right. I'm sorry," Diane blubbered in the auditorium of Lily's arms, still sobbing.

She pushed her head out of her mother's clutches and saw Peter again. Peter looked much younger than she felt. She seemed to be a middle-aged woman and he a teenager.

It had been a terrible mistake. She liked schedules. They made sense of life, pushed you ahead to make decisions that otherwise would be stuck in place by the ultimate quagmire—the meaninglessness of everything. It had come time to have a child. And so she had done it, Peter's reluctance notwithstanding. She'd left the diaphragm in its case, smearing some jelly on her fingers and vaguely on her vaginal lips to maintain olfactory consistency. These precautions were almost insufficient; after the great sex (she had really released into the pleasure, her head filled with images of the possible creation below) Peter suspiciously wondered why he hadn't bumped against the diaphragm during her orgasm, like always. He had never before mentioned that that happened, just one of many intimacies that she believed he neglected to share. She shrugged her shoulders and he didn't press the point. For two months she deceived him, and just as she regretted it and stopped, she felt the first soreness and subtle firming in her breasts.

Peter had asked her to consider an abortion—yet another chance to avoid this disaster. They had terrible fights every night for a week, and then he had made his grand speech: "If you insist, then we'll do it. But I'm not responsible for the care. Don't expect me to sacrifice my work, or my social life. If you think I'm going to be a 'new' father, you're wrong." Diane had listened dutifully,

with a sneer on her lips to show him she knew he didn't really mean
it.

She looked at him now, quavering in her watery vision as her
unstoppable sobs shook her: Peter was young, embarrassed, and
pitying. It was a terrible mistake, she thought. I've destroyed my
body and my marriage. And sooner or later I will destroy my baby.

NINA LAY ON THE BEACH, NAKED, THE WATER RISING HIGHER ON
her belly with each wave, the bright sun glowing through her eyelids, insisting on her consciousness. . . .

"It's starting," Eric said. What was he doing here? He was supposed to be back at the summer house, making calls.

The water was lapping at her mouth, insinuating at the corners,
draining down into her throat. Move up, she told herself. But her
body was paralyzed. And it was raging now, the gentle surf churning up her legs. She had to move. Soon the water would overwhelm
her completely and she'd die.

"Nina! Nina! Do your breathing!"

But I'll drown and die if I open my mouth.

From the endless expanse loomed a huge iron hook, driving
straight at her baby-full belly, sure to tear her apart—and she was
awake, back in the tiny birthing room, machines beeping, Dr.
Ephron's cold black eyes staring at her. "Breathe, Nina!"

Her back broke apart. She felt it for sure this time, the whole of
her spine popping out, all of her draining to the floor. She grabbed
at the nearest hand to hold on, to keep at least her head as part of
this world. Eric took it and she saw his face, although knowing it
was him had nothing to do with the way he appeared. He seemed
to be a completely different person. A little boy she'd known in
school, or passed in the streets.

"I can't stand it, I can't, I can't—"

"Stay with it, Nina," Ephron said. "This is the worst it will
be."

"I need more stuff for the pain!"

"I don't want a sleepy baby! Breathe! Breathe!" Ephron grabbed
her cheeks and forced Nina to look her in the eyes. She did the
breathing for Nina to imitate and Nina found herself panting along
stupidly.

She was merely a head now, floating in space, carried about by
Ephron and Eric. They'd lost the bottom of her forever. "I can't do
this anymore. We'll go home and come back later," she pleaded.

"Okay," Ephron said approvingly. "Rest now."

"It is over?" Nina asked, and she was back on the beach, baking in the sun. Her lips were so dry. But something cool slid over them. Sleeping was so beautiful, so simple, so gentle and warm. She was too close to the shore. The tide was rising again, lapping up over her belly, splashing on her mouth. Move up, move up, get away from it.

"Nina!" Eric the little boy shouted. "Don't push!"

"Breathe, Nina! Breathe, Nina!" Ephron's hand passed over her eyes, rubbing her forehead. "Breathe with me!"

She huffed and huffed and huffed and huffed, thinking each moment was the last she could sustain life.

Ephron said, "I'm going to take a look, Nina."

"No!" Nina tried to gain control of her body. Why couldn't she get up and run? Why was she helpless? "No! No!" she begged. That bastard Eric was holding her down. Was he? Was he hugging her?

"Oh, my God!" The doctor had pushed her insides like pressing a balloon. She was going to explode, pieces of her would be everywhere. . . .

"Okay," Ephron said. "I'm sorry." She came in close, her face huge. "We're going to push now. I want you to push out, push from your rectum, like you're having the biggest bowel movement of your life. Don't push from here"—she made a gesture—"push from your rectum." She turned to Eric and spoke.

The sky was black. Ice cream fell in the sand, breading it for broiling. She was inflated—grown big, big enough to fill a building, blot out a sun.

"It's starting!"

Eric poked at her, his arms fussing with her. What was he doing? Was she beginning to float?

The beeping, the room, Ephron slapped into her consciousness. "Breathe in, breathe out," Ephron said, and the horrible surge of heat and force mushroomed inside. "Push!"

She clenched herself. I am iron, I am iron, she thought.

"Push, Nina! Push, Nina!"

I am God come to create! I am steel!

"Push, Nina! Push, Nina!"

PETER STOPPED AGAIN AT THE NURSERY WINDOW BEFORE LEAVING the hospital. He couldn't pick out Byron immediately; that distressed him, although he knew it wasn't a fair test. Outside of visiting hours, the infants were almost totally covered in their Lucite bins (flattened really, by their fiercely tucked-in blankets), faces down, leaving only hair, ears, and a glimpse of nose to distinguish one from another. Byron's head, bald but for a fine down, was similar to four others, and Peter could remember nothing unusual about his ears to look for.

Peter squinted at the goofy blue- or pink-bordered labels, trying to pick out the *B* of Byron and the *H* of Hummel; the initials were all he could hope to spot through glass smudged by the anxious vanities of a dozen set of grandparents. He found Byron at last: at the far end, against a wall, next to a vacant incubator. Byron was still, the little form of his body visible against the taut cotton blanket. His big, slightly protruding eyes were shut; the lids had the lifeless dignity of cool marble.

Peter stared at Byron, transfixed. His son was unmoving, except for an occasional worried pursing of his lips. Peter thought nothing. He felt a proud sadness, pleasure in Byron's existence, but dismay at the expanse of his uncertain future. After many minutes, Peter found himself thinking it was hard on Byron to be in that big, bright room with all those other babies. One of them was screaming its head off, and although that didn't seem to awaken the others, Peter couldn't help imposing his adult sense of how frightened Byron must feel: to be thrust into the world and find it a place flooded with fluorescent light, crying creatures, and giant black women in stiff, rustling garb who, from time to time, would toss one about, removing things, wiping things, adding things. And soon someone would come and slice off part of his penis, probably while chatting about the stock market or the traffic on the FDR Drive.

The last thought, of the circumcision, obsessed him. Everybody knew it was unnecessary. Diane, however, had been adamant. She had accepted his refusal to tolerate a *bris*, but the notion of an uncircumcised son actually caused her to laugh scornfully, as though Peter had proposed something pretentious and ludicrous, such as giving Byron a gold crown to wear at the playground.

When Peter forced Diane to discuss it seriously, she had found several books on child rearing that maintained although there was no medical benefit to circumcision, father and son should be similarly outfitted, lest the difference cause anxiety in the child. It had been done to Peter, so—

Yes, it was done to me, Peter thought, so how bad could it be?

He wanted to wave good-bye or blow Byron a kiss (just walking away after such a long communion seemed almost rude), but he was made self-conscious by the sympathetic and slightly patronizing gaze of the nurse. Peter waited until the nurse turned her back before waving his farewell to Byron. Peter kept up the wave so long, however, that the nurse caught him at it anyway. In response, made mute by the glass partition, the nurse mouthed, "Good night, Daddy." Peter was disgusted.

He left humiliated and stood uncomfortably in the peculiar carton-shaped elevator (we are eggs, he thought) next to a lot of pale, puffy faces that housed enervated eyes. Peter held his breath, convinced the air must contain an infinity of deadly germs. With each stride across the marble lobby, Peter hurried toward life, through the swivel doors, and trotted out of New York Hospital's cul-de-sac for First Avenue, where the cars rode a concrete conveyor belt in awkward starts and stops.

Peter was late for his dinner at Rachel's and these days it was a mistake for him to give her any cause for complaint. And he wasn't lucky in catching a taxi, so that by the time he entered the somewhat dark vestibule of the town house and rang the buzzer for Rachel's apartment, he suspected (as always seemed the case with him and women) that things would begin badly.

Indeed, when he had finished trudging up the four flights, he found Rachel waiting at her door with a sad tilt of her head, biting her lower lip. She said immediately, despite the pretty green dress and heavy makeup, "I think we should have canceled."

"Nonsense," he answered, and led her in, shutting the door before embracing her. Her wide mouth remained closed and dry, although she arched her body into him pliantly. "I've missed you."

"Oh, God," she answered, and buried her head in his chest.

He looked down at her curly head of black hair, parted severely on one side. The white of her scalp gleamed in the tangle and reminded him of his son's small head: both were fragile and in his care. He didn't feel unhappy, disgusted by his desires and absurd immorality. He felt exuberant. "Cheer up," he said, pulling her out from hiding against his body.

She looked shyly into his eyes and her chin quivered. But she spoke sharply: "That's a pretty hopeless request."

"No, it isn't," he insisted, and leaned forward, kissing her lightly, backing away, and going in again, this time pressing harder, staying longer, parting the lips slightly. "You're sweet," he whispered.

"Yeah, yeah," she whispered, and ducked her head down to avoid another kiss. "What do you want to drink?" she continued, and walked away from him, down the short, narrow hallway, into her one-room apartment.

Once, presumably, the Chelsea town house had been a family residence and this small box of a room had belonged to the maid, the nanny or served as the nursery. The small brick fireplace still remained; but what must have been detailed moldings were now covered by featureless plasterboard, and the pretty lead-glass windows had become blank squares of Thermopane, their metal casings painted white in a futile effort to conceal their modernity. The first time Peter had seen the apartment it had been in a state of college-girl disarray. The sleeper couch was still open from the previous night (embarrassed, she had immediately closed it up, not bothering to straighten the sheets, so that one end continued to wink out even after the cushions were replaced), there were clothes everywhere, and a portable typewriter and a portable television were sharing space on the round butcher-block table. Beside them were an overflowing ashtray and several take-out coffees, one of them still half full.

Tonight, however, everything was in order or, at least, in the order it would appear for a social evening. The couch was a couch, the butcher-block table was set for two, and both the television and typewriter were put away on the white shelving that framed either side of the fireplace. Even the last was dressed for the occasion; several small, gray pieces of wood were stacked, unlit, inside. The results might have seemed pathetic to most, but knowing Rachel, knowing what it cost her to admit she wanted his good opinion, to masquerade as domestically female in any way, Peter was impressed with her bravery, no matter how small the tangible results.

"Do you want wine or scotch?" she asked.

Wine.

"How's Diane?" Rachel asked after his wife's health with a remarkable absence of tension, hostility, or curiosity.

"Ugh." The memory of that scene in the hospital room weighed him down onto the couch. "She's got postpostpartum blues. Raging hormones."

"Who doesn't these days?" Rachel said, her quick comic timing running smoothly. "God, I'm horrible. I can't open this," she added, bringing the bottle of red wine to Peter with the cork only slightly lifted out by her primitive opener. Peter had to hold the bottle between his feet and pull with both hands before succeeding in an almost explosive release. He looked absurd right afterward, hanging on to the corkscrew for dear life, the bottle still between his feet, a monkey botching a man's job.

"Cheers," Rachel said. "Let's see if you can get it to your mouth like that."

"Why don't you get a decent corkscrew? This is a joke."

She held out a glass for him to fill. "What should we drink to—

your newborn baby? Or maybe to a second child?'' She looked at him coldly, her black, black eyes challenging him. ''Isn't this fun?''

He started to pour. ''It's going to be.''

ERIC FELT LIKE A MURDERER, A POISONER WHO HAS ADMINISTERED a dose strong enough to kill, but not kill quickly, and is forced to watch his victim's death agony, the killer's remorse and terror mounting even as he knows he cannot undo the deed. Nina had fallen apart in front of him, an exhausted, cursing, delusional wreck, and he was reduced to a wide-eyed child, speechless with fright.

Eric's duties as a coach had been superseded hours before, first by one of the nurses and then by Dr. Ephron. Nina had shown absolutely no respect for Eric's instructions. At one point, she answered him, ''Fuck off. *You* breathe!'' Not that she spoke to Ephron any differently. ''Get your hands off me, asshole!'' Nina had screamed during one of the internal examinations. My God, she was a tough lady underneath all that dreamy contemplativeness and girlish yearning for cuddles and hugs.

During transition Eric changed his evaluation. Nina wasn't tough. The cursing, the wildness of her desire to be free of the pain showed a remarkable lack of endurance. Although he understood that she was going through the worst kind of delivery, over twenty hours of severe back labor, nevertheless her endless requests for painkillers (that had eventually provoked Ephron, he suspected, into overdosing Nina, since she was way too sleepy, passing out in between contractions) seemed cowardly and immature to him. Although Eric hated to think that—to criticize someone who is dying horribly of a poison you've injected didn't strike Eric as polite—still, along with his awe at Nina's free expression of rage, he was disappointed by her lack of guts.

Eric had another preoccupation while he waited in the trench for the next round of shelling—namely, whether Gomez was back asleep in his chair or lying dead in a pool of blood on Ninth Street. Along with that came the humiliating memory of his own cowardice and passivity. He had been impressed with Nina's behavior on the street, until, in a discussion while they waited for the nurse to give her an enema, he discovered that Nina had never seen the switchblade; indeed, she argued vehemently that it didn't exist. Until then, because Nina and the cabdriver had been so casual at the scene, Eric assumed he had exaggerated Gomez's jeopardy. But if Nina didn't know about the knife, then perhaps they *had* made a fatal error. Eric didn't want to bring his child into the world already owing God one life.

Such thoughts were driven from his mind by the increased pace of Nina's agony. He had a mounting dread of the end result. Ephron seemed nervous now. At first, her reaction to Nina's pain had been impatient and stern. Ephron pushed Eric out of the way and took over coaching Nina, shouting at her, holding her head so she'd make eye contact, even scolding her. Eric got angry at Ephron, wanted to fire her on the spot, but of course, that was impractical. For a while Ephron's brutality worked. Nina did the breathing, and it seemed to distract her from the pain. But when the internal heart monitor (a clear disk smeared with a sticky ointment) was inserted inside Nina onto the baby's head—the thin multicolored wires running out of Nina to the beeping machine made it seem as though she had a phone inside—Nina had to lie flat on her back to avoid disconnection. The pain then overwhelmed everything, and Ephron started administering drugs.

They'd been warned repeatedly that hospital procedures such as the internal heart monitor made back labor worse, that painkillers didn't really stop the hurt; they simply disoriented the patient, making the memory less vivid in time, but not soothing it at the moment. Ultimately, what they had learned merely made it clear that with back labor everything would conspire against them. Eric told himself to insist to Ephron that they disconnect the machine and let Nina get on her feet so the pressure on her spine would be lessened, but he knew that the counterargument would be the danger of not tracking the fetus's heart—that if something did go wrong, and the baby died, Eric would have to live with the responsibility for a lifetime.

This situation, which made all the childbirth advice and training useless, reminded Eric of his work as an investment counselor. What was Nina's pain worth? It seemed like a stock decision in the midst of a panic. If you hang on, you can come out a big winner most of the time, but there is always the once-in-a-lifetime catastrophe to fear, the slight chance whose consequences are so grave that no victory is worth the risk.

So he let events topple on him, not wanting the burden of decision to fall on him, preferring someone else to take the responsibility of disaster. But he hated himself for this, knew that it was his worst fault, that it had been his father's weakness, that it was what held him back from being a great man.

And reliance on anyone else was always wrong. He could see Ephron's confidence and resolve weaken. Nina's wild thrashing and incoherent pleas got stronger and more urgent, rather than diminishing, and Ephron's predictions of when the end would come, when Nina could begin to push, kept being wrong. It was over an hour longer than Ephron had originally guessed, and Nina hardly seemed human. Her skin was like translucent china; her pupils were huge, filled with terror and confusion; her rich brown hair was soaked, a colorless wet mop stuck to her skull. She seemed so weak, barely able to lift her head, that to expect her to have enough strength to push out the baby was absurd. Always, always, it had been Eric's assumption that Nina's giving birth was safe, that there were no real risks—he hadn't even really considered that the baby might be brain-damaged or malformed—and he had certainly never worried that a nineteenth-century event such as Nina's death might occur.

But now Ephron's nervousness, the sudden appearance of a resident, and two other nurses opened an abyss he had never looked into or guessed might be in his path. He saw Nina dead and him alone.

Now, at last, Nina had been told to push. He tried to brace her as he was supposed to, but she had no muscularity to buck up, she seemed made of clammy, boneless flesh. Her attempt to push was pathetic, all of it coming from her neck and face, rather than from below as it should.

Out of the corner of his eye, he saw a red light flash on the monitor, followed by rapid beeping. Ephron and the resident exchanged looks, but what they said to each other was lost because Nina was hoarsely begging him, "Is it out? Is it coming out?"

"You're doing great, honey," he said, and let her slip back into a delirious sleep. I've killed her, he realized. To have a stupid replica of myself, I've killed this good woman.

DIANE THOUGHT: THEY'VE LEFT A SCALPEL INSIDE ME. MAYBE A clamp. There is something large, mobile, and sharp in my intestines. In the night of the hospital—hushed talk from the nurses' station, occasional laughter, the whisper of a patient's slippers en route to the lounge for a cigarette, the soft flop of an orderly's mop—she became certain that the rippling movements in her belly and the stabbing jolts in her bowels couldn't simply be gas built up by an inactive system.

They asked, "Any flatulence yet?" every time she complained, but their persistence didn't persuade her. Farting couldn't possibly relieve this. Her headache was gone now—evaporated by a sweaty afternoon nap—but this was worse, pressure building inside, a thick rope twisting against raw skin, pushing on her sore incision, appearing in her dreams as a snake she had swallowed, weakening her legs, and dismaying her appetite.

She was awake when they brought a wailing Byron in for a 2:00 A.M. feeding. This time he clamped onto her nipple immediately, a fierce warm sucking engine for a few seconds, desperate, thirsting. Then he lapsed into sleep, his lids shutting as if weighted, his little nostrils resting on her swollen skin. She depressed the point of contact with her finger so he could breathe and nudged his cheek to rouse him. He sucked again a few times, but then his body shuddered into sleep, overwhelmed by pleasure. She cuddled his littleness in her arms. His mouth, open with exhaustion, slid partly off her. The sight of her expanded breast, the thick nipple projecting like a bullet at his little face made her feel big, potent, and full of affection.

Byron started suddenly. His mouth closed to find succor. In that half-off position his hard little gums bit right onto the nipple. Diane screamed from the pain and yanked him away. Byron's eyes and nose collapsed together, his mouth opened wide in silent agony, and then a piercing cry of betrayal and loss shattered the hospital hush, while his little arms yearned out clumsily, pleading for something to hold. She clutched him to her, frightened and humiliated.

"Oh, baby, baby, Mommy loves you, Mommy loves you," she begged him, embarrassed, convinced his cries had exposed her to the whole maternity wing, to every mother in Manhattan as incompetent and insensitive. "I'm sorry, I'm sorry, I'm sorry," she pleaded, filling his open, agonized mouth with her nipple to alert him that his desire was still there to be had. He finally got the message and gnawed away frantically for a while, before he sighed deeply and passed out again.

She kept at it faithfully, rousing him, careful now to make sure her nipples weren't in danger, tapping him on the back with a finger to keep him awake, and, as promised by the books, slowly, but surely, he seemed to get the idea, that persistence was rewarded with actual milk. After a while, her unused breast tingled, abruptly and uncomfortably alive, numbed nerves prickling to consciousness—and the leak of moisture that quickly followed proved she had at last succeeded.

He was feeding! He was getting real milk; the transfer of her life, the illnesses she had fought off, every genetic asset, was flowing from her to him—she had succeeded. The heavy weight of dismay, discomfort, and despair lifted off; at last, her energy surged, lights and heat turning on in the family home after a long absence.

She leaned forward and kissed his little brow—soft, raw with newness. His lids opened; his jaw stopped working; the wide, unfocused liquid eyes peered unknowingly at her. And then they came together; the pupils narrowed; he seemed to see her.

"Hello, baby," she said gently. "I'm your mommy."

His eyes shut and his mouth worked again, at a regular pace now, no longer wanting, but taking it in, taking from her, with the calm of trust and love.

NINA WOKE UP COLD BENEATH HER BEDROOM WINDOW. AIR BLEW on her uncovered legs. She had fallen out of bed. She heard them laugh downstairs, parents enjoying a mysterious life, unknown to her. She couldn't move. She called out. She was freezing to death. Somehow she got up and started to run, run down the hallway to the staircase, but it receded with each step, the walls lengthening, the floor buckling. . . .

"Okay, Nina, okay, Nina! Let's try again. It's starting."

I'm here in the hospital. I'm about to have a baby. She found Eric's face, a nervous smile. "Breathe in, out."

"Push, Nina!" Ephron shouted. "Push hard!"

I can do this! It felt so good to explode out, to finish.

"Push from your rectum! Push hard! Okay, breathe in, breathe out. Here comes another."

I can do this, I can do this, I've made it, I've made it.

"Big push now, Nina!"

Come on out, baby, come out of my life, free me, free me.

"All right, dear. Cleansing breath." Ephron looked sorry. She said something. "We're going to move into OR. We may have to do an emergency C section."

"Is it all right?" There was such sadness in Ephron's voice, such loss and confusion on Eric's face.

"There's some fetal stress. I don't think we can wait for you to push baby out. You'll sleep through it. Everything will be fine."

"Eric—" He grasped her hand. What was he saying? "They're putting me to sleep?" What did he say?

"All right," Ephron said. "Let's try one more time, Nina. It's happening again. Push hard, baby's almost out, let's push him out."

"Come on, Nina!" Eric said, so sadly, like a good-bye.

She felt the horrible quaking below. I have to do this, I have to do this.

"Push, Nina! Come on, push!"

Finish! Finish! Finish! Finish!

"Good, Nina! Push! Push hard!"

I'm doing it. Come on, baby! Finish!

It was over!

She didn't feel the awful pressure, the draining weight. She was so happy. She looked at them.

Eric kissed her hand.

"Let's go," Ephron said. "We'll do a C section."

"It's not out?" Nina pleaded. The room started to move. There were so many people around her and the light got bright. "It's not over?"

"Everything's fine," Eric said.

I couldn't do it. I never finish, she realized, and fell, fell down onto the cold floor, beneath an empty window. I never finish, she called out to the merry voices below. I can never finish.

RACHEL GAVE HIM A DINNER OF LINGUINE AND PESTO. WHILE Peter mixed them together, dyeing the white pasta green, he talked of Byron and Diane, coloring his true feelings dark, not black, not melodramatically miserable, but the brighter tones were absent: pride in Byron's existence, and respect for Diane's competence, tinted with fear of responsibility and boredom with staid values.

"Isn't the baby going to hurt her chances for a partnership at Wilson, Pickering?" Rachel asked, focused, as always, on women's careers.

"I thought it might, but she says no, that's old-fashioned, and anyway, she's only taking six weeks' leave."

"Does she like being a lawyer?"

"Rachel, I don't want to talk about my wife."

"Not talking about her seems to me like being in combat and not discussing the enemy."

He laughed, picked up his glass of wine, smiled at her over the rim, took a sip, pursing his pale lips slightly after the swallow. "You're too clever for me." He said this with conviction, no hint of irony or sarcasm.

"That's a nice way of saying—shut up."

"Hey!" He put the glass down hard and it wobbled uncertainly.

"I mean it. You have the nicest way of deflecting anger. It's amazing. Makes me angrier and angrier. More determined than ever to get a rise out of you." She ducked her head, bit her lip, and mumbled to her plate, "No pun intended."

"I don't have the right to get angry at you. Anyway, you're not telling the truth. You're angry at me."

"Oh, please! No messages from Freud. God!" She shook her head, shaking off his irritating remark like a fly.

"You deny you're angry at me?"

"Do you know what Ted Bishop said about me and men?"

"He doesn't strike me as an ideal expert on heterosexual relations.

"I don't know. Sometimes I think the homos see this junk clearer than the rest of us. Anyway, he said all my relationships with men are a copy of me and my brother. I worship at the feet of smart men who only want to play with me occasionally. A heartbroken prepubescent girl chasing after her tolerant, but slightly bored, big brother."

"Well, well. That's not a Freudian insight, is it?" Peter turned his head, frowning with disgust at the fireplace.

"I thought it was very smart of him."

"Have you told him about us?" Peter peeked at her fast, an interrogating cop hoping to catch her in a lie.

"No!" she insisted, but she lowered her head and brought an index finger to her mouth to chew on the nail.

"You have," he said quietly.

"I haven't!" she shouted. "I wouldn't! I'd be humiliated to tell him. My God, I'm supposed to be a feminist writer. It's a joke, a bad joke, written by a vicious male chauvinist satirist."

"No, it isn't. Where does that come from? You're a much better playwright than simply a feminist. And anyway, what's that got to do with the price of fish? What's so humiliating about it?"

"I'm sleeping with another woman's husband while she's lying in the hospital having his baby. Somehow I don't think Simone de Beauvoir would approve."

"No, but she's probably done it."

Rachel burst out laughing, raucously, almost sexually delighted by his cynicism. She couldn't stop and she covered her mouth to dam up the flood.

He wanted to put his cock there, in that amazing mouth, always full of words—words that cut through the world, that said exactly what is, words without compromise or modesty or shame. Peter always felt obliged to keep up with her, to be just as witty, just as honest, just as perceptive. One of the reasons he felt no desire to live with Rachel was the exhaustion he felt after several hours of their bantering. He might as well have played three sets of squash against an intimidating opponent. At least, this return of serve was a remarkable success. Peter could count on one hand the number of times he had made her laugh so hard. On the evenings he'd spent with some of her playwright friends, all of them homosexual, they had done it regularly, with ease. She'd break them up and they'd return the favor. But their wit was merely cruel or fantastic or perverse—never honest, abrasive, or insightful like hers. He and Rachel had slept together four times, each occasion followed by agonized guilt on both their parts (their nonconsummating dates had no unpleasant residue; somehow just seeing her, even necking with her, didn't make him feel he had betrayed Diane), but she had never made a move for his penis. He wished she would. He wanted to dam up her mouth with his hard-on, to live inside her words, to be kissed and sucked by their manufacturer.

Actually, their lovemaking was a disappointment, a tedious anticlimax to their feverish, hungry talks—sluggish digestion following a delicious meal. Rachel, for all her lively wit and energetic body, seemed frightened to death when he made love to her. She looked pale, her eyes were solemn and earnest, she made no sounds, her body was in constant retreat from exploratory kisses; even after penetration, her hands lit on his back reluctantly, as if the gesture might be too bold. He liked her thin body, flattened pillows that hinted at real breasts, a puff of jet black hair covering her hard pubis, slight thighs meeting muscled calves with big, quizzical kneecaps joining them. She wasn't a beauty; but she was distinctive, and if she would only bring the wit, energy, and fearlessness of her conversation to bed, she would be a great lover. Partly, he was grateful she wasn't. He wasn't terrific in bed either, a fact he had long ago resigned himself to. And he found her personality, her talk, her being, so interesting, so addictive that if she were also sexually thrilling, he'd have no control, no brake to stop from utterly surrendering his will to her.

That was being in love, he supposed. It had happened to him once and he hoped it would never happen again. Things were better this way, Diane and Rachel satisfying different longings. Rachel enlivened the mind, warmed the spirit; Diane kept order and regularly exercised his sex. At least, the last was true until Diane got pregnant. In the beginning he hadn't minded the physical changes, the breasts gelling, Diane's belly swelling into womanhood, her olive skin ripening, but then things got out of hand: the breasts laden, the belly explosive, the skin strained and exhausted. He found himself fearing the sight of Diane's body. Toward the end, a glimpse of her nakedness could almost stop his heart with fright. And the fantastic growth within seemed to have taken its energy from her brain, drained her of the light in her eyes, of the desire to talk or even the capacity to think. Her personality became nothing but complaints, yearnings, and moody silences. When she moved to embrace him, he instinctively shied away from her size and awkwardness, as though a city bus had come too close to his position on the curb.

It was then he first slept with Rachel and converted their friendship into an affair. He knew now that had been a mistake, but he didn't regret it. In human relations, Peter believed, error and failure were unavoidable.

I won't sleep with her tonight, he decided.

"THIS IS . . ."—AN UNINTELLIGIBLE NAME FOLLOWED—"THE anesthesiologist."

The narrow face of an Asian woman loomed in Eric's way. Her eyes had a lifelessness that seemed hostile. "When did the patient last eat?"

Eric looked down at Nina, her skin bleached by the bright operating-room lights. Although her eyes were closed, she gripped his hand with unrelenting force and her legs shifted uneasily from side to side. When did she last eat? That soup.

"Soup," he said. His mouth worked slowly pronouncing the word.

"*When?*"

"Oh," he said. He tried to look backwards through the night, rewind to their arrival at the hospital, but the tape got stuck and froze the images. He looked at the wall clock. Six-fifty. In the morning? No, night.

"Was that more than twenty-four hours ago?"

"Yes," he said.

All around the room there was activity. They had been wheeled from the labor room to the operating room so rapidly that Eric had no memory of the move, except that with each step they were joined by someone else, dressed, as he was, in a gown and mask.

"Another one's starting," a nurse said. Eric followed Ephron's glance to the two monitors, one counting the baby's heartbeats per minute, the other measuring Nina's contractions. The red digital numbers of his child's heartbeat flashed: 80, 65, 77, 58. He knew, although no one had said anything, that they were too low. All through the long labor those numbers had been much higher, 150, 166, 188 during one powerful contraction. Nina and he, before she completely lost the ability to notice details, had commented on it and the nurse had reminded them that a fetal heartbeat was supposed to be between 150 and 180 beats per minute. Eric had known that, but only as a fact. To hear the wild, rushing noise of the amplified heart, pounding on the door, racing to be born, made the fact new. He had been frightened by it, first the sound, then later, when they turned the volume off, the numbers. The sheer speed, the mad rush, the wildness—they implied so much need, so much ~~wanting~~, so much longing.

Now he wanted that back. His baby was in trouble. He could see in all their eyes (the masks showed nothing else) the concentration of people in crisis.

"Don't put her under," Ephron said. "We'll try one more time." The anesthesiologist stopped from putting a hypodermic into Nina's IV. A nurse lifted the upper torso of Nina's body. They put her feet into stirrups. "Come on, Nina! One more time! We're gonna push baby out."

"Baby's almost out!" the others said, like fans at a ball game.

Eric looked at Nina, her head rolling from side to side, yearning for sleep. She moaned. He knew if she could talk, she'd beg them to let her alone. Does she know that our child may be dying? Her pain was so great she probably wouldn't care—but later . . . Nina would never recover from that tragedy.

"One big push! From your rectum!"

"One big push," others said.

Someone grabbed Nina's chin and shook her. Her eyes opened; the pupils were blank moons.

"Push, Nina!"

She tried. Dutifully, an exhausted animal, she strained her limp muscles. The baby monitor changed to a steady tone. The red numbers flashed—50, 44, 31.

Stop it, he begged them.

The words were unspoken.

He grabbed their instruments and cut, rescuing his child.

He stood still while the fingers of his left hand turned purple from Nina's grip.

"Fetal stress," a nurse said with casual emphasis, ordering a slice of pizza at a crowded counter.

"One big push, Nina!" Ephron pleaded now, panic washing over her authoritarian tone. "Baby wants to come out!"

"Baby wants to come out!" others parroted.

Nina's eyes focused briefly, her dry, cracked lips came together, and she strained, her neck swollen, its interior anatomy visible, like a snake swallowing an animal whole.

A bell rang from the monitor. The red numbers held steady now: 31, 31, 31, 31.

Breathe my baby, Eric yelled into the corridor of his mind.

"Put her out!" Ephron shouted. There was no pretense of professional calm. "We'll use forceps!"

The anesthesiologist's thumb pushed down on the hypo.

"Eric?" Nina whimpered.

He said, I'm here, my darling, I'm with you forever.

But his lips were stuck together with terror.

"Come on!" Ephron yelled to no one and to nothing in particular.

Nina's legs went first, sagging in the stirrups. Then her shoulders lost the tension of life; her head rolled back; the mouth yawned open. Still, her hand clutched Eric's; her fingers were rigid and cold, like steel. Her upper arms died. Ephron shouted something and he heard the word "episiotomy." Nina had dreaded that inevitable nicety, he knew, and no wonder. They were going to cut the tenderest, most private part of her body. They shoved a large plastic funnel into her mouth; it looked so long, Eric thought, it must go all the way down her throat.

Her hand died. The ferocious taut muscles sighed away into a limp stillness.

A hose was put into the funnel in her mouth. Her skin was white, absent of the color of life; her muscles were dead, helpless against gravity; only her chest rose and fell slowly to indicate her continued existence.

Now he hung on to her hand because *he* needed to feel her presence, to know she lived. There was still warmth in the delicate fingers and narrow palm. Around him many people made noise, hustling about frantically, but a silence enveloped him. He felt the center of his head yawn queasily from fatigue. He was exhausted by the fight to get to this finish, a climax he had assumed would be triumphant, beautiful, ecstatic. Eric looked at her destroyed body and he knew he was looking at death.

"Okay, I'm cutting," he heard Ephron say, and he winced.

The monitor's numbers were unforgiving: 32, 40, 33, 31.

"Baby's down. We won't do a section. I'll use forceps."

A nurse approached with enormous metal hands; they stretched from her arms like the grotesque fingernails of a monster robot. He realized only a second before Ephron put their wide scoop-shaped ends into his wife that they were the forceps. Surely they would tear Nina to shreds and squash his infant's head. Why were they killing them?

He closed his eyes, finally unable to look, beaten even in his passivity as an observer.

"Head's out!" someone yelled.

He looked. Growing out of Nina like a melon was a huge, slimy skull. Around its neck, thick as a hangman's noose, and just as tight, was the umbilical cord.

"Cord! Cord!" Ephron screamed as though it were a ghastly creature. "Clamp! Clamp!" Someone instantly put a metal clamp on the umbilical cord. "We'll cut now!" Ephron was handed what looked like shears, and she angrily cut the umbilical cord right behind the baby's neck, freeing it of the stranglehold.

"We'll clear the shoulders."

"Left," said someone.

"Right," said Ephron, and the baby was out. Two huge testicles, discolored and explosive, dominated Eric's vision. It is a boy, he thought, utterly unexcited by the fact.

"Baby's out!" someone said.

Others, who had been standing behind Ephron like spectators at an accident, grabbed his son and rushed over to a table at the rear. Ephron and the rest turned to watch. He couldn't see, couldn't imagine what so many people could even do to a tiny thing like that. It must be dead, he thought. Of course, it's dead, he argued.

A fragile wail, a squeak of discomfort broke the suspense. He sighed, but Ephron and the others showed no relaxation; they continued to look over.

The cries got louder. He saw two of the people move away, tossing cloths into pails. A glimpse of his son: skin bluish, face distorted with pain, a huge, distended belly overwhelming tiny limbs.

There's something wrong with him. He's crippled. He's brain-damaged. I have a broken son.

"Placenta," a nurse said. Ephron returned her attention to forgotten Nina, her body dead, her mouth violated by the medical equipment.

"Baby's good," a man at the table said. "Six, ten."

"Your baby's fine," a nurse repeated to Eric.

Eric nodded. Ephron looked at him. Her eyes peered into Eric's. He tried to smile at Ephron, thinking she needed a sign of his gratitude, but then he realized his mask covered his mouth. Ephron continued to stare at him. She pulled her mask off. Her mouth opened. Then closed. Around him the others seemed embarrassed, lowering their eyes. "What are you doing here?" Ephron asked sharply.

The question baffled Eric with its existential possibilities. He didn't know what he was doing there. He was holding Nina's hand, clutching the narrow palm and long fingers, stuck to its weakness in the hope it could give him strength.

Ephron's face changed from irritated surprise to her professional manner. "You're not supposed to be here when the mother is under total anesthesia." He didn't answer. Ephron relaxed some more, coming close to her office manners. "Now that you can see mother and baby are all right, could you wait outside?"

He nodded stupidly, agreeing. But Ephron talked nonsense. His wife was ruined on the table. His son might be breathing, squalling, but he had come out blue, starving for sustenance. How could they know he was all right?

He let go of Nina's hand to leave.

Nina's arm dropped like a weighted pendulum to the floor.

"Strap her arm down, for God's sakes!" Ephron shouted at a nurse. Nina's fingers touched the floor: limp, killed. Eric walked out rapidly, through the metal doors into an empty hallway, the corridor narrowed by unused equipment pushed against the wall.

He closed his hot, swollen eyes, feeling weak. His stomach was so empty the middle of his body seemed ready to collapse under the weight of his ribs. He turned around and watched the operating-room doors. There were windows placed high on each of them, but at six-six he could easily see. They had put Nina's arm on her belly, not strapped as ordered. They were fussing with her vagina, sewing up the episiotomy. His son was hidden from view, however, by the tall body of what he assumed was the pediatrician on call. A nurse came out and walked past him as if he didn't exist.

And he felt invisible. Stripped of all his possessions, of all his faith in life and the future. He waited stupidly, blinking his sore eyes at the smudged metal of the doors, sure that bad news was going to issue forth.

AFTER DIANE FARTED ONCE, SHE COULDN'T STOP. IT WAS COMICAL, walking back and forth in the dreary private room, from the sink to the foot of the bed, releasing gas like a vulgar practical-joke cushion.

Visitors were allowed now. They arrived, filling the room with flowers, little boxes with little clothes, blue balloons saying "Happy Birthday," and always with big smiles, exclamations of praise and wonder. "He's so cute!" "He's gorgeous!" "He's so tiny!" She got candies and fruit and kisses and encouragement and attention, endless attention to everything she had experienced or felt over the last few days.

There were flowers and messages of congratulations from Wilson, Pickering but no visitors—"I'm buried by the Hobhouse case," her peer and work friend Didi said on the phone. Diane's boss, the brilliant Brian Stoppard, included a note with a basket of fruit—"A trumpet of welcome to your new associate." That, along with Didi's call, reminded Diane of the risk she had taken in her goal of partnership. Diane reasoned that if she had her child while still an associate and proved that it didn't affect her work, then instead of motherhood's being a fault, it would be seen as a virtue, an event the partners would still have to fear with a childless associate, but not with her. Diane reasserted to herself the cleverness of the plan to soothe her nerves.

They were jangled again when she got her first view of the gap Byron's existence would create with her female friends. Most were childless, although they all had plans or ambitions in that direction. She told them little or nothing of the painful agony following the operation and spoke of the necessity of the procedure itself (which had been a relief) as a disappointment. She didn't know why she lied, except possibly out of altruism and feminist bravado. Most of them were squeamish about pain.

To her friend Betty Winters, her one close friend with a child (although they had seen little of each other since Betty's delivery three years ago), Diane immediately told the truth. They had a long, happy, gossipy talk, of the kind they used to enjoy in college.

"Breast feeding is so boring!" Diane said to her.

"I know! You can't do anything but watch television—"

"I can't even concentrate on that—"

"I know—"

They rushed to finish each other's sentences, in a hurry to establish their unity of feeling. Betty reassured her about the future. "You'll see, it's hard, but you'll love it," she answered to every query. She recommended one child-care book: "It's my bible, I've worn out two copies." Betty left, repeating as she backed out the door, "Call me anytime, day or night, if you need advice or a shoulder to cry on."

Peter's mother, Gail, and his stepfather, Kyle, were depressing visitors. They sat on chairs at the foot of the bed, overdressed in formal clothes, their faces stilled by polite smiles. They looked like wealthy tourists who had been mistakenly booked into a seedy hotel for the night but were determined to make the best of it. Diane thought she was used to Gail's coldness—shocking in a mother—but that Gail maintained her reserve even about the birth of her first grandchild startled Diane anew. Peter's father, Jonathan, and his stepmother hardly improved matters by phoning to say that they had a partner's wedding to attend ("Second marriage, you know, he's sensitive about our support") and couldn't come up from Philadelphia until next week. All this made Diane pity Peter, as she had years ago when they were first dating.

Of course, Peter had been reluctant to have a child. Look at the parents he had: divorcing when he was five, his mother an iceberg, his father obsessed with his law firm, hardly able to squeeze Peter in between cases and business dinners. It was a miracle Peter had ever gotten married.

On the day they left for home, Diane checked the room to see if she had packed everything. Out of the corner of her eye, she watched Peter hold Byron. By hospital rule Byron wore a cap on his head. Lily had given Peter a puffy insulated baby bag from L. L. Bean to carry Byron. It was more suitable for winter than May. Little of Byron was visible, but Peter stared at that bit: big eyes closed, flat little brow, bright lips pursed, open at the center, ready for a nipple. Peter stared at all that with a frown, puzzling over the arrangement of features, possibly searching for a missing item.

"He has no eyebrows," he said finally.

"Yes, he does!"

"Hardly. Just an outline."

"He's a newborn."

Peter frowned again. Given the way Peter carried Byron—his arms stiff, holding Byron at a distance from his body, as if he were a bomb—Diane was relieved when the nurse arrived and, official procedure again, took Byron until they got outside the hospital.

Diane was exhausted by the short trip home. Byron slept through it all, even the exaggerated delight and interest of the doorman and the two elderly women who were regular fixtures in the lobby.

Diane was startled when they arrived at their apartment door, because it opened by itself. A broad-shouldered middle-aged woman, dressed in a white uniform, stood there, her eyes immediately focused on Byron. "He'll be too warm in that, my dear," she said, and took Byron away before Diane even got in the door.

"This is Mrs. Murphy," Peter said.

Of course, the baby nurse, Diane reminded herself.

"Hello, ma'am," Mrs. Murphy said.

Diane nodded in response, unable to talk. She wandered into her apartment, studying each room and its possessions with the curiosity of a stranger.

"When is he due for a feeding, ma'am?" Mrs. Murphy asked, appearing with Byron. She had taken off Byron's outer clothing. He squawked, a bony arm stretching blindly at Mrs. Murphy's bosom.

"Four o'clock."

"You should be resting, ma'am. You don't have much in reserve after a Caesarean. I'll bring the little one in at four."

"Thank you," Diane said sweetly. Where was Peter? She heard his voice in the study, talking on the phone. She smiled graciously at Mrs. Murphy, just as she imagined this woman would expect a spoiled young mother to react to the competence and subservience of a baby nurse. You have no idea who I really am, she thought to herself as she walked by, pausing to kiss Byron. He was so soft! Like the soft hot interior of a muffin. The toothpick fingers pulled at her chin as she withdrew.

"We'll have a nice talk while Mommy rests," Mrs. Murphy said to Byron.

Yeah, she's nice in front of me, Diane thought. She'll probably smother him with a pillow the minute I'm out of the room. By the time Diane reached her bed, she was almost staggering. She felt lumpy and stretched, a sweater worn by a fat person. It was good to be in her room.

Peter looked in the door. "Tony Winters is on the phone. He wants to congratulate you. And then he'll put Betty on."

Diane listened to the eager voice on the phone. "Congratulations! I know you're exhausted. So don't talk. Betty and I are very excited. She wants to say hello."

"Thank you," Diane said, and sounded hoarse, weak, just as she should. But her mind was clear, for the first time in months. The core of her intelligence glowed with energy. I'd better write a thank-you note to Stoppard right away, she thought.

"Diane? It's Betty. How's the baby nurse?"

She laughed. "Weird."

"I hated mine. She barely let me handle the baby. Always hinting that I didn't know what I was doing."

"I can hardly move, so I guess it's good. It's better than my mother being around."

Betty made an appreciative noise. "That's true. I'll let you rest. Call me anytime."

"Okay, thanks." That was strange. Betty's friendliness was so ready, so eager, the relief of someone used to solitude at last finding a sympathetic ear. Was motherhood like that? Isolate you, leave you feeling alone, unappreciated?

She heard—faintly, faintly—her son complain. Peter looked in the door. He seemed happy. "Good, you're resting," he said. "Isn't Mrs. Murphy great? She knows just how to handle him." He left, shutting the door behind him. What the hell did that mean? That I don't know what to do?

Diane closed her eyes and felt herself going, her strong, clear mind turning off.

I know what to do, was its last thought before sleep.

NINA ROLLED ON ICE CUBES. EVERYWHERE SHE LET HERSELF FEEL, there was cold, freezing through her like razors, shattering her bones.

"Wha—"

"You had a beautiful baby boy!"

She couldn't climb out. The blue cold strangled her. She twisted her neck to break the grip.

"Wha . . . happen?"

"You had a beautiful baby boy!"

I'm dreaming, I'm freezing.

"Wake up!"

I'm dying in the cold.

PETER WAITED IN HIS STUDY FOR RACHEL TO CALL.

He thought back to his earlier conversation with Tony Winters, the playwright. "You'll see," that infinitely sophisticated man had said, "the baby will turn you into sentimental mush. And it's good. It's really good. Like being young again, but without the foolishness. Like getting married, but with the commitment real, the product tangible, instead of impossible romantic ideals."

Peter had wandered into the nursery afterward and watched Mrs. Murphy expertly change Byron's diaper. Peter looked away while she changed the bandage on the reddened circumcised penis, but he forced himself to glance at the blackened stub of the umbilical cord. Mrs. Murphy wiped it with a cotton ball dipped in rubbing alcohol. At first, Byron cried at these ministrations, but she handled him so well, lifting him by his feet and sliding the diaper underneath in one graceful motion, that Byron soon stopped and stared blindly at her.

Mrs. Murphy kept up a running patter. "Do you see your daddy, watching, learning? So he can do this, too. And then he can take care of his little one, his treasure."

My treasure? Peter remembered while he waited by the phone. He could initiate the call to Rachel, but she had said she would be hard to reach.

Earlier, Mrs. Murphy had put Byron in Peter's arms and warned Peter to support the neck. Byron pushed his head at Peter's breast, hoping.

"There's nothing there," Peter told his son, feeling bad about it.

My treasure? What can I give him? I don't know anything. I don't have any idea why I've lived the way I have, or what I hope for, or even what I wish had happened. I don't love his mother and I didn't want him to be born.

That was the simple truth. Horrible, unspeakable. It was the truth Peter was rejecting, fighting off like a horde of insects, frantically, hopelessly. Could he change it? By an act of will, by sheer determination?

The phone rang. He grabbed for it.

"Hello," Rachel said. "Everybody safe at home? Can we talk?"

"I'm sorry," he said. The effort made his voice harsh. "We can't do this anymore."

"Talk on the phone?" Her voice stayed cheerful, fought to maintain it. "Or anything?"

"Anything," he intoned.

"Okay," she said casually, and hung up. He was surprised at her easy surrender.

Later he walked into Byron's room, told Mrs. Murphy she could get herself coffee, take a break. "I'll make myself some tea," she said. "He's an angel," she commented while exiting.

Peter knelt at the side of the baby carriage. Byron had two fingers between his lips, his eyes closed, his mouth working. He had his mother's olive skin. A vein ran across his bald skull, pulsing as he sucked. Peter realized Rachel thought his resolve wouldn't last.

He knew it would.

When Dr. Ephron appeared, joining Eric in the slovenly hallway, she had a timid look on her face. Eric thought this was the natural companion to bad news.

"Everything's fine," Ephron began. "As you could see, the cord was wrapped three times around the neck. Doesn't make any difference until pushing. Then it tightens. She'd gotten him so far down I thought we might make it through without a general. But you saw. I had to get baby out quickly. At least we avoided a C section."

He waited. Now for the bad news.

"Okay? I'm sorry if I yelled. I was startled. Fathers aren't supposed to be present at a general. Hospital rule. In the confusion— in the rush, I forgot you were there."

"They're both okay?" he asked meekly.

Ephron blinked. She smiled, not at him, but to herself. "Absolutely, Mr. Gold! They're both fine. She's still under, but she should be coming out of it soon. Your son is fine—you haven't seen him!" Ephron, her manner now self-assured, opened the doors and whispered something inside. She turned back to him. "You can go in for a second to see him." She held the door open.

Eric moved into the operating room slowly, his legs advancing, although his mind wanted to retreat. Nina lay on the table, killed. He didn't look at Nina for more than a second. The sight terrified him. A nurse blocked his vision anyway. She held a mass of white and offered it to Eric with a smile of expectation.

Then it was in his arms. Light, nothing to hold, nothing like the weight it had been in his heart. He looked at the little face, at the little face of his son, his heir, his firstborn.

There was hair everywhere, a black down covering a monkey face. He was squashed; his cheeks, nose, forehead compressed. The eyes were shut, the mouth twisted in a complaint, and he meowed unhappily.

"Oh," Eric said, miserable for him. He thought of the cord twisting tighter and tighter, desiring his death. Eric rocked his arms back and forth. The features smoothed; the mouth smacked open and closed. "Hello," he whispered. The eyelids were red, swollen, weary—a battered fighter.

They opened. Just slits. Pools of blue. The red skin winced at the light and closed again. Eric wanted to hide him from the world, the poor thing—hurt, attacked by life.

"Okay," the nurse said, her arms out to take his son back. "We have to wake up your wife. You can wait for her in recovery."

Eric glanced at Nina as he turned to go. She was spread out on the table under the lights, her mouth open stupidly, her skin white, a dried-out fruit withered by the sun. He wanted to hold her, to rouse her, to tell her what she had accomplished.

He's alive, Nina.

And Eric was back out in the hall again, pushed up against the wall, another discarded piece of equipment.

Through the doors, he heard them try to bring her back: "Wake up, Nina! You've had a beautiful boy!" Pause. Then, louder: "Wake up, Nina! Time to get up!" It was a joke. This is modern medicine? "Wake up! Wake up! Time to get up! You have a beautiful baby boy! Get up!"

He tried to convince himself that he was tired, that he had panicked unnecessarily about his son, that he was incapable of judging whether Nina was really in trouble.

"Time to get up, Nina! Wake up! Wake up! You had a beautiful baby boy!"

He knew Nina had never had a general anesthetic before. He knew that every once in a great while perfectly healthy people never awoke.

"Time to get up! Wake up! Wake up!"

"Wake up," he whispered. He forced himself to move closer so he could see through the glass in the doors. Someone held Nina's face, shaking her head. Her eyes rolled open for a second.

"Get up, Nina! No more sleep! You have a beautiful baby boy!" Their shouts were abrasive, hostile. "Time to get up!"

He hated them. They had saved his child. They were taking care of his wife, preserving her. He hated them.

Nina's all right, he told himself. He thought of his tiny son, the red, swollen eyelids opening . . . excitement came up from his soul, rising over the fatigue, the terror.

Eric walked down the hall, back into the labor rooms, past the other worried fathers, and out into the general hallway, up to the pay phone next to the elevators.

His father answered on the first ring.

"Hello, Grandpa," he said.

Silence at first, then a worried voice: "When?"

"Just a few minutes ago, Dad. You're the first I called. It's a boy."

"Is he all right?"

"He's fine. He took a beating, but he's fine."

"What do you mean he took a beating?"

"They had to knock Nina out and use forceps. They've left his face a little puffy and bruised. Like he went fifteen rounds with Joe Frazier."

"Is she all right?"

"Fine. They're fine. He's a beautiful baby boy. He's got blue eyes."

He heard his father call out, "A boy! It's a boy! He has blue eyes! What?"

His mother's voice said something in the background. "What is she saying?" Eric asked.

"They all have blue eyes when they're born, she says."

"Tell her, thanks a lot. I better go. Congratulations, Dad."

"Call me," his father pleaded.

"I will."

Eric took out the crumpled paper in his pocket with Nina's family's phone numbers. He had intended to tell all four of her brothers and sisters, but he didn't have time. He wanted to be in recovery when Nina woke up. He dialed her parents. Nina's mother, Joan, answered.

"Hi, it's Eric," he spoke quickly. He had always felt uncomfortable talking to Nina's mother. "It's a boy."

There was a long silence. He heard something, a material, a fabric rustle. In the background, Nina's father said, "Who is it?"

"It's Eric," Joan said. "Congratulations," she said into the phone, and he could hear her voice tremble.

"He has blue eyes," Eric said, not caring that the information was meaningless.

"He has blue eyes," she repeated. "Is Nina all right?"

"She's fine. They had to knock her out and use forceps, but everybody's fine."

"Why did they have to—" She hesitated, shying away from using his phrase. "Why did they need forceps?"

"He had the cord around his neck—"

Joan gasped.

"But he's fine. They just needed to get him out quickly. I'd better go. I want to meet Nina in recovery."

"She's not in her room yet?"

"No, no. It just happened. I'm in the hallway. I'll call you later. Can you tell her brothers and sisters?"

"Sure, Eric. Give her my love. Call me when you can."

"I will." Joan had said his name so sweetly, unlike her more typical formal tone. He had never heard any emotion in her voice before.

He walked back, through the rooms that an hour ago he had thought would be witness to a great tragedy. They looked small, dirty, unimportant now. A nurse waved him into a room with several beds separated by curtains. "She's over there."

Nina was asleep, her head rolled to one side, her lips cracked and dry.

"You can wake her," the nurse said. "She won't remember, but you can wake her."

Eric shook her shoulder. Nina's eyes opened. They were large pools of blue, unfocused. "Hi," she said, her voice lilting, although hoarse.

"We had a boy," he said softly.

"Really?" She sounded happy.

"You had a beautiful baby boy!" the nurse called out. "He's big like his daddy."

"Is that true?" Eric asked. The nurse nodded. He looked down at Nina. She was asleep again. He took her hand, the IV still plugged into her thin arm.

Her eyes opened. "What happened?" she asked.

He started to laugh, then realized she didn't know. "You had a boy."

"Really?" The same wonder and happiness and surprise.

"She doesn't remember?" he asked the nurse.

"The anesthesia. You had a beautiful baby boy! Lots of hair! Big!"

"Have you seen him?" Nina asked.

"Yeah, I held him! You did great, Nina."

She shivered. "I'm so cold. Can I have a blanket?"

She was already covered by two. He turned to the nurse, who answered before he asked: "The anesthesia. She doesn't need a blanket."

When he looked down at her, she was asleep again. He moved to go, but her eyes opened. "Eric?"

"I'm here."

"What happened?"

"You had a baby boy. He's fine."

"Really?" Pure happiness. Then sleep.

He waited. The nurse said, "Go home. You need rest. She'll be out of it for a while." But he waited.

Nina opened her eyes, her teeth chattering.

"Eric?"

"I'm here."

"What happened?"

"We had a baby boy."

"Really?"

Finally, he left, convinced his presence was pointless. The walk home was tedious, dreary, and made him feel his almost hallucinogenic fatigue. There was no noise of congratulation. There should be a parade, a crowd of welcome. People went about their business as if it were just another day.

But he knew it wasn't. His son was born. His missile into the future. Eric had to make his fortune for him, ready the world, beat it down if necessary, so his boy could tread on a smooth surface into glory.

Ramon, the small, plump doorman, was on duty. He pumped Eric's hand. *"Un muchacho!"* he said. "A boy! You must be happy."

Frances, a mother of three (she was explaining to the eldest that

Eric and Nina had just had a baby), interrupted: "Now, now, a girl is just as good."

Ramon nodded solemnly at her and then winked at Eric.

Eric went upstairs and walked into their empty apartment. Then he remembered that he had forgotten to ask if Gomez was dead.

He went into the bedroom that tomorrow he would have to set up as the nursery. Next to the phone was the list of friends he was supposed to call.

After four conversations, he quit. The tone of them was hollow, routine, drained of the pleasure he felt and wanted to go on feeling. The memory of that little face, scratched, puffy, needing him, came back over and over.

He left the phone off the hook and went into the living room, searching for the right cut on the *Messiah*, and gingerly put the needle down. He did something that Nina never allowed—he turned the volume all the way up:

"And unto us a child is born . . ."

The thrilled voices drowned everything, the traffic, the vague echo of conversation from the courtyard. He climbed on top of the coffee table, shut his eyes, and swayed, embraced by their exhilaration and his joy.

"And unto us a son is given . . ."

Yes, he had almost died. He was a gift snatched from death.

"And He shall reign forever and ever . . ."

Beyond their deaths. Beyond their love. He would go on forever.

"For unto us a child is born."

He had survived to be theirs, to be the perfect product of their union.

"For unto us a son is given."

A gift from the heavens, from the pure universe. A chance to be perfect. He held his invisible son in his arms, the music cascading in the apartment, his eyes shut, seeing the little bruised face, and exulted: his son was born and the world would be changed forever and forever.

3

THEY NAMED HIM LUKE THOMAS GOLD.

Nina had wanted to honor her uncle Lawrence, Eric his grandmother Tessie. Eric's religion, although he didn't practice it, forbade Nina from using the actual name, so she settled for the same initial (choosing Luke from the New Testament), and Eric didn't object. That was typical of his erratic obeisance to Judaism. "Luke was a Jew, wasn't he?" Eric said. "All the early Christians were Jews." Eric chose Thomas for Tessie—the connection seemed dim to Nina—and Luke won out as the first name because he was a son after all and was going to bear his father's surname forever. Eric himself made that point. All in all she was pleased.

When Nina came out of the anesthesia, she phoned everyone she felt safe disturbing at midnight. They all said, "You must be tired," and she agreed, she was, but she had no desire to sleep.

She told the nurse to bring Luke in—he wasn't called that yet; he was known as the "Gold baby," summoning an image of a statuette—but she was told that he was under the incubating lamps as a precaution, given his traumatic birth, and was supposed to remain there until 6:00 A.M. Did she want to be disturbed then or left alone until 10:00?

Surely she would be asleep by 6:00. She spoke with Eric. They settled on the name. He sounded dead. His voice was empty, bereft. He kept asking, "Are you all right? You sound fine," sounding disappointed by her answers. She tried to explain. Her muscles hurt, she dared not move, touch, or even think about her vagina (when the nurse changed the bandage, a glimpse of the blood-soaked wad made Nina queasy), and Nina worried about Luke, replaying the doctor's assurances, yet fussing over the fact that he had to be under an incubating lamp. Nevertheless, in spite of it all, she felt free, young,

64

alive again. The mass was out of her stomach, she had had a boy (something about that was a relief, she couldn't say what), and she knew, for the first time really, that it was going to be all right, that she had made it through, succeeded in the only things that really counted, the production of a child and the preservation of her life.

She tried to sleep; but the room was hot, and her sore body needed coolness. The air conditioning, Nina discovered, wasn't working. She summoned a nurse, who impatiently said, "They'll fix it in the morning. You should sleep."

"I can't! It's too hot. That's why I want the air conditioning fixed." Nina let out a noise of nervous laughter, a habitual punctuation mark to any expression of anger.

"We'll open the window," the nurse said, moving to it.

"It doesn't open," Nina said.

The nurse worked at it anyway, pulling and groaning at the narrow metal handle. No one believes me about anything, Nina thought. I have no authority in my voice, that's what it is. If it was deeper, they'd believe me.

"It doesn't open," the nurse said.

Nina's snort of laughter pushed the words out: "That's what I said."

"Do you want a pill to sleep?"

"No! I want the air conditioning to work."

"I'll call maintenance, but they won't get to it until the morning."

"Fine," she said, hard on the *n*, as though it weren't.

The exchange had been unlike her. Not unlike how she wished to behave, but different from her usual suppression of any challenge, or demand of authority; knowing the hopelessness of requests, Nina generally didn't bother to make them. But she had lived through hell, through a test of endurance and terror that now made disapproval from a nurse seem as trivial as it in fact always had been.

She lay in bed, hot, her skin chafed by coarse thin sheets, the bed too pliable, its height in the small room disturbing. She felt like a suitcase shoved onto the back shelf of a closet.

And her mind was awake—a lingering head cold decongested. She could breathe straight to the back of her skull, to places in her brain that had been dark and musty for months.

Luke, Luke, Luke, Luke, she recited, picturing boys, beautiful boys with hairless skin jumping into Walker Pond near her family's summer home in Maine, their voices trilling in the rustling birches, dancing through the sun-splotched forest. She kept a hand on her deflated belly as if she could freeze it back into solidity, and saw herself slim again, dressed in a loose white blouse and worn jeans, walking hand in hand with an eager blue-eyed boy, her Luke, her creation, the living tissue of her pride and power.

She still hadn't seen Luke. She wanted him.

What was she celebrating? Her ecstasy shuddered and crumbled like old plaster. She hadn't held Luke to her breast, to welcome him to the world, soothing him for the squeezing horror of the birth canal. Luke's first sensation had been cold steel, gloved hands, suction—Eric's vague description of the scene allowed for endless nightmarish inventions.

Newborns don't remember anything, she reminded herself.

But she didn't believe that; she knew Luke's body would remember, that inside him something would always flinch at the world, at a world not of warmth and love but of brutal technology and simple survival. What had she done to him? She wanted to hold him, to apologize for her clumsy work as an usher, hold him tight, press him with reassurance.

She decided to go to the nursery and demand to see him. She lifted the sheet off and swung her legs over. The pain was searing! Hot. The skin pulsed, outraged. It stung right through her, in two lines running up her torso, the movement of her legs pulling her apart, ripping her skin like paper.

She didn't dare look. She must have torn the stitches; the blood would be flowing. "Nurse!" she tried to call out, but tears, tears of pain, exhaustion, and failure, drowned the cry. She pressed the call button. She shut her eyes against the pain that glowed below, radioactive with hurt.

The nurse appeared, impatience in her stance, a hand on a hip, her body only halfway in the room. Nina raised her face, slack from hurt and tears.

"You're in pain?"

Nina stared at the nurse with hatred and enough rage to incinerate her.

"You're due more painkiller," the nurse said. "I'll get it."

"I want my baby," she said, blubbering like a kid about a lost toy. "I want to see him."

"Can't now. He's under the heating lamp. I'll bring him in at six. Let me get you something for the pain." She disappeared.

Nina breathed. In sharply, and out slowly. She inched off the bed, easing into the descent. The white support socks the hospital had given her to wear made her feet look frail. She watched them slowly slide across the big squares of white linoleum, crippled enough by her wound that the tall, wide door of her room seemed an impossible goal.

But she got there. From its half-open position Nina could see the nursery only ten feet away. The halls were empty, asleep. The nursery (divided into two sections, with a nurses' station in between) had the shades drawn over the windows. Nina saw a different nurse walk across the station into one of the nursery rooms. Nina shuffled herself toward the open door of the station, moving faster, although her pelvis felt cut in two, tearing more with each step, and as she approached, Nina heard exhausted wailing: groaning squawks, high-pitched, easily recognizable as a deserted baby, abandoned, alone. She knew immediately it was her son.

Nina moved into the nurse's station. The nurse was inspecting some charts in the quiet nursery. Nina shuffled to the other nursery, filled by the agonized cries, and looked in.

That was Nina's first look at her son: Luke baked under a big lamp, a chicken warming on a delicatessen counter, nude, his thin arms and legs clawing blindly for help, his face distorted, so that his toothless, open, agonized mouth seemed huge.

Her mind closed against the cruelty and horror of the sight. She felt panic. She moved into the room—echoing with her son's cries of outrage (what monster could ignore them?)—but hesitated to grab him. She had no doubt the baby was Luke. It was the technological setup that intimidated her. What if removing him from the lamp was dangerous?

"Miss! You're not allowed in here!"

The nurse had spotted her.

"He's crying!" Nina pleaded.

"You're not allowed in here," the nurse insisted, and took Nina's arm.

Nina looked down at the nurse's hand and saw two circles of bright blood on the white floor. They came from her—leaked from her wounded heart.

The nurse followed her eyes. "You shouldn't be out of bed, Mrs. Gold. You might tear your stitches."

Nina looked at her gown and saw a dull ooze of red at the groin. Who is Mrs. Gold? she thought as the world swayed away from her and she fell after it—into the nurse's arms.

DIANE STUDIED HERSELF IN THE STANDING VICTORIAN MIRROR BEside her dresser. She was framed by its dark wood, like a portrait. Her apparel was inappropriately modern, however, dressed as she was, in L. L. Bean slacks and a green polo shirt that emphasized her enriched breasts. The pants belonged to Peter, an old pair she had borrowed earlier in the pregnancy. Diane's body was now going in reverse, a much more reassuring process, and she followed the loss of weight, the tightening of skin, with minute fascination and satisfaction.

She heard Mrs. Murphy's voice, lilting, singsong—phony— talking at Byron outside in the hall. Diane walked there and she found Byron cradled by Mrs. Murphy's meaty arms against her puffed, upholstered bosom. "Oh, the eyes are getting heavy now. You'll be sleeping soon."

"I'm going to take him for a walk."

Mrs. Murphy stood in her tracks and tilted her head. "Now?"

"I have to mail some letters, I—" Why am I explaining to her? she thought. "Here." She broke off, holding her arms out. "I'll take him."

"It's windy today."

"He'll be fine. He'll be in the carriage." Diane gathered Byron gingerly. Mrs. Murphy had swaddled Byron in a thin cotton blanket and one arm shot out as Diane took him. Diane kissed the tiny wrinkled fingers, sucking on the soft buttery skin for a moment. Byron's big bald head flopped against Diane's chest, and immediately his mouth opened, jawing at the cotton of her shirt.

"He might be getting hungry," Mrs. Murphy said. "He's due for a feeding."

"In a half hour. I'll be back by then." Diane hated this, loathed accounting for her every move and decision. It was just like being with her mother. Lily always demanded constant justifications for every action, laying the groundwork for a cross-examination that would devastate the opposition's rationale.

Mrs. Murphy held out her arms. "He needs to be changed. I'll get him ready."

"No, thank you," Diane said, and walked past her into the nursery. Behind her, she heard Mrs. Murphy make a noise. Diane ignored her, found the white cap in the carriage, and put it on Byron. Byron opened his large gray-blue eyes wide, staring fixedly at some point in between him and her, observing the approach of an astonishing spectacle. Diane put him on his back, tucking in the thin blanket on the sides of the mattress, and raised the hood. Byron started at that; his eyes blinked twice, and then he again fell into a profound stare. Diane covered his exposed lower half with a heavy plaid blanket, deferring whether to protect him totally until she got outdoors. It was mid-June, after all, and although not hot, already muggy; the slivers of sky she could see from Byron's window were yellow with haze.

"Here we go," she said to Byron—still, frozen Byron, gaping at the world. Maneuvering the bulky carriage out his door required care, so Diane's vision was concentrated on clearing the sides. Diane didn't see Mrs. Murphy standing in her way, a matronly blockade, arms folded, eyes narrowed in disapproval. She only felt the motion stop.

"You can't take a newborn out like that, ma'am," she heard Mrs. Murphy say, without her pleasant lilt, without the insinuation of command. Her authority rang clear, undiffused.

"Excuse me, Mrs. Murphy. I didn't see you."

"That's all right. Let me dress him for you."

Mrs. Murphy hadn't moved from her position. "No!" Diane said, and gently butted her with the carriage.

"I'm here till the end of the week, my dear," Mrs. Murphy said, her hand on the hood to prevent a repetition. "Then you can do things your way. I've taken care of hundreds of infants. I think I know what I'm doing."

What is it about older women? Is crushing us their only chance at power? Mrs. Murphy had been insufferable during the past two weeks, silently correcting everything Diane did, by either changing her selection of outfit or taking Byron away, claiming Diane or he was tired. Mrs. Murphy gave Byron a bottle one night without discussing it in advance, and used the defense that Diane needed rest. Mrs. Murphy's arrogance amazed Diane; after all, she was an employee, a servant. Peter didn't seem surprised—and he was the one who had grown up with help, a string of nannies and mother's helpers. Peter accepted Mrs. Murphy's arrogation of authority over their son, taking Mrs. Murphy's side whenever Diane had tried to argue.

"Mrs. Murphy, I'm taking my son outside." Diane pulled the carriage back to free it of the woman's grip and then began to move forward, determined, if necessary, to bowl her over.

Mrs. Murphy didn't move. The carriage jerked to a halt on impact, the front end tipping up. Byron let out a protest.

"What are you doing?" Diane sounded like a teenager to herself, an angry, but ultimately helpless, adolescent.

"I cannot be responsible, I cannot work here if you don't listen, if you don't take my advice."

Diane pulled the carriage back. Mrs. Murphy seemed to expand with pride at this apparent victory. Diane walked around the carriage and took hold of Mrs. Murphy's fat arm, just under the elbow where the flesh was soft and loose. "Do you know who I am?" Diane said. "I'm a lawyer." Mrs. Murphy blinked, puzzled. "At a top firm. I'm not some dumb rich housewife. I can sue your agency's ass off. I can make life miserable for them at no cost to me except my time. I can make sure you never work again.''

"Take your hands off me!" Mrs. Murphy said, and yanked her arm free. "How dare you speak to me like that! What do you know about being a mother? Nothing. You don't love that baby. You don't know what loving is.''

Diane pushed Mrs. Murphy, her palms out flat, each one on a shoulder. "Get out!" Mrs. Murphy staggered back, blinking her narrow, wrinkled eyes. Diane slapped Mrs. Murphy's shoulders again, her own legs trembling. "Get out of my house!" Mrs. Murphy grabbed at Diane's hand, catching a pinkie. It twisted painfully. Diane pulled back. She was so angry she felt the narrow hall expand, Mrs. Murphy shrink, and lost any sense of her own body. "Get out of here, you ugly woman! You ugly, ugly, ugly thing! Get out!"

"Don't you dare raise your hand to me." Mrs. Murphy's puffy cheeks wobbled with fury. "I could break you in two.''

"Oh, shut up!" Diane hated herself, felt ridiculous and incompetent. She should have been able to handle this woman without emotion, the way Brian Stoppard would, freeze her with a glance, a chilly word. Diane trembled while she walked back to the carriage and pushed it toward the door. Mrs. Murphy, this time, not only didn't attempt to stop her, but held the front door open.

"I want you out—" Diane began.

"I'll be gone! Don't you worry.''

Diane's legs were still uncertain, her knees liquid, when she reached the street.

Although Diane had ventured forth without Byron and had taken a brief stroll with a gang (Peter's father, stepmother, Mrs. Murphy, Byron, and Peter), this was her first solo tour with Byron, her virgin appearance as mother and child. She was conscious that she looked right, a yuppie mother, walking down lower Fifth Avenue with the proper brand of baby carriage, her outfit durable but preppie-chic. She looked the part, but she was a fraud. Diane was a peasant: her skin dark, made for field labor, not office fluorescence; her features big, with the strong jaw and deep-set, mournful eyes of her dead father.

A pair of old women stopped Diane and Byron on Tenth Street. They placed their bodies in the way of the carriage and clucked like grandmothers even before they got a view of Byron. Byron looked at the old ladies with his staring, challenging eyes. Byron's face was like Diane's—humorless, strong, immobile. He wasn't cute. Diane could hear in their exclamations a certain reserve. Byron wasn't quite the pretty, fragile, soft thing they expected and wanted.

After the old women let her continue, Byron finally moved his head and made complaining sounds. Mrs. Murphy had been giving him a pacifier, he seemed dependent on it already, and Diane had forgotten to bring it. He groaned, moved his head from side to side. His arms reached out. I'd better go back, she thought, dreading an early return that would put her face-to-face with Mrs. Murphy.

And then, almost by accident, Byron found his hand and practically punched himself in the mouth with his little fist. He sucked on the closed thumb and two fingers. His eyes shut contentedly.

Soothe yourself, she thought with pride. You and I, we don't need them. We can comfort ourselves with our strength.

PETER STUDIED HIS MOTHER'S THIN, ELEGANT BODY. GAIL WAS dressed in a tight black turtleneck; her breasts made small, almost circular lumps against the material, whitish lumps, the hue presumably caused by a bra.

"Did you breast-feed me?" he asked.

"Nobody did in those days. Are you hurt?" Gail teased Peter with the question, her thin, bloodless lips (pale even with red lipstick) pressed together, holding back a smile.

"Diane says, or, rather, the books say, that some chemical is transferred which helps brain development—"

Gail caught up to him quickly, as always. "So I'm at fault for your bad LSAT's."

"I guess *you* were breast-fed," Peter parried. "You're too clever."

"I gave you good genes, Peter. It's up to you to make something of them. And you have. I'm proud of you." Gail turned her head, apparently to search for a waiter (she raised her unadorned hand in the air to attract attention), but Peter felt she meant to avoid intensifying her words by meeting his eyes. A waiter appeared. "I'd like some ice water please." Gail loved cold water, was the first in the Hamptons to brave the spring ocean, kept a pitcher of fresh water, loaded with ice, to drink as a cocktail years before people gave up hard liquor, and liked, when sailing with her second husband, to stand with her face vulnerable to the spray, not wincing at its cool spit. The hand with which she had gotten the waiter's attention went to her undyed hair, gray (although not stiff or yellowed) and brought back in a simple bun. Her hand smoothed hairs that were not out of place, arranging the arranged. "How's Diane?"

"Fine. She's bounced back from the C section."

"Strong girl," Gail said, with a nod to herself, confirming previous knowledge. "I admire her for planning to go back to work so soon. I should have."

Peter closed his eyes and sighed. Since women's liberation had made such talk fashionable, Gail spoke this way, in little phrases of sacrifice, about her now-defunct ambition to be a painter. Even the recent trend toward praising women for staying home, for the benefits of a nonworking mother, hadn't discouraged the subtle complaints. Peter's irritation made him provocative: "You're chief fund raiser for the most important museum in New York. If you'd gone back to work earlier, you couldn't have accomplished anything more. You merely would have done it sooner."

Gail smiled to herself. "I meant my painting. You can't not garden for ten years and expect to have fertile soil when you return."

"What about Grandma Moses?"

"What are you saying, Peter?" Gail picked up her ice water and took a healthy gulp. There was nothing dainty about her physically; she might push her emotional food about with a reluctant appetite, but she swallowed the real meal with gusto.

"Since Diane fired Mrs. Murphy, I haven't gotten a solid eight hours. I must be cranky."

"You're saying I'm a dilettante," Gail commented.

"If you're a dilettante, what does that make me? No, I'm saying, if you had wanted to paint, you would have. You didn't sacrifice it for your children."

"Well, thank you. I'm glad to find that out. Why did Diane fire Mrs. Murphy?" Gail moved on, but without rush, her tone not making a point of changing the subject—simply altering it.

Peter laughed. "I'm sorry if I hurt your feelings."

"That's nice of you. Did they have a fight? Was she a nuisance?"

"Diane likes things done her way."

"Good for her. But she's going to get some help?"

"She has to. To go back to work."

"Trying to make partner means late hours," Gail said. She squinted at the bright light coming from the restaurant's windows. "I remember that much from being married to your father. Are you going to take the load?"

"No. Now that I've convinced the foundation to commit more money to theater, *I'll* have to go more often. We're funding six theaters in the city and maybe one particular production. That means a lot of cocktail parties and openings."

"When is my grandson going to see his parents then?" Gail asked without emotion, despite the accusation of neglect.

"On the weekends. You're not making sense, Mother. You regret giving up your career, but attack—"

"There's a difference between going to work from nine to five and never being there."

"I've never done anything right in my whole life. You know that. Why should this be any different?" Peter smiled pleasantly, held his head still, his eyes returning her irritated glance evenly. The bluff seemed to work. She opened her mouth to speak, but then shut it, looked off, and frowned. Peter's heart beat loudly while waiting to see if she would fold, but taking in the chips seemed a lonely victory after all.

"When you screw up with children," Gail said, her head still turned away, the small diamond in her earlobe washed out by the strong light, "you mess up a person, not a project." She looked at him. "And you're faced with your failure for the rest of your life."

"Are you—"

"No, I'm not," again faster than he could be. "But I came close. I think it's my duty to warn you. I've told you many times, there are no hidden meanings in what I say. If there's something I don't want to admit to, I say nothing. I don't believe in lying. People always know, or can guess, or, worse, find out."

She doesn't have to lie, he thought. She can contradict herself with absolute conviction, sometimes within a sentence. "How old was I when you and Dad split up?"

"You don't remember?"

"I don't know how old I was."

"You were five. Your fifth birthday was the last party we hosted together."

"I presume that was when you came close."

Gail blinked her eyes. "Came close to what? Are you done? Do you want more coffee?"

"Yes. I mean, no, I'm finished."

She signaled to the waiter, again the hand up, assertive, but casual, and made a writing motion. She looked back at him, with cocktail cheerfulness. "Going back to the office?"

"Yes. Was it the divorce?" Peter asked.

"What are you talking about?"

"Was it the divorce that came close to screwing me up forever, is that what you meant?"

"What gave you that idea?" The waiter handed her a leather case with the check inside. She opened it and frowned. "Outrageous."

"Let me put it on the foundation," he offered.

She laid a platinum American Express card down. "Let your stepfather pay."

"He has a platinum card!" Peter couldn't suppress his horror at this foolish ostentation.

"He likes to remind himself he's rich. I think he worries it's all a dream and needs to pinch himself."

"Never thought discounting electronics would bring Gimbel's and Macy's to their knees?"

"Exactly. He chuckles every time he sees one of their sales in the *Times*."

"He *does*?" Peter was again unable to keep disdain out of his tone.

"Kyle had to struggle for everything he has—you wouldn't understand."

"I know, I know. I'm spoiled, privileged."

"Well, you are privileged, Peter. You can't deny it."

"I was admitting it." He felt the exhaustion of being with Gail; he had spent the lunch shoring himself up against the surf of her critical and whimsical tide, but erosion was inevitable. Time to move away from her ocean.

He put Gail in a cab and walked back to his office in the humid, smelly midtown streets. Only when standing above the central air conditioning vent under his office window, feeling the cool billow his shirt, did he remember that he never got an answer.

Was it the divorce, Mom? Did that almost crush me?

Why wouldn't she answer? Habit?

She didn't want to answer. She admitted that herself.

The cold air snaked up his arms and chilled their hollows. He shivered. I am crushed, crumpled in her pocketbook like a forgotten phone message. Your son called.

Like a recalcitrant city agency, she just never got back to him. So what? He inspected himself for damage. He didn't feel a thing. His mother was a vain woman who took out his father's desertion on him. She neglected Peter to cater to her new husband, making sure she didn't lose another. So what?

Diane would never do that. She loved Byron. Couldn't stand anyone, not even Mrs. Murphy, handling him. Diane was ferocious, a lioness. There was no danger. At least he'd done that one thing right: found a real mother to his son.

"I'M GONNA DRIVE YOU HOME FROM THE HOSPITAL," ERIC'S FAther had insisted on the phone that morning. "I don't want some schmuck cabdriver killing my grandson." Eric had tried to dissuade him, knowing that Nina would want their first experience at home with Luke to be private, but lost the battle.

Later he and Nina sat together, ashamed to look each other in the eyes, while they knew Dr. Ephron was doing the circumcision in the nursery next door. Nina's mother, Joan, interrupted with a phone call. She wanted to fly in for the weekend, along with Nina's youngest sister, and "help with the transition home," as Joan put it.

"I can't talk right now. But I think you should wait until the following weekend. Give us a chance to settle in." Nina listened for a second and insisted, "I can't talk right now," and hung up. Faintly they heard a baby wailing. Eric looked at her. Nina dismissed his silent question. "Could be anyone. We should walk around. Do something."

Eric swallowed. He felt so stupid. The picture of his son's penis, that pinkie between curled frog's legs, being cut—Eric shuddered at the image, at the ease with which castration could occur. They weren't having a *bris* because of Nina, but Eric was glad for selfish reasons. He could never witness the event, much less celebrate it in a ritual.

There was more wailing.

"Okay, let's walk around."

"No," Nina said.

"But you just said—"

"They're bringing him in afterwards to be fed. To help comfort him. I'd better stay. You go for a walk."

"No," he answered, angry that she could be casual about his presence. "I want to make sure it's still on, for Christ's sake."

"Eric!" she said, laughing, but her eyes teared. "Don't say things like that."

"Well, that's what we're worried about! What's the point in not saying it?"

"Nothing is going to happen," she chided.

"You're so full of shit with your brave act."

"Come on," she said, and offered her hand for comfort. "Shut up."

He took her slim hand in his big, thick palm, disarranging her fingers so they were like pencils stored in a bowl. They waited.

"I can't take this," he whispered.

"Shhhh," she said.

"How are you feeling?"

"Fabulous." Her voice was listless.

"Seriously. How are the stitches?"

She winced at the mention of them. "I lied to them."

"What?"

"I told them I had taken a crap. I haven't."

"You have to take a crap?"

"Before they let you go."

"What? They won't let you go until you take a dump? What kind of country are we living in?"

She tried to smile, but her worry weighed her mouth into a sorry grin. "They just want to make sure everything's working okay. That the stitches and everything"—She shut her eyes, as if she could see the wound.

Eric nodded. The wailing could still be heard. "Maybe you shouldn't be lying to them."

"It's nobody's business whether I go to the bathroom!" Nina sat up with outrage, her back stiff with rebellion.

"Yeah, I think that's in the Constitution." He winked at her.

"That's right," Nina agreed. She tried another smile. Her skin was exhausted; even her freckles had paled into virtual nonexistence.

There was a knock on the door. A nurse looked in. "Put on your smock," she said to Eric. "Baby's here."

Eric took the cloth gown from the hook on the door. It was wrinkled and stained with coffee from yesterday's visit. "This is dirtier than my shirt."

"There are laundered smocks at the nursery," the nurse said, opening the door for Eric to pass. Beside her in the hallway, asleep in his bin, was Luke. Nina peered at Luke, an alert deer. "He's sleeping," the nurse told Nina. "How are you feeling? Haven't done any more fainting, I hope?"

"Fainting?" Eric stopped on his way out, next to Luke. He looked down at his son. Luke's exhausted head lay on its side. The eyelid looked puffy, worn-out.

"Nothing," Nina said. "First night I was here, I got a little dizzy. Did they do the circumcision?"

"Didn't the doctor come by?" the nurse asked with surprise.

"No," Eric asked, afraid. "Why?"

"Supposed to," the nurse said with disdain.

"Is everything all right?" Nina asked.

"He's perfect," the nurse said. "He'll sleep for a while and then want to eat."

Eric left and went to the nursery, finding a clean gown in a basket at the entrance. On his tall body, it looked like a short dress. The nurse on duty laughed at the sight. "You could use two of them," she said.

He smiled pleasantly, but he wanted to punch her out. With their faint air of contempt and amused anticipation of nervousness and incompetence with children, the nurses made Eric feel he was a baby. When Eric got back to the room, the other nurse was lecturing Nina on how to change Luke's diaper until his penis healed. Eric forced himself to listen. Some Vaseline had to be put on a gauze strip and placed on the wounded tip, "to prevent the raw skin from getting stuck to the diaper," she said casually.

The image pushed Eric down into a chair and he crossed his legs. He wanted to laugh at himself, but couldn't. His eyes went to Luke. Circumcision is insane, he judged, despite the ghosts of thousands of his forebears. More Jewish insanity, he thought. An image of the local Washington Heights temple, a tiny ugly modern building squeezed between two tall apartment houses, answered Eric unconvincingly. He remembered the first time his father took him to services. He was squeezed, like the temple, between the tall men, pushed along will-lessly, overwhelmed by their heavy smells and frightened by their low, rumbling voices. When the rabbi spoke of his people wandering for forty years in the Sinai, Eric imagined shuffling slowly amidst a crowd of the Washington Heights devout. He thought of the wandering as a rush-hour subway ride on the IRT, rather than a lonely journey in an immense desert.

"Poor baby," Eric heard Nina say as she pulled the bin beside her. The nurse had left. Eric couldn't speak. He watched Luke; his head rested heavily on the tiny mattress, revealing only a profile to study. The mouth worked from time to time for invisible succor. The bruises of birth were almost gone; Luke looked pretty, the small skull covered by a chaotic mass of black hair, curling up on the compressed fat nape of his neck. His back rose and fell with effort. His eye winced at a memory.

"Sorry," Eric heard himself say.

Nina looked at Eric with remorse and affection. "He won't remember," she said, sounding unconvinced.

"How do you know? Now I feel like I remember."

"No," Nina protested, but uncertainly.

"And with me they had some schmuck do it. 'The *mohel* is very safe,' Dad said, trying to get me to do it with Luke. 'Much safer than some *schwartzer* intern.' "

"Shhhh," Nina said.

"Dad wants to drive us home," Eric said casually, praying for an easy passage of this bill.

"Okay," she said. "The doctor said they can't feel it."

"Oh, yeah? Fuck the doctor. What's she been doing, interviewing the newborns?"

"Something about the nerves," Nina said. She put a protective hand on the bin. "They aren't really developed."

"Oh, bullshit. They say that to make us feel better."

"Eric, calm down."

He tried. He shut his mouth and folded his arms, but his leg hopped up and down nervously. Luke shuddered and that quieted Eric—he froze in position. Luke's head moved, and then, abruptly, his mouth opened, his face reddened, and he let out a pained squeal.

They reached for him simultaneously, but Eric backed off at the last moment. Nina picked up Luke. He curled in the air, his legs drawn up, his head falling forward, a spineless creature shrieking in pain—an outraged, betrayed series of squawks that terrified Eric.

"Oh, poor baby," Nina said. But her tone was confident, casual. She cradled Luke in one arm while slipping her gown off with her free hand. She brushed her mane of brown hair off her shoulder and exposed her breast; it was expanded, puffed like a torpedo, her nipple thick and dark red—unrecognizable to Eric. Luke cried, helpless, and flopped in her arms, muscleless, his delicate features twisted by his agony.

Hurry, hurry, Eric thought, disgusted by her slow movements, her calm. "Yes, baby, yes, baby," she said, picking up Luke again (his body curled pathetically, impotent in her hands) and speaking to his distorted face. "Mommy's going to feed you."

"Hurry up, for Christ's sakes!" Eric shouted.

Nina was startled. She stared at Eric for a long moment, deciding how to react. She frowned, finally, and then brought Luke, now a sobbing wreck, to her monstrous tit. Luke opened his tiny lips, the cavern of his mouth yawned, and somehow, despite being over-matched, he surrounded the giant nipple. Luke clamped on it, *hard*, sucking madly. His eyes closed with a desperate satisfaction, his puffy cheeks rippling from the suction within.

"Yes, baby," Nina whispered to Luke. Her hand, fragile and slim in Eric's grip, encompassed the whole of his son's skull, forceful and dominant. Luke sighed. The breath of relief shook Luke's entire body, despair and loneliness trembling out of him like a fever passing. She had drained him of his despair and sorrow, applied balm to his wounded and betrayed soul, with the ease of someone flipping a light switch. All she had to do was bring Luke to her breast.

What could Eric do? Hold that tiny head to his chest? To his hard, hairy breast? What a fucking joke.

Nina looked big, an ocean liner docked on the hospital bed. Luke was quiescent at her breast, hardly longer than half the length of her arm, the dark hair of his head even blacker against her white skin. The gown slipped off her other shoulder. She was nude from the waist up, her beautiful long neck and wide shoulders as balanced, as delicate, and as graceful as a dancer's. This was a sight that normally would have made Eric hard. Her breasts had always been big and firm: ripe for him. Now they seemed monstrous, the free nipple inflated so that the porous holes were visible, the swollen base of her breasts so free from their origin they might be glued on; they were the exaggerated boobs of a pornographic magazine, of an adolescent boy's nightmarish wet dream.

Luke, abruptly, pulled away and shrieked.

"Shhh," she said, and pushed Luke's head toward her, butting his mouth with her rubbery nipple. His mouth yearned for it instantly, cutting off the scream of pain in mid-note. He jawed at her with unabashed greed, lustful, comically desperate.

"I'm going to check on the market," Eric said, nervous and irritated. He stood up. And waited.

Nina didn't look at Eric. She was absorbed by Luke. She stroked his black mess of hair, petting him.

"Okay?" Eric asked.

Now she looked up slowly, her eyes liquid with pleasure. "Sure," she said in a bedroom voice.

"Want me to get you anything?"

She frowned at him. "Where are you going?"

"To check on the market."

"Why don't you use the phone here?" Luke yanked away, angry again, his face protesting, screeching. She shushed him, urging his head back, poking him with her nipple, its magnetism overpowering him once again into intent chewing.

Eric watched, stunned. Absorbed.

"Why don't you call from here?" she said.

"What? Oh. I want to get myself some coffee. You want anything?"

"I need cigarettes."

"And you a nursing mother."

"Give me a break."

He kept watching. "He seems okay."

She stroked his head. "He's perfect."

"That's what the nurse said."

"Did she?" Nina smiled with innocent delight. "Well, she's right."

"Good-bye," he said, and walked out into the hall briskly. Eric passed two Orthodox Jewish women wearing babushkas, shuffling along. Behind them were, he presumed, their husbands, hot in their black suits, their fat, fleshy faces covered with thin, kinky hairs. The men spoke rapidly, their voices gruff and arrogant. The two women were silent and serene together, their duties fulfilled; the two men battered each other with words about business. Eric wanted them all dead.

Downstairs in the lobby he found a quiet, old-fashioned booth and dialed Sammy's private line. "Hi, how we doing?"

"You fucked up again," Sammy said, with enthusiasm. "Telecom went into the toilet. Everything got stopped at seven."

"Fifteen percent. So what? That's the rule."

"Yeah, fifteen percent loss, fifteen percent loss, fifteen percent loss, and pretty soon Mrs. Shwartz is actually trying to live on Social Security."

"What about ITT?"

"Flat! That's a dog. You should get them out."

"Do you have any good news?"

"Dad's play short on the oils netted twenty percent. You were wrong again, bozo."

"You didn't tell him I disagreed?"

"Disagreed! You went along with your clients. That's the only reason you didn't lose them all today."

"Yeah, yeah." Eric sighed. He closed his eyes and tried to visualize the accounts. He couldn't. "Look. I'm gonna take off the rest of this week. I can't handle things—"

"No commissions on our ideas if you're not in the office."

"I know, asshole. Tell your papa. I gotta go."

"How's your baby?"

Eric opened his mouth to answer—but what? The great feeling he had for that insensible creature: how to describe that? "He's perfect."

"Must have gotten it from his mama."

"Good-bye," Eric said, and hung up on Sammy's laughter. He had no spirit for their competitive banter today. He had been wrong again on the oil stocks. He had been wrong on Telecom. ITT had done nothing. He was a jerk. He had tried hard the last three years, read all the material, taken Joe's (Sammy's father and Eric's boss) principles to heart, but nothing worked. Eric had done better when he went on instinct, buying stocks without any knowledge of their fundamentals.

That baby up there needed money. Needed to be free of the jokes of Sammy, the advice of Joe, and the whimsy of the market. Luke needed money. I have to do better. Go back to daring hunches if necessary. I have to do better. Money, money, money, money. That was the milk he could give Luke to quiet the screeching pain of life.

4

DIANE HAD INTERVIEWED NINE WOMEN SO FAR, ALL NO good. Her once-clear picture of the ideal nanny to take care of Byron was now blurred by reality's greasy fingers.

She had begun the search confidently, had set down (in her organized fashion) the qualities she wanted: speak English well (so as not to retard Byron's language development); forty years old or under (for vigor), either childless or with grown children (Byron should not have to compete for the woman's heart); reside within fifteen or twenty minutes by subway (in case of emergencies); have references (appearances are deceiving); and look attractive (since appearances are important).

Diane would sit with Byron beside her in an infant seat, a legal notepad listing her requirements in her lap, and question the prospects, checking off how well they met them. Not long into the process she added more things to her list. One woman, eager, like all of them, for the job, chatted nervously and let slip that she supervised her invalid mother's care. When Diane warned her that the hours might be irregular, considering both her and Peter's jobs, this woman, unconvincingly, maintained that her sister could always stay with their mother in the evenings. Another said she would be happy to stay late but would need cab fare home, or have to sleep over, because her neighborhood was dangerous. Therefore, flexible hours became another item, along with no responsibilities to anyone else, not even a husband.

Although Diane decided against the woman with the sick mother and the other living in the scary neighborhood, they were the only two whom she had seriously considered. The others were looking for green-card sponsors, Caribbean women in search of American citizenship. Diane was convinced they would quit the moment that glory was achieved. She also distrusted the low wages they were willing to accept. Two hundred and fifty a week was the going rate; some of the illegal aliens would take one fifty. Although that was an incentive to go through the hassle of sponsoring them, nevertheless, "You get what you pay for" was more than a cynical aphorism to Diane; it was observed truth.

Diane realized, baffled by the similarity of the nannies (sweet and obsequious, but with proud remarks on how good they were with children, and lots of smiles and coos at Byron's great bald head and unsmiling countenance), that the one essential fact, how well they could take care of an infant, was unknowable. Diane was haunted by the fear that once out of her sight, the nanny would watch soap operas all day, leaving Byron's brain to rust from tears at sentimental melodrama.

Diane feared intellectual and physical neglect despite the consistent theme each woman voiced: that she would take Byron to the park every day the weather was nice, to the museum during the winter, to infant swimming classes, and so on. The woman with the invalid mother even claimed she had done Suzuki violin (a method of teaching two-year-olds how to play) with her last charge.

How to know? The references? That meant relying on the judgment of other women, who might be wrong or have lower standards.

The New York Times, as it had so often, rescued her with a snooty piece on nanny stealing. A reporter had sat with the nannies in Riverside Park and discovered that new mothers often spied on them, picked out the best, and stole them away from their current employers by offering more money. The story was disapproving, but Diane understood too well why those mothers did it and promptly took Byron to Washington Square Park with her notepad.

There were two children's areas in the park, quarantined by chain-link fences from the drug dealers, the bums, the necking students, and the quarrelsome teenagers of Washington Square. The smaller of the two was for infants and early toddlers. Its sandbox was modest; mostly the place was for sitting with carriages and strollers. On the other side of the square the children's area was four times larger. Besides having a much bigger sandbox, there were swings, slides, a climbing dome, a pole, and two wooden structures ideal for hiding, climbing, or sleeping—the last done not by the children, but by the homeless who, at night, scaled the four-foot fences and left in their wake a pungent odor.

Diane reasoned that to observe nannies with immobile babies was uninstructive, so she made for the more grown-up playground.

There, at ten o'clock in the morning, she found few possibilities. Half of the caretakers present were the actual mothers. Two mothers came over to look at Byron, their faces glowing with affectionate memory, their questions amazingly precise. "Does he sleep through the night? Really? You're so lucky. Janie's four and she still doesn't." This mother, who seemed to laugh at every problem, to admit to being overwhelmed, was young, dressed in sloppy jeans and a wrinkled New York University T-shirt (the park was surrounded by that school; presumably she was a faculty wife); the other woman, although she seemed to be a friend of the cheerful incompetent (as were their daughters), was dressed casually, but in fashion: red Reebok sneakers, black tights, a loose white-and-red pin-striped oxford shirt, her haircut short on the sides, long in back, hinting at punkishness, but still arranged enough to allow entry to Lutèce. The fashionable mother made casual fun of her friend's confessions that she couldn't get her daughter to obey her at anything, and had definite opinions on every aspect of child rearing.

Diane told them she needed a housekeeper-nanny and asked if they knew of a good one. The fashionable mother seemed to distance herself immediately. Her back straightened, and a close-mouthed smile of uncomfortable formality appeared, as if she had donned a mask. The incompetent laughed, inexplicably, and said, nodding at her chic friend: "Karen's got the best in the world. She even irons her husband's underpants." The comment wasn't sarcastic, and Karen seemed to withdraw even more, as if she were mentally hastening home to lock up valuables. Diane asked Karen whether she worked (she already knew that the slob did not. "I've done nothing for four years but watch cartoons," the woman had said at one point) and learned that Karen was an art director at *Newstime*, which meant she got Mondays off—hence her presence at the park.

Since there were few actual examples of hired child care to watch, Diane concentrated on interrogating Karen about her prize nanny, Pearl. To Diane's surprise Pearl was described as a southern black who spoke with a heavy accent, was in her fifties, had an invalid mother and a grown daughter who lived with her, was hired without references, and never took Karen's daughter to museums, Suzuki violin, infant swimming, or, indeed, any other activity than to the playground at Washington Square. "What makes her so great?" Diane asked finally.

"She loves Laura, my daughter."

"Pearl carried Laura everywhere for a year," the incompetent said, laughing again. "If it were up to Pearl, Laura might still be in her arms."

Karen nodded. "She did the ironing, the vacuuming, everything, while holding on to Laura."

"Weren't you worried it would spoil your daughter?"

"It did, in some ways. But what would you rather worry about? Spoiling or neglect?"

"That's true," Diane conceded, but later, at home, she couldn't fit the various sociological pieces of those two women and their notion of the perfect nanny into a coherent picture. She returned to the park the next day, in the afternoon this time, having learned that most children in the mornings were in day camps, or tumbling classes, or Suzuki violin, or any of a dozen other activities during the break between the end of the nursery school year and the start of Hampton vacations.

She spotted Pearl, the so-called best housekeeper-nanny, and her charge, Laura, right away. Laura was a self-possessed dark-haired girl who stood in front of Pearl delivering a self-centered speech about her friendships. Pearl smiled and nodded patiently through the talk. "Paula doesn't want to play She-Ra in yard," Laura said. "She doesn't want to share the pretend. She only wants to play with me. That's because I have better toys than Zoey. And Zoey always messes things up in yard."

"All right," Pearl said, nodding while she brushed off the little girl's dress so unobtrusively the cleaning was almost subversive.

"It's clean!" the little horror complained anyway, but she didn't step away.

"I know it is. I'm sorry," Pearl said penitently. "I'm always fussing, you know that."

"Yeah, yeah, you fuss too much. It's not good for you. You need to relax," Laura added, and then skipped off without a good-bye.

Instead of being angry, Pearl laughed with delight and threw her head back, the white of her dentures bright against her golden brown skin. Diane's concentration on Pearl caused their eyes to meet and Pearl cut off her laughter, even covered her mouth, self-consciously. "She's right," Pearl confessed. Then she noticed Byron. "Oh, a new baby!" she exclaimed. "How old's he?"

"Three weeks."

"He's big! My, my. So big!" Her own big hands reached into the carriage. Pearl offered her fat index finger and Byron immediately closed his tiny white hand on it. She allowed him to pull the tip to his mouth, the soft lips closing, sucking. "Strong. Yes, yes, yes," she said, and leaned over his carriage. "You're a strong one.'' Byron froze, his bold stare focused on her. It was the first person Diane had seen him truly notice besides herself. ''Yes, little man, you're strong. You hungry? You always hungry, right?''

Diane heard herself laugh. Her breasts were sore, one nipple had cracked—even when she wore a shield, his jawing hurt. ''He sure is.''

''Well, you're a big one, that's why,'' Pearl continued, her focus on Byron so complete the conversation seemed to be between them. Pearl gently pulled her finger back from his lips. ''My hand's not clean,'' she whispered to Byron. ''I been in the park messing with things. I'm dirty. My hands are dirty. Yes, yes, they are!'' Pearl turned from him, her hand straying on his belly, a comforting paw. ''He's a beauty.''

''Thank you.'' Diane was melted. After all, this wasn't a job interview. Pearl had no motive to praise Byron. This woman loved babies. Diane had to have her. ''When does Lau—'' she stopped herself. She didn't want Pearl to know that she had met Karen the day before. ''What's your girl's name?''

''Laura. She makes me laugh. She's so proud and smart. Wish my daughter was like that. She has no opinion of herself. Not like Laura. She knows she's something.''

''Laura's in school?''

''All morning! I miss her. Have nothing to do. I get my work done in a hour. Do the washing Monday, my ironing's done Tuesday.'' Pearl looked off, couldn't spot Laura in the sandbox (she had crouched beneath the low concrete enclosure), and stood on her tiptoes until she did. ''Wish they'd have another baby.'' She peered in at Byron. ''Right? Like you, strong boy! A baby brother for Laura. That would be good.''

Oh, Diane sagged, disappointed. She *is* fishing for a job. Laura's mother, Karen, knows that, hence her reserved praise. For a moment Diane was quiet and considered abandoning her plan. But after all, even if it was an act with Byron, the performance was excellent. Isn't that what we pay for? she asked herself. I'm a terrific lawyer, I don't really care about my clients, but I work my butt off because I'm a performer. What's the difference? ''Next year,'' Diane said, ''I guess she'll be in school all day.''

Pearl shook her head. ''Don't want to think about it. I'll be so lonely.''

''I have to go back to work soon. I really should be back now.''

''Really? So soon? That's terrible.''

''I need someone to take care of Byron.''

''What?''

"My son."

"I'm getting so hard-of-hearing. I'm almost deaf. I really am. What's his name again?"

"Byron," Diane confessed, embarrassed.

Pearl looked puzzled. "Family name?"

"Sort of. I'd really like to hire you."

"Thank you very much," she said easily, unsurprised by the offer. "But I couldn't leave my girl so soon. Her parents are counting on me, at least for the summer."

"That's not fair to you. Keep you hanging on through the summer without guaranteeing you a job for the fall and winter."

"Oh, when they done with me, I be moving to Florida. Got good friends living there. I can get easy work. I stayed on for Laura." She looked off again to check on her. "If they had another, I'd keep working up here. I don't think they will. Her mother . . ." She trailed off. "She has an important job. Don't have time, I guess."

Diane listened. She was convinced all of it was merely negotiating. She nodded seriously and thought about how Brian Stoppard handled such matters; dealing with this poor black woman was probably no different from handling a corporate vice-president. "I'd appreciate it if you could recommend someone. We live right there on Fifth and Tenth, in a three bedroom co-op. We can pay three hundred a week, maybe more if she can work at night sometimes."

Pearl said, "Three hundred?" immediately.

"Is that too little?"

"I never was good at arithmetic. How much is that an hour?"

"Seven-fifty an hour."

Pearl smiled. "No, ma'am. That's not too little." She looked into Byron's carriage again. His eyes blinked rapidly at the spectacle of her face; his legs rippled the blankets; his arms waved at the air. "Hello," she sang to him. "Oh, you're cute. Can I pick him up?"

"Sure," Diane said. A smile of triumph welled within her, although she kept her lips tight, her manner casual.

Pearl lifted him from the carriage. Her hands were enormous, the fingers meeting around his torso, smoky brown against the white stretchy. Pearl lifted him into the air. His mouth formed an O; his tiny feet kicked at the absence of ground; his eyes bulged at the big bright world.

Diane sighed. She had Pearl hooked. Things were under control.

ERIC AND NINA LEFT THE HOSPITAL WITH LUKE ON A BEAUTIFUL spring day. They were driven the twelve blocks home by Eric's father, Barry, who never went faster than fifteen miles an hour.

Miriam, Eric's mother, sat next to her husband in the passenger seat, twisted around to keep her eyes on Luke, talking to Nina throughout the ride. Nina held Luke in her arms. She winced at every pothole (the episiotomy, the episiotomy, she thought, will there ever be an end to my pain?) and only occasionally heard her mother-in-law's chatter.

"Eric was so big when he was born! I couldn't carry him."

"Oh, yeah!" her husband, Barry, said.

"He was over ten pounds!" she argued to him.

"Please!" he answered.

A truck rattled past Nina's window, the unevenly paved section of Second Avenue shaking its cargo. Luke squealed. His sleepy eyelids squeezed together unhappily. "It's okay, baby," Nina said to him. "Just the crazy city."

"No place to raise a child," Miriam argued.

"The *only* place to raise kids," Barry answered. "You want him to be some schmuck Westchester kid who wouldn't have the smarts to pump gas?"

"That's right, Dad," Eric said. "Kids who grow up in the suburbs are almost unemployable in this country."

"Please!" Barry said. "Their rich fathers give them jobs. They couldn't get anything on their own."

"Sure, sure," Miriam said sarcastically about her husband's remarks, although she kept her eyes on Nina and Luke. "Even if we had made the money to move to the suburbs, we wouldn't have done it. For Eric's sake! So much better for him to grow up playing in between cars, being chased by the blacks in the park."

"There were no blacks chasing us in the park, Mom," Eric said quickly, hoping to cut off his father's angry response.

He failed. "Money had nothing to do with it! We could have moved to the suburbs on our income."

Miriam smiled at Nina. She shook her head and closed her eyes sadly. Then she brought a hand to her lips, kissed it, and put the hand on her husband's cheek. "No excitement! We have our baby grandson in the car."

They're kooks, Nina thought, not for the first time, but without a shudder of revulsion. They were gutted fish on a dock; their innards quivered in public for all the world to see. She looked down at Luke, asleep, his face a mask: the bridge of his nose flat, the beautiful lips sealed, lying in state like a sculpture on a bishop's tomb, the occupant done in cool marble, making him perfect and timeless. But he was a Jew, this baby, this son, this person from her and yet not from her.

Nina had told Eric not to let his parents come upstairs, just as she had prevented her parents (or her mother at any rate) from being there. She didn't know why she had felt that she and Eric being alone with Luke the first time was important—until now. She didn't want Luke to know anything of the world but them, the two of them, so different, her interior hidden, his exploded; she wanted Luke to make himself out of their incompatible materials, to fashion himself new, created by none of the old forms.

"Will you raise the baby Jewish?" Nina's mother had once asked.

"Do you even know what that means?" she had answered.

"You know what I mean."

"He will be raised by us," Nina had said.

Her mother had frowned and said, "These things have to be thought about. I don't care what you decide. But confusion isn't good for children."

"You think being raised Jewish isn't confusing?"

"Being nothing is more confusing," her mother had said.

"My baby won't be nothing," she had answered, furious.

The car pulled up in front of their building. Ramon, the afternoon doorman, rushed out to open the door, the cheeks on his fat, round face puffing up with his broad smile. *"¡Hola!"* he shouted at Luke.

"He's asleep!" Nina snapped.

"You don't want us to park and come up?" Barry asked.

Nina froze in position, her legs out of the car, her torso inside, thinking: I swear, I'll never forgive you, Eric, if you let them.

"We can be a big help," Barry sold himself. "We raised a kid, you know."

"Uh . . ." came out of Eric.

"Let them be," Miriam said. "They need to rest. We'll visit tomorrow."

While negotiating the lobby—Nina moved slowly, giving an impression of protective motherhood, although it was her sore wound that needed the care—Nina reflected that Eric was incapable of saying no to his father. That task always fell to Miriam. Father and son were overpowering men, not only physically and vocally, but in their vibrant, expressive faces. Refusing them was to hurt a bear: a huge, warm, gentle creature shocked by cruelty, his pain and fear made more pathetic by the size of the suffering. Eric feared disappointing his father's expectations and love as much as Nina feared failing Eric.

She thought of this as a problem not in relation to herself. She didn't mind. After all, she had no desire to let Eric down. He demanded only affection and attention; there was nothing brutal in his wants. She thought of it for Luke. Sons have to say no to their fathers, she argued to herself in the elevator, the tower of Eric beside her, Luke unconscious in her arms. The shadow of this man could forever block the sun from her child, obliterate from Luke's sight much that was not in Eric's vision but existed in hers. The world, for Eric, was composed of things: gadgets, money, luxuries, ways of doing. For her the planet had life: in its changing sky, in the aging of faces, in the dirt of buildings, in the brisk efficiency of winter and the languorous sex of summer.

Eric believed people and the things they did were important; sometimes Nina could contemplate the end of humanity not only with calm but with a kind of relief. She didn't bleed at every horror on the news; she didn't weep while passing the homeless, covered, like forgotten cars, with grime; she didn't rage at all the blood-thirsty bigotry of the international world, black against white, Jew against Arab; she didn't despair at the great listless heads of the starving. Instead, she felt hopelessness keenly in all the world's activities.

Nina stood in the hallway while Eric fumbled with the keys. He was nervous; his body moved ahead of his intentions and left him uncoordinated. He had stumbled in the lobby when he simultane-ously moved ahead to the elevator and then reversed direction to help her. He had raced to press the buttons inside, mistakenly hold-ing the door open button until she pointed it out. Now, in his haste to get the right key in the lock, he had dropped the ring. There was silence throughout the building. Everything he did echoed in the stairwell near their door.

She felt dread at this waiting. In the hospital her intimacy with Luke seemed apart from the world and its ghastliness. When they crossed the doorsill to their apartment, the struggle to raise Luke in the mad world would begin. She wanted Luke to know, really know, there was a place of beauty for him, not the decorated pret-tiness of an apartment, but the warm, messy love of home, as she had felt with her brothers and sisters in that rambling house in Brookline, Massachusetts. The noise of dinner, the soft fabric of nightclothes, the games of Christmas, the excitement of Saturday morning, the regret of Sunday night—all the joys of her childhood she wanted to be Luke's. She suddenly felt this life for Luke, here, shelved horizontally in the storehouse of New York, reared by a huge father obsessed by possessions, was pregnant with disaster.

They entered.

The apartment was still. An open window in their bedroom lifted a white curtain, billowing like a sail on Blue Hill Bay. "We're home, baby," she said to Luke, and moved the hand she had supporting his bottom. The diaper felt softer than usual. She pressed it again. There was something slippery underneath. "I think he's taken a crap," she said to Eric.

"You're kidding!" he said as though an astounding and disastrous turn of events had occurred.

"They do that, you know."

"The changing table's all set up," Eric said, again in a rush to do things his body wasn't ready for. He tried to put her bag down and motion her toward the baby's room in one gesture and nearly toppled himself as a result. He had to put out one hand on the floor to prevent a complete spill.

She found herself laughing uncontrollably, her body quaking from it, shaking Luke. Luke moaned. "Shhh," Nina said to Eric, but she meant it for herself. "Don't make me laugh."

"I'm not trying to!"

"Relax."

"Okay. I'm fine. It's in here. I've set everything up." Eric pointed to Luke's room. She moved to have a view of it. The crib was badly placed, against the far wall between the windows. The changing table, which was really an antique dresser inherited from her grandmother, was in the middle against a wall. All quite wrong: the arrangement lacked any sense of flow; the objects were merely plunked down. She regretted again that she hadn't redone the whole apartment while pregnant. "We'll have to move the changing table by the window and put the crib here." She gestured to indicate the wall farthest from the windows, where he had put the inexpensive white shelves, intended for the toys Luke would inevitably acquire.

"Why?" Eric objected. "We can hear him better over there," he said, meaning that the crib was next to the bathroom, which was also connected to their bedroom.

She shook her head no. Explaining was too complicated and she didn't want the bother of reasoning Eric out of it. She knew anyway he argued merely as a point of pride, irritated he had displeased her. Now Luke added to the disharmony. He woke up, with immediate angry cries.

"What's the matter?" Eric pleaded, his face bewildered.

"He needs to be changed."

"He knows that?"

Nina walked to the dresser and put Luke on his back. Luke's face turned red. His hollow mouth yawned with screeching objections.

The sound quickened her heartbeat, made her feel she had to be fast: that Luke was a ticking bomb she had to defuse. "Where are the diapers?" she demanded.

"Diapers?" Eric said slowly. "Oh, my God."

"The hospital package," she said, nodding at the paper bag the nurse had given her with free baby supplies.

Luke's cries raged on as she unsnapped his tiny outfit. A dark mass showed through the diaper material, and had spread across the bottom to ooze from the side onto his thighs. The gook looked like oatmeal. She heard tearing sounds from behind her, and a glance revealed Eric, frantic, unable to open the stapled bag, ripping it apart. The sample package of four diapers also frustrated him. He pulled its top off in one motion. She knew his actions were funny, but she felt only impatience.

When she took another look at Luke (his chest now heaving with frightened, angry bewilderment), she noticed the oatmeal had gotten onto his clothes, and was squashed up his back, messing the plastic of the mattress and staining the bottom of his undershirt. Luke would have to be totally stripped and lifted off the mattress, which would then need wiping before clean clothes could be laid down. She had done all this several times in the hospital, but then Luke had been quiet, his arms maneuvering in the air awkwardly, his unfocused eyes peering with studied wonder at lights and shadows. To take the time now, with his wailing, seemed impossible.

Eric brought a diaper over. "What's the matter?" he said, not to her, but to Luke, as if he were sensible, capable of response.

"The wipes!" she said, pronouncing the words hard. She could barely keep from screaming.

"Right here!" he said, shouting to be heard over Luke's cries. He lifted a blue plastic container of moistened cloths beside Luke's kicking feet. It had been right in front of her eyes.

She lifted Luke's legs, gripping his toy feet so hard they went red. "You're hurting him," Eric said.

She pulled the diaper, a pot overflowing with the hot cereal, from under him, folded it—the stuff squeezed out the sides—and handed the mass to Eric. He took it manfully, but then stood there watching, while the slop in his hands threatened to drop on the floor. "Throw it out!" she yelled over Luke's now-rending cries, broken by gasps for breath. She had Luke's lower half in the air, his feet together in one hand, like a trussed chicken. She looked at the smeared mattress and realized she would need more than simply the wipes to clean it off.

"Where?" Eric asked.

"In the kitchen. And get some paper towels!"

Eric ran to the kitchen. She heard him banging the cabinet doors, opening and closing them violently.

A look at Luke: eyes gone, mouth a pulsing cavern of agony, fingers scratching for help. She put a hand on his bony, throbbing chest. "Shhhh! Shhhhh!" she hissed, intended as a comfort, but her voice sounded scared and angry.

Eric rushed in, sweating, carrying a huge roll of paper towels still in its plastic package. He couldn't get it open; the wrapping clung to his fingers. In desperation, he knelt beside her, furious, and dug through it to the paper towels, but at the cost of many sheets, torn apart by his method. He handed her a wad of fragments.

The stuff, at first, only spread out more, sliding from under the towels. Some of it splattered on her dress. Some oozed through the holes Eric's fingers had made and squeezed through onto her hand.

A wave of nausea hit her stomach. Luke's gasps for breath seemed to go on longer. Could he be choking?

She began to tremble.

Eric appeared. He banged against her hip. There was a flurry of paper, flags of it waving over the changing table, covering everything. A section fluttered on top of Luke's face. She heard herself scream. She pulled it off him.

"It's fine, it's fine!" Eric yelled. He was tossing gobs of soiled paper towels onto the floor. The mattress was clean. "How do I do the diaper?" he shouted, aiming it under Luke. Now Eric was holding Luke's legs up.

She pushed the diaper into position. Eric dropped Luke's legs. Together they pulled the fasteners out, sealing them across the front. Eric instantly picked the wailing frog to his massive chest and swung his body from side to side.

"Please baby please baby please baby, it's all right, it's all right, it's all right." Eric's brow, covered by sweat, furrowed comically, his eyes wide, like a boy holding back tears.

She took a breath. There was a stabbing soreness at the bottom of her body, at some mysterious place around, beside, above, below her vagina and anus. She felt the floor undulate.

I won't faint!

"Give him to me," she said.

"He's all right!" Eric shouted. Luke was quiet. Eric rocked his body from side to side so fast that she thought Luke's brains must be rattled.

"I have to feed him," she said softly.

Eric stopped his movements. He looked at her dubiously. What was wrong with him?

"Give him to me," she repeated. "He has to be fed."

She looked at the room, so beautifully in order only a minute before. There were papers everywhere, colored with the strange soupy muck of her son; there were slain boxes, their entrails scattered across the floor. Eric rose like a ruined tower amidst the chaos, his shirt out, darkened by nervous continents of perspiration, his mouth open stupidly, his huge arms crossed, impaling the little creature to his chest, fiercely gripping Luke to protect him from the barbarians.

"Are you okay now?" he asked.

"I'm fine!" she said. The question made her ache with irritation. What the hell was the matter with him?

"Are you sure?"

She looked at the mess. She began to laugh, from her belly. From her punched-out middle, laughter trembled.

"Look at the room," she said.

"I'll clean it," he said humorlessly. "Are you all right?"

"Goddamm it! Yes! Stop it! Stop saying that!"

He made no answer. He looked down at Luke and kissed the strange confused head of hair. Eric's lips puffed out to make the contact gentle. He kissed Luke over and over. The sight was mesmerizing. Eric looked like an ape grooming his baby. From Luke there came sounds: peeps, sighs, moans, and then a squawk.

"He's hungry," she said, exhausted, almost unable to speak. She eased herself into the rocking chair under the window.

"Here we go," Eric said, approaching with Luke.

She glanced at her watch to note the time of the feeding.

They had been home ten minutes.

PETER ANSWERED THE PHONE EAGERLY. HE GRABBED THE RE-ceiver—reaching for salvation. Rescue, anyway, from the tedium of home. At nine o'clock Diane was already asleep, exhausted by her solo care of Byron. This was the final week of her housebound status. She still had no assurance of a nanny. However, she claimed she was close to hiring away a terrific woman for the amazing fee of three hundred a week. Three hundred a week! The amount wasn't a problem. Between them, Diane and Peter earned one hundred and sixty thousand a year, and his trust fund yielded him an additional after-tax income of fifty thousand. But Peter thought of their resources as exceptional. How in God's name were all those other people paying for it? And there were so many! Since the birth of

Byron, he had noticed the streets of New York were abundant with children: well-dressed, alert toddlers overseen by black, brown, and coffee-skinned women. Everywhere he saw little white boys and girls pulled reluctantly by large dark hands, their pale, smudged tear-stained faces wiped and kissed by thick lips, or their limp, exhausted bodies carried by plump, sweaty peasant arms. Children of the rich raised by the poor.

It gave him pause. Why?

Peter's childhood—after the divorce—had been the same, although his caretakers had been white: a fat, affectionate Polish woman, a dour young Swedish graduate student, a cheerful middle-aged English nanny dressed in starched white. Weren't they merely versions of the current phenomenon? He had grown up intelligent, well educated, socialized. He was no finger-licking, drug-taking street tough. He had no urges to have a few beers and go bowling.

He began to laugh. All these thoughts were so deliciously unliberal, unprogressive, bigoted. And as he laughed, the sleeping silence of his tedious home was broken by the ringing phone.

"Hello?"

A pause. Not a broken connection. There was someone there. Rachel? He hoped.

"Hello," he repeated, gently, to encourage her.

"Uh . . . hello, this is Pearl. Is this the Hummel residence?"

The black southern accent told him this was Diane's hope. "Yes, it is."

"I met your wife in the park. I take care—"

"Yes, yes," he said eagerly. "She told me."

"Is she there?"

"She's asleep. I can have her call you tomorrow, or—"

"She said you needed a baby-sitter for your boy. He's so beautiful! A strong head. I think he's gonna be a big boy."

That pipsqueak? My son? Peter was five-seven, Diane five-five. The chances Byron would be big were small. "Thank you," he said.

"I can't leave my girl right now. Wouldn't be fair to her parents. But my friend—I don't know whether you need to hear about other people—but my friend Francine is looking for work. She's taken care of many children. I never recommend people, you understand? I would be ashamed to recommend somebody who wasn't any good, who might not be good. Oh, I would die if something bad happened because people had trusted me and I had to recommend someone who wasn't good. My friend, I've known her since I was young, she's taken care of many, many children—"

Peter had opened his mouth several times to answer, but she kept on, her pauses unexpected.

"—she knows what she's doing. And she's ready right now, just like your wife needs. But you don't even have to see her or talk to her. I just felt obliged to help out, you understand?"

"Yes—"

"And my friend, she's good, just as good as me. Although I like to think I'm the best, you understand; we all think we're special in some ways. I may not be much—I didn't get much schooling, I'm no good handling doctors or Con Edison, but I knows children. I love them and take good care. My friend's the same. But let me tell you something, you can never tell my friend I said so, but there's no need to be paying her three hundred dollars. She'll be happy with two hundred and fifty."

"Oh?" Peter said, at last with something firm to grasp.

"Oh, my, three hundred! You don't need to be paying nobody that much. But now don't you be telling Francine I said so. She'd kill me! But really there's no need to be paying anybody that much."

"I see. How do I—how do we get in touch—how do we call—"

"I can give you Francine's telephone number. She knows all about the job. Hope you don't mind my talking. Course, I didn't tell her nothing about money. I don't be talking money with my friends. That's not something I do. Her number is—"

"Hold on." He got a pad and pen and wrote down the digits. She repeated her speech again about how rarely she recommended anyone because of her fear that she would feel ashamed later. And once again she referred to the money, asking for an assurance that Peter and Diane wouldn't tell Francine how much they might have offered if she, Pearl, hadn't told them otherwise.

The call left him laughing. The intrigue this black woman had gone in for, on the one hand getting a job for her friend, on the other making sure she wasn't paid more than herself, reminded him of New York theater people, allies who pulled for each other as long as none of their separate boats got too far in front. When Ted Bishop, head of the Harlequin Theater, had lobbied Peter to get the Stillman Foundation to put up money to help relocate the Uptown Theater (in theory a rival of Harlequin), Peter had done so and reported back to Ted his success: a hundred thousand for the move. Peter had forgotten to calculate that that was twice the foundation's contribution to Harlequin for the past two seasons. Consequently, for the next six months he had to listen to Ted slight the Uptown Theater (now in midtown) until Peter convinced the foundation to liberate additional funds to give Ted one hundred thousand to refurbish Harlequin. Indeed, he reflected, this ignorant southern black had, unlike Ted Bishop, known in advance she would be jealous if her friend was paid more. What a thought. What if education and a privileged rearing only resulted in more self-deception rather than extra generosity?

And who had taught Peter his lessons? His mother, with her pretense of artistic talent? Or sad-eyed Swedish Gertrude, too shy to look his stepfather in the face, but able to read bedtime stories with such passion and fervor that Peter fell in love with being an audience? Or was it his English nanny, Betty? Betty had a taste for the theater and talked his parents, or at least his pretentious mother, into permitting her to bring Peter along for her weekly excursions to Shakespeare in the Park, Broadway matinees, and even several baffling Off-Broadway works.

But that was different from these black women caretakers. Surely they wouldn't be taking Byron to see Kevin Kline at the Public or hear Mandy Patinkin sing Sondheim. Maybe *Dreamgirls*, he thought, and broke up again.

Shouldn't I be horrified? Allowing my son to be raised by ignorant, overweight women? Spending forty, fifty hours a week in their care—that must have an effect.

He tried to remember his mother, Gail, caring for him—young, embracing him, taking him to the park, bathing him, holding him, reading a story at night.

But there were few memories.

Gail *had* held Peter's head over the toilet one ill night, sick with dreams of grotesque creatures, wakened by vomiting. Later her elegant hand had tilted a crystal glass of ginger ale to his lips. He remembered the pale bubbles dancing on her wedding diamond.

It must have been a Sunday. The nanny's day off.

Otherwise the images were of Gertrude's thin, straight blond hair, so stiff the edge of her ear split through it; or the Pole's sauerkraut lunches; or the little heaves of Betty's shelf of a bosom, sighing over romantic lyrics, swelling with the brassy Broadway overtures.

Then, later, in real childhood, in the limber elasticity before the voice changed, Peter's life was school and visiting his friend Gary. Dinner after dinner with Gary. Summer camp with Gary, overhearing fights between Gary's parents, sleeping in Gary's upper bunk on weekends.

Peter must have spent time at his own home.

But he couldn't remember it.

"Do you remember that awful woman Paula?" his mother said idly at one interminable Thanksgiving dinner.

"Gary's mother? Of course."

"She liked to tell people that we dumped you on them. That you were constantly at their house."

"I *did* spend a lot of time there."

"Because you wanted to! And because Gary refused to stay over with you. Remember? He was too sensitive."

Peter thought about it, tried to recall. He just naturally seemed to end up staying for dinner at Gary's. Adding him wasn't hard. After all, Gary's parents almost never cooked. Mostly it was a diet of pizza, deli, Chinese food.

"They didn't seem to mind," he had answered.

"No! She loved it. Kept Gary out of her hair. And she could brag we were neglectful parents."

But you were, Mother. Children didn't interest you.

"Peter! Peter!" Diane's voice, hoarse and angry, called out. Behind it, a background noise: he heard a siren wail. Not a siren. His son, crying.

Peter got up from his desk, opened the study door. "What is it?"

"Give him a bottle!"

"What!" he said, shouting to be heard above Byron's siren.

"There's a bottle of formula on the counter!" she shouted from the dark of their bedroom. "Give it to him!"

Peter had heard the first time. He considered reminding Diane that he had warned her—he wouldn't help take care of Byron. He listened to Byron's wail, rising to a pitch, fading out, rising again. It didn't bother him.

"Hurry up!" she said.

Why not? Peter walked into the kitchen. A bottle—it looked like a missile to him—stood on the counter. He took it into Byron's room.

Byron's body was thrashing in the crib. He grunted and farted and then let his siren sound. There was something frightening in the activeness of his activity. Arms flailed. He bumped his face into the mattress repeatedly, trying to lift himself.

For a moment, Peter puzzled over how to pick up Byron *and* hold on to the bottle. He put it on a shelf beside the rocker. When he grabbed Byron, the siren was cut off. Peter lifted him by his bird's chest, puffed with bone. Byron arched his back when Peter took him in his arms, his head thrusting for escape. But when Peter brought the bottle into Byron's vision, the little boy went still. His eyes widened.

With delight at the sight.

With suspense at the pause.

His mouth opened in an O. Peter put the bottle nipple inside and the lips clamped, the cheeks puffed, his jaw worked.

"You like this," Peter said, chuckling.

"What?" Diane called out.

Byron's body started. "Shhh," Peter said. "Nothing," he called out.

"Is he okay?" she screamed.

"Yes, he's fine." Byron's eyes closed, the lids wrinkled and tired. But his jaw worked and a stream of little bubbles running up the bottle showed he was drawing formula. Byron's legs, emanating heat from the soft material of the stretchy, pushed out with pleasure at the onset of getting liquid. His body, taut with desire moments ago, sighed in Peter's arms. The weight of Byron's neck pressed against the crook of Peter's elbow, and then Byron's legs sagged at the knees and his plump arms dipped into the air, like idle oars. Peter envied Byron's pleasure. He admired Byron's passionate desire—wailing to be fed—and his equally fervent satisfaction—the tiny body absorbed, obsessed, by a single longing.

Once there must have been such lust in himself, an ache which, frustrated, caused rage and despair. Diane had taken to complaining that babies were so selfish, so completely unaware of everyone else's feelings. How marvelous that very quality seemed to Peter.

Byron fell asleep. His mouth, that pink hole of suction, sagged open, the bottle nipple sliding out. Peter put it back on the shelf, half empty. Byron lay relaxed in his arms, romantically enervated, like Hamlet borne offstage. He touched the puffy jowl. Soft.

Peter carried Byron to the crib. Byron's body started at being let go, but quickly loosened into unconsciousness again.

"Sometimes," an exhausted Diane had said over dinner, "I think he looks at me and thinks: food."

That's right, Byron, Peter thought to the sleeping figure of his son. Fuck 'em. Get what you can.

ERIC PUSHED THE CARRIAGE BACK AND FORTH. BACK AND FORTH. A little less far away, then a little less back. Back and forth. He measured the distance by the darker edge of the floorboards at the living room's doorsill. The white wheels had been crossing them, then they only touched, now they failed to reach.

Luke's body was still, a hump underneath the baby blue cotton blanket. His head, covered by soft curls of black hair, was on its side, treating Eric to a view of his profile. The eyes were shut—at last. But his back still heaved rapidly, panting. Back and forth on the silent wheels, slower and slower. Eric let his eyes stray to the television, tuned to an idle cable television channel that ran that day's closing stock market prices. ITT rolled by . . . 35½. Fuck.

His options had five days to go. They were still in the money, but each day closer to expiration without a further move up meant an erosion of his profit. Bulls get rich, Bears get rich, Pigs get nothing. He should have taken his profit last week. Now he would barely clear 10 percent. If ITT were unchanged for three more days, even that would be gone. Why the fuck wasn't there a confirmation on the buyback rumor? It would push the stock by five points. That would quadruple his options; he'd clear a hundred thousand. If something didn't happen tomorrow morning, he'd have to sell. Couldn't afford a loss now.

He had lost track of the motion of the carriage. The quiet rubber wheels had shifted, so the hood was pointed at the wall instead of the open doorway. Eric looked away from the television just as he gave a push forward. He saw, only a second before it happened, that he had aimed the carriage and its sleeping occupant into the wall.

"No!" he said, but it was too late. The carriage recoiled from the impact, its springs bouncing. Eric yanked the carriage back. A spasm went through Luke's body—the legs kicked out, his head jerked. The mouth opened and the groaning squeaks began again. "Dammit." He rolled the carriage back and forth quickly again. "Pay attention!" he lectured himself. Luke continued to complain, his body tense, fighting the motion. "Come on," Eric said. "I'm sorry. Forget it happened." Back—forth—back—forth, fast, the vibrations diminishing Luke's squalling into musical moans, until finally they subsided into smacking sounds of desperate suction on his pacifier.

Eric looked toward the hallway, wondering if Nina had been disturbed by the wails. She was wrecked. They had been home twelve hours and Luke was still up. Other than momentary lulls, unless he was being fed or rocked, he had cried—horrible, protesting screeches. Like a soldier back from a ghastly war, Luke seemed to be reliving some horror, pained by unseen hurts. They had tried everything. Changed him, fed him, rocked him, played music, walked with him clutched to their bosoms, kissed him, pleaded—nothing really soothed him. Movement made Luke quiet, but not relaxed, or asleep. He couldn't be set down in the carriage unless they pushed it; he couldn't be put on the couch or the rug or their bed; he couldn't even be held in a chair. Unless there was movement, he screamed. And even when there was motion, his mouth still worked on the pacifier, and at the bottom of his heavy-lidded eyes, open slits remained, peep-holes, filled by suspicion, ready to protest any change.

By nightfall Nina couldn't hold out. She went to bed with instructions to be roused in four hours if Luke was awake. She said Luke could be given two ounces of distilled water in two hours.

Eric stayed on his feet, rocking Luke back and forth for those two hours, sure that his son would fall asleep any minute. Many, many times Luke's eyes had closed (completely, no hermit peeping out) and his body had lain still. But the moment Eric let go of the carriage handle, the head would bang, the legs kick out, the mouth open, the pacifier sliding away, and a cry—screeching at the world, enraged, betrayed, inconsolable—would splice the silence, tearing Eric in two.

Twice he let Luke bawl for a minute, a minute that cost Eric years from his heart, from his soul. A minute that damned him: passive monster, voyeur of suffering. He accepted the purgatory, thinking that would work (Luke'll cry for a minute and collapse), but all that strategy accomplished was utter chaos. Luke's body thrashed, his mouth yawned with complaint, and it would take much longer, much faster rocking to restore the uneasy quiet and suspicious rest of the back-and-forth motion.

Eric got angry. He felt stupid. Incompetent. This tiny thing, this insignificant creature, had only two needs, hunger and rest, to satisfy. Eric could do nothing for him. No effort was enough.

At last the two hours were up. He maneuvered the carriage to where he had put the bottle of distilled water. (He daren't let go or stop the motion.) It was packed with a metal top, like a hat, no doubt to accommodate the nipple inside. Nina, while passing out on the bed, had said, "You pull off the top, it already has a nipple." He tried to wedge the bottle under the arm he used to rock the carriage, but of course, the push movement meant it would fall. He tried to think of some way to open the bottle without letting go of the carriage.

With despair, he realized there wasn't one.

He readied himself. He let go. The bottle was already in his idle hand. The free one grabbed the metal top. Luke screeched. Eric pulled.

Nothing.

Luke banged, kicked, squawked. If he got much louder, Nina might wake up.

Eric pulled. Nothing. He grabbed the top and twisted. He grasped so hard his fingers went white, using enough strength, he knew from experience, to open the stubbornest of jars, with sufficient pressure and strength to bend thin metal. The thick muscles of his arm rippled, tangling under his skin.

Luke screamed, the pacifier loose in his gaping speaker of complaint.

Eric pulled. Nothing. Eric twisted. Nothing.

"Goddammit! Goddammit!" the room yelled. He heard a repeated noise, an object smashing.

"Eric! Eric! Eric!" Nina's hoarse voice called out.

Eric became aware of himself: he was shouting at the bottle, smashing its metal top against the wall. Even that accomplished little, merely denting the cover. He stopped and took a deep breath. Luke's cries were out of control again, a relentless staccato of high-pitched meows: a cat being squeezed to death.

"Eric!" Nina called out. "What's going on?"

"I can't open the fucking bottle!" he yelled, but there was hopelessness in the volume. He had wanted so badly to take over, to relieve her of the burden. To be beaten by this silly bottle top, to have his altruism turned into buffoonery humiliated him.

"Don't try to pull the whole top off!" Nina shouted from her bed. "Just the tip. It's serrated."

Luke wailed, gasping for air in between his raging sorrow. Eric stared at the beaten-up metal top. He had been grasping the larger lip where it met the glass. Now he could see the serration where the stove top widened out. Slowly, in disbelief that this would work, he gently pulled the tip to one side.

Magically, it came off in his hand, revealing the translucent brown of the nipple.

Eric gave the water to Luke who accepted the liquid ungraciously. Luke moaned and squealed from time to time, nagging Eric about his long delay in providing decent service. I'm not giving *you* a tip, Luke seemed to be saying.

Eric thought: this is the first night home. It won't be this way forever. Luke's eyes closed while he sucked. The rigid board became flesh again. Eric leaned his head back on the rocker. He was so tall it provided little support. Eric moved his ass forward so he could catch wood for his head to rest on. Luke started and moaned during Eric's shift, and then relaxed again. At that, Eric allowed his own eyes to close.

The numbers of the ticker rolled by. The symbols were magic: they marched the world to poverty or wealth, executing dreams and tiring reality. Eric knew this wasn't his life. In time, when he was stuffed with money, his body calm, his boy grown, his wife respectful, his name would roll by on the ticker with the equanimity of the numbers, the assurance of place. "One million," he mumbled. "One point six million," he whispered, a lullaby. "Two million five hundred thousand. Annual income. Net assets, forty to fifty million. The Wizard of Wall Street." He would be picked up each morning at the door of their town house by a sleek limousine, its smoky glass revealing to the curious only their own ignorance and, inside, him, invulnerable, pampered, envied, his ideas (conceived in the quiet of his graceful life) assuaging panics and igniting booms.

A weight fell into Eric's lap, startling him. The bottle had slid out of his hands. Luke was asleep, his mouth open, his body flat with relaxation. Success had come at last and Eric had missed the moment of its achievement.

But what had Eric achieved? If he got out of the chair, to place Luke in the carriage, wouldn't the movement waken Luke?

I could stay here, holding him in my arms, lean my head back and sleep. He tried that. But Luke, despite his smallness, weighed in the crook of his arm. And keeping still was a distraction; the doing of nothing became an effort. He decided to risk moving Luke. He started to sit up.

The initial motion forward, the tightening of his stomach muscles produced an immediate reaction. Luke moaned, his head twitched, and his lips pursed. Eric froze in position, his back no longer leaning against the chair, and held his breath. Luke quieted, settled in; only now Eric had lost even the relative comfort of his former posture. He had begun the process of rising from the chair, and to give up, sagging back, would be as much of a jolt as continuing.

If I do this fast, with confidence, sure of myself, sure of my control of him, he will stay asleep. Eric committed himself to this notion and after a pause to ready himself, rose in one quick movement.

Although Luke's head rolled in his arms and Eric tightened his grip around the body, there was no reaction. Luke remained passed out, his toothless mouth open, his neck retracted, the lids of his eyes shut, tiny blue veins made distinct by the translucence of his freshly made skin.

Luke sighed.

Eric stood in front of the carriage. How could he put Luke into it smoothly? Nina had said Luke must be put on his stomach—so as not to choke from spitting up—and that meant flipping him, like a pancake. Surely the splat of contact would rouse him.

But if Eric simply laid him down as he was, faceup, removing the mattress of his arms only a second before the real one, the transition would be less felt.

Could Luke really choke if he slept on his back? Eric had asked Nina that before, and she'd answered, irritated, "I don't know! At the hospital they put them on their back sometimes, but the book said they should be on their stomachs. Just do it that way."

He was exhausted. He couldn't face another round of back and forth, back and forth. He leaned over the carriage, his arms extending, lowering Luke. Eric released Luke's bottom and paused. No reaction. With his free hand he supported Luke's head and slipped the other arm out. Luke's eyes twitched, then were still. Gradually Eric allowed the head to rest and Luke was asleep in the carriage. Faceup. But asleep.

Eric covered him with the blanket and turned out the lights in the hall and in Luke's room. Then he carefully maneuvered the carriage from the living room to the nursery.

There was a blissful quiet. A rest in the household that had had no peace since they arrived.

Could he really choke, I mean, choke to death, because he's on his back? To risk flipping him seemed insane. Luke was at peace, at last; why bother him?

Eric went to bed. Nina slept stretched out, sunning herself in the night, a position she had gotten used to while big from the pregnancy. She used to sleep curled up, shrinking into infancy. Now she lay like a continent, floating on the world. One leg crossed onto his side. He nudged it to get room. She stirred, angrily (that day everything from her was either angry or hysterical), and he turned on his side, hugging the pillow.

He listened. He would hear choking.

The ticker began. ITT ANNOUNCES BUYBACK, TRADING CLOSED, ITT REOPENS AT 50. The options would be worth fifteen hundred each and he had paid two. They would be worth a hundred and fifty thousand dollars. Silly. A boy's dream.

Nina woke him with a yell. "Eric! Eric!"

Eric stumbled on his way out of bed, his hand on his soft penis. He usually wore his underpants to sleep.

"Eric! Come in here!" She was screeching in a high pitch.

"What?" he asked, coming into Luke's room. The sunlight glowed in Nina's hair. She was crying.

"I can't wake him!" she screamed, tears streaming down her face.

And there in the carriage was Luke. Dead.

Eric woke up.

He woke up gasping for air, his head thrust forward.

It was still night. Outside he heard a car alarm wailing for its owner. His heart pounded in his chest, rapping out its criticisms: put Luke on his stomach, you selfish pig.

There would be no rest anyway, he realized, lying there, his ear aching to hear sounds from Luke.

He got up, went inside, and stared at the motionless body. For a moment he thought the nightmare had come true: the chest was still. But he finally saw a slight rise and fall.

He pulled the blanket off.

He put his hands under the little arms.

He turned Luke. The legs curled; the head nosed into the mattress. For a moment Luke rubbed his face sideways, settling in.

Then the little empty mouth opened. A silent yell.

Eric nodded to himself with dismay.

Now came the scream.

Luke was up again.

5

NINA ACHED FOR BED. SHE BEGGED HER BODY FOR MORE energy. She peered past the nursing head of Luke to look at her thighs, studying the flab squashed out by the hard wood of the kitchen chair, and wondered if all her muscles were gone. She closed her eyes, her hot eyes, watering to relieve the harsh sandpaper lids, and felt her neck go liquid, her weighted chin sag. One deep breath and she would be asleep.

Sleep.

Dark.

Warm.

The dance of dreams. The storytelling of memory and desire.

Luke's hard gums slid down onto the nipple and pressed together, pressed together with slow cunning.

"No!" She was awake again, her poor boneless body in retreat from her baby's evil intent. She pushed a finger into the corner of Luke's mouth. The hard, mean little gums were closing. "No!" She forced him off with her finger. He wailed immediately. "Don't bite!" she said to the senseless creature, its face nothing but a gaping mouth. "Goddammit!" She got to her feet. Luke's head flopped back, screaming. The thing had no understanding: it yelled with the conviction that it was entitled to all her energy, to all her milk, to all her love. It had no inkling that her servitude was voluntary.

She paced, letting Luke screech in her arms. She paced, cursing the walls. "Shut up, shut up, shut up!" She passed her reflection in a little mirror, seeing a flash of her own face. Her eyes stared with rage and hopelessness; her jaw was slack, her mouth open, her hair dull and disarranged. She looked wild.

"Okay, okay, okay," she said to the screams of her son. Calm down, she told herself. She walked rapidly to the couch, sat, and offered her breast again, holding his head fast against her so he wouldn't clamp on her red and tender nipple.

Sighing, hiccuping, farting, jawing, Luke settled in. His rage ebbed, his eyes closed, he relaxed. She did not. Her head pounded from the suppression of the pulsing blood of her anger. She tried to fix herself in time, to remember where she was by a logical procession of events. But the disjointed sleeping schedule made her stupid.

Luke never slept. Her mind fought to understand how that could be. How could an infant sleep only four hours out of every twenty-four? How could this baby stand to be awake, fussing, crying the second his body wasn't being rocked or moved? She had read explanations: he had colic, he was in pain, an almost continual pain that kept him awake; the motion soothed him, reminded him of the womb, calmed him. He did need sleep, but his digestion wasn't permitting him the rest. The book said he couldn't wake himself up any more than he could prevent himself from falling asleep; those perverse abilities came around eight months. This was out of his control. It was not Luke's fault; he was an innocent in pain and all her patience was required.

"Let him cry if you can't take it," her pediatrician had advised over the phone. She had called the doctor a few hours ago, in a desperate state, exhausted by five hours of walking Luke in the Snugli. The Snugli was a womb made of fabric, a carrying pouch which put Luke's face into her chest, and curled him up against her stomach. Inside it, Luke was quiet and even got snatches of sleep. But the Snugli gave her no rest; on the contrary, its cross straps bit across her back and strained muscles which had escaped the ravages of pregnancy. "I feel like I'm losing my mind," she had said to the doctor. This was the first week Eric had gone to work and left her alone with the baby. Today she had broken down and called Eric to ask if he could come home early. Eric said no, the market was very active, and suggested she phone his parents, but she declined. This was the first goddamned week. She couldn't ask for their help so soon. "I feel like I'm going crazy," she repeated to the pediatrician. "Isn't there some medicine you can give him?"

"Colic lasts three months. And then it goes away. It doesn't do him any harm. His digestive tract needs time to mature. Comfort him as much as you can, but let him cry if you can't handle it."

Let him cry! Who raised these people, these doctors? she wondered. Did they all go to military school?

So she went back to pushing the carriage, harnessing herself into the Snugli, rocking Luke in her arms. The moment, the instant, the split second, sometimes even a fraction before she stopped the various movements, he cried, he raged, his legs pulled up, his face distorted in pain, his rear end expelled gas, his stomach compressed into a tight ball. Why does it only hurt him when I stop moving? She began to suspect Luke. He knows. He knows. If he pretends to hurt, I'll pamper him. He knows.

Can't he tell he's killing me? He's breaking me; he's making me a failure.

Tears came from her as she sagged into despair. I can't even be a mother. The simplest goddamned thing in the world. A peasant, an idiot can do it. While Luke sucked, tears collected at Nina's jaw and formed a large drop, which then fell on his stretchy. Luke chewed away, unconcerned.

Nina studied him. He was content now. His curly black hair was damp from the humidity; the oppressive weather, the hot gray stifling days, drained her energy.

Luke peered blankly at her while he sucked her dry. There was no apology in his eyes. No sheepishness in his chewing. No fear of reprisal. Only suspicion, a wary surveillance of her. Don't you make a move, his expressionless blue eyes seemed to say. You stay right here for me.

She hated him; from her soul a loathing for Luke's selfish little body arose. Her disgust shot through her like a current. She could feel the rage in the metal taste of her mouth; she could spit her fury at him. She wanted to bash sense into him. "You have to go to sleep," she said, leaning into his face.

Luke blinked and pushed into her breast for protection from her looming head.

Luke's neck, creased by rings of baby fat, attracted her attention. Maybe he was damaged. Maybe the traumatic birth had done something. The doctors might even know that was the explanation of Luke's behavior but not want to tell her yet.

Maybe there's something wrong with him.

Luke pulled off her breast, yelping. His legs retracted to his stomach, his face went red, and he shrieked.

"Okay, baby," she said, and put him to her shoulder, patting his back (so small, and his bony spine was spineless), patting hard to force out a burp. Luke squawked, squealed, complained. No burp. He never burped. Almost never. Sometimes she thought that was his problem: three weeks of gas trapped inside. He's got a Jewish stomach (Eric burped as often as he breathed) with a Wasp throat (Nina's mother had made her feel burping was as bad as murder).

Luke's stomach convulsed and she felt gooey liquid on her shoulder. "Oh, God!" she moaned, and glanced to see what she already knew was there—white and sticky spitup.

Vomited on, she thought—this is my life. Her mind spun through the days and nights. Up at 4:00 A.M., unable to send Eric in with a bottle since formula might make the colic worse, her head nodding into sleep while Luke chewed, then punching Eric (sometimes quite hard) to rouse him so he could walk Luke around, lying in the dark desperate for sleep but constantly wakened by the noise of the carriage in the hall or Luke's squeals whenever Eric would try to stop or had to change Luke's diaper. And finally out of bed at 8:00, again to be gnawed on, then showering unhappily with an ear listening to the moans and squeals that soon would be her problem, showering with hot water even in this heat, to soothe the sore breasts, burning eyes, dented back, and puffy, swollen feet. To have the luxury of a quiet bath, not a bath with distant sounds of screeching and complaint, but a restful stay in a warm pool and a silent apartment, seemed like a distant memory of youth. So she showered hopelessly, with eight hours ahead, eight hours of fighting the urge to kill herself or Luke or both, eight hours of facing her inadequacy, her son's misery, the apartment's mess, and a world filled with smiling faces that assumed she was an ecstatic mother blessed with a glorious child, and not being able to tell, to say: this is hell, this is prison, and I may die from it. Or kill to escape.

She had tried to maintain a semblance of competence for the first few days. She made the bed, pushing the carriage until he quieted, tucking in one side (by then Luke was screaming), and then pushing the carriage to gain more calm, only to lose it while tucking in the other side. She learned to load the dishwasher with him in the Snugli, one hand covering his head, the other rinsing plates and stacking them. She closed cabinets and doors with her feet and elbows; she got used to reading while jolting back and forth in the rocker, willing to accept the nausea that caused for the relief of information, distraction—anything that wasn't about babies. Goddamn babies. Today, however, she had left the bed unmade, the food gelling on the plates, clothes impaled on chairs, and the *Times* sprawled on the kitchen table.

Whenever she took Luke out, he fell asleep while they moved, so that the neighbors, the doormen, the storekeepers, other mothers, all believed Luke was wonderful. Asleep, his fair skin (like hers), his tall brow (like Eric's), his perfect little nose (like hers), his thick, arching eyebrows (like Eric's), his jutting strong chin (like hers), all spoke of beauty, calm, assurance, lovableness. And the moment she got home, once the motion stopped, Luke was back to yelping and whining.

The joys of motherhood. Are they all one great lie?

Are the other mothers that much stronger than I am?

Are they all so much more giving?

Is there so little love in me and so much in them?

By the time Nina had cleaned her shoulder of the spitup and switched Luke to the other breast, her tears had stopped, but her eyes hurt, as usual, from the aftermath of her sorrow. They would swell up until the morning and she'd look ugly. The dark circles were bad enough; now, with her eyes puffy, she'd truly seem to have gone fifteen rounds and lost.

And she was losing this fight.

She put Luke in his crib after he was fed. He had fallen asleep and stayed that way, his beautiful face composed and saintly. Luke stirred when she laid him down, then sighed and relaxed again.

Maybe it was over. The doctor had said, contradicting the books which warned colic lasted for three months, that it could end any day.

She left Luke's room. She sat outside in the hall, rigid with tension, and lit a cigarette.

Luke cried. A little cry at first. Then he cried big. And he cried loud.

Wait it out. She looked at her watch. He wailed. His voice went hoarse with desperation. He wailed. He choked.

"Goddammit!" She got to her feet. She stormed into the room, yelling. "Goddammit! What is the matter with you!"

Luke's cries echoed hers, soaring with her rage, waning with her despair. "I can't stand it! You have to stop!" She put on the Snugli, grabbed Luke roughly, and pushed him in, yanking his legs through. His head bobbed against her, his open mouth wet, his feet kicking as she fought to zip him up.

She wanted to smash his hard tiny head. She wanted quiet.

She carried him outside in the Snugli, frightened to remain alone with him. She went to the nearby church, not to find God but to find the peace and order of her childhood.

Grace Church was beautiful, quiet, the dark wood benches empty, but alive with the wear of generations, the marble cold and white, but soothing, the ceiling high and vast, but protective, the glass bright with color, but dark with age. Balance. Peace.

Against her chest, Luke was awake but still, chewing on the pacifier. He craned his neck to peer up at her, his perfect blue marbles querying her. Going someplace? he seemed to ask. Even there, in the house of God, he was shameless, concerned only with himself and her submission to his wants.

"You have to calm down," she whispered to him. A prayer to Luke. "I love you, but you have to relax," her voice hissed in the cool dark of the church. "Please," she begged to Luke's little face, his brow wrinkled by the effort to look up at her. "Calm down," she prayed to the new demanding god of her life.

DIANE STOOD AT HER APARTMENT DOOR AFTER FINISHING WORK, key in hand, ready to enter. She had arrived home in the same condition for years: her back ached; her neck was stiff; her legs were bloated; her head was dull, ready to throb with a headache. She was bloody but unbowed from the struggle of work, from the pressure of producing for the partners, a pressure made more intense by the recent absence of her maternity leave, ready to enter her home, her haven, to rest, to recollect herself, to catch up on unfinished paper work—but now she came home instead to more work, to a husband who expected food, to a four-month-old baby who had to be fed, changed, bathed, played with, and put to sleep. At the end of her ten hours at the office she had four more hours of labor at home.

She understood now why there were so many magazine covers about working mothers.

But she would not be beaten. Not by sexism, circumstance, or tradition. She held the key to her apartment and gave herself, her body, a moment to feel the fatigue completely, surrendering to it. She closed her eyes and rolled her head back. She let her leather briefcase drop. She listened for sounds from her apartment. It was quiet.

Diane had had a bad day. Stoppard hadn't liked her draft of the brief. He had put his criticisms gently, acknowledging her currently difficult conditions, but it was the gentleness that worried her. Stoppard was usually brutal with those he treasured, unself-conscious in his attacks, as though the victim were a part of himself. When he treated an associate in a sympathetic and kindly way, you could be sure his trust and approval were at a low ebb. Stoppard liked the intimacy of the team where there was no ego but the group's; if he had to think about you, he didn't want you around.

"Maybe this is too much for you right now," Stoppard had said at one point. "I can bring Didi in." If he had meant that as a threat, Diane wouldn't worry. But Stoppard had been serious, was concerned. He thought about Diane as a "special situation," a new mother who had to be pampered, which meant, of course, that she couldn't be relied on. Disaster. She had to stay up tonight and revise the brief, knock Stoppard out with a rewritten draft first thing in the morning.

The decision to take on more work, to give up sleep entirely, energized her. She couldn't stand the effort of her life as a lawyer and a mother if she were merely going to be good at it. She had to be the best to attempt the task at all.

Diane entered her apartment. She heard Francine (despite some misgivings, Diane had hired Francine because of Pearl's recommendation) laughing at Byron. Byron was on his back, a fine down on his head (like a boot camp marine), kicking his short, chubby, powerful legs.

"You ticklish?" Francine was saying. Byron answered her with a throaty chuckle. He kicked at Francine, excited. His mouth opened wide. He hooted at her. His chubby cheeks widened. His lips spread farther and farther apart. Francine signaled to Diane to look. "Yes, you're smiling!" My God, he was. Smiling his head off, his stomach convulsed with laughter. His eyes, which had dulled from blue to gray in the early weeks, were now rich with brown; they still stared at objects with intense concentration, but people were greeted with sparkles of interest. They glittered at Francine, speaking to her. Byron's entire body yearned to communicate: his legs thrust forward; his mouth opened with the ache of pleasure; his small fat hands, like pats of butter, slapped at the air; his stomach, ballooned with milk, rippled at Francine's playful fingers.

"Abba, abba, dabba, dabba," Byron cheered, thumping his heels on the floor.

"Your mama's home," Francine said, and pointed to Diane, who moved into his vision and knelt in her gray skirt beside his head.

He blinked at her appearance with momentary confusion. Then he recognized Diane. He very clearly saw who she was.

At the realization that it was Diane, Byron stopped his animated delight. His legs stiffened, his open, welcoming, joyful mouth closed, his hands rested at his sides, his eyes were dulled by hostility, his melodic voice shut off, and he turned away.

Diane couldn't believe it. She looked at Francine for confirmation, as though they had both witnessed a supernatural event. How could a four-month-old baby reject a mother? How could Byron even know enough (recognize Diane, be aware that her absence had been long, realize what a turned head meant) to hurt her?

Francine was embarrassed. "He's getting tired," she said, but that was an obvious lie.

Diane reached for Byron and lifted him. His face was solemn. Byron glanced at Diane when she put the tip of her nose against his and pursed her lips to kiss him. At the offer, Byron turned his head and gave her his cheek. Then he looked at Francine and once more the miracle happened.

His eyes glittered, his legs kicked, and his hands, the fingers spread wide, groped for Francine's face; his mouth gaped, the nude gums exposed, the soft pillows of his cheeks puffing out into an enormous smile: a welcome from his entire being, from the tips of his toes to the rippling veins of his almost bald head.

"Hi!" Francine couldn't help responding.

Byron's stomach trembled and the musical laughter echoed from the deepest part of his soul. Laughter of delight and love. All for Francine.

Diane turned him sideways so his beaming face would confront hers. Byron arched his back in protest. "Hi, Byron," Diane said in a high, pleasant tone. "Mommy's home!" Again Byron averted his head, his mouth closed tight, and a dull glaze, like translucent lids, covered his shining brown eyes. He was rejecting her.

She stood up. Byron tried to escape from her arms. He leaned his head back, arching away from her, his hands out to reach for Francine. "Where's Peter?" Diane asked Francine.

"He called to say he would be late. Said he tried to reach you at the office." Francine was sweating. She was dressed in a dingy white T-shirt and in washed-out blue jeans that were pulled tight across her big ass and bloated stomach. The middle of her body was much wider than her legs or upper torso. She looked as if she were walking around with a flotation doughnut. Nevertheless, Diane had been glad to get her instead of Pearl. Francine shared her friend Pearl's cheerful voice; but Francine's accent was New York, not southern, and her tone was casual, without a trace of Pearl's deferential modesty. She made Diane feel less like a plantation owner and allowed her to be demanding, since she knew Francine would complain if the requests were unreasonable.

But Francine wasn't pretty; she stood there like a badly made sausage, her kinky hair dyed a strange orange that was meant to be blond, her skin a filmy, uneven brown, her face dotted with pimples, and sweat oozed from her forehead, neck, and underarms. How could Byron prefer Francine? He doesn't. He's just punishing me.

Byron whined, his little hand out for Francine, the fingers calling for her. Diane kissed his stomach, rubbing her mouth into his navel, knowing that would tickle him into laughter and cover the embarrassment of this scene. His stretchy was soft and smelled of Byron's life—formula, Francine, and baby powder.

Byron did laugh, but only reflexively. The moment Diane pulled back to look at his delighted toothless mouth, he stopped, his cherubic fluted lips closing tight. He pushed out with his legs and arms, trying to swim away from Diane. He groaned with the effort as if to say to Francine: take me back, take me away from this witch.

Francine smiled at him and shook her head. "Oh, you're a bad boy. Now don't tease your mommy like that. She has to work just like everybody. She'd stay home with you if she could."

"No, I wouldn't," Diane said.

"No?" Francine laughed, uneasy, but pleased by Diane's honesty.

"I'd go crazy stuck home with a baby."

"I don't mind," Francine said, patting the protrusion of her stomach, upholstered in denim. "Only problem is it keeps me too close to the refrigerator." Throughout all this Byron continued to squirm recklessly, willing to hurl himself out of Diane's arms to reach Francine.

The doorbell rang. Francine answered it and Peter entered, his voice loud with greeting, walking in wide paces, steadying himself on a rocky boat. He's tipsy, Diane thought. "Hello, hello!" he called to them.

Byron jerked himself in Diane's arms, attempting to sit up. His feet moved rapidly, walking in the air. His hands shot out in spasms of excitement.

"Hey, fella!" Peter said, and once again, the glorious sunrise of happiness dawned in Byron, his head rolling from side to side, his mouth open with ecstasy.

"O! O! O!" Byron hooted.

"He's saying hello!" Peter bragged to Diane, obviously expecting this would delight her. "He's saying hello to me!" he repeated with naïve pride. "Hey!" Peter said to Byron, rubbing the little ball of a stomach with his hand. Byron arched with pleasure, hunching his shoulders, his chin doubling, his mouth smacking open and closed as if Peter were a delicious food Byron hoped to eat.

"Well, since he's saying hello to you, why don't you change his diaper?" Diane snapped, and offered the squirming, chuckling Byron to Peter.

Peter stepped back, alarmed, shying away from Byron like a timid man confronted by a wild animal. "I just got in."

"So did I," Diane answered.

"I'll change his diaper," Francine said.

"No." Diane sneered at both of them. "I was just kidding."
She marched out of the hallway to Byron's room. The baby's quarters were the smallest in the apartment, twelve feet by six feet,
designed three generations ago to be used by a maid. Byron really
ought to be in the second bedroom, she thought for the millionth
time. Peter had insisted on keeping that space to himself for use as
a study. Peter's study, she repeated to herself contemptuously. *I'm*
the one who has the real work and I get a small desk in our bedroom.

Byron had moaned while she carried him away from Francine
and Peter and, as she laid him on the changing table, continued to
grumble with complaints.

"Let's find you something nice to sleep in," she said.

Byron averted his face, turned to the wall, and groped it with his
left hand, cooing at the shadows.

"Bye!" Francine called into the room. "Good-bye, Diane. Bye,
bye, Byron!"

Byron swiveled his head and bounced his legs. "Hoo! Hoo!
Hoo!" he went on and on, an owl high on speed.

"Good-bye, Francine," Diane said, and lifted the excited Byron
by his feet, sliding a fresh diaper under his pink bottom, leaving it
open and unfastened for the moment to let him air—the best protection, she had read, against diaper rash. She bent down to open
the drawer with his outfits and found herself at a level with his
body, staring directly at Byron's genitals.

His pencil stub of a penis was rigid, pointed at the ceiling, framed
by his tightly packed testicles. The hairless arrangement was white
and pure, unlike the muddy, overgrown garden of semen-bearing
men. And yet this prepubescent creature was erect. Usually, his
penis was soft, the head hiding like a turtle, melted into the pillows
of his balls. Not now. It was straight up, divining to the heavens,
while he thrust his legs out, his arms also rigid, the fat hands, with
dimples for knuckles, grabbing for things out of reach—the edge of
the diaper, the blue box of wipes, the pink bottle of powder. He
seemed fierce with desire and strength, comical in such a small
body, but impressive also for the same reason.

She told herself the erection was caused by the cool air, a physical
reaction to temperature, not a sexual statement. But she was frozen
in position, her mouth only inches from his little flag of sex. I'm
here, I'm here, it seemed to say. I'm also this, his wide brown eyes
and pursed lips insisted. I have a cock, I have a cock, the tough little

body proclaimed. Absurd but frightening, too. Does it begin that early?

Who is this erection for? she wondered. Me or Francine?

She shuddered at herself. And then quickly fastened Byron's diaper. She closed him up so hard she got an image of the stiff penis snapping off, an icicle yanked from the eaves.

Wanting to obliterate these pictures, she searched for the softest and bluest of his stretchies. Her favorite, a deep navy blue outfit with red feet and a bear stitched on the chest, was getting tight on Byron. She had to bend his thick thigh forcefully to get his second leg in, and even then, when Byron stretched full out, the material was pulled taut at his groin—the puffy front of his diaper gave him the look of a sumo wrestler wrapped in a loincloth.

Byron whined impatiently while she closed the snaps and picked him up. She hugged him close. She put a hand on the back of his bobbing head and tried to urge him into the crook of her neck, to snuggle him, to feel the quiet warmth, to caress what he had once been: tiny, adoring, senseless.

But his strong neck pushed against the hand. His feet kicked at her belly, thumping her like a drum. A hand reached for her mouth, pushing open her lips. The fingers grabbed her teeth, the nail digging into her gums like grappling hooks, and his toes poked her ribs, feeling for a foothold—she was the mountain he wanted to assault and conquer, the height he would use as springboard to leap off into the world.

"Diane!" Peter called from the living room. "Diane!"

Byron kicked harder at the sound of his father's voice, excited, his legs bicycling as if to power her forward. Diane carried him out. "Yes?" she said on seeing Peter.

"What are we doing for dinner?" he asked. Peter had a glass of ice water in his right hand and a copy of the *Times* in his left. He had taken off his blue blazer and looked resplendent, although plump, in his pink Brooks Brothers shirt. Peter's body had begun to show the effects of his sedentary life. A belly had formed, a soft wave ready to splash over the brown leather belt, and his cheeks had settled, thickening his jaw, giving his face a placid appearance of self-satisfaction. His reddish blond hair seemed to grow reluctantly at his forehead; there was no longer enough of a mane to sweep across his brow and a portion stuck out, waving for help.

"I don't know," she answered, keeping the irritation she felt out of her tone.

"Do you want to go out? To Il Cantinori?"

"With him?" she said, ducking away from another of Byron's swipes at her mouth.

"We can't take Byron there. Can't we get a sitter?"

"I haven't seen Byron all day, I'd like to be with him. No, it's too big a deal. Let's order pizza or something."

Peter frowned. He pursed his lips. Then he looked down at the *Times* and seemed to become absorbed in an article.

"Hello!" she called.

"The theater's dying," he said. He looked up at her. "I was hoping for a romantic evening. Dinner. You know."

He meant, she knew, that they had made love only once since Byron's birth. Peter had brought up the subject recently and she had told him that after a day at the office and four hours of caring for Byron she felt tired, and certainly not sexy. Presumably Peter hoped a meal out, just the two of them, would put her in the mood. She hated to think about making love. Before the baby, they had often made love after evenings out, sometimes briskly, even perfunctorily, but that was all right. Planning was not. She hadn't enjoyed the wait, the pleasantly nervous anticipation, of dating; to experience delayed gratification with a husband of eight years struck Diane as ludicrous.

"Peter, if you're horny, why don't you just say so?"

He smiled and blinked at her wonderingly. "Well, well. And they say romance is dead."

"I don't have time for romance. Let's have pizza. We can still go to bed."

Peter smiled and sat on the couch. "Will you order it?"

"Sure," she said, and handed over Byron, who arched and yearned in his father's direction anyway. She looked up the phone number and dialed, going through the schedule: pizza arrive fifteen minutes, half hour to consume, one-hour play with Byron, then bath for Byron, and bedtime rocking, forty-five minutes, sex with Peter an hour (make that half an hour), shower (to avoid rushing in the morning), and then to work on the brief. "I'd like a pie with sausage and mushroom, please." Should be able to get to rewriting the draft by nine-thirty, ten at the latest. Six hours should do it. I'd even get three hours' sleep.

She finished giving the order and hung up. She looked at Byron, held aloft, jumping up and down on Peter's thighs. She didn't feel up to a long-winded sexual exchange: necking, massage, genital foreplay, lengthy screwing—the four-course meal that Peter would want.

I'll give Peter a blow job right after rocking Byron to sleep, she decided. I can always masturbate later.

"MARKET'S CLOSED," SAMMY SAID IN THE MANNER OF A PUBLIC-address announcer at Yankee Stadium.

Joe, Sammy's father, Eric's boss, pushed his chair away from his Quotron. "A good day," he judged. Joe had a pompous voice to accompany his stolid figure and unsmiling face. "I'm going for a walk," he said, and strolled to the door like a king wandering out of his castle. "I'll be back at four forty-five. Sammy, have the totals ready."

"I've already got 'em!" Sammy said, his leg hopping nervously, always the eager son ready to anticipate demands.

That stopped Joe. "Indeed?" he said, "The numbers change right up to close—"

Sammy smiled triumphantly; outperforming his father's expectations was his ultimate satisfaction. "I keep a running total using the spread sheet. Up-to-date every thirty seconds. Want the numbers now?"

Joe shook his head no. "Very impressive. Print them out for later."

Sammy grinned at Eric—exhausted Eric, red-eyed Eric, disgusted Eric, weary of life and of defeat and of these two and their repetitive psychological conflicts.

Joe continued to the door. "Very impressive." He opened the door. "But unnecessary." And left.

"Fuck you!" Sammy said, furious, without any irony or self-consciousness.

Eric tried to explain. "He just pretends he's not pleased, Sammy. He's very proud of you."

"He doesn't want to give me the satisfaction. He's a son of a bitch!"

Irene, Joe's secretary for thirty years, got up from her position at the phones. "Sammy!" she warned, like an indulgent aunt.

"Oh, shut up!" Sammy screamed, a spoiled nephew, casually insulting, confident of clemency. "Come on," he said to Eric. Sammy got up and beckoned Eric to the one private room in the fifteen hundred square feet Joe had leased from Bear Stearns. This private corner room, which had a sweeping view of the southern end of Manhattan, was ostensibly Joe's, although he stayed in the main room with Sammy and Eric for most of the day.

"I have to go home," Eric said, but with hopelessness in his tone.

"Ten minutes!" Sammy said. "The baby can wait ten minutes."

Dutifully, Eric rose. He had been in the chair since lunch. He had to steady himself on the desk for a moment, his circulatory system shocked by the change, and then went into Joe's office. Sammy shut the door. "You know where he went?" Sammy said, his face in a sneer of contempt.

"Your dad?"

"No, Reggie Jackson! Yeah, asshole!"

"For a walk. He's gone for a walk after the close ever since I've known him."

"He goes to get laid."

Eric had gotten his first job at the age of eighteen clerking for Joe at Bear Stearns. It was temporary, a summer job, but Joe had adopted Eric, kept him on as his assistant, and taken him along three years later, when Joe opened his own firm. Thus Sammy treated Eric as if he were a brother and Eric felt obliged to listen to his troubles. But he was tired. Eric rubbed his forehead to keep awake. He had averaged three hours of sleep a night since Luke's birth four weeks ago. He was making trading mistakes right and left. Eric hadn't come up with an idea for his, or Joe's, client list since Nina went into labor. He had been passing along Joe's picks. And Joe was hot, his trades finding fast profits in a sluggish market. Only Joe's belief in family, and especially in fathering a son, had prevented Joe from castigating Eric and confiscating his commissions. Under normal circumstances, with Eric fallow, Joe would demand half of Eric's commissions—all on the days Eric had been absent. Instead, benignly, Joe had let Eric mooch off his brain without compensation, asking careful questions about Luke's health, passing along remedies for colic from his wife, Ceil. Joe's uncharacteristic benevolence toward Eric, a pardon given because of Eric's new stature as a father, had turned Joe's gruff paternal face to reveal a tender profile: he believes in fatherhood, Eric now knew, he really loves Sammy.

Eric used to feel completely sympathetic to Sammy's fits of temper about his father, believing that Joe had crushed his son's self-confidence in boyhood and kept Sammy working in the firm as his final act of sadism. Eric had forgiven Sammy his adolescent behavior toward Joe, the combination of worship and hate, although it was sick in a twenty-five-year-old, because he thought Sammy a victim.

Now Eric wondered—because of the mewing, unhappy Luke at home—whether Joe hadn't merely been an unlucky father, and was doing his best to help Sammy; angry, to be sure, at the weak prod-

uct of his loins, but with a fury that concealed love and protective-
ness. Until the birth of Luke, Eric had perceived the son as the
victim and given him a moral blank check to write punishing
amounts against the father; he wasn't sure anymore and wished he
had never allowed Sammy to confide in him. Eric rubbed his forehead. He wanted to go home. "What are you talking about?"

"Pop!" Sammy said, happy to be full of knowledge, even if the
news was bad. "He goes to a whorehouse every day at four."

"You don't know that!" Eric yelled. Sammy looked surprised.
Sammy was used to the reverse: Eric enjoying it when Sammy spat
at the idol; hating it when Sammy worshiped.

"Yeah, I do!" Sammy exclaimed in an aggrieved teenager's
voice. "I followed him when you were out playing papa. He went
to the same place every day, a dingy little building by the river. In,
out. So I checked. It's a whorehouse." Sammy reached into his
pants, leaned against the door, and took out a vial of cocaine. "Can
you imagine that? Mr. Pious." Sammy lifted a little hill of powder
out of the container with a miniature spoon. A baby's spoon, Eric
thought. Sammy pressed one nostril closed and snorted the drug
into the other, replenished the spoon, and repeated the procedure
for the neglected one. Sammy offered the vial.

Eric shook his head no and tried to picture Joe fucking a prostitute: proud Joe, his big head squashed onto a square, stocky body,
squinting skeptically at the world, like a Jewish owl commanding
a Wasp barn; wise, arrogant, petty, vain, cold Joe—with his pants
off, humping a twenty-year-old in hot pants.

Sammy urged Eric again with the vial. "Keep you up for the
baby."

"No, I'll be too wrecked later."

"Get yourself some for home, you cheap bastard. Keep you going through the night."

"I don't think it's a good idea to raise a kid on coke. Besides, I
can't afford it."

"Oh, this is gonna be great! I'm gonna get myself another job."

Eric thought: ignore him, get up and go. Instead: "Why? 'Cause
I don't want a hit?"

"You need this stuff. You're fuckin' dead on your feet. You
haven't had a decent pick in three weeks."

"Fine. I'll have a hit tomorrow morning. I don't want to go home
stoned."

Sammy looked at his watch. "Pop's probably getting his cock
sucked right now."

"This is sick, Sammy. Why don't you go out and get laid? Stop thinking about your father's prick and take care of your own."

Sammy put the drug back in his pocket. "My poor mother," he said, with eagerness, not regret. "What a husband."

Eric left the office before Joe returned. He rode his bike back home; that had replaced swimming as his daily exercise. Near Canal Street Eric began to feel woozy and almost got hit by a cab when he weaved making a turn onto Sixth Avenue. His heart pounded from the fright and he paused before continuing.

Eric didn't want to believe Sammy's story about Joe. Not that he thought going to a prostitute was so bad. The routine, every day at four for half an hour, although ludicrous on the surface, seemed the worst thing about it—treating sex as something which could be regulated, like evacuation, just a necessary daily body function.

Eric resumed his ride, pedaling slowly, walking himself through the intersections. His body was off: his calves ached and his hand movements came several seconds after he ordered them, as if his brain were making a transatlantic phone call. Nothing was right with him.

Nothing was right with Luke.

The thought that he, like Joe, was stuck with a lemon—yes, there was no other word for Sammy—haunted Eric. He thought of himself as loving and kind, very different from the pompous, selfish Joe. Eric assumed his character, his desire for a strong, healthy son, would guarantee him success as a father. He hadn't considered it a speculation like the stock market—he had gone into the pregnancy confident of a certain minimum of control. He hadn't believed in that control consciously; he realized the expectation only now, after it had been shattered. Now he could see how foolish he had been. Having children as something you could control: obviously idiotic.

Absorbed, Eric overshot Ninth Street and had to turn off Sixth at Eleventh. A shopper darted out between two parked cars. Eric swerved away from the pedestrian, scraping his right leg against one of the cars. The shopper hurried on. "Look out next time!" Eric called after him.

A cabbie who was stopped at the light, snickered, saying through the open window, "You gotta be crazy to ride a bike in the city."

"Yeah, and driving a cab makes sense, right?" Eric answered.

The cabbie's thick face set, hardened into challenge. "Fuck you."

Eric got off his bike. That put his huge frame beside the cab's window. "What did you say?" he asked grimly. Eric felt his strength return with the flow of his anger. The rage filled his body, air inflating a float, and forced out the limp sensation of abstraction he had felt for weeks—powerful Eric back in contact with himself.

"Take it easy," the cabbie mumbled, looking away from Eric's body. The light changed and the cab hurried off.

For a moment, Eric was relieved, rid of the oppressive thoughts, that he was a failure as a broker, and a failure, genetically, as a father. He looked down at his pants. There was a tear on the right leg. He lifted it; a broad line, oozing crimson, made a stripe below his knee. He hadn't felt the scrape at first. Now it hurt. He walked his bike onto the sidewalk, ignoring the curious glances of several people, and leaned it against a concrete wall.

Eric held his hand against the wound and studied the block while he waited for the sting to pass. Like the other streets between Eighth and Fourteenth, Eleventh was a row of red brick town houses, interrupted occasionally by a brownstone, a stunted white brick version of the typical postwar high rise, and, an exception to the other blocks, by the tacky glass and concrete structure of the New School.

Behind Eric was a curiosity, however: a small triangle of cleared land, protected by a concrete wall made forbidding by the addition of spiked iron bars. At the middle of the open space was a locked iron gate. Eric walked to it and glanced in; the triangle was a cemetery. There seemed to be about a dozen worn tombstones.

A cemetery in the middle of Manhattan? And so tiny!

The area inside the wall was no more than ten feet deep and thirty wide. Eric read the plaque on the wall next to the gate:

THE SECOND CEMETERY OF THE SPANISH
AND PORTUGUESE SYNAGOGUE
SHEARITH ISRAEL IN THE CITY OF NEW YORK
1805-1829

A stillness surrounded Eric. The line of cars honking at the corner, the noise of pedestrians seemed to diminish as he looked into this hallowed strip of land. Against the rear brick wall, covered by ivy, the letters of one of the washed-out and faded white tombstones could still be read: ISAAC HENRY. Beneath the name were Hebrew letters blurred by erosion, and below them, writ large in English: SACRED.

This little plot of land had survived, had endured all this time, and even won out over the greed of New York land development.

Eric peered at the other stones. He could make out another name:

Phillips. He read the plaque again. A chill shivered down his spine. He didn't know why.

A young woman's voice startled him. "Look at this!"

"What is it?" a young man answered in a southern accent.

Eric looked at them. Probably NYU students. She was beautiful and tall. She pushed her long blond hair over her shoulder, it draped gracefully down her long, straight back, and she read the plaque out loud in a tone of wonder.

"My God," the young man said when she finished. "There were Jews here even then."

"Shhh," she said, glancing at Eric. The young man followed her look.

"That's what makes it a great city," the southerner continued to her, although the apology was for Eric's benefit.

"That's right!" Eric said to him.

The couple smiled nervously and moved on. Eric watched them until they disappeared, turning the corner at Fifth Avenue. At one point the young southerner looked back, saw Eric, and turned away again. The couple quickened their pace after that. He thinks I'm gonna punch him out, Eric thought, amused. He thinks I'm a New York crazy.

When Eric got back on his bike, he was almost too tired to push the pedals. He prayed that Nina would be calmer than she had sounded on the phone, that the house would be clean, that there would be something home-cooked to eat.

But Eric wasn't surprised when he found the opposite. Nina's eyes were red, the beds were unmade, the sink filled with dishes, dirty ashtrays were everywhere, the apartment had a vague odor of baby shit, and Luke—Luke was crying.

"I can't stand it anymore," Nina said breathlessly. "I'm just letting him cry. The doctor said—"

Eric walked past her into Luke's room. The cries were heart-rending. Luke was arching his back, then falling forward, smashing his face into the mattress, trying to escape the weakness of his muscles and the torment of his loneliness. "How long has he been crying?" Eric yelled at Nina.

"Ten minutes," she pleaded, tears filling her eyes. "He's been like this all day—"

"Lie down!" Eric shouted. "Rest! I'll take care of him."

"Okay," she said, leaving the room, hanging her head.

Eric picked up his son. Luke wheezed with gasping cries; his little body flailed in Eric's arms, so frantic that it took awhile before

Eric calmed enough to realize he had what he wanted—comforting warmth and steady motion.

Luke's breathless panic slowed. His bobbing head stopped and he leaned back against Eric's supporting hand to look at his savior. The curious blue circles stared into Eric's eyes. Although the air conditioner was on, sweat poured off Eric's brow; Eric's body wept onto Luke's clothes. Eric wanted to smile at Luke, but he couldn't. He was worn out. His back ached sorely, as though he were a field laborer at the end of the season's harvest. His leg stung from the scrape. His body felt hot and yet he shivered from the chills where the sweat had oozed.

Eric rocked Luke from side to side.

Calm down, my son. Feel my love. You are safe. You are safe. Rest with me. Rest with me.

Luke leaned his head against Eric's shoulder and sighed. The plump baby legs stretched out; the small feet dangled.

You are with me. You are safe.

Eric reached into the crib and picked up Luke's pacifier. He put it to Luke's lips. They opened greedily. Luke chewed, rested his head against Eric, and sighed.

Eric sat in the rocker and began the movement that had become second nature, losing his self to the motion, his arms pressing Luke firmly, not tight, but close.

Eric's body ached. It told him: you can't keep this up.

I will.

You will lose your clients.

I won't.

You will get killed on your bike.

I won't.

This will make no difference. Your son will always be like this.

He won't.

Out of the corner of his eye, Eric saw Luke's eyes begin to close, the lids rocking open and shut with the motion, each time, shutting tighter, opening less.

No matter what it does to me, Eric said to the fate that tormented him, I will fight to make this work. I will give every drop of my soul to rescue my son from your evil.

Eric vowed to himself: he will never cry again. I will rock him even if I drop dead doing it. He will never cry again.

In the silence of the room, he rested his thoughts, his worries. He felt his son's warmth and relaxation. From time to time Luke started in his sleep. Eric yearned to let go of him, to be free to sleep himself. Eric's stomach cringed for food. The sun went down, darkness seeping into the apartment. There were no sounds from Nina's room. Luke's body finally went so limp that his head slid gradually down into the crook of Eric's arm.

It was night. Hours had passed.

Eventually Nina began to make noises. He heard sheets rustling. Then footsteps. Dishes loaded into the machine. The garbage can being lifted, a bag tied, the front door opening. Finally she appeared at the doorway, peering cautiously into the dark room.

"Is he asleep?" she asked.

Eric couldn't speak to her. He nodded.

"Why don't you lay him down?"

"You know why," he said.

"I can't handle it," she said. "I'm sorry. I'm going to need some help."

"Fine. Hire someone."

"We have the money?"

"No. But I'll get the money."

"Are you sure?" she asked. "Maybe my parents—"

"I'll get the money."

"Do you want something to eat?"

"No."

Nina stood there. Eric felt nothing but rage at her. "Are you angry?" she asked.

"Don't ever let him cry like that again."

"I just couldn't—"

"Don't!" he shouted. Luke started in his arms. Eric began to rock again. "Don't!" he whispered from the darkness to his wife. "Call me if you have to. But don't ever let him cry and be alone again. Don't ever leave him alone and unhappy."

Nina covered her face with her hands. "Oh, God," she said.

"That's all I ask. You can get help, you don't have to cook. You don't have to even think about me. But he must never be left to cry."

In the night of their apartment Eric continued to rock his son. Nina slumped to her knees slowly. He heard her sob.

He didn't care.

PETER LAY ON THE COUCH IN HIS STUDY, THE BOOK FOR A NEW musical in his lap, and listened to his just purchased compact disk player, a clever machine hardly larger than the disk itself, through his new earphones. He had on a recording of the *Follies* concert and was enthralled.

There was so much genius in the world.

Writers, actors, composers, designers, painters, dancers, directors—geniuses everywhere, it seemed to Peter (at least sometimes), even though the arts were dying financially, even though serious work was rarely popular. But that sad fact was what made Peter necessary. And important. And worthwhile.

Peter was today's commissioning Borgia, today's Pope ordering Michelangelo to paint the Sistine Chapel, today's Theo supporting Vincent. He stood, like a breaker wall, against the surf of mediocrity, the foam of vulgar nonsense. If Peter hadn't funded *The Titan*, its brilliant score might never have been heard, certainly not on Broadway, and then there would have been no Pulitzer, no big-budget movie. That gem, that work of genius, would never have shone so bright without Peter's quiet support. Quiet? Invisible, rather. Oh, to be sure, there was a little note in the program: the producers thank the Stillman Foundation for its help, blah, blah. But no Peter Hummel was identified as having talked the foundation into writing the check. Among his colleagues, Peter was credited. To the theater producers, to the major artists of today, Peter was known to be an angel, a true angel, his money not a lien against future success, nor an unthinking pretension of a rich widow. But of course—and recent cutbacks had made Peter feel this fact keenly—the money wasn't Peter's.

Diane had promised sex. Peter glanced at the clock. She had wanted to take a bath first. Time was up.

Peter had come home hungry for Diane. But now, after dinner, after Byron's and Diane's baths, Peter was hours away from the titillation of the Harlequin Theater's cocktail party. There, along with the sour wine and dry cheese, were the female hors d'oeuvres that had whetted his appetite. Blond, brunette, black, and red-haired; full-breasted and languorous, small-breasted and energetic; long-limbed and shy, small-boned and bold; wide shoulders and long necks, tiny wrists and red nails; big eyes, warm browns, bright blues, glistening greens; dark skin, white skin, freckles, pimples, shaved armpits, downy arms, the menagerie of women, so various, each reinventing her sex so that they seemed unrelated, loose from their cages, free in the wild to dazzle men. Peter had come home horny, wanting to go out, to seduce Diane, to taste her long-haired vagina and the dark meat of her skin.

That appetite hadn't survived the tepid pizza and the dinner conversation, an hour of Diane's complaint that Byron hadn't greeted her when she came home. The sexual hunger had cramped in his belly and been forgotten.

While they ate the thick-crusted and tasteless pizza, Byron ignored Diane's sporadic and irritated "Hello, Byron!" to coo at Peter. Finally Peter held out his hand to quiet Byron. Byron gripped his father's pinkie in his soft, padded fist and squeezed with an impressive but harmless might.

"He loves everybody but me," Diane said.

"Nonsense," Peter answered. "It's just the opposite. Punishing you for deserting him proves how much he loves you."

"He's four months old! How could he know to single me out?"

"We learn early, my dear," Peter said, and laughed, shaking his pinkie and, with it, Byron's hand. "Right?" he asked his son. Byron opened his toothless mouth and chortled. The baby feet kicked with pleasure.

"Come here," Diane said, and grabbed her laughing son. This time, held aloft, while Diane buried her face into Byron's belly, kissing his chest and then the round pearl of his face, this time, this Byron giggled and smiled at Diane with pleasure. Relieved, Diane squeezed Byron to her, madly kissing his skull, his ear, his brow, his eyes, his dollop of a nose, and then she pursed her lips in front of his rounded, puffy lips and kissed him on the mouth.

The sight was obscene to Peter. "Okay, okay," he said. "You're gonna turn him into a fag."

"Oh, that's disgusting!" Diane said. Byron kicked, reached for her, pulling at the long black hair, latching onto her big nose, digging at the mystery of his mother. "You know, we're very lucky with Byron."

"We are?" Peter asked. Peter liked Byron, even loved him when they communed for a half hour each night before dinner, but he couldn't quite feel that having any son, no matter how charming, meant he was lucky.

"He's a very good baby."

"Why? Are other babies his age stealing cars and dealing drugs?"

"No!" Diane barely smiled. "I know from talking to Betty, from Francine, from my mother, for God's sake. He sleeps through the night, he doesn't fuss—"

"Just like you," Peter said.

Again she ignored his joke. "He's an easy baby."

"Well . . . we get the credit, don't we? They're our genes."

"That's right!" Diane agreed, and held Byron out, regarding him with the possessive self-satisfaction of a prizewinner enjoying her trophy. "We get the credit," she said in a baby voice.

Byron chuckled, his feet paddled, his fingers stretched, and he answered: "Ooo! Ooo! Ooo!"

Later Peter watched Diane play games with Byron's body on the living-room floor: astride him on her knees, she patted his feet together, rolling him from side to side, lifting him in the air, letting go for a moment, and catching him with an exclamation. Byron roared with delight at every maneuver, his excitement continuous, his pleasure in her attention absolute. When Diane would pause, he'd surrender himself to plead for more: arms and legs out, crucified on the carpet, his eyes wide, staring at her with awe.

She is his universe, Peter thought.

Peter remembered that envy while leaving his study to find Diane so they could make love per his request and her agreement prior to the pizza. Peter didn't feel sexy anymore—his lust had boiled away hours ago—but these days to let a payment date pass could dangerously spoil his credibility for future collections.

Diane was at the pine desk in their bedroom she used for night and weekend work. She wore a huge terry-cloth bathrobe, regal in its proportions, but bourgeois in its thick, unrevealing comfort. She had a hand spearing her long, straight black hair, the fingers splitting its shape and pulling at her scalp. A cigarette burned in an ashtray (she had stopped smoking during her pregnancy, but had started again with her return to the law firm) and she stared angrily at several pages of yellow notepaper filled by her small perfect lines of writing.

"How's it coming?" he asked.

She looked startled at his presence. "What! Oh. Okay. You want to make love," she said, checking that off like a momentarily forgotten errand.

"Do you?" he asked.

"I need a back massage," she said.

Good, he thought. That could mitigate the cold-start quality of this appointment. Diane got up, Peter kissed her, opening the robe's belt, and pushed it gently off her shoulders. Her body looked soft from the bath, loosened by relaxation, fragrant from soaking in perfumed water. Her olive skin was still tanned, except for the white-striped reminder of her bathing suit, so that her sexual parts blared from the dark of their surroundings. With Byron weaned, the swollen breasts had shriveled some, the nipples even darker than before, almost brown. Now they sagged, sloping away gradually from her chest with a modesty and calmness Peter thought beautiful, especially in contrast with the terrible explosive look of the milk pouches.

Peter put his hands on her breasts and squeezed slightly to feel their give, new to him, the beginning of middle age for Diane.

Diane pulled away quickly. She shed the half-off robe and lay facedown on the bed.

I've embarrassed her, he thought. But he liked the age of her body. She wouldn't believe that, so he didn't bother to tell her. She was new to him again. The girl Diane, with her tight skin and fully inflated tits, was gone. But this softer, rounded, weathered Diane was just as good—better because she was unfamiliar.

He put his hands on her back and rubbed. She fidgeted at his touch, her undulating spine like hard pebbles twisting under the walk of his hands. When he wandered below to her ass, he felt some decay at the underside of the buttocks, soft pockets remaining from the pregnancy. He liked them too. She tightened while he touched there, again obviously embarrassed at their condition, so he moved off.

I don't need you to be young, Peter wanted to say to Diane. We grew up together. If you are still a child, then so am I.

Young women are for affairs. Peter smiled to himself.

He was erect from the look and feel of her body. By now she had sighed with relaxation; her eyes were closed; the hard board of her back had buckled into soft flesh. He stopped the massage and undressed. Diane's eyes were closed. Peter lay next to her. He was taut; his muscles echoed with the tension and desire of his penis.

Diane sighed and turned her head, resting it against his shoulder. She held his penis like a flute: her thumb propped up the instrument; the fingertips touched its thick vein to play the stops. She reached down with her free hand and gathered his sweaty cascading balls and repackaged the supply with its spout. She leaned forward and looked at the arrangement she had made, her head in a tilt of appraisal. "They get big when you boys grow up, don't they?" she said.

Peter laughed. He felt both pride and triumph at her remark.

"I'm tired," she said. "Do you mind just doing it?"

"Sure," he said, but felt a twinge of disappointment. There was usually an obeisance to his genitals prior to intercourse—just as he courted her body before marrying it.

He moved on top of her. She guided his penis in. Her vagina felt less strange than the last time, when the interior seemed to have been rewallpapered with a sticky fabric. Diane claimed nursing had caused that; he had wondered if she was simply unexcited. But the sensation hadn't been dryness, rather a stubborn lack of elasticity.

Some of that unyielding effect remained this time, even when she was thoroughly wet. The walls had become glacial, their previous living caress replaced by a smoothness that he fancied was indifference. Diane seemed almost asleep while he moved inside her. Maybe her cunt was asleep.

"Do you like this?" Larry asked the little boy Peter.

Peter stopped moving inside Diane at the memory.

"Something wrong?" Diane asked.

"Are you very tired?"

"No," Diane said, and kissed him with warm, sleepy lips. "I'm relaxed. Don't worry about me."

"Do you touch yourself there?" Larry asked. "Do you like it when you touch yourself there?"

Peter squeezed his eyes, tried to squeeze out the husky, lascivious voice (mocking and insistent) from his brain. He kissed his wife's neck, her lean, smooth dark neck, a part of her he loved, a favorite piece, sure to bring orgasm; but his lips felt numb, unable to taste. Peter pushed himself in hard and yanked out, hard in, hard out. He tried to force himself to pleasure. Diane moaned. Her arms came around his back and pulled at him.

Larry's hand reached inside eight-year-old Peter's pants and searched with his mealy fingers for the little penis.

Forget it, forget it, forget it. Peter arched up and smashed inside. Diane sighed and moaned. She made a hissing sound with her teeth.

"Do you do this?" Larry had asked. He rolled the little penis against Peter's flat stomach, rolling it like dough on a board, back and forth, back and forth.

Did I enjoy that the first time? Or was it later?

"Oh! Oh!" Diane's legs hooked around Peter, feet binding his calves, and pressed him to her.

She's coming, Peter realized, amazed. He had been shot with Novocain, dead from the waist down, not weak, but numbly hard. Might as well let her enjoy it, he thought. He dug at her, dug inside, reaching for her center. She bucked with joy, held him tight, and twisted her pelvis against his hard, dead sausage, yelling with release.

And then, over the top of the sound of her orgasm, Byron cried out, the siren on. Mother and son wailed together. I'm lifeless, Peter thought, and saw Larry's cold eyes watching little Peter's scared face.

Diane and Byron can cry and laugh, but I'm lifeless.

"My God!" Diane said, sweat covering her. "You think Byron heard us?"

Peter listened to Byron's distress, unmoved. The wailing sounded like a car alarm.

"I'd better go to him," Diane said. "Did you come?"

"Yes," Peter lied.

"You're still so hard."

Peter pulled out. The base of his penis ached. It looked red and angry. Byron still wailed. Diane got into the robe and rushed to her son's room.

Peter listened to Diane make soothing sounds at Byron. "Yes, baby. You go back to sleep. Mommy and Daddy are okay."

Peter held his thick old hairy prick, hard and unfeeling, in his hand. *I'm lifeless.* He rubbed himself and it was like touching something that didn't belong to him.

He got out of bed and dressed again in his clothes. Only the wet feel of his penis reminded him that he had had sex. He returned to his study and began his memo on why they should fund the Uptown Theater's workshop of its next musical.

"Do you like it when I touch you there?" Larry had asked, and *little Peter couldn't answer. His small throat had closed. He couldn't speak, couldn't defend himself. "Do you like it when I touch you there?"* Larry had asked.

Peter put the paper aside. Why am I thinking of this now? He hadn't worried over his friend Gary's cousin Larry for a decade, hadn't worried about the minor incident (it *was* minor, he reminded himself) of sexual abuse.

Peter decided it was his nerves, the strangeness of sleeping with Diane after such a momentous event, even though this wasn't their first postbaby intercourse, but the second. It'll pass, he told himself.

What can I do about it now anyway?

Do you like it when I touch you there? Larry had asked the choked and mute child Peter.

No, I don't, the man Peter answered.

6

IN MID-JULY, ERIC AND NINA GAVE UP ANY ATTEMPT TO LIVE normally while caring for Luke. Their son's restlessness, the constant discomfort in his belly allowed them no relaxation, even during the brief times they slept. In the back of their minds, irritating and corrosive, was the worry that Luke would never be right, never easy.

Eric and Nina had conceived in hope, convinced that the creation of their child would give life meaning and beauty. By the fifth week after Luke's birth, the treasured mutual joy of Nina's pregnancy, the keen anticipation of birth had become a grim struggle with Luke's unhappy nature. Nina had given up internal hope that day in Grace Church. She was now addicted to Eric's repeated assertions that if they held on, Luke would be all right. In thrall to Eric's assurance that their self-sacrifice would eventually heal Luke, Nina turned off her ego and became an automaton, feeding, cleaning, rocking, her mind a blank, a bulb burning bright, in a race to complete its task before the final blowout.

"Tell me he's going to get better," she'd say each night.

"It's colic. It'll go away."

"My mother says we should let him cry," Nina once said in a monotone.

"If we hold him, he'll be all right," Eric had answered. And then heard himself say, "If we let him suffer, he'll expect nothing from the world." The words floated up from Eric's soul; they weren't a creation of his brain.

"Why did this happen to us?" she sometimes asked.

"I don't know," he always answered.

By the sixth week, Eric feared even their stubborn will to continue to love Luke would collapse and they would crash, their marriage and their belief in life shattered.

They interviewed a few nannies, but knew, in their hearts, that no one would hold Luke for hours on end the way they did. But they did hire a cleaning woman to come twice a week and Eric knew (he had hoped otherwise) that eventually full-time child care would be necessary. Eric put all actual and potential expenses into his computer at work and looked at the last four-week take of commissions and trading in his own account. The gap between expense and income had widened. A year of this trend and they would be bankrupt.

One night, at the end of the sixth week, after Eric got the Snugli off (it had become Luke's second skin) and succeeded in laying Luke down without startling him awake, Eric found Nina at the kitchen table, in the dark, weeping uncontrollably. It was three-forty in the morning. That day, Eric discovered he had neglected to take a four-thousand-dollar profit in options a week ago, because as the result of fatigue, he had forgotten he owned them. By the time he remembered, it was too late, the price had retreated. Eric watched Nina; she cried without pause. He was terrified by her emotional condition. Eric decided he couldn't leave Luke alone with her. Anyway, he had become inept, even dangerous at trading.

The next morning, Eric went into Joe's office before the market opened, and asked Joe for a leave until September and a loan to cover his expenses.

Joe had the *Journal* open on his desk, his bifocals at the end of his nose. Joe closed the paper when Eric finished his plea. He looked at Eric over the flat rims. "Have you considered that your son's colic might be in your mind? Babies cry, you know. Maybe you're being overprotective."

"I don't think so," Eric said. He was used to fighting this point of view. His mother, Nina's mother, the nannies Nina had talked to in the park, a couple of the child-care books, their pediatrician, all of them (when other suggestions had failed) had made the case that Luke's fussing was made worse by their comforting. But Eric knew about experts—the stock market was littered with the torn scraps of their proud ideas. Consistency, riding out the run of luck against you, was the only thing that ever worked. Bulls get rich and Bears get rich and Pigs get nothing. "I've read that the only thing they know for sure is some babies are born with an incomplete formation of the digestive tract," Eric told Joe, the speech tediously familiar. "In three months, they're all right. If Luke isn't better in another six weeks, we'll act differently. But until then, he's blameless. I mean, Joe, Luke can barely hold his head up. How the hell could he know to manipulate us?''

"They know!" Joe said, wagging a finger and smiling at his own wisdom. "They know how to get their hooks into their parents. They learn in the womb.''

Although Eric thought Joe's brand of wit, with its pompous elaboration, unfunny, Eric nevertheless usually flattered Joe with a laugh. But this time, Eric stared at him. "I don't think so, Joe. It's just bad luck. Sure, I could blame it on Luke and run away from the responsibility. You wouldn't do that. And you wouldn't respect me if I did. Nina can't handle this alone. I want to ride it out with her for the next six weeks. All these years I've never taken Fridays off to go to the Hamptons—I must have saved up six weeks' worth.''

"That's not our arrangement, Eric. You know that. I'm not your boss. This is a partnership—''

"Not exactly, Joe. Come on, be fair. You hold the seat on the exchange. I service your clients and your name is on the checks when I score for mine.''

"Neither are you a broker working for me. You get seventy-five percent commission on your clients. I give you ideas and clients and a steady income—a piece of my management free to boot. And as to not taking off Fridays, when have I taken them?''

"I know,'' Eric said, bowing his head, dismayed. He had told himself not to make that point about Fridays. He rubbed his forehead and closed his eyes. He was so tired he could pass out right there—let it all go, the work, the money, the years of staying on Joe's good side, the marriage (his once smoothly functioning, content marriage), and even Luke. Eric could just let go—fall onto the carpet and be carried off.

"This is really Nina's responsibility,'' Joe said. "I know it's none of my business, but despite women's lib and all that, it's unfair of her to expect you to earn money for the family and also take on caring for your son. What you do *here*''—he tapped the desk with his fingers—"*that* is caring for her and your baby.''

"It's just six weeks,'' Eric said in a tired, exasperated voice that amounted to a whine. *Please*, oh, please. Look Joe in the face, he told himself. "After that, I'm here. There'll be no more of the new daddy stuff.''

"Why don't you hire a woman to help her? What about your mother, or *her* mother, for God's sakes?''

"Joe, cut the crap. How about it—yes or no? It's your choice.''

"Eric, I'm hurt by that. I don't ask you questions as a boss. I'm trying to help. Her mother could be a great consolation to Nina now. It's a wonderful time for mother and daughter—the birth of a grandchild. It is, anyway, if they're Jewish.''

Eric covered his face with his hands. ''Oh, God,'' he said, rubbing his fingers into his tired eyes. Eric hated asking for favors because of the intimacy they allowed; they opened up the account books of your life and gave everyone the right to audit your management ability. Now Luke's colic was due to his mixed marriage. ''That's why I need the time off,'' Eric said, lowering his hands. He had rubbed his eyes so hard that Joe looked blurry. ''We're going to her parents' summer house in Maine. They'll be coming up and can help us.''

''Ah,'' Joe said, nodding. He had talked himself into a corner with his criticisms. ''Then why don't you stay here and let them handle it?'' he argued.

''Joe . . .''

''Visit on the weekends. Take a week—''

''I've been useless anyway. I'm no good like this. You don't need me.''

''If she and the boy are away, you'll be getting rest. Then you *will* be of use. Don't ever say I don't need you.''

''My son needs me more.'' Eric's tone was final. He challenged Joe with a stare.

Joe took off his bifocals and cleared the *Journal* away. He lifted the newspaper gingerly, holding its creased middle with his fingers, giving it the respect of a holy text. ''How much will you need?''

''A month's income. Seven thousand.''

''Seven? And how are you going to repay it?''

''Take it out of my commissions when I return.''

''You're going to generate fourteen thousand in commissions in September? I don't want you churning accounts to pay me off. That's how you lose clients.''

''Forget about the money,'' Eric said, and turned to head for the door. ''I'll get it from a bank.''

''No, no!'' Joe put his hand up, rising from his chair. ''You're being very insulting. Making me out to look like a miser. I'm concerned. I don't want you under any pressures you can't handle.''

He had been brusque in his manner, Eric had to admit. Joe's dignity was important to him, even more important than his money. Eric slowed the pace of his emotions, sighing, and said evenly, ''I'm grateful you're giving me the time off. That's the important part. I can borrow the money from Nina's parents or mine.''

''What about your pension fund?'' Joe said with abrupt happiness—delighted at his discovery of an out for both of them. "Why don't you borrow from that?"

"Oh. Yeah, sure. I'll do that. Anyway, I'd like to clear out of here this morning."

Before Eric could depart, Joe repeated his assertion that he valued Eric and would miss his help in the firm. Joe insisted on a solemn good-bye, clasping Eric's hand in both of his own while he looked earnestly into Eric's eyes: "You're more than a partner to me, you know that, Eric. Take care of yourself."

"Thanks, Joe. I'll be back in six weeks and everything will be kosher."

Eric went out to the trading room and told Sammy. "What!" Sammy said with disgust. He listened to Eric's explanation with a stare, his thin lips disappearing altogether into a tight pout. When Eric finished, Sammy nodded, said, "Bye," and turned his back, hitting keys on his terminal.

"Come on, Sammy. Don't be like that."

"You're going away for six weeks—it's no big deal. Goodbye."

Eric packed up various investment surveys and annual reports to read in Maine and said his farewells to Irene and the other secretaries. Sammy continued to ignore him. Irene walked Eric to the door, hugged him, and said, her voice trembling, "You're a sweet man."

Her emotion gave Eric the creeps, made him feel he would never see any of them again, or, worse, that Irene believed Luke really was a burden that would cripple Eric. Eric opened the door and looked back. "Bye, Sammy!"

For a moment there was no response. Then Sammy, without turning around, called out, "Call in every week. I'll tell you what's going on."

"Okay." That made Eric feel better about leaving. It was hot outside, but not humid. New York glowed from the light: peopled by bright-colored clothes; street corners flagged by the umbrellas of vendors; brokers carrying jackets in their wake, dappling the gray buildings with the pinks and blues and yellows of their Brooks shirts; the sallow or black faces of the service workers winked past Eric, and the tanned or burned faces of the middle class glanced curiously at his load of investment books. Eric was suddenly apart from them, free from their concerns. With his job on hold, Eric's dismay at the future shriveled in the sun. He felt excited at the struggle ahead of him, his hands unbound, ready to fight.

Eric hailed a cab and endured the drive impatiently, irritated by what he thought were inept choices by the driver. He dashed into the lobby, got into the elevator, and hopped from one foot to the other at its slow ascent. When the doors opened, he moved out blindly and bumped into Luke's baby carriage.

"Eric!" Nina said. She looked wan, but peaceful. He had been so distant from her emotionally that her appearance, her drained look, astonished him.

"I got six weeks off. We'll go to your parents' place in Maine." She stared at him. Not unhappily. Dully.

"Okay?" he asked, and kissed her.

She didn't move her lips. "Okay," she said, nodding. "That's a good idea."

"The sea air. Maybe that'll help Luke," Eric said.

"Maybe," she said, nodding more vigorously.

"I love you," he said.

"I love you too," she answered, and put her arms around him. She squeezed herself to him and put her head against his chest.

"We're gonna be okay," he promised.

DIANE AND PETER ENTERED BRIAN STOPPARD'S PARK AVENUE apartment at five minutes after eight. Diane was astonished that the door was opened by a uniformed man and woman who took their Burberrys and umbrellas and asked if they wanted a cocktail. Astonished because the presence of servants implied a big, formal dinner—after all, Stoppard had invited Diane offhandedly, no embossed card in the mail, just a casual aside at the office: "We're having some people over for dinner next Saturday, including the unhappy Gedhorn trio. Can you and Peter come?" The Gedhorn suit, insulation manufacturers whose former employees were suing over unhealthy working conditions, had been Diane's primary assignment for a year, assisting Stoppard on the brief; thus she had assumed dinner would be the two Gedhorn senior vice-presidents and the in-house counsel. And she knew from Betty Winters that she and her husband, Tony, were invited, presumably because Tony, being a playwright and screenwriter, knew Stoppard's wife, novelist Paula Kramer. Such a disparate combination of people would make Diane and Peter ideal guests, since Diane could chat up the Gedhorn trio, see a friendly face in Betty, while Peter, Tony, and Paula discussed show business.

But this was a much bigger event. At least twenty people were already in the living room. Stoppard should have warned her. Betty definitely should have warned her. Diane looked at the women's clothes and instantly felt inadequate in her lawyer outfit, worn to soothe the Gedhorn clients. She was in a gray skirt, a white blouse with ruffles at the collar, and a blue blazer. Diane cursed herself for allotting no time to shop since Byron's birth.

Peter waved to a group by the piano at one end of the living room: Tony and Betty Winters were talking to a cluster of movie stars, William Garth, Delilah, and Amy Howell. The women, even the normally dowdy Betty, were *dressed*. Delilah, with her long black hair draped down her back, was almost naked, swathed from her left shoulder to her groin in skintight white, her nipples darkly oozing through the fabric, her legs snaked by gold lamé, like a Roman soldier. Amy Howell looked like a child wearing a man-sized gangster's suit, utterly covered by thick, woolly Japanese-designed clothes, her shoulders padded, her waist bound briefly, then billowing out and down to the ground. Normally cautious Betty had on a red jump suit and a short, unevenly cut hairdo; the look, instead of seeming punk to Diane, reminded her of middle-aged Jewish ladies in their weekend stretch pants. But that group, given its bohemian stature, wasn't Diane's problem. A glance at the corporate wives and dates truly made Diane feel unequal: they looked like Bendel's manikins come to life. In her work clothes dress, with her big nose and horn-rimmed glasses, Diane thought she might be mistaken for—for what? I *am* a lawyer. That would be no mistake.

Brian Stoppard and Paula Kramer stood among the corporate people, their son and daughter huddled between the legs of the grown-ups. The boy was six, Diane knew, the girl three. Paula saw Diane and Peter, and came toward them just as they were handed their drink orders. Paula had her children reluctantly in tow. The boy, especially, hung back, his head down, his mouth closed in a sullen, shy pout. "Hi, glad you could make it," Paula said breathlessly.

"I didn't realize it was such a big party," Diane said. "I wouldn't have come like this."

"Didn't Brian tell you?" Paula was amazed. She shook her head of frizzy hair. "He's perverse. You look lovely. Have you met Sasha and Rachel? Now that you're new parents, I thought you might like to see the future. Sasha, Rachel, this is Diane and Peter Hummel."

"Hello!" Peter said, and put out his hand to Sasha, who regarded it like a loathsome vegetable on a plate.

"How old's your son now?" Paula asked.

"Six months. He turned over yesterday!" Diane announced.

"Uh-oh." Paula laughed. "Your life is over."

"He did?" Peter asked Diane. He still had his hand in Sasha's face.

"Yes, I told you," Diane answered defensively. She might not have. Peter's lack of interest in fatherhood was unfashionable, and it would reflect badly on her if Paula Kramer knew Diane tolerated it. "He's only done it the one time."

"Shake Peter's hand," Paula urged her son, Sasha.

Sasha put out his small hand limply. Peter shook it gently. "Where do you go to school, Sasha?"

Now the boy looked up, sure of himself. "Hunter," he said, naming a free public school in Manhattan specially created for bright children.

Hunter? Diane thought. Stoppard makes six hundred thousand a year; Paula's a best-selling writer. What the hell are they doing taking up a place at Hunter?

"It's great!" Paula said. "You have to get your boy in. Best school in the city."

"Better than the private schools?" Diane asked.

"Sure, you don't get that miserable homogeneous population of spoiled rich kids," Paula said eagerly. "Besides, at Hunter everybody's there on merit. They studied pointillism in kindergarten! It's amazing."

"Well," Peter said diffidently. "You have to be something of a genius to get in. I don't think Byron's in that class."

"Oh, they're not geniuses," Paula said. "Patty! Hi!" she called out to another celebrity, Patty Lane, entering just then. "If your boy is normally bright and you read to him a lot, he'll score great on the test and get in. Excuse me." She rushed on and moved to the door, pulling her children with her.

"Why the hell did you say Byron's not smart?" Diane whispered.

"I didn't," Peter said. "I said he's not a genius."

"How do you know what he is?"

Peter closed his eyes, irritated. "He's not a genius."

"Peter!" Tony Winters called. He waved them over. Diane felt her stomach flutter at the prospect of meeting the movie stars. Because of Peter's job, Diane had met celebrities, although they were of the theater, not film, and she had even witnessed the surprising flattery they bestowed on Peter in hopes of getting money for particular projects, but this group, Garth and Delilah especially, had been world-famous since Diane was a teenager. To see their faces in reality, in her boss's living room, her husband beside her, wearing her boring clothes, was bizarre. Betty made the situation stranger by asking, as Diane and Peter approached, "Did Byron turn over again?"

"No" was all Diane could manage in answer to Betty under Delilah's bored stare.

"I just heard about this," Peter said.

"She didn't tell you!" Betty exclaimed.

Because he wouldn't care, you fool, Diane thought.

Tony made the introductions and added, to get the conversation going again, "I'm trying to convince Bill to return to the stage."

"In a play of yours, I hope," Peter said.

Betty, meanwhile, both to Diane's relief and irritation, maneuvered Diane aside from the stars and began to babble about children. They talked on the phone regularly now, but it wasn't a comfort. To each step in Byron's development, Betty said, "Oh, I remember that. Wait until he starts—" and then she'd name something better yet to come. Like everything else in New York, even mothers talking about their babies were a competition.

"Do you know what Paula told me?" Betty whispered now. "Sasha, her son, goes to Hunter. They were studying Seurat and pointillism in kindergarten!"

"That must be her standard speech to the wives," Diane said. "She just told me the same thing."

"Oh, my God!" Betty said with a squeal of pleasure. "I thought it was directed at me because Nicholas didn't get in."

"To Hunter? Nicholas's old enough to apply to school?"

Betty stepped back and looked at Diane under lowered brows in mock astonishment. "My dear, you have to apply a year ahead of time. And if you want to have any hope of getting your child into a decent school, you must get him into one of the feeder preschools at the age of two."

"You mean this starts at one year old!" Diane said, her astonishment genuine.

"Haven't you been reading all the pieces in the *Times* and *Town Magazine*?"

"I was skipping them! My God, I have a six-month-old! I thought I had time!"

"Are you mad, woman?" Tony Winters said, leaning into their conversation without warning. "One slip now and your child ends up a bum on welfare in twenty years."

"What's this?" Delilah said.

"Oh, the New York private school madness," Tony explained to the movie stars. "The yuppies have made the mediocre education of New York not only more mediocre, but it costs more and the pressure is worse."

"Really?" Peter said. "When my mother moved me here as a teenager, I don't think there was much pressure to get in."

"Maybe for you," Delilah said. "It's tough in L.A. too. No problema if you got a series on the air."

"It *is* different now," Betty said to Peter. "The competition is fierce. Public schools are much worse and also there are all these well-to-do parents who've been told that early education is the most important of all."

"It's all bullshit," Tony said. He lowered his voice. "Paula told me Hunter is great because it's more real than going to a private school. More real? Everybody in the class has an IQ of one fifty or better. That's real? When those kids go out into the world and work for people whose IQs are in two figures, we'll see how well prepared they are. More real. Sure—the world is loaded with black, Hispanic, Oriental, and Jewish kids with IQs of one eighty."

"I guess your boy didn't get in, huh, Tony?" Garth said, and roared with laughter to cover the insult.

"Yeah," Tony said effortlessly. "Now he'll have to become an actor."

Diane burst out laughing, more at the unexpectedness of Tony's return of serve—since he was a screenwriter, she assumed he'd let any abuse go unanswered by a big star like Garth. Delilah and Amy Howell both scanned Diane after her guffaw, noticing her for the first time. Delilah gave Diane a thorough going-over, up and down. "You're a lawyer, I bet," Delilah said to Diane in a sluggish tone. Amy smiled reflexively.

"How did you *know*?" Betty said, delighted, missing the implied insult, her face open with wonder, a child delighted by a card trick.

"Yes, I am," Diane said.

"Did you see *Legal Eagles*?" Garth asked.

"What's that?" Diane asked.

Garth was stunned. Tony laughed, deeply and resonantly. "Grown-ups who don't work in the movie business don't go to the movies," Tony said to Garth. "They don't even think about movies."

"It must be hard having a kid and being a lawyer," Delilah said to Diane. "Do you work, Betty?"

"Not anymore. Our housekeeper left suddenly—"

"Suddenly last summer," Tony mumbled.

"—and I decided to quit and stay home."

"How do you like it?" Amy Howell asked. "I couldn't stand just being home. I need to work."

"I like it fine," Betty said primly, a hint of self-righteousness in the tone.

"How about you?" Delilah asked Diane, her voice tough, almost like a street kid making a dare.

Diane, for a moment, couldn't think, looking at this famous face from her youth, from when she used to smoke grass, protest the war, dream of arguing in front of the Supreme Court, and lived, in general, convinced that she would never imitate the conventions of her parents' generation. If, the first time she had heard Delilah sing, someone had shown Diane her future—married to a respectable, balding Peter, a son home with a baby-sitter, working to defend a major American corporation from its disabled employees, her stomach still puffy from childbirth, the whole dreary list of things and decay that had changed her, changed her utterly from a tough young girl eager for life to a cautious aging woman fighting to hang on to what she had—if someone had abruptly presented the future, skipping all the gradations of the change, using her first sight of televised-Delilah to now in-the-flesh-Delilah, Diane would have screamed, fled college, run to the countryside, and, like some of her friends, raised vegetables, let her armpit hair grow, and scoffed at the ones who stayed.

I'm thirty-six years old, she thought; in four years I'll be forty. I am closer to death than I have come from birth. My life has hardened in the mold. I am riding an express to the glassy-eyed, hearing-impaired, bladder-weary terminus. I am thirty-six years old and my growing is over.

"Diane?" Peter said, looking at his arm.

Diane followed his glance: she had a desperate grip on his sleeve. All Diane could see, for the moment, was the tweed fabric bunched up in her fingers.

"Are you all right?" Peter asked.

"I feel a little faint," she managed to answer. "I'd better—" She stumbled out of the noisy room, back to the foyer. Paula was still there with her children, surrounded by a half dozen new arrivals. Peter and Betty followed Diane, Peter taking her arm, Betty appearing in front, peering at her.

"You look green," Betty said.

"Hey!" said Patty Lane, the celebrity author, tapping Betty on the shoulder. "No hello?"

Betty glanced back at Patty. "Oh. Hi. My friend—have you met?—she's not feeling well—"

Diane looked at Patty's beautiful body, displayed by tight black stretch pants and a loose pink blouse unbuttoned to reveal the tops of her black bra, and she thought: all these women are more famous and more beautiful than I am.

Patty's pleasant party smile evaporated, her big green eyes widening. "We're fainting," Patty announced, and pushed Peter away, taking Diane's other arm. "There's a bedroom this way," Patty said.

The two women half carried Diane to a huge sedate bedroom, all the fabric beige and the furniture made of light, glistening wood. Patty shut the door in Peter's startled face, as if he were a molester.

"That's her husband," Betty explained.

"Who cares?" Patty answered.

"Diane, this is Patty Lane—"

"I know," Diane said. Diane had read and enjoyed Lane's two novels of distressed young womanhood in New York, pitying and envying the main characters' woes.

"This is your friend Diane!" Patty said with recognition. "Didn't you just have a baby? Should you be out in a mob scene like this?"

Betty laughed. "She had the baby six months ago."

"Oh," said Patty. "So? I'd still be in bed." There was a knock on the door. "If it's your husband, do you want him?" Patty asked.

Diane nodded, although she felt much better alone with the two women. Younger, at ease, free from the world's intense demands.

Patty opened the door. But it wasn't Peter. Paula Kramer bustled in, asking questions, suggesting remedies, mentioning Stoppard's concern that Diane rejoin the party to talk with the Gedhorn people. At the mention of the clients, Diane stiffened. Her anxiety at the chaos of the universe focused into tension at the demands of the present. Diane declined Patty's and Betty's suggestion that she rest for a while and instead returned to the party, ignoring Tony, Peter, and the group that she had embarrassed herself in front of, joining, instead, Stoppard and the Gedhorn people.

Diane felt sure of herself the moment she was back in her element, making fun of the way opposing counsel had deposed the vice-presidents, bolstering Stoppard's ego as he became expansive and predicted victory.

Once they all went to the buffet, she was split from the Gedhorn people and found herself beside Delilah. The star winked at her and said, "You feeling better?"

"Yeah," Diane answered. "I'm not getting enough sleep."

"Does your husband help with the baby?" Delilah asked, but in a tone that implied she already knew the answer.

"Of course not," Diane answered, relieved the secret was out. Yes, I am a failure as a feminist.

Betty, Patty, and Paula waved her over to a corner of the dining room and Diane ate ravenously while they talked. Paula continued to praise Hunter, perversely egged on by Betty, and in the cab ride home, the words of the mothers about getting their children into a good school stayed in Diane's mind. Betty had said to Diane, "You don't have to worry—Peter's mom can get you into any of the good private schools."

The baby-sitter reported that Byron had been an angel, playing happily on the rug until nine, and falling asleep without any fuss the moment he was rocked. While Peter paid her, Diane went into Byron's quiet room and stood over his crib.

Paula's prideful remarks—"They get into Hunter on merit"—Tony's envious ones—"They all have IQs over one fifty"—Paula's advice—"If you just read to your boy a lot, he'll score high on the test"—and Peter's infuriating "He's not a genius" were replayed over and over in her mind.

Diane was smart. She had gotten into Yale from a mediocre public school and from there gone to Harvard Law. Her brain was ferocious, alive, calculating. Her mind could concentrate absolutely on a subject, relentless to the finish, immaculate at arranging the details. More than anyone she knew, certainly more than Peter, she was here, in New York's fast lane, on merit.

Diane put her hand down on Byron's back and stroked gently. Then she let her fingers stray on his warm skull.

"He's not a genius," his father had said.

Byron could make do with Peter's connections and become one of those mediocre children of the successful, lazy intellectually and spoiled by physical comfort.

Diane felt her mind pulse with energy. She imagined her tough, active brain could flow down through her arm, into her fingertips, and into Byron, into the soft, impressionable dough of Byron's mind.

Peter made a living because his mother knew the right people. He got into Harvard because two generations had gone before him.

I made it because of my brain.

Diane closed her eyes and released the force of her intellect into Byron's baby brain. She felt her body glow with the transfer.

Get there on merit like me, she ordered.

WHEN ERIC EXITED OFF THE MAINE TURNPIKE AND GOT ON THE two-lane country highway, Nina rolled her window down all the way and tilted her head out, her face to the wind. The cool country air splashed her cheeks and filled her nostrils with the perfume of nature's maturity. Her eyes rested, gazing at the soft greens, the still white houses, the glimpses of shimmering bays and lakes, the winding stretches of placid road. With every mile, there were fewer and fewer things and people—less and less of lifeless cement, more and more of the breathing earth.

Nina glanced back at Luke. He had been peaceful in the car, soothed by the steady hum of the motor and the regular bumps of the highway's seams. He slumped bonelessly in the hollow of the car seat, his veined eyelids were closed, and his long eyelashes rested, like discarded fans, on the white fabric of his face. His black hair was crazy from repeated perspirations and dryings, some locks curling up against gravity, others collapsed on his brow, stuck to his skin.

Eric's thick thighs, naked in his blue shorts, glowed in the late-afternoon sun. Nina put her hand on the muscled mass of Eric's leg, ironing the curled hairs between her fingers, and tried to imagine Luke-the-tadpole growing up to become like his bear of a father. Eric's arms were so long that even with his seat retracted to the maximum, they looked cramped by the short distance from his shoulders to the steering wheel. Eric had to angle his knee to one side when lifting off the accelerator or else he'd bang it. His head almost touched the roof. Some of his kinky hair actually did. Maybe Luke cried at the prospect of all that stretching in store for his body.

They reached her parents' summer cottage by eight. While Eric unloaded the car, Nina stood at the top of the bleached wooden stairs that declined from the lawn to the rocky shore. Luke was awake in her arms, his eyes wincing at the chilly sea breeze. The orange and pink light of the sunset glowed over the curved sky from the west, colors parachuting from the air to die in the water, tinting the cold blue of the bay red and gold. The dark approached them from the horizon, erasing the bright world. At the edges of the night, stars appeared.

"That's the most sleep he's ever gotten." Eric's voice boomed in the trafficless, unpeopled auditorium of the country, his sound abrasive amid the soothing noise of lapping tide, rustling leaves, and complaining gulls. "He'll probably be up all night."

"I'll stay up with him," Nina said calmly.

Eric cocked his head.

"Really," she said, self-assured. Nina held Luke up to the side of her face. "See the stars, baby," she whispered to the little circle of Luke's countenance. "I think that's Venus," she added.

Eric stepped to her side. "Where?" Nina pointed to what she remembered her father had always told her was Venus. She showed

Eric reluctantly, afraid that, with his literal mind, he might know otherwise and correct her.

"Wow," he said instead. Eric looked at Luke and put out his enormous hand, reaching for Luke's miniature version. "Maybe when you're grown," Eric said to Luke, closing on the little fist, "you can fly there."

Luke frowned at his father's big face, as though disgusted by the notion.

"I doubt it," Nina said, thinking that this worried, clutching child would hardly dare the unknown.

"Yeah," Eric said. "They don't have money for the space program. Instead they'll put up lasers to zap him."

"God, Eric," Nina said, disgusted.

Just kidding," he said.

"I know," she reassured him. Eric was bound to reality, she reminded herself, and no matter how far the leash stretched, he would always be yanked back. Nevertheless, the spell had been broken and she carried Luke toward the house.

The four-bedroom cottage, set in a cleared circle at the edge of Blue Hill Bay, shielded from the road and neighbors by white birches and tall firs, was two hundred years old and had been in Nina's family for a hundred and fifty years. Just inside the front door, on a hand-hewn beam, four generations of Nina's family had marked the growth of their children. "Could you get a knife, Eric?" she asked.

"A knife?"

"I'm going to mark Luke's height."

Eric paused for a moment, studying the beam, and then peering at Luke. Nina knew he was about to make some pragmatic objection, something like the fact that Luke couldn't stand up, but Eric must have decided against it, because he went to the kitchen for the knife.

The tradition was to make the first indentation for height at age five on Thanksgiving when all, or most of the family, was usually in attendance. Nina had always found the ritual boring. From age fourteen on, she had refused to participate, believing that it only intensified the endless competition among the siblings—her brother John had chortled over outgrowing dead relatives—and that, as a connection to previous generations, measurements of height were hardly a profound legacy. There were old American families who kept journals, or whose correspondence, when found in attics, spoke down the long hallway of time. And there were old American families who had at least left relics of their taste and interests and benevolence, who had begun institutions, endowed universities, founded museums, and had civic works named in their honor. But Nina's family, the Winninghams, had merely left behind several turn-of-the-century Ivy League championship squash cups; a stuffy painting of Great-Grandpa, the banker; and a grant for Princeton, by a bachelor uncle, to give a graduating senior money to travel in Italy for a year. To what end no one knew.

The family had endured and lived hearty lives—that was all Nina could deduce from the stories of them. They were good amateur athletes; they made money steadily, although never excessively; they were helpful, but not extraordinary, citizens; they gave decent amounts to charity, but never boldly. The blank markings on the wall were a perfect symbol of their mute past: they had grown; they had procreated. Nina had decided instantly on seeing the beam that no matter how dull this conversation with her ancestors might be, she wanted Luke to speak early. None of the Winninghams had ever stepped out of line, made a rude noise, or changed anything they encountered. Luke, at least, would begin his life with an alteration of their tradition even while obeying it.

She had Eric hold Luke while she used the knife. Luke's curved legs dangled like feelers. The gouge she made in the wood was, at best, a crude approximation, but she took great pleasure in writing the date and Luke's name big, so big that no other infant's data would ever have room to fit, unless its size was radically different. The braggadocio of her large writing was also against the diffident family tradition. "Leave room for the next one," her mother would always say. Nina hadn't been polite; there would be only one newborn Winningham on the beam.

The caretaker and his wife had done a good job preparing the cottage. Wood was split and stacked in the two fireplaces, there were fresh-cut wild flowers in every room, and a crib had been set up in the smallest of the bedrooms. Nina took Luke on a tour. For the first seven weeks of his life, Nina hadn't gone in for much talking to Luke. He was unhappy, tired; always awake and fussing. All her efforts had been to keep him calm and quiet. But now, walking through the rooms of her happy childhood summers, she held Luke up, showing him the things and explaining, "This is your room. When Mommy was a baby, she slept here. That's Blue Hill Bay, which goes right into the Atlantic Ocean. See that? That's the mast of Grandpa and Grandma's sailboat. We'll take you out tomorrow if it's nice."

Luke moaned and whined at first. His legs made spasmodic movements in the air, objecting to the lack of support, but Nina kept talking, turning him, her voice soft, like her own mother's, explaining everything.

"That's a spider web. Is the spider home? No . . . Did you hear that? An owl."

She saw that Eric followed them about with a puzzled expression on his face. "Something wrong?" she asked faintly.

"Don't you think you're worrying him?" Eric said.

Luke wasn't crying; he had even stopped peeping with complaints. "He's fine," she answered. "He's listening to me."

"Okay," Eric said, agreeably. "He *is* quiet. But his eyes look worried."

Nina turned Luke, put him face-to-face with her. The blue marbles glowed at her, radiating their wonder. "We're having a conversation," Nina said. Luke seemed to be studying Nina, filling his eyes; they widened more and more, as if he could expand his vision limitlessly. Luke seemed to want to absorb more than merely the sight of her; he wanted to take in the idea, the function of her. He squawked at Nina.

"I'm Mommy," she said to him. She knew that was his question. "That's your daddy. I'm Mommy. This is Grandma and Grandpa's summer cottage. We're going to stay here."

Luke winced. His legs pulled up and then thrust down. He cried.

"Oh, God," Eric mumbled.

But Nina didn't feel the sinking despair this time. She sat down on the bentwood rocker, its arms worn to silver nudity by four generations of use. She told Eric to turn out the light. She bared her breast and fed Luke.

From time to time Luke pulled off to scream at the spasms in his stomach. He shouted up at her; he pushed with his legs, trying to swim away from the hurt. Nina shushed him, held his hot melon head, and kissed the almost liquid softness of his brow.

The moon lit up the bay and the water reflected a shiny blue light on the beams, the crib, Luke's body, Nina's arms. The rhythms dulled her thoughts; amidst the steady lonely sound of the runners treading wood and Luke's smacks of pleasure, Nina abandoned her self—her selfish core that had fought this duty.

She could feel them in the room—the mothers of her family. Silent and benign, Nina felt them enter, dissolve together, and inhabit her.

The women before her were here, their ghosts rocking infants too, their ceaseless care now hers.

Her labor was over. She was born a mother.

* * *

BYRON'S MOUTH CAME AT PETER. BYRON WAS IN HIS WALKER, A little seat with a tray in front and wheels on the bottom. He raced in his walker, powering himself with his feet. He raced madly along the length of the hall, eyes bright, charging his father with a joyous wide-open mouth.

Peter had come home in despair at the tedium of another evening with his wife and son. The nine months of Byron's life, the nine months of diminished socializing, sleeping Diane, and early-morning rising, seemed to stretch back endlessly, covering all of Peter's past. He could no longer remember the days of last-minute dinner dates and leisurely gossiping in bed with Diane. He had long since given up on making love with his wife; a five-minute conversation that wasn't about Byron's motor development was the closest they came to intimate contact. Besides, Peter didn't want to sleep with Diane anymore. The few times they had, she seemed, even when physically pleased, put upon by the request, and dismissive afterward.

"Da, Da! Da, Da! Da, Da!" Byron telegraphed his only word with staccato insistence.

The walker smashed painfully into Peter's shin. Byron was bounced back by the impact. Byron stood up on his legs, sat down in the seat, then got up again. Abruptly he went in reverse, backing away.

"Da, Da! Da, Da!" he claimed Peter.

"Yes, fella," Peter said. He bent over to rub his leg.

Thus encouraged, Byron charged again. His mouth was open, revealing two tiny teeth on his bottom gum. Peter went to his knees and put out his hands to stop the walker.

Braked by Peter's hands, Byron was jolted again. His head whipped back and forward. Alarmed, Peter said, "Are you okay?"

Byron laughed. His fat little round face beamed. "Da, Da! Da, Da!" he answered, his mouth open, his hands reaching for Peter's nose.

Peter leaned forward and kissed Byron on the forehead. Byron grabbed for Peter's mouth. His nails were sharp and Peter had to give Byron his hand to prevent himself from being scratched. Byron took Peter's index finger greedily and slowly tried to pull it to his mouth.

"Hungry?" Peter said, indulgently.

Byron opened his brown eyes wide and pursed lips together quizzically. Byron maneuvered Peter's finger toward his mouth slowly, testing whether he was allowed. Peter let him. Gently Byron put

Peter's finger between his lips, frowning as his tongue touched the adult skin.

Then Byron bit down as hard as he could.

The two little teeth were sharp as razors. Peter yelled and pulled his finger back. Byron looked baffled.

"Jesus! What the hell are you doing!" Peter yelled.

Insulted, Byron's mouth opened to bawl, but no sound came out.

Peter glanced at his finger. There were two little indentations in the skin.

Now the sound of Byron's cry did come out. Peter was terrified by its volume and passion. "Okay, okay, I'm sorry, I'm sorry."

Diane appeared in the hallway. "What did you do to him?" she shouted over. She picked up Byron. He arched his back, his face turned red, and tear droplets appeared at the corners of his eyes.

"He bit me!" Peter complained.

"Did you?" Diane said to Byron, smiling, as if biting his father were a witty action.

"Don't praise him for it!" Peter said.

"He's a baby. He doesn't know what he's doing." Diane kissed Byron's stomach. His crying was instantly churned into gay chuckles. He bicycled his legs, his hands reached for her—a sensual creature, guiltless and rapacious, to Peter's mind, plundering the household's supply of love.

Every night was the same, only more so, Peter thought. As Byron got older, and was more able to stay awake, the disruption of their life got worse and worse. Once Byron learned to crawl, the apartment was under siege by his curiosity. He attacked televisions, video recorders, magazines, books, and records; the floor and all tables below four feet in height had to be constantly policed for dangerous or precious objects.

No one asked about Peter's health anymore. "How's Byron?" his mother and his friends always wondered first. "Is he crawling? Is he eating solid food?" Last week, Peter had felt flush. When Gail, his mother, called about the museum's cocktail party, Peter told her he was ill. "Stay away from Byron" was her response.

Diane had stopped accompanying Peter to theater or other functions. Peter spent four nights a week out alone. Although Peter had avoided Rachel, he had had four dalliances—a result, he believed, of Diane's desertion. But the phenomenon of Peter's sexual abstraction remained even with other women: he was unable to enjoy the intercourse; numbed from the waist down by memory, Peter screwed without a climax, a drama full of tension, but no release. Kissing, cuddling, wooing the woman's body, he was excited and alive—but once his penis was involved, his mind lifted off and looked down dispassionately on him, the woman, and the activity. He was unable to feel pleasure. Somehow he blamed Diane and Byron, believed they had stolen his passion.

Peter had made up his mind to talk to Diane. He needed her back, he needed his wife. So tonight he had come home early from an Uptown Theater fund raiser, canceled his tickets to the new Fosse show, and bought a bottle of champagne to make things festive. Peter lifted the Moët out of its brown wrapper. "Would you like some?"

Diane squinted. "Champagne? Byron's hot," she said, frowning. She kissed Byron's forehead. "Could you get the thermometer?"

"He's got a fever?"

"He's hot," she repeated. "Feel." She offered Byron to Peter. Byron's eyelids were half lowered and had an extra crease. Peter put his hand on Byron's forehead. Byron tried to shake it off and kicked Peter's chest hard enough to hurt.

"He feels warm," Peter agreed, and backed away. This nine-month-old was dangerous.

"Get the thermometer," Diane said.

Peter obeyed, putting the champagne in the refrigerator first. They could drink it later, after Byron was asleep. When Peter returned from the bathroom, Diane frowned at the plastic case and shrieked, "This is an oral thermometer! What's the matter with you?"

"Don't talk to me like that," Peter said. Diane sounded shrewish, the same tone Lily used with Diane.

"What do you think! A nine-month-old is gonna hold a thermometer under his tongue?"

"We don't have any other thermometer!" Peter shouted, and instantly was ashamed that he had lost his temper. Byron, who had been twisting and squawking in Diane's arms, began to cry again.

"I bought a rectal thermometer. It's in the cabinet."

Peter was disgusted. He remembered back to when he was left by his mother, Gail, to stay with his friend Gary for a weekend. They were eight or nine. Both of them had come down with fevers; they weren't particularly high, but Gary's mother had insisted on . . . He shook his head at the memory. Peter had wanted to object, to balk at Gary's mother's request. She wouldn't have forced him, but Gary had somehow intimidated Peter, made him feel he had to. The humiliation of lowering his pants and allowing a stranger (Gary's mother was a stranger to Peter, no matter how well he knew her) to put . . . He felt sick to his stomach thinking about it. Gail always let Peter use an oral thermometer. When Peter made that point, Gary's mother had said disdainfully, "It's not accurate." Peter remembered the pleasure Gary's mother seemed to take in their discomfort: "Don't move around! Lie still. You're such babies!" Gail would never have done that to Peter. She never offended his dignity. Why didn't I object, why didn't I—

"Peter! Will you please get the thermometer?"

"No," Peter said, backing away, her request a tangible menace stalking him.

Diane peered at Peter in amazement. Byron's hand swiped across her mouth. Byron moaned and squawked. "Why not?"

"Okay," he said, and walked to the bathroom quickly, found another plastic case (with that horrible word "rectal" written on it), and brought it to her, tossing the thing on the couch. He turned to leave.

"Where are you going? I need some Vaseline."

He remembered that as well, the cold, slimy feel of it, the ooze afterward, and Gary's continual talk about the residue of the sensation. In school, a few weeks later, Gary told their classmates. Why he exposed them both to ridicule Peter never understood. As he told the story to their classmates, Gary giggled with mean delight while he described the look on Peter's face as the thermometer was inser—Peter closed his eyes, as again his mind was overcome by the clarity of the memory, Gary laughing, Gary's mother saying, "You're such babies," the whole horrible—

"Peter, I'm going to need your help, all right? He's getting hotter. Get some Vaseline and a towel."

"I'm not having any part of this," Peter said firmly, and left the living room. He went to his study and closed the door. He sat at his desk. He was trembling.

I'm an adult. He's my son. I must defend him. Women like to destroy our pride, to make us into babies.

Peter shook his head, physically trying to free his mind from the strange mesh that had captured his reason. Byron *is* a baby. He tried to cut through to common sense. He's not an eight-year-old. Diane's perfectly correct. What other choice does she have?

But I don't have to participate. I told her. I won't help.

But the issue here wasn't help; it was intercession.

I can't allow Diane to do anything she wants. He's my son. One day, he will turn to me, grown to equality, and ask me why.

Will I pretend I didn't hear?

Through the closed door, Peter heard wailing, dreadful wailing.

"Goddammit!" A faint version of Diane's voice carried in.

Byron's outrage, Diane's frustration—they stood beside Peter, mocking sentinels. Aren't you going to do something? they asked.

"Peter! Peter!" Diane's shouts for help were both desperate and furious.

Peter covered his ears for a moment, but the raging voices of his wife and son reached him anyway. He surrendered, rose, opened his study door, and marched back to the living room.

Peter glanced briefly at the spectacle on the rug. Apparently Diane had been unable to keep Byron still enough to put the thermometer in. "Hold him!" Diane said. Peter maneuvered himself so he was beside Byron. Peter put his hands on the little shoulders, flexing to gain mobility, and held his son down.

For a second, Byron stopped fussing. Peter looked into his son's brown eyes, warm and curious at Peter's appearance; light glinted through them and their color shimmered from hue to hue.

A big smile reversed the angry sorrow. "Da, Da! Da, Da!" Byron claimed triumphantly.

"That's right," Peter said.

"Okay," Diane said. "Here we go."

Byron was about to reach for his father's mouth, to play with the spectacle of his Da, Da. But the thing went in—and Byron s eyes shut, his head bucked forward, his shoulders fought to get up. Peter held him down. Byron screeched his complaints. Peter laid his head next to Byron's and kissed his cheek.

"Only take a second," he apologized.

Byron tried to fight again, but as he lost, his complaints became cries, cries of frustration, cries of defeat.

Afterward, Peter held Byron while Diane cleaned up and went to the bedroom to call the doctor. "A hundred and three," she told Peter. Byron still tried to move, to play, but sighed and relaxed in Peter's arms after a minute of Peter's resistance. Byron's body was hot. The soft, plump thighs radiated his body's distress. The white skin took on a pink hue. The usually restless Byron leaned his sweaty head against his father's shoulder and looked into Peter's eyes with mournful contemplation. There seemed to be no memory of Peter's collaboration in the outrage, no grudge borne.

Diane appeared, her coat on, with a sweater for Byron. "The doctor's still in the office. He'll see Byron if I take him right now."

Byron peeped as Peter handed him over. Byron's fantastic energy, evident only an hour ago, was gone.

He's dying, Peter thought. The heat from Byron's body had made a wet circle on his shirt. The hard candle of his life-force was melting.

"Are you coming?" Diane asked, finished with dressing Byron.

He thought about that, remembering Diane's description of taking Byron to the doctor—the wait in a room full of crying children, the pompous posturing of the doctor, the brutal need to restrain Byron for examination.

"Are you coming? I have to hurry."

Peter shook his head no, scared, ready to give in if she insisted.

"Fine," she said, and left, carrying Byron, who lay limply in her arms, his eyes almost closed, whimpering pitifully.

Peter sat for a long time after they were gone, not moving, unable really to think of what to do. He should be hungry. He wasn't. He could use a drink. He considered opening the champagne. Took too much effort.

He felt sorry for Byron.

Peter tried to imagine what it would be like if Byron died.

Diane would mourn for a while. Would she want another?

Peter tried hard to convince himself Diane would not. The pain of one loss might make her shy of a second creation.

But he knew Diane would never accept defeat. She would go right back and do it again, even more determined.

Peter touched his cheek, where the feverish Byron had rested against him, gazing sadly, giving up the struggle, moaning and peeping from the hot ache. The wet of Byron's sweat had dried; the warmth of his body had cooled. But touching there, Peter felt his son return.

He wanted to cry. The feeling was unfamiliar—a slab of loss; incomprehensible, impossible to chop up into manageable pieces.

Of course, Byron was going to go on living. And growing. And of course, time and time again Peter would fail him, collaborate in his oppression, and have nothing but an apology as an explanation.

He was still in the chair when Diane and Byron returned. Byron was asleep in Diane's arms, his head lolled back, his lips parted, breathing heavily. She put Byron in his crib and returned to say that the doctor had diagnosed Byron as having an ear infection. Peter was to go out and get a prescription for liquid penicillin filled and she thought they ought to have extra baby Tylenol.

Peter listened, saying nothing. When she finished, he got up. She peered at him for a moment and said, "What's the matter with you?"

"I don't know," he said.

"Well, I think you'd better find out," she snapped, so angry that she had to turn away and pretend to be interested in something on the rug.

He thought for a while about answering. What could he say? He hated her as a mother, wanted her as a wife? He loved and pitied Byron, but wished Byron didn't exist at all? That something awful in the corner of his mind had come to life, some shadow had been cast, and now seemed animate—a terrible lurking monster which no night-light could dissipate?

"I think I'd better see a shrink," he said finally.

"You'd better do something," she said harshly, but cut herself off, interrupting a longer exposition of criticism. After a moment, she sighed, and spoke quietly. "You acted really weird. He was sick. I have to take his temperature."

"I'm squeamish," he said.

Diane squinted, puzzled, trying to bring him into focus. "Squeamish about taking his temperature?"

"Yes."

Diane shook her head, her eyes wide, her mouth open. She sat down, collapsed by his incredible remark. "You'd better see a shrink," she said, nodding. "You're nuts all right."

Peter swallowed. Her comment, presumably just the residue of her anger, hurt. He believed, suddenly, that if she really knew him, that would be her serious judgment, not a hostile remark, but a final conclusion.

He went to the drugstore. While waiting for the prescription to be filled, he decided to tell Diane that he couldn't stand what had happened to their life. He didn't want things to continue this way. They would have to get sleep-in help. She would have to accompany him in the evenings. Her centering on Byron had to be shifted. Either that, or he'd leave.

This decision calmed him. He went home with the medicine, cured of his anxieties.

Diane was on the phone with Betty Winters. Diane sounded happy, laughing, and she called out to Peter while still on the phone: "You're not going to believe this! We didn't have to do a rectal—"

Peter blanched at her shouting the word.

"—there's a thing called a Fever Strip. You just hold it on their"—Diane listened to the phone—"hold it on their forehead for fifteen seconds. Can you believe it?"

Diane sent Peter out again to get this modern miracle. The Fever Strip was nothing more than a few inches of plastic with a color band to read the temperature; the druggist said it was just as good as any other method. When Peter returned, Diane kissed him enthusiastically and then eagerly opened the Fever Strip, testing it on Peter's forehead and then her own.

Byron woke up, complaining. They cooled his body with washcloths, used the Fever Strip, gave him his dose of penicillin, and he fell back to sleep.

Peter opened the champagne. Diane had a little, he drank most of it. Before Peter got around to his speech, Diane said she was exhausted. He let her go to bed.

Thinking about his earlier upset, Peter thought it was just a case of bad nerves. There's penicillin to cure the infection; there's a Fever Strip, a thin plastic device, that makes parenting easy. It would all work out. He had to relax and be patient.

He loved them.

Presumably they loved him.

He would have to wait his turn.

7

DIANE'S VISION MOVED AHEAD OF HER, A CAMERA TRACK-
ing, divorced from her mind: the sight of the bedroom, the look of
the hallway, the closed door of Byron's room, loomed and then
passed, seen through a stranger's eyes.

But when Diane opened Byron's door and saw her eleven-month-
old baby, standing in his crib, hands on the bars, head cocked
curiously, sandy hair in a wave across his brow, she woke up. Woke
up with pleasure.

"Ma! Ma!" Byron shouted, crying Hosanna at the appearance
of a miracle.

"Hello, baby!"

Byron bent his knees and then jerked up. He opened his mouth
and showed the two miniatures of teeth on bottom and a stub of
another on top. He grinned and chuckled. He hooted and squealed.

She rushed to get him, to capture his happiness in her. Byron
grappled onto Diane, nuzzled his head in her neck, his little but
insistent fingers touching, poking, patting, stroking. His delight in
her presence was electric in his body.

She changed his soaked diaper, again accompanied by babbling,
laughing excitement. Byron tried to roll this way to get the fresh
diaper, then that way to grab the tube of ointment. He rolled his
bottom up and made his legs accessible to his hands. He grabbed
his toe and pulled it to his mouth. He burst into resonant giggles at
the cool feel of the wet wipes. His brown eyes glistened at Diane's,
as though only they shared this profound joke: the hilarity of his
body functions, the absurdity of cold and cloth, the silliness of feet
and diapers.

Diane had her coffee after she put Byron down on the kitchen
floor with his bottle. He finished it quickly, and with gusto. He

smacked his lips at the last drop, and hurled the vessel contemptuously to the floor. While she mixed formula into the powdered oatmeal, Byron immediately swiveled on his bottom to face the kitchen cabinets. "O!" he shouted to the stainless-steel handles. He flopped forward, palms out. Diane smiled at his adept movements, a baby tank on the move, knees and hands mastering terrain. In a flash he scurried to the cabinets and began his assault. Byron braced himself with one hand and reached for the handle with the other.

Byron took hold of the handle with his right hand. His weight pulled the door open. It swung out, and took him along, tipping him over backwards. . . . Diane dropped the box of oatmeal. With a hiss, its contents spilled over the counter and stove. She caught Byron's head only inches from the hard tile floor. For a moment, Byron looked worried by his sudden upside-down placement. Then his cheeks puffed out, and he laughed.

"You're gonna kill yourself," she said, smiling at his amusement.

Byron groaned in an attempt to get up.

Diane righted him. She took out a pot from the cabinet for Byron to play with. She looked at the scattered flakes of cereal. "Shit," she said. Byron had grabbed hold of the pot handle and now banged it on the floor. Steel on tile: a terrible clatter.

Diane's timing in the morning was precise. Cleaning the cereal would stretch its limits. She hurried: pulled the metal tops off the stove, dumped them in the sink, grabbed a sponge, and went to work on the counter.

She heard a thud beneath her. Then a piercing, although muffled, scream from Byron.

Diane looked at her feet. Byron had fallen forward, right into the pot, his head submerged, his ass up in the air.

Diane shrieked and picked up Byron by his waist, half expecting the pot to be permanently wedged on his head. It did stay on briefly, carried up a foot or so before it fell to the floor with a ringing bang. Byron's face emerged crimson, his neck retracted, his mouth gaping while he wailed, terrified.

"Okay, okay," she said. Diane tried to lean her head back to get a view of Byron's face. But he clung to her shoulder and pressed his nose into her neck. "Let me see," she said, prying him off. "Let me see." Byron's head jerked at hers and he cried right into her eyes. There weren't any cuts.

"Diane!" Peter's voice came from behind her. "What happened?"

"He fell into a pot," she said, turning to face Peter. Byron's wails were cut off by the sight of his father. He lurched forward, arms out, to Peter.

"Da! Da!" he announced.

Peter's hair was askew from sleep. He was in his underpants. He blinked at Diane and Byron. "Try and keep things quiet. I didn't get to bed till four." With that, Peter returned to bed.

Byron's arms stretched for the departing Peter, a plea for Daddy to stay. "Oooh!" he called.

"Forget it," Diane said to Byron.

Byron's brown eyes queried her, his thin eyebrows bunched together above the bridge of his nose: "Da, Da?"

"Da, Da would rather sleep," she answered.

Byron leaned back and clapped. He patted his pudgy hands together and watched her curiously. "Mama! Mama!" he said, explaining his applause.

She laughed. Although each night left her tired and disgusted by the workload of job and baby, these mornings were delights, full of hugs and cuddles, the warm comfort of Byron's soft cheeks, and the flattery of his adoring eyes.

And his growth! His amazing acquisition of skills, subtle at first, but now explosive, were put on display by his morning energy. Byron greeted life with joy, so different from the adult attitude to a new day. Only half a minute after Byron's disaster with the pot, he was back on the floor, crawling to the scene of the calamity, and rerisking its dangers.

While Diane quickly finished cleaning the stove and mixed a new bowl of cereal, she noticed Byron lowering his head down toward the pot, reenacting the crime. He let his forehead touch the rim, and then jerked back at the contact, as if the pot might grab him. At his escape, he would hoot, clap, grab the handle, and thump the pot on the floor, announcing his triumphant mastery.

She put Byron into his high chair, and reflected on his calling for Peter first, then saying her name. "Ah! Ah!" Byron spoke, while she strapped him in, his eyes going from the bowl of oatmeal to her, his hand pounding the table impatiently. "Ah! Ah!"

"You're ready to talk," Diane informed him. She picked up the bowl and used the silver baby spoon given to them by Peter's mother, Gail, to sculpt out a small wave of cereal. Diane offered the stuff to Byron's already open mouth—his narrow tongue out in the air, curled in anticipation. "Food," she told him. "Food."

Byron's eyebrows went up, inquisitive, while he closed his soft red lips over the spoon and suctioned the mush inside. "Mmmm, rowrr, mmm, O!" he commented on the texture and taste.

"Food," she said, and spooned more from the bowl. She held it up for him to see.

Byron banged his hand on the table, startling Diane. "Owff!" Byron exclaimed, and lunged forward to capture the spoon with his mouth. She gave him another portion.

Was he saying "food"?

"More?" she asked, gesturing with the spoon at the bowl of oatmeal.

Byron was grinding the mush, his fluted elastic lips pursed, his eyes almost crossed from concentration on the taste. "Mrrr, awrr, grrr, oof! Mrr, awrr. O!" Byron said to her.

"You're saying something complicated. Compliments to the chef?"

"Diane!" Peter was at the door again. He had put on yesterday's shirt—wrinkled from a night on the floor. Peter looked absurd, his hair shocked upwards, his thin legs shadowed by the billowing curtains that his belly made of the shirttail.

"What is it, Peter?" she snapped, ready to yell at him if he repeated his complaint.

"Did you say he fell into a pot?" Peter rubbed his eyes and peered at Byron.

"Da! Da!" Byron hooted.

"Yes," she answered coolly. "He's all right."

"He fell into a pot on the stove and he's all right!"

"No, no, no." She laughed and lost track of the spoonful of oatmeal, dangling it within reach of Byron's hand. He knocked the dollop of beige matter onto the table. "Byron," she chided. She scooped more cereal and gave it to Byron while describing the accident to Peter. Her husband listened soberly at first, and then scratched his head sleepily.

"I think he's psychotic," Peter judged.

"That's nice," Diane said. "Nice way to talk."

Peter shrugged. He opened the cabinet full of cereals and squinted inside. Peter switched on the overhead lights to see better but was startled by a hoot from Byron.

"Oooh!" Byron lurched forward, his fat arm hailing the light. His eyes narrowed, his mouth scrunched with effort. "Da! Da!" he shouted at the light.

"Daddy turned on the light," Diane said.

"Da! Da! Oooh! Oooh!"

"No, Da, Da. Light," she said.

"He thinks everything is called Da, Da," Peter said.

This galvanized Diane. She unbuckled Byron from the high chair seat belt and put him on her hip. She turned on the globe over the table. "Light," she said.

"Oooh." Byron squinted from the glare.

"Light," she repeated.

Byron queried her with his eyes.

She carried him into the living room. She turned on the standing lamp next to the couch. "Light!" she said. She walked to the end table on the other side and turned on that lamp. "Light!"

Byron put his fingers on her lips, a gentle, curious touch. "Laaa," he said awkwardly from his throat.

"Light," she repeated. She moved to the hallway and flipped the switch. "Light." She pointed to the ceiling fixture.

"Laa! Laa!" he screamed, arching out of her arms, reaching to embrace the bulbs.

"Light, light." She had to pull to carry Byron off (although he was in her arms, his attraction to the fixture seemed to have the force of planetary gravity) and went to the bedroom, flipping the wall switch. "Light, light."

"Diane!" Peter called.

"Laaa . . . t!" Byron broke through the weak muscles of infancy, pushing the sound out. "Laa . . . it!"

She felt a rush of joy, a terrible chill of happiness. "That's right! Light!"

"Laaait!" Byron stretched the sounds in his throat, grappling with them, muscling them to the right shape.

"Light, light!"

"Laait! Laait!"

"That's right, baby!" She kissed his cheek, his puffy pillow.

Byron ignored the affection. He pointed to the illumination and masticated the sounds, his voice piercing: "Lahi-t! Lahi-t!"

"Diane!" Peter appeared at her side, exasperated. "Have you gone mad? The poor kid just woke up."

"He knows!" Diane felt the energy of her pleasure surge to her face, her eyes tearing. "He knows, Peter. He can talk."

"Da, Da!" Byron said, and reached for his father.

Peter took him. Byron's little body was hot, his eyelids were creased. Byron leaned his head against Peter's shoulder. "He's tired," Peter said.

"Watch," Diane said. She turned the light off and then on. "What is it?" she said to Byron.

Byron lifted his head, his back tight with attention. "Laa-hit! La-iht!"

"That's right," escaped from Peter's lips, his face beaming.

Diane went to Byron and held his cheeks with her hands, looking into his eyes. "You're so smart. My beautiful baby boy. You're so smart."

ON BYRON'S FIRST BIRTHDAY, DIANE CELEBRATED WITH A BIG party, inviting everyone she knew who had children under five, the grand- and stepgrandparents, Peter's half sister and half brother, as well as his stepsister and stepbrother. They all came, even the merely legal relations, despite the fact that many had to journey from afar.

Peter was disturbed by their presence. He hid behind his Nikon camera, escaping from conversations that were dull, demanding, or dumb, by claiming a need to photograph the instigator with Byron. Peter ran out of film before Diane had even brought out the cake, and that provided him with an excuse to run outside to buy more.

"I can't believe you didn't buy enough film" were Diane's parting words.

The awful thing, Peter realized, once out on the street, was that none of those people fought to get him to pay attention, to belong, to engage in the party. They were happy to let him be obscured by Byron, by the event, by the camera. Diane? They surrounded her, questioned her, praised her. Because of the existence of Byron, his relations seemed to retract their skepticism of Diane.

"You married well," his stepsister had commented out of the blue to Peter when they passed in the hallway. "Diane's a terrific mother."

"Are you surprised?" he asked pointedly.

His stepsister had two kids and had never had a job. She looked defensive, but answered truthfully. "Yes. I thought Diane was too wrapped up in her career to have a baby. I don't know how she does it."

Peter felt flustered, almost accused, by that answer. For a reply, he took her picture with Diane and Byron.

While he walked to the film store, Peter had a strong desire to hail a cab, take it somewhere, midtown perhaps, and shop in the Fifth Avenue stores. He passed a pair of phone booths. A young man of college age occupied one, talking animatedly. Peter entered the free booth and called Rachel. He dialed without considering the why or the consequences. He needed her sensibilities, her oxygen.

"Hello!" Rachel answered with the enthusiasm of a teenager.

"Hi. It's Peter."

Despite the year that had passed, Rachel didn't hesitate, or seem surprised. She didn't even bother to conceal her delight. "Peter! It's so great to hear your voice. How are you? I've been wondering."

"I can't talk long. I want to see you. Is that possible?"

"I'm always here! What have I got to do? You want to have breakfast tomorrow?"

"How about theater tomorrow? I've got tickets to *Sincerely Yours*."

"Oh, it's supposed to be good!"

"I'll meet you at the box office. We'll have dinner afterwards. All right?"

"Lovely, darling," Rachel said grandly.

Peter returned home with a loaded camera, more at ease and ready to join in the applause for Byron. Diane had Byron on display, set down in the middle of a circle of admiring adults. Peter's son stood among the tall trees, hooting to their tops. He stood boldly, planted on the rug, his fat little legs stiff, his eyes open wide, his mouth pursed with excitement. He shouted to them. He lifted his arms and hailed them. He clapped at their sounds of pleasure.

And then, just as Diane hoped, Byron showed his new trick. Out went his right foot—out forward into space—and then down, firmly, on the rug.

"Oh . . ." mumbled his relatives.

Byron wobbled for a moment.

"Uh-oh." The relatives worried with him.

With a shout of effort, Byron jerked his left foot to join the right, his toes pointed out, a penguin on the ice.

"He's walking!" Lily, his grandmother, shouted.

Byron met Lily's eyes and laughed to her. He put his hands up to her.

"Come to Grandma, baby," Lily called.

Byron, his head bobbing, stepped out into dangerous air, his right foot forward, knee locked, arms out for balance. He wobbled as his foot landed, and then snapped his left leg forward to even things up.

"Yes!" Lily shouted.

Again. Right, teeter, left.

"Wow," said someone.

Right, rock, left. Now faster, ahead to the astonished grown-ups, sounds of triumph pouring from him.

"Homo erectus!" Peter called, and shot picture after picture.

Byron dove at his grandmother Lily when he got close enough, hurling himself recklessly to gain the last few inches in one movement. Lily rescued Byron from smashing onto the rug, took him in her arms, and whirled him around. She clasped him to her breast and began to dance with him, to the amazement of Peter's relatives. That plump old Jewish woman made herself dainty. She twirled Byron, prancing on her tiptoes, covering his face with smacking kisses, taking possession. "My bubeleh, my beautiful baby doll," she sang to him, unashamed of her passion.

Peter looked at his mother. Gail's genuine smile at Byron's steps was left over on her face, the warm sauce of her amazed pleasure jelled into cold glop.

Then, as if to torment Gail further, Lily danced Byron over to Gail and showed him off, a bride flashing her big diamond. "Isn't he gorgeous!" she demanded of Gail. "Isn't he a big gorgeous boy!"

Gail nodded cautiously at Lily, the way she might have responded if she were cornered by a raving bag lady. Gail put on a mollifying smile to veil her embarrassment and desire to escape.

"He can walk!" Lily pushed herself on Gail. Byron grabbed for Lily's huge eyeglasses.

"Sort of," Gail demurred.

"What do you mean?" Lily protested.

"He collapsed there at the end," Gail said.

"What do you expect?" Lily demanded. "He's one year old. That's very early to walk." Distracted by her outrage, Lily allowed her eyeglasses to get within reach of Byron's grabs. The tiny fingers hooked the frames and sent them flying.

"I could see that was about to happen," Gail commented.

Diane retrieved the glasses and offered them to her mother. Lily, however, ignored her daughter, attempting to focus on Gail. Lily's nearsighted squint creased the wrinkled skin into hundreds of new breaks. "He can grab my glasses anytime," Lily said.

"I'm glad," Gail answered. Lily studied Gail's expression to find evidence of sarcasm, but Gail showed a calm and pleasant exterior. "That's what grandmothers are for," Gail added. She brushed Byron's cheek with her tanned hand, lean and long compared with Lily's plump paws.

Byron, relaxed and laughing in Lily's arms, fussed at Gail's touch. "Unhh," he groaned, and averted his face.

"Don't be frightened," Lily cooed to Byron. "She's your grand-mother too. Don't be frightened of her."

"Ma!" Diane said. "Take your glasses. Give me Byron."

Gail turned away and met Peter's stare. He had been fascinated by her cool reaction to Lily's insulting behavior. Gail returned his look for a moment. Then she winked.

"Peter!" he heard his stepfather, Kyle, say only a moment before laying a heavy hand on his shoulder. Peter tightened at the touch. "You have a CD player."

His stepfather didn't ask questions, he made accusations. Peter nodded sullenly.

"You didn't get it at the store."

"You're right," Peter answered.

"You paid two fifty."

"I don't remember."

"I've got them for two hundred. Sell the disks for eleven bucks. They're as much as fifteen elsewhere."

"How do you do it, Kyle?" Peter's father asked this. Jonathan stood a few feet away, his wavy gray hair combed back from his high brow, worn long in the back, bumping over his shirt collar. Jonathan was half sitting, half standing against the radiator cover in front of the window. His chest and stomach were pushed forward by this pose. Jonathan could be living in the Philadelphia of Franklin, with the big belly, thin legs, and the noble, yet intimidating, features of a hawk.

Peter tried to remember the last time Kyle and Jonathan were in the same room—Peter and Diane's wedding?

"The old joke. Volume, volume, volume."

"It's not boxes falling off trucks then," Jonathan mumbled into his scotch and soda.

"No. That's how I got started," Kyle answered with a sarcastic snort. "Now I play fair and square, Mr. Hummel." Kyle's usually subtle western accent—he grew up in Arizona—got thicker from Jonathan's challenge.

"A rare man, indeed," Jonathan said, his tendency to affect an English enunciation worsened by a desire to sound equally distinctive.

Peter felt the old anxiety, the short worried breaths of his child-hood, the spiritual yearning to escape, wrenched by the stronger magnetism of the drama. Peter used to think that his father would go too far with his teasing and say something unforgivably con-temptuous, that Kyle might punch Jonathan at any moment, that suddenly one of them would blurt out—what? Their true feelings? Those were clear.

"He's a fine baby," Kyle said. He smiled at Jonathan as best he could, his broad jaw yielding reluctantly. "You have a fine grandson."

"Say, Peter," Jonathan called to him as if he were across the room.

"Yes, Dad?" He knew from the smirk on Jonathan's face a witticism was coming.

"Do you know why grandfathers and grandsons get along so well?"

"No, Dad."

"They're united against a common enemy."

Peter lowered his head, looked down, down, down. He felt smaller, battered by the hubbub of sounds in the room, wanting to be alone, afraid to move. Jonathan laughed at his own joke.

"Don't get it," Kyle said. "Who's the common enemy?"

"Me," Peter said. He looked up from his shy, oppressed childhood—looked up through the sullen fog of adolescence, up to the equality of armored adulthood. He met their eyes bravely, a grownup again, and they were old. "Me," Peter repeated with the knowing smile of a teacher's brightest student. "Both son and father. I'm the common enemy."

THE LIGHTS OF THE CAR SHONE AGAINST THE LEAD-GLASS WINdows and glared into white circles on their distorting surface. The chug of the engine sounded loud against the country silence. Eric worried that Nina and Luke would be wakened by it. He turned on the driveway floods and went out the door.

"Hey!" called Brandon, Nina's older brother. "How ya doing!" Beside Brandon, in the passenger seat, was his second wife, Wendy. She sat staring ahead in a daze.

"Shhh," Eric said.

"Ah, *il bambino*." Brandon remembered. He shut off the engine. "Asleep?"

Eric nodded. "Probably not for long. Where are your parents?"

"They stayed over in Ogunquit. Be here tomorrow."

From the house they heard Luke's unhappy squawks. "Excuse me," Eric said, and dashed for the door.

"My nephew! That's my nephew!" Brandon called out.

While he rocked Luke, Eric heard Brandon and Wendy enter, find their room, talk in whispers so dramatic they were somehow louder than low voices, until finally Nina's sleepy talk joined them.

Go to sleep, Eric said to Nina in his head. Luke was restless in his arms, the eyes closing with each rock back and opening with each rock forward, a doll perversely designed for suspense, never completely awake or asleep. In Maine, Eric and Nina alternated night duty, to allow the swing shifter to make up the rest in the morning. If Nina stayed up to chat with Brandon and Wendy, she wouldn't be able to handle her morning child care. When, because of exhaustion, she lost control, Eric couldn't sleep. He'd hear her yell or allow Luke to cry, and Eric would get up, take Luke, and order her back to bed. He'd learned that much: Nina was a fine mother as long as she had energy. They would need a housekeeper. How much would that cost? Two hundred? Two fifty?

The whispers got closer. "Eric?" Nina called from outside the door. "Is Luke asleep?"

Luke peeped and arched his back, a hand clawing the air.

"No," Eric admitted.

They came into the cramped nursery, an invasion of giants. Brandon insisted on taking Luke.

"Hey, fella, how ya doing!" Uncle Brandon shouted into the miniature eleven-week-old face.

Luke's eyes shut in horror, his mouth gaped, and then he wailed.

"Great lungs!" Brandon said to Wendy. She stood beside him, her shoulders slumped, her eyes blank.

She's stoned, Eric decided. "Oh, baby," Nina said, and took Luke from his uncle.

"God, look at those feet! He's got your dogs, Eric. They're huge."

"Aren't they!" Nina said, excited. She had been alone with Eric and Luke in Maine for a month. Before that Nina had been dead to happy sensation. This was her first exhibition of maternal pride. Dammed up for so long, a flood of anatomical praise burst from her while she showed Luke off: his long fingers, his straight black hair, his almond-shaped eyes, his strong chin, his soft white skin. Nina looked beautiful as well, her thick brown hair flowing wildly down to her broad shoulders, her pale blue eyes soft from sleep, her skin as white as Luke's. She carried her baby into the living room—he squinted and mewed at the light—and raved about him to an enthusiastic Brandon and an impassive Wendy.

"And he's smart," she said while Eric tried to make a fire, worried that Luke was cold. "I talk to him and he listens."

"We should have a baby," Brandon said to Wendy.

"Yeah," she said to the floor. She looked over at Eric. "Do you have any cigarettes?"

"I don't think you should smoke around the baby," Brandon commented.

"It's okay, Brandy," Nina said. "I smoke around him all the time. I'm terrible."

"Hey, let me," Brandon said to Eric, going over to the fireplace. He removed an unsplit pine log from the top of the smoking pile. "This is choking it."

"It's almost going," Eric protested.

"Let Brandy," Nina said. "He's the champ firemaker."

"Family arsonist," Brandon said. "You know how to make money, I know how to make things burn." Brandon pushed the remaining split birchwood apart and blew gently on the smoldering mass of newspaper and kindling beneath. They burst into flame. "Gotta breathe to burn," Brandon commented. He took more newspaper from a pile and started to roll it into a tight twist. "Lasts longer this way." He nodded at the sooty pine log. "We'll dump her on when she's going good."

"Cigarettes?" Wendy said to Eric.

Eric rushed to get them, even though he felt Wendy's tone was arrogant, an order to a waiter. She didn't thank him. "You want something to drink?" Eric offered.

"I know where it is," Brandon said. "You want any?"

"No," Eric said. He felt reproved, convinced Brandon had meant to remind Eric that *he*, not Brandon, was the guest. The slight hadn't been in his brother-in-law's tone, however. Eric sat down on the couch beside Nina and Luke. He told himself to relax. He felt like a big awkward Jew with Nina's family—ungainly, at war with himself, his emotions either hostilely squelched or naïvely blared, never expressed with their even, self-confident voices. For them, life was an easy chair; for Eric, a hard bench.

Brandon poured two big glasses of Rémy Martin, giving one to Wendy. Although she hadn't asked for it, she took it greedily. "You breast-feeding?" Wendy asked, and swigged the Rémy like soda.

"Of course," Nina said. "I think they passed a law that you have to."

Brandon laughed. "Everything in nature is good."

Luke squirmed in Nina's arms, hiding his face in her bosom, his hands reaching blindly into the air. "Maybe he's hungry," Nina said.

"He's sleepy," Eric snapped.

Nina seemed to miss the point. "I'll feed him. That'll put him to sleep."

"It's not the schedule!" Eric protested.

"Give my nephew a break," Brandon said casually. "He's not an airline."

"Eric's right," Nina said quickly. She must have guessed how provoked Eric would be by Brandon's comment. "Just to relax him." She excused herself to Eric. "He won't really eat." She unbuttoned her nightshirt.

Brandon and Wendy both stared at her blimp of a breast, the spreading purple of her areola, the chubby projection of her nipple. Nina revealed it unself-consciously; they watched without shame. Eric was appalled by both attitudes.

Luke latched on eagerly. "What a deal, kid," Brandon said.

There was a silence while they intently watched Luke's absorption and satisfaction. The little hand reached up to Nina, yearning for something to hold. She lowered her chin and the fingers caressed it.

Brandon took another long drink from his glass and belched. "Sorry, Mom," he said to the beams.

Nina laughed with girlish pleasure. It annoyed Eric that he hadn't gotten that good a laugh out of her since Luke's birth.

"Did you hear about Father's windfall?" Brandon asked.

Nina shook her head no. Eric was alert. The family money had never been discussed in his presence.

"Grandpa's land in California. Someone bought the whole six hundred acres to develop. Father made a killing."

"Grandpa's land?" Nina wondered. "I thought he sold that years ago."

"You mean the Virginia stuff. That was peanuts. This is six hundred acres. Sold for ten thousand an acre."

"You're kidding!" Eric said in an explosive challenge, sitting forward, apparently ready to pounce on Brandon if he confessed it was a joke.

"Thought that'd get your attention."

"How much is that?" Nina asked, very calmly, just curious.

"Six million," Eric spat out, staccato. "Six million dollars."

Brandon let his head back and laughed to the ceiling. "You love money, Eric. 'Six million, six million dollars,' " Brandon imitated Eric, exaggerating the rapid delivery into a breathless, lustful pant.

Eric cringed. Brandon had a knack for seeing through people's little social hypocrisies and enjoyed rudely announcing his insights. The more Eric tried to camouflage his true nature, the more naked he was to Brandon's eyes. Eric understood this, but the instinct to attempt concealment was too powerful to fight.

"Money's his business," Nina said, not ashamed. "Eric hears

six million dollars and he starts thinking of investments." Somehow she made it sound natural and harmless.

"That's why I brought it up," Brandon said. "I told Father to get Eric's advice."

"Isn't he handled by someone at First Boston?" Eric said, in a rapid, almost hostile tone, as if he were conducting a verbal ambush.

Brandon answered, but he spoke to Nina. "Old Puffer died last year—"

"He did?" Nina sounded puzzled.

"Cancer. Father doesn't like the man they turned him over to. Anyway, Puffer was awful. Obvious stuff. 'Good solid returns,' " Brandon imitated, his chin thrust forward, his teeth clenched. "In fact, old conservative Puffer lost tons of Father's dough. This six million is the lion's share of what's left of our inheritance. I'd like to make sure Father doesn't blow it. That's why I told him to talk to Eric. If he doesn't, you should bring it up." Brandon finished this by leaning forward and tapping Eric's knee, the first time he had looked at Eric during the speech.

"He can't," Nina answered, pushing Luke off her breast. His little face was slack, the mouth open, his limbs collapsed. "Daddy has to bring it up."

"I'll remind him," Brandon said.

Luke startled awake and immediately wailed. He was angry, inconsolable, his stomach tight, his legs pulled up to his belly, his mouth screeching with complaint.

"I'll take him." Eric was furious. Everything had been messed up. "You should go to sleep," he said to Nina while gathering Luke.

"All right!" she snapped.

Eric carried his unhappy son back to the small dark nursery, chilled by the damp Maine night. The treads of the rocker squealed at Eric's weight and the floor groaned when he began the motion. Luke sighed and nestled into Eric's chest. He sucked on the pacifier with desperate insistence.

Eric watched him. This nervous, fragile baby—could Luke stand the fight to make money? With that six million, Eric knew he could make a fortune for his son. He felt the stock market growling, ready to awaken. It had been monotonously ticking up and down, a timid metronome, without a decisive move either way for almost a decade, but interest rates were falling, foreign money was pouring in, average volume on the exchange had doubled in the last two years. Even with fairly conservative buys, if the trend kept on (and he knew it would, knew it as if he were in spiritual contact with the gods of money), Eric could double the six million. Then play with the winnings, play looser, and maybe triple that.

He rocked his baby in the night and watched his numbers, incandescent, glow about his head. Bright, bright numbers—fireflies enchanting the gloom with magic. He kissed Luke's sweet, soft forehead.

The staring eyes closed.

He kissed their lids.

Eric Gold, the Wizard of Wall Street, rich beyond fear, held his heir with hope, eager for his in-laws' arrival.

Two things belonged to Nina: Eric and Luke. They were all she possessed of her own making. All her other attempts, her painting, her photography, all her aborted careers, had ended in her boredom or worldly failure. She felt this keenly on her parents' arrival. Her pride pushed her forward, holding Luke in her arms, serving a spectacular platter, and heard in her head, thumping in rhythm, See what I've made, Mom and Dad. She looked at her husband's tall, powerful body, striding ahead of Brandon, shrinking him by contrast, and felt her accomplishment. See my husband, see my baby, see what I've made. She knew her mom had never expected this success. At their wedding, Nina had felt her mother's unexpressed skepticism of her marriage, her mother's doubt that it would last and produce. Nina's older sister had disappointed thoroughly, living with a series of radicals, never marrying, and had aborted three "accidents," not only without guilt but with political pride. Her younger sister had satisfied, for a time, wedding a Harvard classmate, moving to Ohio, joining the country club, but that had ended in divorce, and hints of drink and beatings. Quiet Nina, never first at anything, married to a Jew (not even a particularly successful Jew at that), had managed to find happiness and provide the first heir.

Nina felt all this, but didn't think it. She would have been embarrassed to discover competition in her love. She had been dazzled by her sisters, had felt puny beside them, an indecisive flickering yellow in between the elder's fierce red and the younger's warm green. As her mother and father and Brandon and Wendy gathered around the mute, watchful Luke, Nina, for the very first time, was at the center of her family. That was all she knew of her pleasure.

"Hello, beautiful," her father, a man who usually didn't bestow adjectives on his children, said to Nina.

Her mother took Luke. Joan didn't even ask for her grandchild.

She opened her arms and Luke seemed to float into them. Luke's brilliant blue eyes beamed light, cracking the frozen surface of his grandmother's thin face and rejuvenating her pale eyes. Joan closed her hands on the little body and brought her face close to the new skin, to the puffed and open red lips.

Luke screamed. He shut his eyes, opened his mouth, and complained from his soul with all his might. His disorganized arms reached out for rescue, his legs went stiff with resistance, and his mouth blared protest.

Nina took Luke from Joan quickly, too quickly, she realized when she glanced at her mother. Joan seemed disappointed and offended. "You frightened him," Joan said.

"Other way around, I think," Brandon said with a laugh.

"He had a bad night," Eric mumbled. Nina noticed he looked mortified.

"Is he colicky?" Joan asked.

"No!" Nina said. Eric had begun to nod yes and got stuck in mid-motion by Nina's vehement denial. Meanwhile, at the energy of Nina's answer, Luke cried louder, his legs kicking, his beautiful features demolished by the elastic expansion of his toothless well of sorrow.

"Let's get the bags," her father said, and walked away. Eric hustled after him (like a bellboy, Nina couldn't help thinking), Brandon grinned as if it were all a practical joke, Wendy stared at Luke, and her mother frowned at her.

"Maybe he's hungry," Joan said, with no love in the word "he." The pronoun was said coolly; she might have used "it" for all the warmth in her tone. Luke had failed to please her, so Joan's love had retracted behind her country-club leathery face, lost to view.

Nina cringed for a moment, ready to apologize or resist sullenly. The instincts were familiar, although Nina couldn't place them. But she resisted the reactions they urged. "How was your trip?"

"After forty years, it's pretty boring," Joan said. She was again drawn to the beautiful form of her grandson. Luke sat stolidly in Nina's arms, his great blue eyes evaluating Joan, the trees, Wendy, the men unloading the luggage, each scanned with a deliberate scrutiny that seemed masterful and dispassionate.

"Unnn," Luke commented, and made a gesture with his hand at Joan.

"That's Grandmother Joan," Nina said.

"Hello, Luke," Joan said cheerfully. He had gotten a reprieve. "Hello, baby." She put her hand on his curled foot and squeezed gently. He watched her closely, his body still, like a cat studying prey.

Joan, encouraged nevertheless, moved closer. Again Luke seemed to gesture at her, his hand reaching out in a spasm. Joan opened her hands to him. He arched in her direction. Nina offered and Joan took him.

Eric came toward them, carrying two suitcases. Her father had only a small overnight bag. "Hey, hey," Eric said to Joan. "He looks good on you, Grandma."

"Grandma!" Brandon said to the trees, with a sarcastic tone.

Joan nodded self-consciously at Eric. Luke glanced at his father. Nina moved away from Joan and Luke to open the door. At this, Luke wailed, his arms out to Nina.

Joan stiffened, held him away from her, and said, "He wants you," to Nina.

"He doesn't like you, Joan," Nina's father, Tom, said casually as he passed on his way to the house. Brandon laughed, with energetic malice, and followed Tom.

"No, no," Eric argued even though Tom and Brandon went on inside without listening. "He just doesn't know her."

Nina felt stuck at the door as she watched Luke's distress become hysterical. Joan didn't hug him, or rock him, or distract him. She held Luke in the air like a squealing pig, her mouth closed, her eyes startled and wary.

"Get him!" Eric said in a whisper, but with urgent emphasis.

"She's here." Joan finally spoke. She took a few steps toward Nina and held Luke out, his legs kicking, his face red. "He needs to be fed," she repeated as Nina at last broke her paralysis and accepted Luke.

"No, he doesn't," Nina heard herself say in a wondering tone. "He doesn't know you."

"Well, I only saw him once before. Why would he know me?"

"That's right," Eric said. "He needs time." He carried the bags in.

"Maybe he's cold," Wendy said.

"Hello, Wendy," Joan said. "I haven't greeted you."

"I'm fine," Wendy answered.

Joan nodded as if this were very gratifying news. "Good." With that she went inside the house.

Luke's screams had become muffled moans and whimpers. He nuzzled his face into Nina's breasts. His tears had primed them. But it was an hour before his next feeding, and what's more, Nina felt her pride was at stake. She had said to Joan that Luke wasn't hungry.

"Are you going to feed him?" Wendy asked. She was the only one left outside.

Nina's breasts dripped. Luke squirmed and moaned. He could probably smell their sour residue. Her left nipple throbbed. She gave in, opened her shirt, and lowered the flap that covered her left nipple. Luke latched on.

"Can I touch them?" Wendy asked.

"What?"

Wendy put out her hand and held it only an inch or two from Nina's right breast. "Can I touch it?"

"They're sore," Nina answered, too thrown to know what else to say.

"I'll be gentle," Wendy said with a hint of irritation that Nina might think otherwise. Wendy lowered the flap and cupped the breast, holding the thick knob of Nina's nipple tenderly between her index finger and thumb. "What does it taste like?"

"I don't know!" Nina said, wanting to pull away, but frightened to. What if Wendy didn't let go?

"Come on," Wendy said. "You must have tasted it. Eric must suck on it sometimes. Does he like the taste?"

"He does not!"

Wendy, her face only a few inches from Nina, smiled knowingly, and shook her head no, almost with pity, as if Nina's attempt at lying were too foolish even to merit a contradiction. Then Wendy lowered her head—Nina watched unbelievingly, sure that Wendy would stop, couldn't mean to—and put her lips around the nipple, licking its tip with her tongue. Luke moved his feet out of Wendy's way, but was otherwise unperturbed, staring up at Nina with his serious blue eyes and sucking lazily.

Nina, panic in her throat, grunted to stop herself from screaming, and put her free hand on Wendy's blond hair, gathering a bunch of it. Nina yanked hard.

Wendy screamed, backing away, her hands protecting the top of her skull. "Jesus! Are you crazy! That hurt."

Eric opened the door violently. He looked agitated. "What was that! Is he all right?"

Wendy walked through the open door, and then glanced back, her look resentful. "You're not very motherly. *I* don't think. Maybe you don't like people needing you."

"You're crazy," Nina said without energy, merely stating a fact.

"What's going on?" Eric pleaded.

"Maybe that's why he cries all the time," Wendy said, her face made small by vindictiveness, the eyes, nose, and mouth coming together in a blur of squints, twitches, and frowns. "He knows you don't mean it."

Nina instinctively turned Luke away from Wendy and her accusation. She wanted to cry, although she couldn't bring the sorrow to precipitation. The unhappiness floated inside her chest like a heavy, heavy cloud—the dark swollen cloud of her lifelong failure to please or impress anyone.

THE CONCRETE AND INSULATION MANUFACTURERS FILED FOR FInancial reorganization under Chapter 11, claiming that the outstanding lawsuits, if decided against them, would be an economic catastrophe and that since no insurance could be obtained to protect them, they had to go "out of the insulation business" because every day they continued manufacturing exposed them to more litigation. This shifted the issue from their culpability to their liability (what they would pay on all debt included future debt such as negligence judgments), even though their guilt was still not settled. The maneuver was Stoppard's invention, but Diane was essential in finding a precedent to allow the bankruptcy filing to begin before a judgment was in existence. Threatened with the possibility of winning their suits, but having no one to pay them, the ex-employees agreed to settle en masse for a quarter of what Stoppard and Diane had thought a court would be likely to award. She knew making partner at Wilson, Pickering had become a certainty. Stoppard would sponsor her wholeheartedly and he was the firm's brightest star.

Peter said, when she bragged of her achievement, that it was a swindle, no better than, after you've blinded a man, robbing him of his beggar's cup of coins. Of course, that had been her reaction when she had been brought onto the case. But it *was* true that the company would have been destroyed by the ex-employees' suit. Thousands would have been thrown out of work, work that was now safe anyway, or at least met federal safety standards. The villain, the owner who had buried the warnings of the medical data, was dead. The law would be punishing his grandson, who had watched his inheritance halved by a rapid decline of orders and an even faster increase in insurance payments, along with wage raises, legal fees, and general Wall Street dismay. Most of the lawsuits were not from the victims, but from their heirs. Was it justice to punish today for yesterday's sins? Stoppard had asked the court. And the victims did get some money. Anyway, someone else would have contributed the legal know-how she had. The end result would have been the same.

They took Byron to the park the weekend of her triumph. She had persuaded Peter to spend Sunday afternoon with them. Although Byron had first walked only a week ago, he was already competent, striding pigeon-toed, his full melon belly forward, a miniature sumo wrestler, his mouth open, exclaiming at the pleasures of his mobility. "Ahhh! Ahhh! Ohhh? Da!" He pointed to the trees and yelled: "Zat!" He grabbed the black iron bars of the playground gate and shook it. Byron teetered from the recoil and then tried to get a footing on a low rung, intending to climb it.

"Just like you," Peter said. "He has no sense of boundaries. No responsibility."

She didn't know what he meant. She didn't think Peter knew either, except that he resented Byron's joy, Byron's vigor. She looked at the other parents, all fascinated by her son, some with smiles, others with worry. They were in the small park at Washington Square, full of immobile babies, and only a few toddlers under two. The other one-year-olds were still crawling, or able to walk only a few steps before they wobbled and then crashed with a whoosh on the puffed bottoms of their diapers. They cried at every obstacle, at every frustration.

Not her Byron.

He stood at the edge of the sandbox, arms out at his sides in an attitude of command, erect on his chubby legs, still and steady, the Captain of Babyland.

The other parents were forever having to pick up their children, encourage them to try again, to dig in the sand, to leave their side, to engage life.

Not Diane.

She could sit on the bench beside Peter. She had to get up only to stop Byron from walking off with the pails and shovels of two-year-olds, who, despite their size and age advantage, lost tugs-of-war with Byron. Byron had mastered the technique. He closed his fat fingers tight around the plastic treasures, held his balance, and yanked hard. His calm will to win gave him extra strength; the two-year-olds, made anxious by the possibility of defeat, already half looking for a parent to help them, had their attention divided and their power diluted.

"I'm sorry," Diane would say to the scrunched, embarrassed, irritated face of the bawling two-year-old's parent. "Give it back, Byron."

"Ohh!" he'd say, and loosen his grip at Diane's request, unperturbed by the loss of red shovel or yellow pail, ready for another conquest, a good grab of sand, a stamping, hopeless chase of the pigeons, another assault on the gate. Byron took defeat and victory as one.

Diane could breathe deeply and smell her satisfaction. She had the best baby in the park. She was a success.

PETER SLEPT WITH RACHEL AGAIN. AND AGAIN. AND AGAIN. FOR the past month they had had a regular date each week, going to the theater and retiring afterward to her apartment of convertible furniture.

Their lovemaking was sad. Done silently, quickly, the copulation seemed mostly to be an excuse to hold each other. He felt hopeless about life and the world. The foundation had cut its arts funding to a third of what it had been two years before. He saw Diane alone for a mere hour a day during the week and little more on the weekends. And during those few hours, she yawned, undressed, bathed, complained, and wanted nothing from him but casual chatter and a brotherly kiss.

He knew, he knew, he knew—he knew all the psychological clichés. He'd lost his mother again, he felt competitive with Byron, and on and on. The problem was that they were true. His son grows up while he grows down. Byron moves into the future, Peter into the past.

He called Gary. He hadn't spoken to or seen Gary, the best friend of his childhood, for a decade. "Peter!" Gary exclaimed, and began to babble, asking questions and giving information before he even heard the answers.

They met for lunch. The ghost of Gary's slightly goofy, pale, boyish face hovered in fat and manly features. Gary wasn't married, although he lived with a woman.

"I can't believe," Gary said, "of the two of us, you're the one with a wife and kid."

"Why?" Peter asked, worried, possibly even offended.

"I don't know. I just thought you'd think it was bourgeois or something. I really expected you to be an actor."

" 'Cause of high school?"

"Yeah. You loved it! And you were good."

Peter couldn't concentrate on the conversation. He was lurking behind pleasantries, hidden in ambush with his real question. "Whatever happened to Larry?" he asked casually when the check came.

Gary answered with suspicious rapidity, as if he'd been waiting to. "He doesn't talk to us anymore. Broke off completely with my mother five years ago."

"How come?"

"You know we put him up for a year, when he was—when you knew him. He was a mess. Mom kept him together. And, I don't know, I guess when he got to be a success again, he must have decided we were beneath him. He's become rich, you know."

"I always thought he was."

"Well, he put it on. Got a big PR firm now, does work in Washington, Philly, L.A. I think they even have an office here." Gary changed the subject, talking again about the old days, the games they played, what had happened to other friends. Obviously Gary didn't want to discuss the child abuse and Peter let it go without a fight, although that was his only purpose in the meeting.

At the park with Diane and Byron, Peter listened to his memory's recordings of everything he and Gary had said to each other, as children and teenagers, about Larry's fondlings. There had been few. Gary always insisted Larry didn't mean any harm, hadn't meant it to go any further. The one time Peter challenged that point of view, Gary was flustered and upset. "Yeah, so he's queer. Just 'cause we didn't know to stop him doesn't mean we are."

Clichés, clichés, clichés.

Gary's fear wasn't what Peter had wanted to know. He wanted to know if Gary's mother had suspected anything while it was going on, if she had in fact known. If not, hadn't she thought it odd that a forty-year-old bachelor spent so much time in the children's room? She had known Larry was homosexual; that much he had gotten out of Gary. Hadn't she wondered about all the gifts he bought Gary and even Peter? Why hadn't Gary told her what was going on? Why hadn't Peter told his own mother?

It was so boring in the park. All these anxious middle-class parents, all these lawyers, professors, so-called painters, actors, writers, doctors, accountants, pretending they cared. All with the same MacLaren strollers, the same Nuk pacifiers, the Snuglis, the Fisher-Price toys, some kind of strange herd instinct, a weird consumer fascism.

Peter noticed a man wander into the playground area without a child or a baby. The stranger nodded at various parents. They nodded back, but obviously didn't know him. He was dressed in a suit. That seemed odd. Peter wanted to point him out to Diane, but she was off somewhere saving some poor child from Byron's imperialism. The stranger didn't hook up with any of the mothers or kids already there. He had a long face, his complexion pale, small lips underneath a big nose, wide-set eyes, and a broad forehead. He settled on a bench and watched the children. He smiled benignly at their activities and laughed out loud at something.

Peter felt uneasy. He glanced at the park's border to see if a police car was about. There was. Then Peter realized he couldn't say anything to the cops. Or could he? The sign on the gate read: ONLY FOR CHILDREN AND THEIR PARENTS OR GUARDIANS. If the stranger was alone, the police could ask him to move on. Peter simply didn't have the nerve to do something so presumptuous, so rude.

He got to his feet without thinking and looked for Diane. She would have the nerve. He couldn't see her. He glanced at the bench to check on the stranger. He was gone. But he saw Diane, sitting right near where the stranger used to be, talking to a woman, intent on the conversation.

Peter walked over. Diane just glanced at him and continued talking. "Where's Byron?" Peter asked, not because he missed him, but because he didn't know how to bring up the question of the strange man.

"Here," Diane said, and pointed to a sandy area near her feet. But her gesture froze. "Where is he?"

An elderly woman rocking an infant in a carriage called out, "Is this your husband?" and pointed to Peter. Diane nodded. "That man is—"

Peter sighted him, the pale man in the suit he had worried about. He saw the stranger walking away, outside the children's area, holding Byron in his arms. The man walked casually, Byron quiet in his arms, approaching the arch, heading for the park's perimeter.

Peter heard the thunder of his heart. Felt a sharp bang on his leg. Saw faces, startled, nervous, go by. "Byron!" he called into the thunder.

The world was moving. The stranger turned and glanced at Peter.

"Byron!" Peter shouted into the roar. His shoulder whacked against someone.

The stranger stopped and waited for Peter. The man was calm. He watched Peter approach.

Peter kept running, but he felt dread as he got near, awed that the stranger had stopped and was waiting for him, apparently unafraid.

"Put him down." Peter meant this to be a command. It sounded tentative, almost a question. Peter stopped himself several feet off, frightened to go closer, although he kept telling himself: Byron belongs to you—take him!

"I'm his father," the stranger said, and kissed the side of Byron's head.

The sight made Peter sick. He felt his stomach bend in a hard place, somewhere that was supposed to be inflexible. His mind, too, was hurt—stalled by the stranger's lie.

"No, you're not," Peter said, like a baffled child, unable to fight the lie.

"Yes, I am," the stranger said.

"Get your hands off him!" Diane was screaming from somewhere, screaming with all the rage and assertion that Peter felt, but couldn't get past the dam in his throat. "Police! Get your hands off him! Police!"

The stranger, rather gently, put Byron down, and broke into a run.

Byron held up his arms to Peter.

Diane rushed past, past Peter and Byron, and ran after the stranger.

"Da, Da," Byron said to Peter.

Peter's shoulders got heavy, made him collapse. He fell to his knees and put his arms out. Byron waddled into them, chuckling, gurgling laughter, delighted by his father's reduction in size.

"Don't, don't, don't, don't," Peter heard himself mumble while he kissed the sweet soft cushions, the ice-cream smoothness of his baby's cheeks.

People stood around, watching Peter, broken to his knees on the sidewalk, clutching Byron. Diane had returned, saying, "Jesus! Jesus! Jesus!"

"Da! Da!" Byron said to Peter, his thin brown eyebrows curved into a worried architecture above his eyes.

Peter was crying, felled on the pavement, embracing Byron, and crying. He got to his feet, Diane was saying lots of things, talking breathlessly, but Peter got to his feet, not listening, and kept his face, his wet face, pressed against Byron's. Peter carried his son home, directly home, his arms a steel embrace, his heart panting with love and terror.

ERIC DECIDED TO SAY NOTHING TO HIS FATHER-IN-LAW, TOM, ABOUT the money. He wouldn't have to anyway: Brandon had volunteered to remind Tom. But a week went by, a miserable seven days and nights, without Brandon saying a word, at least not in Eric's presence.

Maybe Brandon had discussed it in private with Tom and been told to fuck off. Maybe Brandon was intimidated. Eric certainly was. Tom Winningham was a tall, elegant man, his undyed hair still mostly black, still distinguished by the waves and sheen of youth. His posture was like a column's; it was a shock to see that he could bend over. His blue eyes were pale and lifeless. They hovered in his skull without purpose, rarely focusing on anything, and when they did briefly catch Eric's eye, their boldness pushed Eric's face aside, a gentle but tangible blow.

Eric had been alone with Tom only once that week. One night, Eric wandered into the living room at 3:00 A.M. after a session of rocking Luke back to sleep. He found Tom seated in the dark, looking out at the bay, his thin face silver from the moonlight. Tom moved his head slowly at the sound of Eric entering, like a movie ghost, with a gradual ominous turn. "Excuse me," Eric blurted, horrified, and skulked out.

Meanwhile, Luke's colic, even though he was almost three months old (supposedly the age when colic goes away), seemed to get worse. Maybe it was the presence of the others. Luke wailed if any of them touched him. He woke up every two hours at night, taking as much as forty-five minutes to fall back to sleep, as if he feared that Eric and Nina would leave him with these strangers.

The second morning after Joan arrived, she walked into the nursery ahead of Nina, thinking she could give Eric and Nina extra sleep. At the sight of Joan, Luke let out screams of horror that shot Eric from the lowest level of sleep to total consciousness with the G force of a rocket blast into space. "I scared him," Joan confessed as Eric and Nina rushed past her into the nursery. "I'm sorry," she mumbled, and left them to clutch the trembling baby to their bosom.

The household was heavy from Luke's rejections. Nina's sisters arrived and got the same treatment. The family began to look at Eric strangely, he thought. They blame my genes, Eric believed. The little Jew in Luke, like a Satanic strain, was what made Luke hate them—Eric fancied he could see those thoughts in their eyes, their cold blue eyes.

But those eyes were in Luke's head, those same evaluating terrible eyes. And Luke's distance from them—was it any different from their own estrangements? These are your genes, Eric wanted to scream at the polite breakfasts and dinners. He's yours! This unloving child comes from you!

Was he unloving? Not to Eric or Nina. Luke had taken to stroking his father's chin while he sucked on his juice bottle, the hot fingertips dotting Eric's face with tenderness and wonderment. When Eric got him from his crib, Luke's body adhered to his, curving with the shape of Eric's pectorals. He rested his heavy head on the shelf of Eric's shoulder, sighing into his neck. And those eyes, those large blue eyes of Luke, they considered Eric, the huge guardian, at leisure, scanned the big face carefully, making sure nothing had been altered, that it wasn't a phony, but the same patient giant of yesterday.

"Has he ever smiled?" asked Emily, Nina's youngest sister. Emily the bitch, Eric called her.

"They don't smile at this age," Nina lied. "It's just gas."

"Oh, no," Joan said. "They have real smiles." And an argument—a disagreement, rather; no voices were raised—ensued. The real point of it was that Luke was an unhappy, miserable exception to the usual joyful cherubim that the rest of the world gave birth to. Nina was restrained for a while, chatting casually, as if the subject had nothing to do with her child. But finally she responded to the subtext—and blew up at her mother and sisters. Tears streamed down Nina's face. She yelled that they were egomaniacs, people who only wanted to be loved and had no patience for loving others. That was exactly the conclusion Eric had come to about Nina's behavior in New York, that her unreasonable fury at Luke was for not adoring her immediately.

Joan and her sisters at first stared through Nina's tirade; then Emily got up and left the room, not in a huffy attitude—she walked past Nina like a pedestrian avoiding a madwoman. Joan began to clean. Luke made it all into an embarrassing farce by wailing in Nina's arms. Nina, her charges unanswered, carried Luke into the nursery and began to rock him violently. Eric followed her in.

"Shut up, shut up, shut up!" she said into her son's melted face in a whisper of rage.

"Okay, okay, give him to me," Eric said.

"Get out of here!" she snapped.

"Don't talk—"

"Get out of here!"

"You're upset." He began, he thought, in a reasonable, reassuring tone.

"He belongs to me! Stop trying to take him away! I know what I'm doing! Get out!"

"Belongs to you?" Eric was collapsed by her remark, his understanding of her, of Luke, of the world, deflated into shapelessness.

"Goddammit! Are you ever going to listen to me?" Nina's face trembled from the force of her shouts. Eric backed out of the room, although he wanted to punch her, although he feared for Luke's safety, because he feared more for her; she seemed ready to explode, not figuratively, but actually blow open—skin, eyes, bones ready to fly off.

He stumbled out backwards and bumped into someone waiting just beyond the door. "Excuse me," Tom said, catching Eric and turning him slightly.

"I'm sorry," Eric said, horrified that Nina's father had overheard. But she had yelled so loudly that probably they had all been able to listen in. Now I'll never get the money, Eric knew, and felt despair and rage at Nina. He knew, and Nina knew, that her brother and sisters were envious that she had had Luke. All she had to do was to be as much of a Wasp as they, and keep a good face on Luke's condition, but she had failed, failed as miserably as a Jewish wife would have.

"I need some help with the wood in the barn," Tom said easily, free from self-consciousness.

"Sure," Eric mumbled. He felt as if he were being called to the principal's office. He followed Tom to the barn. There was a stormy wind coming off the bay, the late August air thinned by the hint of fall, and its chill bowed Eric beside Tom's rigid, unaffected body. Eric felt smaller, younger with each step.

Tom got busy once inside. He didn't talk or explain what he wanted. Tom carried several large birch logs from the pile. Eric hurried and took most of them and set the biggest on the chopping block. "Hurt my hand on the boat yesterday," Tom said. "Could you split these?"

Eric had been schooled by Brandon to split wood, but he wasn't nearly as skilled as his brother-in-law. Clearly this was an excuse to talk. Eric wielded the ax. He hesitated before taking his first chop. He suddenly felt his ability to split the birch straight through was at issue, that he had to do it to win back Tom's confidence.

Tom watched him casually, one hand resting on a smooth worn beam.

Eric kept his eyes on the break in the wood. He raised the ax, brought it down hard, but steady. The blade passed right through, thudding into the block below, the now split halves of birch fainting away from each other.

Without skipping a beat, Tom said, "I wanted to discuss some business with you."

"Un-huh," Eric said, and put another log on the block. He pretended to study its surface for a good fissure.

"I've sold some land recently—"

"Brandon told me," Eric said. Tom might be accustomed to

circumspection when it came to money, but Eric believed Wall Streeters were supposed to have the blunt intimacy of doctors about a client's financial condition. "Six million, he said."

Tom frowned. "Go ahead," he said, nodding at the log.

This time, Eric's ax got caught halfway through. He split it on the second blow. Brandon would have thought that a failure.

"Actually, it's closer to ten million. Brandy overheard only part of the sale. I wish he hadn't heard anything. I'd like you to keep this to yourself. I would rather, given how much the children talk among themselves, that even Nina not know."

"Fine with me," Eric said, and meant it.

"Usually my cash assets are managed by First Boston. But my man there died and I'm not happy with the new people. I wondered if you had any suggestions?"

What was this? A way of saying he didn't want Eric to handle it? Or an opening, to see if Eric was bold enough to go through? Fuck it, he didn't care. "Yeah. I'd like to handle it. I doubt you'd get anyone who would take care of you better. After all, in the long term, it's in my interest to make sure your capital grows. Churning your money is gonna hurt me. Other managers might not care."

"Exactly my thought," Tom said, and seemed relieved. He moved away from the beam, approached Eric, and looked him in the eye. Eric felt the compulsion to glance away, to be faced down by those curious, judging eyes. But he understood those eyes now, now that they also belonged to Luke. Eric knew they masked pain and fear. Eric stared back and this time Tom lowered his eyes. "But that isn't all I have to consider," Tom mumbled.

"You mean, how good am I? Treat me the way you'd treat any other broker. Give me some of it, see how I do, and then either give me more or take it away."

Tom nodded. "What do you think would be a fair start?"

"It's up to you. Give me at least six months before you make a judgment—unless I'm losing a ton. I won't, though."

"How about two million?" Tom said.

"Fine." A tremble of reality shot through Eric. He was in the presence of his dream; it had become solid, food offered to his hungry mouth.

"How do we handle this—this arrangement in terms of the children?"

"Usually I would only tell Nina. I don't gossip about my clients. But I don't have to tell her."

Tom held his neck with his left hand, leaned his head back, and stretched, a doctor feeling for tumors. "You should tell Nina if that's what you would normally do. But ask her not to discuss it with the others.''

Eric explained the mechanics of the transfer of the money, that his fee would be the industry standard of 1 percent annually of the two million, with a 20 percent performance incentive on any profits, and that for the time being he would only charge the commission that the floor broker takes, adding nothing for his own pocket. With that out of the way, he could speak confidently. Tom became almost childlike as Eric expounded his current view of the market, interrogated Tom about his tax situation, made gentle fun of Tom's previous broker's strategies (they would have been fine, actually, if the double-digit inflation and bond collapse of the mid-seventies had not followed hard upon the death of the go-go sixties' stocks; it was the classic position of its time, the shoals that almost every financial adviser had crashed on), and recounted some of his own triumphs, musing on how much money Eric would have made for Tom if he had had the money then.

When Eric returned to the house, he felt okay, even though the Winningham summer house had taken on the aspect of a funeral home. They all talked in hushed voices, averted their eyes when Nina walked past like a widow out of her mind with grief, unapproachable and pitied, Luke still in her arms, his eyes watching everything, moaning from time to time, one little hand clutching his mother's sweater. Even with all that, Eric was calm. What he'd lacked his whole life was a chance, a shot at the big time. At last, he'd landed a big fish, a client with real dough. And if Eric performed, there would be more, and the best part, the best part was that it would all one day come back to his son. He looked at the sisters and at Brandon.

Let them make Nina miserable for now.

Those weaklings would never create any grandchildren.

The money would go to Luke.

And swelled by Eric's genius, his son would be rich.

NINA COULDN'T BEAR THE STUFFY NURSERY ROOM, THE MUMBLE of voices from various bedrooms, the shrill sound of her blood in her ears, the desperate moths thudding on the windows, and the squirming, restless movements of her baby.

She bundled Luke in a heavy blanket and walked out of the nursery, through the living room, ignoring the startled looks of her family, and on out into the night.

Here there was air and refreshment. The tall birches swayed against a bright sky jammed with stars. Luke was silent the instant the real world surrounded them. The bay, a gray presence behind the trees, swelled and contracted gradually, like a body breathing in sleep. She felt so much better away from the shelter of home, much more safe in the wild. She wished Eric and Luke and she could become pioneers, travel away from the prison of everything and into the free nothingness.

"Look at the stars," she said to Luke, and her words were scattered by the outside. Luke seemed to study them anyway, his body absolutely still, awed by the earth's vast ceiling. She felt sure that he also wanted to be away, apart from people and their crowding, their nagging, their criticisms.

"Nina!" Eric called, in a whine despite the volume.

She walked around the corner toward the shore, away from Eric. It was silly—he would be sure to follow.

"Nina?" She heard him and then his feet cracking branches, stamping the grass like an outsized creature, a brontosaur of a man. "Here you are!" he said, running up to her. "It's cold. Is he—"

"He's covered with a blanket!" she snapped.

"Okay. Okay. Okay." Eric faced the shore, took a deep breath, and gazed at the bay. "Looks so beautiful. Almost makes me wish I could swim in it."

"Why don't you?"

"At night?" Eric squeaked. "I'd hit my head on a rock and die."

"I guess you'd better not," she answered.

He looked at her. She couldn't make out his expression, he was half in the shadow of the house. "I haven't had a chance to tell you. It's a secret. You're not supposed to tell your brother and sisters. Your father has given me money to invest."

"Do you get anything out of it?"

"Of course," Eric answered with a laugh.

Nina's experience with her father and money wouldn't make that answer automatic. Tom seemed to regard himself as a good-works opportunity for his children.

"It was weird. He did it today right after—" Eric stopped himself.

"My fit?" Nina supplied the description for him. "That makes sense."

"It does?"

"Just Father's way of apologizing to you."

"Apologizing?"

"Yeah," Nina said, and began to walk. When she glanced at Luke, she was surprised to see he was asleep.

Eric hustled beside her. "For what? I thought he was giving me the money because he thought—"

"That too, of course. He wouldn't take a chance otherwise. I mean, the timing." Shut up, Nina, she told herself. But she couldn't. It was a bitter fact, and who else could share the sour taste but Eric?

"Wait," he said to stop her from entering the house. "This is important. I have to know about this. Don't be mysterious. If he gave me the money for some personal reason, he might take it away suddenly. I have to know."

"He gave you the money to apologize for being stuck with Luke and me," she said, popping the cork on her bottle of sorrow. With the plug out, she felt her strength leak as well. She wanted to cry.

"Oh, no," Eric said, his voice soft, hurt, like a boy's. "No, you're wrong. Maybe he did it because of Luke, because I'm more a part of the family. Not 'cause he thinks badly of you."

"Your parents love you, Eric. You can't understand what I'm talking about. It's like a sin to you, a taboo."

"No! It's his way of being closer. He talks with his money. He's saying he's on your side."

She leaned her head onto Eric's shoulder and closed her eyes to squeeze the tears back.

"Believe me," Eric pleaded. "Your father loves you. So does your mom. And your brother and sisters are just jealous. That's part of love too."

He was so foolish, so naïve, so loving. It made her want to cry all the more. And now she was crying. Dammit. When she went inside, they would see. The tears were loose. Her brain shook from the pain, and rained its aches.

"Believe me," he kept repeating, a little boy consoling his mom, frightened by her emotion. "Believe me," he begged.

"I do," she lied. Anyway, Eric loved her. And he loved his son. If only she could be alone with them and leave the rest of the world out. If only Luke was happier. If only she could fix her baby. She was crying again.

"What is it?" Eric mumbled into her weeping face. "What is it?"

"He doesn't smile," she said.

"He's not even three months!" Eric shouted. Nina shushed him. "He'll smile," Eric whispered. "Don't worry."

Luke stayed asleep. Her arms hurt from his dead weight. She told Eric to go in ahead of her, tell the others she was coming in with an unconscious Luke, and turn the lights off while she passed through. That way they wouldn't see her red eyes.

It worked all the way around. They couldn't see her face, and Luke, other than sighing and retracting his legs, stayed asleep after the transfer to the crib. Nina sneaked off to their bedroom and undressed. She turned out the light, not wanting to squander a minute of the precious hours of Luke's rest—his record for consecutive hours of sleep was two and a half—but she couldn't rest.

She opened a window, despite the blocks of cold it let in, and listened to the night earth, the watery, leafy dark earth. Her muscles ached and her brain couldn't make order out of things. She hadn't been in the comfortable rewarding embrace of sleep for so long that the real world seemed like a dream, a half-awake world, something she imagined while dozing off on a train ride.

She was almost afraid of real rest, of deep, warm sleep, afraid of the regret and rage she would feel when Luke interrupted it. Better never to have another taste, to forget that delicious fruit existed, than to have it yanked away after a few bites.

Eric entered. He always waited awhile to make sure Luke had settled in, if two hours could be called settled. "Whew," he said, on feeling the cold.

"You can shut it," she said, and he did.

She lost the world. The room's human air corrupted the clean, cool atmosphere of nature. She again heard the sounds of things, the hum of appliances, the clink of a glass; someone's tread.

Eric took off his clothes. The last three months he hadn't exercised or slept much more than she, but his body was still smooth, the long ropes of his muscles taut, his chest expansive, decorated by a small patch of curls, his narrow hips without an ounce of fat, the cheeks of his ass like chunks of smooth marble. Clothed, with his frizzy hair and open face, he could almost seem meek; but when he was nude, the graceful power of his six-foot-six frame, upholstered by two hundred pounds of muscle, made Eric a warrior, a young chief ready to lead his tribe.

They hadn't made love since Luke's birth.

Her body felt dead, not passionless, but flattened by exhaustion. It took thought to rise, to sit; it hurt even to lie still. An embrace only made her sleepy.

But in the dark of the country night, watching the only man who had loved her tenderly, the shimmering stars and faint moon glowing on his strong body, she felt her skin awaken, the surface tingling, covering the fatigue of her bones, dispelling the despair of her muscles.

She beckoned to him. He came over and she pulled him on top, pressing his wood-hard back to her, her hands touching the hump of his thighs, the smooth of his neck, the span of his underarms. He tried to get to her body, but she urged his head up, not interested in knowing herself. She didn't want to sense her own decay and weariness, she wanted to feel his vigor.

She fell asleep after he had spent.

She fell into the dark, the absolute rest. In her dreams Eric and she made love on the lawn under the sun. She played in the backyard at Brookline. She rode on Brandy's shoulders. She made cookies with her mother. She kissed the head of Eric's red penis and drank wine. She laughed. And she slept deep. She watched her father walk through the woods. She saw him steer the car, the length of his face quiescent, in command.

Her eyes opened. It was day.

Her body was still and warm and relaxed.

It was day? She looked at the clock. Seven-thirty. Eric, his face buried into a pillow, had his mouth open, his eyes blanked by the closed lids.

Had he gotten up with Luke and let her sleep all night?

No, he was still naked. If he'd gotten up—

Like a stab, the thought split her brain.

She pulled the covers off, her heart back in the real world, the world of anxiety. Crib death.

She pulled on jeans, rushing, reached for her bra. Then she slowed down. If Luke was dead, she was in no hurry to find out.

Eric sat up and peered around. He looked stunned. "Wha—"

"I'll go," she said, and finished dressing. Eric scanned the room. She knew he was figuring it out.

"He slept?"

"Shhh," she said, and began the walk, every step heating her blood, widening her vision. She had images: holding a limp body; standing beside her mother in black. She stopped right outside Luke's door.

She heard Eric dressing. The sounds were frantic. He had arrived at the same terminus of terror.

She didn't put her body in the doorway, but let her head peer about the edge.

Luke's little body was still. Deathly still. And in the same position she had put him the night before.

She stared so hard at his back, searching for movement, that her eyes watered.

And she saw it. A slight rise and fall. His eyes twitched. She waited for him to cry. But he slept on.

The joy of this discovery was almost as awful as the earlier fear.

Eric came thudding toward her. "He's asleep," she whispered, stopping him with her hand.

"He slept through the night!" Eric said, his mouth open stupidly.

"Three months," she said. "He's three months old today."

"You think it's over?" Eric said with such simple trust in her, so sure that she would know.

She felt a chill of pleasure.

She could move. She could dance! She was rested, her son was normal, life was going to be life again, not war, not misery, but life.

They heard Luke peep. Then a rustle. And another peep. Not a complaint, but a noise of curiosity.

They looked. Luke's head, resting on its side, was turned in their direction. The blue jewels of his eyes peered at them. He fought to move, to rise up.

"Hey, fella," Eric said, and entered. "You slept, baby."

Nina followed. She got ahead of Eric and picked Luke up. His face glowed from warmth and newness. He stretched his arms and wiggled his body. The long black hair was askew. She put him down on the changing table and unsnapped his stretchy.

His mouth opened. The tiny fluted lips widened. And widened. The semicircles of his gum appeared.

"You're smiling!" Eric said.

Nina couldn't speak. She didn't dare break the enchantment, but she found herself leaning down and kissing his white belly.

And she heard a laugh.

A laugh she had never heard before: the first laugh of Luke's life.

Her core of joy exploded. Everything was beautiful. She and Eric began to babble at Luke. He smiled again. He winced at the cool wipes, but didn't cry. Eric, almost hopping with pleasure, went to get coffee. She heard Eric brag shamelessly to whoever was in the kitchen: "He slept through the night! And he's smiling his head off."

She didn't care that Eric showing off his happiness to her family would be an admission they had been right to be critical.

Luke was feeding heartily. His eyes stayed on her, and when she smiled at his glorious beauty, he paused and smiled back. When she grabbed his foot and squeezed, he giggled. Even his eyes glittered cheerfully.

The colic was gone. This was a beautiful, happy baby.

After Luke ate, he beamed at everything. She carried him into the kitchen and showed him to the family. Luke watched them all calmly. He laughed when Brandy made a silly face. He touched her mother's hand and let her hold him without a whimper of protest.

"Let's take him out," Nina said to Eric.

She showed Luke the pretty, pretty morning, the new golden light of this glorious day. She put Luke's face to feel the shore air. He closed his eyes and rolled his head in rapture. She felt so good, so proud that she began to twirl.

Luke chuckled; his feet kicked. Eric began to laugh, his eyes tearing with joy. And then Eric joined her dance.

They twirled in the growing sun of the morning, spinning beneath the trees, Luke exultant, laughing, happy, exquisite. They danced with the wind and the grass and the water and held their son between them, their perfect baby for the new day, their final bond of love.

Eric collapsed after a minute, but Nina persisted. She offered her beautiful son to the world, and the beautiful world to him, spinning her Luke, her new planet under the ancient sun.

Part Two

8

"**N**o!" BYRON SHOUTED.

The big floor was cold. Ice floor. Byron slid his feet along until he saw his house. He loved his house. Your house is beautiful, Grandma said. Beautiful. He could make it more: he took a long block, a smooth block, ice block, and balanced it sideways on the roof. Another floor.

"Byron! Breakfast!"

"No!" He was a big boy. "No breakfast!" he said with the resonant voice of a hero.

Mommy's feet thumped. He grabbed another block fast. Do it fast. Byron put the long, smooth, tall block straight up on the roof. "Look, Mommy! Look, Mommy!"

"Byron, what are you doing? I told you to come in for breakfast. I've made cereal for you."

"No—" He couldn't make the sound. What was the sound? "No sea! No sea!"

"You don't want to eat? Fine. Then you're getting dressed."

"Look at house, Mommy. See the ant-enna?" Byron pulled on his penis, the pleasant rubbery attachment, stretched the hose at her, as if it could extend forever and entwine her. "Look at my ant-enna!"

Diane slid open a dresser drawer. It floated on air, mouth agape, tongue out, and displayed undigested clothes. "An*tenna!* An*tenna!*" Diane corrected, her back to Byron, selecting a white turtleneck, blue overalls, socks, and sneakers for him. "Put this on," she said, holding the turtleneck out.

Byron moved at her with his quick feet, small hand out, his wide mouth parted, showing tiny, brilliant teeth. He had a look of pleas-

193

ant obedience as he grasped the turtleneck. He lowered his head and bent his knees, bowing, and joyfully flung the turtleneck away.

It flew on the air, a ghost person, and died on the crib, crucified by the bars.

"Byron!"

"Look, Mommy. It's dead."

"It's not dead. Stop saying that."

Got Mommy angry. "It isn't living."

"It was never alive, that's why it can't be dead. Now put the shirt on. We have to go out and meet this nice woman who you'll play with."

"I wanna play with Francine."

"Put on your clothes."

"I don't like them!" No winning with Mommy. She made everything always wrong.

"Byron, that's ridiculous! Okay, fine. Then *what* do you want to wear?"

"My pj's."

"Oh!" Mommy's body looked ready to jump, jump like Grandma's cat.

"Pee, pee, pee," Byron said. Pulling on himself had made him tingle. He danced from one foot to the other and his voice pierced his skull.

"Go ahead!" Diane motioned to the door to the bathroom.

The floor inside was colder. He bent his back and shot the juice out. "Apple juice!" he said. "I'm going to drink some," he said, and waited.

"Don't you dare!" Mommy called.

There wasn't much in him. He skipped out on his toes. He didn't want to touch the cold with all of his feet.

"What do you do after you pee?"

"Drink more," Byron said. He laughed like Mommy, whooshing the air out between his teeth. His lips buzzed and felt fat.

"Go and flush the toilet and then put this on." The turtleneck was in her hands again.

Byron grabbed it and had a good idea. One of his funny ideas. He ran. She called him. He ran onto the colder floor right up to the toilet, its pelican mouth open and filled with yellow. He threw the shirt at the bowl with all his might, but the turtleneck only floated on its way in—a graceful white kite fluttering down into the foamy sea.

DADDY HELD HIM, HELD HIM IN THOSE BIG WARM ARMS. HIS BLAN-ket pressed against his cheek, soft and smooth. He twisted the shiny edge, pulled it away from the fuzzy part. The blanket was bright skin. Luke unwound it to see the always skin of his finger.

Then Luke placed his finger on top of Daddy's; there were all the same things, only smaller. Same lines on his knuckle, same nail tips. But Daddy had little hairs. Luke brushed them. They were limp, curled to sleep on Daddy's skin. Luke brushed them up and watched them cascade down.

"What's this?" he asked.

Daddy looked away from the TV. "What's what?"

Luke brushed the hairs again.

"Hair," Daddy said.

"What's hair?"

"That's hair."

"Hair on a finger?"

"I have hair in lots of strange places. I'm kind of an ape."

"Noooo!" Luke arched forward with pleasure. Daddy was big like an animal, but he was a daddy.

"I have hair on my chest, hair on my legs, hair on my back, hair on my airs—"

"Hair on finger!" Luke shouted, laughing but a little scared too.

"Even hair in my nose."

But that was really silly. He fell into Daddy's lap with pleasure at such idiocy. Daddy squeezed him and turned him, the TV rolling in the air, the lamplight going up, the coffee table twisting on the rug. Daddy kissed him, hot and wet, on his forehead. Luke looked up at Daddy, at the big round face, open and cheerful, and saw into his father's nostrils.

He couldn't believe what he saw. There *was* hair in Daddy's nose!

PETER WENT INTO THE LOBBY AND SEARCHED FOR THE COMPANY name in the directory. The security guard watched him. "Barrow & Company 8th Floor Lawrence Barrow, President"—then other names. It seemed quite unreal. Apparently, just as Gary had said, Larry the child molester was a respectable businessman. Possibly a role model for eager yuppies.

How old was he now? Sixty? Sixty-five?

Probably doesn't do it anymore.

Gary had said Larry's headquarters was in Washington, but even so Larry might visit the New York office, might walk through any moment. Peter turned to go.

"Can I help you, sir?" the guard asked.

Peter, as if he were fifteen and cutting school, almost jumped to hurry his escape. "No, no," he mumbled guiltily, and spun through the revolving door into sharp, clear New York, the stone and brick of Madison Avenue bleached into adobe towers by the fall sun.

An image of the time Larry, of the one time (remember, Peter, it was just once) that Larry, well, that Larry took Peter's peter into his mouth—he laughed. Peter's peter. A bully at school used to call that out in gym. Peter's peter, peter eater. The bully stopped after the first football scrimmage; Peter knocked him down on an end reverse.

I liked football, Peter remembered, surprised at himself. Gary had urged him to play. Maybe I had been afraid I was a fag; maybe that's why I did it.

I have to get off Madison Avenue, Peter thought, sure that if he were on Park, or Lex, or Fifth, all these crazy memories would stop. He would be late for the staff meeting if he didn't hurry.

But he stopped at a phone booth and called Rachel.

"Hello, honey." She answered his greeting sleepily. "I miss you," she said plainly, without the elaboration of passion or the disguise of irony.

"I think I'd better see a shrink," he said.

"I'll ask mine for some names. What's the matter? Are you all right? Why don't you come over?"

"I'm lost, love," he shouted into the cool receiver. Peter hid himself behind the Plexiglas panel that shielded his upper body from the wind. But it curled up the legs of his unguarded pants until it reached his briefs. He felt X-rayed by the wind. It wasn't cold, it was cool, like a doctor's examination. "I'm just a lost person," he shouted against the wind into the plastic.

"Oh, baby," Rachel said from the warmth of her bed. "Come over. I'll take care of you."

NINA WAS EMBARRASSED TO ASK PEARL. SHE KNEW PEARL NEEDED a new job. The little girl Pearl had cared for since birth was now seven and in school full-time, and her parents had finally decided not to have a second child. Nina had spent many a morning in Washington Square Park with Pearl, her charge, and Luke. Although Pearl was black, middle-aged, not well educated, and clearly of a different social class, Nina had spent more time chatting with Pearl than with the few other mothers who, like Nina, weren't working.

Besides, Pearl was one of the few people Luke seemed to trust. He loved to talk to her. Several times Luke had allowed Pearl to push him on the swings. Once Luke had agreed to let Nina go for a cup of coffee (only a block away) and stay with Pearl. Pearl had even made Luke's first friend for him, a little boy only six weeks older, named Byron. Byron's nanny, Francine, was a good friend of Pearl's; if Pearl took care of Luke, they could be a regular foursome. The harmony, both adult and child, seemed like such a rare opportunity.

And yet, now that Nina had decided on a career and Eric had agreed to hire someone to take care of Luke, now that Eric was making such good money they could afford any price, now that she had had the luxury of nearly two years observing Pearl and other housekeepers, Nina felt it was rude to ask. She and Pearl were almost friends. Might an offer of employment be taken as an insult?

"Pearl, did I tell you that I'm going back to school?" Nina tried as an introduction. She had to force herself to jump, eyes closed, into the shock of worldly talk.

"No!" Pearl said. She bent forward a bit and then straightened abruptly, as if the news were a spring she had sat on. "Who's going to be taking care of Luke?"

"Well, I have to get someone."

Pearl looked to Luke, solemn, hardworking Luke. Disappointed that Byron wasn't in the park, he concentrated on building his sand castle, but glanced up every minute or so to make sure Nina was there, even though she had been there, always there, for every minute of his life. "He's not gonna like that," Pearl said.

"No, he isn't!" Nina said, laughing at the dreadful prospect.

Pearl smiled. "No, I don't think so." She chuckled with thoughtful pleasure. "No, he won't want his mama to be anywheres but with him."

"Is there any chance you might be free to—" She had exhausted all her will in going this far. Nina couldn't complete the sentence.

"—be his sitter?" Pearl asked in a tone of wonder, as if it were too good to be true.

"Yes!" Nina said. "I can't think of anyone who would be better."

"Don't think I'd be better than his mommy," Pearl demurred. "But he does know me. And he's such a sweet boy. Really, he is, and so smart! I can't believe what he knows already."

"I just think it would be so great for Luke and me if you could do it."

"Well, I'd like to. But I'd best discuss it with my woman first and then come and meet your husband."

"Sure."

"Would you be needing me full-time?"

"Yes," Nina said softly, hoping this wasn't a problem.

"Good, because I don't like to have time on my hands. My mama says I'm crazy. I just can't stand to be doing nothing."

Nina heard a wail from the sandbox. Luke was in tears. He was still seated cross-legged in front of his sand castle, but his shovel was gone, in the hands of a self-possessed dark-haired girl of four, who walked away quickly with her ill-gotten tool. Luke's head bobbed as he cried, chest pulsing, mouth broken open at the corners, his hands rising to cover his eyes.

Nina got up. Pearl said, "Oh, I know that girl. She's always causing trouble," but Nina had no time to answer. Her heart, as always, quickened at the sound of Luke's broken feelings. By the time she reached Luke, his long black eyelashes were wet. They held tear droplets at their edges, glistening, like jewels, in the sunlight. Nina glanced about for someone who might be the girl's mother or nanny, someone to intercede and get the shovel back.

"What's the matter?" she heard herself ask Luke, even though she knew what was wrong.

"I wanna go home," Luke bawled. He was shattered crockery.

"I'll get your shovel—"

"Don't want my shovel!" Luke said, for the moment not wilting anymore, his back straight, his eyes open.

Why does he do this? Nina asked herself. Why does he deny the simple truth?

"Oh?" Pearl's resonant voice came from behind Nina. "Well, I happened to get it." She put Luke's shovel beside him. "Is it all right if I leave it here? In case you be needing it?"

Luke, surprised, looked up at Pearl with his great blue eyes. "Don't want," he said, but not sure anymore.

"Course you don't. My, my, is that a castle?"

Luke nodded slowly, his face relaxing.

"Of course it is!" Pearl said. "Looks all done."

Luke stared down at his creation. He had carefully sculpted the dirty sand (here and there were stray pigeon feathers, a cigarette butt, the top of a soda can) into walls and made little towers at the corners.

"So you won't be needing the shovel," Pearl said. "But it is yours," Pearl added. "So let's keep it here beside you."

Luke nodded. "I made a tower," he said, pointing.

"Un-huh," Pearl said earnestly, studying Luke's little structure hard. "That's for the guards."

Luke laughed. "To see!" he corrected.

"Oh, of course it is!" Pearl said, shaking her head at her stupidity. "I should've known that."

Luke laughed loudly, his voice healing, his character reglued. "Yeah! Course, it's for looking. What else could it be?"

"That's right," Pearl agreed, her dentures gleaming. "I must be crazy to think it's for guards."

"Yeah!" Luke said, getting to his feet to walk around his creation with pride. "Too small for people!" He roared at this and looked at them with joy, but his face, just as suddenly, went slack.

The girl was back. She stood a few feet off, hands on her hips, staring at Luke's castle with an envious conqueror's rage.

Pearl glanced at the little girl, lowered her voice to a threatening growl, and said, "Don't be thinking of playing here. We're playing here now. There's plenty of room over there." The girl shrugged her shoulders and moved off.

"I want to go home," Luke said anyway, and reached for Nina's hand.

"All right," she agreed, the relief Pearl had brought, its refreshment, so quickly dissipated. "Thank you," she said to Pearl. "How can I reach you?"

"I'll call you," Pearl said, and wrote down Nina's phone number. "I'll talk to my woman tonight," Pearl added when they left.

At home that night Nina hesitated again, this time with Eric. She hesitated even though the idea of hiring Pearl wouldn't be a shock. Eric knew that Nina planned to return to school in a month and he knew all about Pearl (although he'd never met her). Still, Eric, despite his apparent calm, would be nervous at the actual event of turning over Luke's care to someone else. She worried he might balk at the last minute. Perhaps, on meeting Pearl, he would find fault with her to prevent Nina's departure.

Luke, despite the miraculous cure of his colic, had never become an easy child. He remained serious and careful, even his best moods diluted by a wary distrust. But he was a sweet two-year-old, very loving, and very smart—sometimes it seemed like a terrible intelligence to Nina, that it was the intelligence which made him difficult. Luke slept through the night, he didn't fuss about his food, or going places, he could be taken anywhere, restaurants, movies, trips, he showed no signs of the terrible twos, and yet he was completely dependent on Nina—or Eric. He almost never played by himself. He asked constant questions. He wanted to know the name of every object. He noticed every street horror. He feared the crowd of other children at the playground. He let his pail and shovel be taken from him without a protest, preferring to be stripped of his possessions rather than fight for them. He seemed to want and need a limitless supply of love, not things, not showy attention, but real contact, conversation, reading, play, intimacy, and patience. He could detect even a subsonic whine of irritation in response to a request and would then refuse to accept the giving, like the Jesus of her childhood sermons, wanting only pure love, not grudging duty. But granted generous love and ungrudging devotion, he was a miracle of happiness: easy, laughing, witty, and kind.

Most maddening of all, Luke never showed his good side to others. Adults expecting the usual performance by a baby—gurgling laughs at funny faces, easy clowning at his own infant clumsiness, automatic pleasure at their friendliness—were shocked by Luke's obvious suspicion of them, his unforgiving self-critical attitude at his own failures, his anger at being teased, his obvious desire to be their equal.

"Do you remember me? Give me a kiss. I brought you a present. Would you like me to play with you?" All those offers (always made, Nina noticed, with every expectation by the adults that their generosity was special, impossible to refuse), offers made by grandparents, uncles, aunts, neighbors, friends, were answered by Luke ducking his head and mumbling: "No." He would give them nothing, no matter how high the bribe. It almost frightened her; his lofty lack of self-interest sometimes seemed inhuman.

To have found Pearl, someone whom he did like, someone who gave to children without vanity, without expectation of reward—that was Pearl all right, a woman of apparently limitless self-sacrifice and patience—to have found her and for Luke to already know and like her . . . it was a miracle. Surely Eric would understand that.

So—nervous—Nina told Eric about her conversation with Pearl. Eric had begun to watch a videotape of a cable show about the stock market and he asked her to wait until it was over. She sat patiently while Eric shouted answers to the people on the program, applauding or booing as if the opinions were base hits or errors. Finally he listened to Nina. Eric nodded, said great, and that he would arrange to be home early any day that Pearl could come by. But Eric's legs jiggled up and down, his eyes became solemn (like Luke's thoughtful, worried look before nap time), and it was obvious to Nina that Eric was scared by the prospect of leaving his son in the care of a stranger.

She finally understood, after two years, that Luke was a possession of Eric's. Not one of many, but THE possession. Eric loved only through ownership, so for him the emotion wasn't false, it was real love. Nevertheless, it required performance, that Luke, like some stock, gain in value and popularity. Eric ended every night with a prayerful litany: "Luke remembered such and such, Luke can say such and such, he listens when I read, he's so handsome—'' and so on. All of that was true, but this wasn't pleasure, it was pride.

She almost hated Eric for the way he loved Luke. She felt jealous of the admiration, fearful of its hubris, and worried by the implication of pressure in the future. Eric had already begun to fuss about Luke's education, clipping articles about the IQ test used for admittance to private nursery schools. He assessed the motor and language skills of other children in the park, noting that Luke was taller than others his age, and had a much larger vocabulary. He bragged about Luke's remarkable memory to their friends, and worst of all, Eric's conversations with Nina were always about Luke. Eric laughed about Luke; he hugged Luke as if he were clutching a life preserver; he taped the financial TV shows to have more time to play with Luke and watched them during the few hours she and Eric were alone. All of Eric's energies were directed at the stock market and at Luke; there was nothing for her.

"He's just like me," Eric would say about anything Luke did well.

"That's the Wasp in him," Eric would say about Luke's shyness or his passivity in fighting off other children in the sandbox.

And Luke adored his daddy. Daddy came home with toys, freed Luke from gravity, carried him into the atmosphere, high above the world on his broad, thick shoulders. Daddy never yelled. Daddy never said no.

But Nina had to say no. Nina was always there. Nina yelled. She was vain enough to think that her parenting was better, her love more genuine. But did Luke know that? Did he seem happier with his father because he really was or because Luke knew that Daddy couldn't take anything else? When Luke crashed into something and cried, the look on Eric's face was more pathetic. When Luke lost a pail to a marauding toddler, he seemed even more humiliated than usual if Eric was around. Luke would burst into tears, not at the loss of the object but at Eric's painfully slow method of recovery or, even worse, Eric's monologues of advice to Luke about how to handle the next confrontation. Luke would listen, head bowed, his chin tight, hating himself, hating his father's supposedly reassuring tone, eyes darkened in their pain. In dreadful pain, she knew. She knew. She knew how much the kindly advice of a disappointed father can bruise and bruise and then bleed later.

But how could she tell Eric? Eric would never believe her conviction that if he blew up at Luke and yelled with all his might, told Luke to bash the next grasping two-year-old in the face, that Eric's rage, for all its apparent brutality, would be better for Luke than Eric's labored critique, delivered in a compassionate tone.

Luke had taken to refusing to go to the park on weekends, something Eric encouraged, it seemed to Nina, and she believed their twisted relations with each other about the other kids was the cause. She wanted to correct Eric, to get him to behave like a father, to push Luke, out into the world, to open his big arms and let go.

But every attempt to introduce her observations provoked immediate defensiveness: "I said that to him! But he gets too upset. I can't. I think—I mean, he's two years old, he's got plenty of time to learn how to defend his things. I mean, I think he's kind of noble—not worrying about his possessions, but worrying over the other kid's feelings."

Eric's attitude, his casual acceptance of Luke's lack of aggression, seemed bizarre and self-contradictory. All Eric cared about, in his own life, was money. The gathering and growing of money. How could he accept Luke's passivity?

And her own disgust with Luke's meek, selfless manner, Luke's horror of argument or disapproval, his total absence of competitiveness—wasn't that like herself? Nina never cared when one of their friends bought a new car, got a house in the Hamptons; she was never provoked by others bragging or teasing, by their accomplishments, honors, possessions. Like Luke, she preferred to sit with nothing, to have herself and the universe, rather than squeeze into the squashed planet of things. Why shouldn't her son, with her blood, her bones, her eyes, be the same?

She knew the answer. Because he was a man. She hated the answer. But the answer was in her heart, not her head. He was a man and they would take things from him if he didn't fight. Maybe feminism had changed things for women (she doubted it, but she hoped so), but for the men? No. They still slaughtered their own.

Look at those boys in the park. Carrying swords or whirring, flashing guns. Planting their feet, little hands on little hips, chins out, fists in the air: "I have the power!" Humming cartoon sound tracks, smashing castles with their feet, chasing pigeons with murderous delight.

Soft, sweet Luke, with his milk skin and dark mop of hair, his big bay water blue eyes, resting his head against her breasts, just wasn't mean enough for the big boys. He had a year or two before having to face them, before her protection would no longer be reasonable, before he would be considered weak.

Someone had to push him, push him out into the world. Luke couldn't afford to be like her. He needed big Eric, angry, hungry, greedy Eric, to darken Luke's skin and cover those vulnerable eyes with the opaque shine of ambition and callousness.

"No!" BYRON SHOUTED. THE GLASS THAT WASN'T SLID UP AND down easy. But it wouldn't stay. How funny. Push it closed. Let go. It dropped!

"Byron. Stop it."

"Taxi! Taxi! Taxi!" Byron said, and dove into his mother's lap.

"Do you know what that's for?"

"What's for?"

"What you were playing with. You put the money in there."

"There?"

"Yes. So the driver can take it and give you change."

"Silly," Byron said. He slid down, down, down into rubber depths where it smelled of the dark. Mommy pulled at him. He grabbed the rope of her arm and swung, monkey in a tree.

"Byron! Stop it. You have to sit up here."

Her fingers dug into the pockets under his shoulders. Felt like they poked through. Hurt. "Owwww!" She put him back onto the seat. He kicked at the glass that wasn't. He kicked at the money drawer and banged it up. Bang! It fell back right away.

"Stop!" Mommy held his leg down. He pressed against her a bit to feel the strength, the firmness of her grasp.

"Is that glass?" he asked.

"What?"

"That!" He flung his arm in the direction of the partition.

"No, it's plastic."

"No, it isn't!" he shouted. Plastic was a toy.

"Yes, it is. It's plastic."

"Plastic has colors!" Mommy never told the truth.

"This is clear plastic."

She sounded fast. Running away. "What's clear?" Byron shouted, and bounced against her, bounced against the mommy wall.

"No color." She pushed him away. "We're here. I have to pay."

"I wanna pay!"

"No!" Mommy shouted.

MOMMY AND DADDY WERE GOING TO LEAVE HIM. LUKE KNEW. HE knew suddenly. Mommy and Daddy were going to go outside. But not with him. Outside into the dark. The glowing dark. He knew. Grandma and Grandpa were there because Mommy and Daddy were going.

"Hey, Luke. Can Grandpa hold you?"

No, Luke thought. He turned away. The sea rug floated between him and Daddy. Daddy wants to go. Luke ran to stop him.

"Luke," Daddy said sadly.

Luke ran into the arm basket, jumped into the elevator, up in the air to Daddy's big face and got a kiss. But that was bad. Daddy's arms held him tight. Too tight. "Nina!" Daddy called, his voice crying.

Grandpa was next to him. Holding a stuffed bear. "What's his name?"

Luke pressed against Daddy's shirt. It smelled hot and flat and new. Daddy was going.

Mommy came. Her shoes crashed on the hallway floor. They weren't her staying-home shoes. They sounded like spoons crashing. She was leaving.

"Mommy!" Luke put out his arms.

She took him, tossed him, rolled him in her arms. She wore smooth clothes, like his blanket, soft and slippery. She smelled like Grandma and stores and bathrooms—not home Mommy. She was going out. Out into the glowing night.

"Play with me," he said.

She kissed his stomach, his neck, his cheek—warm, liquid, soft bites. Then she held him up to her face. Her lips were crayon red; her eyes glowed like the night. Outside.

"Play with me," he said.

"Mommy and Daddy are going out. Grandma and Grandpa are going to stay—" Mommy sounded hard, like television.

"We're gonna have lots of fun," Grandpa said, close, very close, his big daddy face and white head a bright light, a scary bright white.

Luke ducked into Mommy, into her smelly blanket, her soft pillow chest. He wanted to be wrapped in her, and sleep warm in her bed.

"Should we do the bedtime things before we go?" Mommy asked, the real mommy, her voice like the sunny day, clear and lit, not glowing. "Daddy can read you a story—"

"You read me," Luke said, and felt his eyes hurt and squeezed and wet. He knew he was lost now. They would leave.

"Okay," Mommy said like a kiss.

PETER TOLD RACHEL. AT LEAST, HE TRIED TO TELL HER ABOUT Larry. She tilted her head and listened with open, wondering sympathetic eyes. But Peter felt she was puzzled. After all, what did it amount to?

When Peter was eight and nine, Larry, taking advantage of opportunities created by living with Gary, asked Peter a lot of leering questions, made suggestions about masturbation, reached in Peter's pants and rubbed his penis, once put it in his mouth; the incidents were all brief, never brutal, and when Peter finally was able to refuse, Larry stopped. Peter told this to Rachel guiltily, his eyes averted, his voice low, halting, summarizing the items, a sinner confessing. She looked puzzled when he came to the end. Was that all? her look seemed to say.

But then Rachel hugged him for an answer. She put her hand behind his head and pressed his nose into her shoulder. "Poor baby," she prayed over him. "You must have been so scared."

She trapped him in the embrace, as if he were slipping away and had to hang on.

He felt awkward in Rachel's arms, irritated by her motherly softness, although that's what he had come for, that's why he had called the office to say he would miss the staff meeting. That's why he had told her: to be petted, to be soothed. But once in her arms, he wasn't a sad little boy anymore; he was a disgruntled teenager. He wanted to shake free, peel off her sticky affection.

"It's okay," he said, and pushed his way out of her spidery love.

"It must have made you angry."

"I'm not angry," Peter answered, and looked at his watch. He wanted to leave. The nervous morning, going to Larry's building, coming to Rachel's, had made nonsense of his day. He had told his secretary he had family business to take care of—how could he show up now?

"You're not?"

"No," he answered, surprised at her perceptiveness. "I'm not angry at you—I just needed to breathe."

"At me? Why would you be angry at me? I meant at that man."

God, what a mistake. No, he wasn't angry at Larry. He didn't believe Larry still existed; that's why Gary's account of Larry's current activities was a surprise; that's why he had gone to the building lobby, to see if Larry really had such a company. Larry was a fossil of his past. Like *Tyrannosaurus* standing gaunt in a museum, Larry was a bone-dead terror; this abrupt growth of muscle and skin was more weird than anything else.

And there was another worry, something he felt constrained to tell Rachel, because she was his mistress and Peter didn't think he should talk about his son with her. Byron, when he was grabbed in the park by a pervert, brought home the implication of Larry's continued presence. There must be other boys, other lives being— what? Ruined. No, hardly. But touched, touched forever. Not merely the temporary contact of lust, but the lingering interrogation of the past. Not merely the cracks it made in sexuality, but also faith in parents, the trust of authority, and the vague, but persistent, disgust with intimacy. Other boys. Other boys. Happening now. Peter could see their faces, and (he had to admit this) what happened to them was partly his fault.

Wasn't it?

He could stop it, couldn't he?

Couldn't he? Well, perhaps—

Couldn't he?

NINA KISSED LUKE'S SWEET SOFT CHEEK AS SHE LAID HIM DOWN into his crib. He had grown so big that letting go of him was a relief.

"Ma, Ma," he said through his pacifier.

"Shhh," she whispered. "If you need anything, Grandma and Grandpa will get it."

Luke whimpered. He pressed his face into the mattress, his legs curled up, and he sucked hard on the pacifier.

Nina inhaled, held her breath, and turned. She walked out purposefully (she heard Luke sit up and make a sound of protest) and did not look back.

Eric confronted her in the hall, his body worried and inquisitive. She shushed him before he could speak and made for the door.

"I didn't say good—" Eric began.

Nina took his arm. "Just go," she said. This wasn't their first departure from Luke, but it was the first Luke knew of. Their other dates—they felt like dates, arranged in advance, dressing up, having a time limit—had been when Luke would fall asleep at six-thirty or seven. They would read him his bedtime stories, give him his bottle, rock him to sleep (Luke almost never woke up during the night, and when he did, it was in the early hours of the morning), and only then would the sitter arrive and Nina and Eric leave. In his infancy, when they were most confident Luke would stay asleep, they used a widow who lived in their building. The widow knew Luke only from encounters in the lobby or elevator, not from her vigils in their apartment. Luke had never stirred, had never known she was there. But finally, as he got older, his bedtime later, his consciousness of the world keener, Nina had decided the deception was too risky, even though they had begun to use Eric's parents, whom Luke knew well. He might guess, he might delay going to bed just long enough to make them late for an eight o'clock show. He had a tendency to lie awake for up to an hour before falling asleep; if he called out (as he sometimes did) to ask for water, or tell some observation, and Grandma or Grandpa walked in . . . Well, it was a betrayal, a horrible betrayal, and Luke would be shocked, unforgiving, inconsolable. However difficult telling Luke in advance might be, that honest hurt would keep more important feelings unbruised.

Luke knew Eric's parents, even had something of a relationship with them, especially with Eric's father, Barry. How bad could it be for Luke? Leaving him with his grandparents, surely that was nothing, nothing, nothing. Everything was going to be fine.

They got outside, onto the lively Village street, full of students in their wild outfits, full of gays in their wild outfits, full of tourists looking at the wild outfits, full of yuppies in dull outfits not looking at anyone. There were so many people strolling, laughing, on their way to something, that the street had a party atmosphere, a late spring night in New York, too early for the desertion to the Hamptons, or the return to provincial homes after graduation. The Friday release made the gray week of law, banking, publishing, psychiatry into a memory. The black night changed the monochromatic day to fuzzy glowing reds and yellows, winking pinks and blues, bouncing lights everywhere, the city a torchlight parade of celebrants, some decayed, some naïve, some earnest, and some mad. Nina was glad to be back among them, in the free world, released from the dress gray of motherhood.

"What should we do?" Eric asked. A group of college kids, in torn bulky rags, their young cheeks red with excitement, came bounding by, splitting Eric and Nina.

"Sorry—" one of the girls called back.

"What can we do?" Eric wondered.

They hadn't made a plan in case Luke's reaction caused a delay. Now it would be hard to get into a good restaurant without a reservation. "A movie?" Nina asked, thinking of the early days together (only three years ago in fact, but eons in memory) when a movie and late dinner were their coziest, happiest times.

Eric looked doubtful while they rushed around the corner to the stationery store (about to close its doors) and bought a paper to see what was showing. They were out of sync with the local theater's starting times, but Nina figured out they could go to midtown, grab a bite, and get into a nine o'clock show of a movie they both wanted to see. "Let's go," she said, excited, pulling Eric's large, thick warm hand to get him to the corner.

He hung back, his weight a dragging anchor. "I don't think we should," he said, after almost toppling them both.

"Why not?"

"Shouldn't we stay close by?"

"It's ten minutes by cab."

"Should we be in a theater? We can't call—"

"Sure we can! Eric, he's with your parents."

"Some recommendation. Look what they did to me."

"What did they do to you?" Nina demanded. She thought his mother and father odd, but mostly in a good way, protective, concerned, loving.

"Made me a nervous wreck about my son."

"Eric, I don't want to spend our first night out in three months in the lobby of our building."

"Okay, but." He sighed. Eric turned his back to her and looked downtown. The World Trade towers could be seen standing alone in the distance, two fat boxes of dotted lights. "Let's just have dinner. I don't want to rush uptown."

"We have plenty of time," she argued, but with a hopeless feeling. For a moment, among the other partygoers, she had felt young, abrupt, unscheduled.

"We can go to that new restaurant in SoHo."

"We'll never get in."

"Come on," he said, his big hand pulling her in tow.

She thought: we'll end up eating crummy bar food, Eric'll talk about Luke and the market, he'll say we should get home early to make love, we will, his parents will stay for an hour raving over Luke, Eric will enter me and push in and out tediously until I come, and he'll come, itching to get out of bed to watch his tapes of the business show, to read his research, fiddle with his numbers, and start that late-night mumble, the chant of dreams—"Low earnings multiple, half book value, possible takeover."

Try to be cheerful, she ordered herself.

Nina tried. She put her arm through Eric's, she talked about going back to school, she walked among the others, the ones with real parties to go to, trooping down Broadway past the winking, leering lights, and pretended it would go differently.

But it didn't.

THE WOMAN CAME DOWN, HER ROUND FACE CAME DOWN, A BALloon floating right into Byron's eyes. "Hello, Byron. My name is Tracy. We're going to go in here and play some games. Your mommy'll wait for you out here."

"Okay." Big boy Byron, big feet forward! He marched on the shiny floor. Foot slaps.

The room was big. There were white hot dog lights way up. Like the big tunnel. Big tunnel to Grandma.

"How many eyes do you have, Byron?"

Big balloon head. One. Two. "Two. Like you."

Smile. "How many ears do you have?"

"No ears," Byron said. Cups on ears, his hands covered them. The hair tickled inside.

Bigger smile. "How many ears do you have?"

Dance, big boy. Tunnel sound. His hands were glue, his head a teacup. See my handle, see my spout. "No ears! No ears!"

"Sure you do, Byron. How many?"

Dance! He spun and spun and spun, covered ears, covered hair, hands stuck. "Can't hear! No ears, no hears, no ears. No hair! Don't have hair!"

"Let's make a picture, Byron." Balloon head floated down. "Draw a picture of your family. Here's some paper. Want to pick out a crayon?"

She pushed him like a stroller. There was a yellow table. She smiles, but her voice frowns. He stood still. The crayon box was right in front. He looked at the balloon head.

Smile. "Pick out any color."

"Draw!" he shouted. "Draw!" he shouted again. His voice came out like water from a faucet. Whoosh! He picked up a red crayon and danced it across. Broken red. Big X. "There!" he said, and pushed the paper, pushed the box, sliding off the table. "There!" he said.

The balloon head bobbed, up and down, no smile anymore. Just the frown.

"Where's my mommy?" he asked. Balloon head was no fun.

THE DOOR CLOSED. NIGHT. GOOD NIGHT MOON. LUKE FELL. DOWN on the blanket, yellow and soft.

Mommy and Daddy went out into the glowing night.

He sucked hard and smelled the bakery of sleep, warm and pungent.

Listen. Grandpa's voice. Rumble, rumble. Like Daddy—underground.

I'm alone!

I'm alone!

The room was dark and empty. Out—out—out in the glowing night.

He wanted to grow up, grow up huge out of the crib, out of the dark, big and bigger, to be in the day, to be in the day with Mommy and Daddy.

I'm alone!

I'm alone!

He cried. He cried. And heard a baby cry. And screamed.

There was a crying baby in the dark.

The rumble, the feet came, and scared him.

Press into the blanket and hide. Hide from the crying baby and rumble feet.

"Luke?" Grandpa brought the light, the hot light in, and with him, Daddy's voice. "Luke? Can I read to you?"

"Yessss!" It hurt to talk. Water was everywhere.

Grandpa caught him. Luke went up, big and up, out of the dark and the crib, into the warm light.

Luke squeezed into the hot body, fell against the pillow chest, and rested.

There was no crying baby.

There was Luke and Grandpa.

Grandpa opened the book and read.

" 'In the great green room,' " Grandpa rumbled, thundered inside, " 'there was a telephone. And a red balloon.' "

Balloon in room. Luke laughed.

Grandpa looked at Luke. His face, his bright white face, got so big. Luke squeezed into the hot. "I love you, Luke," Grandpa sang.

Grandpa glowed in the night. Safe and hot and big. Glowing in the night.

"What's going on?" Grandma said, and with her came more light.

"We're reading," Grandpa said.

"Can I listen?" Grandma asked.

"Sure," Grandpa said. "That's all right, isn't it, Luke?"

He sneaked into the warm, against the rising, falling chest. Grandma took his hand and held it—smooth and cool she was, calm and gentle.

Grandpa rumbled like the outside: " 'Good night moon. Good night room. Good night cow jumping over the moon. Good night air. Good night nobody.' "

Grandma kissed Luke's forehead. Soft and cool. She left.

But Grandpa stayed and rumbled on, rumbled on, rumbled on. Luke put his ear to the thunder and the heat. In Grandpa's white bright glow, Luke baked to sleep.

9

THE TESTER LOOKED AT DIANE WITH THE DEAD EYES OF A bureaucrat. Eyes without the possibility of appeal. "I don't think he's ready for this yet," she said.

Byron hopped across the linoleum floor, slotting his feet in each black and white square as he moved, an unguided pawn in New York's educational game.

"You should have him tested again in six months," the tester continued, returning a form to Diane. The woman's body was already half turned, ready to dismiss any complaint, or deflect any inquiry.

"What happened?" Diane asked anyway.

"He doesn't want to answer any questions."

"No! No! No!" Byron sang, hopping his way on the squares. "No, no, no!" he chanted.

This brought a smile to the tester's face. "Don't worry. That's very common with bright two-year-olds. Give him another six months." And now, having expended the full supply of her goodwill, the tester did show her back to Diane.

Diane would have liked to have the woman arrested. She wished she could say anything, anything at all, to disrupt the tester's control and self-confidence. "I was thinking of enrolling him in Suzuki violin," Diane said abruptly.

"I would wait on that too," the woman said, and then gestured at another anxious parent.

"No!" Byron hopped on one square. "No!" Byron hopped on another square. Then back and forth, rocking and chanting. Diane noticed the stares of the other adults, followed quickly by averted eyes, and felt her red-hot rage at this humiliation. She had come to

211

test Byron's IQ early, just in case he needed tutoring. Obviously he would.

"Come on!" she yelled at Byron, and grabbed his squirmy hand. Byron's body instantly went limp, the weight pulling down on her hand. "Stop it!" she yelled.

She felt her brain levitate and separate from her body, and she saw this foreign Diane's behavior: a privileged, aggressive woman furious at her child for not being perfect.

But that wasn't Diane, not the real Diane. She loved Byron. He was the embodiment of vigor and energy and courage, everything she admired and wanted. Byron was Diane at her best. There were times when she looked at his beautiful naked body, the perfect muscular miniature, legs flexing as he climbed on tables, chairs, beds, closet shelves, kitchen sinks, refrigerators (no mountain too high, no cliff too sheer), and she rushed to grab him and kiss the hard loaves of his buttocks, the soft swelling of his belly, the sweet wrinkles of his neck and felt she would be happy forever, permanently, invulnerably proud of the achievement of Byron's existence.

It wasn't that she wanted Byron to be the best: he *was* the best.

When Diane watched her brave son master things so easily—walking sooner than others, talking sooner, climbing sooner, becoming toilet-trained in a day, absorbing knowledge like a sponge, fearless of adults, shaking his mass of sandy curls, his wide mouth stretched in an impish smile, brown eyes glistening, hungry to swallow the world and make it his—and then looked at grown men—men like her husband, conservative, worried they wouldn't please, lazy in the face of knowledge, unable to care for themselves, their hair crushed and dulled, their asses bloated, their eyes corrupted by fear, their mouths cautiously pursed—she wanted to know what had happened, and what terrible thing could happen to her Byron.

She thought she knew: soft mothers, envious fathers, brain-dead teachers, lazy friends, a culture of television, status, and possessions.

She wanted Byron to get into Hunter, into a school of hungry kids, poor kids who not only wanted what the other fellow had but whose parents couldn't buy it for them. She had persuaded Peter to move the television into his study, hidden by a cabinet, out of sight and access. She had disposed of the crib when Byron was fifteen months, and following her pediatrician's advice, when Byron was two, she showed him that the shit in his diaper belonged in the toilet.

"See?" she said, holding the turd (in its diaper cocoon) above the bowl. "It goes in here." He got the message right away and was trained. Except at night. He couldn't hold his pee in that long. But during the day he would often just go off to the bathroom, lower his own pants, and do his business without fuss.

Of course, people would laugh if they knew she felt intense pride about such simple things. The articles in the *Times* and *New York Magazine* whined about children being pushed. It was fear, that's all, Diane believed, fear by her generation that the sloppy educations, the diluted culture, the spoiled, dependent childhoods, the values of acquisition, all of it, if it were thrown out, would produce superior people, better than themselves, smarter, surer, and with an elegant, discerning taste. She wanted a son who was afraid of nothing and no one. She wanted a responsible, self-sufficient, educated, and strong man to flower in the corrupt soil of New York, to defy the tradition of neurotic, self-absorbed, veneer-educated, spoiled middle-class kids that, more or less, described herself, her husband, and all their friends.

So she was angry at Byron's failure to take the IQ test. She tried not to be. She pulled him out onto the street, and reminded herself that she had taken him to it at the early age of two and two months precisely because she wanted him to have several cracks at it, that this fiasco was merely a preliminary hearing, not the trial.

"Mommy, Mommy, Mommy," Byron said, speaking in triplicate, a maddening habit he often fell into. "Ice cream. My ice cream."

She had promised him some before they went to the test, a simple reward for being good. "You're going to meet a woman and play with her for a while. If you're nice, you can have some ice cream afterwards." That's what she had said. It had never occurred to her that Byron might balk completely and thereby call into question whether this treat should be granted. Even if he had done poorly, although Diane wouldn't know that for many weeks until the test results were sent to Byron's prenursery play group, she had meant to give him the treat, to suggest the fact, possibly untrue in this society, that good work was rewarded. But should she compensate him for utter failure? Was that something she wanted to encourage?

Keep your promises, advised one book.

If you make a reward conditional, keep to the conditions, admonished another.

Which had she made? And did Byron know the difference? What did "if you're nice" mean? Maybe he thought he had been nice. But he hadn't been. That much needed to be made clear.

"Ice cream, ice cream, ice cream," Byron said.

"No," she mumbled, not out of fear at his reaction but afraid of her anger.

"I want ice cream, I want ice cream, I want ice cream."

"Don't say that over and over. You only have to say things once."

His face closed, like a door shutting out light and noise. His eyes dulled, his body went stiff, his mouth tightened, and he raised his shoulders, retracting his neck. "You said I have ice cream after."

"If you were nice to the lady. I mean, to the woman. If you were nice to the woman, I would give you—"

"I was, I was, I—"

"Byron!"

"Oh!" he grumbled, and tossed her hand back, a gift refused. He stomped off, lifting his feet and slapping them down, a comical exaggeration of a manly huff. When he reached the curb, Byron turned back to her, put his chubby hands on his swaying, elastic hips, and compressed his fair eyebrows so that the subtle undergrowth of black hairs darkened his brow. Angry, he looked more like Diane. "I want ice cream!" he trumpeted,

A passing man laughed. "So do I," he said, and moved on.

She felt the lava bubble below and push against her crust. Stay calm, she warned herself. She decided to ignore him for the moment, keep the refusal silent, fearful that articulation would become rage. Diane hailed a taxi and moved to its door. "Come on," she said.

Byron looked at her, his head upturned. The curls of his sandy hair were innocent and beautiful. His lean torso—she could picture the washing board of his ribs ripple as he stretched—sat uncertainly on his bowed legs.

"He's so adorable," Diane could hear her mother, Lily, say.

"Come on!" she shouted, her hot core steaming through.

Byron sat down on the sidewalk. He crossed his legs underneath him, closed his eyes, and put his hands over his ears.

"What's the story?" the cabdriver said.

"Start your meter," Diane said. "I'll get him." As she moved toward her little Buddha, the crust cracked, nothing could stop the rage flowing up through the faults in her hardened pride. "Byron! Get up! Get up right now!"

He shook his head and made the curls dance. Everything was black for a moment, her head filled with the smoke. She found herself carrying Byron, a dangerous thrashing fish, in her arms. His feet, his hands, kicked and slapped her. There were blows to her face and stomach, and her ears were scraped by the coarse edge of his screams. They were right in front of the testing facility, around them people were watching, but she felt great relief at dropping the pretense of calm about her disappointment.

She hurled him into the taxi's back seat, a final statement of her power, her strength. He landed awkwardly and bounced off the upholstery, falling to the car floor. She got in, told the driver the address, and left Byron hunched down there, holding the side of his face that had hit the floor. She ignored the cries, no longer willful yells, but pathetic and tearful. She left him alone, sitting rigidly. She left him to cry without her comforting arms—without her love.

ONCE ERIC WAS IN HIS CHAIR, SIPPING HIS HOT COFFEE, SURrounded by the sounds of Joe's rustling newspaper, Sammy's nervous leg flexing the leather of his seat, the secretaries sorting and carrying account statements and confirmation orders, once Eric could feel he had safely arrived at work, had made it through another weekend of being Daddy, he felt whole. His puffy eyes were mesmerized by the frozen numbers of Friday's closing prices. He listened to the faint pillowed whoosh of distant cars. He sipped more of the coffee and nestled his tired back (he had carried Luke on his shoulders for hours over the weekend) into the crannies of the chair's cushions, and felt at home.

For the first time in his life, he was at ease at work.

Two years ago, when Eric returned from those months of combat with Luke's colic in Maine, he had found a rival in his chair. Joe, in his unsubtle way, had hired another broker, named Carlton, during Eric's paternity leave.

"If you were going to be gone for a long time, I needed someone," Joe explained. "Carlton was available, our business has been growing, I thought: why not? Be less pressure on you." Joe went on to say that he thought there was room for Carlton to remain, and then hit Eric with news that Joe must have expected would be killing—namely, that almost half of Eric's clients wanted Carlton to continue to handle their accounts even after Eric's return.

Eric doubted that his clients had come to this decision without prodding. Joe's message was clear: you are on probation. I've cut your salary in half, and if you pull anything else on me, you're gone. Probably Joe expected Eric to react with terror, contrition, and a plea for restitution.

Instead, Eric told Joe that he would be handling two million dollars of Nina's father's money and that although he would pay the floor commission rate, Eric didn't feel obliged to pay Joe a premium rate since Eric wouldn't be using Joe's investment advice.

Up until Nina's father, almost all the clients Eric worked with had been given to him by Joe. The few whom Eric had brought in were lured by Joe's past performance record. Eric's job, in essence, was to be there to answer the customers' questions, keep them happy, and occasionally make a choice among several possibilities selected by Joe. Eric had, and could, submit stock selections of his own to Joe. He was permitted to pretend to the clients, and he had often enough, that many of the stock picks were his own. But Joe was in charge, he owned the firm, he could take the clients away, he could reduce Eric's cut of the profits, he could fire Eric.

Tom's two million gave Eric a weapon. Eric might be able to afford to quit. He didn't want to. To continue with Joe, even if it meant staying on the phone all day with Joe's clients, would save Eric thousands in commission costs. Besides, he needed the base income, since Eric couldn't be sure he would succeed with Nina's family money. Also, Eric knew that if he stayed, he wouldn't be cut off from Joe's ideas. Joe was too vain and pompous to stop himself from allowing Eric to pick his brain. Besides, if Eric continued to handle half the clients, he would know Joe's movements anyway.

After a good half hour of amazed questions, about Nina's father, the amount of money, and so on, that problem was what Joe addressed. "Eric, if you put any of that money into my portfolio, it's unfair for me not to benefit from the gains."

"I'm sorry, Joe, if you buy IBM for your clients, that can't stop me from doing it."

"You're being unfair. I've trained you, you participated in my clients' money. I deserve at least, at the very least, to get the retail commission profits. You're collecting an incentive fee from your father-in-law and a percentage of my profits. You're being very greedy."

"You did not train me in any of the important things, Joe. Sammy's been taught how to analyze a company, how to arbitrage. I've been taught how to schmooze."

"That's not true! You didn't want to learn. You're not interested in the tedious work of discovering value. You want the action."

"I'll settle for the action if that's all there is. If you'd made it easy for me, if you'd opened the door at all, I—"

"Nonsense. I'm here. I'm available. You didn't ask."

"What's the point of arguing?" Eric said. "We're both so full of shit we couldn't tell the truth if someone paid us to."

This put a stop to the sputtering, outraged Joe. His thin eyebrows disappeared into his forehead; his dull brown eyes seemed to shrink and gleam. Then he burst out laughing, and pulled on his thick red wool tie, as if grasping a leash to keep his head from bolting off his torso. When Joe was through laughing, he cleared his throat, looked at the ceiling, and said, "I'll work more closely with you. I'll get rid of Carlton. But I must participate in the profits."

They worked it out. Eric told Joe to keep Carlton. He calculated (correctly, as it turned out) that Carlton would become Joe's whipping boy, relegated to handle the most wearying and least ambitious of Joe's investors. Eric gave Joe half of his incentive fee in return for no reduction in his base salary, and kept for himself the significant premium between the wholesale cost of the floor broker and the retail commission charge that would be levied against Tom's account. But it was understood that no actions could be taken in the account without Eric's approval and that Eric was not obliged to suffer ridicule if he made losing picks. For the first time, in the true sense, he and Joe were partners.

The year and three-quarters since this arrangement had been Eric's happiest time at work. Joe began to invite Eric along on lunches with his bigger investors and with some of his old cronies from the large brokerage houses. And once a week Joe would have a strategy session with Eric, from which even Sammy was excluded. It was a deep, warming broth to the lifelong chill in the belly of Eric's self-esteem.

All these changes didn't happen at once. When between them, Eric and Joe increased the value of Tom's portfolio to a little over three million dollars in the first nine months, Tom gave Eric another two million to handle. Now Eric was managing a five-million-dollar portfolio, small potatoes to the big boys down the street, but a thick, aromatic steak to Eric. It was then that Eric became Joe's favorite son, power-lunch companion, and tactical confidant.

"Fifteen minutes," Sammy said, and turned on the electronic ticker. Sammy looked thinner. He had taken up jogging, or so he claimed, and his starved face now had the look of a greyhound's. Since the change in Eric's fortunes, Sammy was cool to Eric, although more respectful.

"Where's Carlton?" Joe said.

"How the fuck should I know?" Sammy mumbled, and threw himself into his chair. "Convincing some widow to buy Telephone."

"Fred Tatter for you," Irene said to Eric. In the days before Tom's money, she answered only Joe's phone. Now she doubled as Eric's secretary.

Eric put his finger under the receiver and pushed down, flipping it like a pancake in the air. He caught the floating phone in his left hand and brought it to his ear. "Hello, Fred. You're my first call."

"I should be working," Fred said.

Fred was a best-selling novelist. After the second of his successes, Fred had opened a quarter-of-a-million-dollar account with Joe, who had been recommended to Fred by his father. There would be long stretches when Fred wouldn't call, presumably while he was at work on a new book, and then months of frantic activity (happy months in a way, since Fred was easy to churn, and even if he lost money, they made a lot on the commissions), orchestrated by many infuriating calls. Fred had been inactive for a while. Recently, with his newfound confidence, Eric had initiated a trade for Fred. When Eric persuaded Fred to buy an over-the-counter computer stock, New Systems, that was a first for Eric—because he had discovered the stock himself. Fred was reluctant, but had finally agreed to let Eric buy five hundred shares at nine. Now, three months later, the stock was up ten points to nineteen. "Well," Eric said. "If you'd bought more of New Systems—"

"I know, I know. Don't tell me. I've been kicking myself."

"You're making money. You bought five hundred—that's five grand."

"Yeah, but if only I'd really trusted your judgment. I'm not trusting enough! You get so fucked around in my business, everything's so—uh, uh, compromised."

"Well, you know the old saying about Wall Street. All we've got is our word. If there's no trust, there's no trading."

Sammy swung his chair to face Eric and began to masturbate an invisible penis in the air. His hand moved in long strokes and he made a mocking face of an ecstatic expression. Eric smiled at Sammy, but Joe, his face reddening, whispered furiously: "How dare you! Do your work, instead of making fun."

Meanwhile, Fred was almost shouting in Eric's ear. "I know, I know, that's the way it is in the real world. Just my crazy business. Anyway, why don't we buy some more? Say five thousand shares."

"Whoa! That's almost a hundred thousand dollars."

Fred sounded firm, manly. "Well, no risk, no gain."

"That's no pain, no gain. And this could be painful. Stock drops five points and you're out twenty-five grand."

"I thought you liked this stock."

"I liked the stock at nine. It's more than doubled."

Joe looked, somewhat fiercely, at Eric. Joe waved off Irene, who was indicating she had a call for him. "Don't you think it's going up more?" Fred said, innocent confusion in his voice.

Eric said, "Could you hang on for a second?"

"For my favorite broker, you bet."

Eric covered the receiver and said to Joe. "What?"

"He wants to buy, let him buy," Joe said.

"We're looking to get out," Eric said. "I'm ready to close out half the Winningham account if it gets to twenty."

"That's five thousand shares," Joe said. "This is a thin stock. His order could get it up to twenty. Then you get the Winningham account out."

"What's the point? If Fred ends up losing."

"We don't get an incentive fee with Mr. Tatter. We get commissions. He trades on and off. He's small fish. You protect your own. Winningham is family." Joe, evidently convinced he had closed the subject, took his phone call.

"He's big family!" Sammy said, rubbing his fingers together to indicate money.

Eric returned to the phone. "Fred, can I call you right back?"

"Uh, well, I want to make the trade at the opening."

"I'll get back to you in five minutes." Once off, Eric sat and waited for Joe to finish his call.

Sammy watched Eric waiting. After a minute of this silence, he said, "You're too nice."

"What's nice? It's not good business. I'm making money for Fred—"

"*We're* making money for Fred," Sammy lectured.

"No!" Eric shouted.

Joe frowned at him and said to the phone, "I have to call you back."

Eric continued at Sammy: "I'm making money. New Systems was the first decent gainer he's had. I gave it to Fred because I thought he was getting fed up with us. He needed a big winner. To turn it into a loss is stupid."

"I see," Sammy said. "You make the bold move of getting your father-in-law to invest and now you're an expert on keeping clients."

"I can't have this kind of disruption in the office!" Joe shouted. "What did you tell Mr. Tatter?"

"I said I'd call him back," Eric answered. "I'm satisfied with the gains in New Systems. I bought it on the basis of their accounting software for IBM. They've won that market. We've had a hundred percent gain. I don't want to go in deeper."

"You're not trading for Mr. Tatter. He's making the decision.

You don't have to work that hard for him. You warned him it's risky. That fulfills your obligation."

"I don't know," Eric said, doubt creeping in. Joe understood these matters. He had built up a remarkably loyal list of investors, most of whom had given him discretion, didn't complain when they were churned, hung on during lean or flat times, and were grateful when there were gains.

"That's right!" Sammy shouted. "You don't know! Do what you're told!"

"Samuel!" Joe pressed so hard on the desk that he partially lifted himself up. "Apologize immediately! What is this? We're partners," Joe said, gesturing to Eric. "Eric is free to tell his client what he wants. I was merely advising him."

"Oh, please, Papa!" Sammy swung his head from side to side, almost moaning. "Please stop the bullshit. You don't have to put on this act. Eric doesn't have the guts to leave."

Eric felt a shock, his fingers electric, the comfortable chair vibrating him out of his comfort, back to the hard and lumpy world of dissatisfaction.

Irene and the other secretary, Carol, both looked away. Sammy sat panting, his thin body pointed forward. Joe's owlish square body and big head became still. Only Joe's eyes blinked, flashers on a stalled car.

Eric tried to speak, but he croaked instead. He cleared his throat.

"Don't even bother to answer him," Joe said softly.

But Eric managed to find his voice. "I'll walk out right now," he said to Sammy. "If that's what you really believe."

"Yeah," Sammy said, shaking his head. He glanced at the ticker. "Market's open."

"Either apologize to Eric," Joe said, "or get out."

"No, no," Eric said, and tried to wave Joe off, but he could barely lift his arm. His muscles were unstrung, limp in the chair. "If you believe it, you've got nothing to apologize for. Do you believe it?"

"*I* know it's nonsense," Joe said.

Sammy had kept his eye on the ticker. "You were right, Papa. The oils are getting a play."

"I want an apology," Joe said. "I'm not as nice as Eric. You accused me of being a hypocrite."

Sammy kept his eyes on the restless stream of numbers. "I'm not afraid. I *will* leave."

"Sammy," Irene said, low, an oboe playing beneath the melody.

"Then please do so," Joe said. He glanced at Irene. "Who's on hold?"

"Mr. French," she said. "Sammy," she repeated.

Joe picked up the phone. "How are you today, Mr. French?"

"Are you serious!" Sammy screamed without warning, twisting his body away from the stock quotes, leaning forward across the table, his face thrust at Joe.

Joe swiveled, giving his back to Sammy, and continued to the phone, "I can't recommend it on the basis of what I know. What did your friend say was going on?"

"I'm only going to ask you once!" Sammy screamed. His volume tore up the words' coherence, ripping them to pieces. "Are you serious!"

"Pardon me," Joe said, and put his hand over the phone. He turned to face Sammy. "Yes." Then he swiveled back. "I'm sorry, go on."

Sammy slammed his hand on the table. Irene jumped back. Eric, horrified, got up and pleaded, "Sammy, forget it."

"Get out of my face!" Sammy said, slapping at Eric's outstretched hand. "You stupid fool! Errand boy! I could stand you when you were just a nice schmuck, but Eric the Great Stock Adviser is just too much bullshit."

He walked out. Eric looked stupidly at the door and, after a few moments, turned back to check on Joe's reaction. Joe pretended nothing had happened. The owl was still on his perch, talking in a pompous mumble, apparently unmoved.

Sammy and Joe had had many terrible fights. Eric and Sammy had often screamed at each other. But no one ever walked out, or was asked to, for that matter. Sammy spoke his contempt for Eric with thorough conviction. He hadn't meant his words simply to hurt; he believed them.

"It's Fred Tatter again," Irene said.

So I was just a nice schmuck, an errand boy. And now I'm a fool.

Eric took the call.

"Well?" said Fred. "The market's open. You said you'd call back."

"I can't recommend it, Fred."

"What about two thousand shares?"

"Okay, if you want." Eric hated him, this fool whom he had tried to protect. What did it get him? Nothing but the misery of truth. "I'll call you back with the price."

Eric placed the order, then sat back in his chair, his eyes closed, and waited for a confirmation. Errand boy. Eric the great stock picker. He tried to tune the words out. Errand boy. But they had music in them—Schmuck! Errand boy!—a persistent, irritating jingle that couldn't be forgotten.

BIG BOY. BIG BOY. BIG BOY.

Byron sucked on his soft thumb, washing it with his saliva. He ironed the liquids back into the mushy skin, pressing them out with his tongue and the roof of his mouth. Up and down, trailing his teeth on the knuckle's hard bump. First cool, then hotter inside, soft on top, hard on bottom.

Big boy!

Mommy pulled him through the lobby. He swung on her hand, felt himself bottomless, heavy, but loose anyway, free in the world tied to the mommy swing.

"Are you tired?" Mommy's dark, dark face stopped the easy, loose world.

"Tire?"

"Tired. You're sucking your thumb. Do you need a nap?"

"No!" Angry Mommy wants me away. Look—behind the leaves. A man.

"Hello, Beerun!"

It was Jesus, the doorman. Peeking through the leaves.

"Hello, Beerun!"

Byron scurried across the forest floor to catch the lion Jesus.

"Can't catch me, Beerun!" Jesus hopped back and forth around the plant, the gold buttons of his blue suit rattling, his feet dancing on the grass floor.

So funny! The green world shook, tables, chairs, all hopping around the lion Jesus. He pawed the air and meowed. "I kratch you, Beerun. I kratch you," Jesus said as Byron dived for his silky pants. "Oh, no!" Jesus said. Big boy had caught him. Big boy had won.

"Byron, the elevator's here."

"Okay. Up now, Beerun. You big boy," Jesus said, lifting him up from the green rug. "Go catch your mommy."

"Rrrrr," Byron said, and grabbed Jesus's legs again.

"No, no, big boy Beerun. Your mommy's waiting." Jesus's hands pushed him gently toward Mommy. Byron paused and looked at Mommy's body, tilted sideways, holding up the elevator switch.

"Can't catch me!" Byron sang and ran, his hair floating, big boy on the fly. "Can't catch me! Can't catch me!" He ran into the gold box and looked up at the lighted numbers. Home was six. He jumped at the buttons. Press the button—see the light.

"What are you doing?"

"Want to press, want to press, want to press."

"I told you. You only have to say things once!"

Big boy jump. Couldn't. Mommy hands could. "Lift me, lift—" only once, say only once.

"Okay, okay."

Press and light. "Six!" he called to the light. "We're home!" he called to Mommy. "Can we play?"

"We're in the elevator."

"I know, I know—"

"Byron!"

"I know," he mumbled. "Can we play in my room?"

"I have to go to work. Francine will play with you."

"I hate Francine."

"You do not!"

"Francine fat!"

"Bryon! Don't you dare say that to her! That hurts people's feelings."

"Fat, fat, fat." The elevator doors opened. Byron ran out. "Francine fat!" he shouted at the tall wall door with the symbol of home—6A.

Diane grabbed him by the elbow. The floor fell away. "Stop it!" she yelled.

Home—6A—jumped. "I'm not bad!" he answered, once the 6A stayed still.

"Stop it! I can't stand it when you're like this!"

"You don't love me," big boy called up to her, to the dark face.

"I don't love you when you act like a brat!"

Brat is bad. Not bad. "I'm not!"

"You are! I don't love a brat. I love a boy who is good."

The 6A dripped, the floor got big. Mommy's hand felt hard. Not bad. Too big for the bad. His face got squeezed and hurt. He cried.

"Oh, no," Francine's voice said. She was fat and big in the home door. "What's all the crying? You hurt yourself?"

"I have to go, Francine," Mommy said. "He needs a nap."

"Don't! Don't need!" The squeezing face hurt more. Mommy don't love me.

"Now, Byron," Fat Francine said. "Don't cry. Babies cry. Big boys don't."

Big boy. Big boy. Big boy not bad.

"Good-bye," Mommy said. The dark face came at him, a shadow sun darkening the squeezed hurt.

"No!" he cried, and turned into Francine's big warm fat.

"Byron! You bad boy. Give your mommy a kiss."

"Forget it," Mommy said, and the shadow went away.

Big boy run, big boy sleep. Big boy bad.

I AM DADDY'S HEAD. I AM HIS HAIR. HIS EYES. HIS EARS. HIS NOSE. His mouth. I walk on Daddy's head. Walk through the sky. Walk through signs.

"Don't pull on my hair, Luke." Daddy's forehead rolled up and under his hand.

"Okay." Luke made his hand flat and felt the rumpled skin.

"Duck," Daddy said.

The building cover moved at his eyes. He felt himself lowered; he put his head next to Daddy's. The sun went dark for a moment and then he was going up again, up again to the windows, above the grown-up heads, big and bigger in the world.

"That was a low awning," Daddy said.

"Why?"

"Didn't you see how low it was?"

"Why low?"

"Compared to the others, it was low."

"No, no." Luke wanted to burst out of words, to yell. "Why make it low?"

"Oh, I'm sorry. I didn't understand."

Luke felt the inside jail open and laughed away the worry. "You didn't!"

"No, I didn't." Daddy's hand went around crazily to pat Luke's back. "I don't know why they made that one so low. Maybe the only place to attach it—do you know what 'attach' means?"

"No."

"Like glue. Sticking something to something."

Daddy was happy. Luke patted the hard ball of Daddy's head to feel his happiness.

"Anyway, maybe the only place to attach it was low."

"I see." He felt the wet air and the dry light. The song played in his ear: "I like you just the way you are. Not the clothes you wear."

"Is this your neighborhood, Luke?" Daddy said with happiness in his voice.

"What?"

"Welcome to your neighborhood, right?" Daddy said with

laughter in his happiness. "This is your neighborhood. Mr. Rogers has his neighborhood and this is yours."

The worry was back, confused sound and dark light. "What?"

"Do you know what 'neighborhood' means?"

He put his hand on Daddy's fur and grasped it to hold on, hold on to the big and bigger world. "No," he said, and wished he could pull the hair.

"It means the place right around where you live, the stores, the park, these streets. And 'neighbor' is someone who lives right around where you live. In the same building, or one nearby."

The air was wet again on his face, the light dry and warm. "I see," he said, and then watched the people, the stores, and, ahead, the wonderful and terrible prospect of the trees and grass of the park. They belonged to Luke now, like his toys, his room, his bed. "This is my neighborhood," Luke sang. "Welcome to my neighborhood." He laughed.

Daddy's happy head bucked under his hand. "That's right, Luke."

As Eric approached the playground gate, he felt more in control than usual, because he had been so clever at wooing Luke to the park. When Eric first made the suggestion they go to Washington Square Park—he wanted Nina to sleep late, undisturbed by their noise in the living room—Luke had lowered his head, his bright blue eyes darkening as if the source of their energy were on the blink. Eric said, "We'll go to the park, I'll put you on the swing until you're tired of that, then I'll catch you going down the slide—"

"I don't want to slide," Luke mumbled, afraid of both the slide and of Eric's attempts to get him over the fear.

"Okay, we'll build a sand castle together. Then we'll come home for lunch with Mommy."

It had worked. For the first time in a month since an incident with a brat who took Luke's shovel, Luke agreed to go to the park with Eric. Eric knew now he had been wrong to lecture Luke to make a more vigorous defense of his possessions, that his speech had backfired, increasing Luke's fear of the random world. Luke didn't want to order the mess himself; he wanted it made safe.

Eric forced himself to talk in a cheerful, hearty voice while he carried Luke to the park on his shoulders, obliged to push the stroller with only one hand, the other grasping Luke's plump, dangling leg. The sharp edge of Luke's heels bruised Eric's chest, Eric's hand cramped from the tight grip he had to maintain on the stroller handle in order to steer straight, and his neck felt permanently dented by the relentless weight of Luke's behind. But it had been worth it. When Luke began to sing the theme song of his favorite television show, *Mister Rogers' Neighborhood*, Eric hit upon the idea of explaining to Luke that the park and the streets and the strange people around them were Luke's neighbors. This worked too. Luke arrived at the playground singing. He moved eagerly toward the swing area and, once on, asked to be pushed faster.

"How fast?" Eric asked.

"To the moon!" Luke answered.

"That's fast," Eric said, and sighed with relief.

Eric made his hand into a metronome and watched the back of his son loom and then recede. He listened to two mothers chat about their children's moods and sleep habits as if their kids weren't right there, swinging in the air. What do they think? Eric wondered. That the rush of wind in their children's ears makes them deaf? He remembered his mother's dismaying habit of discussing his school problems with her friends while he and his buddies played at their feet. Miriam insisted to Eric that he shouldn't worry about his academic difficulties, but she talked of nothing else with her friends.

Well, that was all part of the garbage of his past, mistakes that he wasn't going to repeat.

"Luke! Luke! Luke!" a sandy-haired two-year-old stood on a bench outside the swing area. He waved his fat little hands in the air, his broad mouth revealing a row of widely spaced teeth.

"Who's that?" Eric asked.

"Oh," Luke said, a touch of worry and excitement in his tone. "That's Byerun."

"Brian?"

"Bye! Run!" Luke's voice was at once loud and restrained, like someone shouting through a closed door.

"Oh, Byron." That was Luke's friend, Eric realized, introduced to Luke by his soon-to-be-baby-sitter Pearl.

"Hello, Luke! Play with me! Luke! Play with me!" Byron jumped up and down on the bench joyfully. He looked so open, this kid with his tousled hair, big smile, and pug nose. Byron's body, smaller and leaner than Luke's, seemed to quake with energy. His presence was the ideal of boyhood: electric and sunny. Even the playground adults, battered daily by the happiness of children, took notice of Byron and smiled at his enthusiasm.

All at once, Eric felt afraid of Byron, envious of his parents, and proud of the fact that Luke was the focus of his attentions. "Do you want to get out of the swing?" he asked.

"Yes," Luke mumbled, very low, ducking as he answered, as if he expected a refusal to be hurled at him.

He's never been refused anything. Why is he so timid? Eric punched himself with the question.

"Play with me, Luke!" the happy Byron called. "Play with me!" Byron yearned.

Behind him, a dark Jewish yuppie appeared. She was dressed in L. L. Bean clothes and, at first glance, looked nothing like her son. Her hair was black and straight, and her deep-set eyes hid in a cave made darker by wide black circles of fatigue. Her face was long and dour, her mouth closed, her body still and enervated. But she had Byron's bold look as she took in Eric and Luke, and when she spoke, she had Byron's loud, confident tone: "Are you Luke?"

"That's Luke!" Byron said. "Play with me, Luke! Play with me!"

"Yes." Eric answered Byron's mother for Luke, afraid that Luke would never do so. Eric hurried to get Luke out of the swing, influenced by Byron's repeated chants. "I'm his daddy."

"I've heard so much about Luke. My name is Diane."

"Hi, I'm Eric." Eric's hands encased the box of Luke's chest to lift up Luke, out of the swing, over the fence, down next to his friend. Eric could feel his son's heart beat with the excitement of this encounter. That was a terrible relief—to know there was someone else Luke wanted to be with, that he had not inherited his mother's hermitlike disdain for friendship—but there was also loss, both of his son and of control. He was letting the fluttering bird go, but to what?

Byron took Luke by the hand, like a lover, like a parent, and pulled him toward the sandbox. "We play, Luke," Byron said.

And Luke spoke instantly, clearly and confidently as he would at home. "I have a shovel. And a pail. Daddy, can I have my shovel and pail?"

"Here they are," Eric said.

"You speak so well," Diane said to Luke, her compliment aggressive, almost acquisitive.

"I do too!" Byron said.

Luke, of course, lowered his head, away from the blinding light of being addressed by a stranger. "Come on," Luke said to Byron.

Byron violently took Luke at his word. He grabbed Luke's hand and hopped across the playground toward the sandbox. Byron pulled Luke so hard that he fell, nosing forward into sand like a helpless puppet.

Eric jumped forward. "Byron!" Diane called. "Don't pull him like that!"

Eric reached Luke and lifted him to his feet. "Are you okay?" Luke nodded.

"Play, Luke!" Byron called from the sandbox. Luke went toward him, in his slow, careful walk, distrustful of the earth.

"How old is Luke?" Diane asked the moment Eric returned.

"Two years two months."

"Six weeks younger than Byron. He speaks really well. Did he start talking early?"

"About nine months."

"Really? I've heard a few girls speak that well at his age. But no boys. I thought Byron was the most precocious, but Luke makes real sentences."

Eric was pleased she had noticed, and surprised she had so quickly, from merely one exchange. "From what I heard Byron speaks well," Eric said.

"Yeah, I thought he was the best. But Francine had told me that Luke was amazing."

"Well, he likes to talk, although he's shy. But his mother and he have long, long conversations. Even when he was a little infant, it would calm him if we talked to him."

"Byron won't stand still long enough to have a conversation."

Eric sat down on the bench next to Diane. She didn't have the small pillow of maternal belly; her thighs looked lean; even her posture, despite the exhaustion in her face, suggested girlish energy. "Look at them!" Eric said in a reflex of surprise when he glanced at the sandbox.

Luke and Byron were digging a hole together. Their bowed, concentrated heads almost touched, and even from that distance, the music of their voices—Byron's, piercing, upper register, Luke's, low and sweet and melodious—could be heard as one song played harmoniously by two distinct instruments. "Isn't that great?" Diane agreed. "Francine told me they were real friends, but—it's very precocious of them. Usually, it's parallel play at this age. They look like they're cooperating."

Luke isn't so frail, his wings are strong, Eric thought.

"You work on Wall Street, right?"

"You can tell just by looking?"

"No." Diane wasn't amused. "I gossiped with Francine. She told me your wife has been at home, but she's going back to work."

"Well, to school first. She wants to design clothes, so she's taking some courses at FIT."

"Oh," Diane said, her eyes doubtful. "Did she used to do that before?"

"No, she dabbled in photography. Did some work as a graphic designer. Flirted with acting when she first came to New York. You work?"

"I'm a lawyer."

"Criminal?"

"Corporate."

"And your husband?"

"He's in charge of the Stillman Foundation's funding to the lively arts."

"Really? That's interesting." Diane named her and her husband's jobs in a casual tone, as if they were unremarkable and ordinary. Since, in fact, they weren't, her manner made Eric feel that she must believe herself and her husband to be very successful, perhaps too obviously successful, so that an open show of pride would be redundant. "Is he at work?"

"He's asleep," she said with a grunt. She poked her hands into her jacket, slumping down on the bench, like a benched ballplayer enviously eyeing his active peers. "And your wife?" she asked, turning her head for the first time to look directly into Eric's eyes.

Reflexively, he couldn't face them. "She's asleep too."

"Well, aren't they lucky?" Diane said with another disgusted grunt.

"Yes, they are."

"And how did we get to be such suckers?"

Eric laughed and with the laugh let go of his succession of worries—how can I get Luke to the park? how can I get him to be less shy? how can I get him to be less afraid? how can I make more money? how can I learn to make it on my own? How? How? How? He laughed them out and up, ugly pigeons on the wing, soaring into the open patch of the New York sky.

THAT MISERABLE DAY WHEN DIANE TOOK BYRON TO THE IQ TEST, expecting triumph and ending instead with hurling Byron into a cab, that miserable day, like so many others, found her happy to return to work. She had noticed long ago that the parents of young children were happy to be at the office on Monday mornings. That afternoon she was grateful for the obligation to get out of the house, away from her cranky two-year-old.

She settled at her desk, returned the accumulated phone calls, and finished the memo she had to prepare for Stoppard, all in record time, more than making up for her absence in the morning.

Then her mind wandered. She knew she should go home. Peter wouldn't be there; he had a fund raiser and then a show. Peter had asked her to come along, she could call the baby-sitters, but the prospect of getting to bed at midnight or even later, only to be roused at three or four in the morning if she was unlucky (the nights they went out Byron tended to wake) or six-thirty if she was fortunate had defeated her. She should go home, deal with Byron. Maybe all the absences of parents had made him temperamental. She had to force Peter to develop a closer relationship with Byron. Maybe another child would help. Sure, Byron would be jealous, but he would have a companion.

Companion in misery?

It wasn't that bad. She remembered last Saturday in the park, watching Byron play with that boy Luke. He was happy. And they were the two smartest kids there, she knew that. The parents around her and Luke's father, Eric, stared openly when Byron and Luke returned from building their sand castle and went into a kind of elaborate duet of speech, their words fashioning the turrets their small awkward hands could not, their language sculpting details that the crude sand couldn't define.

"How old are they?" one mother asked.

"Two," Diane said.

The mother shook her head in unhappy confirmation and her eyes went to her own kid, a lummox, his eyes dull, his mouth hanging open moronically. He had pathetically tried to horn in on Byron and Luke's creation. Luke had immediately backed off, Diane had noticed. She had felt Eric tense beside her, but her Byron had saved the situation.

"We're building! Not you!" Byron had commanded and the dullard had stumbled back on his heels, as if pushed.

If only Byron had cooperated with the tester! What a show he would have put on! Diane had learned the various questions and tasks the IQ test put to the children and she knew Byron could manhandle them.

She liked Luke's father. He was a huge man, well over six feet, with big, broad shoulders, his face wide and cheerful, his kinky hair glowing in the sun. His big, meaty hands were warm—he had touched her on the arm to emphasize some story—and he had a bearish love for his son. He gathered Luke into his thick arms when Luke finished gabbing about the castle and thus miniaturized Luke. Luke was swaddled like a newborn infant against Eric's powerful chest. Eric's full lips kissed Luke on the forehead unselfconsciously, with none of the shy affection Peter occasionally gave to Byron, with none of the false, presumably male heartiness of the typical American dad, but with a strong desire, fierce and desperate and comforting. "You're great, Luke!" Eric had said, almost wildly, a stage character bursting into song.

She imagined going to bed with Eric, made small and warm and protected by his body, swamped by his wet lips, her hands on the tight engine of his ass. . . . "You're great!" he might sing at the end.

She felt contempt for Peter.

Of course, Peter still shone bright; he was smooth, a polished precious gem, a jewel compared with other husbands. Eric might be good for a night, but probably the brain was oafish, his ability to understand her limited.

Yet she felt disdain for Peter. He was a jewel, but what use was it? What real value did she get out of his refinement? His wit? His charm? His impeccable taste? If Peter could take her to dinner and a show and then become a bear in bed, a hungry mammal, instead of a self-conscious civilized man, then . . .

That wasn't it. It wasn't sex. Peter didn't feel passion, not for his child, not for her, not even for life. He felt only ironies. He understood when someone portrayed passion on the stage, but he'd flee from the roaring reality.

Byron had passion. He had energy and the love of doing, and his mind had the refinement to make something of life.

She missed Byron. Diane called home.

"The Hummel residence," Francine's obviously black accent answered.

How weird, Diane thought, at the picture of her life that was summoned by having a black servant answer with that antique phrase. "Hi, Francine, it's Diane. How's it going?"

Francine lowered her voice. "He's playing in his room. Seems happy, but he keeps talking about"—she laughed, embarrassed—"keeps talking about how you don't love him."

"What?"

Francine whispered. " 'Mommy don't love me, Mommy don't love me,' that's what he keeps saying. I told him to stop." She laughed again. "He told me I was fat."

"I'm sorry."

"I don't mind, I just gave him a good hard pinch, told him he was too short to be telling me I was fat. That stopped him. He's all right. Just likes to get his way. Who doesn't?"

"I'm coming straight home," Diane said.

"Not if you have work. He's fine."

"I'm done. That's why I called. I'll be home in twenty minutes."
She hung up and moved quickly, as if her house were burning
down. I was wrong, I was wrong, she thought, clearing her desk.

Didi walked in just as Diane was ready to go. "Get your coat.
We're going for a drink with our mentors."

"I can't." But she stopped still, waiting for permission to leave.

"Something wrong at home?"

"I have to go," Diane said, but not moving.

"Half an hour?"

"It's never half an hour."

"Maybe they want to tell us we're making partner."

"They wouldn't do it like that."

"Harold said he'd take us to the Century Club."

"I've been there," Diane answered.

"Me too," Didi said in a little girl's whine, and stuck out her
tongue.

Diane laughed. She let her shoulders sag and laughed. Didi's
eyes twinkled. Diane envied her freedom. Didi hadn't steered into
the wife and mommy expressway, with only a narrow breakdown
lane for divorce, its next exit middle age.

"Have Peter take care of the kid," Didi said. "He can order a
pizza for dinner."

Again, Diane laughed at this picture. Didi tilted her head, curious, the way she looked when listening to an important but self-
deluded client. "Peter's not home," Diane answered.

Brian Stoppard looked in. "Ladies?"

"Diane has to go home," Didi answered.

"Just for half an hour," Stoppard said. "My car will take you
home. Won't be much longer than if you fought that." He nodded
toward the traffic below. "Take you half an hour to find a cab or
get there in the subway."

His argument was specious, but he had appealed, like a good
lawyer should, to Diane's self-interest. She went, and quickly
downed two drinks, talking too fast, squeezing in everything, conscious that, once she left, Didi would have Harold and Brian to
herself, and besides, she noticed how they both looked at Didi,
especially Harold, that old fart, his watery eyes lingering on the
swell of Didi's blue blazer, dazzled by the small diamond earrings
uncovered by Didi's boyish haircut. She's much prettier than I am,
Diane thought, seeing Didi through her whitened liquored vision:
young, self-assured, a movie actress playing a lawyer, some kind
of capitalist wet dream, a killer associate with tits. Didi had high-
lighted, or dyed, or hennaed, or something'd, her hair. It was red-

der, fresher. Sure, Didi had time for hairdressers and Saks and winter vacations, and late sessions at the office.

"I gotta go," Diane said. The sentence came out as a single slurred word. I'm high, she thought.

"I'll walk you to the car," Stoppard said, and by God, he took her arm, as if she might not be able to walk.

Stoppard held her elbow as they walked down the gloomy Century Club staircase to its gloomier lobby. The old black men who took the coats, stood guard at the front desk, and opened the door seemed funereal, only recently freed by the Civil War, still mourning President Lincoln's loss. The thought made her giddy. She turned to Stoppard. "Are Didi and I gonna make partner?"

He smiled. "You're drunk," he said cheerfully.

"Be responsive. I don't care anymore. I'd just like to get over the suspense. I hate suspense."

Stoppard just smiled, that fucking poker smile, slight, ironic, tasting some future delight, contemplating some past triumph. He went to get her coat. Diane tried to make eye contact with one of the black retainers. Her glance made him uncomfortable.

"Good evening, ma'am," he said at last, somewhat desperately.

Stoppard helped her on with her Burberry. She was so tired of it and the rest of her lawyer uniform. She missed the frayed oversized army coat she had worn in college. Inside, the army had felt like a comfortable blanket, but she looked tough in the mirror. "No answer, huh?" she said when Stoppard took her outside to his limousine.

Stoppard paused this time, his face dark and aged, his eyes glowing black in the amber haze of the street lights. "Are you seeing a therapist?"

"No!" She was insulted that he would think she might. Therapists were for people like Peter, for all those spoiled princesses. Therapists were there to console people after their defeats.

"I think you should."

"Huh?" I must have heard him wrong. Stoppard recommending a therapist? Would he make someone a partner who had cracked as an associate?

"Before you had your baby, you would never have blundered and asked me a question like that. And then I give you a chance to think it over, and you repeat the mistake. You never would have shown that you had any doubt you'd make partner in the old days. That's the kind of insecurity I expect from Didi. If you doubt it, maybe I'll start to doubt it. I don't know if it's motherhood or your marriage or what, but something's got you off-balance."

She felt her stomach contract on the day's emptiness. Taking Byron to the test had been her lunch, the cocktails her only sustenance. Her mouth went dry. She tried to replay Stoppard's speech even as he was finishing; she tried to calculate whether he was advising, admonishing, or dismissing. Was he friend or foe now? "I think you're overreacting," she said quickly, knowing, from somewhere, that that response was the perfect camouflage for confusion.

Stoppard surprised her. He lifted his chin and laughed up at the buildings. When he was finished with this exhibition of hilarity, Stoppard looked at her with pity. "Go home, dear. Think about what I said."

She was baffled and found herself inside the car, without remembering getting inside. She sat stupefied, her brain stuck on the last exchange. Why did he laugh? "I think you're overreacting." What's funny about that?

DADDY HOME. DADDY HOME. DADDY HOME.

Luke was free of gravity again. He twirled in the air, the long wait over.

"Look, Luke, I brought you something." Daddy pulled out a shiny package, a toy in a bubble, with bright-colored letters all around.

It was He-Man!

"Do you know what this is?" Daddy said. "Byron's mommy told me about it."

"Is that one of those action figures?" Mommy said.

"Yes, it's He-Man!" Luke said. She didn't know, couldn't know. "That's He-Man!" Luke said loud, very loud, so she would know.

"He's pretty special, huh?" Mommy said.

"It has a story with it," Daddy said, holding a bright square of still cartoons in his hand.

"Read it to me," Luke said, worried it was too soon. Daddy still had his coat on.

"Sure. Let's see, 'He-Man meets Ram Man.' "

"Why don't you take your coat off first?" Mommy said.

Daddy looked at Mommy.

"Hello," Mommy said to Daddy, as if they'd just met.

Luke laughed. Mommy knows Daddy.

"Hi. How was your day?" Daddy said to Mommy.

"A little tiring," Mommy said.

Mommy didn't tiring. She didn't sleep. "Sorry," Daddy said.

He began to bump and shake. He-Man danced in Luke's hands. He-Man's body moved! Just like Byron's He-Man. It was the same!

"Look." Luke showed them. The arms punched. The legs walked. The stomach twisted. He-Man was the same as Byron's, but brighter, his colors everywhere, not missing like Byron's.

"I think you'd better hang it up," Mommy said.

Luke clutched He-Man. He wanted to keep it. "It's okay here," Daddy said, and pushed his coat away. How did he get it off?

Daddy read about He-Man. He could smash walls. He made friends with Ram Man, who had a metal head and legs that jumped. And there was an evil, which means bad, man made of bones. When Daddy finished, he said, "He-Man has his own TV show. Did you know that?"

"Yes," Luke said. But what is a show?

"It's on in the morning. We can watch it together." Daddy looked at Mommy. She nodded at him. "Did Mommy tell you about Pearl coming tomorrow to play with you?"

"No." Why here? Why not in the park?

"Pearl's gonna come here and play and help Mommy."

"Help Mommy?"

"You know, clean. And stay here with you if Mommy has to go out."

Luke looked at Mommy. She had her sad mouth, her chin smashed in, her eyes sideways.

"You know how Francine sometimes stays with Byron," Mommy said.

"She always stays with him," Luke said. Daddy's body got hard. Byron's mommy was never there, Luke wanted to say, but Daddy's body got too hard, Mommy's mouth too broken.

"Not like that," Mommy said. "Not all the time."

"Just for part of each day," Daddy said.

"Each day!" Luke knew now. Mommy was leaving him, like the other mommies. Pearl wasn't Mommy. She wouldn't know how to do things.

"Nothing's gonna happen for a while," Mommy said fast. "Pearl and I are both gonna be here for a long time. I won't go away until Pearl knows everything about you and how you like things. Okay?"

Mommy was leaving. Her broken chin told him the truth. She was leaving.

"Look at what He-Man can do!" Daddy said, and made the tan body twist and punch.

Luke closed his eyes to escape them, Daddy's toy, Mommy's worried face.

Daddy's body got soft, his arms hard, and he squeezed.

Luke cried. He let his worries go into the shake of his chest and the wet of his eyes.

"Don't worry, Luke," Mommy said.

"Let's play with He-Man," Daddy said.

"No!" He wanted to be away from their leaving. He shut his eyes and wept. He wanted to be free from their going.

"Don't worry, Luke," Mommy said.

"Everything's all right," Daddy said.

"No!" Luke tried to yell, to break away, but they wouldn't let him go—go away from their going.

THE WATER LOVES ME, BYRON THOUGHT. THE THUNDEROUS FALL from the faucet blasted the bubbles. He looked into the hole.

Water washed his head. Water everywhere, in his mouth, in his eyes, warm on his chest.

"Byron! Watch yourself!" Francine said.

Hard. Hard, it hit his head, like the sky smacking him. He felt his skull break open.

He screamed at it! He screamed at the pain. Francine's hand closed on the hole. He could feel her hand on the skin. He still had his head.

"I told you! Now, it doesn't hurt that bad. Just a bump on the head. You got a hard head. Poor baby. Told you! You got to keep away from that faucet."

"What is it! What is it! What is it!" Mommy was there. Dressed in the door.

"He hurt himself on the faucet," Francine explained. "Ducked his head under, then came right up, bang!"

"It hurts, Mommy."

"Sweetie." She came and picked him up from the warm water and held him against her. He pressed into the paper of her clothes, his wet lips into her black hair.

"I love you, Byron," Mommy said. "Don't forget. I always, always love you."

10

PETER WENT FOR A CONSULTATION WITH A PSYCHIATRIST. THE doctor was a squat old man whose big, watery eyes stared back, unmoved by Peter's attempts to be, by turns, witty, earnest, lively, calm, self-confident, querulous. Peter hinted at a full deck of childhood traumas for the psychiatrist to choose from, and none was taken. The enervated listener didn't push Peter to give more particulars. He watched Peter coldly, a reptile observing prey with unblinking eyes. When they did move, it was to the clock on his desk. The sight of time prompted the doctor's longest speech. He suggested analysis. That, in practical terms, meant five sessions a week on the couch at a hundred and fifty an hour.

Peter said he'd think about it, and he did, only with outrage and despair, and then went on, at Rachel's insistence, to see a mere psychotherapist recommended by a friend of Rachel's. This time, maybe because this doctor, or Ph.D. anyway, was a mere female, an elegantly dressed, heavily perfumed nice middle-class lady in her late forties, this time Peter blurted it all out, his parents' divorce, the child molestation, the affair, his sexual numbness with Diane, and even his elaborate fantasies, admitted to no one, that Diane and Byron would die in some accident and leave him free, tragically and gloriously free.

"Free of what?" Kotkin, Ph.D., asked.

He was so sure of his answer—the tedium, the responsibility—that Peter was surprised to hear himself say instead, "The guilt."

"What are you guilty about?" Kotkin asked.

"I don't know. Of the affair?"

"But you said these fantasies started when you had stopped seeing Rachel. Before you resumed the affair."

"That's true. I don't know. The guilt of failing them?"

"How have you failed them?"

"The affair?"

"But the fantasies started while you weren't having the affair."

"Right. Well, of not loving them."

She nodded, almost bored. "What can I do for you?"

This question baffled him. Somehow, he realized, he thought he was supposed to do something for her. "Cure me?"

Kotkin smiled. "You're cured. What else can I do?"

He stared at her and then laughed. Her flip answer made him replay his confession and hear how solemn, how dreadful he had made his life sound. But was it really? "I don't know," he said at last.

She said she thought they could work together, that she could help him explore his past. My bothersome past, he thought, and missed hearing the rest of her soothing vision of their future. Twice-a-week visits to this nice lady to chat about his feelings. That's somehow the way it came out. Her perfume, her long dress, the quiet earth tones of her furniture—the reality was softer than the cement blocks of abstract words she spoke.

He suspected this feeling was transference. Because he knew both too much and too little of analytic theory to be sure if he was right to prefer her to the psychiatrist, he ignored his doubts and let the abrupt suffusion of protection and warmth he felt afterward flow into his chilled, timid arteries.

Peter went to the next few sessions eager to be a good patient, his mouth yawning words, emptying himself of all the evil, yes, evil in him. I hate my wife. I hate my son. I'm getting bored with Rachel. I want my mother to beg my forgiveness. I liked Larry playing with me. I hated Larry playing with me. I want to know why I let him. I let him because I liked it. I let him because my father left me. I want to leave New York, and live alone in another city, sleeping with lots of pretty girls, who aren't smart and mature like Diane, or funny and loving and wise like Rachel, but silly with big tits and fatless hips. I wish I were an artist. I'm glad I'm not. I love Diane. I love Byron. If they were dead, I could be happy.

Gradually, Peter became aware that the sessions were making his time at home with Byron and Diane easier. Diane asked only perfunctory questions about the process, her interrogation atypically brief and vague. Presumably she was afraid of what Peter might discover. Rachel, on the other hand, was nosy. Eager, too. And she got increasingly frustrated by Peter's answers.

"You know, I'm at exactly the age my father was when he left my mother," Peter commented to Rachel a month into his therapy.

"Does Dr. Kot think that's significant?" Rachel asked, with a worried brow and concentrated frown.

"Kotkin, her name is Kotkin."

"I know, honey! I think it's funny to call her Dr. Kot. I like to think of you on Dr. Kot's couch."

"Making up cute names about authority figures strikes me as a way of making them even more intimidating, rather than less so."

"Peter, you're being defensive."

"Darling, there's one thing I've definitely learned from my therapy—I'm defensive about *everything*. I'm defensive when I'm on the offensive. I'm afraid that inanimate objects are going to leap at me—"

"Me too." Rachel laughed, leaning toward him, touching his arm, trying to move in closer. "Me too," she kept saying, unloading her furniture into his emotional apartment, claiming the drapes, the rug were just like hers. "Me too," she said. Peter had talked about Rachel's claims of duplication in therapy.

("She wants to be close to you in every way," Kotkin said.

("Yeah, but it's so adolescent, like teenage love, or even teenage friendship," Peter answered, expressing a judgment he hadn't known he felt.

("You prefer distance," Kotkin said.

("Give me a break. I prefer difference. Isn't that what the relationship between men and women is about? Difference?"

("I hope so," Kotkin said with a mock sigh of despair.

(That was funny. Was therapy supposed to be funny?)

"You're not defensive," Peter argued to Rachel. "You're insecure."

"It's the same thing," Rachel complained, hurt, grabbing her furniture protectively.

"Yeah, the cause, I guess. But mostly you want approval. I want to hide."

"What does she say about me?" Rachel asked.

"Nothing. She doesn't say things. She asks questions."

"I love you. Have you told her I love you?"

"Now you want approval from my shrink."

This degenerated into a fight. Rachel ended up crying. "I can't go on seeing you until you straighten out whether you're going to stay married or not."

Peter agreed. That made Rachel angry. He had seen her act resentful, dented, her head drooping, her arms closed, hiding her chest, but this was different. Her shoulders, usually slumped, got square, her arm gestures strong—she looked unpleasantly masculine. "Diane's your mommy. You're scared to leave her because she takes care of your life. Keeps everything in order. I'm your bohemian fling."

Peter understood now that Rachel hoped for marriage or a commitment like it, that she had expected his therapy to make him feel that his marriage to Diane was an illness, or a symptom of an illness. This discovery had none of the shock of revelation; rather, was like noticing a color in familiar wallpaper, seeing something close by, always there, but previously ignored. He was offended by Rachel's presumption.

("Aren't you flattered?" Dr. Kotkin asked.

("Flattered?"

("That a bright, successful, attractive woman wants you?"

("She's not that attractive," Peter said, and laughed sheepishly at his cruel joke.

("If she were more attractive, would you be flattered?" Dr. Kotkin asked, suddenly stripped of her sense of humor.

("No. Of course not. I'm just not flattered.")

He was bored. Rachel believed she was very important in his life. Obviously that was her problem. Unless Peter gave her absolute confirmation, she would forever be unloading her things into his soul, matching her fabric to his, lighting the same areas, completing his set of china. If she couldn't possess the thing of him—marriage—she wanted to own his feelings.

Rachel yelled at him. She told him she couldn't see him for a while. Peter looked downcast, but was secretly thrilled. One less cloying person.

("I want you to get rid of them."

("Get rid of who?"

("In our first session you asked what I wanted from you. I want you to get rid of all of them. My mother, my father, my stepmother, my stepfather, Larry, Diane, Byron, Rachel. Get rid of them."

("And then what will happen?"

("Then I'll be happy. I'll buy a Winnebago and drive to Wyoming and live free and wild."

("How can I get rid of them?"

(He took that one seriously. His legs felt stuck to Kotkin's couch. His head sank into the pillow. He closed his eyes and the lids burned. "Make me not care about them. About what they say. Or what they want. Or what I owe them."

("And if you didn't care about all that, then you'd be free of them?"

("Wouldn't I?"

("I don't know. Is that what you're saying?"

("What do you think? Or will you really never tell me what you think?"

("I think all of this talk about getting rid of them are made-up feelings."

(Peter tried to raise his head, but the weight of his soul held him down, vulnerable to her omniscient voice. "You do!"

("I don't think you want to be free of them. I think you make that up. You bring it to me because you think it's naughty, and that's fine. You can come here and say naughty things. You want your wife and son dead. You don't want to see Rachel. Maybe some of these things you do want. But that's not why you're saying it.")

That was thrilling. Therapy was more fun than life. He was glad not to have to see Rachel for a while. He could see Kotkin instead.

NINA TOLD LUKE THE TRUTH. SHE EXPLAINED THAT SHE HAD TO go to school to learn how to make designs, that she wanted to do something, the way Daddy did something.

"But you take care of me," Luke said.

She didn't tiptoe. She said she had to do something besides be a mommy. She contradicted Eric's halting, guilty speech of the previous night. Eric had told Luke that Mommy had to work, that people worked to make money, and money was needed to live. That wasn't the truth. Nina couldn't bear to hurt Luke—and pretend the hurt wasn't intended. She didn't bother to explain her logic to Eric; it wouldn't be logic to him.

Luke's blue jewels, shimmering with emotion, bravely held her in their light, wanting to know more. "What kind of designs?" he asked.

She showed him the dresses in her closet to illustrate. Luke made a game of it. He ran into the ocean of hanging fabrics, their hems washing over his head, waves of silk and wool and cotton. "Soft," he said for the silk.

"Right, that's silk."

"Scratchy!"

"That's wool."

Luke paused under the cotton dress. His head popped inside, then appeared again. "Soft and scratchy. Like a towel."

"Right! Very good description, Luke. That's cotton. Towels are made of cotton."

Luke ran into her legs and hugged her knees. "Mommy," he said in his sweet, high trill, singing to her. "Mommy."

"You want to see where I'll be going?"

Luke looked shocked, as if she had offered something forbidden. He nodded cautiously, afraid of the admission. She took him to FIT and pointed to the featureless, undesigned buildings where her classes would be. After that, they ate in a coffee shop, a room of trapped air that had been heated and reheated. Its only color was a dull red—the vinyl booths, the pointless glass-colored panels, even the waiter's jackets. Nina thought it funny that this masterpiece of ugliness was so near the Fashion Institute.

Luke adored the coffee shop. He smacked his lips with each sip of his chocolate milk shake, and exclaimed about each glass horror, each phony wood panel, and was delighted by the plastic container of artificial maple syrup made in the shape of a bear.

They took a taxi home. Luke's energy waned, and with it, the props for his courage collapsed. The blue jewels' glint was dulled by water; he leaned his head against her soft breasts, no longer hard with his sustenance, no longer able to soothe every hurt. He cried softly into her lap. She stroked his head and said nothing. Nothing she could say would be true.

Her head throbbed. She loved him, but she wished he would stop. Each tear burned her skin. Each sob punctured her heart.

And was it worth it? Was she really going to make something of her attempt at a career? The chances she would land any kind of job were probably slight. She had never really finished anything. Except for Luke, what crop had she sown and harvested?

And now I'm abandoning him, she thought, sighing as Luke stopped crying and fell into coma, his mouth open, his pacifier falling out. He was still such a baby: still in diapers, still with a plug in his mouth, still clutching his favorite stuffed animal in his crib.

If only Eric's lie had been true. If only they needed the money. What a good, solid excuse for leaving.

Anyway, the value of a mother staying home, that was in the heads of men, magazines, talk-show-segment producers, and the women who wanted to stay home anyway. From the park she knew plenty of children whose mothers worked, and with lousy nannies as caretakers to boot. Still, those children functioned. They had problems. But Luke has problems. Maybe he's got them because I stay home, she thought. A few weeks ago, Eric had come back from the park raving about Byron's gregariousness. Nina admired Byron's boldness too. Byron's mother, whom Nina had never seen with Byron, worked. What harm had that done Byron? Apparently none. It was all blather. The mothers who left their children to work, and the mothers who left work for children—both groups claimed reasons beyond their own interests, as though nothing in life were done for the self.

I have to work. We need the money.

It's better for my child, during these formative years, to have my full attention.

We're having another child because I think it's better not to be a precious only child. Studies have shown that—

The park was littered with women who talked like that. Nina held the limp soft pad of Luke's hand in hers. It was still an exquisite miniature. Of course, sometimes, she wanted to make another baby, another finely worked masterpiece from the forge of her womb. Nothing she had ever done was like it. To repeat the triumph, why, it was pure ego, pure power. It's better not to be an only child, indeed. She kissed the sleeping Luke's hand. No, in this great big greedy world, it was impossible to find people who did things to satisfy their own desires.

Luke was a dead weight as Nina carried him out of the cab and into the building lobby.

"Ah, sleeping," the old ladies of the lobby said. At the sound of their voices, Luke nestled against Nina's breasts. They were smaller now than before she got pregnant, a percentage evaporated forever into his mouth. Another kid, and someone might consider her small-breasted. Three or four, and she'd be almost flat. Maybe not. Maybe there was some irreducible size, an invulnerable core. Luke stayed asleep all the way into his crib.

She hurried to clean the apartment. Pearl was due to come at noon. She hoped Luke would still be asleep. Pearl was supposed to start today, spend the next two weeks while Nina could stay at home, and let the transition to full care proceed gradually. Pearl arrived ten minutes early.

"He asleep?" she said right away.

"Yes," Nina said.

"Well, I'd better start cleaning up," Pearl said with an eager look at the living room Nina had just straightened, as if it were going to be a formidable task.

When Luke woke, he was, as usual, reluctant to embrace consciousness; his eyes rolled unmoored in his head, his body felt hot and boneless. Nina carried him past Pearl without making anything of her presence. Luke startled immediately. His back stiffened, his eyes docked on Pearl, and his fingers took hold of Nina with an insistent, and somewhat desperate, grip.

The truth, the truth. "I'm not going anywhere," she whispered.

"Mommy," he answered.

Pearl was so smart. She waved a mute and gentle hello to Luke and then went on cleaning.

They sat together in a clinch for a long time and watched this big black woman work. Pearl disassembled the couch and vacuumed its naked bottom. Luke's eyes got wide at the sight. Pearl found many lost pieces of his toys. She carried them to the sink, cleaned them, and then placed each one on the table in front of Luke, laid out in a line, evenly spaced, like jewels on Tiffany's counter. Luke was delighted.

"That's He-Man's sword!" Luke said, his voice soaring up, octave above octave.

"That's a sword!" Pearl said, shaking her head in wonder. "It's not dangerous, is it?"

"Noooo!" Luke laughed, although his eyes teared. "It's made of plastic," he said.

"Plaster?" Pearl said, not used to Luke's babyish pronunciations, sometimes chewing hard consonants into softness, sometimes stretching already long vowels into marathon journeys.

"Plastic!" Luke shouted, but the volume didn't make his enunciation clearer.

"Plastic," Nina said to help.

"Plastic!" Pearl understood. "You know what that is?"

Luke was still unaware that his vocabulary was precocious. He learned the words to understand and express himself, not to gain adult praise. Nina had done her best about that, shushing Eric, and Eric's parents for that matter, when they began to exclaim at one of Luke's sentences. Luke stared at Pearl with a puzzled frown. "Actually," Luke said, although to anyone but Nina's or Eric's ears the word would sound Achtyewally, "it's colored plastic."

"Of course he does," Nina said to begin Pearl's training— namely, that the acquisition of knowledge was to be taken for granted. "Luke knows about wood and metal and plastic and tile and cotton and wool and silk. Everybody knows about those things."

"And Formica," Luke said.

Pearl queried Nina with her brows. "Formica," Nina translated.

"My, my," Pearl said, and looked into Nina's eyes with a startled and impressed expression.

"We saw fake Formica today," Luke said. This sentence took awhile to produce and obviously baffled Pearl.

"We went to a coffee shop where they had tables made of Formica, but the Formica was made to look like wood," Nina said.

"That was good," Luke judged.

"Uh-huh," Pearl said. "Could you help me with something, Luke? I don't know where you keep your toys, you know, where I should be putting all these things so you can find them. Would you show me?"

"Mommy," Luke said, and grabbed her.

"Let's go to your room and show Pearl where everything belongs."

"Okay." Luke relaxed at the assurance that Nina would also come.

Pearl smiled at Nina over Luke's head as they flanked him in his slow waddle to his room. Once they were there, Luke's energy surged, happy in his role of guide. Pearl knelt beside him and listened earnestly. She missed every third word, but each time asked Luke to repeat it. Then Luke began to misunderstand Pearl's southern accent, her abbreviated vowels and softened consonants. Pearl sounded like a soothing mellow saxophone; Luke trilled above her restful melody, his song faster and gayer as he gained confidence in Pearl. They had to repeat a lot to each other, but Pearl began to make fun of her own pronunciations and somehow convinced Luke that the reason she had trouble understanding him was that she spoke so poorly.

Nina retired to the back of the room. At first, from time to time, Luke glanced in her direction or addressed his comment to her. Each time, Pearl answered before Nina could.

Nina felt herself start to disappear. She could imagine a day when time would pass faster than the second-by-second creep of Luke's infancy; she could imagine a time when Luke might not need her. He talked and talked to Pearl. Now Pearl let him go on without asking for clearer repronunciations; she let his talk streak, his comfort increasing as they built a huge wood-block castle for He-Man. Nina knew Pearl had his confidence entirely when Luke said that Pearl could pretend she was She-Ra.

"Luke," Nina said.

He almost gasped. Luke swiveled on the cushion of his diaper and looked scared. "What!"

"I'm going to take a nap. Do you want to take a nap with me?"

"No," he said, his face darkening.

"Would you rather just keep playing with Pearl?"

"I'd like that," Pearl said.

"Okay," Luke said, reluctantly.

Nina walked out. She held her breath as she went into her bedroom—my God, to be alone in her own bedroom in the middle of the afternoon—and lay down.

There was a silence, ominous she feared, from Luke's room. He might follow her any second.

Please, Luke, enjoy yourself.

"I have the power!" She heard his little voice soar. "I am He-Man!"

BIG BOY BYRON GRABS HOLD OF THE STEEL BAR, COLD TO HIS touch, and swings at Mommy. He lets go and flies. The branches of the trees catch him.

Below Mommy calls, "Byron!" She is angry.

Byron drops at her, Big Cat Byron, claws out, ready to tear her; she collapses like an empty dress. And he can't see, he can't see!

Byron woke up into the dark. "Mommy," he said.

Voices rumbled in the hallway. His penis was pressed on. He let go. The warmth spread everywhere; a hot bath like a hug kept him company. Daddy was home; that was his voice talking to Mommy.

You have to be changed, Byron.

Byron pushed at the blankets. They didn't move.

Big boy Byron push. He used his special powers and kicked the bricks off him. He could break walls; he could smash buildings.

The warmth was going away. The floor was cold.

Mommy doesn't like diapers. Dirty diapers. Byron pulled at his soft blue fur. It was wet at the rubber band. Get off me, slime.

His hands could be strong, made of metal—

He heard a baby cry. What baby? Mommy and Daddy have a baby?

He pulled them off, the pj's, and his claws ripped the diaper Band-Aids out. The fluffy white was now damp. His penis and bottom felt cool and happy.

The baby cried. What baby?

"Mommy," he said. No answer. Byron walked to his door and looked at the hallway. The floor was black in spots; the open door to the kitchen disappeared into nothingness. It was a long way to Mommy.

"I can't," his daddy said.

There was light around their door, glowing yellow, yellow pee door. Mommy was the baby. She was crying.

"I can't," his daddy said.

Byron felt fear. His body chilled; there were things behind him, reaching with their claws for his cold little body, for his little penis and bare behind.

"Mommy! Mommy! Mommy! They're going to eat me! Mommy! Help!"

The door exploded into light. Daddy came at him, making crashing sounds. "Byron, what is it?"

"I'm scared! I peed! I'm scared! Help me!"

Daddy picked him up; his clothes felt rough, but warm. Mommy was behind. Her face was right at his, meeting him at Daddy's shoulder. Byron couldn't see her eyes.

"What's the matter, baby?" Mommy asked. "You had a bad dream?"

"What's dream?" Byron asked.

"While you were sleeping," Daddy said.

"Did you think something bad was happening?" Mommy said.

"Monsters. Tigers want to eat me." There were big cats, everything. Look in the kitchen! Yellow monster cat! "I'm scared." He screamed to chase it away.

"There's nothing there," Mommy said, and kissed his hand, the hand he had pointed at the kitchen darkness.

"In the kitchen?" Daddy said, and turned, Byron turning with him. "I'll show you."

"No! No!" Byron squeezed Daddy to make him stop.

"That's all right," Daddy said. "I won't let go of you. Turn on the light, Diane."

The hall blew up white and orange. It shrank. Nothing but the dumb hall. Mommy lit the kitchen. The same. Nothing but the things, the cooking things.

"You took your diaper off?" Mommy said.

Mommy's eyes had cried; her mouth was down. "You cry?" Byron said.

Mommy closed her face on his, shutting out light. Her cheeks were slippery like ice, but warm like pillows. "Do you want me to lie down with you?"

"Yes," Byron said, and leaped from Daddy to Mommy. She put him in a new diaper and new fur, red now, like the picture of Daddy's burning tiger. Mommy carried him to bed.

"I'm the baby," Byron said.

"Yes." Mommy laughed.

"Only babies cry," Byron said.

Mommy got under the sheets with him. He put his feet on her stomach and dove his head into the hot cave of her arms. "I'm in the mommy cave," he told her.

"Go to sleep now," Mommy said.

Don't want to. But the hot lowered his eyes, only the top of his head was cool and not sleeping. Deep in the mommy cave, everything clean and dry, he was a baby and safe. Safe. And a baby.

* * *

"I THINK WE SHOULD"—MOMMY SAID MORE THINGS TO PEARL LUKE couldn't hear—"the park." Luke took his pacifier from the table and pushed it in. That made his mouth feel happy and full, but his body was too big. He climbed on the couch and snuggled into the corner. He pulled his blankey up to his chin and rubbed against the smooth. Mommy would go away, really away, today.

His eyes hurt.

"Luke." Mommy's voice was too fast and too high. "Luke, we're going to get dressed—"

"No!" he said, and then hid behind the blanket, frightened by his own angry voice.

"To go to the park," Mommy said. She wouldn't let him say no. "I have to go to school today. I thought you'd walk me to the bus and then you and Pearl can go on to the park."

"No," he said softly this time, and hid, thinking: If I stay home, then Mommy can't go.

"Really?" Mommy was dressed like a going-out night, a grown-up night. "I have to go soon. I thought you'd like to walk me to the bus."

Luke stared at Mr. Rogers. He was painting his swing yellow. Daddy had made the tape. Luke could remember Daddy pointing to the recorder button: this is how you turn it on in case Pearl doesn't know. Why wouldn't she know? What's wrong with her?

"Luke?" Mommy was over him now. Her knees were dark from the nets stretched over them. "It's beautiful out. I don't want you to stay here all day watching television."

He held on to the TV with his eyes. Don't look. Her smell covered him. Soft lips kissed his head. Don't look.

"Luke?" she whispered. "Let's get dressed."

Mr. Rogers was showing a film. A film of how they make yellow paint. "Look," Luke said.

"What's that?" came Mommy's voice, like the rain, everywhere and above.

"Making yellow."

"What? I can't hear you with your pacifier."

No. Keep it.

"Oh, I see. Yellow. So that's how they do it. I'll bring your clothes and get you dressed while you watch."

He kept his eyes on the TV. He got the Feeling and moved his bottom to rub it in and away. You press the power and it pops up. The tape goes in—which way? Which way? Pearl won't know. Remember which way the tape goes, Luke. Pearl won't know. Why not?

He saw something at the living-room doorway. Pearl stood there with her jacket on.

No no no no no no no no no no.

The color was dust; the paint was milk. Together they make yellow.

Mommy carried his clothes in. She flipped him back on the couch. Luke held on to the TV with his eyes and didn't look, not at her, not at Pearl.

No no no no no no no no.

Mr. Rogers talked about yellow. Yellow flashing lights, yellow crayons, yellow curtains. Yellow blankey. Smooth on his cheek.

It hurt when Mommy turned off the TV. The world got quiet and small and sad. His eyes closed against the pain, the weakness. Mommy picked him up. Pearl had the stroller waiting.

No no no no no no no.

He pressed his face into her, but felt only the rough clothes, not Mommy. "I want to go with you," he said to her.

"I have to go," she said, soft, but angry.

"I want! To go with you."

"You want me to go?"

The stroller was going, he was going.

No no no no.

"I want to!" he yelled, and lost his pacifier.

No no.

He let the crying come out.

All the noes were crying out.

"I'm sorry, honey." Mommy was everywhere and above.

The elevator sank through the floor. She gave him his pacifier back. He felt it fill his mouth, wet inside, outside.

The wall door popped him out into the lobby. There were all those legs and clothes. Voices: "What's the matter, baby?"

Ramon bothered him. "Watch you cry."

He hid his face. Don't watch.

"Watch matter? Big boy don't cry."

"Yes, they do," Mommy said. "Everybody cries sometimes."

The yellow covered him, hot and smooth and rough.

No.

PETER THOUGHT: I'VE BECOME A CHARACTER IN A POORLY WRIT-ten play. Recently, he had seen several with scenes just like the one he was suddenly playing himself. Diane had called out to him when he came home. He had been at a late dinner with a lively group after an Uptown Theater premiere. They had been at Orso, a de-lightful place, jammed with his favorite celebrities, theater people, and he was smashed. What a good word for it. Smashed, all the little fearful repressions repressed, the opaque partition between outward and inward self smashed by gin. He came home feeling young, relieved the affair with Rachel was over, looking forward to tomorrow's session, and to a weekend of interesting theater and ballet—and then Diane called to him.

He went into the bedroom, bobbing happily on his sea of alcohol. Diane was in a long nightshirt from L. L. Bean, surrounded by papers, the room filled with cigarette smoke. Maybe she'll die of lung cancer, he thought with disinterest, wondering, not hoping.

"Peter," she said in the fake formal tone people adopt when they're about to speechify. And she went on about her worries. Incredibly obvious worries. Horrible clichés that should be cut from any good drama. She was aging. Byron was becoming precious. He could use a sibling. A sibling? That set off his alarms.

He watched her talk on; he stopped hearing. Her head levitated in his slowed vision. "You want to have another child," Peter interrupted.

She paused before she answered. "I wanted to know what you think about it."

He laughed, he couldn't stop himself, there was no repressing the nonrepression. "Bullshit. You want me to say yes, you don't want me to think about it."

"Does that mean no?"

"I don't want to have another child."

Diane seemed surprised. How could she be surprised? He had never wanted to have a child. Had he made any speeches that having a kid was great? How could she be surprised? Diane glanced down at her papers, intent on them for a moment. "Has being a father been that bad?" she asked with a sudden look at him.

"No," he said with a groan, although why he was positively negative was a mystery.

"Would you rather we hadn't had Byron? Sometimes I think about you asking me to have an abortion—"

"Wait a minute!" He couldn't stop himself; she was insane, she was out of touch, spinning in the solar system. "Are you saying if I don't want to have another child, it means I want to kill my son?"

Diane pushed the papers off her lap and pulled her legs up in a crouch, like an aggressive animal, a cat poised. "Are you listening to *me*? Or are you talking to someone else?"

"What?" He felt drunk, stupid. Maybe he wasn't understanding her.

"*I'm* in this room. Not your shrink."

"Maybe we should talk about this in the morning."

"No! That means we'll never talk about it. Yes, I want to have another child. Not only that. I want you to be a father. Your son is suffering. Do you hear me? *He is suffering.*"

God, the words hurt. They could punish. He remembered noticing that when a scene becomes emotional, the words could be physical, hit you, even in your comfortable aisle seat, whack you in the chest, and knock your breath out. He thought suddenly of Byron, like himself, abandoned without acknowledgment of hurt, living with a ghostly parentage, seen but not felt. Her words transmitted that image.

"I can't," he heard himself mumble. "I can't," he pleaded.

"You can't what?" Diane persisted.

Peter stared at her. She isn't afraid of me.

"You can't be a father to that wonderful boy? That's too hard for you?"

She doesn't want truth; she wants to be righteous. "I'm not interested in any of this," his voice answered. He was banging inside his body, swelling up to the edges of the shell—hatching. "I don't want to be married to you. I don't want to be a father. I told you that. You didn't listen. You never really listen to me. You think I'm someone to be manipulated, you think everyone is to be manipulated, so the world works the way you want it to work. I can't be what you want. I can't! I can't!" His face had burst through, pressed out into cool world, hot and alive against the chill.

Diane sat still. She looked girlish. Her long nose and dark skin gave her face a tough edge, but her eyes got big, her mouth trembled. She looked ready to cry. "I don't want to manipulate you—"

But Peter was out of the shell; he was born again, new-feathered and strutting in the sun. "Yes, you do. You think your desires are good and my desires are bad. So you ignore my desires, like I'm a two-year-old and you know better. It's a vanity all middle-class women have. They live their lives with the unexpressed conviction they are more moral than men. That they care about real things and men don't. All the men believe it too! But I don't. You're just as selfish as I am! You want to control Byron, you want to control me, you want us to meet your schedule. Well, I can't! I can't! No matter how much you badger me, I can't! I can't!"

She was crying. In a strange way: her head was still as stone, her forehead, her cheeks, her lips didn't move, but a stream of water dripped straight down, a statue weeping. "I love you—" she started to say.

But he was free; he was born whole again; no matter how bad

he was, he was real. "I don't love you," he said quite happily. "I don't give a damn about you."

Diane bent forward, wailing. Peter was surprised. He reached toward her, reached for the words, to put them back, put them back into his ugly mind. He hadn't remembered that she was real too.

"I'm sorry," he said. "I don't mean that." She went on crying. "I just can't be what you want. I can't. I can't. That's all. I can't."

Diane cried. Peter watched. He tried to think of what he might say.

"I can't," he repeated.

From the next room, Byron screamed. Byron screamed the scream of innocence murdered. Byron screamed right into his father's bones. A cold scream of murder that whistled through Peter. Peter ran to save him.

NINA DIDN'T LIKE THE FEEL OF SCHOOL AT FIRST. THE BUILD-ings were too big. The people were too big also. She wasn't used to being around such large people: competent, talky, able to do things, argue, have opinions, look her in the face, or down at her—everything oppressed her senses.

Each frustrating day at school began as a tragedy at home. Luke's anxiety would start as soon as Pearl arrived. That first week, Luke saw Nina off with an utter collapse into bawling despair. Nina assumed the worst was over. But the second week, Luke took to grabbing Nina's ankles and begging her to stay. It would have been comic if it weren't so crazy. What was wrong? Nina came back home at the time she promised; Luke had no complaints about Pearl. There were many things Pearl didn't get quite right, but they were trivial and soon corrected. Pearl reported Luke was basically happy. Nina stood in the hallway one morning after she left, and listened for fifteen minutes. The tears stopped after five. She heard laughter and shouts of play after ten. She came downtown at lunch-time one afternoon and watched Luke from a distance while he played with Byron in Washington Square Park—the kid was happy! So why was he clutching her shoes, screaming, "Don't leave me, Mommy. Don't leave me, Mommy"?

Maybe it was because of Luke's gender, she thought one day as she eavesdropped on three students before the start of a color-design class. The trio was in their late teens, a boy and two girls. The young man was a handsome Italian. The girls called him Sal. Sal teased the girls. He complained that women were faithless. Sal's long eyes were like Luke's in their shape, and while he moaned that women always did him wrong, those eyes looked wise and clever and in control, the way Luke's did now when he pulled on her ankles. Maybe it's a genetic code in men, Nina thought. Shout your dependence on women, complain of separation, and have a ball while the women slink off miserable in their guilt.

Sal was so self-aware that he noticed Nina for the first time, because she was staring at him. "Look at her, she's another one," Sal said, his eyes making fun of himself. "She's deciding right now if she'll bother to break my heart."

"No, I'm not," Nina answered without thinking. She hadn't spoken to any of the students yet, didn't want to, wanted to stay outside, just learn, not become one of them.

"She was thinking you're full of shit," the stupider of the girls said, and then giggled hard, quickly ashamed of her blunt remark.

"Probably," Sal said, "just thinking I'm a jerk, right?"

"I was thinking you're like my son," Nina answered, again saying something she hadn't meant to.

It got quite a response. The girls roared, as though Nina had put Sal down, really embarrassed him. He seemed to think so too. He got red in the face.

"I mean, your eyes," Nina apologized. "The shape of your eyes is like my son's."

"Yeah?" Sal wasn't convinced. He wanted to know, but he asked in a sarcastic tone so he wouldn't be risking his dignity again.

"Really," she said in her hopelessly thin, earnest voice. All those Jews, blacks, Italians, Greeks, their voices boomed or sang or moaned—even the rest of her family had music in their throats— but she had this dumb unmodulated monotone, like a public-address announcement.

"Well, that's nice." Sal relaxed.

"How old's your son?" the stupid girl asked angrily, presumably irritated by Nina's success in complimenting Sal.

"Two and a half," Nina answered.

The girls broke up again. "Yeah, a two-year-old! That's you, Sal," the stupid one said. Sal looked confused and then hurt.

The teacher came in and began to talk. It was interesting, but Nina couldn't stay with it; her mind went back to Sal's reaction when Nina announced Luke's age. Sal didn't understand the compliment Nina had given out. In fact, it was such great praise Nina had regretted its escape. Luke's eyes were probably the most beautiful in the world.

Later, Nina caught Sal looking at her. Nina had lost the logic of the teacher's remarks and her eyes lit on Sal. Sal's eyes were judging her, studying her hips and middle. Looking for the sloppy fat of pregnancy, she thought, and sucked in. But she was in good shape. Sure, the hard board for a belly had warped, but she wasn't fat. It was obvious that Sal worked out. His shoulders almost had wings; his ass was tight and hard. When he moved his arms, the muscles sighed and rose under the skin, undulating gently but suggesting force. He had a pretty face, his beard was very light, and his chin came to a delicate point. He was a half man, a young buck. He had no stomach. Not even a suggestion of roundness. Flat. His neck was thick, though, and a little short. If he lost his hair, let his belly go, he'd become a slovenly middle-aged man. This was his prime, his youth. Luke would grow into that. And she would get old.

Did she mind? No, she wanted to see Luke become that beautiful mix of man and boy, arrogant and shy, a brand-new machine, its clean engine full of power, its driver both reckless and scared.

Sal lifted his eyes from his inspection of her figure and met her eyes. He almost fell over, he was so quick to break the eye contact. He even turned his body away, desperate to erase any evidence that he had been curious. At his age, Nina would have been the one to pretend she hadn't noticed. In fact, she would never have returned the glance at all, watching him watch her out of the corner of her eye, hoping, wondering, resenting, and longing. Not now. There was nothing to fear from men. They always stayed boys, no matter what. They were gentle; even the brutal ones were frightened, she knew that from Luke. Women bend, men break, her mother once told her. It was true. They thought it was all up to them; they had no humility in the face of nature; they actually believed some sort of triumph or defeat was possible.

She looked at Sal's lap, at his tight jeans. There was a large oval formation at his groin, as if he were wearing sports equipment. Is he stuffing it? she wondered. There was a kid in high school who did that. He had had some calamity—it shifted at a dance? She didn't remember. It was hilarious and quite a shock. Only the girls were supposed to be faking size. Another myth: men were not only frailer than women but vainer too.

She imagined a long white penis, hairless, a giant version of Luke's.

The image embarrassed her. She shook it off and concentrated on the lecture.

She was able to pay attention toward the end; she even got an idea for the line she would have to draw for her leisure-wear class. She stayed back and quickly made notes of the color combinations the teacher's principles inspired. She noticed Sal dawdle a moment too, and she felt his breath on her neck, and his voice whispered into her ear, "Do you really have a two-year-old kid?"

"Yes," she answered, puzzled.

Sal also seemed baffled. "I thought it might just be a put-down."

"Why?"

"Why not? Everybody puts me down."

Nina assured him she hadn't and then left. Not quickly or coolly, she certainly didn't want Sal to think she didn't like him—obviously anything less than admiration would kill the fellow—but she didn't want to have to flatter him for ten minutes so his confidence could be completely restored.

After all, she had to get home. There she had two boys who would need all the praise she could spare.

HE HAD THE FEELING. GO AWAY, GO AWAY. HE RAN INTO THE living room, head down, butting the air like Ram Man, past Pearl, past Skeletor. "He-Man! Help me!"

"I help you," Pearl said.

"No! You're not He-Man."

"I'm sorry. It's so nice out today, isn't it, Luke?"

Want to stay. "I don't know. I haven't been out."

"Well, why don't I help you get your clothes on?"

The Feeling. Twist and squeeze and go away. Push it out, Luke. You'll feel better.

"You have to go?" Pearl said, very soft.

"No!" Luke jumped at the sound of his voice.

Run! Head down, butt them down, smash! "I'm coming, He-Man!"

"Byron's gonna be at the park today." Pearl's voice followed him. "I talked to Francine. She said they'd be there at eleven. It's half past now. Byron be so sad if you don't come."

Luke saw his new figure—Sy-Klone—twisting arms, tornado man. He could show Byron. Byron said he's gonna get it, but I already have it now. But Byron would play with it.

"Look." Pearl's voice was with him in his room. "I ironed your favorite overalls."

"I want to go to the park," Luke said.

"You do!" Pearl acted so surprised. "That's a good idea, Luke."

The Feeling was gone anyway.

"FRANCINE!" BYRON YELLED. "FRANCINE!"

"Go," said the stupid boy behind.

Byron felt the metal. He could bend metal. He was big. "Francine, watch me!"

She didn't look. "Go!" said the stupid boy.

"No!" Byron pushed his face at the boy. Stupid. My eyes can deeestroy! Where's Luke? "Go away!"

"It's my turn, poop head!" Stupid said.

"Poop head!" Byron laughed in Stupid's face. "Poop not on head."

"You're a poop head!" Stupid said.

Byron's legs felt small. Stupid laughed. Laughed at Byron. "I am not," Byron said.

"Poop head, poop face, poop eyes, poop nose, poop head!"

Byron wanted Francine! "Francine! Francine!"

"What?" Francine called up, her funny hair orange in the sun.

"Watch me slide!"

"Go, poop head!" Stupid said.

Byron's face hurt. "Don't say that!" he yelled.

"Go!" Stupid pushed. Byron felt the metal melt. His legs flew. The slide slapped his cheek. He held on and cried and cried and cried.

"What's the matter with you!" Francine yelled at Stupid. "You don't push people down the slide. Byron, honey, let me look, come on—oh, it's okay, Byron. Don't hurt that much."

"He pushed!" There, Stupid, you are bad. You hurt me.

"He's a baby!" Stupid said.

"Am not!" Byron yelled, and cried again.

"That's right," Francine told Stupid. "And you're too old to be pushing little babies on the slide. You're big enough to know better."

"What's wrong?" said a grown-up.

"Your boy pushed my baby." Francine was not scared of grown-ups.

"He wouldn't go!" Stupid said.

Byron cried hard. "He hurt me!" There, Stupid. You bad. "He said I was poop," Byron yelled.

"Did not," Stupid said. "I said he was a poop head. And he is. I'm going." Stupid ran down the steps and out to the sandbox. His grown-up left too.

Byron put his warm face into Francine's pillows.

"Okay." She put him down. "You're okay. Don't be crying so much about it. You're not hurt. Big boys don't cry. You see he called you a baby 'cause you were crying."

"He pushed me."

"Next time he push you, you push him right back."

Byron is big. Grab Francine leg, tree leg, and pull. Swing on the tree, Big Cat Byron!

"Go on, now. You're all right. Go on and play."

"I'm hungry"

"Hungry? You had a snack just ten minutes ago! You're not hungry."

"Yes, I am!" Hold on to the dinosaur leg. Big Cat Byron, claw!

"No!" Francine push. Push away. "Go and play now. We'll have lunch later."

"I want—"

THERE'S LUKE!

"Luke! Luke! Luke! Luke!" Hop, hop, hop. He doesn't see. "Luke, here! Come here! Luke! Luke! Luke!"

There. He comes, he comes with the grown-up Pearl. He has Sy-Klone!

Twist and twist and twist, arms flying.

"Hi," Luke said. "See? I have Sy-Klone."

"Let me see." Byron big and bigger takes the toy and makes it go, arms flying, smacking bad guys. "Let's play He-Man, Luke."

"Okay."

Byron takes Luke's hand. "You know, Luke, you're my best friend. I love you."

"I know," said Luke.

BYRON DIDN'T KNOW HOW TO WORK SY-KLONE. "Byron—" Took so long to say. Byron was gone already. In the sandbox, burying Sy-Klone. "That's not—" Luke tried to hurry there.

Byron was talking. "I can tunnel. Find Skeletor and beat him."

No, no. He doesn't tunnel. Sy-Klone flies. He makes a tornado and flies. "Byron—"

Byron grabbed Luke. Luke tried to get his hand away. Byron squeezed too hard. "Let—"

"There's Stupid!" Byron put his face right up to Luke's, blowing at him. "He called me poop head."

The Feeling. No. "What?"

Byron pulled Luke down. His knee hit Sy-Klone. It hurt. Byron pointed to a bigger boy. "That's Stupid. He pushed me."

"What did you say about poop?"

Byron whispered. "He called me poop head."

"Poop head?" Luke thought of a head covered with—He laughed. "That's crazy."

"You're a poop head!" Byron called out to the bigger boy.

"Shut up," the bigger boy answered.

Byron twisted and twirled. He was being Sy-Klone!

Luke reached to stop Byron. "Don't—"

"Whee." Byron whirled across the sandbox. His shoes dug holes; his arms flashed around and around. "I am Sy-Klone!" Byron said to the bigger boy.

"Shut up!" The bigger boy picked up sand and pulled his hand back.

"Watch—" Luke jumped, Ram Man, ready to butt away the sand.

The wind hit. Rough rain splattered on Luke's face.

Eyes! It's in eyes!

Luke fell, he wasn't Ram Man, he yelled for Pearl, put his hands on his eyes and tried to get the rough lumps out.

He couldn't open his eyes, he rubbed—something stuck his eye. He yelled and let go, pushed his head down, to hide, to go to sleep, to be away from this.

"He did it! He did it! He did it!" Byron yelled.

Pearl was there. "No, I didn't," Luke said to her.

"Did it get in your eyes?" Pearl's voice came in between the hurt.

He tried to open them—the roughness tore at his head—he screamed again and kept them shut.

"I want to go home!" Luke yelled. "I want to go home!"

"I'm sorry," a child's voice said.

"He's a big boy, he should know better." Pearl sounded deep and heavy. Luke smelled Pearl, he was in her arms.

"I want to go home!" Luke yelled to her. "I want Mommy!"

His eyes were wet, smooth and silk now, covering the roughness. He tried to open them.

No! No! It hurt, it hurt, it hurt.

"You just rest, don't rub. We going right home."

Home. Home. He cried, he cried, he cried. It felt so good to cry.

"Luke, Luke, Luke." Byron jumped at him. "Don't go, Luke!"

Press against Pearl. Take me home.

"Byron, leave him alone."

"Luke, Luke, Luke." Byron jumped at him. "Don't cry. Big boys don't cry."

No, no, no, no.

11

FRIDAY AFTERNOONS WERE THE HARDEST FOR ERIC. THE weekend was ahead. The restless, worrisome weekend, with the market closed and the TV and newspapers full of conflicting opinions on the economic future. Three nights and two days to remember the week's mistakes and missed opportunities, three nights and two days of relentless child care, his body always all on the move, his mind wandering again and again through the bearish article in *Barron's* on the oil group, recalling Rukeyser's guests' comments on *Wall Street Week*, refighting arguments with Joe and Sammy, winning them this time, booting up his home computer and studying Tom's portfolio, dreaming of the numbers going up and up—

Was it time to raise the stops?

Should he double that position?

Should he leverage more? Trade the futures? Or hedge with the options?

He asked and reasked, with no market open to engage his attention, to contradict, to confirm, to react to, nothing but hour after hour of ghostly combat with greed and fear.

You've done so well so far. Relax.

But had *he* done it? Or was it Joe? Was the success merely due to Eric's being leashed to Joe's firm hand, Joe's guidance in control: 10 percent down and out, trailing stops, minimize losses, maximize profits, keep it simple, don't diversify so broadly so that you're always losing somewhere, pick the hot areas and stay with them. The trend is your friend.

But were Joe's tactics so great anyway? These days they weren't making money fast enough. They had stayed only a few percentage points ahead of the averages, and they were riding one of the great bull markets. Yet every day picking winners got tougher.

Joe had talked Eric out of two gambles, on bankruptcy turn-arounds, that would have worked. Four hundred percent returns, maybe enough to get Tom bragging in Boston, pull in some of his country-club buddies' money.

Why couldn't Eric become another Gabelli, another Peter Lynch? Why couldn't Eric manage a billion dollars? It wasn't that hard, it was just knowing the right people, getting the dough and doing what he had been doing—

But again, ask yourself: do you deserve the credit for the success of Tom's portfolio?

Sammy had returned to the office a week after the fight with Joe in which Sammy had implied that Joe kept Eric employed only because of Tom's money. Hoping for a retraction, Eric pressed Sammy about the argument, although Sammy seemed not to want to discuss it. Eric prevailed and got an apology. Sammy explained that he had been upset for weeks, convinced his father had little faith in him, and so he'd taken that out on Eric. Eric believed that was the truth.

But Eric didn't think Sammy believed his own apology. It was the obvious excuse and so Sammy said it. The retraction, once extracted, made Eric feel worse.

So what do I care what Sammy thinks?

What do I care what *I* think if I'm making money?

But it wasn't enough. This market might be a unique opportunity. Wall Street was awash with geniuses, dozens of people in their twenties and thirties casting huge nets into a harbor fluttering and shimmering with millions in salaries and bonuses. By comparison, Eric wasn't doing that well. Eric was still on the street corner, the hustling end of the business, leafleting the suckers to get them inside the casino. The Harvard M.B.A.'s and lawyers, with their merger and acquisition magic, their junk bunk financing, their respectable pimping—they were making the real money. Wall Street was on a bender, and it would come to an end, it always had before, and Eric might come away with little more than a hangover. He had to steal some of the valuables, stuff his pockets, make enough of an impression on the host to be invited back for the quiet gatherings that hard times would bring.

Eric became obsessed with catching the wave just before all those flopping, gleaming fish were sucked back to the ocean depths. Eric went to the Strand, a secondhand bookstore, and bought a load of books on the 1929 crash. What everyone forgets, Eric told an attentive but bewildered Nina, is that you can make even bigger money when everything falls apart. Actually, the biggest fortunes were made in the year following the '29 crash.

Eric tried to talk to Joe about his desire to be prepared to short the market, to ride the wave out to sea, and smile gaily back at those fishermen, their nets suddenly empty.

"Are you crazy?" Joe answered. "This bull market is a runaway train. I can understand considering getting off. But stepping in front of it?"

"If you think it's a runaway train, then why are we still in the first car?"

"We have our stops to protect us."

"That's just avoiding losing money, Joe. We make money when the market goes up, we're aggressive, why can't we be aggressive when it goes down?"

"We will be! I made plenty of money in 'seventy-four. I did all right in 'eighty-one. But you have to wait until the trend develops. We're not in the business of picking tops and bottoms."

Joe was content with the money they made. To Joe, his income of half a million a year was extraordinary, way beyond the expectations of his youth. Joe, naturally, thought a young man Eric's age should be happy with two hundred thousand per annum. Certainly, if a seer had come to Eric five years before and shown him his present circumstances, Eric would have assumed his future self would be happy.

But he felt diminished by his surroundings, a town house shadowed by skyscrapers, a doorman hustling tips while inside the luxury apartments twenty-nine-year-old Ivy Leaguers made millions.

So quit. Contact the brokerage houses and try to land a job as an equity fund manager. Call Tom and ask him to arrange a luncheon of his rich friends for me to pitch to.

Or—more to the point—take off the leash. Buy the S&P futures, take a big position in the biotechnology stocks, double up sometimes instead of getting stopped out, be bolder, be bolder, be bolder!

But this was Nina's family's money. Her future presumably. Eventually, his son's. He had to take care, go slow, listen to Joe—

Fridays faced Eric with an uninterrupted weekend of these arguments. And then, after only a month at FIT, Nina's work impressed one of her teachers, one of the many on the faculty who also ran businesses, and he asked Nina to apprentice three afternoons and occasional evenings a week, in order to work on the spring line. That meant Wednesdays, Thursdays, and Friday nights Eric had almost all of Luke's care to himself. Nina urged Eric to ask Pearl to stay late, but Eric felt it was wrong to sit in the house and let some black woman be with his son while he was right there, perfectly able. Besides, wasn't that one of the benefits of his work? The market closed at four. He could be home by five, five-thirty at the latest; he could read his material after Luke was in bed. On the nights Nina had to stay late, Eric could be alone to dream, to yell at himself, to question his ideas, to get tough, to get ready for the day that was coming soon when he would catch the wave and ride away laughing on a sea of money.

The third Friday he was alone with Luke, Eric had, over Joe's objections, bought a small position in one of the new genetic-engineering stocks, DNA Technology. DNA had dipped on an overall down day for the market, and Eric wanted to jump on at the low price. Joe argued, and whined, and teased. But Eric bought anyway, and then Joe said his worst: "All right, have it your way. But you're on your own. Just your father-in-law, nobody else."

Joe's words were like a curse, a poisonous cloud hovering about Eric's shoulders. Eric went home in this gloomy atmosphere. Pearl greeted him nervously.

What? She's worried I don't have her money?

Eric immediately produced her salary, two hundred and fifty dollars, to forestall any concern, counting out the bills and placing them on the kitchen counter.

We should pay her more, he thought. It's too much already, he also thought.

"We went to the park to play with Byron. You know, he's a rough boy, not like Luke. So sweet. Well, Byron was teasing this other boy—"

Eric looked into the living room for Luke. Usually, at the sound of Eric's key in the lock, Luke was at the door, little man, way down below, his head tilted up to see Daddy, his bright blue eyes open with excitement and wonder. No one had ever waited for Eric with such longing or hugged Eric with so tight an embrace of joy.

"—and he threw some sand. It got into Luke's eye."

Eric saw Luke. He was huddled, collapsed really, into a corner of the couch. Luke's blanket covered half of his face. The television was on, but Luke had only one eye open.

"I put some water in it. My, he didn't like that. But, you know, to clean it out—"

"Hi, Daddy," Luke said in a sad, small, tired voice.

"Let me see your eye," Eric said, in a calm voice, but he was terrified to look. Luke lowered the blanket reluctantly.

It was wet. The surrounding skin was red. Eric reached to lift the lids, but Luke pulled his head away.

"I just want to look," Eric said.

"I put some salt in the water and boiled it first to make sure it was purified," Pearl said.

"Salt?" Eric thought: that's got to be wrong.

"He says it feels better now. I think it's all washed out," Pearl went on in a hasty tone of apology. "This big boy threw sand in his eyes. I yelled at the woman taking care of him. I've seen her. She's no good. She don't pay no mind to what he does."

"I'm sure it's okay," Eric said. He prayed it was. He had no idea what to do. Call a doctor? And say what? He'd sound like a fool. Take him to a doctor? On Friday night? They're all heading to the suburbs. He kissed Luke on the forehead. The skin felt soft and weak and moist—newborn again.

Pearl kept talking. Eric repeated over and over, "I'm sure it's fine, I'm sure it's fine," made nervous by the account of her nursing. Pearl only made things worse when Eric finally got her to the door. "He didn't poop today," she whispered. "That'd be the fourth day now."

Eric didn't know that. Why hadn't Nina told him Luke's constipation had returned?

Eric returned to the living room and sat next to Luke. Luke rested against Eric's body, the blanket once again covering the wounded eye.

He's not right. He's not moving; he's not asking me to toss him in the air, play catch, pretend to be a horse; he's not standing in the middle of the living room and telling about what happened in the park. Nothing about Luke was normal. He didn't yell with pain, he didn't moan—but the whole personality was different from usual on a Friday afternoon. This was the quiet, mournful Luke awaiting a separation, the frail Luke-flower closing his petals in the twilight just before Eric's parents arrived to baby-sit.

Luke laughed at something on *Mister Rogers' Neighborhood*. Eric turned and saw Luke's face open up and relax . . . and then Luke brought a hand quickly to his eye, his face contorted, and he moaned.

"Let me take another—"

"No." Luke groaned and hid his head in the blanket.

"—just to see if there's any more sand." Luke didn't stir. Eric put a hand on Luke's back and patted. It was a miniature of a man's, swelling with Luke's life, so small and so strong. "Let me see. I won't put anything in it."

"Okay," Luke said in a dying voice. He let Eric look, wincing when Eric pulled back the lids.

Eric couldn't tell. How could he? How would he know if there was a microscopic grain? It wouldn't survive Pearl's eye bath, could it? If she was thorough. What about that salt? Well, she said she boiled the water with the salt. Maybe it had boiled away.

Maybe constipation was Luke's real complaint. That was getting worse with each month. Their pediatrician had prescribed a mild laxative, some kind of chocolate stuff, the consistency of pudding, to give Luke before bed. That helped for a while, but it seemed to be getting worse again.

After Eric gave up looking for the invisible grain of sand, he saw Luke squirm, rub his behind back and forth.

"Do you have to go to the bathroom?"

"No!" Luke shouted. That was so rare it startled Eric. The vehemence convinced Eric that the constipation was the real villain.

It's because he's sitting still, Eric decided. He got up and turned off the television. It was obscene, a child watching that much. Luke looked alarmed. "Wanna play He-Man?" Eric said, on his knees on the rug. "I'll be Skeletor."

Luke was so pale. He smiled a little. "Okay."

Eric put his heart into the pretend. "I will destroy you, He-Man!"

"No, you won't," the tiny, bowlegged, soft-faced two-year-old answered. "I have the power!" Luke raised his plump arm to the ceiling and thrust his ballooned belly forward.

Eric jumped to his feet and ran. He made Luke chase him from one room to another. After a few minutes, Luke stopped, his head lowered slightly, his legs coming together. Eric charged him, made Luke keep moving, keep the system going. His eye's fine. He just needs to take a shit.

Luke's face suddenly went red and he stopped again.

"Daddy, I have the Feeling."

"That's okay. Don't worry about it."

"It hurts."

"Come on, He-Man. I'll get to Castle Grayskull before you do and tear it to pieces."

"No, you won't!" Luke forgot his bowels and ran again, his miniature body rocking from side to side as he tried to imitate strength. Luke got ahead of Eric and put his arm out. "Stop, Skeletor! I won't let you pass!" Luke beamed with pride at his successful defense. He smiled into Eric's face, full of his triumph.

Then Luke closed his mouth. His knees buckled slightly; he lowered his chin. He scrunched his neck down. He began to strain, his skin reddening.

What a life, Eric thought as he remembered his dream of managing hundreds of millions of dollars. What a pathetic life, he thought, while he watched his son try to empty his bowels. What a fool I am to dream of millions, he thought, as he cheered Luke on with the intensity of a fan rooting for the home team to score.

* * *

THAT PETER MIGHT NOT DO WHAT DIANE WANTED WHEN IT CAME to major decisions, such as having a second child, was an unexpected discovery.

"You're really surprised?" Betty Winters said over lunch, a few days after Peter had spoken so cruelly on the subject. "He didn't want to have Byron."

"I thought he loved Byron. I thought he'd gotten to like being a father."

"I'm sure he loves Byron."

"I think he hates us," Diane said. She felt so beat. The landscape had been utterly changed. She had worked so hard to make a home, and she'd found too late that the foundation stood on muddy ground. "I've been kidding myself about Peter. I've been telling myself that all his negative talk was just talk, that deep down he wanted me to push him forward, push him to grow up and be a man. He doesn't. He wants to spend his life going to the theater, to museums, talking pretentious nonsense with his artist friends. I thought all that was just being young, you know, something you do when you have the time to do it—"

"But it's Peter's work to go to the theater," Betty said, her sympathetic expression gone. She sounded impatient.

Of course. Betty's husband's a playwright; she thinks it's a worthwhile life too. Diane didn't. Although it was fun meeting the behind-the-scenes people, going to opening night, not merely following the cultural lemmings of New York, but helping to lead them to a nice cliff, nevertheless, it wasn't the real business of life. Although Tony Winters's plays were amusing, they were quite silly. His movie scripts were pleasant, reminiscent of the great old romantic comedies; however, those classics were inconsequential and Tony's modern versions were adolescent. There wasn't a single play that Diane had seen during the ten years she had accompanied Peter to the theater which she could, even for an instant, consider in the same class of seriousness with Shakespeare or Chekhov. And if such a genius was out there, Diane doubted that Peter would be of any use to him. Deep down, did they really think what they did was important, was real in any way, that it was somehow worth a life of childlessness, worth discarding the very tangible result of child rearing? Was Tony Winters ever going to write a play as extraordinary as his handsome, intelligent six-year-old son, or as brave and beautiful as his one-year-old daughter? No matter how many theaters Peter funded, no matter how many lunatic gays or depressed straights he helped with the foundation's money, nothing could equal the glory of creating Byron.

It was so obvious to Diane, a truth glowing in the sky as big and bright and warm as the sun. How could Peter find shadows in this brilliant light?

"Peter's like Tony," Betty said. "He has the sensibility of a creative artist. They go through moods; they can't stand to think that they're married and have kids. Makes them feel ordinary—"

"They *are* ordinary," Diane said, relishing the reassurance of common sense, of what she loved in the law, its ruthless disregard for the distortions of self-delusion, its insistence on fact.

"Well, they're not your average men."

"Feeling that having kids is a drag on your freedom ain't exactly a sophisticated or unusual male reaction," Diane said, enjoying her denigration of Peter and Tony, pleased to irritate Betty's pride in her husband. Tony was worse than Peter, Diane thought. Tony not only ignored his children and, according to Peter, whined about them privately, but also put on a public display of loving them, waxing sentimental at parties on the joys of fatherhood, even exploiting the current rage for involved fatherhood in his recent play. The hero, a thinly disguised portrait of Tony, was shown as a brilliant and charming but adulterous and insecure man, who is finally redeemed when circumstances put him in sole charge of his child during a dangerous illness. "Unconvincing," the *Times* had said about the play's final scene. But the stupid thing ran for almost two years, flattering a city full of yuppie men and reassuring their maltreated, eager-to-be-fooled wives. Like me, Diane thought, suckers desperate to believe they had bested their mothers, had gotten their men to be different.

"You really feel bitter about Peter," Betty said.

"Yeah, I do. I gave him all the room in the world. I got up with Byron every morning, even though my work is hard. Peter has a staff meeting a week, he has a lunch date. That's his workday. The rest of it is going to openings, eating at Orso—some tough life. But I get up with Byron, I make sure there's food in the house—" Diane damned the flow and swallowed the rest of her complaints.

"It's too hard," Betty said quietly. "There's too much stress in your work—"

"My work isn't stressful."

"—Along with having a baby? Diane, it's too hard."

Betty, of course, had downgraded to part-time employment after her first child. With the birth of her second, she had quit altogether. People always believed, no matter what they said, that everyone should copy their life choices. Even if they were miserable. And whether Betty admitted it or not, Tony's play was a public humiliation for Betty, an advertisement that he was consistently unfaithful to her, that he stayed in the marriage only because he loved his children. This point of view was a lie. Diane knew it was a lie. Tony would collapse without Betty; the stuffing would come out of his bright suit of clothing like a scarecrow rotting in an abandoned field. But Tony had manufactured this falsehood into a play, and everybody took it to be true and felt sorry for Betty. Diane wanted so badly to say this to Betty, to make her know the fucking truth. "I've been thinking of quitting," Diane said instead.

"You have." Betty nodded with an obnoxious, knowing air. "You can afford to, right?"

"Peter's rich." That was another thing wrong with Peter, another free pass he'd been given that had made him spoiled and selfish. "Maybe I should do what he's probably doing. Go out and get myself a lover."

Betty, to Diane's surprise, laughed. She looked off musingly. "I'd do it too. But aren't you scared of AIDS? God, when I read those articles, when Tony tells me about—you know Raul Sabas has it?"

"Really?" That was sad. Even in her rage at theater people, Diane got an image of Sabas dancing across the stage and singing of love, his face happy, looking to the sky. "Poor man," she said.

"Yeah, they're saying it's lymphoma, but it's AIDS."

"Well, I might get it anyway," Diane said, determined to be hard, to be truthful. "How the hell do I know who Peter's screwing?"

"Diane, stop it. That's horrible." Betty fussed with her napkin and then tossed it on the table. She picked up her purse and opened it nervously, then stopped. She looked puzzled. "I don't smoke anymore. Can you believe that? I was going for a cigarette."

"Maybe he's gay," Diane said, bored by Betty, especially by her quitting smoking.

"Tony gay!" Betty arched in a funny, cartoon leap, cat on a stove, paws in the air, voice screeching.

"I don't know, but I was talking about Peter. Be just like him—being in the closet. He's in the closet about everything else, every other feeling. Christ, he's got the biggest closet in New York. He lives his whole life in the dark."

"Calm down," Betty ordered, obviously made uncalm herself by Diane. "Have you thought about seeing a therapist—"

"Not you too!"

"It's helped Tony," Betty stammered.

"Maybe instead of my quitting," Diane answered, "you should

get your old job back. Everything is in terms of Tony.'' Betty stopped fidgeting, a deer frozen by headlights. Betty's look of shock and hurt slowed Diane down, but Diane couldn't prevent a furious mumbled afterthought: "Tony, Tony, Tony."

Betty stared at Diane, her mouth tight. "Why are you so angry at me?" she asked in the tone of a judge challenging a defendant to express remorse about his crime.

Last chance for mercy, Diane thought. What the hell, I'll make it. "I guess because you're happy, because Tony is happy, you got two kids, you don't feel any conflict about work."

"Sure I do!" Betty said, at ease again. "I go out of my mind when Tony goes to L.A. for script conferences and I'm stuck with the kids for weeks. I don't have anything to say when I'm at parties except that Gina is now talking, and Nicholas is starring in the Lower School Music Assembly. Maybe I should start working part-time again and you should cut back."

"Betty." Diane couldn't help chuckling at her naïveté. "There's no way to make partner and work part-time."

"Is it really that important?" Betty asked gently.

"Making partner?"

"Yeah."

"You're just a clerk if you don't make partner. You take orders."

"I didn't realize it was that important to you," Betty said quietly. "Obviously, I knew you wanted to practice law, but—"

Betty was right, Diane decided later, making partner wasn't that important. Diane went back to the office and ran into Didi, who was bursting with office gossip. One of the middle-aged partners had left his wife and shacked up with a first-year associate. Everybody was shocked at the partner's many blunders: he hadn't closed out the joint financial accounts; he hadn't bothered to conceal that he'd moved in with the young associate; he hadn't discussed it with Stoppard or the other powerful partners who might disapprove. And as for the first-year associate, well, her career was finished. "They're both crazy," Didi said.

But they were in love. Maybe they had flipped, but if not, if it was passion, then why should the senior partner care if he got screwed in the divorce settlement, if he got hassled by Stoppard, why should the first-year associate worry about a possible partnership seven or eight years hence? Why should a career block happiness?

Yes, Diane no longer believed that justice would prevail in the world, that blacks would ever be given equal opportunity, that there would be peace, that the rich would get poorer, and the poor richer, or that any of the dreams of her college days would come true—but to go to the other extreme, and decide that making partner in a law firm was more important than her own peace of mind, that was madness.

Diane said none of this to Didi. She merely nodded at the titillated Didi and thought: I don't even need the money. Once alone in her office, Diane called Peter.

"Do you care," she asked her husband without a preliminary, "if I look for other work?"

"Like what?" Peter said.

"I don't know, teaching, maybe even public-interest law. No, that could be a heavy caseload. Anything that leaves me more time to be with Byron."

Silence. What was he calculating? The cost to him?

"Are you worried about the money?" Diane asked.

"Of course not," Peter snapped, with the true contemptuous dismissal of inherited money. She believed him. "Is this your way of preparing for a second child?" he asked.

"You don't want another child," Diane answered.

"You don't always pay attention to what I want," Peter said.

He's prepared a final argument against me. For a moment, she couldn't swallow or talk. He's ready to divorce me, Diane thought so coldly that she chilled herself.

"I think it's a good idea," Peter said before she could answer. "I still don't want to have another child. But I think it would be good for Byron if you were around more."

"Fine," Diane said, and hung up without a good-bye. She waited for Peter to call back. He would have in the past. Even if he didn't mean it, Peter would call back and say, "Are you angry?" listen to her bill of indictments, and then say, "I'm sorry, I've been bad. My mother's driving me crazy. I don't know what's wrong with me. I love you. I'd fall apart without you." Even if the words slid out of him too fast, soda cans dispensed indiscriminately, sugar bombs for a little girl, that effort of insincerity showed he still cared.

Now he doesn't even bother to lie, she thought coldly, and again shivered with dread.

It was gone! It was gone!

Luke's belly was full of air again, his legs no longer heavy, and back there, though it stung and pinched, he was empty, he could breathe, he could move because it was all gone, pushed out—

But the eye. He couldn't get rid of the eye. He tried not to move it. Look still, don't go fast to see.

It hurt hot. It stabbed. Go away, please.

"Don't you feel better now?" Daddy said, coming with a new diaper.

Don't say no. They put things in it. "Yes."

"Did it hurt a lot?"

"Yes," he said softly. No! He moved it. The hot. The poke. Hurt! Hurt!

"Do you have to go again? Do you want to go on the potty?"

"No, no." He pushed all the things away with the word, with his body. The potty, pooping, his eye, looking at it, the hurt, the hurt, the hurt. Go away, please. The soft, smooth water came in his eyes. Sting around the thing, burning, but making it soft, the hard spot in the eye, get soft, go away, go away.

"All right, all right." Daddy hugged him. "Forget the potty. Let me get your diaper on in case you have to do more."

I don't, I don't, but up he went, a pillow in the air, little in Daddy's big hands.

"Whee," Daddy said, and made him fly. "Luke the jet, coming in for a landing." Daddy's face worked hard putting on the diaper. Then Daddy looked at Luke's eyes, and woke up to Luke, smiling. "I love you, Luke," Daddy said, and it was like walking out into the sunlight, everything bright and warm.

"Whoosh!" He-Man raised his arm, his jets firing him up and down, big legs on the ground. "I have—" The thing was back in his eye. Stand still, don't look at fast things.

"Luke . . . ?" Daddy watched him.

No, no.

"You have to go again?"

"I want to watch television."

Daddy sat quiet, a pigeon watching. His chest puffed and sank. His head lowered.

"I won't," Luke said, and the tears came again, soft on the burning hurt, melting it away, go away, go away.

"What's bothering you?" Daddy said to the ground.

"My eye," Luke said, and he covered it. Don't touch, Daddy, don't look.

"Okay, sit on the couch. I'll put on the TV." But Daddy carried him, gentle, and kissed him. Blankey covered the hurt eye. Dark and cool, he kept still. It's okay. Don't move.

Don't look at the fast things. Go away. Go away.

"WE'RE GOING TO GO OUT," MOMMY SAID. DADDY TOO.

"To Grandma's?"

"No, to a restaurant."

"Yah! Yah! Yah!" Byron danced like they liked. Daddy smiled. Mommy rubbed his head.

"So you told Stoppard," Daddy said; he kept talking all the time to Mommy. About the dumb work things. It was bright in the night. Only people's faces were light. They flashed on and off. And greens and reds and yellows dripped and stretched on everything. Only big people were out, big boys like Byron, like Stupid poop head.

"Luke got hurt."

"I'm amazed, Diane. I can't believe you just went ahead."

"Luke got hurt! Luke got hurt!" Bounce up, bounce ball up. Too see me! See me!

"What? Who got hurt? He-Man?"

Daddy don't know. "No! Luke got hurt!"

"Shhh! Byron!" Mommy said hard. "We're going into the restaurant now. Other people are eating. You have to be quiet. I want you to talk in a whisper."

"Talk in a whisper?" Daddy said, and laughed.

"Ha! Ha! Ha!" Bounce up at Daddy. "Whisper! Whisper!"

"Shhh!" Mommy pulled him down. Like the elevator sinking, sinking. "Here we are. Now be quiet. Or we'll go right home"

"I want go home!" Byron pushed, pushed at Mommy's leg, fall on her, to give.

"Okay." Mommy pulled away from the glass door, from the stretching lights.

"Diane—" Daddy called.

"No!" Byron pulled back to the door, to the fun. "No! No! I be quiet."

"Byron'll be a good boy and be quiet?"

"Yeeeesss." The noise spun and tickled in his mouth. "Yeeeessss," he sounded.

"Want to sit next to me, Byron?" Daddy had the glass door open. Balls of light bounced over the tables. There were men with doormen buttons.

"Who are you?" Byron asked a big one.

"Marry O—bats you name?"

The chairs had red behinds and black backs! There was a cake on the windowsill!

"What's your name?" Mommy shouted in his ear.

"You know," Byron said, and got his ear away from her hot noise.

Daddy laughed. He was happy. Daddy put him up, up over the black backs, and down on a red bottom. In a grown-up chair!

"Byron," Mommy said to the big stomach man with buttons.

"Hat name?"

"Byron," she said again.

"Surrey?" Stomach mumbled.

"Byron," she kept saying.

"I'm Byron!" he shouted to stop them. "Me!"

"Like the great poet!" happy Daddy said. His cool fingers squeezed Byron's neck.

Stomach had a little chair, a baby chair.

"Pick him up," Mommy said to Daddy.

"No! Wanna sit here."

"Shhh!" Mommy said hard. "It's a booster seat. To make you taller."

"No! Don't want!"

"How are you going to reach the table?" Daddy asked.

Knees are feet. Byron showed them. He could get everything now. "See!" He picked up the salt. "What's that!"

"Pepper," Daddy said.

"Okay," Mommy said to Stomach. "We don't need it." Baby chair go away.

"Ha, ha, ha, ha!" Byron laugh like Skeletor.

"Byron," Mommy said, angry.

"Okay, okay." Lean against Daddy. Daddy's soft hand touched him, cool tips, like water, down the face. "What's pepper for?"

"Food," said happy Daddy. "To add flavor when the food is yucchy."

"Yucchy food!" Byron choked loud. Grown-up laughed over there. "Yucchy food!"

"Peter, don't encourage him."

"Hey, Byron," Daddy said, so happy. "I'm very good at going to restaurants. Did you know that?"

"Good?" Daddy must be good.

"Restaurants love me. Know why?"

"You quiet?"

"Yes, I'm very quiet while I put pepper on my yucchy food."

Byron laughed. The lights squeezed, Mommy got bright, her mouth wide and white, Daddy's arms shook with happy bounces, and Byron put his head, shaking and laughing, into Daddy's chest and let himself be held.

"I love yucchy food," Byron said.

Mommy looked so bright, her face white under the dancing lights. "You're so cute, Byron," she said, and kissed the air. Daddy caught her kiss and placed the cool love on Byron's happy hot cheek.

* * *

HE'S FINE, ERIC ABUSED HIMSELF. WHY DID I CALL NINA AND TELL her to come home? She's going to think I'm an idiot. Or worse, that I wanted to mess up her work.

He was desperate not to interfere. FIT and this part-time evening job had made Nina happier than Eric could remember. Her short temper with Luke—well, it wasn't so short—but that buildup of resentment, culminating in a sudden switch from tolerance to shouting, no longer happened. Nina tired more easily, but she seemed to remember her gratitude at having Luke, not to feel as put-upon. Eric knew why. He shared that reaction, even though he was exhausted coming home from work, his body reluctant, his mind fainting at the prospect of an hour's play the minute he was through the door. But after the roughhousing was over, even though his skin was boned and his muscles unstrung, the fatigue was housed in satisfaction. He knew why he was tired. The happy face he kissed good night told him why. Luke made the reason he worked clear, made everything in life immediate. Important. Aimed.

I am a father, he would catch himself thinking at odd moments, an announcement of worth that nothing could diminish.

He could look at Joe and feel superior to him, despite the gap in their knowledge of the market. My son is loved, his is not.

He could look at Sammy and care less about his insults, because he knew what a terrible thing had been withheld from Sammy.

On every street, in the park, on the television, in the papers, everywhere there were fatherless men or, worse, failed fathers. Everywhere, everywhere, were abandoned sons, neglected sons, misunderstood sons; everywhere there were failures. Not Eric. He loved Luke. And Luke loved him. And they were going to endure.

That's why the constipation bothered Eric so. He couldn't handle it, couldn't really help. What was Eric going to do when Luke was sixteen? Run Luke around the apartment so he could take a crap? And the eye. Eric should have called the doctor and gone. Instead, like a baby, he phoned Nina, interrupted her work, and begged her to come home.

And now Luke seemed fine. Sure, he was quiet, sitting in the corner of the couch, holding the blankey to his eye, but he talked and laughed. He even got up and ate his slice of pizza. Luke was very sensitive; that's why he still worried over his eye. Eric was convinced that by morning it would be forgotten.

Nina came home, dashing in from the hallway. Eric expected resentment, but she stopped at the living room and looked at them with pleasure. "How are my boys?" she said.

"Mommy," Luke said softly, but the relief was loud in his tone.

Nina kissed Eric quickly and, with her coat still on, went right to Luke. "Put your head back, I won't touch your eye, I just want to look at it."

Luke's eyes watered immediately. "Okay," he said, almost blubbering the words.

Nina did as she promised. She rolled her eye and told Luke to do the same. He yelped when he tried. "Do you still feel like something's in there?"

"Nothing!"

"Probably nothing is. But does it feel like something is? Not telling me won't make the hurt go away, Luke. I spoke to the doctor and he said sometimes sand can scratch an eye, and even though it's not there, the scratch can hurt. It'll heal itself. You'll be fine. But I have to know. Does it feel like there's still something in it?"

Luke covered his face with his blanket, like a criminal broken down, and he confessed, "Yes! It hurts a lot!" And he bawled with relief, collapsed by pain.

My God, Eric thought. I've been here for two hours. He's been in terrible pain. And I thought it was the constipation. For two hours Luke's suffered, and I thought he was fine. My God, I'm an idiot. I'm not even a good father.

DIANE WAS AMAZED BY THE RESPONSE. ALL HER ENEMIES WERE confounded. Stoppard, who had become progressively cooler and irritating since the birth of Byron, increasingly picky and dissatisfied with her work, almost pleaded with her to reconsider.

"Diane, you're a superb lawyer. Don't do this. You'll regret it later. Byron's going to grow up and leave home to date girls with paisley hair. I can ease your caseload for a while."

"I'm a superb lawyer?"

Stoppard frowned. "Of course you are."

"I haven't had a compliment out of you in a year."

"Your work hasn't been good."

"Then you should be happy I'm leaving."

She was delighted to see Stoppard squirm, compliments wrung from the sponge he had used to soak up her talent and energy. Give me more, she said, and he twisted and squeezed out praise. "I can guarantee you you'll make partner this year," he said with a final squirt, his hands out as if to say: there, I'm dry now.

"Thank you," she said graciously. She meant it too; the acknowledgment of her abilities was what she had always wanted. She knew now *that* was the important value to her, not the money, or the public prestige. She didn't like to fail. She liked to be the best. "Partnership would mean even more work. I have a family. I want to take care of them."

Stoppard then appealed to Diane's duty to her sex, asserting that her sudden departure because of children would only confirm the chauvinist partners' worst fears about women. God, that was funny.

Of course, Diane's mother was delighted. "Oh, that's so much better for Byron. And for you, dear. I'm so happy!" Yeah, I won't be topping you anymore, right, Mom? Now you don't look like such an unaccomplished, spoiled woman. "I'm coming up this weekend to celebrate," Lily insisted. Diane couldn't talk her out of it. To celebrate. Diane's quitting made Lily want to party.

Peter? That surprised her. He got loving. He got passionate. Ran his finger over her body, shaping, dancing, scratching, squeezing, molding. Put his mouth on her, swallowed her sex.

I cut off my balls, so now his are bigger.

But she didn't feel the bitterness implied by her intellectual observations. She knew she hadn't failed, even if those closest to her were relieved that she had given up. She could have kept going, made partner, raised Byron, blown them all out, Supermom caped and flying onto the pages of *New York Magazine*. She chose not to. She could have climbed the wall. She had decided to turn away.

There was something secretive in her pride that she had rejected her work, a closely held mirror in which she could peek without being observed and see herself superior, a nun renouncing the pleasures of the world, an artist spurning celebrity, a purist, choosing life over ego, choosing her family over vanity.

When Diane told Didi, at first she wasn't believed. Then once Diane convinced her, amazingly enough, Didi began to cry. Diane held her. Didi sobbed like a girl. "What is this?" Diane said.

"I feel so alone," Didi said.

The world is nuts, Diane thought. Nobody knows what they want. She invited Didi to dinner, something she had never done before. "I couldn't," Didi said. "I'd go home later and want to slash my wrists."

"No, you wouldn't. You'd go home and thank God." I've guaranteed her partnership, Diane thought. I've changed four lives: mine, Byron's, Peter's, and Didi's.

They had a great time that night, Peter and Byron and Diane. Something terrible had left the house, something that had had them by the throat. That was obvious. Peter was her lover again, Byron obeyed her, got sweet and loving, and she could breathe. All that, all that, all that—just for killing her career.

* * *

WE'RE GOING TO GO SEE A DOCTOR,'' MOMMY SAID.

He cried. His head, heavy and sad, fell forward. Couldn't stop it. Mommy, her body swishing in her blanket coat, touched his face.

"He's just going to see if there's anything there and give you something to feel better. It won't hurt so much. Now, we're not seeing your regular doctor—"

Help. His nose ached from the tears. "Why? Why?" The water washed in his throat. Help me. "Daddy!" Help, Daddy. "I don't want to!" He called to them, he screamed to them to be Mommy and Daddy again. "I'm okay!"

"Are you sure?" Daddy said.

"Eric!" Mommy yelled at Daddy.

Cover up. Hide in her. He pushed against the swish coat. The eye! Don't yell. They take you if you yell.

"Okay. Where is it?" Daddy said, scared. Why is Daddy scared?

"Fourteenth Street and First."

"And First!" Daddy worry, Daddy don't want to go.

"The Eye and Ear Infirmary. At night you go to the Fourteenth Street entrance."

"Jesus, we might have to walk back, I don't think there'll be cabs—"

"Then we'll walk back, Eric. Get his jacket. Let's go."

Don't look. Stay in, Mommy. Eyes closed, he was nowhere. No doctors, no poking. Nothing in the eye. Go to sleep.

They had his arms. Take my hands off. Take my leg, take me away, I stay here in Mommy.

"Come on, baby," Daddy said.

No! He pulled for Mommy, swim to her. "I'll carry him," Mommy said.

Face on her, press against the eye. Go away. Go away before the doctor.

Mommy pulled, pulled on his head. "Luke, look at me. Look at me, Luke."

Can't look. Close on the burning hurt. Be away, away.

Mommy came inside his eyes, a huge doll. "Luke, don't be so scared. We're going to a different place than your regular doctor, but they're nice there. And we'll be with you the whole time. They just need to look in your eye."

Don't want my eye. Don't want to see. Let me sleep, let me go away.

"Okay? Shhh." Soft kisses. Daddy, in his coat, turns on the light. The hall glows.

"The elevator's here."

Sleep. Sleep. He leaned on Mommy and held the worry in, poking in his chest to get out. In, in. Good-bye, home.

GET READY TO BE A MAN.

Eric Gold, Wizard of Wall Street, walks boldly, people moving out of his way at the mere sight of his imposing body.

In the street, his long arm signaled for a taxi. A couple on the other corner dropped their competing hands when Nina appeared behind Eric, Luke loose in her arms.

"Fourteenth and First," he said, fully in command. "It's the Eye and Ear Clinic. The entrance is on Fourteenth."

Eric reached for Luke's hand. Luke's fingers fell into his palm, drooped leaves soaked with fear. Nina kissed Luke on the forehead over and over, a steady patter of love.

The stupid traffic made the ride endless. He could have walked it faster. *If anything really serious ever happens, I could carry Luke to the emergency room. Remember that.*

This is what it means to be a man. Don't hesitate, don't doubt, get it done. You sat with him for three hours doing nothing. Luke's doctor would have still been available. You've made enough mistakes for one night.

"He's asleep," Nina said when the clinic was in sight.

"Oh, no" escaped from Eric. *Don't whine, don't worry. But Luke's so cranky just after he wakes up. Is Nina angry at me? I should have handled this. Better for him. Better for her.*

I should have bought four times the amount of DNA Tech than I did. Either make a bold move or don't make it at all. What's the point of a little position?

On Monday, I'll quadruple Tom's exposure.

Luke looked so small, his head decapitated on Nina's shoulder, the big eyelids closed, their tiny veins showing purple through his pale skin.

Eric Gold, discoverer of undiscovered values in the OTC market, a frequent panelist on Wall Street Week, *rated number two among money managers for the last year, moves past the lingering bums at the clinic's entrance and holds the door wide for his beautiful wife and wounded son.*

Out of my way, out of my way. An Indian nurse stood beside a security guard at a reception desk. "Yes?"

"My son has something in his eye."

Luke woke up crying. "Shhh, shhh," Nina said.

"Oh, the poor baby," a gigantic black woman said. She was seated in a row of plastic chairs. Around her, sprawled in funny positions, like discarded clothes, were five children.

"Geuss?" the nurse said to Eric.

"Excuse me?"

"It was geuss?"

"No, not gas. Sand."

The nurse laughed at Eric as though he were a cute child. "Oh, sand. Not geuss. You have to wait. Fill this form out, please."

Luke wailed. His arms arched into the air, grabbing for what he already had—his mother. He grabbed for Nina as though she were incorporeal. "Mommy! Mommy! Mommy!" he screamed. "It hurts! It hurts!"

"You take the baby first," the black woman as big as the Stock Exchange said to the nurse.

"I see if Doctor can see him now," the nurse said to Nina.

"Thank you," Nina said. "Thank you very much," she added to the black woman.

Why are you thanking her? She's not running this place, Eric thought. He answered the questions on the paper. Glass, the nurse meant glass, he realized and wondered if many people got examined for wrong things in their eye. Of course, a nurse who can't speak English well is perfect for the job of emergency room triage. And she laughed at me for misunderstanding her. The world is mad.

"Shhh, shhh, it's okay, okay," Nina kept on saying over Luke's cries of pain. Eric wrote quickly. His answers on the form looked like the scrawls of a maniac.

"Car? You have a car?" The nurse was back.

"Yes, I have a car."

The nurse laughed at him again, as if he were just the cutest and silliest thing she'd ever seen. "Medical car-d!" she said, and smiled.

"It hurts! It hurts!" Luke's voice scratched the air. All the waiting people hunched their shoulders, fighting the cold wind of his cries.

"Can he see us?" Nina said.

"You're necks."

Next, next. "I'll pay cash," Eric said. He was tearing his wallet apart; he couldn't find the fucking Blue Cross card.

"Oh. No car? Need a boucher. Wait."

The black mother tapped Eric. "Don't give 'em no cash, mister."

"Here it is!" The Blue Cross card. It was old. From when he first married Nina.

"There you go," the black mother said. Her children looked as if they'd been there several weeks, their eyes crossed with boredom, their hair flattened in odd spots by their using the chairs' plastic arms as pillows. The girls' skirts were pushed up, the boys' shirts pulled out. None of them seemed to have anything wrong with their eyes other than a dead hopelessness, a glaze of enraged resignation.

Thank God I'm not her, Eric thought. Thank God those aren't my kids.

I'm going to buy the shit out of DNA Tech on Monday.

"Eric!" Nina was following a pretty Asian woman wearing a doctor's clothes.

"Sweet baby," the black woman said as Eric turned to go.

I should give her some money, Eric thought, but that was ridiculous. "Thank you," he said.

He rushed after Nina and Luke. Luke's eye looked bad now, swollen, red, and he was gasping from tears, choking, whimpering, blind, clutching Nina's clothes with arched fingers, a cat climbing a tree.

Nina was talking over him, reciting the chronology, the Asian doctor nodding as if the information were familiar.

"Can you open your eye?" the doctor interrupted, speaking to Luke. She had no accent; she was like a TV anchorwoman, her pronunciation without geography.

"He fell asleep in the cab. It seems to be—"

"He's probably scratched his cornea," she said casually, and moved to a tray, getting implements. "There's probably no sand still in there, but the pain of the scratch gets worse, especially if the lid is closed for a while. We'll take a look. Could you turn the lights out?"

"Is that permanent? A scratch?" Who asked that? Eric thought. Me. That's who.

"No, no. I'm guessing. I shouldn't. You'd better hold him."

"Mommy! Mommy! Mommy!" Luke screamed to be saved, a condemned man pleading for mercy.

We're helping you, Luke. We really are.

"The lights?" the doctor said to Eric.

With the room dark, Luke's desperate cries were horrible. Three giants eating him alive in the dark—

"Let me look!" The doctor's fingers tried to spread Luke's eyelid, squeezed shut by terror. "Let me look!"

Luke's flailing arms whacked Nina in the face. "Ow!" she yelled.

"Mommy! Mommy! Mommy!"

The black woman looked in. "He all right?" she said to Eric.

"Please leave!" the doctor said to her. The nurse appeared and led the black woman off. "You'd better hold him," the doctor said to Eric.

Eric Gold, the first to realize DNA Technology was the IBM of the future, profiled in Barron's—

He took Luke from Nina. Luke fought his grip, his arms up, his body wriggling like a slippery soap in his hand, the feet kicking at his stomach—"No! Daddy! No! Daddy! Hurt! Hurt!"

Eric felt tears yawn in his eyes. It was so dark Nina and the doctor couldn't see them. Nina got out of the examining chair. He tried to drown out Luke's pleas.

Eric Gold made a bold investment four years ago, buying nearly 2 percent of the outstanding shares in DNA Tech at an average price of nine. The stock has since split five times—

Eric got into the chair and lifted his head back, away from Luke's butting head and wild arms.

"Hold his arms," the doctor said. What was that in her hand? A swab, she's going to swab his eyeball.

Eric grabbed the little arms, put them against Luke's chest, and folded his thick arms on top, pressing hard to keep Luke still.

I'm holding my son to be at the torturer's mercy.

"Daaaa! Daddd! Daaayyy! Hurt! Hurt!"

Eric Gold, Wizard of Wall—

The doctor came right at the eye with that thing—

I have to hold him still. She might pop his eye out if he moves.

Luke's muscles went stiff and he screamed out everything, even the soothing fantasy in Eric's head.

"It's okay! It's okay! It's okay!" someone shouted over and over. "It's okay! It's okay!"

The doctor moved away, studying the swab. "There was sand still in there," she commented.

Luke screamed, "You're hurting me, Daddy!"

"I'm just holding you, Luke. The doctor's done—"

"You're squeezing me!" Luke yelled.

"You're holding him too tight," Nina said.

I am, he realized. He let his muscles go. Eric had pressed Luke hard enough to push him inside his own heart.

I'm out of control, Eric thought.

"There was a lot of sand in there," the doctor said. "It must've really hurt. How long ago did this happen?"

"Five or six hours," Nina said.

"Brave baby," the doctor mumbled.

"It's all out now, Luke," Nina said.

"Go home!" Luke said in a lonely whine, an abandoned pet.

"I need to look—" the doctor began.

Luke pushed at Eric's looser net of arms. "No! No!"

"Just to look! With this. See the light." The doctor held out the tool. "I'm going to shine it on you. Not touch."

"It doesn't hurt anymore!" Luke yelled.

"What?" the doctor said.

"He says it doesn't hurt anymore," Nina said, doubt in her voice.

"I'm sure it doesn't. I put an anesthetic on. Last him for, oh, a few hours. But I couldn't see if he has a scratch. I need to look again. I won't touch."

"No, no, no, no, no."

Eric thought: Tell Luke it's okay. Take charge. But he had nothing left. Luke had been in terrible pain for hours while in Eric's care. And then Eric had practically crushed Luke, held him helpless while he suffered. It was nothing, it would be forgotten, anyone might have made the same mistakes—but it wasn't Eric's idea of being Daddy. He felt the ache of tears in his eyes, stinging to be free. *I can't even do this right.*

If these two women find me in tears, I might as well spend the rest of my life in bed, under the covers.

"Come on," the doctor said, coming in again with the penlight. "Roll your eye up. I won't touch you."

"Hold him, Eric," Nina ordered. *The bitch, she'll be remembered as the angel of mercy. I, the monster.*

The screaming started again. Hopelessly, Eric tightened and shut out everything except modifying his grip to be firm but not painful. *Eric Gold, the Wiz—*

"Daddy! You're hurting me! You're hurting me!"

"Yeah. He's scratched his cornea. If he was a grown-up, I'd put on a patch. You'll have to put drops in every four hours."

"Oh, no" escaped from Nina. "For how long?"

"Three days."

Eric loosened his grip. The weekend. The wonderful weekend. *I get to spend my weekend crushing my son in my arms while Nina drops things on his naked eye.*

If I'd acted faster, maybe he wouldn't have scratched it.

"How's the baby?" the black woman asked Eric as he carried Luke, calm now, already half asleep, out of the examining room.

"He's okay," Eric said.

She smiled. "But you ain't, right?"

12

MINE. I GET MINE VIOLIN. MY FRIENDS CAN'T PLAY WITH it. Do *not* belong to anybody else. Mine.

Byron felt the case, smooth and bumped, soft-shaped and hard. Daddy smiled. Mommy was at the metal stand, stick man, clean and new. Grandma and Grandpa were on the couch, still as chairs. Old. People get old and die, Mommy said. Hair get white, skin get mushy, bones get old, and people die.

"Oh, it's so cute," Grandma said. "Like a real violin."

"It is real!" Byron told her with everything, all his body.

Daddy laughed. Grandpa too.

Don't believe me. "It *is* real! It *is* real!"

"Shhh," Mommy said. "Now show them the right way to take it out of the case."

"There's a right way?" Grandpa said.

Byron knows. He flipped up the locks. They made a satisfying noise. Open. The violin shone in its green bed, shaped to hug itself. Nothing else could go in there.

"Oh, it's so cute," Grandma said, and she laughed. "My friend Paula must see this!"

Watch Mommy to see I'm okay. Hand under neck—so smooth and hard—other hand under its belly. Where do my feet go?

"Byron," Mommy warning. "Rest position."

Mistake. Put it at your side. Laser gun.

"Is there a bow?" Grandma said.

"Yes!" Byron let go with one hand and pushed the case so Grandma could see the bow—stuck onto the top, held by little belts. He pushed so she could see, but the case spun on its lumpy under-belly, spun and spun around on its funny stomach, spun right off the coffee table!

282

"Whoa!" Grandpa caught it.

"Byron!" Mommy hard. "You're not holding—"

Quick, quick, back to your side. "I wanted to show the bow!"

"Mother, you're messing him up," Daddy said to Grandma. But he smiled.

"Don't confuse me," Byron said to Grandma.

They laugh again! Why? She made me do it.

"Is it broke?" Byron asked.

"No, no, no," Daddy said. He showed the case. The bow was still there.

"I want the bow," Byron said. It was so special. Bent, but not broken, with its loose white hairs that weren't loose and weren't hairs.

"You're not up to the bow yet. That comes later," Mommy said.

"I know!" Not what I asked. Want the bow. "Just hold it!" he said.

Mommy didn't answer. Mommy pointed to the music book. Little feet with scarves hopping up and down the ladder. Notes. I can read music. Well, a few notes.

"He can read music?" Grandma loved that.

"A *few* notes," Mommy said.

"More!" Byron answered. "I know all these!" He showed with his finger.

"Byron! You're going to drop the violin!"

Back at your side! Watch Mommy. "I know all these!"

"They're just two notes, Byron," Mommy said. "You know a lot, but not all the notes."

Mommy pointed to the first note, G, first string. "Play position," Mommy said, and gestured to the drawing of feet the teacher had made.

"Look at that!" Grandma said, noticing the ghost feet. Byron stepped into the invisible shoes and brought the violin up. The black thing, the rest, dug into his skin.

"More under," Mommy said, and pushed.

Too cool. Tickle, tickle. Don't show it! Under the fingernail and pull.

Not right, not right.

Grandma clapped once. "Very—" Daddy shushed Grandma like she was a child. Ha-ha. Grandma old.

"There are two and then a rest," Mommy said.

Two? Under the nail, don't pull! No sound.

"Try again," Mommy said.

Under the nail and pull medium.

"Good!" Mommy excited.

Again.

"Good!" Mommy happy.

Byron heard them. They were pleased. He turned to smile. "See!"

"Byron!" Mommy warned. "You have a lot more."

Under the nail, pull. Under the nail, pull. Too hard. Try again. Tired. Under the nail—that hurt. The string stayed on his skin, even after going away. Still there. Look. The string is still on my skin!

"I'm tired," Byron said.

"You only have another line," Mommy said, her finger on the next hopping foot. Her face dark, her eyes burning.

"It's wonderful, Byron," Daddy said. "Keep going."

"Can I hold the bow?" Byron asked.

"After you finish the line, you can hold the bow for a little bit. But it's not to be played with."

Under the nail—pull!

It's inside my skin, still pushing in on it, pushing in.

Byron used the fatter part of his finger and didn't pull so hard. The sound was wrong.

Look at Mommy. About to say—

No, her finger went to the next one.

Fatter part. Wrong sound. "I want to stop!" Byron said fast.

"Just one more."

Brush it softly. Wrong, wrong, wrong sound.

"Very good," Mommy said, but she wasn't excited.

Grandma and Grandpa and Daddy clapped.

"Yah!" Byron hopped and laughed. "Yah!" He danced at its end, showing his prize. Mine!

"Byron!" Mommy grabbed the violin. "You can't do that. If the violin breaks, you can't learn it."

"You said I could hold the bow."

Mommy didn't answer.

"Here," Daddy said. He pulled the bow out from the belts.

Byron took it. Sword. He-Man sword. Don't let Mommy know.

"Well, that was great," Mommy said. "Aren't you impressed?"

"Must take ten years before they can play a song," Grandpa said.

"I played a song!" Byron said.

"Of course you did," Grandma said.

"Yes, you were very good," Grandpa said.

Mommy kissed his head. "Okay, let me put the bow back."

"I want to!"

"Okay."

Sword away. Through the belts, into the case. Close. Click, click. Mommy kissed his head again. "You're a good boy, Byron."

I'm a good boy.

"When you give your first concert," Grandma said, "will you invite me?"

"Are you old?" Byron asked her. Maybe she was a child.

Grandpa laughed. So did Daddy. "Yes, I am," Grandma said with a broken mouth, her voice quiet.

"Then you're going to die," Byron told her.

NO MATTER HOW FAR THEY WENT, NO MATTER WHICH PATH THEY walked back into his memory, Peter and Kotkin ended up face-to-face with Larry, stroking Peter's flat stomach, digging under the belt, under the elastic of his briefs, reaching for the little penis to make it tickle and tingle, like peeing, but not peeing, like resting, but not resting—

The more Peter discussed the events and the harder Kotkin worked to get him to be clear about the details—how old were you? how long after the divorce? did you say no? what did Larry say?— the fuzzier they got. Peter had gone into therapy with clear images. Larry standing next to a little version of Peter, Peter's head just clearing the sink in his friend Gary's bathroom. Larry had, under the pretext of peeing, taken out his erect penis. Only it wasn't an erection to Peter; it was a huge, angry, pulsing creature, a blind, breathing sausage, a blank-faced snake, a hairy worm—

"You want to touch it?" Larry said. "You can touch it."

"No" from out of his little mouth, echoing out of the chasm of his past. "No," he stammered.

Larry didn't argue. He took Peter's hand and pulled it toward the impossible gravityless thing. "It feels good when you touch. People want you to touch it. Hasn't your father ever shown you his? He'd like you to touch it."

"He said that!" Kotkin asked. She sounded outraged, amazed, disbelieving, disgusted.

"I don't know, I don't know," he stammered. He had always been afraid to say. What was real, what was not? It seemed incredible even to him. People would be disgusted to know. He had never told details. Were they real?

"You don't know?"

She wasn't outraged, that's in my head. "I can't talk about it." Sour and choking, bitter and lumpy, the memories churned in his chest, bubbled in his throat. Was it real? Why didn't I say no the very first time he reached in my pants? Why didn't I tell someone?

But I did. I told Gary. Larry said he had done it to Gary.

"Yeah, he plays around with it," Gary had said. Or had he then? Was it years later? "Tell him you don't like it. He'll stop and give you a present."

"I don't like Gary as much as you; that's why I don't touch him anymore," Larry had said.

He won't stop with me.

Did I think that? I pulled my hand away—even if this memory is false, even in the lie, I didn't touch him. It. Red and pulsing, a blind face. Or is that the block? Did I touch?

No.

"What were your parents doing?"

"They were divorced!"

"I know," Kotkin said with a trace of impatience. Or did she? "Where were they? Were they around? Had you been dumped at Gary's?"

Yes. No. "I don't know. I just don't know. I should see Gary and find out."

"You've never discussed this with your mother or father?"

"No." Peter laughed.

"An absurd question?" Kotkin said warmly. Or was it? Was it sarcastic?

"No, I guess if I were healthy, that's what I would do, I would ask the grown-ups what the hell was going on. I'd find how exactly old I was, where they were, and how much was done. The whole cast is still alive, just waiting for my questions."

"But you don't want to ask them?"

"No, yes, no, yes."

Kotkin chuckled. "Are you scared?"

Flat on his back, peering into eternity. What was scared?

Who am I?

There was one time, the time when Larry invited Gary and Peter to a matinee of the road company of *Hello, Dolly!* Later, Larry took them to his office. Peter felt safe because Gary was with them and Larry had never touched Peter without sending Gary away and in the office that would be impossible—

But Larry's secretary needed a hand with some packages, just to carry them downstairs. Larry insisted Gary, just Gary, go. "I'll help," Peter tried to say, knowing, knowing. . . .

Still stuck in his throat, hundreds of years later, lying on Kotkin's couch, still forming in his mouth—"I'll help too." Peter's eyes still pleaded with Gary: take me with you, take me with you.

"What are you thinking about?" Kotkin asked.

And during the fifteen minutes that the secretary and Gary were gone, Larry lowered my pants and put it in his mouth.

"Are you remembering something?" Kotkin asked.

"No. Yes." The couch was heavy. Too heavy for the floorboards. Its dense weight cracked them, crashing down, down. I want to sleep. "I don't want to talk about it anymore."

"Okay," Kotkin said with the sweet, soft voice of forgiveness. "You don't have to talk about anything you don't want to. But you can tell me anything you want to. That's what I'm here for."

"I know." He wanted to cry. Somewhere, maybe below the couch, beneath the floorboards, were all his tears.

"Do you feel you can talk about anything here without being judged, or made fun of, or—not believed?"

"Yes," Peter said, just rising above the pool of sorrows.

"Good," Kotkin said, like a mom pleased with her little boy.

THE LOBBY WAS DREARY. ITS MOSAIC TILES WERE DULLED BY YEARS of tramping feet and coarse mops. Low-wattage bulbs glowed through globes that were either heavily frosted or very dirty.

"God, I used to think this was so big," Eric said.

"What, Daddy?" Luke asked.

"I grew up in this building," Eric answered. He picked up Luke, and kissed him on the cheek. Luke was so beautiful these days that neither Nina nor Eric could come near him without bussing him. His face was in transition from the padded cushions of infancy to the elastic trim of boyhood. His blue eyes radiated curiosity and wonder. His bow-legged walk had straightened, his neck had lengthened, his recent haircut had shaped his straight black hair into manly layers, his fluted baby lips, although still red against his pale skin, had widened, and when he opened them to laugh, there were bright little teeth. The toothless smile had become a boy's grin. His voice was musical—a relief to Nina that Luke hadn't inherited her monotone—and he spoke into the air with unrestrained volume and excitement, a trumpet waking the world. Except for the constipation, his disposition was excellent: he was loving, smart, and compassionate. Still afraid, though, to say what he wanted in the face of opposition.

Like me, relying on others to make him happy, Nina thought.

"Remember?" Eric said to Luke. "I was a boy just like you in this building. I thought it was so big."

Luke smiled that smile, broad and full, showing all the happiness in his soul. "Because you were small," he said.

"Right!" Eric agreed. "See what a funny elevator they have, with a porthole like a ship?"

Everything was so dreary. The elevator buttons were eroded at their centers by stabbing fingers; the doors shuddered when they opened and closed; the cables squealed; the whole thing sounded ready to collapse. And the smell. Billions of stews and soups and roasts were everywhere, especially in the hallway. The smells made Nina feel full.

"They're here!" Eric's father, Barry, shouted from the door. Barry already looked ragged, his shirttail out, his forehead sweaty. He threw out his thin arms, and opened his long fingers to Luke. "There's my grandson!"

Eric handed Luke right to him, and that skinny old man danced in the tiny foyer, his arms made into a seat, and put his forehead on Luke's, their eyes locked together. "You're so big now!"

Nina tried to imagine her father, Tom, doing this jig and she laughed. Somehow the contrast almost made her forgive Tom. It must be exhausting to be Barry, always full, and always emptying, never a still body of contentment.

The apartment was hot with cooking. Voices, the loud, sour voices of old relatives, clanged down the hallway like rattling dishes. The relatives topped each other, in a hurry to remember the best part of the story first, competing to shout the greatest appreciation.

"They're peasants, that's what makes them like that," Eric once said to Nina. "It's not being Jewish. My old neighborhood, I had two friends who weren't Jewish. One Italian, one Greek. Same thing at their house. That's when I knew. These people are all peasants."

"They're very loving," Nina had answered. She thought it again now, as a gaggle of the old folks, jewelry rattling, wrinkled masks hovering, gathered around Luke. Luke clung to his grandfather, averting his face, hiding in Barry's neck, his eyes taking account of them with cold suspicion.

"So beautiful!"

"Look at his eyes!"

"So cute!"

They appraised Luke, as if Luke weren't there, weren't an intelligence. He probably understood more about the world than they; certainly his sensibilities were finer. There was something corrupt in growing old, something that got stuck in a groove. Luke showed what he felt without the civilizing dishonesty of adulthood. Right now he exhibited his loyalty to his grandfather, to Miriam, to Eric, and to Nina, unself-consciously, free of the pressure to pretend delight at the presence of others.

"Come on, come on, I'm gonna introduce you to someone special," Barry said.

"Give him some room!" Aunt Sadie shouted, although she was the one most in the way.

"This," Barry said, "is your Great-uncle Hy."

"Great-great-uncle," someone said.

"Hi?" Luke said.

"Not like hello," Eric said.

Everybody laughed, much to Luke's confusion. He cringed at the harsh collective sound.

Hy, only a few years ago, when Nina had first met him, had been a tall, strong old man, his back straight, his busy white hair neatly combed, his eyebrows black with passion. Now Hy was stored in a wheelchair, his shoulders bent, hands resting like dead paws, his hair dirty and shapeless, the eyebrows white.

"Four generations," someone said.

Hy attempted a smile for Luke. His head bobbed with effort as he tried to bring welcome to his gaunt cheeks and scared eyes.

Hy's eyes were pale blue, Nina realized. That's the recessive gene that made Luke's blues possible.

Barry offered Luke to Hy like a pet. Luke squirmed, looked away, his body fighting, but the protest was silent.

"Oh, he's scared," Aunt Sadie said.

"Okay, Barry," Hy croaked. "Don't frighten him."

"Daddy," Luke peeped. Eric took him.

"What's that?" Luke asked, pointing to the wheelchair.

"It's a chair," Eric said.

Tell the truth, Nina thought. "Like a walker, Luke. It helps Uncle Hy get around."

"My legs aren't so good," Hy said to Luke, again trying to lift the tired muscles of his face into a smile. He wanted so badly not to frighten Luke.

The gaggle froze in their positions, now silent in unison. What are they scared of? Nina wondered. That Luke might realize Hy is dying? That Hy will? Surely they both, in their hearts, already know.

"I'm the oldest Goddard," Hy said. "You're the youngest." Goddard was Hy's name, the blood relationship was through Miriam, Eric's mother.

"Not for long," Aunt Sadie said. "Julie's pregnant." That started them up again. Sadie had mentioned the branch of the family that had made good. Julie's mother had married well, to a national shirt manufacturer. They lived in California, and the rest of the family, left behind in relative poverty in Washington Heights, talked about them the way their ancestors in the shtetl might have spoken of those who had gone to America. Sadie, who kept up with the shirt manufacturer's brood, came back tanned from visits to L.A., speaking of Rodeo Drive as though it were a temple, and she sneered at any improvement in the lives of the Washington Heighters by citing better possessions in Los Angeles. Nina saw Eric's face darken at this new one-upmanship. She could hear Eric think: so now even my son is shit 'cause Julie's having a kid.

Did he marry me because I come from a rich Boston family? But Eric didn't know how much, if any, money my father had. Did he marry me because I was a Wasp? Julie's mother had married into money, but the man was a vulgarian. Nina remembered him at their wedding, taking out thick folds of cash and deliberately selecting large bills to tip the waiters. "Get a bottle of imported champagne," he said, making the point that Tom had skimped on the liquor.

"The schmuck doesn't know that less is classier," Eric had said later about the incident.

"My father's cheap," Nina answered.

"No, he isn't. He isn't new money, that's all," Eric answered.

He hates his own people, Nina thought, watching Eric hunch his shoulders against Sadie's attack. "Julie's got such fancy doctors," Sadie said, "she already knows the baby is a girl. Can you imagine that?"

"Everybody's got that!" Aunt Rose answered. "Nothing to do with fancy doctors. They do that with everybody now."

"You didn't have that!" Sadie argued to Eric.

"That's cause my wife isn't over thirty-five," Eric answered, laughing cruelly. "If it hadn't taken Julie so long to find someone to marry her, she wouldn't have needed amnio."

"Eric," Nina said to stop him. She knew he didn't mean any of that. He just wanted to fight Sadie with like weapons.

"Julie's very beautiful," Sadie protested, with her peculiar logic.

"Especially with that nose he bought her," Aunt Rose answered.

"That was years ago!" Sadie said. "She was a little girl."

"Stop," Hy croaked. He looked agitated. One paw had lifted from its cushioned rest. The bent fingers trembled. "Sadeleh," he said to Sadie, in a tone of command. "You talk too much about money."

"Hy," she complained, tossing her head. "I'm talking about medicine, not money."

"Don't talk about medicine either. I'm sick of both money and doctors."

He still has his brain. Nina worried for him. To be stuck in that broken body with a clear head must be awful. "How do you like where you stay, Hy?" Nina asked him, kneeling beside his contraption. The huge wheel came into her vision, reminding her of the paddle wheel on an old steamboat ride that ran the river Charles one summer.

"I don't like it," Hy said quietly.

"They take good care of you," Sadie almost yelled at him.

Nina looked into Hy's eyes. They were so old, the white almost yellow, but in their large, peering worry, open and curious, blue and fragile, they could be Luke's. She wanted to cry. It was unfair. "I'm sorry. We'll visit you," she stammered.

"Too much trouble," Hy said. "Your baby is beautiful."

"Let's get started," Miriam said.

Uncle Bill leaned into Barry. "I hope you're going to do the short version."

"Is this the baby's first Passover?" Sadie asked Nina. They almost bumped heads when Nina got to her feet.

"No, we were here last year."

"Are you raising him Jewish?" Sadie went on. "Because Israel doesn't think he is. They say it doesn't count if it's just the father."

"They're a government," Hy said, his voice disintegrating, the sounds crackling like bad radio reception.

"The religion too, Hy," Sadie said. "He may even have to convert." Sadie peered at Nina. "You plan to have him bar mitzvahed, don't you?"

The guests were in awkward positions, half out of their chairs, partially out in the hall, en route to the dining table. So Sadie's equally awkward question, stiffening the group in their uncommitted postures, hung in the air, causing both physical and intellectual paralysis.

"He's two years old," Miriam said, and laughed. "Can we worry about this some other time?"

Sadie abruptly grabbed Nina by the elbow and pulled her down (Sadie was a very tiny woman) to kiss Nina's cheek with a loud, wet smack. "Just a question, dear. I ask a lot of questions because I want to know everything."

"Me too!" Luke said in his piercing voice.

Everyone turned to look at him, surprised by his existence.

Luke ducked his head in Eric's chest and hid.

* * *

"WHICH ONE?" DADDY ASKED.

"Here." Luke showed him, 6A, that was Byron's apartment. "Don't you know?"

"Daddy's never been here," Mommy said. "You visit here with Pearl when you have a play date with Byron. This is our first visit."

Luke felt good. He knew more than Mommy and Daddy about something. "I'll show you," he said, and took Daddy's hand. Luke pulled him to the door. "You push the button," he told Daddy.

Daddy looked funny. His face was sad, no smile. Daddy looked at the door. Then at the button. Daddy pushed his pants legs down. "I've got to get these let out," he said.

"Ring the bell," Mommy told him.

"Yeah!" Luke told him. The hallway's no fun.

He heard Byron. "Yah, yah, yah, it's Luke. I'm here, Luke! I'm here!"

The door opened. Byron came right out, almost through the door. "I got Castle Grayskull!"

"Uh-oh," Mommy said.

Castle Grayskull! Luke ran with Byron, past legs and books. There!

"See the trap," Byron showed him. Skeletor fell right through!

"Daddy!" Luke called.

"No," Byron said. "Don't."

"Daddy, look!" Daddy's face came down from the ceiling, right next to him.

"So this is it, huh? Fantastic." Daddy likes toys.

"See the trap?"

"Can you believe this horrible stuff," a deep voice said. Luke leaned against Daddy and looked up. A smiling man was above him.

"Introduce your friend, Byron," Byron's mommy said.

"My daddy," Byron said. He reached for Luke's hand. "Let's take Castle Grayskull to my room."

Where are we? The hallway.

"And what's your friend's name?" Byron's Mommy said.

"My name is Luke," Luke told her. She forgot?

"You're supposed to introduce him," Byron's Mommy said to Byron.

"Hello, Luke, I'm Peter," said Byron's daddy. "I've heard a lot about you."

"Let's go to my room," Byron said.

"Yes, take Grayskull to your room. Brunch will be ready soon."

"Don't wanna eat!" Byron said. "Right, Luke? We don't want to eat."

"Yeah, I'm not hungry," Luke said.

"Of course, you have to eat," Diane said.

Byron pulled Grayskull. The weapons rack fell off. The trapdoor went crazy. It was going to break. Luke wanted Byron to stop.

"Here, I'll help you," Daddy said to Byron.

"I can do it!" Byron said.

"Byron, that's not polite," his daddy said.

"Come on, Luke, we can carry it."

But it was made of stone, Luke thought. He got himself strong, like He-Man. Put his hands on the wall. It was plastic! Like nothing. Like air to push.

Byron pulled too hard. It came in half. He was holding half, only half, it was broken, no, no—

"It's okay! Don't cry!" Byron's mommy said.

What? "It comes apart, Luke," Daddy said, and took the two pieces of Grayskull. There were things that—Daddy pushed it together. It was fixed.

Luke wiped his sore eyes. "I thought it was broken."

"No! No!" Byron said. "Comes apart. See?" Byron showed him, pulling.

"Don't!" Luke begged him. "Reattach it!"

"What did you say?" Byron's daddy said.

Luke fought to say the long sound harder: "Reattach it!"

"My goodness. That's a good word, Luke," Byron's daddy said.

"See?" Byron's mommy said. "I told you."

"I'll help you carry it, Byron," Daddy said.

"We can!" Byron yelled.

"Byron!" his mommy yelled.

Stop. Stop. He tried to stop them with his body, but they wouldn't.

"Why are you crying?" Daddy asked.

"Leave it alone," Luke told him.

Daddy looked sad. "Okay."

"Let's go," Byron's mommy said. "We'll leave them to play."

The grown-ups walked off, down the hallway. Deep voices got small, talking about me and Byron. They're so far away. "We'll leave," she said. There's a door in the kitchen. They could go out that way.

"Daddy," Luke called. Daddy had looked so sad when Luke told him to leave Grayskull alone. Luke was sorry to make Daddy sad.

"Don't call for them," Byron said.

"Where did they go?"

"In the kitchen! Come on, let's go!" Byron dragged Grayskull. Everything kept falling out.

"I want to see Mommy and Daddy," Luke said. Byron's room was even farther away.

"No!" Byron yelled. That hurt Luke's eyes, like the sand, scratching. "We don't want to be with grown-ups! We don't like grown-ups, right, Luke?"

"I want to," Luke said, the soft water coming. He walked into the strange silent room, following the voices, deep and kind.

"No!" Byron pulled him. "The grown-ups don't like us! Don't go to them! They don't like us! And we don't like them!"

"Daddy," Luke tried to call. I'm sorry, Daddy. I'm sorry I made you sad.

"No." Byron pulled him away from the warm, the soft voices.

"Let go," Luke tried to tell Byron, but the water drowned him.

"No grown-ups!" Byron pulled hard.

Luke fell. His elbow hit something very cold and hard. He yelled and cried. I'll never get to them, I'll never get back to Mommy and Daddy.

"What is it?" Mommy's voice.

"Luke?" Daddy's voice.

"What did you do, Byron?" The scary sound of Byron's mommy.

"I want to be with you," Luke tried to say to Mommy's ear.

"Of course you can."

"Do you want me?" Luke asked.

"What do you mean?" Mommy said with a kiss. "We've already got you."

"TIME TO PRACTICE," MOMMY SAID. BYRON KNEW SHE WOULD say that. Now that she was home mostly, every day just before lunch, she said, "Time to practice." And then the talk:

"Your teacher says you must practice every day and that the best way is to pick a time—"

A clock from the shelf. Peel the green numbers from the video recorder.

"—and practice at that time every day. Then you can have a cookie."

The cookie was good. But what if he never got a cookie except when doing things like practicing?

"Other children don't know how to play the violin. They would like to know. You have a special chance to learn something they don't know."

And it was something Daddy liked. Daddy would always stop his reading to listen. "I want to practice with Daddy," Byron said.

That worked. Nothing else had ever stopped Mommy. But this time she stopped.

"You do," she said.

"Yeah, yeah, I wanna practice with Daddy."

"Why don't you want to practice with me?" She looked funny. She was stopped.

"Don't like to practice with you." Byron turned away and grabbed a block. Make noise, make noise. "Brrrrr!"

"Why not? What do I do wrong?"

"You yell," Byron said.

"I do not!" Mommy yelled.

"Yes, you do!" Byron yelled back. Make noise, make noise. "Brrrrr! Brrrrr!"

Mommy took the block. "Stop that."

"I'm playing!"

"Not while we're talking. Okay, I won't yell. But you're supposed to practice with the person who takes you to the lessons—"

"I want Daddy to take me to the lessons!" That stopped her again. This was good. "You take me everywhere. Daddy doesn't. Why can't he take me?"

"Daddy has to work," Mommy said, but she said it slow, like not really saying.

Work was hard. A wall. A big stop. "No, he doesn't," Byron said, but didn't like it, like falling on a slide.

"What do you mean? Of course, he has to work."

"You said!" Byron remembered. Mommy in the park. She told Luke. No, somebody. "You said Daddy doesn't have to work."

"No, I didn't. Stop lying, Byron. Daddy has to work at the time you're having your lessons. He can't come to them."

"I want Daddy!" Byron shrieked. He had to get through the wall. He couldn't stop. "I'm not lying!" I remember. No mistake.

"I must have been saying something different and you misunderstood."

"I don't lie!"

Mommy laughed at him. Like blowing in his face. "Oh, not much. Anyway, it's time to practice."

"No!" Arms folded, melting into his skin. Without arms I can't practice.

Mommy went and got the violin case. She put the sheet on the stand.

I can stay like this forever. That will stop her.

"Byron," Mommy said.

Don't move. No sound.

"Byron," Mommy said. "No cookies, no park, no television, no more He-Man toys."

"I don't have arms!" Byron said.

"No M & M's."

"No arms!"

"That's right. No M & M's."

"I don't have!"

"That's right. We can just stand here all day, doing nothing."

There was Francine carrying his clothes. "What you doing?" Francine asked. Francine would play with him. "Being a statue?"

"Monster!" Byron growled. He opened wide to eat her.

"Byron!" Mommy angry. "Francine, Byron is not allowed to do any playing until he practices his violin."

Byron was on Francine, hungry cat, mouth ready to drink her fat. She pushed him. Can't fight the cat.

"Your mama say you can't. Stop now, honey."

"Byron!" Mommy thunder. Mommy pulled arms back. His feet went up. The floor hit his back. Mommy pushed him on the floor into his room. "You have to sit there and do nothing! Unless you practice, you're going to sit and do nothing!"

I could cry. The body wanted to cry. Byron got up and charged at Mommy. "Give me! Give me!" He pulled at the violin case.

"You're going to practice?"

"Yes! Yes! Yes!" Like hitting. "Yes! Yes! Yes!"

Mommy gave him the case. She stood at the stand, her finger pointing to the first note. Click, click. Open. His hand went around the neck.

Put your hand under the belly and lift with both hands.

But he knew he was strong. Strong enough to pull the violin out by the neck. Strong enough to wave it in the air.

He looked at Mommy. She smiled, her finger pointing.

Pull—

"Byron, that's not how—"

He put his hand under the belly. Smooth and hard. It was going to hurt the skin.

"You have to be careful or you'll break it," Mommy said. "It's not a toy."

That's what's wrong with it. Can't break it, can't play with it. It was scary, not giving, always hard. Not something that he would overgrow, make his, do what he wanted.

"Get your feet into play position," Mommy said, nodding at the drawing of shoes on the floor.

Brown, hard, silver strings, little but always bigger, in his arms, but always far away.

"G," Mommy said.

Pull—hurt! Cutting his nail!

Byron let his strength go, let it go, right into the air, flying, spinning, smashing.

When the violin struck his dresser, there was a crack. Not the bang Byron expected, but a crack, a quick break, like an egg.

He looked at Mommy. She stood still, her eyes on the broken violin.

"It hurt me," Byron explained.

He didn't see Mommy's hand. It hit the side of his face like a moving wall.

BYRON JUMPED UP AND DOWN. "HELLO, DADDY!" THE SIDE OF Byron's face was swollen and blue. He bounced cheerfully, he smiled his impish grin, but he looked as if he had had a terrible accident.

"What happened to your face?"

"Mommy hit me," Byron said, and Diane appeared in the hall from the kitchen entrance. She had no marks on her, but her eyes were dead, her chin slack, as if grieving.

"You did?" Peter asked, his throat drying up. He swallowed, hoping it wasn't true. Byron had taken to telling lies, outrageous lies that were hardly real untruths, since they were too preposterous to be able to deceive.

"He threw his violin and smashed it. I lost my temper." Diane's tone was flat, a news report. She put a hand on the flowing sandy cap of Byron's hair and brushed the flopping curls down. She watched them rise again, untamed, with a thoughtful, sad stare.

Peter's legs were taut, so rigid that he felt the need to sag to his knees, as if the muscles would explode from the tension of keeping him up. That brought Peter face-to-face with Byron. The skin on the side of Byron's face was a swirl of yellow and bluish colors. But Byron's eyes twinkled as he said, "I threw it. It got all broke." He lowered his head and shrugged his shoulders in a poor imitation of disappointment. "Can't play anymore."

I'm supposed to mediate this, to find out what's right and what's wrong. I can't leave Diane's misbehavior to her own supervision.

The responsibility was almost as frightening as the evidence that

Diane had lost control. Byron could be maddening, was getting more and more infuriating, but—

"Why did you smash the violin?" Peter asked Byron gently, hoping to get the truth by not implying in his tone that there was any threat of punishment in response to honesty.

"It hurt me." Byron put out his index finger. "See?"

There was nothing wrong with Byron's finger. Diane looked at it with a curious expression, as if she had never seen Byron's finger before. Peter got her attention and raised his eyebrows in silent inquiry, hoping she would explain. But her body sagged in response, her eyes looked vacant—I'm not here, they said.

"Your finger looks okay," Peter said.

"It hurts!" Byron yelled with a whoosh of air into Peter's face. The speed and fury were startling. Peter rocked back on his heels.

"I'm not arguing with you. I just don't understand. How does it hurt your finger?"

"He's lying," Diane said in a listless voice, gazing off at some view, something mysterious and beautiful that wasn't there.

"Am not!" Byron's eyes got red and he was crying. His dissolution into tears happened so fast that logic told Peter the unhappiness must be fake. But Byron wept with conviction. Byron stood between them, making no move to be consoled, standing independent in his deserted sorrow.

And then the truth came to Peter, clear as a message from God. The simple truth shone through the pleasant fog of Peter's assumption that Byron was a privileged, even spoiled child, doted on by his mother, and loved by Peter, if somewhat casually. After all, Diane had given up her career only a few months ago for Byron; even Peter had taken to staying home three or four nights a week. There were layers and layers of evidence that Byron had an especially charmed life: Francine, his nanny, was there for him as well as Diane; Diane's mother made regular visits and brought all the newest and most expensive toys, such as that disgusting castle; Diane had applied to put Byron into the best private schools; Byron had swimming classes, violin classes, tumbling classes, summers in the Hamptons, a trust fund set up by Peter's father, even a friend, that little boy Luke, who lived a block away. Surely this was a childhood that would amaze Charles Dickens. Peter had often said to Kotkin, "I envy him. I resent him having a happy childhood." But now, suddenly, watching this creature, this baby, stand alone in the well of his despair, his face mottled by Diane's rage, Peter knew: this is not a happy child. We are raising him badly. He is suffering. And it's up to you, his father, to make it right.

"Come here," Peter said, and opened his arms.

"No," Byron interpolated in his sobbing. Byron hugged his arms to his chest and swung gently from side to side, rocking himself.

He only trusts his own love, Peter thought, and a nauseating wallop of fear and self-disgust hit Peter in his gut. "Come on," he said, and reached for Byron, not only to comfort his son, but to find a bottom for his own sinking hopes. Byron fought the embrace. He pushed against Peter's arms and averted his kiss.

"Let go," he moaned.

"I love you," Peter said. The words almost hurt his throat.

Diane grunted. Peter looked up at her, but she had no expressiveness on her face. She leaned against the hallway walls, her head resting on a poster of *The Titan*.

I didn't make that show, Peter thought, I made this misery. Kotkin wouldn't approve of that judgment, Peter scolded himself. Byron eased in Peter's arms, accepting the hug. The sobs went from a gallop to a trot, slowing, quieting. Byron's rigid resistance melted into a limbless bundle of warmth. If only Peter could hold Byron forever, in this simple unity of love and good intentions, then being his father would be easy.

"Are you okay?" Peter said.

"Yeeessss," Byron moaned.

"Does your face hurt?"

"No," Byron mumbled.

That had to be a lie. Was he scared to complain of Diane's . . . abuse?

This can't be happening to me, Peter thought. She just hit him once, for God's sakes. Calm down. Again, he looked at her for something, an explanation, help, consciousness.

"I told him I was sorry," she said this time. There was no apology in the tone, however.

"Mommy got angry," Byron said. He looked at Peter hopefully, wanting his answer to satisfy.

What do I do? If I don't say she's wrong, am I approving it for Byron? If I criticize her, am I wrongly faulting her for a minor incident?

What about the violin playing? Is that lost forever? But Byron was so proud, so handsome when he practiced. Wasn't Byron going to reject any attempts in the future to apply himself to the demands of art if this calamity is the only memory of an attempt?

"Can I see the violin?" Peter asked. He wanted to inspect the one tangible thing in all this.

"It's broke," Byron said, lowering his head.

"Does that make you sad?"

"Yeesss," Byron sobbed. "Mommy says I can't play anymore!" he wailed.

He wants to play? Maybe it was just an accident. No, she said he threw it. Or did she? "What happened?" Peter said bravely to Diane. "He dropped it?"

"No! Don't you listen! He refused to practice and he threw it—" Her exasperation was too great. She closed her mouth and stamped her foot. Byron startled in Peter's arms. "I can't talk about it," she said, and leaned back against the poster, shutting her eyes and sighing. "I'm an asshole," she mumbled. "Just forget it!" she shouted at the ceiling.

"I don't think anyone's going to forget it."

"Fine. You deal with it." Diane went into the kitchen. She banged something. Byron jerked again in Peter's arms. He's terrified of her. How could that be? He adores her. How could one slap destroy all that, all her sacrifice, almost three years, month after month, week after week, hour after hour, of love and care and pride—gone? From one slap?

Maybe Byron and I want too much.

"Daddy," Byron said.

"Yes?"

"Would you play with me?"

Peter felt trapped. He didn't want to be with Byron. He wanted to pursue Diane, to correct her, reengage her attention on Byron. She seemed ready to resign from her role as a mother. That had to be prevented. Peter couldn't substitute for her; that would be even worse for Byron. "Show me the violin," Peter said.

"No!"

"Maybe it can be fixed."

Byron opened his eyes wide. He looked normal. Active, his body ready to perform, full of hope. "Okay." He pulled Peter into his room. The violin must have been left where Byron had thrown it. Diane must have been too upset to do anything about it.

It was finished, all right. The neck had been severed, its back thoroughly cracked, and a strip about an inch wide had caved in.

"We could tape it," Byron said, excited now. A project, a repair, an erasure of his wrong and Mommy's anger: attention, correction, and forgiveness all in one package. Peter had given him hope. That was stupid of me, Peter realized, holding the dismembered instrument in his hands.

"I'm sorry, but it's too broken."

Byron stared at the corpse for a moment, then his cheeks puffed, his mouth got tight, and he cried. "I wanna play it," he wailed in harmony with the sobs.

"We'll get you another one," Peter said, hugging him, hugging him hard.

"Mommy said no," Byron blubbered.

"We'll get another," Peter said, and felt much better. Forgive all this. He had his motive right at last. Forgive it all, his mischief, her rage. "We'll get another. You'll play."

"No, we won't." Diane was there, like a ghost, appearing whole, from silence to full volume. "You can't fix everything with your money for him. He broke it. That's it. He has to learn that what he does has consequences."

Byron shivered in Peter's arms. He pressed himself against Peter's chest, an animal hiding in a cave.

"You can't just appear and make everything magically perfect," she said to Peter. Her eyes burned black in the ringed hollows of her dark face.

Peter clutched Byron and made no answer.

She's declared war on us, he thought, and his throat dried up again.

"You'd better get me something to read about being Jewish," Nina said, watching the streaming lights of the West Side. The car bucked and slid on the patchwork repairs of the decaying highway. Their roughness had done nothing to prevent an exhausted Luke from immediately passing out in his car seat. His head lolled to one side as if partially severed.

"Huh?" Eric said. He glanced away from the road to show her, in the glowing half-light, an incredulous face.

"Or you'll have to explain to Luke what the stories are."

"What stories? The ovens? How Woody Allen became a sex symbol? What are we talking about?"

"God, Eric. I mean, Passover"—she hesitated before pronouncing the word—"Hanukkah. The stories of the holidays."

Eric didn't answer. He nodded to himself, with a sneer on his lips. "Okay," he said after a bit.

"I'm going to tell him about Jesus."

"You are?"

"Yes. So you'd better give Judaism equal time."

"Why the hell are you gonna tell him about Jesus? You don't go to church."

"It's part of who he is. He's half Jewish and he's half Christian—"

"This is 'cause of fucking Sadie! I could kill that woman!" Eric lurched forward in his seat. He took his hands off the steering wheel and made as if to strangle the windshield. The car weaved slightly out of their lane.

"Eric!" Nina reached for the wheel.

He grabbed it back. "Calm down. I'm not gonna kill us. God, that woman is a walking migraine. She's just trying to get under your skin with all that crap about whether—"

"It's got nothing to do with Sadie. I've thought—"

"Of course it does! She's the Howard Cosell of Passover. She goes to aggravate people!"

Nina laughed. "Eric, you know Luke. He heard all that talk. Tomorrow he'll start asking questions. I have to answer them. And even if Sadie hadn't done it, sooner or later it would come up. You can postpone it for a while, but eventually you have to tell him who he is and what it means."

"He's our son!" Eric shouted as he wildly switched from one lane to another to pass a sluggish car. "He's not a kike or a goy. He's our goddamn son."

"Eric, you can't teach Luke to hate himself because he's Jewish."

"What?" Eric looked hurt, not that surface turbulence of irritation at Sadie, but the deeper worry, the look of self-doubt, that he often brought home from the office.

"Sometimes, from the way you act with your family, it makes me think you married me because I'm not Jewish."

"That is one of the reasons I married you."

Nina let this hang in the air for a moment, sniffing it for malodorousness.

Eric glanced at her. "What's wrong with that? Isn't one of the reasons you married me because I'm not a Wasp?"

"I didn't think about it," Nina answered.

"Oh, come on, you must've."

"Did you also marry me because of my money?" Nina felt brave asking this; she felt reckless.

Eric sat up and straightened his usually hunched shoulders. He didn't look at her and his tone was clipped and formal. "What money? You didn't have any. And you still don't."

This evasion disappointed Nina. Made her angry. "You know what I mean. My family money."

"When I met your family, I thought they had to be broke. They wore crappy clothes, they complained about every nickel, they bragged about how cheaply they got things—"

"You're not being honest, Eric." She got that out, but then turned away to look out her window at the bouncing city, long and dark, secret and shining.

"I've made more money for your family in the last year than any of them have for two generations," Eric said, in a rage. The rage of the guilty, Nina thought. "They never gave us a nickel! We're the only one of their children who remember their anniversary, who've given them a grandchild, and the only money we get is a percentage, a tip, a gratuity, for making them millions. My parents, who have nothing, *nothing*, gave us twice as much money when we got married—"

"I don't want to talk about it anymore," Nina said, still watching the city, dark and glowing on the water—

"I see. You insult me and then the discussion's over. Great."

She wanted to cry. This wasn't the funny, excited boy she married. He was as ugly as these concrete streets, dirty and unchanging, lit up for show, but dark and lonely, the welcoming glow nothing more than a lie.

"All right," Eric suddenly said as if answering a question, although they had been silent for a while. "The truth is I married you because you were completely different from all the girls I had ever met. I didn't marry you for your money, but I knew money and you were connected, that one way or another it would come along."

Of course, he knew I would one day inherit, he knew that Father's cheapness only meant there was lots of money, he must have known, and that's why he wanted a child, an heir, the only grandchild so far, the firstborn.

MOMMY. MOMMY. WARM IN THE COOL, WHISPERING, "SHHH, we're almost home."

"Do you want the stroller?" Daddy's strong voice asked.

"Shhh," Mommy said, and Daddy sang to her.

In the great green room there was a telephone, and a red balloon—

Way, way up, in the slice between the buildings, floating on the sky, was the moon.

"Moooon," Luke tried to say in his sleepy throat.

"Yes," Mommy whispered. "It's a full moon."

So big to look at. He closed on her soft pillows, pressed his nose on them, and felt her blanket arms cover him. . . .

Byron says: come on Luke, stay with me. We don't like the grown-ups. And they don't like us.

No!

Come with me, Luke. We don't like the grown-ups. And they don't like us.

No!

Byron dances in the sand. He calls from the top of the slide. Always faster. Always stronger. Come with me, Luke.

"Mommy!"

"Shhhh, we're just in the elevator. You'll be in your nice crib soon."

"I love you, Luke." Daddy scratched a kiss.

Press into the pillows and fall on the arms.

"I like them, Byron."

Come with me, come with me. We don't need the grown-ups.

Good night, Moon.

Good night, Luke.

Part Three

13

DIANE LET GO. SHE OPENED HER CLENCHED FINGERS AND watched her identity float up, away from impossible standards, smaller and smaller against the passive blue sky of her surrender.

Peter said, "I'll take Byron to the violin lessons," and she dared him, with a release: "Good."

When Byron appeared at the bedside, rubbing his eyes, saying, "I peed in my bed," she said, "Good." And turned on her side, away from him, back into the dark, the private night of sleep.

Her mother said, "I'll come up, stay with you for a few days and help with Byron's birthday." And Diane said, "Good," a spectator while her mother ran the house for the week.

I quit, she had told Stoppard.

I quit, she told Peter.

I quit, she told Byron.

I'm glad you came, she told her mother.

Diane made the bathroom her pleasure palace, retiring there almost every night with a paperback mystery, a glass of wine, a pack of cigarettes, a box of something to munch, cereal, popcorn, M & M's, anything little and crunchy, and treated herself, her stomach, her mind, her clitoris, climaxing with closed lips, surrounded by the paper wreckage of her snacks, the low moans drowned by the thumping water.

She shopped, the horizon of her wardrobe widened to infinite distance by her escape from the legal compound. She could dress like a Greenwich Village wife, or a suburban bourgeois, or a bag lady for that matter. She was shy at first, and needed a girlfriend for company and permission. Diane took along Betty Winters, or Didi, or her old friend from summer camp, Karen, whom Diane had seen less and less of with each passing year of marriage to

Peter; but now Diane reversed that trend. Each was good for prodding Diane to experiment with different looks—Betty bourgeois, Didi seductive single, Karen outright weird. Diane spent uncounted thousands (she refused to total up the credit-card bills) and, after ruthlessly discarding her old clothes, put the new things in her closet. Each morning, she was tempted into wearing one of the new outfits, but more often than not, she ended up in her comfortable worn jeans, a soft cotton T-shirt, and a loose sweater. Only those incredibly expensive boots Karen had talked her into buying got real use. Even at self-indulgence, she was a failure.

Diane stayed clear of Byron. When he refused an order, she walked away and left him undressed, the toilet unflushed, the meal uneaten, the park unexplored, the toys strewn on the floor. During the week there was Francine to do those things and, on the weekends, she noticed that every once in a great while, like the appearance of Halley's comet, Peter would actually straighten the living room, take the bag of cookies away from Byron, take Byron to the park (well, that happened only once), or charm Byron, as if he were a reluctant foundation board member, into another bite of vegetable.

But the applications to schools were due soon. Diane waited for Peter to volunteer. She mentioned the fact.

"You'd better get going," he said.

She was so beaten, so fearful of insisting on anything, she said meekly, "Will you help?"

"I don't have time," Peter answered. "I think you do," he added, the closest he had come—yet—to a complaint about her sloth.

She set aside one day, and groaned herself up to the task. It was like starting a car that had been idle all winter. She needed seven cups of coffee in succession to clear the sludge in her system and make the phone calls. She hired a limo for the day, an insane extravagance, and went by each institution to get its forms. Her hand trembled when she filled out the application for Byron to take another IQ test, a prerequisite for all these fancy schools. The first try at that had been the birth of her rages at Byron. Peter's got to take him to the test, she said to herself.

When Diane stopped by Hunter to get its application, she felt old hopes rise, but sickeningly—a rich meal gone bad in her belly. All the parents Diane knew were obsessed by Hunter and the other top schools. When Luke's parents came to brunch, that was all they talked about, Hunter, Dalton, Trinity, Collegiate—and whether the Grace Church School in their own neighborhood was good enough. If Byron gets into Hunter, she thought, clutching the forms as the hired car pulled away from the curb, then no one will know I'm a failure.

Hunter wanted something none of the other schools did: "Please write a description of your child's accomplishments and abilities. If more space is needed, you may attach additional sheets."

What? My child's accomplishments? Well, he forced me to face the fact that I have no endurance. He can break a violin in a single gesture. He's the only person in the world who had the nerve to inform my mother-in-law that she is going to die. I think it was news to her. He also knows the network scheduling of cartoon shows by heart, now that I've given up discipline and let him watch hour after hour after hour.

Abilities? Well, he can eat three slices of pizza and top that off with ice cream, but a stalk of broccoli makes him full. He can climb up slides, he can come out of a bath dirtier than he went in, he can program a compact disk player to repeat the same cut of *Cats*, but he can't put on underpants.

What if she didn't hype Byron on the applications? What if all the mothers and fathers told only the bad rather than the good? Could Hunter still pick out the best and brightest? Were there brilliant bad qualities?

She sat at home, Hunter's blank page in front of her. I could call his brattiness independence, his stubbornness determination, his knowledge of television schedules a sign of concentration and memory. I could say he's honest and forthright for telling his grandmother she's going to die, and his refusal to dress shows a love of nature.

"Mommy!" Byron pushed in the door, no knock, self-assured, a prince with run of the castle. "Can I have a cookie?"

She nodded. She had resigned her authority, but she couldn't actually speak the words of acquiescence. Her head was forever bobbing, like one of those dolls, semidecapitated, a spring allowing the head to bounce when touched ever so lightly.

"Mommy says I can!" Byron shouted to Francine, and he skipped off, humming a cartoon-show theme.

I could say that his ability to sleep in urine-soaked pajamas shows a brave disregard for personal comfort. And the way Byron orders his one friend, Luke, around, insisting he build everything, turning Luke into a mere spectator, pushing Luke like a cart from one spot to another, thoroughly dominating him, shows leadership qualities. Never mind that it's the same kind of command Hitler mastered.

And now he hits adults if you say no to him. Bunches up his little hand into a bony fist and whacks you on the shoulder. That shows a sense of equality with authority.

The tip of her pen inadvertently touched the paper and a little squiggle appeared. She was exhausted from her ride around the city. I quit my job so I could do more with Byron and instead I do less. The pen kept on sliding, like Byron, with a mind of its own. The squiggle went down the page, a thin blue river running on the white landscape to nowhere.

UNCONSCIOUS. A BASKETBALL PLAYER HITTING THREE POINTERS. A home-run hitter on a streak. Beating every stoplight on a drive through the city. Being high. Closing your eyes, and becoming the music, your body moving to the rhythm with the sound—even before you heard the notes.

Every stock Eric picked, every sale, even on prices, he got right every time. The words in the business pages burned into Eric's consciousness, and sparked immediate decisions. He could glance at a headline and see a stock result. He could listen to an economist and know whether he was right or wrong. The air itself was full of nourishment. Unconscious. Don't wake me. Don't let this reality become a dream.

Oh, to be sure, the market had rallied across the board, everyone was doing well, but not as well as Eric. Between the second and third year of handling Tom's money, with the market up 40 percent, Eric had tripled his father-in-law's portfolio, his own, and those of Joe's clients who let Eric trade for them. In effect, that was the entire clientele, since Joe now tagged along with Eric's choices, still making some moves of his own, but few, very few. Joe went with the hot hand.

Eric almost woke up when he realized that all the discretionary money of the firm, fifty million dollars, danced from stock to stock at his tune. Sammy nicknamed Eric the Wizard, duplicating Eric's fantasies. Of course, Sammy said it with a sneer, but a thin one, and he listened respectfully when Eric talked, his previously hectoring tone erased by Eric's profits.

Everybody loves a winner.

Everybody but Nina.

For eight years Eric had felt shame, embarrassed that he hadn't produced for Nina, that he wasn't a figure of success for her to be proud of, and now, now that he stood gleaming in triumph for all the world to see, she walked past him as though he were a familiar statue covered with pigeon shit.

She's jealous 'cause her family is so proud of me, Eric decided, and thus forgave, or at least ignored, Nina's cool behavior.

Eric didn't have time for Nina anyway. Eric's success with Tom's money was bragged about at Boston dinner parties, and country-club foursomes. That meant nights out with prospective and current clients.

It changed his relationship with Luke. Luke sadly lowering his head as Eric approached for a good-bye kiss, Luke pretending another evening without Daddy was okay, Luke talking while Eric tried to read the endless flow of business reporting, tried to brand himself with more information—yes, yes, yes, Luke, okay, Daddy has to read, Daddy has to think—Luke's watching Eric go with baleful eyes became almost a nightly event.

But Eric had to keep on. The money rushed in, what he most wanted, what he had thirsted for, waves of it, and he needed new ideas, he couldn't just keep buying the same stocks. Tom's friends gave Eric even more than Tom had originally. These days, if Eric tried to take a position in a thinly traded stock, his own buying would send the price up 3 to 4 percent.

And then one day, one innocuous day, Eric's luck hit the wall.

The averages all went to new highs. But three-quarters of Eric's stocks didn't move at all. The portfolios—their daily value printed out with ruthless accuracy at the market close and put in Eric's hands to study at home—showed a slight loss.

Okay. Not serious.

The next day, another record for the Dow Industrials, for the S&P Five Hundred, third-highest trading volume in Stock Exchange history. The few picks Joe had stuck with, boring, obvious blue-chip stocks, went wild. Eric's stocks, the high-flying OTC growth issues, just died, dumb spectators at the carnival.

Sammy was on Eric immediately: "Your stuff's looking constipated."

The word enraged Eric. Constipation was Luke's one flaw, a problem that had gotten worse with every solution, a single malfunction that threatened the entire mechanism. The doctor's chocolate laxative did nothing. Days went by with nothing coming out and Luke got less active with each one, until finally Luke sat immobilized, frightened to do anything, because—

Because why? Whose fault was this difficulty? Luke's anatomy or some mistake that Eric and Nina had made?

"Get off my back!" Eric shouted at Sammy. Eric had been too good, too strong, too brilliant to be the meek Eric anymore.

Joe sternly glanced at Eric's noise. Eric stared that old man down.

I am this firm, Eric thought. They would have lost most of their clients if we'd stuck with Joe's lemminglike picks, buying whatever the institutions did, a coattail investment strategy that a six-year-old could imitate. "You want to look at my performance compared to the S and P over the last year?" Eric yelled in answer to Sammy, but he looked at Joe.

"Whoa!" Sammy teased. "Hey, Wizard, don't turn me into a toad!"

With the growth of their assets, the firm had new employees, two additional secretaries, Carlton still there to handle the smaller clients, and a solemn Conservative Jew, Aram, who ran the computer programs that kept their books. Everyone was seated at the circular table and they all laughed or smiled at Sammy's mockery.

"I can't work like this! I can't handle this kind of money if I'm gonna have everyone in my hair all the time!" Eric shouted at Joe. It was like working in a subway car, everywhere you turned a face. No silence, no rest, phones always tweeting like sick birds, Quotron keys clacking dully like lamed crickets.

"Take it easy," Joe said, and glanced at Sammy with something like a private exchange.

"What does that mean?" Eric demanded. "Take it easy! I'm a big winner for two years. And two fucking days! Two lousy goddamn fucking days my stuff doesn't move and this asshole's on my back! I don't have to come in here, you know. I can sit at home and phone in the trades. Hell, I can call the floor myself, I don't need Sammy to do it for me." He was blasting into the atmosphere, breaking up gloriously, sparks flying into the night sky, free of their gravity, ten years of their drag, free and alone—

"I was kidding!" Sammy squeaked. Sammy was scared.

He should be, Eric thought. I could insist Joe send Sammy home to his mother.

"I'm sorry! Jesus Christ! I'm sorry," Sammy pleaded.

Why, the little prick was almost begging.

"I'm going for a walk," Eric said. Eric knew the liquid fuel of his rage would burn out and he'd feel stupid, crashing to earth with stammering apologies. He wanted to go before humiliation followed righteousness.

He went outside during the trading day. When had he ever done that, except for a quick bite to eat? He loved the numbers of the Quotron, changing with a little blip, a quick dance, never still, a new game every day. Now that he had a past to live up to, they were terrible, but once the promise of tomorrow had been his friend, a consolation.

What a relief to be away, away from the possibility of erosion. What should he do? Close out his positions? Had the market topped? Was this October 1929?

He could lose it all: the income, the respect, the control of Nina's family money. Tom had even talked of creating a trust for Luke. Eric was so close to victory.

On the street, he was lost. Away from the money, he was confused. Eric bought a hot dog from an Asian on a street corner, even though he had already eaten. It tasted horrible, nothing like the kosher franks Eric used to get as a kid from the neighborhood deli in Washington Heights. The deli was owned by a white sausage of a man: Morris. Morris made the franks behind the tall glass display of his meats and handed the buns over the top of that cliff. On his wrist, stretched bluish black numbers were tattooed. "Enjoy," Morris said. God, they were good. Hot and thick and juicy, the mustard tangy, the sauerkraut warm and crunchy, the bun crust firm.

And Eric liked the numbers on Morris's wrist—an 8 on the end undulated as the skin flexed to lower the food.

Eric was seven when his father told him what the numbers meant. Their color was uneven, faded here, greenish there, their shapes twisted—a consequence of attempts to erase them. Before Eric knew better, he thought they were a spy's secret code.

Once Eric knew the truth, the next time he got a frank, Eric's hand trembled when he took it from Morris.

"Enjoy."

"I'm sorry," the little confused Eric answered.

What a schmuck, Eric thought, throwing out what was left of the Asian's hot dog. Morris didn't need my pity.

Were the Quotron's numbers going to betray him also?

Why can't Luke move his bowels?

Luke screamed and screamed while huge, impossible turds came out, usually only halfway. Pearl had told Eric and Nina that sometimes she had to pull them out—

Ugh. It was disgusting. Three o'clock. The last hour. Eric went back to the room with no privacy, to the endless scoreboard.

Joe was happy. His stupid, obvious Dow stocks were soaring—look at them go, the owl seemed to say, blinking at his Quotron. Big multiple point gains, setting new highs.

"Your positions are down," Aram said dispassionately.

Eric stared at the sheet. How could they be down? The fucking Dow was up forty points! How could he have found withering trees in a forest of winners? Eric stared at the black numbers, tattooed on the page, and instead saw Luke scream at nature's release. Eric didn't look up, afraid lest the others see on his face the fear he felt.

Make a decision, for God's sakes. Don't be like your father. Dad stayed in that bad location with his little shoe store, sat there while his business dwindled. Move, Mother told him. He didn't. And Dad went under, ended up as a clerk at a rival's store, bankrupt in the midst of the go-go sixties.

"Sell," Eric said.

"Sell what?" Sammy asked.

"Let's start clearing out the lowest gainers. Bottom half of this." Eric stabbed the page with a pen, drawing a line to show what should go. "I'll take this group." Another stab. "You do them."

"Don't panic," Sammy said.

"Don't tell me what to do," Eric said. He looked around. Everyone's head was down except for Joe's, the owl head still and huge on its shrinking torso.

"Those OTC stocks," Joe said. "They lag the blue chips sometimes. Maybe you should hold a day or two. Get better prices."

"I'm just clearing out half, taking some profits. We'll reposition on the next sell-off."

Joe nodded. "Don't panic. That's beneath you."

Sammy looked at Eric, a hand ready to pick up the phone.

"We'll wait," Eric said.

PETER HELD BYRON'S HAND. BYRON REPEATEDLY WITHDREW HIS fingers from Peter's grip, corks popping free. Byron ran up to a store window; or to chase stray, magically fluttering garbage; or to pretend he was some horrible cartoon character who could fly or run very fast. But Peter always recaptured the little hand, smooth and warm, partly for the pleasure of holding Byron's energy close, but mostly to hang on. Peter worried that on one of these trips to the violin lessons he would somehow, through an insane random event, lose Byron forever.

Peter had never expected Diane to agree when he offered to take Byron to the violin lessons. It was the first and only task of Byron's rearing at which Diane admitted she was incompetent and Peter might not be. Diane had conceded defeat for the first time.

Since then, she seemed to do nothing else besides surrendering to every challenge, living a perpetual Appomattox. Peter understood that this meant Diane was very unhappy; sometimes he wondered if she was breaking down. But he didn't press an investigation because Peter discovered that Diane's collapse, although irritating and inconvenient in practical ways, was an emotional relief for Byron, as well as for him.

Peter's first task, when he took over the music lessons, was to inform the school about the destroyed violin and replace it. That was easy. It cost a fortune, but it was only money.

Taking Byron to the lesson was another matter. Peter was nervous the first time. He would have been fearful anyway, left in charge of his son; the fact that it was an activity Diane hadn't been able to handle scared Peter all the more. But the dreaded event had turned out to be almost boring. Byron's teacher was a young thing, no more than twenty. And Byron wasn't rebellious. Although Byron did everything incorrectly, he worked hard to impress Peter. "See, Daddy?" he kept saying.

What should Peter do? Criticize or encourage? He picked the latter. No matter how poorly Byron followed the instructions, Peter smiled, and said, "That's great, Byron." It seemed to work, not in the sense that Byron improved, but he continued to try. Later, Peter decided that must have been Diane's mistake: she hadn't encouraged Byron; she kept pushing relentlessly, like a mad Olympic coach. Poor Diane, she wanted perfection now. But even the teacher let Byron slide. She gave up correcting Byron's improper positioning of his feet to concentrate on the violin grip. When Byron reacted testily to those instructions, his teacher gave up on that also and, as a last resort, merely insisted he play the correct two notes on the exercise.

"At home, I want you to practice your foot positioning and how you hold the violin." The teacher spoke to Byron, but glanced at Peter, to signal it was really his duty.

Of course, Peter realized. They dump the mean part on the parents. That's why poor Diane had worked so hard, responding to the violin lessons as if she were the student being tested. He felt sorry for her.

"They really expect the parents to do all the work," Peter commented casually the evening after first taking Byron to a lesson. Peter introduced the topic, hoping to soothe Diane's feelings, to let her forgive herself.

"Yep," she said, and kept her eyes on yet another murder mystery. She read them constantly these days, a perpetual mask in front of her face, skulls and daggers, pistols and dark shadows.

"I didn't do that when we practiced," Peter said to Diane's murder mystery. The teacher had suggested they practice right after the lesson when the instructions would still be fresh.

During the practice, Byron had again done everything improperly. But Peter didn't harass Byron. Peter reminded Byron about his feet, about the proper hold of the violin, before Byron started to practice.

That was the first sign of revolt. "I know!" Byron shouted.

"Don't shout at me," Peter said gently. "I'm only going to tell you once. If you do it wrong, I won't bother you about it. It's up to you to remember." For the first few notes, Byron was in order. Then he was chaos: changing positions, the violin sometimes under his chin, sometimes his cheek, sometimes almost floating in the air. When Byron asked to play with the bow—a no-no—Peter let him. Byron soon got bored and gave it back.

"I told him what he had to do at the start," Peter reported to Diane, still trying to break through the spine of her paperback, to tell her it wasn't her fault, "and then I let him make mistakes. When it was over, I told him what he had done incorrectly."

"I'm sure that made it a lot easier." Diane answered neutrally, and turned away, cuddling with her book.

Again, at being corrected, Byron had balked. "I know, I know," he whined. "You don't have to tell me." He then asked for a cookie.

"It did make it easier," Peter said, pleased Diane hadn't argued. "He asked for a cookie when it was done."

"Un-huh." Diane read on.

"I told him he could have a cookie after dinner every day whether he practiced or not, whether he did it well or not."

"Guess we'd better buy more cookies," Diane said, and laughed. "I'm going to take a bath," she added, and fled the room.

For months Peter had successfully taken Byron to the lessons and practiced with him every day. Diane never listened—she deliberately went away if they got the violin out in front of her—never asked about Byron's progress, never responded when Peter raised the subject.

And Byron enjoys it so much, Peter complimented himself, while they walked to yet another lesson. Peter held the eager, twitching little hand and smiled back at a woman who, while passing them on the street, beamed at the sight of father and son and tiny violin case. Diane should feel that way, Peter thought. She should be proud.

She's just jealous that I'm doing it so well, Peter decided, and squeezed Byron's warm fingers. Well, to hell with her, Peter thought, his heart full of happiness.

* * *

THE WORK WAS GREAT. NINA WAS GOOD AT IT. SHE KNEW, NOT simply because Tad, her teacher and part-time boss, told her so, but because she could feel her own mastery.

Of course, it was nothing, coloring the designs, making a suggestion here and there about hue—very, very gently, creeping through the lair of a sleeping monster. Tad never woke to roar at her. But he sure did yell at the others, especially the pretty young men. Tad would push the loose, bulky sleeves of his sweater up to his elbows for emphasis, and his reedy voice, ill suited for the sounding of anger, squealed up to the fourteen-foot tin ceiling. But never at her. "No, dear," was the worst he would say.

Is Tad gentle with me because he's gay? she wondered. Couldn't the reverse be true just as easily? She mentioned this question once to Eric.

"He's a fag?" Eric said, chewing the word up in several tones of disgust. He sounded like a real New Yorker then; the word came out of his mouth unvarnished from the raw prejudices and fears of his adolescence. "Of course, he's a fag," Eric added. "He's a dress designer. That's a relief. I was worried you were having an affair with him."

"You were?" Nina was amazed. Not at the idea that Eric would be jealous if she had an affair, but at the discovery that he had the imagination to think she might. "You were, really?"

"Yep."

Nina was pleased for several hours, until it occurred to her that maybe Eric didn't think any man would want her to work for him unless she was putting out.

"Why didn't you tell me he was a fag?" Eric asked the next night.

She was angry by then. "Stop calling him a fag."

Eric laughed, with the indulgent laugh of a parent. "Sorry. Why didn't you tell me he's gay?"

"Why should I?" Nina asked. I don't like what he's become, Nina thought. Eric was dressed in a suit because he had had to have drinks with a potential client. Eric's kinky bush of hair was pressed flat, his eyes were circled by fatigue, he spoke loudly, probably from the alcohol—everything smelled of business and money and grown-up maleness. Nothing soft, nothing imaginative, nothing natural, nothing beautiful.

"I don't know." Eric flipped through a copy of *Forbes*—he always had some money publication in front of him. "Just gossip."

Eric peered at an article and then spoke abruptly. "Aren't you worried about AIDS?"

Nina wondered where that came from. She stared.

He tossed the *Forbes* away. "You know, with all that sewing, if he's gay, couldn't there be some blood—"

She stared at him. He was kidding. He had to be.

Eric paused and looked nervous, aware he had said something stupid. "I just thought—you know there might be—"

"He doesn't do any sewing!" Nina shouted. She chuckled at the thought. "You think I'm sitting in a room sewing?" She burst out laughing. Is Eric so out of it, so totally uninterested in me, that he thinks I'm sewing in a sweatshop?

"No, of course not," Eric said, a grave mask lowering over his innocent bewilderment.

"He sketches designs. I help color them sometimes, draft variations on his instructions. He lets me try out a few little things. Tiny, tiny things—you wouldn't even notice the changes."

"Why does he need help coloring them?" Eric asked.

"He doesn't." Nina shook her head. She must have explained this before. "He doesn't want to go through the tedious process of trying different shades. These are just for him to look at, rough sketches, and it's a way of us learning about the unity of color and design—the whole creative process."

"You mean, this is the school part?"

"No, not exactly."

"Is his company publicly traded?" Eric said, and reached for a copy of the *Wall Street Journal*. He flipped to the stock listing noisily, an animal rustling through a bed of leaves.

"I don't know," Nina said.

"Could you ask him?"

"No."

"No?" Eric raised his eyebrows. "Nothing to be embarrassed about. Tell him your husband manages fifty million dollars—he'll be happy to tell you whether there's stock for me to buy."

"Un-huh," Nina said, and tried to think of something to do or say that would end this. She couldn't. She stared back at Eric and tried to smile pleasantly, but her chin felt tight, defensive.

Eric leaned forward and spoke with eager condescension. "Really. You see, if he has a publicly traded company, then he'll own a lot of shares himself, and if I buy for my clients, that'll send the price up, which increases his worth. Understand?"

"Yes," she managed to get out. She willed herself to smile

brightly, but her muscles rebelled and restrained that desire into a regretful pout.

"You'll ask him?"

"Un-huh," she mumbled, convinced that this evasion wasn't as bad as a direct no.

Eric nodded. He glanced at the stock listings and let the newspaper drop to the floor. "Did Luke take a crap today?"

Nina shook her head. Not this again. What could she do about it? She followed the doctor's impossible directions: get Luke to take this chocolate pudding stool softener, but don't make a big deal about his constipation. How could she do both? Luke had never been told to do a particular thing and had the reason why withheld from him. "Just tell him it's something to make him grow," the pediatrician said, irritated, wanting to go on to the next patient, to give another quick answer to someone else. But that would be like Luke's vitamins and she never made him take his vitamins. This laxative had to be administered every night or it wouldn't work. So she told Luke what it was for and he was scared.

Luke doesn't want to go to the bathroom, she admitted to herself. Luke's not constipated. He doesn't like the sensation, and so he holds it in and then becomes constipated.

"Don't make an issue of going to the bathroom," the doctor had told Nina. "If you make it a test of wills, things will get worse."

"It will make it softer," she told Luke, and offered him a reward if he took it.

Luke took the chocolate pudding softener and, for several months, it helped. He would move his bowels every three or four days with a lot of complaining and straining, but he'd manage it at last. Afterward he was so happy, racing everywhere, hungry for activity and very hungry for food. But by the next day, she could see him occasionally flex his buttocks tight, pushing it in, stopping his actions, his mood changing. . . .

She hadn't told Eric her observation. He would argue. Because Nina had once confided to Eric that she was constipated as a child, he was convinced Luke's problem was genetic. Her fault, more to the point.

"How long has it been?" Eric asked.

The intervals were lengthening, and so were the stools. "Five days," she said.

"We have to take him back to the doctor."

"I'm not taking him back to the doctor," Nina said instantly. "He's examined him and there's nothing organically wrong."

"There has to be!" Eric pleaded. He got up from the chair and removed his suit jacket, ready to get to the dirty work. "How could he be holding it in?"

"He just holds it in!" Nina said.

"But how?"

"Don't you ever hold it in?"

"No," Eric inhaled, his chest puffing. "Why would I?"

"You're not near a bathroom! You have to hold it in. What would you do, go in your pants? Of course, you can hold it in."

"I go every morning, right after my coffee. Unless my stomach's upset."

"Terrific. Let's get your mother to toilet-train Luke. She did a great job with you."

"I'm not saying it's your fault."

"I know you're not. But you could try and think of what Luke is feeling and can do, rather than what you feel and you do. You and Luke are different people."

"Look." Eric sighed, and glanced toward the hall, as if he were being summoned away. After a moment, Eric turned back, stared at Nina out of the dark hollows of his exhausted face, and sighed again.

"What is it? Say what's on your mind."

"You understand it better because you had the same problem—"

"I did not have the same problem!" Nina slapped the couch. He was impossibly stupid, a clumsy city car spinning its wheels in the mud of real life. "I was a little constipated. This is different."

"There has to be something wrong with him."

"He doesn't like doing it!" Exasperation forced the truth out of her. "I can see him holding it in. So it gets harder and hurts more, so he holds it in more! And on and on, worse and worse."

Eric frowned. He said timidly, "You've seen him hold it in?"

Nina stood and imitated Luke's flexed buttocks squeezing closed the hole in his dam. "That's what he does! Even Pearl sees him do it. He does it in front of you."

"Jesus," Eric said, and sagged back down into the chair. He looked shot, his arms limp, his head forward on his chest, his face still and solemn. "Jesus," he mumbled again. "What are we going to do?"

"I'm not doing anything about it, Eric," Nina said. "Everything I've tried makes it worse. I've talked to him, explained to him, but he won't let go. I've taken him to the doctor—I've done everything. It's up to Luke. He's suffering. It's up to him to get out of it."

Absorbing this news, Eric looked a little bit like the Lincoln Memorial. His great body was squared by the chair, his legs and arms massive, his head quiescent, his eyes mournful, seeing ahead to the future.

"He'll be fine," she tried to reassure Lincoln.

"You can't leave it up to him," Eric intoned. A house divided against itself cannot stand. "He can't deal with it. He's a three-year-old baby." Deep and grave. A severe judgment of history.

"There are some things people learn on their own. It's his body. He has to be comfortable with it—"

"That's the goy in you," Abe Lincoln said.

"Goddammit!" Nina thought him so ridiculous she gave up being gentle. "How would you like it if every time something didn't go perfectly with Luke, I called you a kike?"

"Oh, come on!" Eric complained. At least that broke his marble pose.

"It's the same thing!" Nina said. "Goy! That's an insult. This isn't my fault! It's not because I'm a goy! Maybe it's your fault! You never challenge Luke to do anything on his own. When you take him to the park, you still stand by the slide and catch him."

"He won't go down unless—" Eric protested.

"He goes down the slide with no one catching him all week. On the weekends, with you, he has to be caught. You're a patsy for him. He knows you'll do anything. So he asks. He's manipulating you!"

Eric was her boy again, sagging in his suit, his big face opened by pain and amazement. Help me, Nina, his eyes seemed to call out. She felt sorry for him. Unless he was puffed up, pursuing money, he really didn't know anything about life.

"You know, Eric," she said, seeing her chance to get through. "You have to stop making everything ugly. Fag, goy. You're really a sweet man." She felt her love for Eric waken from its overtired sleep. Maybe she could restore him, restore them—

"What are you talking about!" Eric said. "Is that what this is about? 'Cause I called your boss a fag?"

"No," she said sadly. He was slipping away; the connection was loose.

"You're not gonna help Luke 'cause I called your boss a fag?" Eric was a peacock again, still tired, but swelling, confident in his silly fan of colors. "Is that why you won't ask him about his stock?"

"I told you I would. You're—"

"You won't. You were lying."

"I was not!" she lied. She had to get away. "I'm going to bed—"

"No!" Eric reached for her. "No, don't go to bed angry. Please. That's the worst. I can't sit here alone, worrying about Luke, with you pissed off at me."

If only she could stay and he would stop badgering, but he would never let go of his troubles, never let Luke work his own way out of something, never leave her alone to succeed or fail in the world, always wanting himself there, helping, bragging, nagging, like some massive overcoat, sweltering, tripping her, its heavy cloth blocking her mouth. "Don't worry about Luke," she said to him. "I'll call, I'll try to get another doctor—"

"Who?"

"Something. Let's go to sleep now," she said with motherly sternness.

Little boy Eric turned away, his frame expanding in the chair, still and great, Lincoln again. His jaw set. "I had a bad day. I got to read some stuff. Pick new stocks."

So that was it. Money. He hadn't made money today. So he had to fix her. Fix Luke. Fix something.

"Good night," she said, and put him out of her mind.

DIANE CARRIED THE ENVELOPES TO THE MAILBOX.

"Let me! Let me!" Byron barked up at her.

She groaned at the effort of lifting Byron, her arms trembling from his weight while he lowered the lid and put the letters in. She had filled them out, the school applications for Byron to begin his life on the New York assembly line, so he could get a reservation at Orso, so he could pass the co-op board at the San Remo, so he would know which beach to lie on in the Hamptons, and finally so he would know to pretend that none of that knowledge mattered.

I'm being unfair. She smiled into the sun. What a pretty day. This Saturday was made by a god in love. The city glowed. The air was mild. Beautiful pedestrians ambled on the concrete river in a gentle flow, passing the cliff walls of iridescent, sandblasted buildings capped by blue sky, occasionally fishing at the sidewalk stands of food, art, clothing, and incomprehensible souvenirs.

Peter had done the job for her, written the page describing Byron's abilities and accomplishments to send to Hunter. Diane understood Peter's success as an arts funder from the fluent, quite convincing bullshit that he had streamed onto the page. She read it over several times and wished she had a son like the one Peter described. There wasn't a lie in it, that was the amazing thing, not a single falsehood, and yet there wasn't any truth in it, just facts garbed in sentimental adjectives—well, maybe it was true, after all. Bright children. Didn't they always seem to be brats to anyone but their relatives? Weren't men like Brian Stoppard really grown-up brats? What's Peter if not a spoiled, articulate manipulator? Look at me, thousands spent on my education, and I sit at home, with a woman to clean and keep my child occupied, surrounded by services, dry cleaners, restaurants that deliver, taxis—

"Hello!" It was Luke's father, Eric.

"Luke!" Byron shouted into Luke's face, pulling at his hand. "Come to the park with me!"

"We're going to the park," Diane said.

"So are we," Eric said.

Diane felt self-conscious. She brushed a stray hair off her forehead. I look crazy, she thought, regretting that she hadn't put on makeup, or dressed in something interesting. She had a closet full of clothes! She tried to smile (remember how ugly you look when you're serious) to hide the fatigue, the sluggish despair. Eric seemed so energetic, especially for ten in the morning. He had a copy of *Barron's*, already wrinkled, under his arm. He asked if she wanted a cup of coffee. She said yes. They stopped and got the boys chocolate doughnuts—Byron couldn't believe his luck, but Luke seemed to take it as a matter of course—and Eric convinced Diane to get a Linzer torte.

"Used to get them in my old neighborhood," Eric said. "I love them!" She asked him what his old neighborhood was. Washington Heights, he said gravely, and then went on and on about the place, interpolating apologies for its being (what did he call it?) lower middle class, whatever the hell that was. He talked about delis and bakeries and grandmothers who lived with their children and spent their days leaning on windowsills to supervise the grandchildren playing games below on the sidewalks—the memories brought a smile to his face. He talked about delivering papers, going to the movies on Saturday, being chased by gangs, and chasing others with his own gang, smoking his first cigarette under the lobby stairs because on the streets there were too many grandmothers, too many uncles, too many friends of his parents who might see.

"You sound like you wish you were a kid again," she said. By then they were settled on the park bench, the torte gone, their coffees almost drained.

"I hated it," he said with a big smile.

The surprise got her to laugh. She forgot her unwashed hair, her boring clothes, and leaned her shoulder against him. "Come on," she said.

"I did!" Eric was so pleased by the admission. "The whole universe was seven people. They made up their mind about me before I was walking and that was it: I was strong Eric, not too bright, always to be relied on for doing errands or helping out—I don't know. They loved me, my family, my friends, their parents— but they didn't respect me.''

"There's a difference," Diane asked, thinking it over, "between love and respect?''

"Very feminine to think they're the same. Girls looked at me and they saw a husband. When they respect a man, they look at a man and see a lover.''

"Really?'' He was so open, so unafraid of saying something offensive or stupid, so uncalculated. What a relief to talk to him. "I think you're wrong. It's the other way around. Women respect the men they think make good husbands.''

"They don't love them?'' Eric's big face, his wide-set eyes innocent as a deer's, scanned her. Eric's eyes weren't blue, but they were the sweet, wondering eyes of his son.

"They love them too, but they respect them a lot, much more than the irresponsible bad boy.''

"Maybe Jewish women,'' Eric said wistfully.

Is he having problems with his wife? She's not Jewish. Diane had forgotten their shoulders were still touching until his comment made her self-conscious. I'd rather be in bed with him than watching Byron bully his son, Diane thought.

"Come on, Luke! You're Ram Man—''

"I don't want to be—''

"You have to be Ram Man! He helps He-Man.''

Eric saw. He didn't like it. His lips were tight, holding his displeasure in.

Go ahead, tell my kid he's a tyrant. Go ahead.

"How's your work?'' he asked instead.

"I quit my job.''

"You did!'' She had gotten his mind off his son. He was openly astounded.

His amazement brought a smile to her face. "You don't approve?''

"I'm sorry—''

"Don't apologize. Tell me. You don't approve?''

"Weren't you at some fancy law firm?''

Fancy law firm. Eric was like an uncle at Passover, but made young, made her own age. So comfortable to be with. "Yeah, it was pretty damn fancy.''

"They were being too tough?''

She shook her head. She could say this to him. "I was good. That wasn't the problem.'' Eric nodded encouragement, so she went on, "I was going to make partner. I was a real prize.''

"I bet you were. So why did you quit? Not for Byron's sake?" Eric wondered aloud. "He was already past two—you're pregnant!" Eric was inspired. He snapped his fingers and pointed at her, happy at his guess.

"No." She couldn't help smiling. His lips were moist, his forearms thick and firm, smooth on the underside, furry and undulating on top.

"I don't get it," he said.

"I couldn't handle the stress. Going to work, coming home, taking care of Byron, no stopping—ever. The schedule was too relentless. I had to give up something. Couldn't give up Byron. I didn't like corporate law anyway. It's just junk in the end. Glorified clerking and for what? You don't accomplish anything."

"Except making money. A partner at a top New York law firm makes six, eight hundred thousand a year."

She thought of what she told others—money isn't that important, there are other ways, blah, blah—but this man, like an uncle at Passover, would accept only one answer: "My husband's rich."

Eric nodded. He understood. "That's nice," he said.

She laughed. He looked baffled. She put a hand on his wonderful animal arm and squeezed to reassure him. His wide eyes took her in without judgment or expectation. They looked at her lips and then back to her eyes with a touch of shyness. So he's thought it also. She smiled at him, a smile of years ago, a smile of acceptance and seduction.

"I didn't mean to—" he started.

"You're right," she said. "It's the only nice thing about my marriage."

That got the message across. He looked solemn. A little afraid. Well?

He was considering whether to back off. He glanced away, to get some privacy. But he returned fast.

"Sometimes," he said with a heavy Passover sigh, "sometimes, I think money's the only reason I'm married."

ERIC SAW LUKE'S HAND WANDER AGAIN AND AGAIN TO HIS ASS, touching the narrow valley to push something invisible back inside. Sometimes Luke squeezed his legs together and pushed back, sealing the pee that might crack the other dam. He managed to fight the urges off by concentrating on Byron's orders; but every few minutes, there was another call from nature, and his hand and legs worked quickly, furiously, to disconnect the frightening summons.

Eric saw it all. He had before, he had to admit, but he'd looked through it. Nina had forced Eric to see. Luke was holding it in. But how?

Why?

Wasn't this a sign of some illness in Luke's personality? What had they done wrong? Wasn't there stuff about this in Freud? They hadn't rushed toilet training; they hadn't begun until Luke was two and three-quarters. Anyway, the constipation had started when Luke was still in diapers.

Pearl. It must be Pearl. She must have done it.

Or Nina. She said her constipation wasn't as bad as Luke's when she was a child, but that chocolate pudding softener had been given to her, she admitted that—

It was genetic! Goddammit, it had to be. There was nothing psychologically wrong with Luke.

While Eric made these observations, he kept talking to Byron's mother about Washington Heights, hoping to get his mind off the subject. His babbling brought the old neighborhood back: Eric could see the bleached concrete sidewalks, the bright Saturday mornings with a long day of slug and running bases and war on the Danger Rocks in Fort Tryon Park; with Monopoly to play in the afternoon; with four quarters in his pocket to buy new pinkies if he hit home runs over the wall in stickball.

The stocks he had kept two weeks ago had continued their slow decline into soft mud. The Dow stocks, Joe's chickenshit Dow stocks, they were out of the earth's orbit, spinning silently up and away. . . .

I won't make any more money if my son is fucked up, Eric thought, as he caught Luke doing it again, the hand quickly, guiltily, going back and pushing. If my son is screwed up, I won't make any money.

What have I done wrong? Why isn't he okay?

I think this woman likes me.

Her eyes were awake with intelligence, twinkling with mischievous sarcasm, a pleasant change from the bold and clear, yet wondering and shy light in Nina's eyes.

Eric said whatever came into his head to Diane, confident she would accept him. This woman admitted money was important, instead of that Wasp horseshit of Nina's. No matter that Tom was a cheapskate: Nina, her brothers, her sisters, they never lacked for anything. When they were kids, did they have to worry about getting into SP classes in public school, or whether they could get into Bronx Science? Going to an Ivy League college was the ultimate triumph in Eric's neighborhood, the scholastic equivalent of making the major leagues. One kid, one kid in the whole fucking neighborhood, got into Harvard. One kid, one pale, friendless, unsmiling drone, got in.

Money. Nina went to Europe when she was eight. When she was ten. When she was thirteen. Their family went on a trip every summer. They went skiing in Switzerland during Christmas vacations. Yeah, sure, money doesn't matter.

"My husband is rich," Diane said.

Of course, Eric had known the moment he met Peter at brunch. The guy was snobbish about everything, even the kid's toys. Peter groaned, not about their cost, but about their warlike bias. Well, what the fuck are little boys going to pretend? Eric wanted to ask him. That they're wearing camel-hair coats and telling their secretaries to put somebody on hold?

Byron was more of a man than his father.

"Stockbroker," Peter had said with a neutral look on his face that day at brunch. "That must be nerve-racking."

And dirty. Not like helping to put plays on, or whatever it was Peter did. Dirty, dirty, dirty.

Peter was an anti-Semite. Probably Nina would be if she hadn't fallen in love with Eric.

Dad would always say, "Remember, they're all anti-Semites. Some of 'em are just polite about it."

Diane wants to fuck me. She has a good body. And she's easy to talk to.

Eric looked away from Diane's inviting glance and felt her shoulder on his. He saw the jammed park, the sloppy, tired faces of the parents, Luke squeezing his groin, the stock quotes in *Barron's*, the Quotron ticking down, Nina turning off, shutting him out, Mom and Dad, worried when he told them Tom had given him money to invest—

"Don't lose it," Mom had said. She thought he would fail. Just like Barry.

Forget all that. Eric looked into Diane's welcoming eyes.

"You're a stockbroker?" Diane's husband had asked, his eyes cool with disdain.

It would be a pleasure to cuckold that guy.

THE MUSIC SCHOOL WAS A HAPPY PLACE. PETER LIKED THE sounds—rhythm, pianos, violins, cellos, horns—echoing through the wide institutional halls. Parents were everywhere, lurking outside, carrying cases, or coats, or schoolbooks, or their own briefcases. Bright, earnest children, armed with their instruments instead of plastic guns, walked confidently to and fro—an army of culture to fight the world of junk.

On their way up to the third floor, where Byron took his private lesson, they passed a large room in which a quartet of nine-year-olds were struggling with a charming piece—and doing well to Peter's ear. Byron pulled Peter to the doorway and they paused to listen.

"They're playing together," Byron called out.

"Shhhh. That's called a quartet," Peter whispered. "If you learn the violin, you can play in one. Or you can play in an orchestra. That's when all the instruments play together."

"I want to!" Byron said as if Peter could snap his fingers and make it so.

If only I could. "Well, you practice hard and you will." Byron's natural competitiveness will serve him well, Peter thought.

Peter fancied Byron went into his lesson with an eager step this time. At the start, Byron listened carefully, not fussing, trying to put his feet where they should be. But when he had to shift his attention to a proper grip on the violin, he lost track of his feet. And when his teacher diverted his attention to that, his grip on the violin went awry. Back and forth the corrections came. Like displacement of water, when Byron did one right, the other went wrong. His teacher didn't give up today; she continued to insist he correct the mistake.

Byron's open face got tighter and tighter, his bright eyes darkening. His body stiffened. He pulled away from his teacher's touch. "I am!" he shouted at last.

"No," she insisted, pushing the violin more under his chin, "it's—"

"Leave me alone!" Byron pulled away and plucked the notes wildly, digging his finger under the strings, and yanking them up.

"Don't do that!" His teacher, an overweight, unattractive young woman hardly out of her teens, said this with real anger in her voice, not simply the dispassionate cool of a stern educator.

Byron dropped the violin like a stone and walked to the door. "I wanna go home," he said boldly.

He was so little. He looked absurd standing at the door, the top of his head beneath the handle, too small to be in this situation.

And yet would Mozart have become Mozart without his father's relentless demands?

Peter said nothing. The teacher looked to him to intervene.

I won't provoke him, that's what he wants.

"I think you should consider stopping the lessons," the young woman whispered to Peter.

"He's frustrated," Peter said softly. He was outraged that she was willing to quit so easily. I'll go to the administrator, he decided.

"He hasn't learned anything. I wanted to go easy and so I haven't, you know, made him do it right. But now he's gotten into bad habits and he obviously doesn't want to do it right. Maybe he should switch to another instrument, or take the music appreciation classes, and then pick this up again in a year. He's been to twelve lessons and he hasn't learnt anything."

"That's not true," Peter protested. Byron had made some progress. At least he practiced.

"Well." She lowered her head. "It looks bad for me if I lose a student—so I don't mind continuing." She regarded Peter. "I just don't want him to be turned off forever. He's bright and outgoing. He'll come back to it. Right now, this might be a waste of his time."

Peter turned away from Byron, who still stood at the door with a grave look. Peter whispered, "I thought he was getting better at it."

"Well, he hasn't been practicing, right?"

"Every day! We do it every day."

"Oh." She smiled regretfully. "He might as well be at the beginning. I'm happy to keep trying. Byron?" she called to him. "How about we just play through the notes once?"

"No," he said with remarkable clarity and conviction and confidence.

"Okay," she said cheerfully. "I want you to practice differently. Just getting your feet right and holding the violin in play position. That's all. No notes."

"Okay," Byron said. The gleam of triumph in Byron's eye gave him away. To Byron this was a battle of wills, not learning a musical instrument. He wanted to beat the adults.

And I've been a perfect sucker, letting him do what he wants.

"Let's go, Daddy," Byron said.

Byron chattered on their way home, growing happier with each step, his energy up and surging with his victory.

"I'm getting good," Byron said. Peter grunted.

"I'll be able to play with the big kids," Byron went on, happy and happier.

At home, Diane was arranged cozily on the couch, a cup of tea beside her, a mystery clutched to her bosom. Byron ran to her, ran into her arms. "Mommy," he blessed her.

"Mmmmm," she said. "What a nice hug. Did you have a good lesson?"

"I'm really good," Byron said.

Diane smiled. Byron's head was facing away from Peter. Over the bowl of sandy hair, Diane looked at Peter for confirmation. Peter shook his head back and forth, contradicting Byron.

She saw. But she kissed Byron and said, "I'm glad, honey."

14

"IT'S NIGHTTIME!" BYRON SHOWED LUKE. HE PULLED THE string down. The shades went crazy with a loud shaking. Half the window was uncovered.

"It's nighttime, Daddy!" Luke called out.

"No," Byron said. He grabbed Luke's hand. "Don't tell them. They'll make us go to bed."

"But, Byron." Luke sighed. The effort of arguing with Byron was so great, sharp and hurting, like when the poop was stuck. "They know it's nighttime."

"No!" Byron shook his head back and forth. Then back and forth harder. "Oh, no! My head is loose! Ram Man, help me, my head is loose."

Luke liked that joke. "Okay." Luke put his hands out and stopped the crazy head. "Don't move!" he ordered the evil head.

"Oh, no, it's coming off, it's coming off!" Byron danced on his tiptoes, his hands pressing down on his head.

Byron always goes on and on. "No, it isn't," Luke informed him. "I saved you. I stopped it."

"You didn't, you didn't." Byron's arms spun out, out and out, like Sy-Klone.

"Byron?" His mommy was at the door. Daddy was behind her. "What's going on?"

"My head is coming off!"

"I saved him!" Luke said to Daddy.

"No! No!" Byron spun himself to the ground, holding on to his head.

"Shhhh!" Byron's Mommy said to Byron. "It's late. You have to play quietly."

Luke held his body still. Please, Byron, don't fight. We can go on playing if you don't argue.

"I *am* being quiet!" Byron shouted.

"Why don't you play with your new Play-Doh?" Byron's mommy asked.

"Yea!" Byron was up on his feet. He jumped up and down at his mommy. "Yea!"

Luke also tried to act excited. He wanted them to know he liked the idea. "Yes, Daddy," Luke said, and hopped up and down, but less than Byron. He didn't want Byron's mommy to end the play date because he was acting too happy.

"Okay, okay, quiet down. We'll set you up at the kitchen table."

Byron had a lot of Play-Doh. Every color. He had yellow, blue, red, green. Byron took all those to his side. He gave Luke the white Play-Doh. "I'm going to make something terrific," Byron said.

"Me too," Luke said. He stared at his one can. White was boring.

"Mine's going to be lots of colors," Byron said.

"I'm going to use the blue," Luke said. He took hold of the blue Play-Doh.

"No," Byron said. He pulled the blue can out of Luke's soft fingers. "You use the white." Byron pointed to the white Play-Doh. Byron opened the blue can and shook it hard to get the Play-Doh out.

Where was Daddy? He was talking to Byron's mommy in the living room.

Tell me if there's anything wrong, Luke, Daddy had said. Tell me how you want it to be and I'll fix it.

"Daddy!" Luke called.

"Don't!" Byron said.

"What is it, Luke?" Daddy answered, but didn't come in.

"Here." Byron pulled a chunk of blue Play-Doh off and put it in front of Luke.

I have it. Luke touched the small chunk of blue Play-Doh. Byron had all the cans open. He was rolling colors, making shapes. Already doing everything. Luke thought about what to make.

"I'm making He-Man," Byron said. "You make Ram Man."

"I don't want to," Luke said softly. He hoped Byron wouldn't hear.

"You have to!"

Daddy's head appeared at the edge of the wall. "What is it, Luke?"

"Nothing!" Byron shouted.

I wanted the blue Play-Doh. But I have it. What can I say?

"I asked Luke, Byron, let him answer me." Daddy sounded angry. He doesn't want me to need help. "What is it, Luke?" Daddy asked.

"Are you cooperating, Byron?" Byron's mommy called out.

"Yes! I'm making He-Man, Luke is making Ram Man. We'll show you when we finish!"

"What was it, Luke?" Daddy's voice got close, right in Luke's ear.

"Nothing," Luke mumbled. Daddy left. Luke held the Play-Doh in his hand. He wanted to make a sailboat, like the sailboat in Maine, just right outside his window, quiet and tall, slicing the sky. He pushed the cool, soft Play-Doh, watched his fingers disappear. Shape round and smooth here and long there. He pulled a piece up—

"This is good, you know why?" Luke explained to Byron. "I'm making a sailboat, like the sailboat in Maine. And it's blue and white. And those are the colors I have!" This was great.

"No," Byron scolded. "No, you're not. You're making Ram Man."

The sail rose up thin and blue from the chunk of PlayDoh. Luke let it go—his boat was ready!

"You're doing it wrong!" Byron's hand crushed the sail, smashed the boat. "You have to make Ram Man."

It was gone. He had made it so great. And now it was gone. He hated Byron. He wanted to throw him in the garbage and put his many colors in there too. "I—don't—I—don't—" but Luke couldn't move the words through his feelings, couldn't push them out.

The tears were here, hurting and pushing his eyes, poking and hurting, everything wanting out—

"Byron! What have you done?"

"I was just playing and Luke smashed his thing and cried!"

"Luke." Daddy in his ear, pushing to get in, but everything wants to come out. "Luke, what is it?"

"Byron!" His mommy was going to yell and yell and break everything. "Are you—"

"Really, Mommy, he cries. He cries a lot. Like a baby."

"Oh, and you never cry," Byron's mommy said.

"Luke, what happened? You couldn't make what you wanted?" Daddy in his ear, buzzing like a loud television.

"I wanna go home," Luke said to push them away. "I wanna go home!"

"Don't go home, Luke," Byron said, and he began to yell and cry. "I want to keep playing."

"It's past your bedtimes," his mommy said.

"No!" Byron cried now.

Good. Make him cry.

"I wanna go home," Luke said, now clear, able to push them away.

"Okay," Daddy said. "We'll go home right now."

"No!" Byron smashed his stupid He-Man and pushed all the Play-Doh off the table.

"Byron!" His mommy grabbed him and pulled him away.

Good. Good.

"Let's get your jacket, Luke."

Good. Daddy and me. We'll go home. Mommy will come late, and even if I'm sleeping, she'll give me a kiss, and tomorrow I can make my sailboat alone.

"YOU GET SKINNIER EVERY DAY," SAL SAID WITH A SNEER ON HIS lips. He must think it makes him look sexy, Nina thought. Where did he get that idea? Elvis was before his time.

"Thank you," Nina answered. Where to go to eat? She had exhausted everything nearby—she'd end up at that coffee shop Luke had thought so magical. The food was terrible, but being there brought the memory of Luke along for company.

"But enough is enough," Sal said. "I'm going to lunch with you to make sure you get some fat on you."

"So I can look like your mother?" Nina asked.

Sal seemed bewildered by her joke. Nina could throw him so easily. He was funny, with his tough manner and skin so thin he might be a two-year-old. "What does that mean?" Sal complained.

"You said your mother was a fat slob."

"I did?" Sal blanched as if she had reminded him of the commission of a sin.

"I guess you were kidding," Nina said.

"I don't want you to look like my mother," Sal said, his swagger back. He had a gleam in his eye. He means that to be a come-on. But he means everything to be a come-on. She knew, just knew, that if she ever took him at his word, he'd panic. She was a safe dangerous game.

They were outside. Sal moved in front of her. "Where do you want to go?" he bluffed, pretending confidence she would go to lunch with him.

"I didn't say—" She stopped herself. She didn't want to play teenage games. "I'm going to the coffee shop."

"Ugh. How about Japanese? It's good for you. This is New York! You have to be adventurous."

"I've had Japanese food before, Sal." She laughed at him. He worked so hard at this male mastery. "You can join me at the coffee shop." She walked off. He didn't come along.

At the corner, she looked back for Sal. Sal was still where she had left him, caught between his pride and his desire to come. When Luke balked at where Nina wanted to go next, Luke would do the same: bluff and stay back until she moved decisively away, and then he'd come running.

The light changed. Nina almost didn't cross, forgetting that she could abandon Sal, he wasn't a three-year-old. So she moved on and, once in the coffee shop, felt some regret after all.

The coffee shop was jammed and noisy. She got herself a tiny table, and as she opened the menu, Sal appeared.

"Jesus, you're stubborn," he said. "What are you gonna have? Burger, right?"

Then he was off and chatting, talking about his fat pregnant sisters (that's what he called them) and about Tad. Tad seemed to be his main concern. Sal was obviously envious of Nina's job. He repeatedly asked what she had done to get it and flatly didn't accept her answer that Tad had simply offered it to her, presumably on the basis of her work in class.

"Come on, you must have asked him if he had any jobs?"

"No, I didn't. Never occurred to me."

"Come on!"

"Okay, I paid him to give it to me."

"That's what Rosalie thinks. That you offered to work for free."

Rosalie was one of the pair of girls who hung on Sal's every word, trailing him through the hallways, giggling from the thrill by his presence. Nina smiled at the thought of Rosalie's envy. She enjoyed its novelty. When was the last time someone was jealous of what she had?

"Don't tell her I told you," Sal said.

"Oh, she must have wanted you to tell me."

"No! She likes you."

Nina laughed. Sal seemed so familiar to her. He shouldn't—was he like Luke? Like her brother?

"Really, she does! She just said that 'cause she's jealous."

"It's okay," Nina reassured him. He was fascinated by competition, but didn't want to admit it caused bad feelings. Who was that like? Eric?

"Is it true?" Sal asked.

"Is what true?"

"That Tad doesn't pay you?"

Nina again laughed at him. He waited for her to stop, as if it were a commercial message interrupting his favorite show's denouement. "He pays me. Minimum wage. He doesn't have to pay me. Some of them aren't paid, they're interning. But they get school credit for that."

"That must be what Rosalie meant." Sal ate his hamburger in four bites, his jaw dropping like a crocodile's and swallowing chunks. Ketchup appeared at the corner of his mouth. "What a rip-off."

"Sal, if you want to, you can look at everything as a rip-off."

" 'Cause everything is a rip-off."

"Then nothing is a rip-off."

"Huh?"

"Something has to *not* be a rip-off for everything else to be. If everything is a rip-off, then everything is equally fair."

"Oh, that's bullshit. That's something rich people think to make them feel better 'cause they're doing the ripping off."

He was like Eric, just like Eric when Nina first met him: hungry, eager to make an impression, intrigued by her, disgusted by the rules of the game he so desperately wanted to win. Only then, Nina was young, and Eric's view of life was new, and seemed refreshing: a forest cleared of the dead brush of her family's hypocritical values. Her family pretended winning didn't matter to them; but they talked of nothing but who was best skier, best squash player, best sailor, and they believed winners always deserved their victories.

"Never thought of that, right?" Sal said, pleased with himself, convinced he was teaching poor naïve Nina the way of the world.

"Are you going to hate your life if you don't make money?" Nina asked.

"You mean, if I starve?"

"No. If you don't become rich."

"You mean, if I have to live in the Bronx like my parents and have fat babies who grow up to have fat babies?"

Nina laughed while she nodded.

"I'll kill myself."

Nina shook her head. "Give me a serious answer."

"That is a serious answer, beautiful. You know, you are beautiful."

"You don't have to flirt with me, Sal."

"Hey—I mean it. I'm not playing. You *are* beautiful."

Sal was thrilled to be saying this. He sat straight up, at attention, his eyes glistening, his nostrils open, his mouth grave. She watched him, fascinated. He was a visitation from her past—Eric wooing her. Nina had utterly believed in Eric's passion, had believed his romance was inspired by pure love for her. She thought she had won an old-fashioned chivalrous adoration.

"I've never met anyone like you," Sal said, high on his feelings, skimming on pure sentiment. "I think about you all the time. I don't want other women; they're impure compared to you. I wish I could touch your hair, lie next to you in bed, and hold your hand. I close my eyes and see you." He closed his eyes and kept them shut while he talked. "It's like you're not even human. I've never seen skin like yours—and your eyes! They glow like a cat's and see right through me." He opened and gazed at her. "Your eyes catch me and I have to follow them. I'm yours. I love you. I used to dream about making love to you. But I think I'd be too scared. I'm not good enough. But I can't lie. Not telling you what I feel, just pretending everything's normal. I love you. It's so great to say it. I love you."

Sal sat there, erect, awaiting her judgment.

But all she could think of was Eric. Young, bedding her. Young, marrying her. Young, impregnating her. And now, in only a few years, old and harassing her. Sal just wants to fuck me, Nina thought. Confirm his escape from his neighborhood, get a visa to somewhere else. She hadn't thought that for a second when Eric courted her. Was the difference Sal? No, Nina was older, and knew better.

I wish I didn't, she thought. I wish I could fall in love with this boy and be fooled all over again.

WHEN DIANE CALLED TO INVITE ERIC AND LUKE OVER FOR A LATE-afternoon play date, and suggested they stay and order pizza, so the boys could have their first dinner together, for a moment, Eric thought, she wants to see me alone. En route, he dismissed that idea. Sure, Diane knew Nina would be working, Eric had told her about Nina's schedule the other day in the park, but probably her husband would also be there.

He wasn't. Although Diane was dressed casually, she was made up and looked alluring. She immediately offered Eric wine. There was a spread of cheese and crackers out on the coffee table. There were fresh-cut flowers in several vases, there was music playing, there were no toys strewn anywhere, and she told Byron to take Luke into his room and show Luke his new toy, Snake Mountain.

"Peter working late?" Eric asked as coolly as he could.

"Yes, there's a big opening tonight. I guess I should have gone, but I didn't feel like it." She had a keen edge to her voice when, as Eric knew well, by the end of the day most mothers would have given up on cheerfulness. What was so exciting about having the father of your three-year-old's best friend over for pizza?

But it made no sense. What were they going to do—plunk the boys in front of the television, turn on a tape of He-Man, and screw in the bedroom?

Eric was grateful that Luke had managed to take a crap a few hours ago. God, what a mess. First, huge, impossibly long turds oozed out, in a slow agony, accompanied by screaming and tears, and then diarrhea followed. Luke had been stopped up for a week this time. Something had to be done. After it was over, Eric turned on the television to distract Luke and sneaked off to the bedroom to call Nina at work. Nina was irritated by the interruption. "I'll take him to another doctor. I have to go." And she hung up without a good-bye.

Yeah, I'd be happy to sleep with Diane. Why not? I'm just a servant for Nina, taking care of her kid, her money, her family's affection, you name it. I make sure he gets enough sleep, I make sure Luke knows he's loved—what if I behaved like Diane's husband? Then we'd have an aggressive brat like Byron.

Nevertheless, Eric wished Luke had some of Byron's public self-assurance. He didn't think Byron was *really* more self-confident—he knew what Byron was, remembered Byron's type from his own childhood. Byron was a shrimp who needed to be in charge or his ego would crumble. Yeah, but those shrimps always ended up dominating everyone—like Joe. They were completely concentrated on besting everyone—so they did.

No more. Eric wouldn't allow it this time. Joe was pushing Eric at work, taking back control of the accounts merely because, for the past quarter, Eric's stocks were down and Joe's were up. He thinks he can just grab it back, take it out of my hands, and I won't say anything. Well, he's wrong. I'll walk. I'll walk with the fifteen million I control.

But you're losing it, you can't keep your grip, you may need Joe. The whispers of doubt were terrible, sickening.

I'll go mad if I don't shake it. Make a decision! Leave, that's what I have to do. Go out on my own. Otherwise Joe will always eat away at my confidence. I would have sold earlier if it weren't for Joe—not Joe, Sammy, standing there beneath me, as I'm scared shitless on the ledge, saying, Jump! Jump!

"Do you mind Nina leaving you alone with Luke so much?" Diane asked.

"No. Most of the time, the only person I really have fun with is Luke." Except for the constipation. If only that would go away—maybe I should ask her advice.

"Really?" She smiled with approval. "I wish Peter felt like that. I think he would if he spent more time with Byron."

"You must enjoy it."

"Yeah?" She laughed sarcastically.

"Well, you gave up your job to be with him."

"No. I gave up my work to have fun. To slow down. I just blame it on Byron."

"Smell the roses?"

"That's right." Diane lowered her head. "Only I don't have anyone to smell with me." She looked up, right into Eric's eyes, asking the question.

He held her look.

She moved to the couch, sitting next to him, always keeping her eyes on his, bold, like Byron, demanding: I'm here, I'm here. Eric's thoughts sped by, the ticker going wild, overloaded by volume: what do I owe Nina, do I love her, the boys are in the next room, when could I see Diane anyway, every second of my life is accounted for, I'd figure out something, but it's crazy, right, and her tits are great, we could live together, the boys would always have playmates, but it would be bad for Luke, why am I worrying about that, this is just a lay, maybe she's kidding—

Diane's eyes went down, purposefully, to Eric's lips, kissing them with her glance.

Oh, for Christ's sakes, for once in your life, make a decision without tiptoeing through fields of bullshit—

He kissed her. Her mouth was soft. He hadn't expected that. With her black hair and sharp chin, her dark, bold eyes and lean, angled body, he had anticipated meeting something hard and solid, charged with energy. But she was soft, melting at his contact, absorbing him. He could taste her lipstick, smell her perfume. She was fresh-baked, not yesterday's roll; he wanted more.

"No!" Byron shouted.

Eric pushed Diane away, his body shocked, jumping back. He lost his balance, his ass sliding off the edge of the couch, and fell like a bulky package, thudding onto the rug. He looked to see—

But there was nothing in the doorway.

"No!" Byron shouted. The voice came from the other room. The boys were still safely ignorant. Eric looked up at Diane, who seemed dazed. "They're playing," she said.

She should be laughing. She must be pretty far gone if she's not laughing. "This is crazy," Eric said.

"They're allowed to be crazy," she answered. "Why can't we?"

" 'Cause we're the parents," Eric said, and he laughed.

But the laugh didn't escape his throat, and he saw himself, big and clumsy and old, bussing a married woman on her couch, and he coughed, needing to laugh, and then he did laugh, again and again, until there were tears in his eyes while he laughed, and he didn't stop laughing until the boys ran in to ask what was so funny.

For weeks Diane had used Eric to stimulate her bath orgies. Night after night Eric lifted her to the ceiling and consumed her from the bottom up, swallowing her below and raising her above, until she flew up to the yellow globe, the bowl of popcorn quavering big, then little, the orange bowl squeezed to red, then white. Eric took her in the hallway with Peter just in the other room, and she had to press her lips tight to hold the freedom inside, gulping back her pleasure, Eric moving over her, restless, loving, frantic, ravenous—

Diane hadn't expected her fantasy to become real.

Night after night she loved Eric's image, until she found herself inviting him over on impulse, as if reality had become soft and she could, at will, puncture it with her dreams. She used the boys as a beard, picked a night when she knew Nina and Peter would be elsewhere, dressed up for Eric, bought wine and cheese and flowers, picked out music, restraightened the living room, as if it were a date, a special night, assuming all the while: of course, I won't do anything.

And then she made him kiss her. She couldn't stop herself, didn't even think about the risk that he might not, and thus expose her desire to ridicule.

Only when Eric fell off the couch, frightened by the mere sound of children—she hadn't heard the noise that startled him, at least not consciously, although she knew why he broke off contact—only when Eric fell off the couch and was so scared that he became hysterical, only then did Diane pause and think.

When the boys discovered Eric on the rug, they were delighted by his collapsed position. Luke jumped all over Eric with a familiar joy, shouting references to games they must play every night, Byron stood and watched for a moment, amazed by the giant daddy toddler. Peter never lowered himself. Eric played like a kid, diminished in both size and dignity, a huge child shouting back phrases from He-Man, pretending right along with his son, falling over when a little fist bounced harmlessly off his massive chest—she had one fantasy with Eric's chest hairless, another in which she pressed her lips against a soft mossy bed—and he growled fiercely when he counterattacked. Byron hung back, not shy, but baffled, until Eric suddenly grabbed him also—

Byron's face spread open into a wide smile and he tried to play along. However, Byron's punches were in earnest. Diane knew she should scold Byron, but she was fascinated into silence. She watched Eric take the blows politely at first, his face showing confusion, and waited to see how he would deal with it.

"Hey." Eric grabbed Byron's hand, after he had taken two socks on the chin. "We're just pretending to hit. You don't actually do it."

"Yeah, yeah, Byron. You don't actually—" Luke showed him, swinging hard and then stopping his little fist just an inch before meeting Eric's body. "You know what I mean. You just pretend."

"This is what you do," Eric said. "You let Luke distract me and then you jump on me from behind."

"Okay," Byron said agreeably, and that worked. Byron followed orders and the three of them ended up in a heap, the boys triumphant, Lilliputians climbing atop the giant prone body, cheering themselves and proclaiming victory over evil.

Only the arrival of the pizza saved Eric from endless defeats.

This is the kind of man I want, Diane realized. I'm not horny. I'm married to the wrong person.

In all the confusion, Byron's birth, Peter's emotional withdrawal from the marriage, her resignation from the job, her rages, that simple answer had never occurred to her. That she had a bad marriage, yes. That Peter probably didn't love her, yes. That she might not love him anymore, yes. But all those thoughts, and the thousands of others they spawned, were part of a jungle—wet vines and laden ferns obscuring her view of the horizon: I married the wrong man. I wanted someone to be with, someone simple and ordinary like Eric, someone to handle at least half of life. Then I could work. I need a man. A partner. A husband.

I don't want to sleep with him, I want to substitute him for Peter.

Then they were alone again, Eric spoke quickly, guilty and embarrassed. "I'm sorry about—you know—"

"That's okay."

"I guess I'm a little nuts these days."

He's going to back down. That bothered her. Even though she no longer wanted to go on, his doing it first was irritating. "I wanted you to," Diane said.

"You did, didn't you?"

"Yes." He knows that. Why is he pretending he doesn't?

"But we couldn't. How? And—" He looked the point, his eyes going toward the sounds of their sons playing in the other room.

"We can do anything we want," Diane answered, unwilling to let him get away that easily, with the excuse of practicality. Why didn't he admit he was a coward? Or at least claim decency.

Eric sighed. "I just can't handle it. That's all. I'm barely hanging on right now. Anything else and I'd sink." He pointed straight down. "Boom!" He looked at where he had crashed his imagined self, shaking his head over the phantom corpse. "I want to," he said softly. A little bit like Luke, head down, desire spoken to the floor.

"Anytime, I'm here all day, every week. I can always get away." Why not? At least I'll make love. Anyway, he won't do it.

Eric raised his head and stared. "Okay," he said.

"PETER! PETER!" HIS MOTHER CALLED HIM. GAIL'S ANGLED HEAD popped up between the hairdos, her face briefly covered by passing gowns and elegant suits, then exposed just as briefly. She sought Peter in the confusion, pressing flat her already ironed hair with nervous exasperation.

Opening night at the ballet. Peter had forgotten how archaic it seemed, an evening of privilege, of meaningless beauty, attended by a weird marriage of the wealthy and the artistically obsessed. A charming or pathetic scene, depending on one's mood. Some were openly watching the celebrities, leaning over the balcony above, or standing on their level, but away, at the perimeter, all eyes on the center vortex, rich patrons waltzing about the stars.

"Here you are," Gail said when Peter reached her. "This is my great friend Ann. And her daughter Juliet—"

"The cellist," Peter acknowledged, and shook hands with a tall, very shy girl of eighteen. She was a prodigy, an actual success, a proof of early music education.

"Peter's boy, he's only three, is studying the violin."

"Suzuki?" Juliet said. To Peter's surprise, she seemed to blossom at the introduction of this subject. She straightened her shoulders, held her head up. She had a pasty face and thin lips, but her big, solemn eyes, beneath a high brow that wrinkled and smoothed

itself expressively as she talked made her interesting, if n
tiful. "How does he like it?"

Peter thought: being a parent means condensing the truth into a
lie. "He doesn't like the work of it. But he loves it when he can do
it."

She nodded and smiled to herself. "Yeah, I know how he feels."

"Now, now, no complaints," her mother said. "It was worth
it."

Gail rattled off Juliet's accomplishments, although she had told
Peter about them before. Juliet listened to herself being discussed
without self-consciousness or vanity. She was used to it. More people joined them, more arts funders, people whom Peter felt he had
known from the moment of his birth, people who nodded at him
as if he were a boring landmark. I could be stark naked and they
wouldn't notice, he thought. The crowd began to move back in,
and in the flow, Peter found himself standing next to Juliet. She
smiled up at him, a slow, wise, mournful smile.

"Can I ask you a dumb question?" Peter said on an impulse.

She smiled at that too, as if all she had ever been asked were
dumb questions. "Sure."

"I know your mother started you early—"

"Five. Your son's got me beat."

"—but when did you decide you wanted to be a musician?"

"This way, dear!" her mother called, and tugged her into a
different tributary from Peter's.

Juliet looked back at him, very serious, wanting to tell him: "I
never did." And she was carried off, like a piece of paper riding a
current, looking back at him, her eyes still answering.

He moved to his seat, entranced by Juliet's answer. Does anyone
have any choice about what they become? When a steelworker's
son becomes a steelworker, does anyone wonder if that's bad? If I
force Byron to become a musician, is that really so terrible? My
mother never demanded I be anything; she let me drift, so long as
I had the right opinions on politics, on culture, so long as I showed
no interest in things she didn't approve of. Sure, she made no demands of accomplishment, but was that good? I feel useless.
Wouldn't I prefer being pushed, oppressed into some kind of brilliance?

He settled in his seat and thought of Mozart. Peter didn't know
the real story of Mozart's life; he knew the play *Amadeus*, he knew
snatches, enough to sound educated. If Byron were pushed, relentlessly, unforgivingly, made into a freak, an unsociable unhappy

person—but someone who could create like Mozart—would that really be worse than a normal upbringing?

But what if Byron isn't talented? What if all I accomplished was to make Byron a neurotic, imprisoned by soulful despair, and without a key of genius to unlock the sorrow?

Like me? The therapy had taught Peter one thing: there was no escape. He could understand, he could protect himself, he could learn to forgive, he could enjoy what he had; but there was no undoing the divorce, his father's neglect, his mother's rejection, or Larry—

He hadn't thought of Larry for a while, not after the sessions with Kotkin recalled more of the incidents, not after settling them— your parents weren't around, you felt abandoned, and this man touched you, wanted you, and you liked the wanting, but not the touching, but you were scared to complain because no one had ever behaved as if your complaints mattered. Did your complaints stop your father from leaving your mother? Did your complaints make your mother stay with you, instead of her new man?

Child molesters are clever; they have a keen scent for loneliness.

And Larry's still out there, still doing it, still twisting simple melodies of unhappiness into dissonant symphonies of pain.

I have to deal with Byron, with Diane's collapse. Kotkin was no help, said nothing. Why do you think anything has to be done? she asked. No answers; his questions were bounced back.

Maybe I can't deal with Diane and Byron until I deal with Larry.

How many children has Larry hurt? Gary never did anything to save Peter, and denied and lied even to this day. I'm just as bad, aren't I?

But Larry's an old man, he's managed to survive his perversion, to escape, like some Nazi war criminal living in New Jersey, and now, Larry being old, wasn't it merely cruel to—

What? He chuckled at the thought of going to the police to report Larry, he chuckled out loud, right in the middle of a pas de deux that had everyone transfixed. The woman next to him turned her head to stare—what in the world could he be laughing at?

It occurred to Peter that Larry might be in the audience. He scanned the rows from his position in the center ring, to the right, then to the left, studying the men in their sixties, trying to reconstruct Larry's features and decay them appropriately. He might be bald now.

Maybe he'll die of AIDS, Peter thought with a mixture of revulsion and pleasure. The pleasure faded at the memory of his visit to Raul Sabas in the hospital. Paralyzed, bone-thin, wheezing—

You're disgusting, he told himself. And if Larry has AI[   ] might be giving it to young boys. Who knows what he does now, who knows how far he's gone in twenty-five years of perversion? Maybe he does more than merely touch now, maybe he finds runaways, maybe he kills them—

This is madness. The audience applauded. Peter staggered out with them, back into the intermission parade outside, people gawking from above, swirling groups plucking hellos from the air, quick opinions whispered to the floor—

"Hello." Juliet was at his elbow.

"What did you mean?" Peter said.

"Before?" She smiled at him sweetly. Does she ever get to meet any normal boys, or are they all freaks like her? "No one in the history of the world ever decided to be a musician," she said. "Your parents have to decide for you. Otherwise, it's too late. If you start as an adult, you can only be an amateur."

"How do you know you want to do it, then? When does it belong to you?"

"It belongs to me," she said, looking down at her shoes, mumbling, "because it's all I've got."

"And if you had something else, would you give it up?"

"Something else, like what?" She smiled now, looking off, enjoying this. "Husband and kids?" she offered, as if they were a wild possibility, flying to Mars or something.

"Okay."

"Could be." She laughed. "Maybe that's what'll happen. I'll marry some egomaniacal conductor—no, maybe pianist—and give it up to bear his children. Then I could teach my children, push them like Mother pushed me. It's like a bad movie, isn't it?" she said, and giggled.

Peter smiled politely and agreed it was silly.

But her scenario was just like real life, he thought.

I'm stopping the lessons. If I force Byron to be something, it has to be something *I* know, something *I* can teach.

DADDY SAID THIS WAS SPECIAL. NOT A REGULAR THING. SPECIAL for me. No more violin lessons, but that's okay. There'll be special things like this.

"Why?" Byron asked Peter.

"Well, they're showing these cartoons in a museum because, even though they still make Bugs Bunny cartoons, these, the ones we're going to see in here, were made a long time ago, they were the first ones made. See the drawings? This is how they do it."

Up, up. Glass. They were small. I can do that.

"You see they make lots of these drawings and then they use a movie camera to film the drawings one after the other. So it looks like they're moving, just like when you flip the pages of your little book."

"Let me see!" Byron went down. Daddy handed him his special book with the little man, the little line man. Byron made the pages go, whoosh! And the stick man danced across, running at Byron's thumb, right off the page! "Watch out!" But then he was on a horse!

"Okay," Daddy said. "Now stop and look at each page slowly. See? There's one drawing for each page, just moving the man and the horse a little bit at a time. That's how they make cartoons. There are thousands of drawings moving very quickly."

"I wanna make one!"

"When we get home, we'll make one, okay?"

"I have a great idea! Make one about He-Man."

"It's a great idea for you to make one. But you should make up your own story. Something *you* make up will be different than anything else in the world. Anybody can make up a He-Man story, but no one but *you* can make up a story that comes from here—"

Daddy tapped on his head. Daddy looked so close, so happy. Daddy wants me to make up a story. "I can make up a great story!" Byron said.

"I know you can," Daddy said with a kiss and a hug.

THE LITTLE LEGO PIECE, HOT RED, SMOOTH AS ICE, COULD GO RIGHT on top, hold it there, hold it there—the Feeling! Pinching, growing inside, growing with a pain of metal, hard and sharp, twisting inside—

"Luke." Daddy's voice was boxed, something from television, very important. "It's time to go to the bathroom."

"Nooooooooooooo!" Push him away.

Daddy's hand came low, swinging for him. "Let's go." His hand closed hard, squeezing, pinching, like inside, heavy pushing in and down, so big and metal, ready to cut him open. Go away—

Daddy pulled him—

"Noooooo!" What was Daddy doing? "It hurts! I can't."

"Everybody has to go to the bathroom," said the boxed voice, coming from someone else in Daddy.

Daddy pulled Luke. Pulled away from the toys. Nothing could stop it, no strength could stop him, right to the toilet, to the great white bowl, flowing up from the floor—"Daddy! Daddy! I don't

have to! I don't have to! Mommy! Mommy!'' Where wa
Where is the real Daddy!

"Sit on the toilet and push it out," Daddy said, and pulled Luke's
pants down.

The cold air made his hole weak, the metal pushing, hurting him
and everything collapsed, blocks crashing, his eyes falling out,
tears everywhere—"I can't! I can't!''

But Daddy left.

I'm alone. Alone.

"Daddy!'' He tried to move out, but the pants hit him in his
knees, tying his legs, and he fell on the cold floor. "Mommy!
Mommy!''

"Luke.'' The boxed voice was back, harder, metal, and he was
picked up, the pushing inside still there, twisting and burning in
his stomach and penis. "It's time to go to the bathroom.''

"Nooooooo!'' He was being put on the toilet, the hole spread,
the feeling big and bigger coming down. He tried to get up and he
did.

Where was Daddy?

I'm alone. He's left. I'm still crying, but don't cry, Daddy isn't
here, you don't have to, just push it back. He squeezed, maybe it
was too late, he squeezed hard, his stomach closed on it, eating it
back, eat it up, go away, go away!

The pain, the metal twisting up, twisting up, hurt, hurt his chest,
his eyes—I have Legos red and white, and I build beautiful buildings, castles for He-Man, and spaceships to visit the stars in Maine
because in New York there is so much light you can't see the stars
very well so I build my Legos to fly to the stars in Maine, and to
Venus, away, away, away, away. . . .

ERIC WOULDN'T WAIT. HE INSISTED THEY REPAIR LUKE. SO NINA
called and called and called, first a fellow mother, then a friend of
a fellow mother, and another, until she got the name of a behavioral
child psychologist who dealt specifically with problems of sleeping,
eating, and toilet training. The pediatricians had failed her with
their medicines, all that had happened was that Luke was now on
mineral oil, which greased the stuff out against his will, presumably
to convince him it didn't hurt, but he kept saying it did, and the
doses of mineral oil had increased steadily, and she knew what
Luke meant by hurting, he meant he didn't like the sensation, and
no matter how easy they made it feel he would still complain—

She knew because watching him, listening to him, she realized
that's what she had done, that the legend of her constipation as a

child was a myth. She had hated the feeling of letting go, of the stuff coming through, coming out, but she wasn't her parent's first-born and no one wanted or expected her to be perfect, the way Eric wants Luke to be, so she was put on laxatives and left to suffer if she fought them, and to this day, she had to drink four cups of coffee each morning and try several times before relieving herself, grimacing throughout the whole unpleasantness. But Luke has to be perfect or Eric will go mad, so Nina called the psychologist and told him about Luke's behavior.

The psychologist's deep, humorless voice stopped her before she got a few words out: "Has your pediatrician checked him for a physical problem?"

"Yes, there's—"

"And you had no trouble training him about urinating?"

"No. He doesn't wet his bed. His problem is letting things out."

"Okay, I know exactly how to solve this. I need to see you and your husband once. The fee will be a hundred and fifty dollars."

"Do we bring Luke?"

"No. I don't need to see him. I just have to tell the two of you what to do, and if you're consistent, within a few weeks, the problem will be solved."

"Really?" She breathed in his tone of confidence. It was like believing in God. Everything solved, made perfect. You love Jesus and you go to heaven.

"Absolutely. I've dealt with hundreds of cases. All successful. Of the big three, sleeping problems, eating problems, and what I call obstipation, this is the easiest to deal with."

He made an appointment to see them that night.

Of course, when she told Eric, he was so predictable. She had done what he wanted, and of course, he balked at the result. "A hundred and fifty dollars! Who is this guy? God?"

If he can do what he promised, he's God. "Eric, you wanted to deal with this. So we're going. Otherwise, I don't want to hear another word from you about it."

"All right." He sighed, the fate of the Union resting on his shoulders—so many dead, so many lost for the sake of a free country.

Why do I love Eric?

Luke is so wonderful. So beautiful. Skin as sweet and smooth as vanilla ice cream. His eyes shone truth: his love, his fear, his dreams, his sorrows. He adores Eric. And me. He knows he's loved and he loves us. Let him be constipated, Lincoln. Give up. A house divided against itself is the only kind that's built.

But they went and sat in a tiny waiting room, with paint p[ ]
on the walls, while the psychologist met with another couple. When
the couple emerged, they looked beat. They were middle-aged parents; they appeared to be in their forties. They averted their eyes,
but shame glowed from the corners.

Cheer up, Nina thought, we're screwups too. Probably everybody is.

The psychologist had a dour face, his skin pale and puffy, his
clothes wrinkled, his shirttail hanging out, his face greasy. "Come
in," he mumbled. He looked surprised when Nina put out her hand
and introduced herself. "Why don't you take a seat?" he said after
handing her a sweaty palm and limp fingers. She glanced at Eric;
he was furious. He sat down hard on a director's chair and made it
groan. Eric's lips were pressed tight, his feet together, his back
angled forward. He looked ready to spring. Give it a chance, Eric.

"Describe what happens when Luke—is that it?—describe what
happens when you can see Luke needs to move his bowels," the
psychologist said.

Eric looked at Nina. He wanted to leave this to her; then he would
be free to ignore the advice. I can't let him. "You tell," Nina said.

Eric was going to refuse, but the psychologist asked him, "Does
he tell you he has to go to the bathroom, or does he run around
holding it in?"

"No, he doesn't say he has to; he holds himself and races
around." Eric was loud, angry. He picked up the director's chair,
staying in it, and shifted forward. Nina thought the legs would give
out from their squeal of agony.

"Does he talk about it at all?"

"Oh, yes, he can go on and on about how it feels. We've explained to him that it's digested food and that the body has to get
rid of it. He's happy to talk about that—"

"Right, okay, I don't really need to know, I just like to hear.
Amazing how similar the pattern is. There are three major behavioral problems that children develop—problems sleeping, problems
eating, problems of one kind or another with toilet training, and
also going to school, but that comes later, I was thinking of the first
five years. I don't think any parent escapes from one of these. The
problem happens when it becomes a way of getting attention—"

"He gets lots of attention, that can't be it." Eric shifted forward
with such force that the chair moved also.

The psychologist leaned away from Eric, obviously shocked by
Eric's vehemence. He paused and stared at Eric.

Eric was insistent. "We hardly ever go out, I play with Luke for hours, it can't be that. He was constipated, even as a baby."

I've got to interrupt. "I have a theory," Nina said.

The psychologist moved his eyes to her with obvious relief. Eric had scared him. "What's that?"

"I think he was constipated, maybe something he ate, when he was a baby. I remember a couple of times he passed hard turds and strained a lot. I think maybe he remembered the hurt and now tries to stop everything, and that makes him constipated, and it does hurt, so he tries harder to stop it."

The psychologist nodded. "That's very interesting. That could be. You know, I don't care about causes," he said this to Eric. "I'm not that kind of therapist. I only care about solving the problem. In terms of the treatment, it makes no difference why it started. If you're a Freudian, you won't like that, but your son'll have a better chance of getting to a Freudian psychiatrist if he's not sitting at home, holding in his bowel movements."

Eric stared at the psychologist, held himself up, resistant, a stiff sail, for a moment. Then his chest sagged. He leaned back, his chair groaning for mercy. "You've got a point."

"These things happen because the parents are good parents, or are trying to do the right thing. Your son complains about something, you pay attention to it, and your concern becomes a way of having you. Do you have trouble with Luke about eating?"

"No," Eric said.

"What do you do if he says he doesn't want to eat?"

"We say fine."

"Aren't you worried that he'll starve?"

"No," Nina said. "I read in a book that he won't starve. He'll eat."

"Exactly. You know he will, you don't worry, so he doesn't worry. He eats. Sleeping, eating, and going to the bathroom are things that human beings have to do. We're animals, after all, we'll do them, as long as there's no reason not to. You have to act as though you expect him to go to the bathroom. And he will. Because he can. There's nothing physically wrong with him. This is what you do: when you see Luke hold it in, and only then, only when you see him hold it in, you take him by the hand and say, 'It's time to go to the bathroom, Luke.' And you take him into the bathroom. If he talks to you about it, argues or chats or whatever, and this is very important, don't answer him, don't get angry, don't do anything. Just lead him into the bathroom and tell him to go and leave him there. If he comes out and hasn't gone,

don't say anything, don't answer him if he talks about it. Wait unt
you see him hold it in again, and then take him by the hand, say,
'It's time to go to the bathroom, Luke,' and do it all over again.
You may have to do it a hundred times. Now, if he starts to cry,
walk away. Say, 'I don't talk to little boys that cry,' and just walk
away. Don't get angry, don't discuss it. Wait until he stops crying,
then take him by the hand again and say, 'It's time to go to the
bathroom, Luke.' Eventually, he'll go. When he does, give him a
reward. M & M's are good. Don't give him a lot, just a few, don't
make a big deal about it. Say, 'You were a big boy, Luke, so you
get a reward,' and you give him a few M & M's. Eventually, after
it's been working for a while, don't mention the M & M's. If he
does, give them to him. He'll forget after a while. The important
thing about all this is consistency. He will try anything to stop you
from ignoring his problem. You have to be consistent. It's hard, but
it only takes a few weeks, and I'm telling you it will work. He
wants anger, or protection, or talk, or anything, anything but to do
it. That's what you have to insist on. That it's just a normal thing
that everybody does. You can say that if you like. 'Everybody has
to go to the bathroom, Luke,' but that's the only explanation he
should ever hear. Don't praise him any more than I've said when
he does succeed. That's just as bad as yelling at him for failing. It
isn't an accomplishment. It isn't something to be praised or punished for; it isn't something he does to please you. It's a normal
human function.''

They both sat meek and silent in their chairs, mute children,
punished by the truth, frightened by its demand. Nina went over it
and over it in her mind. I can't do this, she thought. To the psychologist, she complained, ''I don't want to say to him, 'I don't
talk to boys who cry.' ''

''Okay,'' the psychologist answered quickly. ''Then say, 'When
you're finished crying, I'll come back,' and leave him. This is also
important, if he follows you, crying, you have to leave, don't punish
him for it, just leave him.''

''I don't like that,'' Eric said.

''I'm only talking about when he cries because you tell him to
go to the bathroom. Not other kinds of crying.''

''I don't know,'' Eric said.

''If you want him to be free of this, this will work. Give him an
opening and he'll take it. It's up to you.''

Lincoln sat. His heavy head fell onto his chest. Nina didn't blame
him. This would be a burden. And it would be Eric's burden. She
knew everything now, knew that Luke's problem was her fault, just

as Eric had believed all along. She had had the same problem as a child and thus she could never insist to Luke that everybody goes to the bathroom, that it was expected of him, because to this day, somewhere, buried under the covers of adulthood, a frightened child continued to hope she would never have to go again.

ERIC SHUT HIS EYES AGAINST THE SOUND. BUT HE COULD STILL hear.

The wails soared in the apartment, flying wildly about the rooms, a frantic, terrified bird, beating its soft body against the hard prison.

Eric opened to look. Nina sat stone still, but her face cracked from unhappiness.

At least she had been honest: "I can't do this, Eric. It's up to you."

I've already made two mistakes. "When you stop crying, we'll try again." What an asshole. The psychologist had said, *specifically* said, just wait until the crying is over and then when he holds it in—I've linked them now, that when he stops crying—what an asshole. I can't handle this. I just can't.

Luke found them. He came stumbling into the living room, drunk with tears. Luke had managed to get out of his pants, so he was bare from the waist down. "Mommy, Mommy" was all Eric could make out of his speech, but he was saying more, about what he couldn't do, and the hurt, and about Daddy.

"Shhh," Nina said to him, and picked him up, holding him in her lap. Eric had a headache. Not a real headache. It was just his brain exploding.

Luke tried to get them to talk. It was obvious now that he wanted to talk, to get them to talk. Nina caved in, she asked him why he cried so hard—Eric shot her a look. How am I going to do this if she doesn't—

"Daddy left me alone. I was going to try, but he left me alone—"

It's bullshit. Just like the doctor said. If I stand in the bathroom, he'll talk to me about how much it hurts—

"Okay, Luke. As long as you don't cry, I won't leave you alone. Okay?"

"I cry because—"

"I don't want to talk about it anymore, Luke! There'll be no more talking about it! That goes for you too, Nina!" Eric shouted. He swallowed. Luke ducked his head into Nina. The walls seemed to ring from the shout. They bounced about, thunder rumbling. Luke stayed still in Nina's arms.

Luke thought it was over. In five minutes, he was calm again, happy. Eric waited. It didn't take long. Luke had cheered up, was telling Nina something, and he flexed his buttocks, began to dance on his toes, holding—

Eric was up, his hand taking Luke's, "It's time to go to the bathroom—"

"Noooooo!"

"I won't stay in the bathroom if you cry." I'm stuck with this position now. He pulled Luke with him. He let himself go dead, absolutely dead. The colors had no vibrancy, the sounds no resonance. Eric looked past Luke's pleas as if he were a bum on the street. Eric drained his heart of emotion, watched his humanity empty out, down the drain, until his soul was as cold and bare as a porcelain tub. I'm a guard at Auschwitz; this is how evil is carried out, numb, everything pale and flat.

"Daddy! Daddy!" Luke pleaded.

"I'll leave if you don't stop crying."

"Okay, okay, okay." Luke gasped, tried to swallow his tears back. He did after a moment. He climbed up onto the toilet seat, his little legs not long enough to touch the floor. His face went red and jumped off. "I can't."

When Luke says he can't do it—the doctor had said when Eric went over all the possible permutations, after Eric had quit arguing—when he says he can't, say fine and go. Don't make trying the issue, only getting it done.

Back out they went, Luke surprised that he had gotten away with so little torture. Back they went to the living room, and a second later Luke danced, buttocks tight, hopping.

"It's time to go to the bathroom, Luke," and now Eric's voice did sound neutral, a dead voice of authority.

"No!" Luke's protest was shorter this time.

Back they went. Up on the toilet, jumping off. Out to the living room. Another minute, then: "It's time to go to the bathroom, Luke."

"Again?" Luke said, like a grown-up, outraged by a mad bureaucracy. Nina actually smiled.

"It's time," dead Eric answered, beyond being charmed.

By bedtime, although they had gone a dozen times, there was still no yield. The next morning, after fifteen more journeys, after Luke tried running away, talking to Eric while he held his legs together on the toilet (I'm not talking, Luke, I'm just keeping you company), after Luke threw one wild crying jag (Eric walked into the living room and sat with the *Wall Street Journal* open in front

of his face), after Luke tried to appeal to Nina, after dozens of little tricks, Luke finally made an effort, perhaps bored by the repetition. His face turned red, his stomach squeezed flat, and he pushed out four enormous turds. Where did he keep the stuff?

"You're a big boy, Luke," Eric said, well beyond feeling any triumph or relief. "You can have a few M & M's as a reward for going."

"Okay," Luke said quietly.

Then, his body empty, Luke was happy. He asked Nina to take him to the park. Eric went along. Luke laughed and went down the slide without asking anyone to catch him. He built elaborate castles in the sandbox, he told Nina stories about his constructions, he asked her to push him in the swing, and to read him all the signs in the deli where they went to lunch, he took his afternoon nap peacefully with her, in her arms, he played in his room in the evening before dinner, he talked to Nina while they ate, he was very, very happy, and he ignored Eric completely.

He asked Nina to read his bedtime stories, instead of Eric, and told her Daddy didn't have to come in to say good night. Eric went anyway, brushed the black hairs off Luke's sweet brow, and kissed the soft chin. "I love you, Luke," Eric said.

"Nighty-night," Luke said in a phony voice. He usually said, "I love you too."

Eric came out, beat. He thought: tomorrow Luke will start to hold it in again.

Eric fell onto the couch, facing a blank television screen, the remote control in his hand, too tired to press the power button. Nina's hand brushed the top of his hair. He looked up and her face was on him. He saw a glimpse of her blue eyes, filled with water, and her lips kissed him. "You were very brave," she said.

"Now I'm his stupid father," Eric said, and he wanted to cry. His voice quavered; his eyes blurred.

"He loves you," she said.

"Now I'm just another stupid father," Eric said.

15

"**N**o!" Byron shouted. "You can't." Luke dropped his mud cake.

"But, Byron, but—"

"No!" Luke does everything wrong. Doesn't listen. "I told you. This is the tower. Nothing goes on the tower."

"Oh, yeah." Luke was being gooder now. "Right. You told me. What kind of thing would go on a tower! Right, Byron? Nothing should go on a tower."

"Yeah, that would be crazy!" Luke'll play right now. "Now, you be Skeletor. And I'll put you in the prison."

Luke pulled back. Byron grabbed him.

"Come on Skeletor. Go in the prison. You're bad." Luke *is* bad. He doesn't listen.

"I don't want to—"

"You have to! I have the power! You have to!"

"I don't want to!" Luke ran away.

Good, I'll catch him. Fast Byron—go! Got his arm and squeeze. "I got you, Skeletor!"

"Byron! What are you doing?" Oh, Pearl. Go away. "We're playing."

"I don't wanna be Skeletor," crybaby Luke was saying.

"Why do you cry all the time?" Bad Luke. Doesn't listen.

"He don't cry 'cept when you being so bossy," Pearl said.

"What is it, Byron?" Francine's big tushy was in his face. So big and blue, her pants stretched like a pillow when you sit on it. "You bossing Luke again? He plays so nice and you don't let him be."

"We were just playing He-Man. Luke was being Skeletor and I was chasing him. Right, Luke?" Byron nodded at Luke, making his eyes talk. He blinked the words at Luke: don't tell them. They're grown-ups and they'll ruin our game. Blink, blink. Don't tell them, Luke.

"You telling the truth?" Francine said, and pinched Byron. Her fingers were mean; they squeezed in your skin and hurt.

"I'm gonna get you!" Byron grabbed the big tush and squeezed the blue bumps on it. Hard! There—you fat poop head! Hurt you!

"It's okay! It's okay!" Luke shouted. "We were just playing. I was being Skeletor." Francine stopped pinching.

"That's right, Luke," Byron said. He loved Luke. Luke was so much funner to play with than anybody.

"Really?" Pearl said.

"Yeah. Yeah!" Luke was so happy, so happy to play with me.

"Luke likes to play with me!" Byron told them. "He knows I'm not bossy, right, Luke?"

"That's right," good Luke said.

"He doesn't have very good ideas about what to play. I do. That's because I'm older."

"Older!" Francine laughed.

"I *am* older than Luke! Don't you know anything!"

"No!" Francine put her fat face in front. Byron reached out, to pinch that face, pinch that laugh off her face. She ducked away. "I'm just ignorant! I don't know anything!"

"I'm older!" Byron told Luke. Luke had to understand. That's why his ideas weren't so good. "I was born before you. That's why my birthday comes first."

"Okay," Luke said quietly.

Good Luke. I love him. "You go in the prison now!"

"Okay," Luke said in a whisper.

DOESN'T MATTER. SKELETOR NEVER DIES ANYWAY. MOMMY SAID, they're pretend, they don't live, they don't die. Mommy said, you tell Byron you won't play if he doesn't want to play games your way. But he is older. And his ideas come so fast. Like a grown-up, always coming, always fast, let's do this, let's do that. Tell him you don't want to.

"I don't wanna do this anymore. Let's go on the slide."

Byron stopped shooting Luke. His mouth was a big hole and he sounded like a radiator making heat. "I'm trapping you!"

"Byron, I know that! I know that! This isn't so much fun anymore. Let's play Super Friends on the slide."

"No! I have a better idea!" Byron hopped. He swung his head from side to side. "I'm so smart. I have the bestest idea! You are

Skeletor, see? And the slide's Snake Mountain. You get on top and I'll come and capture you.''

''Okay,'' Luke said. So he'd still be Skeletor, but at least he'd be on top of the slide, up among the leaves, taller than people, like Daddy, seeing the top of everything. He started up the steps, getting closer to the tree branch hanging over the top floor. I can grab a leaf. That could be a shield. I wish we were playing Super Friends. All we do is play He-Man. He thinks his ideas are so good. I don't think they're good.

''No, Luke! Come down! I have a better idea! That's Castle Grayskull and I'm He-Man!'' Byron had run up, so fast, up the stairs. He pushed Luke. ''Go down. You're Skeletor. Go down and you come up and attack me.''

I don't want to. I don't want to. Tell him you don't want to, Mommy said. Tell him you won't play at all, unless he plays the way you want. Mommy thinks it's so easy. I don't have ideas fast enough to stop him. He won't play my way. Mommy thinks it's my fault.

I want to go up! Up in the air, up to the stars you can't see in New York because it's so bright, up to the other suns and other planets, away, away, away—

''Luke! You don't listen to me! What's the matter with you! I told you, go down—''

''Byron!'' Pearl said. ''You stop bossing Luke now! You hear me!''

''Byron, you don't start playing nice, you be going home for your nap!'' Francine called.

''Why didn't you just do what I said?'' Byron buzzed in his ear, like a part of his head, buzzed angry. ''Do what I say or they won't let us play!''

''Byron, don't be whispering lies to Luke,'' Pearl said.

''I'm not!'' Byron said. ''I'm not!''

One thing Byron doesn't know. He doesn't know how to talk to grown-ups. ''We want to go on the swings,'' Luke said. He saw them, empty, just beyond. They go up, up to the moon, Daddy said, up and away.

''No, we don't!'' Byron said. He squeezed hard.

Let go. Tell him to let go, Mommy said, if he grabs you. You know, you're bigger than Byron. You can push him away it you want.

''Let go,'' he whispered.

''Let go of him, Byron. I'll take you to the swings, Luke.'' Even Pearl couldn't stop Byron. He kept on squeezing.

"The swings are boring!" Byron squeezed. "Stay! I have a better idea!"

"I wanna go on the swings," Luke said. He held himself tight, and prayed: do what I want, please. Please.

"Okay," Byron said. "I know! I have a great idea. We'll get on a swing together."

"Okay," Luke said, happy. He didn't care. Up and down they could go, loose and free, up to the sky and the buildings, swinging in the trees.

Byron pulled him down the steps. He had to hold on tight to the rail so he wouldn't fall.

"Don't pull Luke!" Pearl yelled at Byron.

"You're so bad," Francine said to Byron, laughing. They walked into the slide area.

Pearl picked him up, up and over the bar—

"No! I go in the same one! We're gonna swing together, right, Luke?"

"Right," Luke said quietly. Please just let me swing. No more problems.

"You can't both fit in there!" Francine said, and picked up Byron.

Byron kicked and kicked. "No!" He swung at her. She let him go. "No! I go in with Luke!"

Pearl leaned in and whispered soft into Luke's ear, "Don't pay him no mind. I'll push you."

Up.

Hello, buildings.

Down.

"No! I don't want to! I'm going, Luke! I don't want to play with you!"

"Okay," Luke whispered.

Up. To the blue sky.

Down. To the gray earth.

Byron was off, running out to the sandbox, his face red. He yelled something at Francine. She went over to yell at him.

Hello, branches.

Hello, benches.

Mommy said, Byron has to get his way or he gets angry, but if you let him, then you can't have fun. But I know how to have fun even if I don't get my way. So if I play what Byron wants, there's no more problems, no more yelling, right, Mommy?

No, she said.

Francine slapped Byron and he cried.

"I'll let him stay in my swing," Luke called back to Pearl. "He can swing with me."

"No, honey, he can't fit in your swing. Francine's gonna take him home. He's tired, he needs to nap."

Francine carried Byron off. Luke could hear him crying even when they got too small to see, even when they disappeared behind the bushes. "I wanna play with Luke!" Byron screamed over and over.

"I'll see him tomorrow, right, Pearl?" Luke asked.

Sure.

Tomorrow I'll tell him he has to play some things my way.

DIANE GRABBED THE HARD CHEEKS OF ERIC'S ASS AND PUSHED him to her, his thighs strong, flexing against her skin, his penis filling her, his mouth breathing on hers, saying, "You're so beautiful, you're so beautiful . . ."

"Diane!"

She jerked up from her spread of pleasure and hit her head on the porcelain. "What is it!"

"A call for you." Peter opened the door of the bathroom and looked in. "Friend of your mother's. Eileen somebody."

"Can you bring it in here?"

"It'll reach?"

"Yes." She got herself a cigarette immediately. Why is that busybody calling? Did I forget something? Mom's birthday, the anniversary of Daddy's death, their anniversary—no.

Peter brought the phone. "Don't electrocute yourself."

"Hello?" She began the conversation with innocent curiosity, and found herself in a dark world, inhabited by indistinct shadows and dreadful uncertainties. Eileen was Lily's best friend. Lily had had a bad cold for two months. Eileen kept urging Lily to go to the doctor. She finally went today. The doctor told Lily she has a heart murmur. They're going to do a test, where they take a picture of her heart. She might need open-heart surgery. Lily told Eileen she didn't plan to tell Diane. "Don't want to worry her," Eileen quoted Lily as saying.

Even facing death, Lily wanted to be impossible. She knew Eileen would call me. She knew—oh, what's the point? Mom must be terrified.

Diane got out of the tub, meaning to get dressed before she phoned Lily, but her hand trembled when she reached for the towel. She sat on the toilet seat, pulled a towel down to cover herself, and dialed.

"Hello," Lily answered, a hello of such despair and terror and weakness that Diane would have known something was wrong even if ignorant.

"Eileen called me, Ma," Diane said.

"I'm so angry at her! I told her—"

"She had to, Ma. Listen, what did the doctor say?"

"I have a heart murmur!" Lily said as if the diagnosis were a personal affront. "They have to give me a catheterization. My friend Judy had one. You know they're dangerous? He won't tell me, of course, what it might be. But this is what they do before you go in for open-heart."

"But the doctor didn't say you needed surgery?" Maybe Eileen was exaggerating. Please.

"No, of course, he didn't say. You know doctors. All he's thinking about is not getting sued. I told him you're a lawyer. I didn't tell him you quit." She laughed at herself. "I don't know. I thought maybe he'd take better care of me. He scared me," Lily said in a funny voice, not one Diane recognized from her mother's repertoire. No bark, no whine, no sarcasm, no bitterness, no anger. She sounded like a friend. "I didn't like him," she added, an afterthought, not important.

"Dr. Shwartz?"

"No! This is a cardiologist that Shwartz sent me to. He's not qualified for something like this."

"When's the—"

"This Friday. That's what scared me. He's in a big rush. They don't rush unless—" She laughed again, only it was mixed with tearfulness.

"I'm coming to Philly, Ma. I'll leave in—"

"No, no. Eileen'll go with me. Wait until it's something—"

"I see, I'm only supposed to come when you're dying."

"I hope you *will* come when I'm dying!" Lily answered, outraged, missing the point as usual. "I expect you to—"

"Ma!" My God, I'm yelling at her. "Ma, I'm coming, okay? There's nothing for me to—"

"Oh, and I suppose Byron is nothing. You can't leave him for—"

"I can leave him for two days. In fact, I can leave tonight."

"At this hour!"

"I'll take the car. There'll be no traffic—"

"No, no. There's no point. You'll be exhausted when you get here and me—well, I won't get any sleep tonight. I'll be up making noise, probably disturb you."

Diane had to hang up on Lily in order to get going. She had to be rude to get Lily to allow her to be considerate.

Diane explained the situation to Peter in a breathless rush while packing. Diane was glad to go, to do something; idle, she would be tortured by worry.

"What do I tell Byron?" Peter said. What a response. Not, I'm sorry. Can I help? Should I come? Well, Peter hates my mother. She's just a stupid cartoon to him, a Neil Simon character, something you sneer at from your seat in the theater, someone whom you cry for at the curtain, if the actress is good enough and the playwright sophisticated enough to know the New York audience is full of people with mothers like that, and they don't want to think thoughts that are too terrible. Shut up, Diane! She's sick. Shut up, shut up, shut up.

"Tell him Grandma is sick," she told Peter, "and I'm going to take care of her for a few days. I'll call him in the morning. If everything goes well Friday, you can both come down for the weekend. She'd love to see Byron."

The look on Peter's face! Why, if he were on trial, a jury would hang him for that look. "Um, this weekend is bad—" he started to complain.

"Let's not worry about it now. Okay? I'm going."

Once at the door, after kissing a sleeping Byron good-bye, she added something to Peter: "If she's in real trouble, you're bringing Byron this weekend."

"Okay," he said, chastened. "Give her my love."

Diane softened, kissed him good-bye. In the parking garage, when she started the car, she thought: I don't want his help anyway.

NINA FELT SOMETHING CRAWL ON HER. SHE SAT UP FROM HER BED of grass and looked away from the trees, the long-haired trees that swayed above her, waving hello—

Who was it? Luke? No sound from his room. She turned on her side and gasped with horror.

Eric was upright in the bed, wide-awake, staring out as if he'd seen a ghost.

"Eric!" she cried out. "What's wrong?"

Eric's head moved slowly, a robot activated by her voice. His big face looked at her. "They're too hard. Luke's shit is too hard. It's not just that he's holding it in. He's really pushing now, really trying. I mean, after the first couple times, he gets serious and really tries. I've looked at them. They're hard."

Her heart was still pounding. She coughed, in order to clear out the choking scare, so she could breathe. "Eric, you're gonna kill yourself. Relax. He's doing great. You're doing a great job."

"No, I know, honey. That's okay. But I think there was something physical in it. He did start holding it in because of—well, it's your theory. I'm sure it's right. Did the pediatrician say anything about what he should eat?"

She sighed. She wanted to laugh at him. Or maybe scream at him. Or maybe hose him down. She looked across at the angry red eyes of their digital clock: 2:35. Blink: 2:36.

"Are you worried about something at work?" she decided to ask. Maybe this was a dream. Maybe this was a conversation she wanted to have, but couldn't. Probably this was a dream.

"How did you know?" he said, and his robot head looked back at whatever vision he thought was there, just out there in the dark, ahead of him.

"You always worry about Luke when there's something wrong at work."

"You're right," he said. And then Eric lay down, collapsed onto the bed. He nestled his head into his pillow, like Luke into his blanket, and closed his eyes.

The angry red eyes: 2:36. Nina got herself settled back under the covers. Should I ask him what's wrong at work? Eric's eyes were shut. He breathed heavily. Was he asleep? Maybe I'm dreaming.

The trees waved hello. There was nothing but sky above them. Nothing but blue, happy blue.

I love my husband, she told the trees, the long-haired trees. They nodded and waved hello.

BYRON SHOOK HIM. "WHERE'S MOMMY?"

Peter's head felt big and heavy. Too much Rémy last night. I'm in bed, it's morning, and I'm alone with Byron. "Mommy had to go visit Grandma."

"Why?" Byron demanded.

"Grandma's sick. Mommy went to take care of her for a couple days. What time is it?"

"I don't know!" Byron said, and laughed. "I'm a child!"

Peter looked at his son. Byron's skin was smooth from sleep, his sandy hair wild, up in places, smashed in others. He was at attention, his body alert, ready for the day. "Are you hungry?" Peter asked.

"Yeah!" Byron said with lust.

That got Peter awake. He struggled out of bed. Byron took him by the hand and gently tugged, towing Peter as if he were an ocean liner, into the kitchen.

"Rice Krispies, please."

Peter had never gotten up with Byron before. Never been alone with him in the apartment, except for brief times, such as Diane going out to shop. Thank God he's toilet trained, Peter thought while having coffee and watching Byron maneuver his mouth around bulky spoonfuls of cereal. Then Peter remembered—he glanced at Byron's bottoms. There was a dark patch around the groin. "Did you pee in your bed?" he asked.

Byron cringed. "Yes!" he shouted, as if furious. But his body cringed and seemed afraid.

"Okay," Peter said.

"The sheets'll have to be changed," Byron said.

"Nah," Peter answered. "Let's mail them to somebody."

"What?" Byron smiled.

"Let's mail them to somebody for a Christmas present."

Byron laughed. "Terrible present."

"Okay. Then we'll have Francine put them in the laundry."

"Mommy says I have to put them in. I did it, so I have to clean them."

Right. That was the advice of their pediatrician. Make him take responsibility.

Responsibility. There wasn't an adult who really took responsibility for anything. Not if he had enough power or money to pass it on.

"You want me to do it now?" Byron asked quietly.

"No," Peter said. He liked having Byron there for company. A hungry little man, absorbed by the kitchen television, dangling his feet, his mouth stretched wide to capture food. "Francine'll take care of it."

"No! Mommy said—"

"Hey, Byron," Peter heard himself answer with impatient anger. "I'm your father. If I say Francine does it, then Francine does it."

Byron shrugged his shoulders, lifting them so high they touched his ears. "Okay with me," he said.

Peter opened the newspaper. He glanced at the reviews. His eye was caught by an ad for a children's movie. He could take off this afternoon. Byron had never been to the movies. He proposed the notion and got a bigger reaction than he had expected.

"Oh, yeah! Thank you, thank you, thank you." Byron kissed him and then danced across the kitchen floor. "We're going to the movies!" he proclaimed.

This is my chance, Peter told himself. Let's see if I like being a father.

"IT HURTS, DADDY!"

Eric pressed his fingers into his palm, pushing the nails in to silence himself with pain.

"It hurts, Daddy!"

I know it does. He's not lying. He's gone four times in six days and the stools were still hard. It's not his diet, Eric knew that much. Eric had been copying Luke's breakfasts and dinners and now he found himself barely able to retain anything.

"Ugghhhh," Luke groaned, his face red. There was a loud plop and Luke jerked his legs. "It splashed me!" he said with a smile.

"Don't worry about it," Eric mumbled.

"It feels cold," Luke said. "Ughhhh," he groaned, and his face went red again. Another plop. "I did it."

"Good. You're a big boy. I'll get your M & M's while you wipe yourself."

"You know, now that I'm pooping more," Luke said in a cocktail-party tone, as if he were discussing last summer's trip to Venice, or an interesting exhibit at the museum, or the most recent movie, "I mean, after all," Luke said. "I have gone a lot lately, right Daddy?"

"Wipe yourself. I'll get the M & M's."

"But it still hurts," Luke said. "You told me that when people go regularly, it hurts less and less."

"I don't want to talk about it, Luke. Everybody has to go."

"I know! I know that! But—"

"I don't want to talk about it." He walked out.

Luke's bowel movements were all he thought about these days, except, of course, for the stocks. They had become part of his mind, a piece of his brain, flashing and beeping day and night, in the soapy rivulets while showering, hovering above his bed at night, glaring whenever he closed his eyes for a moment, dancing when Nina kissed him, branded across her breasts, big on the living-room walls, numbers everywhere, betraying him, killing him.

He got the M & M's. He gave Luke the whole bag this time.

"*All* of them?" Luke said, appalled.

"You've been a big boy. You can have them all."

Luke shook his head. "I don't want all of them."

"Okay, then have as many as you want."

A few weeks before, Joe had taken away all accounts from Eric's supervision except for Tom's and Tom's friends, a group they had nicknamed the Boston Beans. In the past quarter, Eric's management was down 3 percent while the S&P average was up 12 and Joe's management up 18. Two of the five Boston Beans had withdrawn their money yesterday. And Tom, who never initiated a call, had phoned that day.

"We're not doing well, apparently," Tom said in that goddamned voice, the tone as soft as a pretty melody, the meaning as cold and hard as a tile floor.

Eric babbled excuses. "Well, we've made our money in the growth issues, and they're not participating at the moment, but they always lag the Dow, they'll come back—"

When Eric finished the call, Sammy mumbled, "Trouble in paradise." Eric wanted to punch him, but he couldn't even manage a yell.

At the end of the day, Joe called Eric into his office for a private conference.

"I'm going to manage the rest of the Boston Beans. Maybe I should do Tom's also? Give you a rest?"

Two of five Boston Beans had withdrawn their money. If Joe had been managing them, they not only would have stayed but might have increased their investment. What could Eric say?

I can say, I'm managing that money. I made it, I can lose it.

But Eric was mute, not argumentative at all. Instead, Eric was uncertain whether he should even continue to handle Tom's money. If he gave up the Boston Beans, why should he continue to handle Tom? And if he continued to handle Tom, then why should he give up the Boston Beans?

He wished they had nicknamed the Boston money something else. With Luke's diet in his belly, the word "beans" made his bowels churn.

"I think you could be a little burned out," Joe said. "You've done remarkably—one of the hottest runs ever—for two years. Maybe you should back off. Give yourself a chance to grow some new ideas."

"It doesn't make sense for you to handle Boston and not Tom."

"Then I'll handle Tom also," Joe said. "Maybe you want a week off?"

What is this shit? He's going to manage them and I'll continue to get my management fee?

"Let me think about it. For the moment, let's keep things as they are."

"I want to reposition the Boston money," Joe said. "You handle Tom."

"No," Eric said. "Tom will be suspicious if that happens."

"I'll explain it—"

"No," Eric repeated, volume climbing in his voice.

"You've lost two accounts!" Joe shouted. "I don't want to lose the rest! At least get out of some of the hi-tech garbage. You told me we were taking profits in New Systems a year ago! You're getting killed. This is a flight to quality. They want—"

"Joe, I read the papers. Everybody is saying the same thing!"

"And who are you suddenly! To disagree!"

I'm Eric, the Wizard of Wall Street. One day I'll duck into limousines, past the hoards of admirers, my camel-hair coat swirling around my legs, my jaw set, my brain a machine that never knows fear, or hesitation, or error.

"Think about it," Joe said. "One week and then if nothing changes, I may have to call the Boston Beans and even your father-in-law and tell them I don't agree with your current approach."

That would finish Eric. They'd either give Joe control or withdraw.

"You know something, Daddy?" Luke shouted. He was dancing across the living room floor, ecstatic now that the sludge was out of his system. "I'll have better ideas when I'm older. Right?"

"Better ideas?" Eric said. He tried to think back to the meeting with Joe again, to continue the rerun, but Luke had said—Maybe I can't adjust on the stocks because I'm busy with his damn bowels. If Nina were a real wife, if she cared about money! If she only knew what money means on this earth!

"Yeah, Byron has better ideas right now—"

"Better ideas about what?" Eric's tone was so sharp that Luke paused, his clear, glowing blue eyes clouding to a deeper, worried color.

"Forget it," Luke said, and swung his arm in the air. "I have the power!"

"No, no," Eric said, and got on one knee. "Say it again, I'm sorry, I was thinking—say it again."

"When I'm older, I'll have better ideas than Byron. When I get to be older than he is."

"I'm sorry, Luke, I don't understand."

"Daddy!" Luke clenched his fists in frustration. "Okay," he said with a manly sigh. "Byron is older than me, right?"

"Not really."

Luke stood still. He stared into Eric's eyes like a deer frozen in the lights, paralyzed by surprise.

"Byron is six weeks older than you, Luke. That's nothing. We call that being the same age. A year, two years, that's older. But six weeks is nothing. And another thing," Eric said, a chill running down his spine as he realized what he was really saying and to whom he was saying it, "age has nothing to do with whether your ideas are good or not. Even if Byron was much older than you, it doesn't mean his ideas are better."

"Yeah," Luke said slowly. "I don't think his ideas are so good. But he said—"

"I don't care what he said, Luke!"

"Okay." Luke bowed his head, shamed. "I'm sorry."

"No!" Eric picked him up so they were face-to-face. "There's nothing for you to be sorry about. Byron is a liar!"

"What!" Nina had been peacefully reading on the couch. "Eric, what did you say?"

Ignore her. She doesn't know. She thinks we're going to survive just because we're good people, because we love each other. Maybe we don't. And maybe we'll go under.

"What did Byron say to you?"

"Nothing." Luke tried to look away. He squirmed in Eric's hand.

"Come on, Luke."

"He said because he's older, his ideas are better."

Nina laughed. "He's not older than you, Luke."

"He isn't?"

"No," Eric said. "He isn't. And even if he is older, that doesn't make his ideas better."

"Okay, Daddy." Luke smiled.

Eric put him down on the floor.

"I have the power," Luke called. Eric watched him run, swinging his invisible sword.

Nina, her face soft, solicitous, said, "What was that about?"

"That Byron is a bully."

"That's what Pearl said today. He's very bossy, but Luke loves him."

"Maybe it isn't love."

"Oh, no," Nina said. "He can't wait to get to the park to play—"

"That might not be love."

"Eric," Nina said, frowning at him. "Byron is pushy, but Luke holds his own, and if he can't, he has to learn to. There are plenty of bullies in the world."

Luke was back. "Watch how fast I fly, Mommy." He ran with his hands out in front. "I'm Superman! I'm Superman!" The little toddler, his legs still chubby, his head still a little too big for his body. "I'm Superman!"

I'm gonna go in there tomorrow and scream at Joe. How dare he tell me he's going to take the Boston Beans away? That's my fucking money to win or lose.

Lose.

Lose.

Lose.

"What did you say, Eric?" Nina asked.

He gasped. Can't tell her. Would Tom call her?

"You were mumbling," she said. "What did you say?"

"Nothing," Eric answered, and lowered his head, ashamed.

DIANE HELD HER MOTHER'S HAND AS THEY WALKED INTO THE hospital. The smell, a mixture of baked institutional food and cleansers, overwhelmed her mouth. She took a deep breath to suck in the despair and sickness all at once and be fast acclimated.

Lily squeezed Diane's fingers at each sight of illness, gasping at each bit of news. Go in there. Undress. The doctor will do such and such. This is a tranquilizer. No, we can't put you out. You get to watch your heart on a monitor.

Squeeze. Gasp.

"I don't need to see that!" Lily said, and managed a laugh, although its sound was brief and pained.

"May I stay with her?" Diane asked Dr. Klein, the cardiologist, when he came in.

He looked astonished at the suggestion. "No. Hospital procedure wouldn't allow that."

"Can I read a book or something?" Lily said in an aggrieved tone. "Just lying there—I'll be bored!"

Lily had come up with these inappropriate statements every few minutes since Diane had arrived in Philadelphia. She was obviously terrified, but she kept up a pretense, not a convincing one, that she was only bothered by the inconvenience and fuss.

Lily maintained this fiction, except for the night Diane arrived.

"They told me everything would be fine with your daddy," Lily had said that night, her hands nervously rubbing the knot in her robe's belt. The translucent skin, stretched across her bony knuckles, looked tired, as if it might peel off. When did that happen to her hands? "They said your daddy would recover from the heart attack if he watched his diet—and then the next morning he's dead. So I don't believe them. Not that they're lying. They don't know what they're doing. And the worst thing is they think they know."

Diane explained to Lily that fifteen years had gone by since then, that medicine had learned and developed a great deal in heart treatment. "It's the most successful area of medicine there is," Diane said.

"You're smart," Lily said. Her chin buckled under her upper lip. "You're my smart girl," she repeated.

Diane felt her heart expand, warm against all the years of silence, hot and red, glowing against the ice age that had formed between them. Diane took the bony fingers, cold with fright, in her palm. "Don't worry, Ma. They do know what they're doing."

"If they make me into a horror," Lily said, "just shoot me. I don't want to lie someplace, drooling all over myself." Lily laughed, a ghastly hysterical laugh, at this thought. "That's all I need—to end up wearing diapers with some *schwartzer* to change them."

"Will you please not call them that, Ma?"

Lily took offense. Loudly proclaimed she wasn't a racist. Her proof: she paid her girl (a black woman of sixty) a dollar more an hour than the going rate for housecleaning.

My mother is dumb. How is that possible? Was Daddy so brilliant? He owned and managed three record stores and made a good living, but he was hardly Einstein. Where did I get my SAT scores from? There must be some intelligence in this woman; there had to be gold buried beneath the layers of conventional attitudes and dull gossip.

Maybe not. I was probably kidnapped from a roving band of intellectuals, hijacked away from a life of the mind and forced to live in the suburbs of Philadelphia.

Diane called home while waiting for Lily to emerge from the catheterization. She had read in the release disclaimer there was a 1 percent chance that insertion of the catheter would provoke a heart attack. The document was pretty good legally, but nothing could protect the hospital from a clever lawyer.

"I'm a lawyer," Diane had heard herself saying to Dr. Klein, just as stupidly as Lily had. Even dumber, Diane had lied, saying, "I'm an associate at Wilson, Pickering." She had been so intent on scaring the doctor with this fact that she had forgotten to say her tentative farewell to Lily, her just-in-case good-bye. "Don't worry, Ma," she had planned to say. "I love you."

After the doctor left, Diane had another opportunity, but Lily distracted her, throwing a temper tantrum about her legs being uncovered because her gown was too short. "I'm a small woman!" she began to shout. "This must be for a child!"

"It doesn't make any difference, Ma," were the last words Diane had spoken to her mother before she went in. "You're not going to a bar mitzvah. Don't worry about your outfit."

That farewell was a far cry from "I love you, Ma!" She's going to be all right, so it doesn't matter. Diane reached Francine at home. Byron was out again with Peter. Diane's absence seemed to be a blessing. Peter had taken off three days in a row, treating Byron to a movie, the circus, and now, although it sounded unlikely, according to Francine, to a play.

Diane sighed and stared out the waiting-room window at the hospital's half-empty parking lot. A drizzle had begun. There was nothing to see but the cars, put in slots like empty shoes in a closet, longing for use. Diane had enjoyed that nighttime drive down from New York. Alone, urgent, scared, music playing out of the darkened hollow beneath her, the dashboard lights glowing like cat's eyes.

If she dies, I'll get in the car and disappear. Drive and drive and drive. If she dies, I'm an orphan. And orphans wander. Alone.

NINA WANDERED THE AISLES OF THE DRUGSTORE UNTIL SHE FOUND the laxatives. She hadn't needed them in years; the worst of her constipation had ended in college when she began to drink coffee.

Maybe I should start Luke's day with three cups of espresso, she thought.

Tad had asked her to work for him on next year's line. He suggested she drop her courses at FIT and work full-time.

"You're not one of these children," Tad had said. "You don't need this. Work for me for a few years and they'll all be going to you behind my back and offering you the world."

She almost believed him. She said yes, she would drop her courses and become his assistant, my number two, as Tad called it. But she hadn't told Eric the news. That was wrong. But she needed at least a few days to think up her explanation of why taking the job was so important. She knew it was, but she couldn't explain why.

There were lots of new twists to the laxatives, so-called natural laxatives, but when Nina studied their labels, they all had chemicals of one sort or another and cautioned that regular use might lead to dependence. Eric wouldn't accept that for his son. Although Luke was getting the shit out, his body wasn't making it easy. She called the behavioral psychologist and he said, "Well, as long as he's trying and doing it, you can continue the mineral oil to make it easier."

But Eric had said no to that. "He'll be on it for the rest of his life," Eric said.

The Perfectibility of Man. But Eric was right. Luke was happier, freer, his spirit blossoming. He played for hours now, no longer comatose on the couch, staring at television. He concentrated on his pretend games, learned the alphabet merely by osmosis, used the slide fearlessly, let go of her and Eric in the mornings with assurance—Luke was tougher, more decisive, surer of himself.

She found something new. Fiber biscuits. She read the package carefully. All natural ingredients. Can be used as a daily supplement without a risk of dependence.

Don't be dependent. Don't need anyone. Dress yourself, fight your own battles, carry your sword into the world and conquer it. There's love at home, but there's happiness outside.

She showed the biscuits to Eric. He read the box three times. "It doesn't seem to have chemicals or anything bad," he admitted, but with suspicion. "What do we do? Have him eat one a night?"

"Why not? It's just bran, that's all. He can have it before he goes to bed, right after pooping." Luke now made a regular trip to the toilet with Eric right before his bedtime stories.

It was all so absurd, so laughable. But it wasn't, not really, she knew it wasn't.

Over dinner, she tried to tell Eric about Tad's offer, but she couldn't let go, sever herself from being Eric's wife, always convenient, always willing to make things easy.

What do I say if Eric says, no, I need you to be here, I'm under a lot of pressure?

Eric *is* under a lot of pressure. His face seemed to be pulled so tight that he couldn't loosen enough to smile. He sat at dinner, staring into space, not hearing Luke's happy monologues: "You know something? It's not so good to build something very tall, because they fall down. Unless you make a bottom—"

"Foundation," Nina said. "A foundation is what goes on the bottom and holds up the building."

"Yeah! A foundation. You have to make a big foundation or something tall will fall down."

Eric stared off. His eyes were big and absent. Their brown color usually had depth, allowing light to penetrate into his soul; these days they were clouded, a muddy pond, no reflection, no transparency, just swirling, stormy dark.

"Are you with us?" Nina asked softly, touching Eric's hand.

"Has your mother called you lately?" he asked, quickly, as if an answer were urgent.

"No. I have to call her. I haven't—why?"

"Nothing."

He was like a baby. Eric said, "Nothing," just the way a petulant child does, a concealment so inept it might as well be a confession.

"Sounds like it's something," Luke said, his broad mouth smiling, his blue eyes shining love at his father.

Eric answered Luke with a confused look, as if he didn't recognize him. "It does?"

"Yeah," Luke said. "Are you winning these days, Daddy?"

When Luke was two, he had asked Eric what he did at work. He had been told that buying and selling stock was like a game, that you won points or lost points each day. For a while, Luke would ask, "Did you win today, Daddy?" Lately, he hadn't.

"No," Eric said, but he looked at Nina. "I'm not winning."

"Well"—Luke put out his hand, palm up, and shrugged his shoulders, an imitation of Eric's cool manner about the pooping—"you'll have to try harder."

"I'm trying as hard as I can," Eric said. Nina couldn't tell if he understood the irony of this conversation.

"You can do it, Daddy. Maybe you need to do more of your reading things. After dinner, I could watch some cartoons and you could do your reading."

Eric smiled a heartbroken smile. Something is terribly wrong, Nina admitted to herself. He must be losing a lot. He's scared. "Okay," he croaked in answer to Luke.

"That'll help you, won't it, Daddy?"

"Yes."

"See?" Luke said with another broad smile to Nina. "I can help Daddy do his work."

"That's good," she answered Luke, and leaned across the table to kiss his sweet skin. Her beautiful boy was good, so good and so beautiful that he could get his father to talk. So good and so beautiful that it hurt to think of it.

"WHO'S HE, DADDY?" BYRON'S VOICE TRUMPETED OUT OF THE enforced silence of the audience toward the legal noise of the stage.

"Shhh," Peter whispered. "Remember, it's not television. Everyone can hear you."

"Okay, okay," Byron answered in his whisper, dramatic and high-pitched. Byron dug his nails into Peter's arm. "But who is he?"

Peter explained that the man was the hero, but he looked different because time had passed and he was grown up.

''Oh,'' Byron said, and his mouth stayed open, slack, astounded by the lights, the sounds, the restless movement of the actors. Peter watched their actions play on his son's face, their sounds animate his short legs, dangling over the cliff of his center aisle seat. When they'd gone to their seats, Peter and his three-year-old son had gotten incredulous, scandalized looks at their appearance on the fifth-row center of a Friday-night performance on Broadway.

''You're bringing a child to this?'' one rude woman had the temerity to say to Peter.

Peter stared at her. He'll probably get more out of it than you will, he wanted to answer. He promised himself he would—the next time. Of course, he never expected Byron to last even for the first act, but what did that matter? He could get house seats and charge them to the foundation anytime—this was his one accomplishment on earth. Why shouldn't he lavish it on Byron? So what if it was *Nicholas Nickleby*? So what? This was a once-in-a-lifetime feast and Byron would have had at least a bite of the hors d'oeuvres.

Peter had to talk constantly, explicating everything. Byron held on to him, as if he were blind and needed Peter to keep him from stumbling. Byron was thrilled. Peter couldn't believe it. He had expected impatient Byron, self-indulgent Byron, center-of-attention Byron to demand they leave after ten minutes. Peter would have thought that a success. But they were more than an hour in, and yet Byron, his eyes tired, fighting to stay awake, was still taking it in, his little body reverberating with every sound, thrilled—

Just like me, Peter thought.

Finally the little head, stuffed with sensation, nodded from the weight. Byron nestled into the cushioned chair like a cat and fell asleep. Peter waited for a well-lit scene to gather Byron in his arms and walk up the aisle. The spectacle—Byron snuggled against his chest—managed to distract the audience, draw smiles, silent exclamations, and pointed fingers.

For one brief moment, Peter had upstaged Broadway.

The car he had hired was ready for them. Byron's eyes opened when Peter had to adjust his grip to get Byron in the car.

''Daddy?'' he called.

''Yes, darling,'' Peter heard himself say in a soft, loving voice. Is that me?

''Home, Daddy?''

''Yes, honey, we're going home. Close your eyes.''

It was quiet and dark in the car, making the city's animation and brilliance into a silent film. Byron was warm and trusting in Peter's lap. Peter could feel Byron's contentment, tangible, aglow in the dark.

He would rather be out with me, uncomfortable, his mind called upon to absorb the difficult, than be at home without me, patronized by some sitter—it's being with me that makes him happy.

Peter was crying. He noticed that with surprise. A tear hung at the bone of his jaw and then fell, splashed onto Byron's sandy hair.

"I'm sleeping, Daddy," Byron said, his eyes closed, but with a smile. He pressed his face into the crook of Peter's arm.

"Good," Peter said. He had considered arranging for a sitter to come and pick up Byron at the theater and then stay himself to see *Nickleby* again, but he had changed his mind at the last minute, and now he was glad.

Peter carried Byron into the lobby. Two old women, irritable, gossipy crones, peered at his package. One said, "Oh, he's sleeping."

"Happy in Daddy's arms," said the other.

They weren't so bad. At least they understood the magic of children. Upstairs, he tried to pull Byron's clothes off, but the attempt provoked groans and Peter finally put him in the bed still dressed.

Remember to have him pee before he goes to bed, Diane had told Peter, or they'll be soaked in the morning.

Let him pee, Peter decided, and draped the covers over Byron. Let him ruin all the sheets in Christendom.

Peter felt solid back in his study, sipping a cognac. He tried to think of other shows, other plans. Maybe they could walk in on a couple of matinees, sneak Byron into a rehearsal or run-through here and there. In a few years there were theatrical camps. His mother had once mentioned something about public library events, readings or something.

Larry. He tried to summon Larry's face. What did Larry look like? Kotkin had asked at their last session when Peter mentioned that he had become curious about Larry now. He felt an urge to see him, confront him.

Peter took out the telephone book and looked for a residential number for Larry. He didn't find one.

What does he do? After all these years? Cruise the docks? Or is that scene dead now? Does he stop at touching? If I'd let him go on, would Larry have stopped at that?

He should have had the sitter come. He felt restless. It was still early, only ten, and he was stuck at home with Byron. What was the point of that? Byron was asleep, for God's sakes. I could have stayed at *Nickleby*, could have called Rachel. Haven't seen her in a long time.

He dialed Rachel's number and got her machine. "Just Peter," he said after the beep, and hung up.

"Daddy!" Byron called at midnight. "Daddy, I peed in my bed!" he shouted, panic in his voice.

What a disgusting mess. Byron's underpants were glued by urine to his skin, the pants probably ruined from the extent of the saturation. And Byron wailed throughout as if he were the victim. No wonder it makes Diane crazy, Peter thought. But Diane had wanted him. She has no right to complain. Peter didn't bother to change the sheets. He covered them with towels and put Byron back in.

The phone rang. Rachel? At this hour?

"Peter?" It was Diane. Cold Diane. "I guess you never planned to call to find out whether my mother was alive or dead."

"What? I thought she was just having a test. I was waiting for you to call." A lie. He simply didn't think of her mother.

"A dangerous test. She's okay." Diane's voice relaxed a little bit. "She's very sick. She needs open-heart surgery. She has to have an aortic heart valve replacement."

Peter urged himself to say something appropriate. "Oh, God," came out. "Are you at the hospital?"

"No. We're back home. I'm hanging up—"

"Wait—" Peter called. I can be better at this. Give me a chance.

"I don't want to talk right now. I'll call you in the morning."

He sat at his desk for a long time. He tried to drink more cognac, but his glass was empty and he had no energy to get more. He grabbed the glass several times and drank air, tried to sip that last little drop, stuck at a small hollow in the bottom. He turned the snifter upside down, but the liquid didn't surrender to gravity. It smeared everywhere, clinging to its container, and never got past the rim. He tried to arch his tongue inside, but it wasn't long enough to reach that last precious bit of flavor. At last he put his finger in, punctured the dollop, and sucked off what he could. A brief pleasure—but tart and good.

He called Larry's office. It was two in the morning. No one answered.

MOMMY SAID, "WE'LL GO TO THIS PLACE, WHERE THEY TEACH children, and a woman will play with you for a while. I'll be there the whole time." *Mister Rogers, Sesame Street, He-Man*, they all talked about it—school. Sounds like a wind. Like running in the wind: school!

Daddy was excited. "Have fun today," he said.

"I don't understand," he said to Mommy while they walked there. There was no sun today. The sky was like the cardboard in Daddy's shirts. Gray. Flat and long and all gray. A sunny sky is different. There's white in places, the clouds. And sometimes the blue is flat and it looks short, but sometimes the blue is deep and curved. Sometimes the sky is gray and blue and yellow and shiny and dull all at once. Not today. A flat gray cardboard sky. Is it going to rain?

"What don't you understand?"

"Don't children go to school and stay?"

"Yes, when they go. This is just a visit."

"Oh." Why visit? Well, it's good. I don't want to stay. Not with the sky so flat and gray.

"Here we are," Mommy said, and they climbed steps, went through tall doors, like the lobby doors, wood and glass. There's a boy with a Transformer. They're not so good. Oh, but look! It looks like a dinosaur!

It was hot in the room. He wished he had a toy. Not a Transformer. Well, maybe. The dinosaur—

Mommy was talking to a woman.

"Hello, are you Luke?" She was smiling hard, kept her teeth turned on for so long without laughing.

Mommy will tell her I'm Luke.

"Yes," Mommy said. "This is Luke."

"We're going to go in this room and play for a while."

Luke moved toward the woman's hand and let her take hold. But then she turned, moving at the door—but Mommy!

"Mommy!" Luke called. She wants to come too.

"Luke," the woman said, turning her teeth on again with no laughter. "Your mommy knows she's not allowed to be with us while we play. She's going to wait here—"

"In this chair," Mommy said, and sat down.

"And she'll be right there when we're through."

Something I can't stop. That hurt, the crying was going to start. I want to stop things sometimes. Well, no arguing. We're just gonna play. Stop crying, Luke.

He pushed the tears back in his eyes. The room was pretty big and had lots of things.

"I have that," he told the woman. She had turned off her teeth at last.

"Yes? I have some shapes we can play with. Would you like to do that?"

She's got a triangle. I bet she asks—

"Do you know what shape this is?"

Oh, this is like *Mister Rogers* and *Sesame Street.* "It's a triangle," he said, and tried to laugh. "You can't play with a triangle. They're too pointy."

The woman turned her teeth on again; only this time, she laughed too.

MOMMY GRABBED HIM. HER ARMS HUGGED HIM TIGHT. HE PRESSED his stomach into her breasts, felt them hug his tummy. He wrapped his legs around her and covered himself in her neck; her hair, smooth and long, touched his cheek. "Mommy," he sang to her.

"My baby," she said into his ear. "I missed you."

"He was a very good boy," Daddy said.

"Of course you were," Mommy said, and bounced him on her hip. "Now let's go in and say hi to Grandma. Give her a big kiss 'cause she's not feeling so well."

She let him down on Grandma's furry rug and he ran, watching the edges of his shoes disappear. He ran down the hall and into Grandma's pink room. She was in bed, way up, sitting up like a stuffed animal.

"Bubeleh! My grandson," she called.

"Hi, Grandma." She looks sad. Say something to make her smile. "I'm much bigger than the last time you saw me," he said. Daddy had told him that.

"You are, darling. Come here and let me give you a hug and kiss."

Byron climbed up the puffy mountainside. Her bony hands took hold of him. She brought him close and he kissed her cheek, her melted cheek. "Mmmm," she said. "You taste so good."

Her breath splashed his face. She smelled like garbage. "You smell, Grandma," he said, and tried to squirm out of her arms.

"Oh, my God!" Grandma said. She let him go.

"Byron!" Mommy said.

"Don't yell at him," Grandma said. "I've got to go to the bathroom. I haven't gargled today."

"Hello," Daddy said.

"Hello, Peter," Grandma answered. "I need some privacy, I'm in my nightgown."

Daddy took him out. "I'm hungry," Byron told him.

"Let's go in the kitchen." The kitchen was yellow and its floor was black and white like checkers.

"Grandma has Oreos." Byron pointed to the cabinet where they were kept.

"I think you should have—"

"I just want one cookie!"

"Okay." Daddy found the box and began to crackle the paper inside.

I'll open it up and lick the sweet white off first. "Why is Grandma still in bed?"

"She's sick, Byron. Here you go." Daddy came with the box. It was full of cookies.

"Is Grandma going to die?" Byron asked.

"No, what gives you that idea? Where do you get that idea?"

He had to pull the cookie pieces in different directions to get them unglued from the sweet white. "Mommy said when people get old, they die. What happens when they die?"

Daddy looked into the box of cookies. He stared at it.

"Mommy said nobody knows for sure," Byron said. "But that's crazy."

Daddy took out a cookie and ate it himself. "When people die, they rest. They rest and they're happy," Peter said.

"Grandma's resting. Is she going to die and rest more?"

"No," Daddy said. "She's going to have an operation to make her feel better. She has to rest for the operation."

"I don't want to die." The white was gone. He put the cookie pieces back together.

A nice sandwich.

Mommy came in fast. She came right down to Byron. "Honey, please don't say anything to Grandma about dying."

"Is she—" Daddy nodded toward Grandma. There were funny noises from the hallway. Noises like Grandma, but not.

"Yeah. She's upset," Mommy told Daddy. She hugged Byron and put her face to his. Her breath splashed him, but it was hot and didn't smell. "Please, Byron. It makes Grandma cry if you talk about dying. Please don't say anything about it."

There's something wrong about dying. Maybe you die if you're bad.

"I won't say anything!" he shouted. He grabbed Mommy. "I promise I won't say anything! I'll be good. I'm a good boy, Mommy."

"I know you are, Byron. It's okay, it's okay." Her neck covered him and he could put his face on her springy breast. "Would you like another cookie?"

Wow. Another cookie for being good. "Yes!" he shouted.

16

LUKE CAUGHT THE WORDS IN HIS STOMACH, STUCK THERE AT the bottom, and blew them up, leaves swirling in the wind, magic appearing from his mouth. "Byron," he said. The words were almost out, almost free from the secret Luke. The Luke with power. "You know, Byron, you're not older than me. I mean, you're a little bit older—"

"That's right!" Byron hopped. Byron pulled at Luke's arm. Come on.

Pull against him. I'm heavy. Too heavy to move. "But we're really both the same age."

"No," Byron said, and pulled harder, now using both hands.

I'm a heavy weight. I'm a big heavy box no one can lift. Byron's face got round. His eyes swelled. He can't move me!

"Yes," Luke the immovable said. "We're both three. That's the same."

"That's right," Pearl said.

Francine slapped Byron's tushy. "Let go of Luke! What you doing!"

I'm the World Trade Center and he can't pull me down.

Byron teetered, a tall pile of blocks, leaning, going—Byron fell at Luke.

Hold him up—I can't—

The cement was sharp and flat and hard. His brain bounced up to the blue sky and down again against the rough and the hard street. The hot sun hurt the ache, warmed the pain.

Pearl and Francine yelled at Byron. I'm not getting up. I can't tell him any more things.

Francine slapped Byron across the face. He cried. Pearl picked

up Luke. She put her hand on the softened part of his head. Her
fingers melted inside and made the hurt more.

"Ow!" Luke told her. Saying that made him cry.

"You pulled me down!" Byron shouted. Francine's hand was
still on Byron's face: red ghost fingers blinking white and red.

Luke fought to get out of Pearl's fat black arms, heavy and wet,
smothering him. "Let go!"

"He's all right," Francine said.

Everybody who's hurt is all right to Francine.

"Now say you're sorry, Byron," Pearl said, and pushed Byron
at Luke.

"I'm sorry," Byron said. "Let's play now."

You're not older than me. You're not stronger than me.

"Come on, Luke!" Byron said, and grabbed Luke's hand again.

"Byron!" Pearl yelled.

I'm not here. Someone else is being pulled. I'm not here.

"Let's play now, Luke, okay? I don't wanna argue anymore."

Someone else is playing. Someone else is being pulled.

THE WORDS CAME OUT TERRIFIED, NOT AS HE HAD WANTED TO
pronounce them. They trembled in the air, fluttering baby birds on
their first flight: "I'm here to see Larry Barrow. My name is Peter
Hummel."

"Do you have an appointment?" The receptionist was neutral.
She didn't acknowledge his scared tone.

("Do you want me to tell you not to see Larry?" Kotkin had
asked at that morning's session.

("I don't know.")

("Then why are you telling me you plan to see him?")

(So you'll tell me not to. So you'll tell me to. "I don't know,"
he answered.)

"Does he know what this is in reference to?" the receptionist
asked.

Does he ever. Imagine Larry at his desk—safe, smug about his
dirty secrets, sure of his invulnerability, and now I've come. I've
come grown. Powerful, able to destroy. At last, on equal terms.

What will he think? Do I have a gun? Do I have a lawyer? Be
scared, Larry, be confused. Like me, feel the dread, the uncertain
sickening doubt.

The receptionist accepted Peter's stammered answer: "I'm an
old, uh, acquaintance. Personal, not business."

What did she mean by that look? That snicker? Does Larry often
have boys visit him in the office?

I'm not a boy.

(''What will you say to him?'' Kotkin asked.

(I'm floating on Kotkin's couch, floating on the sea of my unconscious, buoyant, just above the great dark ocean, giving the back of my head to the depths. ''I don't know.'')

A secretary appeared. She seemed uncertain. ''Hello. I'm Larry's assistant, Maria. He's in a meeting. I don't want to interrupt him. Can you tell me what this is about? Maybe I can be of help?''

Peter felt his anger gather at his brow, a black cloud storming in front of his vision. You can't escape me like this: with secretaries, with the platitudes of business. ''No,'' Peter said, and his true voice, his adult voice, was back. A trace of contempt played in the polite melody: ''I've known Larry since I was a child. He might not remember my last name, although I'd be surprised. I was best friends with his cousin Gary. He'll remember me if you mention Gary.''

''I see.'' She was stuck for a second. ''Well, I don't know how long he's going—''

''I'll wait.'' Peter sat down on the gray modular couch. I'm here to stay.

THIS TIME DIANE WAS DETERMINED TO SAY HER CONDITIONAL good-bye. Lily was scheduled for a 7:00 A.M. operation. Openheart surgery for breakfast.

Diane stayed with Lily until 10:00 the night before, the end of visiting hours, sitting all day in an uncomfortable armchair beside Lily's hospital bed.

Lily was terrified. Her head was propped up by a triple layer of pillows. They diminished her face, held it still, halfway in a cave. She peered out like a cornered animal. Lily's bony hand gripped Diane with relentless pressure. Even when Lily reached for another sip of ginger ale, or for a tissue to wipe away the slow, steady stream of tears, her hand stayed flexed around Diane's palm. Lily's skin was pasty, her forehead as frail as a newborn's, and her lips trembled continuously so that hard consonants were lost and speech became a plaintive whimper of vowels.

''They dope you up—so you don't remember.'' Lily said this every hour or so.

''That's good,'' Diane said.

''But it hurts just the same. You just don't remember later.'' Lily swallowed. ''What about the blood? How do I know they won't give me something in the blood.''

''They check the blood, Ma.''

"They check everything! But things still go wrong!"

"Ma," Diane said softly, hopelessly. Don't worry, Ma. Everything's going to be all right. I love you. Say it. "Don't worry, Ma—"

"I can't help it," Lily said, and she was crying again. "I just wanted to die in my sleep. That's all I asked of God, that He kill me in my sleep."

Lily had never spoken of God before. She was so self-centered that even the most powerful being Lily could imagine was cast as a breaker of promises. Not a savior to humble herself before, but just another disappointment. Shut up, Diane. Shut up.

"Everything's going to be all right, Ma."

Lily sighed to end her weeping, a heavy, almost sexual pause. "I know. I'm a very weak person. I'm scared of everything. I never wanted to be alone, to handle anything by myself. And your daddy left me alone—I should have killed myself when he went."

A nurse appeared. "I'm afraid you'll have to leave in five minutes."

"Can't they make up a bed for you here?" Lily whispered to Diane. She knew that had already been refused.

"I'm going to get you something to help you sleep," the nurse said. She had overheard.

"Drugs. That's their answer to everything," Lily said.

When the nurse returned with a sleeping pill, Diane said, "I'm going to stay fifteen minutes until she's drowsy."

"I'm sorry," the nurse answered, eyes blank, her voice mechanical, "but it's against hospital procedures."

"Just fifteen minutes."

"I'm sorry, it's a rule. You wouldn't want anyone to say later that we had done things wrong. That's the kind of thing—"

"I'm a lawyer," Diane answered. This is my mom, after all. I can be obnoxious. "And I certainly wouldn't want to have to waste my professional time on any of this. So I'm going to stay here for fifteen minutes as a visitor. Thank you." Diane didn't look at the nurse to judge her effect. She kept her eyes on Lily. The nurse remained for a moment, then left.

Lily's face was transformed. "You told her!" she said with a delighted smile, a Byron-smile of mischief and power. "You should have seen the look on her face!"

"I was bluffing. There's nothing I can do about her wanting to kick me out."

"Doesn't matter. You're a professional person. They respect that." Lily seemed to have forgotten all her worries and self-pity.

She smoothed the blanket down and pursed her lips. "My daughter. You told her."

I've sat here holding her hand and talking softly and she got more scared by the minute. Two sentences of bullshit and she's happy. She wants me, after all the years of talk about my marriage, having children, worrying over my femininity, after all that, she really does want me to be in control, to be another Daddy, to be strong.

"When the doctor comes out and tells you about the operation, I want you to get the truth out of him. Threaten him if you have to. I know he's lying. Doctors don't feel important unless they lie to you."

Diane wanted to say, You're crazy, he's not lying, but Diane knew now that wasn't what her mother wanted. "Don't worry, Ma." This was her revised speech, her conditional good-bye. "I love you, you're my mother. If they don't take good care of me, I'll sue them for every penny they've got."

Lily smiled. She put her head back on the pillow. She closed her eyes. She looked dead. She spoke in that pose. The sight of her, still, her head aloft on the pillows, was eerie. "I was very lucky to have you. If you had been a boy, you couldn't have helped me and I couldn't have helped you. If you had been like me, weak and scared and silly, I couldn't have made it through your daddy's death. You didn't need help. You gave it. My strong little girl." Lily opened her eyes and they were swimming with love, with her easy tears of unhappiness, her eyes big and old and, like always, not seeing very clearly.

"Okay, Ma," Diane said, feeling her pretense about to collapse, unable to keep up the calm and strength on her face that was expected. She stroked Lily's hand. "Go to sleep now." Soothing a baby. "Go to sleep now."

NINA WAS READY FOR ERIC WHEN HE CAME OUT OF LUKE'S ROOM, finished with the bedtime ritual. "I've got great news."

"Don't tell me you've been promoted again." Eric said this pleasantly. He hadn't objected to her job as Tad's assistant, but Nina was convinced that Eric's reserve over his own worries had evolved into deviousness. Ever since her mother had called and asked a lot of pointless, atypical questions about the well-being of Nina's marriage, Nina thought something had to be up. Something more than Eric's "I'm having a bad run of luck. That's why I'm in such a shitty mood. I just gotta reposition stuff, then I'll be okay," something more than that was up.

"No," Nina said, excited. Here was a great present for Eric.

She couldn't say it in front of Luke and the wait had been almost unbearable. "I got the results of Luke's IQ test. Well, not the results, they don't give that out. But they tell you what's on it. Here—I knew I couldn't remember it exactly—I made some notes." Nina took out the paper she had kept in her purse since morning. She had always known that Luke was bright, but the tester's comments had astonished her anyway. "They do it by age levels. His vocabulary is at the top of the range, a nine—it goes no higher than nine."

"Nine?" Eric was shot with excitement, standing in the middle of the living room, going up on his toes, and then down on his heels, hands in his pocket, jiggling keys and money.

"Nine years old that means. Vocabulary, his language was at the top. Nine. His math skills were eight. Then, in a category, I forget what she called it, abstract reasoning, cognitive something, anyway, she told me it's very important because it measures ability, rather than acquired knowledge, was also at the very top, nine. Also orientation was nine."

"Orientation?"

"Knowing his name, his address—"

"Right, right," Eric said. "Diane, Byron's mother, told me that was something they did. So I taught him our phone number, our address. Even taught him our zip code."

Nina was amazed. "You're kidding."

Eric smiled. He rocked on his heels and beamed. "I thought I should teach him more than just how to take a crap. Didn't he do badly on anything?"

Of course. Eric wouldn't believe it, couldn't be happy if there weren't something a little wrong. "Well, his motor skills were only between five and six."

Sure enough, that shot Eric down from his floatation up to the heavens. He took his hands out of his pockets, from his excited rattling, and he sank into a chair. "What the hell are motor skills?"

"Folding a triangle, drawing a circle. She said boys are always a little behind girls in that area."

"Folding a triangle! What the hell is the point of that!"

Nina wanted him to be satisfied, to be happy, to know that he was a good man, that he was a successful father. She tried to smooth disapproval out of her answer: "Eric, he was still two to three years ahead of his chronological age. And listen to this." She read from her notes: " 'Luke will make an excellent student. His ability to concentrate and complete a task is well-developed beyond his years. He is in the upper quarter of the 99th percentile of his age-group.

He would thrive in a competitive, challenging academic environment.' ''

Eric looked off, toward their windows. His mouth hung open and his face softened. ''Good for him,'' he said, and then cleared his throat loudly. ''You did a great job.''

''So did you,'' Nina said, although she didn't think it had been a job, didn't think they had done anything, except love Luke.

''No, I mean, you must have done a great job of keeping him relaxed when you took him to the test. I knew I shouldn't take him. He would have sensed how nervous I was about it. Well, now we're in great shape. Every one of those fucking schools will want him!'' Eric leaned back and he smiled. ''I was scared. You know? I was really scared I would fuck him up with my stupid genes.''

No. He can't mean this, he can't be this crazy. ''What are you talking about, Eric? You're not stupid.''

''Well, everyone is always telling me I am. But not Luke. They can all go fuck themselves now, for all I care.'' He let out air, not a sigh, but an explosive release. ''Your parents will always pay for Luke's schooling, right?'' Eric asked abruptly. His face was back to that mask of rigid worry. ''I mean, no matter what. They'll always pay for him to go to good schools?''

Nina studied Eric. He wanted to tell her. ''What's wrong, Eric? Are you losing everything?''

''No!'' Eric was disgusted. He shook his head at the floor, sighed, leaned back, and shook his head at the ceiling. ''That's what's so fucking crazy about it. I've given back some of the profits, that's all. Tom's still way ahead. His friends are still way ahead. These guys. They've never known what it is not to have money. And yet they're so greedy.'' Eric looked at her, with reproach. ''You never told me your father was so greedy.''

''So if you're not losing, what's the problem?'' Nina wanted to stay in pursuit of the disease, not be distracted by all these symptoms.

''Joe has called up your father and the others. He's told them he can't stand behind my investment decisions.'' Eric mocked Joe's voice—prissy, pompous, Henry Kissinger on Vietnam: '' 'We disagree on the kind of stocks, not the direction of the market. And I no longer wish to associate the firm with Eric's selections. Of course, he's still here. I simply wish to give you the option of changing the current management philosophy without going to the extreme of taking your funds elsewhere.' '' Eric cackled. He jumped up from the chair, ejected back into the furious pace of his thoughts. "Funds! Joe can't even say the word 'money'! For God's sakes. Money!"

Nina had never understood Eric's relationship to Joe. She had concluded after many years that Eric's complaints must be pro forma, that the stories had to be exaggerations. No sensible person would continue to work with the Joe Eric described. "That's disgusting," she said. She felt it too, Joe's betrayal was conjured as a dark cloud of villainy, an incomprehensible force of nature; when she thought of it, it had no context in her experience. "Father told you Joe said all this?"

"Joe said it in front of me!" Eric's voice squealed. Eric got up on his tiptoes; his forehead crinkled; his hands spread out and arched to the ceiling in agony. "He made the call right in front of me, in front of the entire office!"

And now, the nameless dread was hers. What was Father's answer? He had her husband's self-respect in his hands, maybe the happiness of her marriage, probably the future of her son. She waited for Eric to volunteer the information.

But Eric said nothing. He brought his agonized fingers to his rumpled forehead. He massaged the skin, as if the tips could push something back into his leaking brain.

Help him, Nina. Help him. He's like Luke, he has no real weapons to fight with.

But Nina had lived to be free of her family. She had married Eric and lived in New York to be away from them. Now, like some nightmare, everything in her life depended on the one thing she had never been able to count on: her father's love.

WHAT IS HE THINKING? THAT HE SHOULD COME OUT AND MEET ME here, in the reception area? That he'd be safer in public? But not if I start talking. What is he thinking?

I've spent the better part of my life wanting to know what he was thinking. Did he think at all, or was it just a physical craving, nothing diabolic, nothing calculated, an addiction, a yearning he couldn't squelch?

The assistant returned. She looked unfriendly. "Mr. Hummel? Come with me."

Peter followed her.

Is this a trick? Will I be led into a room of security guards and thrown out?

They passed the usual lineup of secretarial cubicles opposite medium-sized private offices, the doors open, overdressed men and women on phones talking the friendly chatter of a phony business:

"Bill? Hello, how was London? Yeah, I hoped you could—"

"Are you kidding? I'm fatter than ever!"

"Great. Let's do the Tea Room? I know it's a bore—"

We're heading for the corner office, Peter knew. He rubbed his palms. They were wet. His throat felt thick and clogged. In a moment of panic, he thought he might not be able to talk. He could see himself, a hand on his Adam's apple, choking, mute.

He cleared his throat. He wanted to shout before he entered. There were only a few more feet to go.

Speak! Make sure you can speak!

The assistant stopped a foot or so before the door. It was open. Peter could see an L of couches, empty, cornering a huge black glass coffee table. Larry was out of sight, probably behind a desk. The assistant gestured for Peter to go inside alone.

Alone in an office with Larry. Come with me, Peter wanted to say to this neutral woman. Come with me. Don't leave me alone with him.

"IT'S ME, GRANDPA," LUKE CALLED AT THE DOOR. ERIC KNELT at his son's height, and saw the sight he had seen all his childhood, the door to his parents' apartment towering in front of him, a tall, fat guard with its one circular metal eye, blind and fixed.

"Hey! Hey!" Barry said from the other side, and the police lock clanged. Luke hopped up and down. The door opened and they were in each other's arms, the bookends of Eric's life, his soft-hearted father, his sweet-spirited son.

They don't need me, he thought. No one needs me.

Since Eric had become cruel to Luke, the implacable explicator of life (everybody goes to the bathroom, Luke, it's time), since then, Luke had flourished. Gone were all the moody reactions to new things. The shyness remained, but only a normal amount. The intelligence test proved Luke was more than sound. Nina's success at work proved she was more than sound. Gone were all their difficulties. Luke adored her. Unlike Eric, Nina still got the gift of Luke's tender side, his baby self. "Mama," Luke would say when she got home, and wrap his legs around her stomach, rest his head on her shoulder, and gaze into her eyes with absolute concentration.

Eric entered the home of his parents unheralded, an afterthought, a nanny. His mother and father circled about Luke, chattering over his height, listening to him talk, telling him what he could have, what they might do, and Eric wandered in unnoticed. He went to the kitchen, in search of coffee. He looked for coffee all the time now, because his brain never seemed to reach consciousness, because he never got enough sleep, because only coffee was warm and for him alone, only coffee narrowed his vision to the thing he had to solve.

Which was what, exactly?

The Boston Beans were gone, had moved their accounts to Joe's supervision. Therefore, Eric had lost half his management fee. Tom had done nothing, which was good and bad. Tom hadn't called Eric after speaking with Joe, hadn't phoned to say that he continued to have confidence in Eric. And when Eric discarded his pride and initiated a call to Tom, Tom didn't reassure Eric, didn't say that his refusal to let Joe take over the management was permanent, or merely a final trial of Eric's abilities.

What do they want? Two bad quarters after eight good ones! Do I have three months to keep Tom? Do I have six? Do I have nine? Do I have a week?

Eric could have asked Tom to declare his intentions. But he didn't. He convinced himself that to pretend with Tom that nothing had happened showed self-confidence. Later Eric realized it was an excuse for cowardice.

Nina's response to the situation wasn't helpful. Leave, she said. Open up your own firm. You can work out of our apartment. Next fall Luke will be in school, we can make it on what you earn from Tom's money, and my salary, and soon we won't need Pearl anymore—

Work alone? With no one to tell me what I should think, no one to fight off, no one to give in to, no secretaries, no coffee machine, pay for my own Quotron, pay commissions to some broker . . . it was sickening, impossible. Nina's suggestion caused despair, forced Eric to face himself in a way he had hoped never to.

I don't have the guts. And if Tom left me then, I would be ruined. Maybe we could make it without my salary for a while, as Nina had suggested, maybe I would get some of Joe's clients, the ones who know me, people like Fred Tatter, to come along, but then I would have to produce every day, every week, and—

Eric's father had tried and failed. Barry had left the store where he had worked for ten years, where they had valued him, although that was a low estimate, as a mere floor manager. Eric's mother thought Barry could be more, pushed Barry until he opened his own store; but Barry was too nice, he let the clerks steal, he got bad prices, he let people slide on the layaways, he didn't change locations when he should have—

"Hello, Eric," his mother said, floating into the kitchen on her slippers, her hands out to take hold of his face and kiss him. "We ignored you," she said. She kissed. "That's only because your son is so gorgeous."

"I don't mind," Eric said, and he meant it. He would have hated it if his parents didn't make a fuss over Luke, if they were civilized about grandparenthood, like Nina's parents.

Last Thanksgiving, Nina's mother had finally acknowledged Luke's superiority. "He's very handsome," she had said. "And very intelligent."

"Yes," Eric had answered, pleased that Nina's mother had finally said the obvious.

"I guess all grandmothers think that about their grandchildren," she went on, and spoiled it. Civilized. Sensible. Nina's parents could only see a miserable gray in every rainbow.

Eric's parents neglected him, blind to Eric's dimmer light, a boring streetlamp compared with Luke's fireworks—but that was all right. In loving Luke, they were really loving Eric.

"You look tired," Eric's mother said. "Are you working too hard?"

Eric peered out of the kitchen, past their dull, by now ancient green living room furniture. His father and Luke were gone: probably into Eric's old room, to play with Eric's old toys. "Tell me something, Mom. You think Dad made a mistake going into business by himself?"

Miriam narrowed her eyes suspiciously. She saw criticism everywhere, especially from Eric. "I told him to go into business by himself."

"I know. Think you were wrong to push him?"

That relaxed her. Open attack didn't bother her; she liked that. "He would have driven me crazy if he didn't try. I told him to go ahead, but I was really telling him what he wanted to hear. He would never do something he didn't want to do because of what I said. He's stubborn. He's a stubborn man," she said, and rubbed her stomach thoughtfully. "How are you doing with your father-in-law's money?" she asked.

She always asked. Every visit, "How are you doing with your father-in-law's money?," her anxiety irrepressible, her lack of confidence in Eric almost a nervous tic.

"Okay."

"Just okay?" she said, suspicious again. She opened the refrigerator. "Are you hungry? Did you eat?"

"No. We haven't had lunch. You'll have to get something."

"Luke'll want hot dogs at the deli. Maybe—" She looked excited. "Maybe I can fool Luke into having a good hot lunch here. I could make my crazy lentil soup with the pieces of hot dog in it."

Eric knew that soup well. "He'll love it."

"You'll have some?" she asked eagerly, pleased at the hope she might succeed with both of them.

"Absolutely."

She began to get the makings. She moved with the deliberation of age and her natural carefulness: every gesture evaluated first, then executed with slow pleasure.

Miriam and Barry took very few chances. There had been one big risk, and its failure had shut all the windows and doors. They had locked themselves in their little cave in upper Manhattan, hibernating until the cold, wild world came to an end. In everything there was the old look of failure, the old smells: mistakes and regret unventilated. That was his home, and the frightened part of Eric was glad to be back.

But he couldn't stay in their cave, in their warm misery. To be so doomed, eking out a reasonable but unspectacular existence would kill Eric. Better to take one chance and lose everything than live a slow progress to death.

PETER THOUGHT HIS LEGS WOULD BUCKLE. NEW JOINTS SEEMED to have been created, a leg of knees, each one bending out of sequence, collapsing his stride. He hoped to get to the couch and sit.

Larry was behind an enormous black glass desk that matched his coffee table. It was the worktable of a man who does no work. The sight of Larry was an immediate shock. He was hairless. Peter couldn't remember the color Larry's hair used to be, but he remembered large quantities of it, bushy, thick, waves in conflict, like a romantic painting of a stormy sea.

"Hello, Peter," Larry's voice said. He stayed in his high-backed chair. The tall black leather back rose above his bald head like a tombstone.

Larry was real, after all. Not a nightmare. But real.

Peter got himself to the couch. It put him all the way across the room from Larry. There were floor-to-ceiling windows behind the desk and to its side; they showed a static, sickening view of glass boxes with no ground in sight.

"You sure have grown," Larry said with a smirk. A hand went to his hairless pate. He ran his palm from the forehead back, feeling for what was gone. "Would you like something to drink?"

Larry's socks were too short. Peter could see a stripe of very white skin just beneath the gray fabric of his pants leg. Peter couldn't speak. He shook his head.

"To what do I owe the pleasure of this visit?" Larry seemed to be smirking. He regarded Peter with amusement and contempt. Peter had expected shame, fear, wariness—certainly not arrogance.

"I wanted to talk," Peter mumbled.

"Uh-huh." Larry nodded, encouraging a half-wit. "About what?"

This was impossible. Larry's sham, his show of ordinariness, made the introduction of the topic—"You were wrong," Peter blurted.

Larry got out of his chair quickly. He was shorter than Peter expected. The memory of Larry was different, distorted by child-hood scale. Larry moved right at Peter.

Peter prepared to defend himself. Peter's legs pressed against the couch, his arms flexed. But Larry detoured at the coffee table and moved to the open door, shutting it. He stood with his back to it, looking down at Peter.

Is he looking at my groin?

"Look. In my life, that never happened. I'm sorry. But I don't want to talk about it." Larry smiled. Regretfully. Sorry, kid, can't help. He gestured with his hands, palms up, I've got no weapons, there's nothing I can do, call me next week.

"It did happen," Peter said. He sounded retarded. Questioning and demanding all at once.

"I've dealt with it. I've been in therapy. That's in the past." Larry walked back to his desk, again with energy, abrupt, leading with his belly, like a toddler.

Peter returned Larry's expectant stare. His eyebrows were raised, a waiter attentive to a customer's order. "Why?" came out of Peter.

"Because it was a sickness. I couldn't face that I was gay." He quickly put his hand to his forehead, paused, then slowly moved it over the top of his head, feeling the raw skin possessively.

He's like a giant penis. Fat, reddened, a bulbous head.

Peter sniffed at something. A perfume.

No, Larry's cologne. It was the same, the same sweet odor, the same languorous smell—He's lying. He smells the same, he is the same.

"Why me?"

"You were around." Larry smirked. He looked away and seemed to deliberately remove the sarcasm from his face.

Fuck you. Peter's cheeks and lips felt thick and heavy with his upset. They were too heavy to support his head. He looked down.

"I mean, I was living at Gary's, you were there a lot."

With Peter's eyes closed, the past was now. Larry's slightly raspy voice, a hard whisper, sneaked into the ear, through the unlocked basement door of his brain. Yesterday was still here.

"And"—this came out with a sigh, weary and bored—"you were lonely. Your parents were splitting up. You needed love. You look like you still do."

Peter opened his eyes. Larry was an old man. His skin was pulled too tight—a face-lift. He was artificially tanned, even the dome on top; that's why the leg skin seemed so white. "I wanted it. Is that your excuse?" Peter said. He could say that easily. He had guessed that Larry would try to convince Peter he had been willing.

You like this, don't you?

"I don't know what you wanted," Larry said. "I didn't think about what you wanted." Larry shifted his chair forward. He flipped open a thick black leather appointment book. *Does he own anything that has color?* "I have to go in ten minutes—"

"What did my parents' divorce have to do with it?" Peter felt sure of himself now. This man had no scruples. He wasn't pathetic, trapped by neurosis; he was a villain, a theatrical evil man, the kind Peter so often watched onstage and never believed in.

"Well, I knew all about it. Your mother even confided in me one day. When she thanked me for taking you to the theater." He smirked again.

He can't mean to be this naked about it. I can destroy him. I can ruin him.

"She was quite a woman. Still alive?"

"I don't believe she confided in you. I don't believe she thanked you." Yesterday was here again. Peter stared at the black glass desk, its sharp edge cold and treacherous. His heart was pounding. Even now, he couldn't look Larry in the face. Even now, taller, full-grown, strong enough to twist Larry's perverted hand until he fell to his knees, even now Peter couldn't contradict Larry without wild terror beating in his chest.

"Oh?" Larry was pleased with himself. "She met your now stepfather at some fund raiser and they started meeting in the afternoons. After two months, he asked her to leave your father. And she did. Just like that. Amazing woman."

But that's wrong. Dad had an affair. Mother found out about it and left him. Tell him.

"I was impressed. And I felt sorry for you. She said all the right things about what it might do to you—but she didn't mean them. Just politeness. Mothers should love their sons. Mine did. She adored me. You were lonely. I was lonely. And after all, all I did was masturbate you. Nowadays we call it safe sex. You shouldn't worry about it. Doesn't mean you're a fag if that's what you want to know.''

Tell him he's wrong. He's wrong about everything. How could he get everything so wrong?

''Or—'' Larry put on a new look, thoughtful and soft. ''Or—are you? Is that why you're here?''

I'm not here. Shut the eyes and disappear. I'm not here.

''That's not why my parents split up.'' Peter answered with his eyes shut tight against the bad dream. His chest hurt. It was tight, a drawstring pulled across his heart, strangling him. He cried.

''Hey!'' The raspy voice. ''Hey, come on. It's all right.''

Go away, monster. Mommy and Daddy will come back. Go away, monster, and my mommy and daddy will come back.

THE DOCTOR TOLD DIANE THE OPERATION HAD BEEN A SUCCESS. Lily's heart had become somewhat enlarged, compensating for the valve leak, but not dangerously so. The description made Diane think of car engines. She was told she could see Lily briefly in the intensive care unit, but that she should be prepared for Lily to look bad.

''She'll be on a respirator and she'll be heavily medicated.''

Diane waited more than an hour before a nurse appeared to tell her she could go in briefly.

The moment Diane entered the swinging doors to ICU she couldn't get enough air to breathe through her terror. There were ghastly sights in every bed.

The nurse pointed her to Lily. The first look at her mother wobbled the floor; Diane reached for something to hold on to, but there was nothing. She was adrift in the middle of the white room of wreckage.

Lights flashed on monitors; something beeped repeatedly. Diane forced her eyes to focus on Lily.

Her skin was alabaster. No red, no pink, no blue, no green, no depth, no looseness, no softness. The skin was hard white, drained of any shade or hue. A marble statue—sculptured death. Her mouth was raped—twisted open, jammed full by a plastic device. She looked murdered and destroyed, mocked, humiliated, and desecrated. Tubes ran from machines into her helpless arms or disappeared to horrors underneath the sheets. Bags hung from the sides, for urine, for the bowels, for God knows what else—Diane looked away from those sights. Her eyes were locked, anyway, on her mother's dead skin and butchered mouth. The machine breathed and then forced Lily to.

"Wake up! Your daughter's here!" the nurse shouted.

It was unbelievable. Diane summoned herself to stop the nurse. But there was no answer.

The nurse shook the dead white body. "Your daughter's here. And you're sleeping. Say hello."

Absurd. As if you could communicate with the dead.

But the eyes did open. Slow, not seeing.

"Say hello," the nurse ordered.

And Diane obeyed, like a frightened child. "Hi, Ma," said her voice. It sounded like her, like Diane.

Lily's eyes rolled; her stuffed ruined mouth couldn't answer, of course. The death mask, the white plaster face tried to find life. Lily's hand moved, like a puppet's arm; the string of her fluids bounced in the air. Lily's fingers went up and then, in a movement of terrible unknowable pain, gestured Diane away. Go, they seemed to say. Leave me. I am not here anymore. Leave me so I won't have to exist.

Tell her you love her. Tell her she was good.

"Talk to her," the nurse ordered. "She can hear you."

"I'm here, Ma," Diane said.

Go away, the fingers said. Leave me so I won't exist.

Diane told her brain to stay clear. Fear pressed on her mind.

Go away, the fingers begged.

Diane took hold of them. Cold sticks. Lily's eyes were shut again. She's dead.

I have to leave. In the brilliant light of the room, Diane turned away, blind with terror. She had to find the wall with her hand, and feel her way out of the horror.

NINA DIDN'T HAVE THE COURAGE TO CALL HER FATHER. SHE called Joan instead.

"Hello, dear," her mother answered with a plaintive lilt of surprise.

"Hello. How are you?"

"I'm fine. How's Luke?"

"He's great."

"Really?"

"Yes. Uh, is Father there?"

"No, he's at the office. Do you need to speak to him?"

"Do you know anything about this, uh, uh—" I'm a child. I can't speak.

"About what?"

"Well, Eric told me—you know he works with this horrible man?"

"I thought he works for someone."

"Yeah, I guess. They have some sort of arrangement."

"You said he's horrible?"

"Well, he's always criticizing Eric. Apparently he called Father."

"That's business, Nina. I don't discuss your father's business. Why don't you call him?"

"Well, I, uh—"

"Yes?" her mother said, hissing the last letter, but moaning its interior.

The phone felt hard. Nina gripped its narrow belly. The tips of her fingers met each other. She smelled the plastic of the receiver, the grease of other mouths. A few months and it would be summer. If Eric again insisted on staying in the city the whole season, she would take her vacation with Luke. "I can't ask." Nina sighed the rest of her plea.

"Well." Joan said this and then no more.

"Could you—"

"We haven't seen Luke in a while," Joan said quickly. "I'll speak to Tom. Maybe we can—no, not this weekend. Perhaps, yes, I'll discuss it with him. We'll try for next weekend. I have to go—"

Nina didn't have a chance to say good-bye, only a blurted thank-you. She hung up and returned to her desk: the ghostly dress half drawn, a skirt about to billow.

What did I thank her for? Nina thought. Should I tell Eric? No. Father might refuse to visit.

She despaired of being able to concentrate. She had to have these sketches done by Monday.

If I call Father, it'll be settled. One way or the other, it will clear my mind.

She got up again. The walk to the phone was self-conscious. She heard her shoes on the oak floor, saw her hands wave up and down with her stride.

She took hold of the hard receiver, leaned her head against the harder body of its mother, shut her eyes, and sighed. Breathed in. Then out. She had promised herself never to ask Tom for things. Asking darkened Tom's lean, bright face; the pale blue eyes looked away, his thin lips vanished, and "Hmmmm" was hummed out.

Eric doesn't want me to do this. He would be furious. She imagined what Eric's rage might be: "You humiliated me! I don't want your father's money as a favor."

No. This was Eric's problem. She hung up.

Eric watched Barry listen to Luke. Barry was nervous in his attentiveness, his head tilted down, his body taut, every molecule magnetized toward Luke, to hear what his precious grandchild was saying.

"You know, Grandpa, I think it's not such a good idea to eat out a lot."

They were walking to Fort Tryon Park, the playground of Eric's childhood, down the steep block from Broadway. Luke's voice, at less than three feet tall, was more than three feet away from Barry's ear. "Un-huh," Barry said, but fast, so he wouldn't miss Luke's next syllable.

"For example," Luke said, hand out, palm up, to illustrate the common sense of his point, "I like hot dogs. They're not good for you, if you have them in a deli. But Grandma put them in a soup! And that's good for you, right? I mean, soup is good for you."

Eric laughed. He was sad. But he laughed anyway. His pleasure in Luke grew every day. He had never thought that would be possible. Eric had loved infant-Luke so much, kissed the sweet skin, gazed into the huge eyes, held the warm tiny body against his chest, next to his heart, and thought: I can never love anything more than this. But the growing and grown Luke, smarter and surer every day, his figure lengthening, the rounded fat of his cheeks evaporating, Nina's strong chin emerging, the funny, clever, gentle boy-Luke cleaned a dusty corner of Eric's heart and danced there in a brilliant and solitary light.

They took Luke to the old swings and slide. Now the park was taken over by Puerto Ricans and blacks. Eric didn't like them. He listened to the way they addressed their children: irritation, suspicion, and command in every word. Just like the parents of his childhood. Those Jews and Italians and Greeks and Poles were no different from these people. Immigrants. People without money. People who had to do the thousands of errands the rich never do. It wasn't the benefit of beauty that wealth brought; it was the absence of ugliness. No carrying groceries in the snow, no roaches in the plates, no rides on subways, no vacations on smelly rush-hour beaches, no shared rooms, no classrooms of forty, no denials of gifts to commercial-bombed children, no incompetent doctors, no disrespectful city bureaucrats, no washing dishes, no making beds, no cleaning toilets, no ironing, no noes. Anything ugly, anything repetitive and dirty, could be done by someone else, some anonymous black face.

I got out, Eric said to himself, watching them, their tired, harassed faces, hearing their loud, always angry or confused voices—even the laughter of the poor was unhappy: clanging bells, not happy peals. Their children fought over every toy, every activity, as if they already knew that there isn't enough for everyone on this planet, and for those who don't fight, there isn't even sympathy, just lonely tears.

"What you want?" a young mother, not more than twenty, shouted at a pathetic two-year-old. She was a light-skinned black, probably beautiful, Eric thought, but her hair was angrily out of place, her skin was glossy with sweat, her eyes vacant with exhaustion.

The two-year-old cried out his answer. Eric thought he spoke in Spanish.

"He took it? Miguel! Miguel!" she shouted at a boy of six.

Also hers?

She screamed at the six-year-old Miguel in Spanish. Miguel watched her rage as if it had nothing to do with him. When she was finished, Miguel walked away. He had a bright ball in his hands, the object the two-year-old wanted.

That's why I always take two of everything to the park, Eric thought. Then Eric realized she couldn't afford two of everything, any more than he, as a child, had any recourse if he lost his pinkie early in the weekend and none of his friends had money for another. They would go to the park and hope to steal a ball or find a stray one. The fear of losing his pinkie meant that Eric never tried to hit a home run in stickball. One glorious moment of success brought all play to an end.

The two-year-old burst out with a fresh squall of tears as he watched Miguel walk off still in possession of the ball. "That's what you get for not watching your things," she told him. "Stop that," she ordered her two-year-old after a long, cold stare at his misery.

He didn't. He stood in front of her, his arms hopeless at his side, his features squeezed into formlessness.

"Stop it!" she ordered again.

Here it comes, Eric thought.

And she slapped him across the face. He screamed at this. She picked him up and walked away, her lean young body twitching with fury. She yelled and yelled, not looking at her son, complaining to the trees, to the other parents, to the sky.

Because she's poor. Because she doesn't have another ball. Because she has to do every little thing, change every diaper, wash every dish, make every bit of food, clean every piece of clothing—

"It's horrible here now," Barry said. "Remember how it was? With all the families? You knew everybody. All the kids knew each other . . ." and he went on.

It was the same, Dad. The people were white. But it was the same.

LARRY WAS IN HIS EAR: "LOOK, I HAVE TO GO. PLEASE STOP CRY-ing."

The sweet perfume hugged Peter's cheeks, hot and foggy in his nostrils. Peter put his hands between his legs and pressed. He pressed his eyes tight too. Get small. Get small.

"Jesus," he heard Larry complain.

Calm down, he lectured. You're all grown up now. You have your own apartment, you have a wife and child, you have credit cards. You have a job, you have a secretary. You can get up, go outside, and catch a cab. Maybe you need to nap.

"Are you having some kind of breakdown?" Larry asked.

Peter opened his eyes a little, squeezing a look. An old man dressed in a gray suit was there.

That's the horrible Larry, the gigantic man-penis, whispering, "You like this, don't you?"

"Are you all right?" Larry asked slowly, saying each word with emphasis. "I have to go now. I can't leave you here on my couch, crying."

This is him? This is the monster?

Larry sighed, exasperated by Peter's silence. "I'm sorry I said that about your mother. I'm sure she loves you."

My mother? What did he say?

You're all grown up now. You can get up and go.

"You look better. Do you want a drink? I've got some scotch here—" Larry moved toward a cabinet. "Jesus. Look at the time. Why don't you have a drink? Relax. Take your time. You can leave when you want."

"What did you say?" Peter's voice was a child's, a weepy child's voice.

"Nothing. I shouldn't have—"

"You said mother had an affair. That's wrong. That's all backwards." Peter brought his hands to his eyes. They were wet. He brushed at them.

Larry didn't want to answer. He tapped his foot and nodded. "It was a long time ago. Okay? I'm going to go.'' He opened a cabinet. "The scotch is here. I'll tell my—''

"You said she met Kyle and then—'' Peter couldn't talk. Couldn't think out the sentences.

Who is this old man? Why am I asking about the divorce?

"That's what she told me—I don't know. Look, I'm sorry.''

Larry left. He walked fast. Opened the door with a quick jerk and disappeared.

There's no point to this. Peter took his hands and rubbed his legs from the thighs down. He pressed his fingers into the flesh as hard as he could. He wanted to stretch, to grow out again.

He stood up. Tucked in his shirt. Cleared his throat.

You are all grown up now. What's done is done. All the clichés do apply. You are a fine human being.

Your mother confided in a child abuser. And the child abuser thinks your curiosity is an irritation.

There's nothing wrong with you, Peter. It's everybody else who's crazy.

THE NURSE TOOK DIANE BY THE ARM RIGHT OUTSIDE ICU'S swing-ing doors. "Feeling faint?'' she asked.

Diane shook her head, relieved at her escape. She never wanted to go back and see Lily again.

It isn't my mother in there. They killed my mother.

"I know they look terrible right afterwards. But you'll see, by tomorrow her color will return. She's doing fine.''

Diane got herself back to the waiting room. The internist had said he would meet her there. She lit a cigarette but was nauseated by her first drag and put it out. I have to quit, she decided, thinking of ICU, that human junkyard. My father died of a heart attack and Mom has this congenital problem. Diane had had the internist listen to her heart on his visit yesterday. He heard nothing but offered to run some tests. She had declined.

She felt alone.

Peter seemed to have nothing to do with her; she couldn't really summon an image of his face. And Byron? He had been good with Lily, affectionate, not rambunctious, but somehow she didn't feel he belonged to her.

I'm an orphan with lousy genes.

The parking lot outside was bright that day. For the catheteriza-tion, it had been rainy. Almost every space was occupied. The car roofs glittered in the sun, glowing to her, beckoning. She wished she could drive back to New York and get home. Get into the bath. Have some popcorn. Masturbate. Go to sleep.

If there's something wrong with my genes, then Byron will get it too.

The internist arrived. He was genial but brief. They had put in a porcine valve; the operation was a success. Lily would be in the hospital for two to three weeks, probably the latter because she wasn't in good condition.

Diane walked to her car and thought: I can't stay here for three weeks. But who could take her place? Where was Daddy? Where were her sisters? Her brothers? The whole world had a family. Peter had two sets of parents, stepbrothers, stepsisters, aunts, uncles.

She thought she was okay.

But behind the wheel she couldn't find the ignition. She pushed the key at the black plastic, but there were no holes, no entries.

I have no family. No one to help me. No one to drive me home.

Her eyes filled with tears. Painful tears. And no one could hug them away.

"I don't have anyone to help me," she said to the windshield. "Mommy, please help me," she said, blubbering to the hot silent car.

I AM SO FAST! WATCH ME RUN!

The street shone up at him. Bounced.

"Whoa!" said someone's body. Byron twisted sideways and squeezed through the slow grown-ups.

Boring grown-ups. I am so fast! Watch me run!

There were people everywhere. There were books and magazines on the sidewalk, lying flat, watching the sky. There was an ice-cream truck.

"Francy! Francy! Can I have ice cream?"

"You ain't had any lunch. Later."

I am so fast! Watch me run!

In the park, there were dogs. Big black dogs. Little silly dogs. There were skateboards. Where's Luke?

"You looking for Luke?" It was Pearl. She doesn't like me anymore.

"Yeah! Yeah!"

"He's playing with David in the sandbox."

David. He's that big boy.

I am so fast. Whoosh! "Hey, Luke! Wanna race?"

Luke's face was round; his eyes glowed. He looked at Byron as if he didn't know him. He's so slow. Not like me. I am so fast!

"Luke! Luke! Wanna race!" I'll win.

"Ugh!" Luke acted funny. "I'm building!" he said.

"Yeah," that big boy David said. "We're making a space station."

Luke and David stood over a tall sand building. They had a pail of water. Luke poured a little over the sand. It changed colors! Got dark and solid. Luke made it into a long shape and put it on their sand building. It stayed up!

"I wanna do that!" Byron moved in front of Luke and reached for the pail.

"Byron!"

David pulled the pail away. Some of it spilled.

"You spilled!" Byron told him. He was bad. Obviously, he was bad.

"You can't play. We don't have enough for you."

"I don't want to." Byron took Luke's arm. "Come on, Luke. Let's race."

Luke sat down! His legs disappeared. He fell onto his tushy. "No," he said. He stared up at Byron. His eyes glowed.

"He's making the space station with me," David said. "You can watch."

"Luke, you have to race with me." Byron had to make sure Luke understood. He was bad sometimes, didn't do what he was supposed to.

"I don't want to race!" Luke shouted. "You hear me! I don't want to race!"

"I'll go slow, so you can catch up." I am so fast!

"No," Luke said.

"Here." David gave Luke the pail. "We need more antennas."

"Oh, right." Luke poured a little of the water.

"You're not doing it right," Byron said. Luke poured too slowly.

But Luke didn't stop. He made his little towers. Dark and solid they were, but Luke could shape them anyway and they stayed on the sand building.

"Here," Byron said, and reached for one of them. "This will make it better."

"No!" Luke grabbed Byron's hand. "This is mine, Byron! Go make your own."

I'm too strong. He can't hold me.

Byron, the fast, fast strong man, pulled to get his hand free. Luke didn't let go. "Let go!"

"Don't touch my antennas!" Luke said, and squeezed Byron's

arm. "Okay? I'll let you go now, Byron, but don't touch my antennas."

Pull. Pull.

He couldn't get free. He didn't understand. He was so much stronger than Luke. Why couldn't he get free?

"Byron," Luke said. "Are you going to leave my antennas alone?"

"They're stupid. I don't want to touch them!"

Luke let go. Byron could still feel Luke's fingers, although they were gone. They still squeezed.

I'm not strong today. Didn't have my lunch. Have to eat to be a big, strong boy.

"Come on, Luke. Let's race now."

Luke didn't hear.

"Luke! Pay attention! Let's race now!"

Luke heard. Finally. He moved close to Byron. He put his face right up against his. He could feel the warm tip of Luke's nose. Byron was so glad. Luke's mouth opened.

"NO!"

It hurt so much. The hot, ugly air of Luke. Byron fell down, blasted down. Luke loomed over him, dark against the bright sun. Luke's blue eyes glowed—angry cat, ugly cat.

"I said no, Byron! How many times do I have to tell you? No! No! No!"

17

BESIDE ERIC'S QUOTRON, LYING ATOP HIS IN BOX, WAS THE sheet of all positions in Tom's account. In three weeks, the next quarterly report would be sent to Boston. If Eric couldn't make a dramatic improvement by then, the quarterly statement would show a 12 percent decline in the value of Tom's portfolio. Should Tom buy a *Wall Street Journal*, or a *Barron's*, or any other financial publication, he could easily see that the Dow Jones industrial average was up more than 8 percent during this same period. The S&P 500 had done even better, up 11 percent. And if Joe decided to complete his betrayal, he might send Tom a statement of Joe's performance: up 20 percent. Joe might not even need to inform Tom himself: the Boston Beans, having switched management, might insinuate the facts of Joe's success casually into a country-club conversation with Tom.

Of course, Eric was behind Joe's and the major averages' gains for only the past nine months. A sensible man, with a normal amount of courage, would give Eric more time. After all, Eric had been successful for three years; the money he had lost for Tom over the past nine months was money Tom didn't have three years ago. But Eric knew Tom wasn't a sensible man. Tom had allowed an old Wasp investment firm to mismanage him for twenty-five years without a complaint, and yet Tom had complained to Eric after only nine losing months.

"Shouldn't we get out of some of these small companies?" Tom asked when he and Joan had visited New York two months ago. He said "small companies" with his head tilted, mouth in a sneer, as if small companies were ugly, distasteful things, grubby little delis run by fat, greasy Jews.

Tom's last words were: "I might have to withdraw some money

by the end of the year. I'm considering a real-estate deal out West. I'll let you know ahead of time, of course. I may not. I have to study the situation.'' A warning? A politely worded introduction to the final bad news? A last chance?

Ask yourself, Eric said in the shower, ask yourself: What is the difference between me and Tom's former incompetent money managers? They were old boys, good goyim; I'm a high-school-graduate Jew.

Ask yourself, Eric said to the black gutters, as he rode his bike between the glacial walls of the tall trucks: would Tom question me over a bad nine months if I knew how to wear peacock-colored clothes and could sail a boat?

Ask yourself, Eric said to his morning coffee, staring at the sheet: would Tom keep one of his own on such a short leash?

Then why pick Joe for a replacement? Eric didn't believe the real estate story. Tom would give his money to Joe.

There he sat, that old owl, each day looking more and more like a rabbi. Joe and Sammy whispered to each other all the time now. There were no more dinners with Joe's contacts; there was no more talk of tapping Eric as Joe's successor. Joe smelled blood; he thought he could wrest Tom away and leave the whole operation to Sammy. Of course, they'd keep Eric on, the house whipping boy, the dutiful number two.

Leave, Nina advised. Tom will stick with you, clients will go with you, you'll make money for them, you'll be on your own, you'll be happy.

She didn't understand the danger.

Neither did Joe. Tom would eventually leave Joe also. The old fool doesn't realize that.

Maybe Tom wouldn't, maybe he'd stay with Joe. Maybe it's something about me.

Eric wasn't a good salesman. That's what his mother said of his father's failure: your daddy wasn't a good salesman. When Eric explicated his investment philosophy for clients, he was nervous: he spoke rapidly; he admitted he might be wrong; he didn't possess Joe's pompous air of wisdom and sagacity. Joe's manners were bullshit, of course. But it was bullshit that reassured the customers.

Maybe anti-Semitism is an excuse.

Maybe I'm just a loser.

Eric tasted metal in the hollow of his tongue, tasted the sour fear of a lifetime in a single swallow.

He couldn't stand this indecision, this waiting.

''Market's open,'' Sammy said. The red numbers began their undulation across the ticker.

Eric picked up the phone, their direct line to Joe's two-dollar floor broker.

"What are you doing?" Sammy asked.

Fuck you. Eric stared ahead. "Billy?"

"Hey, Eric. Got something for me?"

For months now, Eric had absorbed the white noise of market opinion, thousands of pages of it, hours and hours of statistics and interpretation. The market was at an all-time high. He was going to sell it. The overwhelming majority of traders were bullish. In history, great fortunes on the Street were made by going against the crowd, exiting against the mob rushing in, or entering while they ran out, shouldering through the babbling herd with no apologies to ease the way.

"I'm gonna sell the market, Billy. In the Winningham account, I want to clear out all positions. I'll give them to you—"

"Eric!" Sammy tapped him on the shoulder. "Eric!"

Eric went ahead with the recital of Tom's positions, ignoring Sammy.

Sammy rolled his chair over, bumping Eric's. "Eric, have you lost your fucking mind? You can't go to cash in this market. Tom can invest in cash by walking to the fucking bank. He doesn't need us to earn six percent."

There was heat in Eric's body, terrible heat. It flashed through him; he put his face at Sammy's pale ferret face. "You shut your fucking mouth! I don't want to hear a goddamned word out of you! Shut your fucking mouth!"

"Eric?" Billy called out plaintively through the phone. "Eric? Is that you?"

The room clicked and whirred into action. Sammy moved; the secretaries looked over; Joe pushed his chair away from his monitor. Eric shielded his eyes, stared down at the list he had made weeks ago, and talked to the phone, only to the phone. He finished reading off Tom's stocks. "Okay? That's the exchange. I'll handle OTC. Now, when you're done getting out, I want you to go short these Dow stocks in thousand lots: IBM, GM, International Paper—"

"Eric!" This was Joe now. "Eric, I'm long those stocks. They're very strong."

Eric continued the recital of his list—

"Use the options! Or the futures! If you want to hedge, that's the right vehicle!" Joe's voice sounded nearby.

Eric glanced up. Joe had left his chair.

I got the old bastard off his perch.

Joe's hand landed on Eric's shoulder. "Listen to me. This is not the way to be short."

Eric stared ahead, down at the sheet with the short list, scrawled in his hand one late night months ago when he had dreamed of this, of a decisive triumph—

"Good evening, our guest tonight on *Wall Street Week* is Eric Gold, chief investment officer of Washington Heights Management, his own firm. Mr. Gold went short the stock market at its all-time high two years ago. We'll find out tonight—"

"Eric," Joe whispered in his ear. "I'm asking you to delay for an hour. Let's have a talk in my office first. I'm sure we can work out a mutual strategy—"

"Hold it, Eric," Billy said on the phone in Eric's other ear. "Let me close out the long positions first, then I'll get the shorts."

"Okay. Get back to me." Eric pushed away from his desk, bumped into Sammy's chair, and got free of Joe's hand. "It's done," he lied. It wouldn't be done until Billy called back. "There's nothing to discuss."

"It's inappropriate for you to be short stocks that I'm long."

"Then get out of your stocks."

"Eric," Joe said, and put his hand out again, gesturing to his private office. His voice was low, seductive. "We need to talk."

If I go in there, he'll manipulate me out of it. I don't have the strength to fight him.

"Forget it. What's done is done. I'm going for a walk." He rushed out, ran from Joe's plea—"Eric!"—and from Sammy's insult—"You're an asshole!"

"Tell us, Mr. Gold," they will ask me. "Tell us, Mr. Gold," they will honor me. "What was it like to go against the crowd? When everyone was sure, when no one had the courage, how did you feel?"

I am strong. I stand alone. I am strong. Nothing was given to me in this world; my father let me go into the world without weapons, with nothing to make me equal to the rest. I stand alone now—Eric Gold, the Wizard of Wall Street, brave and lonely and brilliant.

DIANE DECIDED TO STAY IN PHILADELPHIA WITH HER MOTHER throughout the recuperation. She believed that Lily's health and her own life were inextricable. She offered to take Byron down to Philadelphia during the nursing of Lily, but to her surprise, Peter said no.

"He's started at nursery school, we have the IQ test next week. He can't miss them. We'll visit on the weekends."

Peter's self-assurance amazed her. And she felt relieved not to have to put on a show for Byron. Whenever Diane was away from Lily's sight, she had a tendency to burst into tears. It infuriated her because she didn't feel like crying. There was no gentle lull of self-pity beneath the weeping. It happened at the images: Lily broken on the wheel of modern medicine; the angry stitching down her chest, a zipper branded on her skin; Lily's pale, dead face; her eyes, weak and scared, pleading for everything to be all right. Diane hated the reversal of nature: her mother, the great force she had resisted, surrendered to, run from, railed against, prayed to, was a scared kid now, utterly at Diane's mercy. There were no more criticisms of Diane's dress, or Diane's values, or Diane's eating habits, or Diane's marriage, or anything else—just gratitude, and a pathetic conviction that Diane's reassurances were guarantees.

Lily's doctors told Diane they didn't want to discuss Lily's condition unless Diane was present. Without Diane, there were hysterics, accusations, and misunderstandings. The doctors talked to Diane while Lily listened. She lay smashed on the bed, an oxygen mask over her mouth, her eyes on Diane, trusting when Diane approved, nervous when Diane, by asking further questions, seemed not to be satisfied.

"She's doing well," the internist would say.

"You're doing well," Diane would say to Lily as if the doctor had spoken in a language unknown to Lily.

Lily would nod at Diane with a ridiculous and sad faith.

Back at her mother's kitchen table, Diane cried every time she thought of Lily.

And Diane hated herself for her tears, hated the discovery that she needed her mother's madness, her mother's irritations, her mother's crummy values. They were gravity; without them, Diane clutched at the spinning earth, holding on by her fingernails. She had to save this woman, she couldn't let her go. It meant nothing to Diane, made no sense, that of course, someday Lily must die. It was gibberish. Lily was the world, the never-satisfied world, and she could not die.

Every day Diane woke up with iron in her belly—long, hot rods stuck through her stomach. She had to press in with her fingers to break them; they cracked and she'd belch their metal out.

But new rods were stuck through Diane the minute she relented; they reappeared instantly, burning and sizzling inside her. Only when Diane got into her mother's car, a decrepit and wheezing vehicle, to drive to the hospital did the metal in her stomach dissolve and leave her free to feel happiness. She loved driving. It reminded her of the last two years of high school and her college days. She bought a dozen tape cassettes of sixties music and played them loud. They filled the vacuum of the car with memories and exploded her present, sent her back to the happy past: young and intense, full of energy and hope. No death, no failure, no compromise.

But the drive was short. In the parking lot, Diane was overwhelmed with guilt that she had had such a good time in the car. She sang back to the music, laughed at the snapshots of her past—lovers, arguments, ancient happiness.

Your mother is very ill, she scolded. Today the drive seemed to end even more quickly, the joy of it over so fast. Diane darkened her face as she stepped into the hospital, ready to heap mounds of phony confidence over her terror and hopelessness about Lily's condition. She had hours of vigil ahead, sitting beside her split-open mother. Lily, exhausted and on painkillers, would sleep on and off, always clutching Diane's hand, as if it had life to spare. The linen, the hospital noises, Lily's fear never changed. It was boring. Very scary and very boring.

Diane tried to remember New York. Her real life, she would have said a few weeks ago. But Peter and Byron, their apartment, her old job, her friends—they had no tidal force to draw her to them. It seemed life had always been this way: Lily and Diane, fighting nature.

Peter and Byron didn't need Diane, anyway. According to Peter, this time Byron had taken the IQ test without any problem. He had gone to the prenursery school with typical enthusiasm and come home babbling about the activities.

Last night Diane had had a twenty-minute conversation with Byron over the phone; he rattled off the things they did in school and concluded, "You know, Mommy, I think I'm going to like growing up."

"Oh," Diane said, and held herself back from laughing. "How come?"

"Well, Daddy said I go to school for eighteen years while I grow up. I think I'm really going to like that."

Peter got on afterward and sounded like a competent parent of many years' experience. It was bizarre.

Maybe I was the problem. Me. With my ceaseless demands, my endless criticism.

Whom did I do all that work for? Nobody needed it. Nobody wanted it.

"We miss you," Peter said last night at the end of her conversation with Byron. But he didn't sound sincere. The facts didn't bear him out.

My mother needs me, she answered herself walking into the cardiac care unit. Do I take her back to New York? Insist to Peter we move into a larger apartment with a room for Mom?

That frail, scared, greedy, foolish woman. Diane loved her.

Diane set her face into a strong look of confidence and walked into the room.

The bed was empty.

"Ma?" she called out.

And she was hovering outside the window, looking at the Diane in the doorway: dressed in nice clothes, her hair brushed, her face made up, carrying the newspapers, and a take-out container of coffee.

"Ma?" this nice person called out.

Diane rushed to herself, smashed through the window, across the linoleum floor, rushed up into her own body, became herself, and began to scream: "Where is my mother? Where is my mother?"

Two nurses, both of them familiar faces, ran in and began to talk, to her and at each other. A mistake had been made, they were trying to say, Diane was supposed to have been called.

They didn't have to finish their explanations. Diane had forgotten to worry about this, about a sudden event during her absence. Diane had forgotten to be vigilant; she could have talked them into letting her sleep at the hospital, she could have—but she didn't and so, of course, Lily was dead.

WHEN NINA TOLD TAD'S SECRETARY SHE'D CALL ERIC BACK, NINA remembered the smell of Luke's hair. She had bent down to kiss Luke as she left him at the play group, but he was being called by David, by Katy, by Josh, by Rachel—"Hello Luke!" "Luke! Look at my new shoes!" "Luke! come play with me!"—and Nina's lips managed to catch only the top of Luke's head as he moved toward his friends. Hours later, at work, she could still feel the fur in her nose, the smell of baked life from his scalp, fresh and warm: soft hair, hard skull.

To Nina and Eric's astonishment, according to the two young women who ran the prenursery school, Luke was the favorite of his class, always in demand, chosen by the other children to arbitrate disputes or as a spokesman for their desires. Today's easy separation from Luke was thoroughly different from the first month of taking Luke to the prenursery school. Then he had clung to Nina's side, peering out from a lowered brow and half-concealed head. He was a growth on her body; baby kangaroo in the pouch.

Now Luke woke up early, asking, "Is it time for school?" He squirmed out of her pouch, rushed from her at the entrance, ran to his world. He loved his new friends, their habits, their mistakes, their games. Nowadays Nina had to plan ahead for the weekends, ask Luke which friend he wanted to see, make a date, and then tactfully say no to the others when their mothers phoned, eager to reserve time with her Luke. Solitary Nina had raised a friend to all toddlers. She worried his popularity was merely a by-product of his poor self-defense mechanisms, but it didn't seem to be in practice: Luke had the ultimate threat, that there were others who wanted to play with him, and so he was wooed, given what he wanted, without the need to demand it.

Luke's development gave Nina confidence. When Tad turned over to Nina more and more of the supervision of the line, she felt competent, assured of the future, because her Luke, the mewling, unhappy, constipated, nervous infant, had grown into a strong, smart, loving, and happy child. Why didn't it mean that to Eric? He was responsible for much of Luke's maturation; why had Eric's self-esteem declined?

Eric phoned in the midst of a hassle with two models. One had arrived late for a fitting and said she had to leave early for a shoot; Nina needed more time with her. Nina wanted to concentrate on persuading the model and Eric's call was a distraction. "Ask him if I can call him back?" Nina said, and tried to reason with the model, but she overheard Tad's secretary say to Eric, "Then where can she call you back?" and Nina smelled Luke's hair from the morning: baked and soft and hard.

"Wait!" she called out. "I'll take it."

"Nina?" Eric's voice answered her hello. He called out from the bottom of a canyon of New York noise—trucks, horns, shouting pedestrians.

"Eric? Where are you?"

"On the street." He was desperate. "Can you—are you busy?"

"What's wrong?"

"I've had it with Joe!" The words were strong, but Eric's tone was scared.

"You've quit?"

"No, I—uh—I just told him. I'm going short the market, I can't— I sold out all the stocks, your father's stocks, and I'm gonna go short."

Short meant betting against them, Eric had once explained to her. Over the years, Eric always made going short sound dangerous, immoral. It was something he was tempted to do and feared; he often spoke of it the way teenagers talk of breaking some rule; trying something adult they weren't supposed to: sex, drugs, running away from home. She knew that much; it was a step Eric feared and desperately wanted to take.

He was babbling his financial talk now: "The P/E's are too high, interest rates aren't coming down anymore, everybody's bullish—so who's gonna buy? Everybody's in the market, so there's no one left. All the greater fools have bought. There's the Iran-contra scandal, there's—we've had a great run, but it's over, it's 1929 again. Joe says it's 1928, but that's exactly the way people get trapped, convincing themselves—"

"Eric," Nina interrupted. He could go on endlessly and never state his problem. Like Luke, wanting you, the one he loves, to discover it for him. "Why aren't you in the office? Have you had a fight with Joe or did you—"

"Yeah—I shouldn't have left. I've gotta talk to Billy on the floor. I haven't gone short yet. Just sold the longs. Nina!" he cried out. Music passed by him; a truck roared.

"What!"

"Nina," he said again, this time in a sad, hopeless tone.

"Do you want to come here, Eric?"

"Can you come downtown?"

"No," she managed to stammer out past her feeling that she was wrong to deny him her presence. But she had promised Tad the dresses would be fit today. "I just can't. If you can come here, I can—"

"No, I—I gotta get back. Do you think I should call your father? Tell him what I'm doing?"

She felt disappointed by this. She had thought Eric wanted her, needed her—not her relationship to her father. "He's put you in charge," she answered. "Isn't that right? Are you supposed to consult him on every move?"

"This is a reversal. What if Joe—he could be calling Tom right now."

They were looking at her, the models, the tailor, Tad's secretary. Waiting for her to take charge. Why did Eric have to stir the pot? Their life was so good, they were so lucky compared with everyone else, why couldn't he let their happiness simmer quietly, why did he have to bring everything to a furious boil?

"Why don't you come here, Eric? I'll almost be done—we can go to lunch."

"No. I gotta go. Call you later."

And he was gone.

But, like Luke, his absence was incomplete. His voice inhabited the model's clothes, shone on the tailor's pins.

Months ago, after she had ignored Sal's protestation of love, he had backed her against the wall on a stairway at FIT and pushed his mouth at her. Nina had forced him off and said, "I don't want you." It had leapt out of her, this impolite sentence.

"I want you," he had answered.

"But I don't want you," she shouted back.

She couldn't say that to Eric. She couldn't say that to Luke.

Sal's face reddened. "You're a cunt," he said finally, and walked away.

Rejection met with rejection. The way of the world. Say yes or I'll hate you. She had always said yes to Eric, now she said maybe, or do it my way, and he hung up quickly, cut her off from his confidences, looked at other women while walking with her, and his eyes were pained, wounded, a child without his chocolates.

I don't care if you make money, Eric. She wanted to shout at him: I don't care about money. We have enough.

What would he say?

She knew what he would feel. He would hate her.

THE LINEN WAS THICK. PETER HELD THE CORNER OF THE TABLE-cloth between his index finger and thumb. He felt its solid weight.

Gail was across from him, studying the Four Seasons menu. Peter watched her face consider choices; thick with age and thought, it was the face of a very smart woman. At a cocktail party, Gail showed only a vacant pleasantness in her eyes, and her smooth hair, pulled back, seemed to strip her of weaponry; but in this pose, considering her choices, her eyes were clever and concentrated, her hand strong as it caressed her naked forehead. He imagined kissing his mother's neck, her long, thin neck, and feeling her head lean on his in surrender to the pleasure.

Peter squeezed his eyes shut to dissolve the image, as if it were really happening.

She must have been deliciously sexy, a tempting prize: thin body, arrogant mind, teasing wit. Kyle, his stepfather, had wanted her; he still puffed up proudly when he was introduced as her husband. Kyle had made his money years ago, when Peter was six; that unsophisticated westerner, his millions made by age forty, had come to New York and seen this jewel of the East, daughter of privilege, helpmate of the arts, and Kyle wanted his cock to conquer her, to be more important to her than even her own son.

I'd like to kill him.

("Really?" Kotkin asked. "It's your stepfather you want to kill?"

(Kotkin thinks I'm wrong, she thinks I'm really angry at my mother. "Maybe I hate my father."

("Why? If he didn't have the affair?"

("For not keeping her. For not making her happy?"

("You mean, your father didn't have a big enough cock to keep your mother happy?"

(No. Don't say this. No. Let me be. I don't want to know this. Maybe if I lie quietly and don't speak, Kotkin will leave me alone.

("Did you think you didn't have a big enough cock to keep Larry happy?"

("No, no," he begged Kotkin.)

"What am I having?" Gail wondered aloud.

Me. You're having me. I'm born again, without Jesus, without lies.

("I didn't know!" he shouted at Kotkin. "How could I project my fears of my father losing my mother when I thought my father had left *her*, had cheated on her? 'Your father wasn't satisfied with me,' that's what Gail told me."

("She said that?" Kotkin alert, happy, on the scent of some trail in her notebooks.

("I don't know what she said," Peter despaired. "Give me a break. Gail never tells the truth. How can I know what she said?"

("What do you think she said? Do you remember the night she told you?"

(Mom and Dad sat on the big chairs. Gail smoked.)

Gail smoked?

"Did you used to smoke?" Peter asked.

"Yes," Gail said with a fond smile of remembrance. She raised her hand for the waiter's attention. "I have exciting news, Peter. We'll order and I'll tell you."

"What is it?" Peter blurted with a harsh, nervous laugh. "You're pregnant?"

Gail looked at him as if he were vomit, her lips in a curl of disgust.

("No," he told Kotkin, thinking again. "That was when she told me she was going to have my half sister. They sat me on the couch and told me. She smoked throughout.")

"We'd better order. You must be hungry," Gail said, dismissing Peter's joke. When they were done, Gail leaned forward, eager and happy. "I'm going to be appointed cultural commissioner."

I could sell my story to the New York *Post*. Cultural czar son abused by neighbor. He laughed.

"You find that funny?" Gail blinked at him. "What's wrong, Peter? You're behaving horribly."

("Do you remember when they told you about the divorce?")

("I guess not.")

(Silence. Disapproval. Kotkin thinks I'm lying, I'm blocking, I'm repressing, I'm ruining the session. Her notebooks are full. Empty them, Peter. Make her feel she's a good therapist.)

"Do you remember Larry?"

"What?" Gail seemed distracted. She pushed her plate, scanned the table.

"Larry. Gary's cousin. He was a child abuser. He felt us up."

Gail sat, the screened sunlight trailing across half her face and body. The water glasses shimmered. Her lips parted. The perfect edges of her teeth glowed beneath the red. Her tongue appeared and touched them. "What do—he did that to you?"

"And Gary. Nothing horrible. Just safe sex." Peter laughed again. People use wit to blunt their evil, he thought.

Gail covered her face, lean hands over her eyes and nose and mouth like a mask. She bowed her head.

("What do you think your mother would say if you told her?")

("I don't know.")

("Do you want to tell her?")

("Yes. More than anything else. I want her to know what she did. I'd like someone to know, just for once, what stupid little shits they are. For once, I'd like someone to admit they did wrong and that nothing—nothing—explains it, or makes it right.")

("Is this just your mother we're talking about? Or everyone?")

("Everyone.")

("Including you?")

("Not me." Peter shifted his head and saw Kotkin's shoes. "Not me," he told Kotkin's Reebok sneakers. "I'm perfect.")

("And me?" Kotkin asked. "Am I also a little shit?")

("You're not real. You don't exist.")

Gail moved her hands away, twisting them together above her empty plate, wringing something out of them. "I didn't know," she said.

"I wasn't a bad son, Mother. You were a lousy mother. My father wasn't a lousy husband. You were a selfish, adulterous bitch."

My God, I'm free.

Gail's face trembled. She got small and wrinkled and old.

My God, I'm home. I'm out. I'm out of the sea of lies.

"Peter," his old mother pleaded.

Beg me, Mother. Beg me for my love.

"Peter, that's not true," her voice watered, words sagging out of her throat, drowning in the air.

"You tell lies to protect yourself. I thought it was to hurt me. But the lies are to cover your nakedness. I'm not your son anymore. And Byron will have nothing to do with you. I don't want to be reminded of your existence. It's crazy—"

("What do you think will happen if you say this to your mother?" Kotkin asked.

("I think you'll be out one customer."

(Silence. Kotkin thinks I'm acting out, crazy, escaping from one jail cell into another.)

"It's crazy, I know," Peter groaned to the old woman who was his mother. "But I've never really been your son anyway. So let's make it real. Let's take away the fiction. Why should you have your illusions? I don't have reality! Let's take away your dreams, then maybe I can have some."

He was crying. Happy five-year-old Peter was back in his cheeks, in his mouth, in his eyes, in every part of himself, crying at what they did to him, crying at their stupid, selfish love.

He pushed away from the table, fought to stand on the teetering world.

"I'm going home."

Her face was strange, something old and different. I didn't even know her.

"Home," he sang to her. Maybe the word would tell her. Tell her his regret. "I wanted to love you."

Peter covered his face on his way out. He didn't want to see himself in the stranger's eyes.

Go to the love you've got, Peter. Get there fast.

MOM DIED ALONE.

The doctor said it had happened fast, mostly during her sleep. Lily woke up with the episode already well under way; she suffered little, he claimed.

What bullshit. He was also in bed when it happened.

Diane tried to be rational. She went to the doctor, listened to his explanations, spoke to Lily's friends, asked them where to arrange a funeral, found the director, made all these plans, all to happen quickly, to bury Lily as Lily would have wished: a respectable Jewish woman, with a solemn rabbi and a full house of her peers.

Diane spent the day of her mother's death being a good girl. She made all the right arrangements.

But orphans wander. In Philadelphia she was an orphan.

At first, she tried to stay. She sat in her mother's kitchen, after the long, incredible day, and the event came to the door, entered, and sat at the table: Hello. Your mother died today. How do you feel?

She jumped up. Turned on the television. Cried.

Peter called to check on her and asked, Should we come down right now?

No, wait till the morning. Brave Diane. I'll be all right.

We'll come over, Lily's friends said when they phoned.

No, no, brave Diane said, tomorrow. I want to be alone tonight.

Everyone said, We understand.

But Diane didn't understand why she turned them away.

Because I wasn't there. I didn't save her.

And she cried, moaned in agony on her mother's furniture.

Peter said, "I'm very sorry. She loved you very much."

For a second, she thought he was kidding her. He liked to be ironic, so ironic that the slow-witted took him literally and never knew they had been insulted.

But his voice choked when he repeated it: "I'm so sorry. She loved you very much.

"Do you want me to tell Byron?" he asked later.

"We have to tell him!" Diane had shouted.

"I know. But do *you* want to—or me?"

She cried at that. She saw Byron, sandy hair askew, run in the door—right now; there he was, arms out, belly forward, face stretched: "Grandma! Grandma!"

Lily's fat arms opened for him, hands greedy for him, at last a male she had made, on whom Lily could lavish all her vanity and indulgence. "I have a present for you," Lily always said.

"Where?" Byron cried out, squirming in her arms, in ecstasy.

It was as though they had both died, not just Lily, but also the Byron that existed because of Lily.

And Lily's Diane—she too was dead. Diane was pretend, a gift for Lily: a strong young woman, independent, determined, and efficient. That Diane lived in Lily's mind and, with its death, must also die.

Later she walked into her mother's room to look for clothes to bury Lily in and got stuck there weeping in front of the closet.

Do it right, Diane. You weren't there to help her die; at least bury her right.

But she couldn't stay in that house.

Finally, she gave up the vigil, walked out of the house of her childhood, out to her dead mother's car, put on the sixties music—music of love and betrayal, of idiotic hope, music without any notes for death—and drove away.

Orphans wander. In Philadelphia she was an orphan.

Diane decided to drive to New York.

Mom died alone, she kept thinking.

Diane looked through the skimming cars and could see Lily, desperate, writhing in the pool of light from her hospital reading lamp, could see Lily now, on the highway, reach for Diane as her heart contracted, wringing life out of her. "Diane! Help me!"

Over and over, on the turnpike, car lights floating ahead—behind—hovering over the gray river, Diane could feel Lily's horror: Where are you, Diane?

Why wasn't I there? To hold her through it, to say good-bye, to kiss her away . . .

She pushed the car, pushed it up, faster and faster, away from the mistakes, from the pictures:

Lily, hand frozen in terror, reaching for Diane:

Lily, seated beside Byron, watching her grandson eat with the miracle of it reflected in her face; Lily in bloom, amazement at the presence of Byron's life smoothing her jowls, easing her mouth into a smile: "Do you like it?"

"Un-huh!" Byron nodded at his grandma. "I love it!"

"He's so delicious," Lily had said that just yesterday when Diane told her Peter's report of Byron's happiness at the prenursery school.

Diane and Lily smiled at each other, at their mutual triumph. They had made Byron together, a relay race across the years, two husbandless women; Byron was there in their hands to show the world that they had survived.

Who's going to listen to me brag now? Who'll listen to the worst of me? Who'll make me go on?

How much longer to New York? Diane checked the clock, her mileage, tried to identify where she was on the turnpike. She had to get back to Peter and Byron.

The Beatles sang it now on the stereo: "Get back. Get back to where you once belonged."

But I don't want to be Peter's wife; I don't want his invention. I want my mother's: the brilliant student, the tough lawyer, the Supermom. "You were the smartest girl in your class. The other mothers died with envy."

In Lily's lonely triumphs, Diane was created. Diane had fought Lily hard as a teenager—and lost. Ended up just the way Lily had wanted: married to a rich man, worked at the right law firm, made the male Lily had craved.

The car began to vibrate. Diane felt the rumble run from the front to the back, across the roof, and start again.

I'm going too fast. Mom's old car can't take it.

But in the cave of night, on the gray river, she had to hurry back. Only another half hour at this speed and she would be back, back to Lily's creation. She could go into Byron's room and hold him. She could put her ear on his smooth back and listen.

Listen to a young heartbeat.

Fast. Strong. Brave.

She forgot for a moment. She could feel Byron's skin against her cheek and hear the thuds of his life. She forgot for a moment.

The sound pulled back—a shot, air exploding. The gray river twisted away. . . .

Don't hit the brakes hard, you'll skid. Turn into it, the tire's blown—

There was Byron—get home to him.

I can handle this, the road is empty, this skid will—

The gray river disappeared. Her head hit the ceiling. She knew she was off the road, bucking on the black grass. She knew the shadows ahead were trees—

The seat belt. She had forgotten.

There's Byron—get home to him. How fast am I going? Why doesn't it end? What a stupid way to die.

The shadows came fast now. Dark and huge.

Do something! There has to be something you can do.

At the last second of this eternity, cursing herself, Diane twisted out of the seat and tried to leap back, back to the way she had come, back against the rush to nothing.

ERIC GOLD, THE WIZARD OF WALL STREET, RETURNED TO HIS DESK, ignored the sounds of the pygmies, and made his bold move. "Billy? Here's the short list—"

"Uh, Eric," Billy stammered. "We've got a problem."

What problem? Weeks ago Eric had cleared the borrowing. He had been ready all his life for this triumph.

Sammy's hand came down on his phone. Eric stared at the fingers slashed across his phone, cutting him off. He thought: okay, Sammy, I'll slam the phone on you and break your fingers.

"Eric." It was the owl. "I've told Billy not to accept any orders from you. I spoke to Tom Winningham half an hour ago. He's removed your discretion and turned it over to me. I couldn't do anything about your closing out the positions, I've explained that. Mr. Winningham was appalled that you sold him out of the market. I told him it would be a good opportunity to get him into some quality issues.''

"It's Billy," said one of the secretaries.

So this is why no one looked at me when I came in.

"Tell Billy we'll get back to him," Joe said.

Eric couldn't look up. His eyes stayed on Sammy's white fingers—cutting Eric off from the money.

Joe said, "I begged you to discuss this in the office with me. I repeat my request. We've worked together for many years—let's not end our association too hastily."

Joe was sure of his position. Eric couldn't help himself from guessing what Joe might offer. Half the management fee? Nothing? Raise Eric's salary while lowering his cut of the profits?

Come on, Eric. You can't go back. You can't be the pleasant servant anymore. Joe is relying on your cowardice.

"Sammy," Eric said. "Move your fucking fingers or I'll break them."

"Either come into the office now," Joe said, "or get out."

Eric looked at Sammy. Sammy's thin face, usually nervous, worried, harassed, seemed to be at peace. Sammy's won, Eric realized. Sammy had recovered his father's respect. For a weird moment, Eric was glad for Sammy.

If only I had the courage to go, this would be a happy ending for everyone.

"Sammy," Eric repeated. "I'll break your fingers."

"Who are you gonna call?" Sammy said softly. "Your father-in-law? He's already made his decision. You can't talk him out of it."

Leave, Nina had said. Leave and we'll make it. Maybe she could call Tom, get him to change—but she won't.

He got up slowly. He felt himself grow. He was tall. Much taller than anyone in the room.

I'm so big. I should be strong.

His life was in this room. His dreams, no matter how comatose, still beeped a stubborn rhythm, still danced on the crazy red letters and numbers.

Go.

"Come into the office," Joe said in a sweet, low chant. Joe got up from his chair and gestured inside.

Sammy nodded at Eric. Go in, make a deal.

Him too? He also wants me to stay. Why? Guilt? Or fear?

Leave. You don't need them, Nina had said.

But she knew nothing about it. She didn't know Eric's weakness, she didn't know his fear.

I am so big. So much bigger than them. Why can't I be strong?

A THOUSAND-PIECE SETTING OF CHINA SHATTERED. A HUNDRED drawers of silverware crashed.

Cover yourself. Close up.

Diane was in the womb again. Legs tight, arms folded, eyes shut. She spun in the dark sea and prayed to be born.

Let me live through this mistake. I'll be good. I won't make any more errors.

The angry noise, with a final crash, stopped.

She stayed covered, closed, and awaited judgment.

There was no light. Her eyes saw nothing. The world was soft.

Get out quickly. Death waits here for you.

Out!

The floor cut and crunched. There was a little opening, just a small way out. Squeeze through. I won't fit. I'm too big. I can't get out!

Go quickly—death wants you. Get out!

I'm alive. This is a car. I'm alive. This is the window. Get out! Mom's car will explode.

And she was out—rolling on the earth's mattress, rolling on the unmade bed. But there was no light anywhere.

You idiot—you're blind now. You killed your eyesight. You stupid, stupid, careless girl. You killed—

Open your eyes. You'll see. Everything you want will be there; open your eyes and you will see the world you want.

This is grass. That's the sound of the car engine. Just open your eyes and you will live.

She let go of fear. She opened her heart, stretched her legs, released the grip on her soul. The stars floated up to the ceiling, the blue-black dome of the world, white lights everywhere, jammed with life, crowded with cold confidence, millions of lights, endlessly signaling: we are here for you. We are with you.

The goddamned car, that wreck, may blow up.

She forced herself to her feet. Her legs didn't have enough string in them. She fell forward, like a stupid infant.

Obviously they're broken. Probably you're dead. You're dying and you don't know it. Your arrogance is a joke. To think you could survive that crash. Well, if you get yourself to a hospital, maybe there's a chance. Better get your purse from the car to pay the bill.

She walked again without remembering how.

But where's the car door? The wheels were in the way. Why did they put the wheels like that? In the way of the doors? What a stupid car.

It's upside down. My God, it's upside down. Get away from it, it'll blow up. Survive the crash and die for your purse.

But they won't take me without my Blue Cross card. They'll let me die. Concussion probably. Maybe shock. Aren't you supposed to sit down now? You'll probably die because you're walking.

You're very tired. Go back to bed. Have a different dream.

I'm sorry, Ma. I thought I should be home with Peter and Byron. I'm sorry I love them. I could be happy. I could go to the stars and float, but I love them—I have to have a Blue Cross card so they'll love me.

Okay?

"Are you all right?" a face said.

I've never been right in my life. Maybe my purse was thrown from the car. See, if I didn't need Peter and Byron, I wouldn't have a purse.

"Is there anyone else in the car?"

"Purse."

"Sit down here. You don't look God."

Of course not. No one is God. People make the world what it is: bright stars or unmade beds. People decide that even without their purse. Because they love. That's why. They love and so they die.

I've got to stop crying. This policeman won't take me to the hospital if I'm crying.

Big girls don't cry because they lose their purse; they go to Saks and buy a new one.

"No one's in there. Here, just sit. What happened?"

Don't tell him. If you don't tell him you made a mistake, he'll never know. But please, please stop crying!

"An ambulance is on the way. I'll get a blanket from the car. Don't move, okay? You got that? Don't move."

I hear Byron. He's coming. He peed in the bed again. Well, I'm staying asleep. Peter can deal with it.

I'm not needed.

Just go to sleep. In the morning, I'll be different. I'll go to Saks and get a new mother.

"MAMA!" LUKE SAID. HE JUMPED IN FRONT OF HER, ARMS OUT, grappling for her love, "Mama!"

She took his long body—the feet banged against her hips—and

hugged him. Luke still fit onto her body, a perfectly designed accessory. His head rested on her shoulder, his face into her neck.

"Eric?" she called. She had worried; she had felt wrong all day.

"I'm here," he said from the living room. An admission, and not a happy one.

She carried Luke with her. Eric sat on the couch, staring at a tape of He-Man playing on the television.

"What happened?" she asked.

"It's over," he said. "They're all against me. There's nothing I can do." He gestured at the television and laughed. "Market was down today, down fifty-three points. Tom would have made money. Fuck him."

"Eric!" She glanced at Luke to warn Eric about his language.

"Sorry. I'll shut up."

"What happened?"

"Your father—Joe called your father while I was out. Your father fired me. Joe is generously offering to keep me on under the old terms."

"He what?" Luke said. He smiled as if Daddy must be making a joke. "Grandpa did what?"

"It's an expression," Nina began.

"Nothing, Luke," Eric said harshly. "It's nothing."

"Sounds like something," Luke said. He kicked his legs. "Let me down."

"Okay," Nina said. Luke's body slid down her, fireman on a pole to the rescue.

"How could Grandpa fire you?" Luke asked Eric. "What does that mean? You're not on fire."

"We shouldn't be talking about this," Eric said to Nina.

Not talking about it is how you get to be like Father, Nina thought. She was angry. She stood on a hill and saw the hurt and the rage from a distance, in the past and in the future—the dark, swirling cloud of her family rushing to blot out her patch of sunlight, to rain on her happy meadow. "To fire," she said to Luke, "means to stop someone from doing a job you've asked them to do. Like, if you pay somebody to do something, and you don't want them to go on doing it, and you tell them to stop—that's firing them. It has nothing to do with putting them on fire."

Eric laughed. Not happily: he groaned. "Grandpa didn't think I was making good bets with his money."

"Well . . ." Luke put his hand out, palm up. "Well . . . it's his money, right?"

"Actually, it was given to him by his grandfather," Nina said. "But it's Grandfather Tom's now."

"I see!" Luke hopped on one foot. "It was given to him and now he's supposed to give it to Daddy."

"We really shouldn't be talking about this," Eric said, but he smiled at Luke.

"Why not?" Nina asked Eric. "Why not? You didn't do anything wrong. So Joe called up and Tom just let him do—"

"Yep," Eric said.

"Did you call Tom?"

"No. I left the office without saying anything. Joe gave me a choice of staying on the old terms or leaving immediately. I didn't answer him. I just left. I was a fool! I should have told your father first. I should have left a year ago when I was hot!" Eric lifted the cushions of the couch in his big hands. They came up as if they were small pillows and he flopped them down like an excited infant unable to control his motions.

"I know!" Luke called out. He glanced from the tape of He-Man and to Nina, his attention divided. "If Grandpa Tom's grandpa gave him the money, then Grandpa Tom should give me the money, right? I'm his grandson. Then Daddy can make the bets."

Made sense to Nina. Luke smiled at them, pleased with himself, convinced he had found the answer.

"You left the office," Nina said to Eric. "Where have you been all day?"

"Daddy picked me up from school!" Luke said in a shout of joy.

"We went to the park, we went to Forbidden Planet and got a toy. We had fun, right, Luke?"

"Yep," Luke said. "I got a new space toy." Luke hooked her hand and gently tugged. "I'll show you."

"Why don't you bring it out here and we can keep talking to Daddy?"

"Okay," Luke said in his high trill of good cheer. He skipped out of the room.

"I'm sorry," she said.

"I don't know what to do," Eric said. He didn't look at her. He was ashamed.

"I love you," she said. But that wasn't enough. That wasn't enough for him.

"I guess I have to stay. Can't pay the bills otherwise. I'll go in tomorrow and eat whatever I have to eat from Joe."

Maybe it's for the best, Nina thought. She went over to Eric and kissed his hot and worried brow. Eric leaned his cheek on her hand and closed his eyes.

"I love you," she whispered.

He has us; he doesn't need anything else.

PETER'S FORTRESS OF TRUTH WAS UNDER SIEGE. THEY KEPT TRYING to break in, and tell him lies. But Peter was busy. He had to take Byron to Philadelphia for Lily's funeral; he had to explain Lily's death in advance.

"You'd better tell him," Diane had said. God, she sounded awful. Enervated, frantic, desperate, hopelessly lost, intensely focused on errands—as if her emotional keyboard had no chords, just atonal keys played by a chimp.

Peter's mother called. Peter hung up at her hello.

Peter's stepfather called. Peter hung up at his hello.

Then Peter turned on the phone machine. He ignored Byron's insistent interrogation: "Why didn't you talk? We're here. Why don't you answer?"

Peter shut off the phone machine speaker so he and Byron wouldn't hear the pleas for him to pick up.

He gave Byron a bath. Byron sat in the water on his knees. He poured, he danced toys on the surface, he splashed them under the faucet's torrential waterfall. Byron sang to his pretend things: oh, no, look out! Duck! I've got you now, you evil one! The tips of Byron's mop of sandy hair got wet. The water darkened their color; the curls were glued to his neck and ears.

Do I tell him now?

"We're going to Philadelphia tomorrow to see Mommy," Peter said.

"Yay!" Byron shot up with pleasure, his lean stomach, perfect penis, and strong legs silky from the water. "We're gonna see Mommy!"

"Yes. Won't that be great?"

"Yeah," Byron said, and looked solemn. "She's been away a long time."

"Well, she'll be coming home with us."

"Yea! Yea!"

(*How do I tell him, Kotkin?*)

(*Explain it simply. Don't hedge. Tell him what you know and what you believe, but keep it simple. If it makes him unhappy, comfort him, but let him be unhappy. Don't make him pretend he isn't.*)

"Will Grandma be there?" Byron asked.

The phone rang again. The machine picked it up.

"Well, you know Grandma's been very sick. And she got sicker. She's—" Peter couldn't say the word—such a naked, ugly word.

"She died!" Byron's eyes became circles; his mouth and jaw squeezed. He looked furious.

"Yes."

"Because she got too old," Byron said, his face set, very angry.

"Well . . . and sick too. We're going to miss her." Peter felt his eyes water. He had hated Lily. Well, not hate, but she was a silly woman with stupid values, and her presence was sandpaper on Diane's skin.

"Why are we going there?" Byron complained. "If Grandma's dead, why are we going there?" His body was stiff. He had tucked his elbows in and closed his little fists. Like Diane, he wanted to fight unhappiness.

We made him together. He has my hair. He has her eyes. He loves to be in the audience and watch a spectacular, like me. He wants everyone to do things his way, like her. We made him together and so he's both of us at once. He's someone else, but he's our soup, our brew.

"When people die, it makes everyone who knows them sad. So they get together and . . ." Do I have to say bury? Do I have to tell Byron Lily will be put in the earth, this woman who loved him more simply and absolutely than I did, who loved even the idea of him, do I have to tell him we will put her in the dead ground, alone?

"And cry?" Byron said. He collapsed, broken at the middle, brought his hands to his face, and wailed into them. "I don't want to go!" he screamed. "I don't want to miss Grandma!"

Peter snatched Byron from the water. The body folded in his arms, huddled in his lap. Peter's clothes soaked the water from Byron. Byron cried and shivered. Peter pulled a towel off the rack and covered him, tented Byron within his heart. Peter stroked his back and sang: "It's okay to miss Grandma. She loved you. It's okay to miss her."

The phone rang.

Peter closed his eyes and soaked up his son's water, the tears of life's final betrayal, and waited for happiness to return. He knew it would.

18

A YEAR AFTER LILY'S DEATH, PETER, DIANE, AND BYRON went down to Philadelphia to unveil Lily's tombstone. A similar ceremony had been held for Diane's father a year after his death, and Diane felt she should repeat for Lily what Lily had done for her husband. A rabbi was there, but no one else was invited, just as only Lily and Diane had gone years ago.

Peter gave his arm to Diane for support as they walked on the manicured lawn up to the gravesite. He had gotten into the habit of helping her at Lily's funeral and during the recovery period following her car accident. He continued to, even though she had healed months ago. Diane's leap backwards had given her legs, rather than her head, to the impact. Her last act, at the final moment before contact with the trees, had saved her life. Whenever she wondered about her desire to live, given her suicidal decision to drive home the night her mother died, Diane recalled her dive to the back seat, her twist away from death; she never again doubted her desire to be alive, to be Byron's mother, to be a woman, to feel whatever she must.

At odd moments, when she listened to Byron play the piano (at Byron's own request he had begun lessons shortly after Lily's death), when she watched Byron blow out the candles at his fifth birthday, when she held his hand crossing streets, when she missed him at her job (she had joined a public-interest law foundation to represent women's causes), Diane felt, in a burst of heat in her breast, horror at how close she had come to losing all the happy things that surrounded her.

The accident must have also changed how she saw Peter, because he seemed so different. Peter claimed his therapy had helped. He told her what he had discovered about his parents' divorce and said

426

that knowledge had released him from a prison of conflicted emotions about marriage. He certainly treated his mother differently: he refused to have Gail over to the house, to see her in any way. She took Byron to Gail's every few weeks, and they were received with almost excessive deference and consideration. But the most startling change in Peter was his desire to have another child. Diane, however, didn't believe that Peter's therapy or this reversal of information as to which of Peter's parents had first cheated on the other could really be the reason Peter seemed so changed to her. She was convinced that during the first years of Byron's life she had suffered from her own madness, her own distorted way of seeing things—that in those days, she hadn't really known Peter.

Diane told Peter she didn't want to have another child. She was tempted to repeat all the things she felt she had done so badly with Byron, to get them right, but for exactly that reason, Diane thought she owed Byron sole attention, bandages for whatever cuts she had made.

"He comes from a long line of only children," she told Peter.

"Well," he answered. "We have time."

But she was forty-one years old now and she didn't think she had time. She had boarded the train for good and would ride this trip out to its last stop without any more transfers. As a lawyer, she would fight on behalf of lost or losing causes; as a mother, she would raise her child patiently; and as a wife, she would be a companion to Peter. To have another child would mean a temptation to try to be perfect again. And she knew she wasn't perfect. She was Lily's daughter and Diane's illusions: a combination that was flawed.

The rabbi read what he was supposed to; Diane spoke her lines. They uncovered Lily's headstone.

In the car ride over, Byron had asked if he could make up a poem about Grandma and say it at the ceremony.

Byron stood in his dress clothes, a lean young boy of five, with perfect skin, bold eyes, limber legs and arms, standing at the edge of his grandmother's grave. He looked up into the sun at Diane and Peter with no fear, no awe.

"Now?" he asked.

"Sure," Peter said.

Diane watched the rows of graves and smelled the flowers; it was a beautiful sunny day.

"Good-bye, Grandma," Byron said to the gray stone. "We miss you. We remember your cookies. We remember your hugs. We'll try to be good and love everybody like you loved us."

Diane rested her hand on Byron's head and felt herself drain into him. She closed her eyes, tightened her grip on Peter's arm, and she was strong between them, the three alone and together: a family.

AMERICA HATES CHILDREN, PETER THOUGHT. IT PRETENDS TO IN-dulge them, thinks of itself as so generous and abused, but beneath it all is hate. Hate, neglect, and narcissistic rage.

Peter walked through the crowd of adults and toddlers, through the shuffling mass in the park and listened to the so-called grown-ups:

"No, you've had too much!"

"Why don't you go play on your own?"

"That belongs to the little girl! Give it back!"

"Oh, so they both came down with the flu at the same time. Threw up on everything!"

"My housekeeper says he's an angel. I come home and all I get is complaints and tears."

These parents were spoiled children. Giant spoiled children. Some of them liked to hit. Or threaten to hit.

"I'll give you a good smack if you don't stop!"

"Do that one more time and we go right home and you get a spanking!"

Others suffocated their babies with psychobabble:

"Are you sharing? If you share nicely with your friend, then he'll share with you."

"Mommy and Daddy are tired. Like when you get tired and cranky and need a rest. So we're just going to sit here. You can play next to us."

Peter was sickened by them. Of course, it was the logic of their position: in authority, being imperfect, they made mistakes, and in authority, they couldn't admit their wrongs, their inadequacy. The victims had to bear the blame. Otherwise, society would collapse, children would never sleep, never eat, never learn, never grow up to raise their children just as badly.

"Daddy," Byron said. He spoke clearly and well. He was a solemn, hardworking child; the joy and energy of his babyhood had been replaced by seriousness and concentration. "I want you to understand something."

"What's that, Byron?"

"If Luke comes today, I want to play with him all day I don't want a short play date. I want a long one."

A mother nearby snorted at this. Peter glanced at her. She smiled sarcastically. "Knows his own mind," she said in a flip tone, suggesting Byron was wrong to be like that.

Peter turned away from her and answered Byron. "Well, that's up to Luke and his parents. *If* he comes. His mother said she wasn't sure if he wanted to."

Byron nodded. He stared at the ground for a moment. "Could I go to the same summer camp Luke is going to?"

"Where's he going?"

"I don't remember the name. You could ask his mommy or daddy."

"You like Luke a lot, don't you?"

"Yeah, he plays the most interesting games. I wish he went to my school."

They had had trouble getting Byron into Trinity. Peter, who knew several of the trustees, had asked them to intercede and they had. Peter didn't want to explain to Byron that Luke hadn't been able to get into as good a school. He feared Byron might blurt that out to Luke and hurt the boy's feelings. Luke was a sweet child and, although they didn't go to the same school, was still Byron's most requested playmate. Peter didn't know what to say. He nodded and stroked the sandy mass of Byron's hair. "But you have friends in your class you like?"

"Yeah, they're okay. I'm gonna go on the slide."

"Okay. Bye."

Byron moved off. He climbed alone, slid down alone, watched a group playing, said something to them. They didn't answer. He returned to the slide and went down it again.

Is he lonely? Is he unpopular? He was very creative. He worked hard at the piano and was making good progress. His drawings were terrific: strong lines, good colors, his imagination disciplined and energetic.

He's going to be an artist of some kind. Not like me. Not an audience, but a creator. There will be an easy way for Byron to get the unhappiness out, to shape its chaotic mass into beauty.

Diane appeared at the gate, looked for Byron, and, after spotting him, came over to sit down next to Peter. She offered her lips for a quick kiss. But Peter didn't give her a peck. He put his hand lingeringly on the back of her head. After several seconds she broke off, her eyes shining, and laughed. "They'll throw us out for necking."

She took his hand, twining their fingers together, and looked out at the slide, watching Byron.

"No one here Byron knows?" she asked.

"I'm hoping Luke will come."

She nodded. "Your mother called. She asked if I could bring Byron by today."

("I realize Mom is just a person, Kotkin. She is not a monster. She's just an ordinary person, who made ordinary mistakes. She thought of herself first. Everybody thinks of themselves first."

("Does that mean you forgive her?"

("It means it's not my place to forgive her.")

In front of Peter and Diane, a mother and father were trying to force their two-year-old into a stroller. He arched his back, stiffened his legs—an anti-leaving-the-park demonstrator. "We have to go now, sweetie," the embarrassed, upset mother said over and over. She tried to force the hard body to bend, to break to her will.

("Are you going to see your mother?" Kotkin asked.

("Why do you ask that?"

("Just wondering. Are you thinking about seeing her? How long has it been?"

("A year.")

The father took over, lifted the two-year-old in the air, and pushed him into the stroller fast and hard. The father held his son down with one hand while strapping him in with the other. "We have to go now!" he pleaded.

("She wanted Kyle. Nothing would have stopped that. She was in love with him. That mattered more to her than what I wanted. She's just an ordinary person."

("Does that bother you? To find out your mother is ordinary?"

("Yes. I believed she was extraordinary."

("And now you know she's not."

("How banal, eh?"

("No," Kotkin said softly. "No."

("And Larry. Him too. He was just an ordinary person."

("Do you forgive him?" Kotkin whispered.

("No. I don't forgive anyone.")

"Remember that?" Diane said, gesturing to the parents who had forced their child into the stroller and were hurrying away from the scene of their cruelty. Their child's cries went with them. "Remember that phase? Byron never wanted to leave. Never wanted to stop playing."

"He still doesn't," Peter said. "He's just more polite now."

"Mmmm," Diane said. "You're right."

"If Luke doesn't come, I'll take him up to Gail's."

Diane looked her surprise. She squeezed his hand. "I'll go with you."

"Okay."

She gave him another squeeze and returned to watching Byron. "He's a good boy," she said. "He's survived us."

Peter nodded. He sat and watched. He was an audience again; he was satisfied.

("You know, Kotkin. I'm going to tell you something I thought I'd never say."

(He waited for her to ask. She didn't.

("I'm a happy man."

("I'm glad," Kotkin said.)

Indeed, I am a happy man.

WELL, IF I SHOW BYRON I BROUGHT MY MICROSCOPE, HE WON'T like it. He'll tell me it's boring. I know it's not boring. But I don't want to argue.

We can play a game. We can play Ghostbusters on the slides.

I wish he was interested in nature things. That tree has something on it. Daddy says it's a fungus. But he must be wrong. The fungus is too big for the tree to still be alive.

If I made the universe, I wouldn't make it with a big bang. I would let it start that way. Very compressed. Lots of it, jammed together. But I wouldn't release in a bang. It could spread out, like when a pebble hits the water, spread out slow—what's the word?— gradually. That means slow but regular. That's how I would make the universe. I'll tell Byron.

No. He'll argue. He thinks the universe is the sky anyway. That's all right.

"Mommy!"

"Yes, Luke?"

"I don't want my microscope."

"Okay. Give it to me."

"Well, we should go back and leave it home."

"What!" Daddy laughed.

"I'll just put it away. Give it to me," Mommy said.

Can I tell her? "Okay," Luke said. "But put it so no one can see it."

"You mean so Byron can't see it," Mommy said. "You know why he doesn't like it? It's because he doesn't know—"

"I know that!" She didn't like Byron. He was okay. He could play good games if you talked to him the right way. You had to slip into him, make him think what you want is what he wants. "Anyway, I can find things and look at them at home. Byron will be interested when we're home. I told you I want the play date to be at my house, right?''

"Yes. If that's okay with Byron's parents.''

They won't say no. Byron will want to come with me. There are fewer rules at my house. No cleaning up at the end. Byron hates to clean up. Me too. What's the point? You only mess it up again the next day.

Look at that squirrel.

"Luke! Luke!''

There's Byron.

"I'm Slimer, Luke! I'm gonna slime those bad boys!'' Byron pointed to some boys Luke knew from other times in the park.

Well, I'll play Ghostbusters for a while. Then I'll change the game to the tree with fungus. If I tell Byron the fungus is a ghost and we have to get it off the tree, then I can do some experiments.

If you spread out gradually, you can have the whole universe— without even a bang.

GOOD! LUKE DIDN'T BRING HIS BORING MICROSCOPE.

There's nothing as blue as Luke's eyes. Like the blue in that painting Mommy and Daddy like. Not a real blue.

"We're going to slime them?'' Luke asked.

"We're gonna have a long play date, right Luke? I told my mommy and daddy that we had to have a long play date.''

"Well—okay, but I want to go back to my place.''

Good. "That's good, see? We can make chemicals in the bathroom.''

"No, I don't want to do that, Byron. Those aren't real chemicals. That's just soap and water.''

"Okay.'' Can't argue. Luke will play with those stupid boys if I argue. When we get to his house, I'll do it anyway. "We'll always be friends, right, Luke?''

"Well.'' Luke put out his hand and looked at the sky. Even the sky was not as blue as his eyes. "If we know each other.''

"But we'll try to always know each other, right?''

Luke put his eyes on Byron; they got dark. "Okay. But we can't fight all the time about what to play.''

"But sometimes I don't want to play what you play.''

"When that happens, we'll play different things. Then, when we want to play something together, we'll do it. Okay?''

"But it gets boring waiting.''

"Well.'' Luke lowered his head. His black hair showed the white underneath. How does the dark show the light? "That's the only way I know how to be friends."

"Okay," Byron said.

It's too hard to fight everybody.

"We'll do what you want, Luke."

ERIC, LUKE, AND BARRY LEFT THE APARTMENT TO GO TO THE park. It was early Sunday morning. The day before had been Luke's fifth birthday. They carried with them Luke's present from Nina and Eric. It was a bike, a two-wheeler, to replace his tricycle. Eric had prayed that Luke would ask Nina to teach him how to ride. Luke was still fearful of new physical adventures, a kind of instinctive cowardice that disturbed Eric and reminded him of his own indecisiveness. But Luke declined Nina's tutorial offer and insisted that Daddy teach him. By chance, Eric's parents had asked if they could come downtown for breakfast that morning, and Eric seized on this opportunity to invite his own father along, in the hope that if there were problems, Barry might be a help. After all, Barry had taught Eric how to ride. Of course, Eric was older when he had learned. Eight years old—it had taken Barry that long to afford a bike.

By now Eric understood that Luke was unusually smart. The response of the schools to the results of the IQ test made that clear. Despite Eric's lack of connections, despite the horrendous surplus of applications, despite all the warnings that in order to get into a superior private school, a child had to be specially tutored from age zero, despite all that, Luke was accepted everywhere. Three schools called to urge Nina and Eric to select them. Their experience was so different from other parents that only one conclusion was possible.

Eric wanted to shout the news, to brag at every social function. He wanted every parent to know what they had been told at the nursery school by Luke's teacher, a woman who had taught four-year-olds for thirty years. She said that Luke was the brightest child she had ever had. But Nina clamped down on Eric. Just say Luke is bright. That's enough.

With the limitless choice of schools offered, they had a difficult time making their selection: they spent three weeks revisiting each school; they had meetings with headmasters and headmistresses eager to win them. Even Hunter was eager to get Luke. Eric wanted to pick Hunter, but Nina vetoed that. She thought the kids at Hunter were too grim, made into little adults, urged to acquire knowledge in order to gain applause. Luke loved learning; he wanted to know everything because he loved understanding. Nina wanted to pre-serve Luke's unself-conscious love of knowledge. Eric could see that, so he went along with Nina, and they placed him in one of the better but not the hottest of New York private schools. "He'll get bored," Eric protested. "We'll tell him what he needs to know," she answered. By now, Eric had to read books on evolu-tion, on biology, on the current developments in physics in order to keep up with Luke's curiosity, his memory, and his ability to detect contradictions in the books they read to him. Luke worked with Nina on her designs, he listened with Eric to the business shows, Luke gobbled up all the scraps of information the world scattered about him, and then he played with his friends—there were so many of them—without displaying any of it. In kindergar-ten, Luke managed to keep his teachers in the dark for months, but by the end of the term, at the parent-teacher conference, Luke's teacher said, "You have a remarkably intelligent child. Do you know that?" she asked, quite curious, apparently unsure.

"Yes," Nina said. Eric nodded.

The teacher stared at them. "He knows things about geology, about space, about, well, about most things, that I don't know. I sometimes ask him to answer the questions of the other kids. He used to refuse to answer. He's getting over that. He's more com-fortable with his natural role as a leader."

A leader. The word expanded Eric's nostrils; he breathed in the air, electric with promise. He dared not hope his son would escape the generational curse of failure. The brains must come from Nina, Eric thought, so he prayed that self-destruction wouldn't come from him.

Eric had accepted his defeat a year ago. He continued to work for Joe under the old terms, salary and a cut of commissions. No management fees, no discretion over clients' money. Joe had de-veloped heart trouble over the winter and left each day after lunch, putting Sammy in charge. Once Joe was out of the office, Sammy copied Joe's manner toward Eric, slipping his feet into his father's vacant shoes. Sammy treated Eric amiably, but with an undercur-rent of contempt. It didn't matter. Eric earned a hundred and fifty thousand a year, enough to pay the bills. Tom, perhaps out of guilt, had set up a trust fund for Luke. The money would be there for Luke to go through Harvard, or wherever it was that he would end up. As long as Eric's genes didn't interfere, Luke would be extraor-dinary.

Eric didn't feel bad. He was Luke's caretaker; he was there to guard the jewel until it went on display for the world to gasp at.

And best of all, Nina was eight months pregnant. Only a month and there would be another. Another chance. And this time Eric wouldn't be nervous, he wouldn't doubt it was worth the effort, he wouldn't allow his own struggles to distract him from the pleasure of watching new life grow in his garden.

Luke was excited. He wanted to try the bike on the street.

"No, let's get to the park," Eric said.

"Why?" Luke asked.

"It's easier to ride at the park," Barry said. "The pavement is much smoother."

"It is?" Luke said, and his brain clicked on. Eric saw it happen, knew it was coming. "No, it isn't, Grandpa. It's true this is cement and that's tar, but it isn't much smoother."

Eric looked at his father and smiled.

"Well." Barry tried desperately. "The park has wider streets—"

"No," Luke began gently. He was forced to contradict grown-ups a lot and it pained him. It took Nina more than a year to persuade Luke that if he spoke politely, no one would mind being corrected. "No, Grandpa, actually—"

Eric interrupted. "The reason we should try in the park is because it's your first time and there are people walking around here. If you have trouble controlling the bike, you'll worry about hitting them. At this hour the park is usually empty and you can concentrate on balancing, you don't have to worry about steering."

"I have to worry a little about steering, right?" Luke said, and laughed. "I don't want to crash into trees."

"That's true," Eric said.

They moved on. Barry was quiet until they were almost at the park. Luke had danced ahead to the corner. Barry whispered in Eric's ear: "Why did you tell him he might crash into people?"

"I didn't."

"That's why I said it was smoother in the park," Barry defended himself. "Now he may worry he'll crash."

"Dad, Luke knows he may crash. I'm trying to make it clear that's nothing to worry about."

"But it *is* smoother in the park."

It wasn't, but Eric let that point pass. Why fight?

When they reached the park, Luke immediately got on his new bike. Eric held it by the underside of the seat. Barry stood ten feet off, half bent over. "Just pedal fast," he said.

"I'll hold the bike, Luke," Eric told him, "until you ask me to let go."

"Okay," Luke said, brave and firm and scared.

Eric pushed, keeping his eyes on the little head, aloft on the bike, ready to move on. "Pedal," Eric prompted.

"Pedal fast," Barry said.

"I don't want to," Luke mumbled.

"Pedal as fast or as slow as you want," Eric said.

They moved. Luke stayed stiff on the bike, afraid to move, his arms bowed in the air, gripping the handles desperately.

"Just relax and enjoy the ride," Eric said, huffing and running quickly.

They had passed Barry, who shouted: "Let go of him!"

"Don't!" Luke begged.

"I won't until you say I should."

Eric had to run fast now; it was harder and harder to keep up with his son.

"This is fun," Luke said. His arms relaxed.

"You can see so many things, can't you?" Eric said, huffing. They were close to a turn.

"Yes. I'm higher up," Luke said.

Eric couldn't stay with Luke. They made the turn onto a downward slope and the bike gained speed. One hand came off the bike, briefly.

"Can I let go, Luke?"

"Sure," said the happy voice.

But Eric didn't. He had to run very fast to keep pace with Luke, but he didn't want to let go, to lose the sight of his son's open, joyful face.

"Let go, Daddy," Luke said.

"Okay, I'm gonna let go."

"Okay," Luke sang back to him.

"Remember how to stop."

"I know how to stop," Luke said, impatient now. "Let go!"

Eric opened his hands and watched his son zoom away.

Eric's soul went with Luke—released, fast into the world, the figure, erect and proud and little, getting smaller and smaller, farther and farther away.

I leave him in your care, world. He is the best I can do. Take care of him.

"I'm doing it, Daddy!" Luke called back. "Should I stop?"

"When you want to, Luke. Only when you want to."

The bike wobbled. Luke put his feet on the ground and they skidded. The machine began to tilt. Luke planted his feet hard—and he went over, collapsing into a heap with the bike.

Eric and Barry ran to the fallen Luke. He lay still on the ground.

"Are you okay?"

"My foot is trapped," Luke said. Barry lifted the bike. Luke got up slowly. He looked betrayed. "I hurt my knee," he said.

Eric rolled up Luke's pants. There was a broad patch of skin gone, an angry red rectangle.

Luke winced.

"It's not bleeding. Do you want to try again?"

"No," Luke said.

"Oh, you should try right away," Barry said.

"I don't want to!" Luke said.

"You won't fall," Barry said. "You fell because you were going too fast. Just go slower and you won't fall. It's because you stopped thinking about being on the bike. You know, it's a funny thing, but the better you are at bike riding, the more likely you are to fall."

"What?" Luke said.

Eric knew what his father meant: you get careless.

"Try again and go slower," Barry insisted. He held the bike for Luke. "Go on, get on."

Luke obeyed. But he was reluctant this time. Still scared, but not brave, not happy. Eric became a spectator. Barry took over.

Barry pushed Luke slowly, then let go without warning. Luke immediately put his feet down and stopped. Barry asked him not to do that. Luke said Barry shouldn't let go unless he asked him to. How about I let go after I count to ten? Barry suggested. Luke agreed, but again was reluctant and unhappy. Barry pushed Luke slowly and let go after a count to ten. Luke wobbled on for a bit, then put his feet down and stopped. Barry lectured him: "Don't worry about falling. If you go slowly, you won't fall."

Eric was sweating. His head ached. Watching Luke fall had upset him. Listening to Barry, he was nauseated. He hated the sound of his father's voice: it was insistent and whiny, obviously fake in its protestations of assurance. Eric wanted to get away, to stop hearing Barry talk.

Luke started up again, but immediately quit once Barry let go. It was obvious Luke could ride the bike, but the fear of falling defeated his ability.

Barry lectured Luke: "If you go slowly and think about it you won't fall. If you're careful, you won't fall. It's funny," Barry kept saying, "but the better you become, the more likely you are to fall."

Eric's mouth dried up. His head hurt. His skull bones were falling in, battered by Barry's talk. Stop him, he could hear Nina say. Stop him from talking to Luke.

It's funny, Barry kept saying. The better you are at something, the more likely you are to fall.

At this point, Luke wouldn't even allow Barry to let go of the bike.

Eric got to his feet. He charged over to them. "Okay, okay," he said talking fast, afraid of the rage inside. "Listen to me, Luke." He talked as if he were giving instructions in a crisis, saving Luke's life. "The faster you go, the less you think about it, the easier it'll be. Grandpa's wrong. He's totally wrong. The better you are, the less likely you are to fall."

"That's not what I meant!" Barry protested.

"Yeah," Luke said. He laughed, but tears came to his eyes. "I didn't think it made sense."

"When you decide to stop, use the hand brakes."

"I use my feet 'cause I don't—"

"You shouldn't use your feet—" Barry started again.

"You don't want to tip over," Eric outshouted his father. "I know. I know, but first slow down with the brakes. You won't tip over until you're going slow. Then put your feet down. You won't fall, Luke. Your body knows how to ride the bike. You already did it, remember? Look—" Eric pointed the distance Luke had traveled before the fall. "Look how far you got. You did that all on your own. The better you are, the more you do it, the less likely you are to fall. And if you fall—so what? You get up and go on!" Eric felt as if he were about to cry. It was absurd: why did he feel like bursting into tears? He swallowed them back. "The better you are, the faster you go, the more sure it is that you won't fall. And if you do—" He paused, held his hand out, offered the finish to Luke.

Luke watched him. His mouth was tight, his blue eyes glowed in the sun. "So what?" Luke said. "I can just get back on and ride, right?"

"Right! Let's do it." Eric grabbed the back of the bike. "I'll let go when you tell me."

He pushed Luke fast, his heart racing. Eric saw a look of hurt on Barry's face. Dad didn't mean any harm, Eric said to himself. Barry just doesn't know how to teach.

"Let go," Luke said suddenly.

"Okay!"

Eric let go of the bike and stopped. Luke skimmed away, riding on the world. Eric was between the branches of two trees and the sun was on his head, warming him. He felt a chill shiver through his body. What the hell was all that from Barry? He doesn't know how to deal with kids. I'll tell him I was sorry for interrupting his lesson. Probably it would have worked, but Eric had felt too sick to listen.

Away, in the distance, Luke moved under the trees, in and out of the sunlight. Luke moved in the air, confident above the dangerous ground. He was alone on the path riding his bike with joy.

Eric watched him, the nausea gone, his body strong again. Luke slowed and stopped himself. He turned the bike to face Eric.

"I did it, Daddy."

"Of course you did. You're very good so you won't fall."

"When you're good, you don't fall, right, Daddy?"

"That's right, Luke. And you're very good."

Luke pushed his foot on the pavement to get started, caught the pedal, and came at Eric. The head was up, the blue eyes danced in the air, and he flew past Eric and Barry, alone and proud and very good.

NINA LAY THERE, AGAIN BEACHED ON A HOSPITAL GURNEY. SHE waited for the tide. Eric sat and watched her. The monitor spewed out paper.

She was two weeks late. She was eager for the pregnancy to end. Marge Ephron, her doctor, had ordered this test, a fetal-stress test, to determine if there was any problem.

There just couldn't be a problem. There just couldn't be anything wrong.

Was that a movement? Yes, it had to be.

A nurse came in. "How we doing?" the nurse asked, but she looked at the reams of graph paper for her answer.

"Okay," Nina answered anyway.

"Have you been feeling contractions?" the nurse asked looking up from the paper.

"No," Nina said.

"Are you sure?"

"Why?" Eric said.

"Well, see this?" The nurse curved the paper in their direction. "That looks like a contraction to me. Baby's heart rate is all right. It's responding correctly. Here's another one about ten minutes ago." The nurse showed the jagged break from the norm on the paper, the stabs wounding a graceful curve.

"You don't feel anything?" Eric asked.

"No," Nina said. How could I have contractions and not know it?

"I'll call Dr. Ephron and tell her. I think maybe you should stay on the monitor for a while. Just in case you've begun contractions. No point in going home and have to turn right around.'' The nurse left.

''Well?'' Eric said.

''Can't be,'' Nina said. What was that? The ripple in the ocean, the whale spinning inside. No. That's not a pain. Probably just twisting in his bed.

''Why not? You had back pain with Luke. Maybe you don't recognize a normal contraction.''

Luke. He was so happy. He had flowered so beautifully. What a great boy. Maybe this was a mistake. Maybe you don't try to follow up on success.

She didn't think so. Eric was so good at being a father. And so sad at his own work. How wrong not to have another child.

She wanted to dare the skies again, to ask them for another temporary gift of perfect love.

They grow up and we get old.

Anything, any loss of sleep, any loss of ease, was worth the sweet, and too, too brief time of holding the little ones until they burst out of your arms and into the world.

What was that?

''Is there something on the machine now?'' she asked.

Eric bent over. He was so tall he had to bend almost in half to read the paper. ''No,'' he said. He put his hand on her exploded stomach.

The nurse returned. ''Dr. Ephron says you should stay on the machine until we figure out whether you're having contractions.''

''Maybe it's just the baby moving around,'' Nina said.

The nurse shook her head no. ''That's here. See?'' She showed the baby movements. ''These are coming from you. Just relax.'' She left.

Was that a pain?

''Is there something on the paper now?''

Eric bent over. ''Yes,'' he said. ''It's happening again. You feel it?''

No. Nothing.

''It's going crazy,'' Eric said. ''You sure you don't feel pain?''

''I don't know.'' She sighed. ''Talk to me. After Luke, what did you do when you went home?''

Eric thought. ''I fell asleep,'' he said.

''That's all?''

Eric was embarrassed. ''I played some music.''

She laughed. ''The *Messiah*.''

Eric smiled shyly. "He's a miracle to me," he said, and choked on the words.

Tears were in her eyes also. She put out her hand. "We've done okay."

"Luke did it. Not us." Eric took her hand and stood with his head bowed, waiting, praying over her.

"This one will be great too," Nina said.

There!

"What is it?" Eric asked.

There! Sharp and hard, the message had come.

"What is it?" Eric asked.

Nina smiled.

At last! There it was!

At last, she had felt the pain, the exquisite pain of life.

About the Author

Rafael Yglesias is a member of the successful writing family that includes his parents Helen and José Yglesias, his brother Lewis Cole and his sister Tamar Cole. He lives with his wife, Margaret, and their two children in Manhattan.